READER'S DIGEST

CONDENSED BOOKS

FIRST EDITION

Published by

THE READER'S DIGEST ASSOCIATION LIMITED
25 Berkeley Square, London W1X 6AB.

THE READER'S DIGEST ASSOCIATION SOUTH AFRICA (PTY) LTD.
Nedbank Centre, Strand Street, Cape Town

Typeset in 10 on 12 pt. Highland Lumitype Roman
and printed in Great Britain by Petty & Sons Ltd., Leeds,
Varnicoat Ltd., Pershore and
Ben Johnson & Co. Ltd., York.

Original cover design by Jeffery Matthews A.R.C.A.

ISBN 0 340 18533 3

READER'S DIGEST CONDENSED BOOKS

COLLECTOR'S LIBRARY EDITION

In this volume

THE FEARFUL VOID
by Geoffrey Moorhouse (p. 235)

Three thousand six hundred miles by camel across the Sahara Desert. No one had done it before. To Geoffrey Moorhouse that was challenge enough. Heroism comes in many forms: for him it was simply a blind determination to be maintained day after day, through mounting privations, even to the very brink of death. A determination to survive his chosen hell. His account of his experiences is vivid, unforgettable, and utterly truthful.

JAWS
by Robert Benchley (p. 11)

Sunshine . . . golden sands . . . rich summer residences . . . sparkling waters . . . and beneath those waters a great white shark lurking, hungrily, just beyond the shallows.

Naturally panic was to be avoided at all costs. The prosperity of too many depended on the summer trade. So, while police and powerful business interests wrangled, people died. What the town desperately needed was a man prepared to hunt—and fight—the shark. . . .

PIED PIPER
by Nevil Shute (p. 339)
Never can Nevil Shute have written a more exciting or heartwarming tale than this. In it he captures brilliantly an old man's tenderness, and the innocent preoccupations of children, even in the face of war's bloody ruthlessness. The classic escape to freedom that he describes is a wonder of courage, endurance, gentle humour, and love. . . .

A PALM FOR
MRS. POLLIFAX
by Dorothy Gilman
(p. 135)

Agent most extraordinary — America's answer to Mata Hari —saving the world at the drop of a knitting needle. . . . Mrs. Pollifax rides again.

With a nice line in karate added to her armoury, and a little help from Interpol, she confounds the enemies of the Western Way of Life. Truly, never in the field of human conflict has so much been owed by so many to . . . just one little old lady.

END PLAY
by Russell Braddon (p. 453)

What is family loyalty? How much of it is in *your* family? Would it allow *you* to suspect your own brother of a particularly brutal murder? And if so, would it then oblige you to protect him from the consequences of his crime?

Robbie Gifford found these questions unusually easy. But then, he was an unusual person. And his brother, too, was an unusual person.

JAWS
Peter Benchley

J A

W S

a condensation of the book by

Peter Benchley

Illustrated by Stanley Galli
Published by Andre Deutsch, London

The great white shark lurked just beyond the shallows, raiding the beaches and seizing its victims at random. No one—not the marine experts, the fishermen, or the Coast Guard—could explain why it had appeared off Long Island that summer, or chosen to terrorize that particular town. But there it was, and there it stayed, a presence bringing, in more ways than one, death and destruction to the town.

Police Chief Martin Brody saw his duty clearly: the beaches must be closed to prevent further loss of life. Mayor Larry Vaughan disagreed: it must be business as usual or the resort town (himself included) would be ruined. Meanwhile, to Brody's pretty, discontented wife the shark brought danger and excitement of a very different kind.

Then, as the death toll rose and the town remained sharply divided over what to do, the grim truth had to be faced. The monster must be caught and killed, or the town itself would die.

Part One

1

The great fish moved silently through the night water, propelled by short sweeps of its crescent tail, the mouth open just enough to permit a rush of water over the gills. There was little other motion: an occasional correction of the apparently aimless course by the slight raising or lowering of a pectoral fin—as a bird changes direction by dipping one wing and lifting the other.

The senses transmitted nothing extraordinary to the small, primitive brain. The fish might have been asleep, save for the movement dictated by millions of years of instinctive continuity: lacking the flotation bladder common to other fish and the fluttering flaps to push oxygen-bearing water through its gills, it survived only by moving. Once stopped, it would sink to the bottom and die of anoxia.

The land along the south shore of Long Island seemed almost as dark as the water, for there was no moon. All that separated sea from shore was a long, straight stretch of beach—so white that it shone. From a house behind the grass-splotched dunes, lights cast yellow glimmers on the sand.

The front door to the house opened, and a man and a woman stepped out onto the wooden porch. They stood for a moment staring at the sea, embraced quickly, then ran together to the beach. The man was drunk, and fell giggling onto the sand. The woman laughed.

"You need a swim," she said, "to clear your head."

The man lay back and closed his eyes.

"You go ahead," he said. "I'll wait for you here."

The woman undressed and walked to where the gentle surf washed over her ankles. The water was colder than the night air, for it was only mid-June. She called back, "Sure you don't want to come?" But there was no answer from the sleeping man.

She backed up a few steps, then ran at the water. At first her strides were long and graceful, but then a small wave crashed into her knees. She faltered, regained her footing and walked until the water covered her shoulders. Then she began to swim.

A hundred yards offshore the fish sensed a change in the sea's rhythm. It did not see the woman, nor yet did it smell her. Running within the length of its body were thin canals filled with mucus and dotted with nerve endings, and these nerves detected vibrations and signalled to the brain. The fish turned toward shore.

The woman continued to swim away from the beach, stopping now and then to check her position by the lights shining from the house. The tide was slack, so she had not drifted. But she was tiring, so she trod water for a moment, then started for shore.

The vibrations were stronger now, and the fish recognized prey. The sweeps of its tail quickened, thrusting the giant body forward with a speed that agitated the tiny phosphorescent animals in the water and cast a mantle of sparks over the fish.

The fish closed on the woman and hurtled past, a dozen feet to the side and six feet below the surface. She felt only a wave of pressure that seemed to lift her up and ease her down again.

The fish smelled her now, and began to circle close to the surface.

Its dorsal fin broke water, and its tail, thrashing back and forth, cut the glassy surface with a hiss.

For the first time the woman felt fear, though she did not know why. Adrenalin shot through her body, urging her to swim faster. She was about fifty yards from shore.

The fish was about forty feet from the woman, off to the side, when it turned suddenly to the left, dropped entirely below the surface, and, with two quick thrusts of its tail, was upon her.

There was no initial pain, only one violent tug on the woman's right leg. For a moment she thought she had snagged it on a rock. She reached down to touch her foot, treading water with her left leg. She could not find her foot. She reached higher, and then she was overcome by a rush of nausea and dizziness. Her groping fingers had found a nub of bone and tattered flesh.

Pain and panic struck together. The woman threw her head back and screamed a guttural cry of terror.

Now the fish turned again, homing on the stream of blood. This time it attacked from below. The great conical head struck the woman like a locomotive, knocking her out of the water, and the gaping jaws snapped shut around her torso.

THE MAN AWOKE, shivering in the early morning cold. The sun had not yet risen, but a line of pink on the eastern horizon told him that daybreak was near. He was annoyed that the woman had not wakened him when she went in, and he found it curious that she had left her clothes on the beach. He picked them up and walked to the house.

He tiptoed across the porch and opened the screen door. The deserted living room was littered with glasses, ashtrays and dirty plates. He walked across it and turned right, down a hall, past two closed doors. The door to the room he shared with the woman was open, and a bedside light was on. Both beds were made. He tossed the woman's clothes on one of them, and went to check the bathroom. It was unoccupied. Only then did he allow his mind to consider the possibility of an accident.

Very quickly the possibility became a certainty. He opened the door of his hosts' bedroom, hesitated for a moment beside the king-sized bed, and then placed his hand on a shoulder.

"Jack," he said. "Hey, Jack."

The man sighed and opened his eyes. "What?"

"It's me. Tom. I hate like hell to wake you up, but have you seen Chrissie?"

"What do you mean? Isn't she with you?"

"No. And I can't find her."

Jack sat up and turned on a light. His wife stirred and covered her head with a sheet. "When did you see her last?" he asked.

"On the beach. Then I fell asleep. Didn't she come back?"

"Not before we went to bed, and that was around one."

"I found her clothes on the beach."

"So what do you think?"

"What I'm beginning to think," said Tom, "is that maybe she had an accident. Maybe she drowned."

Jack looked at him for a moment, then glanced at his watch. "I don't know what time the police in this town go to work," he said, "but I guess this is as good a time as any to find out."

WHEN THE PHONE rang Patrolman Leonard Hendricks was at his desk in the Amity police station reading a detective novel called *Deadly, I'm Yours*.

He picked up the phone. "Amity Police," he said. "Can I help you?"

"This is Jack Foote, over on Old Mill Road. I want to report a missing person. Or at least I think she's missing."

"Say again, sir?" Hendricks had served in Vietnam as a radio man, and he was fond of military terminology.

"One of my houseguests went for a swim at about one this morning," said Foote. "She hasn't come back yet. Her date found her clothes on the beach."

Hendricks scribbled on a pad. "What is her name?"

"Christine Watkins."

"Age?"

"I don't know. Say around twenty-five."

"Height and weight?"

"Wait a minute." There was a pause. "We think about five feet seven, between one-twenty and one-thirty pounds."

"Color of hair and eyes?"

"Listen, Officer, why do you need all this? If the woman's drowned, she's probably the only one tonight. Right?"

"Who said she drowned, Mr. Foote? Maybe she went for a walk."

"Stark-naked at one in the morning? Have you had any reports about a woman walking around naked?"

Hendricks relished the chance to be insufferably cool. "Not yet. But once the summer season starts you never know what to expect. Color of hair and eyes?"

"Her hair is . . . oh, dirty blond, I guess. I don't know what color her eyes are. Let's say hazel."

"O.K., Mr. Foote. As soon as we find out anything we'll contact you."

Hendricks hung up and looked at his watch. It was 5:10, and he wasn't anxious to wake the chief for something as vague as a missing-person report. On the other hand, if she was washed up somewhere, Chief Brody would want the whole thing taken care of before the body was found by some nanny with a couple of young kids.

Judgment, that was what the chief kept telling him he needed; that was what made a good cop. The cerebral challenge of police work had played a part in Hendricks's decision to join the Amity force after he returned from Vietnam. He was convinced that as soon as he could get sprung from this midnight-to-eight shift, he would start to enjoy his work. But at the moment it was a drag. Chief Brody liked to break in his young men slowly—at a time of day when they wouldn't be over-taxed.

Eight a.m. to four p.m. was the business shift, and it called for experience and diplomacy. Six men worked that shift. One handled the traffic intersection at Main and Water streets. Two patrolled in squad cars. One manned the phones at the station house. One handled the clerical work. And the chief handled the public: ladies who complained that they hadn't been able to sleep because of the din coming from The Randy Bear or Saxon's, the town's two gin mills; home-owners who complained that bums were littering the beaches or disturbing the peace; and the vacationing bankers or lawyers who stopped in to discuss their various plans for keeping Amity a pristine and exclusive summer colony.

Four to midnight was the trouble shift, when young studs from the nearby Hamptons would flock to The Randy Bear and get involved in a fight, or speed drunkenly along the Montauk Highway; when, very rarely, a couple of predators from Queens would lurk in the dark side streets and mug passersby; and when, about twice a month in the summer, the police would feel obliged to stage a pot bust at one of the huge waterfront homes. The six largest men on the force worked four to midnight.

Midnight to eight was usually quiet. Normally, during the summer, it was manned by three officers. One, however, a young fellow named Dick Angelo, was taking his leave before the season began to swing. The third was a thirty-year veteran named Henry Kimble, who held a daytime job as a bartender at Saxon's. Hendricks tried to raise Kimble on the radio, but he knew the attempt was hopeless. As usual, Kimble was sound asleep in a squad car parked behind the Amity Pharmacy. And so Hendricks picked up the phone and dialed Chief Brody's home number.

Martin Brody was in that fitful state of semiconsciousness before waking. On the second ring of the phone, he rolled over and picked up the receiver. "Yeah?"

"Chief, this is Hendricks. I hate to bother you this early, but I think we've got a floater on our hands."

"A floater? What the hell is a floater?"

Hendricks had picked up the word from his night reading. "A drowning," he said, embarrassed. He told Brody about the call from Foote. "I didn't know if you'd want to check it out before people start swimming. It looks like it's going to be a nice day."

Brody heaved an exaggerated sigh. "Where's Kimble?" he said. "Oh, never mind. It was a stupid question. One of these days I'm going to fix that radio of his so he can't turn it off."

Hendricks said, "Like I said, Chief, I hate to bother—"

"Yeah, I know, Leonard. You were right to call. I'll take a look along the beach in front of Old Mill and Scotch, then I'll go out and talk to Foote and the girl's date. I'll see you later."

Brody hung up the phone and stretched. He looked at his wife, lying next to him in the double bed. She had stirred when the phone rang, but soon lapsed back into sleep.

Ellen Brody was thirty-six, five years younger than her husband. The fact that she looked barely thirty, though a source of pride to

Brody, was also one of annoyance. For despite the strains of bearing three children she had been able to keep her good looks, while he —though hardly fat at six feet one and two hundred pounds—was beginning to be concerned about his blood pressure and his thickening middle. Sometimes Brody would catch himself gazing with idle lust at one of the young, long-legged girls who pranced around town during the summer. But he never enjoyed the sensation, for it made him wonder whether Ellen felt the same stirring when she looked at the tanned, slim young men.

Summers were bad times for Ellen Brody, for in summer she was tortured by thoughts of chances she had missed. She saw people she had grown up with: boarding-school classmates, now married to successful husbands, summering in Amity and wintering in New York, graceful women who stroked tennis balls and enlivened conversations with equal ease, women who (Ellen was convinced) joked among themselves about Ellen Shepherd marrying that policeman.

Ellen had been twenty-one when she met Brody. She had just finished her junior year at Wellesley and was spending the summer in Amity with her parents—as she had done for the previous eleven summers. Though she'd enjoyed the modest wealth her father had earned, she had not been eager to live a life like her parents'. The petty social problems had bored her.

Her first contact with Brody was professional. She was arrested—or, rather, her date was. It was late at night, and she was being driven home very fast by an extremely drunk young man. The car was stopped by a policeman who impressed Ellen with his youth, his looks and his civility. After issuing a summons he confiscated the car keys and drove Ellen and her date to their respective homes. The next morning Ellen wrote Brody a thank-you note for being so nice. Brody telephoned to thank her.

When he asked her out to dinner and the movies on his night off, she accepted out of curiosity. She had scarcely ever talked to a policeman, let alone gone out with one. Brody was nervous, but Ellen seemed so interested in him and his work that he eventually calmed down enough to have a good time. Ellen found him delightful: strong, simple, kind—sincere. He had been a policeman for six years. He said his ambition was to be chief of the Amity force, to have sons to take duck-shooting in the fall, to save enough money to take a vacation every third year.

They were married that November.

There were some awkward moments during the first years. Ellen's friends would ask them to dinner, and Brody would feel ill-at-ease and patronized. When they got together with Brody's friends, Ellen's past seemed to stifle fun. Gradually, as new acquaintanceships developed, the awkwardness disappeared. But they never saw Ellen's old friends any more.

Until about four years ago she had been too busy and too happy to let the estrangement bother her. But when her last child started school she found herself adrift, and she began to dwell on memories of how her mother had lived; shopping excursions (fun because there was money to spend), tennis games, cocktail parties, weekend trips. What had once seemed shallow and tedious now loomed in memory like paradise.

At first she tried to re-establish bonds with friends she hadn't seen in ten years, but all common interests had long since vanished. Ellen talked gaily about local politics, about her job as a volunteer at the Southampton Hospital. Her old friends talked about New York politics, about art galleries, painters and writers they knew. Most conversations ended with feeble pledges about getting together again.

Once in a while she would try to make friends among the summer people she hadn't known, but the associations were forced and brief. Ellen was self-conscious about her house and about her husband's job. She made sure that everyone she met knew she had started her Amity life on an entirely different plane. She was aware of what she was doing and she hated herself for it, because in fact she loved her husband deeply, adored her children and—for most of the year—was quite content. By now she had largely given up active forays into the summer community, but the resentments lingered. She was unhappy, and she took out her unhappiness on her husband.

Brody rolled over toward Ellen, raising himself on one elbow and resting his head on his hand. With his other hand he flicked away a strand of hair that was tickling her nose and making it twitch. He debated rousing her, but he knew her early-morning moods were more cantankerous than romantic. Still, it would be fun. There had not been much sex in the Brody household recently. There seldom was, when Ellen was in her summer moods.

Just then, Ellen's jaw fell open and she began to snore. Brody got up and walked into the bathroom.

IT WAS NEARLY 6:30 and the sun was well up when he turned onto Old Mill Road. From the road there was no view of the beach. All Brody could see was the tops of the dunes. So every hundred yards or so he had to stop the squad car and walk up a driveway to a point from which he could survey the shore.

There was no sign of a body. All he saw on the broad white expanse were pieces of driftwood, a can or two and a yard-wide belt of seaweed pushed ashore by the southerly breeze. There was practically no surf, so if a body were floating on the surface it would have been visible.

By seven o'clock Brody had covered the whole beach along Old Mill and Scotch roads. He turned north toward town on Bayberry Lane, and arrived at the station house at 7:10.

"No luck, Chief?" Hendricks said.

"That depends on what you mean by luck, Leonard. If you mean did I find a body, the answer is no."

Brody poured himself a cup of coffee, walked into his office and began to flip through the morning papers—the New York *Daily News* and the local paper, the Amity *Leader*.

Kimble arrived a little before eight, looking, aptly enough, as if he had been sleeping in his uniform. He and Hendricks had coffee while they waited for the day shift to appear. Hendricks's replacement came in at eight sharp, and Hendricks was getting ready to leave when Brody came out of his office.

"I'm going out to see Foote, Leonard," Brody said. "You want to come along? I thought you might want to follow up on your . . . floater?" Brody smiled.

"Sure, I guess so," said Hendricks. "I got nothing else going today, so I can sleep all afternoon."

At the Footes' house the door opened almost before Brody finished knocking. "I'm Tom Cassidy," said a young man. "Did you find her?"

"I'm Chief Brody. This is Officer Hendricks. No, Mr. Cassidy, we didn't find her. Can we come in?"

"Sure. Go on in the living room. I'll get the Footes."

It took less than five minutes for Brody to learn everything he needed to know.

"We'd better go down to the beach," he said. "You don't have to come. Hendricks and I can handle it."

"I'd like to come, if you don't mind," said Cassidy.

The three men walked down to the beach. Cassidy showed the policemen where he had fallen asleep—and where he had found Christine Watkins's clothes.

Brody looked up and down the mile-long stretch. For as far as he could see, clumps of seaweed were the only dark spots on the white sand.

"Let's take a walk," he said. "Leonard, you go east as far as the point. Mr. Cassidy, let's you and I go west. You got your whistle, Leonard? Just in case."

"I've got it," said Hendricks. "You care if I take my shoes off? It's easier walking on the sand."

"I don't care," said Brody. "You can take your pants off if you want. Of course, then I'll arrest you for indecent exposure."

Hendricks started eastward, the wet sand cool on his feet. He walked with his head down, looking at the tiny shells and tangles of seaweed. A few little black beetles skittered out of his path, and when the wavewash receded he saw minute bubbles pop above the holes made by sandworms. He enjoyed the walk. It was a funny thing, he thought, that when you lived in a place you almost never did the things that tourists did—like walk on the beach or go swimming in the ocean.

Once Hendricks turned around to see if Brody and Cassidy had found anything. He guessed that they were nearly half a mile away. As he started walking again, he saw ahead of him an unusually large clump of kelp. When he reached it he bent down to pull some of the weed away. Suddenly he stopped, frozen rigid. He fumbled in his pants pocket for his whistle, blew it weakly, then staggered back and fell to his knees, vomiting.

Snarled within the weed was a woman's head, still attached to shoulders, part of an arm and about a third of her trunk.

HENDRICKS WAS STILL on his knees when Brody and Cassidy got to him. Brody was several steps ahead of Cassidy, and he said, "Mr. Cassidy, stay back there a second, will you?" He pulled apart some of the weeds, and when he saw what was inside he felt bile rise in his throat. He swallowed and closed his eyes. After a moment he said, "You might as well look now, Mr. Cassidy, and tell me if it's her or not."

Cassidy's eyes shifted between the exhausted Hendricks and the mass of weed. "That *thing*?" he said, pointing. "What do you mean, is it her?" He shuffled forward reluctantly. Brody held back a piece of weed so Cassidy could get a clear look at the gray and gaping face. "Oh my God!" said Cassidy, and he put a hand to his mouth.

"Is it her?"

Cassidy nodded. "What happened to her?"

"Offhand, I'd say she was attacked by a shark," said Brody.

Cassidy's knees buckled, and as he sank to the sand he said, "I think I'm going to be sick."

Brody knew instantly that he had lost his struggle for control. "Join the crowd," he said, and he vomited too.

2

Several minutes passed before Brody felt well enough to stand, walk back to his car and call for an ambulance from the Southampton Hospital. By eleven o'clock he was back in his office, filling out forms about the accident. He had completed everything but the cause of death when the phone rang.

"Carl Santos, Martin," said the voice of the coroner.

"Yeah, Carl. What have you got for me?"

"Unless you have any reason to suspect a murder, I'd have to say shark."

"I don't think it's a murder, Carl. I've got no motive, no murder weapons and—unless I want to go off into left field—no suspect."

"Then it's a shark. And a big one, too. Even the screw on a liner wouldn't have done this. It might have cut her in two, but—"

"O.K., Carl," said Brody. "Spare me the gore."

"Sorry, Martin. Anyway, I'd say shark attack makes the most sense to put down, unless there are . . . other considerations."

"No. Not this time, Carl. Thanks for calling." He hung up, typed "shark attack" on the forms, and leaned back in his chair.

The possibility of other considerations hadn't occurred to Brody. Those considerations were the touchiest part of his job, forcing him constantly to assess the best means of protecting the common weal without compromising either himself or the law.

It was the beginning of the summer season, and Brody knew that on the success or failure of those twelve brief weeks rested the fortunes of Amity for a whole year. The winter population of Amity was about a thousand; in a good summer the population jumped to nearly ten thousand. And those nine thousand summer visitors kept the thousand permanent residents alive for the rest of the year.

Local merchants—from the owners of the hardware store and the sporting-goods store and the two gas stations to the local pharmacist—needed a boom summer to support them through the lean winter. Charter fishermen needed every break they could get: good weather, good fishing and, above all, crowds.

Even after the best of summers Amity winters were rough. Three of every ten families went on relief. Dozens of men were forced to move for the winter to the north shore of Long Island, where they shucked scallops for a few dollars a day.

Brody knew that one bad summer would nearly double the relief rolls. And two or three bad summers in a row—a circumstance that fortunately hadn't occurred in more than two decades—could wreck the town. If people didn't have enough money to pay for clothes or food or repairs, then business firms would have to close down. The town would lose tax revenue, municipal services would deteriorate and people would begin to move away. So everyone was expected to do his bit to make sure that Amity remained a desirable summer community.

Generally Brody's contribution—in addition to maintaining the rule of law—consisted of suppressing rumors and, in consultation with Harry Meadows, the editor of the Amity *Leader*, keeping a perspective on the rare unfortunate occurrences.

If one of the wealthier summer residents was arrested for drunken driving, Brody was willing, on a first offense, to book him for driving without a license, and that charge would be duly reported in the *Leader*. But Brody made sure to warn the driver that the second time he was caught he would be charged, booked and prosecuted for drunk driving.

When youngsters from the Hamptons caused trouble, Harry Meadows was handed every fact—names, ages and charges lodged. When Amity's own youth made too much noise at a party, the *Leader* usually ran a one-paragraph story without names.

But Brody wanted full disclosure of the shark incident. He intended to close the beaches for a couple of days, to give the shark time to travel far from the Amity shoreline.

He knew there would be a strong argument against publicizing the attack. Amity was still feeling the effects of the economic recession. So far the summer was shaping up as a mediocre one. Rentals were up from last year, but they were not "good" rentals. Many were "groupers", bands of ten or fifteen young people who came from the city and split the rent on a big house. At least a dozen of the expensive shorefront properties had not yet been rented. Reports of a shark attack might turn the season into a disaster.

Still, Brody thought, one death would certainly have less effect than three or four. The fish might well have disappeared already, but Brody wasn't willing to gamble lives on the possibility. He dialed Meadows's number. "Free for lunch, Harry?" he said.

"Sure," said Meadows. "My place or yours?"

"Yours," he said. "Why don't we order out from Cy's?"

"Fine with me," said Meadows. "What do you want?"

Suddenly Brody wished he hadn't called at mealtime. The thought of food nauseated him. "Just an egg salad sandwich, I guess, and a glass of milk. I'll be right there."

HARRY MEADOWS was an immense man; the mere act of drawing breath caused perspiration to dot his forehead. He was in his late forties, ate too much, chain-smoked cheap cigars, drank the best bourbon and was, in the words of his doctor, the Western world's leading candidate for a huge coronary infarction.

When Brody arrived Meadows was standing beside his desk, waving a towel at the open window. "In deference to what your lunch order tells me is a tender stomach," he said, "I am trying to clear the air of essence of White Owl."

"I appreciate that," said Brody. He glanced around the small, cluttered room, searching for a place to sit.

"Throw the stuff off that chair," Meadows said. "They're just government reports."

Brody piled the heap of papers atop a radiator, and pulled the chair over to Meadows's desk.

Meadows rooted around in a large brown paper bag, pulled out a paper cup and a plastic-wrapped sandwich and slid them across the desk to Brody. Then he began to unwrap his own lunch: a large meatball sandwich, a carton of fried potatoes, and a quarter of a lemon meringue pie. He reached behind his chair and from a small refrigerator took a can of beer.

"Amazing," said Brody. "I must have had about a thousand meals with you, Harry, but I still can't get used to it."

"Everyone has his little quirks, my friend," Meadows said. "Some men chase other people's wives. Some lose themselves in whiskey. I find my solace in nature's own nourishment."

They ate in silence for a few moments. Brody finished his sandwich and lit a cigarette. Meadows was still eating, but Brody knew his appetite wouldn't be diminished by a discussion of Christine Watkins's death.

"About the Watkins thing," he said. "I have a couple of thoughts, if you want to hear them." Meadows nodded. "First, it seems to me that the cause of death is cut-and-dried. Santos thinks it was a shark attack, and if you'd seen the body, you'd agree."

"I did see it. And I agree that's what killed her. But there are a few things I'm not so sure of."

"Like what?"

"Like why she was swimming at that time of night. Do you know what the temperature was? Sixty. And the water was about fifty. You'd have to be out of your mind to go swimming under those conditions."

"Or drunk," said Brody, "which she probably was."

"You're probably right. There's one other thing that bothered me, though. It seemed damn funny that we'd get a shark around here when the water's still this cold."

"Maybe some sharks like cold water. Who knows about sharks?"

"I know a lot more about them than I did this morning. After I saw what was left of Miss Watkins, I called a young guy I know up at the Woods Hole Oceanographic Institution. I described the body to him, and he said it's likely that only one kind of shark would do a job like that."

"What kind?"

"A great white. Others attack people, like tigers and hammerheads and maybe makos and blues, but this fellow, Matt Hooper, told me that to cut a woman in half you'd have to have a fish with a mouth like this"—he spread his hands about three feet apart—"and the only shark that grows that big *and* attacks people is the great white. There's another name for them—man-eaters."

"What did he say about the cold water?"

"That it's not uncommon for a great white to come into water this cold. Some years ago a boy was killed by one near San Francisco. The water temperature was fifty-seven."

Brody said, "You've really done a lot of checking, Harry."

"It seemed to me a matter of public interest to determine exactly what happened and the chances of it happening again."

"And did you determine those chances?"

"I did. They're almost non-existent. From what I can gather, this was a real freak accident. According to Hooper, there's every reason to believe that the shark is long gone. There are no reefs here. There's no fish-processing plant or slaughterhouse that dumps blood or guts into the water. So there's nothing to keep the shark interested." Meadows paused and looked at Brody. "So it seems to me, Martin, that there's no reason to get the public upset over something that's almost sure not to happen again."

"That's one way to look at it, Harry. Another is that since it's not likely to happen again, there's no harm in telling people that it did happen this once."

Meadows sighed. "Journalistically, you may be right. But I don't think it would be in the public interest to spread this around. I'm not thinking about the townspeople; they'll know about it soon enough. But what about the people who read the *Leader* in New York or Philadelphia or Cleveland?"

"You flatter yourself."

"You know a lot of the summer people subscribe year-round. And you know what the real estate situation is like this season. If I run a story saying that a young woman was bitten in two by a monster shark off Amity, there won't be another house rented in this town. Sharks are like axe-murderers, Martin. People react to them with their guts."

Brody nodded. "I can't argue with that, and I don't want to tell the people that there *is* a killer shark around. You're probably right. That shark has probably gone a hundred miles away. But suppose—just suppose—we don't say a word, and somebody else gets hit by that fish. What then? I want you to run the story, Harry. I want to close the beaches, just for a couple of days, and just for insurance. If we tell people what happened and why we're doing it, I think we'll be way ahead."

Meadows sat back in his chair. "There won't be any story about the attack in the *Leader*, Martin."

"Just like that."

"Well, not exactly. I'm the editor of this paper and I own a piece of it, but not a big enough piece to buck certain pressures."

"Such as?"

"I've already gotten six phone calls. Five were from advertisers—a restaurant, a hotel, two real estate firms and an ice-cream shop. They were most anxious that we let the whole thing fade quietly away. The sixth call was from Mr. Coleman in New York, who owns fifty-five percent of the *Leader*. It seems Mr. Coleman had received a few phone calls himself. He told me there would be no story in the *Leader*."

"Well, Harry, where does that leave us? You're not going to run a story, so as far as the good readers of the *Leader* are concerned, nothing ever happened. I'm going to close the beaches and put up a few signs saying why."

TEN MINUTES AFTER Brody returned to his office a voice on the intercom announced, "The mayor's here to see you, Chief."

Brody smiled. The mayor. Not Lawrence Vaughan of Vaughan & Penrose Real Estate; not Larry Vaughan, just calling to check in. But Mayor Lawrence P. Vaughan, the people's choice. "Send His Honor in," Brody said.

Larry Vaughan was an elegant, handsome man in his early fifties, with a full head of salt-and-pepper hair and a body kept trim by exercise. A native of Amity, he had made a great deal of money in real estate speculation, and he was the senior partner (some thought the *only* partner) in the most successful agency in town. Unlike Ellen Brody, who had descended from summer folk to winter folk, Vaughan had ascended smoothly from winter folk to summer folk. As a local merchant, he was not one of them, so he was never asked to visit them in New York or Palm Beach. But in Amity he moved freely among all but the most aloof members of the summer community, which, of course, was very good for business.

Brody liked Vaughan. He didn't see much of him during the summer, but after Labor Day, Vaughan and his wife, Eleanor, would occasionally ask Brody and Ellen out to dinner at one of the better restaurants in the Hamptons. The evenings were special treats for Ellen, and that in itself was enough to make Brody happy. Vaughan seemed to understand Ellen. He always treated her as a clubmate and comrade.

Vaughan walked into Brody's office and sat down. "I just talked to Harry Meadows," he said. "Where are you going to get the authority to close the beaches?"

Vaughan was obviously upset, which surprised Brody. "Officially, I'm not sure I have it," Brody said. "The code says I can take whatever action I deem necessary in an emergency, but I think the selectmen have to declare a state of emergency. I don't imagine you want to go through all that rigmarole."

"Not a chance. But I don't want you to close the beaches."

"So I see."

"You know why. The Fourth of July isn't far off, and that's the make-or-break weekend. We'd be cutting our own throats."

"I know the argument, and I'm sure you know my reasons. It's not as if I have anything to gain by closing the beaches."

"No. I'd say quite the opposite is true. Look, Martin, this town doesn't need that kind of publicity."

"It doesn't need any more people killed, either."

"Nobody else is going to get killed. All you'd be doing by closing the beaches is inviting a lot of reporters to come snooping around where they don't have any business."

"So? They'd come out here, and when they didn't find anything worth reporting, they'd go home again."

"Suppose they did find something. There'd be a big to-do that couldn't do anybody any good."

"Like what, Larry? What could they find out? I don't have anything to hide. Do you?"

"No, of course not. Look, if you won't listen to reason, will you listen to me as a friend? I'm under a lot of pressure from my partners. Something like this could be very bad for us."

Brody laughed. "That's the first time I've heard you admit you *had* partners, Larry. I thought you ran that shop like an emperor."

Vaughan was embarrassed, as if he felt he had said too much. "My business is very complicated," he said. "There are times I'm not sure *I* understand what's going on. Do me this favor. This once."

Brody looked at Vaughan, trying to fathom his motives. "I'm sorry, Larry, I have to do my job."

"If you don't listen to me," said Vaughan, "you may not have your job much longer."

"You haven't got any control over me. You can't fire any cop in this town."

"Not off the force, no. But believe it or not, I do have discretion over the job of chief of police." From his jacket pocket he took a copy of Amity's corporate charter. He found the page he sought, and handed the pamphlet to Brody. "What it says, in effect, is that even though you were elected by the people, the selectmen have the power to remove you."

Brody read the paragraph Vaughan had indicated. "You're right," he said. "But I'd love to see what you put down for 'good and sufficient cause'."

"I dearly hope it doesn't come to that, Martin. I had hoped you would go along, once you knew how the selectmen felt."

"All the selectmen?"

"A majority."

"Like who?"

"I'm not going to sit here and name names for you. All you have to know is that I have the board behind me; if you won't do what's right, we'll put someone in your job who will."

Brody had never seen Vaughan in a mood so aggressively ugly. He was fascinated, but slightly shaken. "You really want this, don't you, Larry?"

"I do." Sensing victory, Vaughan said evenly, "Trust me, Martin. You won't be sorry."

Brody sighed. "I don't like it," he said. "It doesn't smell good. But O.K., if it's that important."

"It's that important." Vaughan smiled. "Thanks, Martin." He stood up. "We do have one thing going for us. Miss Watkins was a nobody. She was a drifter. No family, no close friends. She said she hitch-hiked East from Idaho."

BRODY ARRIVED HOME a little before five. His stomach had settled down enough to permit him a beer or two before dinner. Ellen was in the kitchen, still dressed in the uniform of a hospital volunteer. Her hands were immersed in chopped meat, making a meat loaf.

"Hello," she said, turning her head so Brody could plant a kiss on her cheek. "What was the crisis?"

"You didn't hear? A girl got killed off Old Mill."

"By what?"

"A shark." Brody reached into the refrigerator for a beer.

Ellen stopped kneading meat and looked at him. "A shark! I've never heard of that around here. You see one once in a while, but they never do anything."

"Yeah, I know. It's a first for me, too."

"So what are you going to do?"

"Nothing."

"Really? Is that sensible? Isn't there anything you can do?"

"Sure, there are some things I could do. Technically. But the powers-that-be are worried that it won't look nice if we get all excited just because one stranger got killed by a fish. They're willing to take the chance that it was just a freak accident that won't happen again."

"What do you mean, the powers-that-be?"

"Larry Vaughan, for one."

"Oh, well, that makes me feel better. Larry tends to take a wider, more overall view of things than most people. He probably does know what's best."

Brody felt the blood rise in his neck. He tore the metal tab off his beer can, flipped it into the garbage can, and walked into the living room to turn on the evening news.

3

For the next few days the weather remained clear. A gentle breeze rippled the surface of the sea but made no whitecaps. Only at night was there a crispness to the air, and after days of constant sun the earth and sand had warmed.

Sunday was the twentieth of June. Families who owned summer homes in Amity had been coming out for weekends since the beginning of May. Summer tenants whose leases ran from June fifteenth to September fifteenth had unpacked and, familiar now with where linen closets were and which beds were softer than others, were already beginning to feel at home.

By noon the beach in front of Scotch and Old Mill roads was speckled with people. Husbands lay semi-comatose, trying to gain strength for the railroad trip back to New York. Teenagers were ranged in symmetrical rows on colorful towels. The little children played at the water's edge, digging holes and flinging wet sand at each other.

A boy of six stopped skimming flat stones into the water. He walked up to where his mother lay dozing, and flopped down next to her. "Hey, Mom," he said, "I don't have anything to do."

"Why don't you go throw a ball?"

"With who? There's nobody here. Can I go swimming?"

"No. It's too cold. Besides, you know you can't go alone."

"Will you come with me?"

"Alex, Mom is pooped, absolutely exhausted. Can't you find anything else to do?"

"Can I go out on my raft? I won't go swimming. I'll just lie on my raft."

His mother sat up and looked along the beach. A few dozen yards away a man stood in waist-deep water with a child on his shoulders. She looked in the other direction. Except for a few couples in the distance, the beach was empty. "Oh, all right," she said. "But don't go too far out." To show she was serious she lowered her sunglasses so the boy could see her eyes.

"O.K.," he said. He grabbed his rubber raft and dragged it down to the water. When the water reached his waist, he held the raft in front of him and leaned forward. A swell lifted it, with the boy aboard. He paddled smoothly, with both arms, his feet hanging over the rear of the raft. He moved out a few yards, then began to paddle up and down, parallel to the beach. Though he didn't notice it, a gentle current slowly carried him offshore.

Fifty yards farther out, the ocean floor sloped precipitously. The depth of the water increased from fifteen feet to twenty-five, then forty, then fifty, leveling off at about a hundred feet until the true ocean depths began.

IN THIRTY-FIVE FEET of water the great fish swam slowly, its tail waving just enough to maintain motion. It saw nothing, for the water was murky with motes of vegetation. The fish had been moving parallel to the shoreline, too. Now it turned and followed the bottom upward.

The boy was resting, his arms dangling down, his feet and ankles dipping in and out of the water with each small swell. His head was turned toward shore, and he noticed that he had been carried out beyond what his mother would consider safe. He could see her lying on her towel, and the man and child playing in the wave wash. He began to kick and paddle toward shore. His arms displaced water almost silently, but his kicking feet made erratic splashes and left swirls of bubbles in his wake.

The fish did not hear the sound but rather registered the sharp and jerky impulses emitted by the kicks. It rose, slowly at first, then gaining speed as the signals grew stronger.

The boy stopped for a moment to rest, and the signals ceased. The fish slowed, turning its head from side to side, trying to recover them. The boy lay perfectly still, and the fish passed beneath him, skimming the sandy bottom. Again it turned.

The boy resumed paddling. He kicked only every third or fourth stroke, but the occasional kicks sent new signals to the fish. This time it needed to lock on them only an instant, for it was almost directly below the boy.

The fish rose. Nearly vertical, it now saw the commotion on the surface. There was no conviction that what thrashed above was food, but the fish was impelled to attack. If what it swallowed was not digestible, it would be regurgitated. The mouth opened, and with a final sweep of the sickle tail the fish struck.

The boy's last—only—thought was that he had been punched in the stomach. The breath was driven from him in a sudden rush. He had no time to cry out. The fish's head drove the raft out of the water. The jaws smashed together, engulfing head, arms, shoulders, trunk, pelvis and most of the raft.

On the beach, the man with the child shouted, "Hey!" He was not sure what he had seen. He had been looking toward the sea, then started to turn his head when an uproar caught his eye. He jerked his head back seaward again, but by then there was nothing to see but the waves made by the splash. "Did you see that?" he cried. "Did you see that?"

"What, Daddy, what?" His child stared up at him, excited.

"Out there! A shark or a whale or something! Something huge!"

He began to run toward the boy's mother, who was half-asleep on her towel. She opened her eyes and squinted at the man. She didn't understand what he was saying, but he was pointing at the water, so she looked out to sea. At first, the fact that she saw nothing didn't strike her as odd. Then she said, "Alex."

BRODY WAS HAVING lunch when the phone rang. Ellen said, "I'll get it," but Brody stood up.

"No, that's O.K.," he said. "It's probably for me anyway."

"Bixby, Chief," said the voice from the station house. "I think you'd better come down here. I've got this hysterical woman on my hands."

"What's she hysterical about?"

"Her kid. Out by the beach."

A twinge of unease shot through Brody's stomach. "What happened?"

"It's . . ." Bixby faltered, then said quickly, "Thursday."

Brody understood. "I'll be right there." He hung up the phone. Fear and guilt and fury blended in a thrust of gut-wrenching pain. He felt at once betrayed and betrayer, a criminal forced into a crime. He had wanted to do the right thing; Larry Vaughan had forced him not to. But if he couldn't stand up to Vaughan, what kind of cop was he? He should have closed the beaches.

"What is it?" asked Ellen.

"A kid just got killed."

"How?"

"By a goddam shark."

"Oh, no! If you had closed the beaches—"

"Yeah, I know."

Meadows was waiting in the parking lot behind the station house when Brody drove up. "So much for the odds," he said.

"Yeah. Who's in there, Harry?"

"A man from *The New York Times*, two from *Newsday*. And the woman. And the man who says he saw it happen."

"How did the newsmen get hold of it?"

"Bad luck. They're staying with people for the weekend. They were onto it within two minutes."

"Do they know about the Watkins thing?"

"I doubt it. They haven't had any digging time."

"They'll get onto it, sooner or later," said Brody.

"I know. It puts me in a rather difficult position."

"*You!* Don't make me laugh."

"Seriously, Martin. If the *Times* prints that Watkins story in tomorrow's paper, along with today's attack, the *Leader* will look like hell. I'll have to use it, to cover myself."

"Who are you going to say hushed it up? Vaughan?"

"I'm not going to say anybody hushed it up. There was no conspiracy. I'm going to talk to Carl Santos. If I can put the right words in his mouth, we may all be spared a lot of grief."

"What about telling the truth? Say that I wanted to close the beaches and warn people, but the selectmen disagreed. And say that because I was too much of a chicken to fight and put my job on the line, I went along with them."

"Come on, Martin, it wasn't your fault. It wasn't anybody's. We took a gamble and lost. That's all there is to it."

"Terrific. Now I'll just go tell the kid's mother that we're terribly sorry we had to use her son for chips."

Brody entered his office through a side door. The boy's mother was sitting in front of the desk, clutching a handkerchief. She was wearing a short robe over her bathing suit. Her feet were bare. Brody looked at her nervously, once again feeling the rush of guilt. He couldn't tell if she was crying, for her eyes were masked by huge, round sunglasses.

A man was standing by the back wall. Brody assumed he was the one who claimed to have witnessed the accident.

Brody had never been adept at consoling people, so he simply introduced himself and started asking questions. The woman said she saw nothing: one moment the boy was there, the next he was gone. Her voice was faint but steady. The man described what he thought he had seen.

"So no one actually saw this shark," Brody said, courting a faint hope in the back of his mind.

"No," said the man. "But what else could it have been?"

"Any number of things." Brody was lying to himself as well as to them, testing to see if he could believe his own lies. "The raft could have gone flat and the boy could have drowned."

"Alex is a good swimmer," the woman protested. "Or . . . was."

"And what about the splash?" said the man.

Brody realized that the exercise was futile. "O.K.," he said. "We'll probably know soon enough, anyway."

"What do you mean?" said the man.

"People who die in the water usually wash up somewhere. If it was a shark, there'll be no mistaking it." The woman's shoulders hunched forward, and Brody cursed himself for being a clumsy fool. "I'm sorry," he said. The woman shook her head and wept.

Telling them both to wait in his office, Brody walked out into the front of the station house. Bixby was at his desk, Meadows by the outer door, leaning against the wall. A young man in a bathing suit and a short-sleeved shirt seemed to be asking him questions.

Two men were sitting on a bench. One wore a bathing suit, the other a blazer and slacks.

"What can I do for you?" Brody said.

The young man next to Meadows took a step forward and said, "I'm Bill Whitman . . . from the *Times*. I was on the beach."

"What did you see?"

One of the others—presumably from *Newsday*—answered.

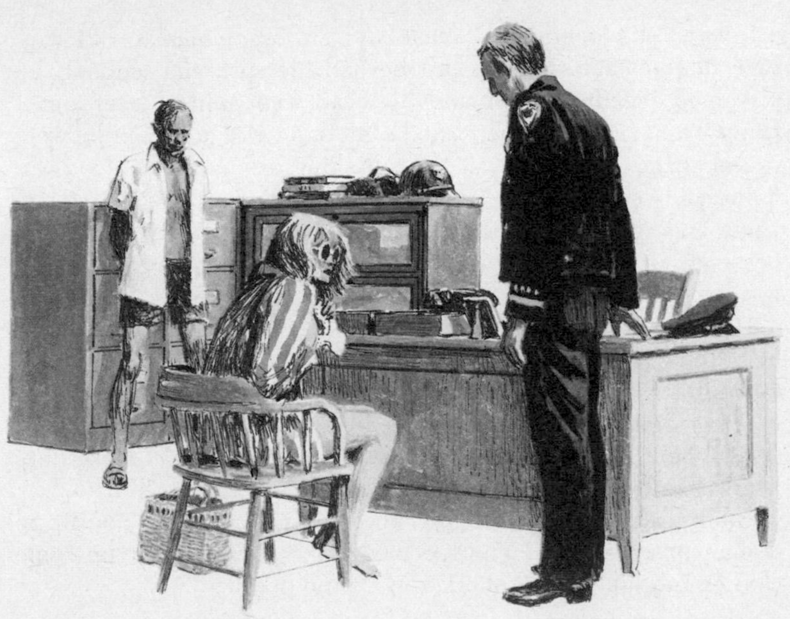

"Nothing. I was there, too. Nobody saw anything. Except maybe the guy in your office."

The *Times* man said, "Are you prepared to list this as a shark attack?"

"I'm not prepared to list this as anything, and I'd suggest you don't either, until you know a lot more about it."

The *Times* man smiled. "Come on, Chief, what do you want us to do? Call it a mysterious disappearance? Boy lost at sea?"

Brody said, "Listen, Mr. Whitman. We have no witnesses who saw anything but a splash. The man inside thinks he saw a shark, but he says he has never previously seen a live shark, so that's not what you'd call expert testimony. We have no body—"

Brody stopped at the sound of tires grinding on gravel. A car door slammed, and Hendricks charged into the station house, wearing a bathing suit. "Chief, there's been another attack," he said.

The *Times* man quickly asked, "When was the first one?'

Before Hendricks could answer, Brody said, "We were just discussing it, Leonard. I don't want you or anyone else jumping to conclusions. After all, the boy could have drowned."

"Boy?" said Hendricks. "What boy? This was a man, an old man. Five minutes ago. He was just beyond the surf, and suddenly he screamed bloody murder and his head went under water and it came up again and he screamed something else and then he went down again. There was all this splashing around, and blood was flying all over the place. The fish kept coming back and hitting him again and again. That's the biggest fish I ever saw in my whole life, big as a station wagon. I went in and tried to get to the guy, but the fish kept hitting him."

Hendricks paused, staring at the floor. His breath squeezed out of his chest in short bursts. "Then the fish quit," he said. "Maybe it went away, I don't know. I waded out to where the guy was floating. His face was in the water. I took hold of one of his arms and pulled. . . . It came off in my hand." Hendricks looked up, his eyes red and filling with tears of exhaustion and fright.

Brody said, "Bixby, call the hospital. Leonard, are you up to doing some work?" Hendricks nodded. "Then go put on some clothes and find some notices to close the beaches."

WHEN BRODY arrived at the office on Monday morning a copy of *The New York Times* lay in the center of his desk. About three-quarters of the way down the righthand side of page one, he saw the headline and began to read:

SHARK KILLS TWO ON LONG ISLAND

by WILLIAM F. WHITMAN

Special to The New York Times

AMITY, L.I., June 20—A six-year-old boy and a 65-year-old man were killed today in separate shark attacks within an hour of each other near the beaches of this resort community.

Although the body of the boy, Alexander Kintner, was not found, officials said there was no question that he was killed by a shark. A witness, Thomas Daguerre, of New York, said he saw a large silver-colored object rise out of the water and seize the boy and his rubber raft and disappear with a splash. Amity coroner Carl Santos reported that traces of blood found on shreds of rubber later recovered left no doubt that the boy had died a violent death.

At least 15 persons witnessed the attack on Morris Cater, 65, which took place at approximately 2 p.m. a quarter of a mile down the beach from where young Kintner was attacked. Mr. Cater called out for help, but all attempts to rescue him were in vain.

These incidents are the first documented cases of shark attacks on bathers on the eastern seaboard in more than two decades.

According to Dr. David Dieter, an ichthyologist at the New York Aquarium at Coney Island, it is logical to assume—but by no means a certainty—that both attacks were the work of one shark.

Dr. Dieter said the shark was probably a "great white" (*Caracharodon carcharias*), a species known throughout the world for its voraciousness and aggressiveness.

In 1916, he said, a great white killed four bathers in New Jersey on one day—the only other recorded instance of multiple shark-attack fatalities in the United States in this century.

Brody finished reading the article and put down the paper. There were three people dead now, and two of them could still be alive, if only Brody had. . . .

Meadows was standing in the doorway. "You've seen the *Times*," he said.

"Yeah, I've seen it. They didn't pick up the Watkins thing."

"I know. Kind of curious, especially after Leonard's little slip of the tongue."

"But you did use it."

"I had to. Here." Meadows handed Brody a copy of the Amity *Leader*. The banner headline ran across all six columns of page one: TWO KILLED BY MONSTER SHARK OFF AMITY BEACH. Below that, in smaller type, a subhead: Number of Victims of Killer Fish Rises to Three.

The victims were Alexander Kintner, age 6, who lived with his mother in the Goose Neck Lane house owned by Mr. and Mrs. Richard Packer, and Morris Cater, 65, who was spending the weekend in Amity. Patrolman Leonard Hendricks made a valiant attempt to rescue the struggling Mr. Cater, but the fish gave no quarter. Mr. Cater was dead by the time he was pulled clear of the water.

The *Leader*'s account of the killings ended:

Last Wednesday night, Miss Christine Watkins, a guest of Mr. and Mrs. John Foote of Old Mill Road, went for a swim and vanished.

Thursday morning, Police Chief Martin Brody and Officer Hendricks recovered her body. According to coroner Carl Santos, the cause of death was "definitely and incontrovertibly shark attack."

Asked why the cause of death was not made public, Mr. Santos declined to comment.

Brody looked up from the paper and said, "What about the beaches not being closed? Did you go into that?"

"You did."

"*I* did?"

"Read on."

Asked why he had not ordered the beaches closed until the marauding shark was apprehended, Chief Brody said, "The Atlantic Ocean is huge. Fish don't always stay in one area, especially an area like this where there is no food source. What were we going to do? Close the Amity beaches, and people would just drive up to East Hampton and go swimming there. And there's just as good a chance that they'd get killed in East Hampton as in Amity."

After yesterday's attacks, however, Chief Brody did order the beaches closed until further notice.

"My God, Harry," said Brody. "You really put it to me. You've got me arguing a case I don't believe, then being proved wrong and *forced* to do what I wanted to all along. That's a dirty trick."

"It wasn't a trick. I had to have someone give the official line. I tried to get hold of Larry Vaughan, but he was away for the weekend. So you were the logical one. You agreed to go along with the decision, so—reluctantly or not—you supported it."

"I suppose. Anyway, it's done. Is there anything else I should read in this?"

"No. I just quote Matt Hooper, that fellow from Woods Hole. He says it would be remarkable if we ever have another attack. But he's a little less sure than he was the last time."

"Does he think one fish is doing all this?"

"He doesn't know, of course, but offhand, yes. He thinks it's a big white."

"I do, too. I mean, I think it's one shark."

"Why?"

"Yesterday afternoon I called the Coast Guard. I asked them if they'd noticed a lot of sharks around here recently, and they said they hadn't seen a one so far this spring but they'd send a boat down this way and let me know if they saw anything. I finally called them back. They said they'd cruised up and down this area for two hours and hadn't seen a thing. So there sure aren't many sharks around."

"Hooper said there was one thing we could do," Meadows said. "We could spread fish guts around in the water. If there's a shark around, he said, that will bring him running."

"Oh, great. And what if he shows up? What do we do then?"

"Harpoon him."

"Harry, I don't even have a police boat, let alone a boat with harpoons on it."

"There are fishermen around. It seems to me—" A commotion out in the hall stopped Meadows in mid-sentence.

They heard Bixby say, "I told you, ma'am, he's in conference."

Then a woman's voice said, "I don't care what he's doing. I'm going in there."

The door flew open, and standing there clutching a newspaper, tears streaming down her face, was Alexander Kintner's mother.

Meadows stood and offered her his chair, but she ignored him, walked up to Brody, and slapped the newspaper across his face. It made a sharp report that rang deep in his left ear.

"What about this?" Mrs. Kintner screamed. "What about it?"

"What about what?" said Brody.

"What they say here. That you knew it was dangerous to swim. That somebody had already been killed by that shark. That you kept it a secret."

Brody couldn't deny it. "Sort of," he said. "I mean yes, it's true, but it's. . . . Look, Mrs. Kintner—"

"You killed Alex!" She shrieked the words, and Brody was sure they were heard all over Amity. He was sure his wife heard them, and his children.

He thought, Stop her before she says anything else. But all he could say was, "Sssshhh!"

"You did! You killed him!" Her fists were clenched at her sides, and her head snapped forward as she screamed, "You won't get away with it!"

"Please, Mrs. Kintner," said Brody. "Calm down. Let me explain." He reached to touch her shoulder and help her to a chair, but she jerked away.

"Keep your hands off me!" she cried. "You knew. You knew all along, but you wouldn't say. And now a six-year-old boy, a beautiful six-year-old boy, my boy. . . ." Tears seemed to pulse from her eyes. "You knew! Why didn't you tell? Why?"

"Because we didn't think it could happen again." Brody was surprised by his brevity. That was it, really, wasn't it?

The woman was silent for a moment, letting the words register in her muddled mind. She said, "Oh," then slumped into the chair next to Meadows and began to weep in gasping, choking sobs.

Meadows tried to calm her, but she didn't hear him. She didn't hear Brody tell Bixby to call a doctor. And she saw, heard and felt nothing when the doctor came into the office, gave her a sedative, led her to his car and drove her to the hospital.

When she had left, Brody said, "I could use a drink."

"I have some bourbon in my office," said Meadows.

Brody smiled, "No. If this was any indication of how the day's going to go, I better not louse up my head."

The phone rang. It was answered in the other room, and a voice on the intercom said, "It's Mr. Vaughan."

Brody pushed the lighted button, picked up the receiver and said, "Hi, Larry. Did you have a nice weekend?"

"Until about eleven o'clock last night," said Vaughan, "when I turned on my car radio driving home. I was tempted to call you, but I figured you had had a rough enough day without being bothered at that hour."

"That's one decision I agree with."

"Don't rub it in, Martin. I feel bad enough."

Brody wanted to scrape the wound raw, to unload some of the anguish onto someone else, but he knew it was impossible, so all he said was, "Sure."

"I had two cancellations already this morning. Big leases. Good people. I'm scared to answer the phone."

"I wish I could tell you different, Larry, but it's going to get worse."

"What do you mean?"

"With the beaches closed."

"How long do you think you'll have to keep them closed?"

"I don't know. As long as it takes. A few days. Maybe more."

"You know that the end of next week is the Fourth of July."

"Sure, I know."

"It's already too late to hope for a good summer, but we may be able to salvage something—if the Fourth is good."

Brody couldn't read the tone in Vaughan's voice. "Are you arguing with me, Larry?"

"No. I guess I was thinking out loud. Anyway, you plan to keep the beaches closed until when? Indefinitely?"

"I haven't had time to think that far ahead. Let me ask you something Larry. Just out of curiosity."

"What?"

"Who are your partners?"

It was a long moment before Vaughan said, "Why do you want to know? What does that have to do with anything?"

"Like I said, just curiosity. No offense."

"You keep your curiosity for your job, Martin. What are you going to do? We can't just sit around and hope the thing will go away."

"I know. A fish expert, friend of Harry's, says we could try to catch the fish. What would you think about getting up a couple of hundred dollars to charter Ben Gardner's boat for a day or two? I don't know that he's ever caught any sharks, but it might be worth a try."

"Anything's worth a try, just so we get rid of that thing and go back to making a living. Go ahead. Tell him I'll get the money from somewhere."

Brody hung up the phone and said to Meadows, "I'd give a lot to know more about Mr. Vaughan's business affairs."

"Why?"

"He's a very rich man. No matter how long this shark thing goes on, he won't be badly hurt. But he's taking all this as if it was life and death—and I don't mean just the town's. His."

4

Thursday afternoon Brody sat on the public beach, his elbows resting on his knees to steady the binoculars in his hands. When he lowered the glasses, he could barely see the boat—a white speck that disappeared and reappeared in the ocean swells.

"Hey, Chief," Hendricks said, walking up to Brody. "I was just passing by and I saw your car. What are you doing?"

"Trying to figure out what the hell Ben Gardner's doing."

"Fishing, don't you think?"

"That's what he's being paid to do, but I haven't seen anything move on that boat in an hour."

"Can I take a look?" Brody handed him the glasses. Hendricks raised them and looked out to sea. "Nope, you're right. How long has he been out there?"

"All day, I think. He said he'd be taking off at six this morning."

"You want to go see? We've got at least two more hours of daylight. I'll borrow Chickering's boat."

Brody felt a shimmy of fear skitter up his back. He was a very poor swimmer, and the prospect of being on top of deep water—let alone in it—gave him what his mother used to call the whim-whams: sweaty palms, a persistent need to swallow and an ache in his stomach. "O.K.," he said, "I guess we should. Maybe by the time we get to the dock he'll already have started in. You go get the boat ready. I'll see if he's given his wife a call on the radio."

Amity's town dock was in a little inlet protected from the open sea by a stone jetty. Hendricks was standing in Chickering's Aqua-Sport, the engine running, when Brody came along the pier and climbed down into the boat.

"What did she say?" asked Hendricks.

"She hasn't heard a word. She's been trying to raise him for half an hour, but she figures he must have turned off the radio."

"Is he alone?"

"As far as she knows. His mate had an impacted wisdom tooth that had to be taken out today."

Hendricks cast off the hawser at the bow, walked to the stern, uncleated the stern line and tossed it onto the deck. He moved to the control console and pushed a knobbed handle forward. The boat lurched ahead, chugging. Hendricks pushed the handle farther forward, and the stern settled back, the bow rose.

Brody grabbed a steel handle on the side of the console. "Are there any lifejackets in this thing?" he asked.

"Just the cushions," said Hendricks. "They'd hold you up all right, if you were an eight-year-old boy."

"Thanks."

The breeze died, but there were small swells, and the boat took them roughly, smacking its prow into each one, recovering with a shudder that unnerved Brody. "This thing's gonna break apart if you don't slow down," he said.

Hendricks smiled. "No worry, Chief. If I slow down, it'll take us a week to get out there."

Gardner's boat, *Flicka*, was anchored in deep water about three-quarters of a mile from shore, its stern toward them. Fifty yards from it, Hendricks throttled down, and the boat settled into a slow roll. They saw no signs of life. There were no rods in the rod holders. "Hey, Ben!" Brody called. There was no reply.

"Maybe he's below," said Hendricks.

When the bow of the AquaSport was only a few feet from the *Flicka*'s port quarter, Hendricks pushed the handle into neutral, then gave it a quick burst of reverse. The AquaSport stopped and, on the next swell, Brody grabbed the gunwale.

Hendricks made a line fast to the other boat, then both men climbed into the *Flicka*'s cockpit. Brody poked his head through the forward hatch. "You in there, Ben?" He looked around, then withdrew his head. "He's not on board. No two ways about it."

"What's that stuff?" said Hendricks, pointing to a bucket in the stern.

Brody walked to the bucket and bent down. A stench of fish and oil filled his nose. "Must be chum—fish guts," he said. "You spread it around in the water and it's supposed to attract sharks. He didn't use much of it. The bucket's almost full."

Suddenly a voice crackled over the radio. "This is the *Pretty Belle*. You there, Jake?"

"He never turned off his radio," said Brody.

"I don't get it, Chief. He didn't carry a dinghy, so he couldn't have rowed away. He swam like a fish, so if he fell overboard he would've just climbed back on."

Brody was standing at the starboard gunwale when the boat moved slightly, and he steadied himself with his right hand. He felt something strange, and looked down. There were four ragged screw holes where a cleat had been. The wood around the holes was torn.

"Look at this, Leonard," he said.

Hendricks ran his hand over the holes. He looked to the port side, where a ten-inch cleat still sat securely on the wood. "What would it take to pull a thing as big as that out?" he said.

Brody walked to the stern and leaned on his elbows on the gunwale. As he gazed down at the transom a pattern began to take shape, a pattern of holes, deep gouges in the wood, forming a rough semi-circle more than three feet across. Next to it was another, similar pattern. And at the bottom of the transom, just at the waterline, were three short smears of blood. Please, God, thought Brody, not another one. "Come here, Leonard," he said.

Hendricks walked to the stern and looked over. "What?"

"If I hold your legs, you think you can lean over and take a look at those holes and try to figure out what made them?"

"I guess so." Hendricks lay on the top of the transom. Brody took one of his legs under each arm and lifted.

"O.K.?" said Brody.

"A little more. That's it." Hendricks began to examine the holes. "O.K.," he said. "Pull me up. I need my pocketknife."

"What is it?" Brody asked when Hendricks was back aboard.

"There's a white chip or something stuck into one of the holes," Hendricks replied. Knife in hand, he allowed himself to be lowered over the rail again. He worked briefly, his body twisting from the effort. Then he called, "O.K. I've got it. Pull."

Brody hoisted Hendricks over the transom. "Let's see," he said, and Hendricks dropped a triangle of glistening white denticle into his hand. It was nearly two inches long. The sides were tiny saws. Brody scraped the tooth against the gunwale, and it cut the wood.

"It's a tooth, isn't it?" said Hendricks. "My God! You think the shark got Ben?"

"I don't know what else to think," said Brody. He dropped the tooth into his pocket. "We might as well go. There's nothing we can do here."

"What do you want to do with Ben's boat?"

"It's getting dark. We'll leave it here. No one's going to need this boat before tomorrow, especially not Ben Gardner."

They arrived at the dock in late twilight. Harry Meadows and another man were waiting for them. As Brody climbed the ladder onto the dock Meadows gestured toward the man beside him. "This is Matt Hooper. Matt Hooper, Chief Brody."

The two men shook hands. "You're the fellow from Woods Hole," Brody said, trying to get a good look at him. He was young—in his mid-twenties, Brody thought—and handsome: tanned, his hair bleached by the sun. He was about as tall as Brody, but leaner.

"That's right," said Hooper.

Meadows said, "I called him. I thought he might be able to figure out what's going on."

Brody sensed resentment in himself at the intrusion, the implicit division of authority that Hooper's arrival had created. And he recognized the resentment as stupid. "Sure, Harry," he said.

"What did you find out there?" Meadows asked.

"I'm not sure," he said. "Come on back to the station house and I'll fill you in."

"Is Ben going to stay out there all night?"

"It looks that way, Harry." Brody turned to Hendricks, who had finished tying up the boat. "You going home, Leonard?"

"Yeah. I want to clean up before I go to work."

Brody arrived at police headquarters before Meadows and Hooper. He had a phone call to make, a call he dreaded. He checked the phone book for the Gardner number, and dialed it.

"Sally? This is Martin Brody." Suddenly he regretted having called without thinking about what he should tell her.

"Where's Ben, Martin?" The voice was calm, but pitched slightly higher than normal.

"I don't know, Sally. He wasn't on the boat."

"You looked all over it? How could he not be there?" The voice was shriller now.

Brody wished he had gone to the house in person. "Are you alone, Sally?"

"No. The kids are here."

Brody dug at his memory for the ages of the Gardner children. Twelve, maybe; then nine, then about six. Who was the nearest neighbor? The Finleys. "Just a second, Sally." He called to the officer at the front desk. "Clements, call Grace Finley and tell her to get over to Sally Gardner's house. Tell her I'll explain later." As he turned back to the phone Meadows and Hooper walked into the office. He motioned them to chairs.

"But where could he be?" said Sally Gardner. "You don't just get off a boat in the middle of the ocean."

"No."

"Maybe someone came and took him off in another boat. Maybe the engine wouldn't start. Did you check the engine?"

"No," Brody said, embarrassed.

"That's probably it, then." The voice was subtly lighter, almost girlish, coated with a veneer of hope that, when it broke, would shatter like iced crystal. "And if the battery was dead, that would explain why he couldn't call on the radio."

"The radio was working, Sally."

"Wait a minute. . . . Who's there? Oh, it's you." Brody heard Sally talking to Grace Finley. Then Sally came back on the line. "Grace says you told her to come over here. Why?"

"I thought. . . ."

"You think he's dead, don't you?" She began to sob.

"I'm afraid so, Sally. That's all we can think at the moment. Let me talk to Grace, will you please?"

A couple of seconds later, the voice of Grace Finley said, "Yes, Martin?"

"Can you stay with her for a while?"

"Yes. All night."

"That might be a good idea. I'll try to get over later on."

"Is it that . . . *thing* again?"

"Maybe. That's what we're trying to figure out." He replaced the phone and looked at Meadows. "You heard."

"I gather that Ben Gardner has become victim number four."

Brody nodded. "I think so." He told Meadows and Hooper about his trip with Hendricks. Once or twice Meadows interrupted with a question. Hooper listened, his angular face placid and his eyes—

a light, powder blue—fixed on Brody. At the end of his tale Brody reached into his pocket. "We found this," he said. "Leonard dug it out of the wood." He flipped the tooth to Hooper, who turned it over in his hand.

"It's a white," he said.

"How big?"

"Fifteen, twenty feet. That's some fantastic fish." He looked at Meadows. "Thanks for calling me. I could spend a whole lifetime around sharks and never see a fish like that."

Brody asked, "How much would a fish like that weigh?"

"Five or six thousand pounds."

Brody whistled. "Three tons."

"Do you have any thoughts about what happened?" Meadows asked.

"From what the Chief says, it sounds like the fish killed Mr. Gardner."

"How?" said Brody.

"Any number of ways. Gardner might have fallen overboard. More likely, he was pulled over. His leg may have gotten tangled in a harpoon line. He could even have been taken while he was leaning over the stern."

"How do you account for the teeth in the stern?"

"The fish attacked the boat."

"What the hell for?"

"Sharks aren't very bright, Chief. They exist on instinct and impulse. The impulse to feed is powerful."

"But a thirty-foot boat—"

"To him it wasn't a boat. It was just something large."

"And inedible."

"Not till he'd tried it. You have to understand. There's nothing in the sea this fish would fear. Other fish run from bigger things. That's their instinct. But this fish doesn't run from anything."

"Do you have any idea why he's hung around so long?" said Brody. "I don't know how much you know about these waters—"

"I grew up here."

"You did? In Amity?"

"No, Southampton. I spent all my summers there."

"*Summers.* So you didn't really grow up there." Brody was

groping for something with which to re-establish his parity with, if not superiority to, the younger man, and what he settled for was reverse snobbism, an attitude not uncommon to year-round residents of resort communities. It gave them armor against the contempt they sensed radiating from the rich summer folk. It was an attitude that, in general, Brody found both repugnant and silly. But he felt somehow threatened by the younger man.

"O.K.," Hooper said testily, "so I wasn't born here. But I've spent a lot of time in these waters, and I wrote a paper on this coastline. Anyway, you're right. This isn't an environment that would normally support a long stay by a shark. On the other hand, anyone who'd risk money—not to mention his life—on a prediction about what a shark will do is a fool. There are things that could cause him to stay here—natural factors, caprices."

"Like what?"

"Changes in water temperature or current flow or feeding patterns. As food supplies move, so do the predators. Two summers ago, for example, a completely inexplicable phenomenon took place off Connecticut. The coastline was suddenly inundated with menhaden. They coated the water like an oil slick. Bluefish and bass feed on menhaden, so all of a sudden there were masses of bluefish right off the beaches. People were wading in and catching them with garden rakes. Then the big predators came—tunafish, four, five, six hundred pounds. Deep-sea fishing boats were catching bluefish tuna within a hundred yards of the shore. Then suddenly it stopped. The menhaden went away, and so did the other fish. I spent three weeks up there trying to figure out what was going on. I still don't know."

"But this fish has stayed in one chunk of water only a mile or two square for over a week. He hasn't touched anybody in East Hampton or Southampton. What is it about Amity?"

"I don't know. I doubt that anyone could give you an answer."

Meadows said, "Minnie Eldridge has the answer."

"Who's Minnie Eldridge?" asked Hooper.

"The postmistress," said Brody. "She says it's God's will, or something like that. We're being punished for our sins."

Hooper smiled. "Right now, anyway, that's as good an answer as I've got."

"That's encouraging," said Brody. "Is there anything you plan to do to *get* an answer?"

"A few things. I'll take water samples here and in East Hampton. I'll try to find out how other fish are behaving—and I'll try to find that shark. Which reminds me, is there a boat available?"

"Yes, I'm sorry to say," said Brody. "Ben Gardner's. Do you really think you can catch that fish, after what happened to him?"

"I.don't think I'd want to try to catch it. Not alone, anyway."

Brody looked into Hooper's eyes and said, "I want that fish killed. If you can't do it, we'll find someone who can."

Hooper laughed. "You sound like a mobster. 'I want that fish killed.' Look, Chief, that shark isn't evil. It's just obeying its instincts. Trying to get retribution against a fish is crazy."

"Listen, you. . . ." Brody was growing angry—an anger born of frustration and humiliation. He knew Hooper was right, but he felt that right and wrong were irrelevant to the situation. The fish was an enemy. It had come upon the community and killed two men, a woman and a child. The people of Amity would demand the death of the fish. They would need to see it dead before they could feel secure enough to resume their normal lives. Most of all, Brody needed it dead, for the death of the fish would be a catharsis for him. But he swallowed his rage and said, "Forget it."

The phone rang. "It's for you, Chief," said Clements. "Mr. Vaughan."

"Oh swell. That's just what I need." He picked up the receiver. "Yeah, Larry."

"Hello, Martin. How are you?" Vaughan was friendly, almost effusive, Brody thought. He's probably had a couple of drinks.

"As well as can be expected, Larry."

"I heard about Ben Gardner. Are you sure it was the shark?"

"Yeah, I guess so. Nothing else seems to make any sense."

"Martin, what are we going to *do?* I'm getting cancellations every day. I haven't had a new customer in here since Sunday."

"So what do you want *me* to do?"

"Well, I thought . . . I mean, what I'm wondering is, maybe we're over-reacting to this whole thing."

"You're kidding. Tell me you're kidding."

There was a moment of silence, then Vaughan said, "What

would you say to opening the beaches, just for the Fourth of July weekend?"

"Not a chance."

"Now listen—"

"No, you listen, Larry. The last time I listened to you we had two people killed. If we catch that fish, if we kill him, then we'll open the beaches. Until then, forget it. What is it with you, anyway? Are your partners on you again?"

"That's none of your business, Martin. For God's sake, man, this town is dying!"

"I know it, Larry," Brody said softly. "And as far as I know, there's not a damn thing we can do about it. Good night." He hung up the phone.

Meadows and Hooper rose to leave. Brody walked them to the front door of the station house. As they started out, Brody said to Meadows, "Hey, Harry, you left your lighter inside. Come on back and I'll give it to you." He waved to Hooper. "See you."

When they were back in Brody's office Meadows took his lighter from his pocket and said, "I trust you had something to say."

Brody shut the door. "You think you can find out something about Larry's partners?"

"I guess so. Why?"

"Ever since this thing began Larry has been after me to keep the beaches open. And now, after all that's just happened, he says he wants them open for the Fourth. The other day he said he was under heavy pressure from his partners. I told you about it."

"And?"

"I think we should know who it is who has enough clout to drive Larry crazy. He's the mayor of this town, and if there are people telling him what to do, I want to know who they are."

Meadows sighed. "O.K., Martin. I'll do what I can. But digging around Larry Vaughan's affairs isn't my idea of fun."

Brody walked Meadows to the door, then went back to his desk and sat down. Vaughan had been right about one thing, he thought: Amity was showing all the signs of imminent death. And it wasn't just the real estate market.

Two new boutiques that had been scheduled to open the next day had had to put off their debuts until July third. The sporting-goods store had advertised a clearance sale—a sale that normally took place in September. The only good thing about the Amity economy, as far as Brody was concerned, was that Saxon's was doing so badly that it had laid off Henry Kimble. Now that he didn't have his bartending job, he could occasionally survive through a shift of police work without a nap.

Beginning on Monday morning—the first day the beaches had been closed—Brody had posted two officers on the beaches, Since then there had been four reports of shark sightings by members of the public. One had turned out to be a floating log. Two were schools of jumping bait fish. And one, as far as anyone could tell, was a flat nothing.

On Tuesday evening at dusk Brody had received an anonymous phone call telling him that a man was dumping shark bait into the water off the public beach. It turned out to be not a man, but a woman in a man's raincoat—Jessie Parker, one of the clerks at Walden's Stationery Store. She admitted she had tossed a paper bag into the surf. It contained three empty vermouth bottles.

"Why didn't you throw them in the garbage?" Brody had asked.

"I didn't want the garbage man to think I'm a heavy drinker."

"Then why didn't you throw them in someone else's garbage?"

"That wouldn't be nice," she had said. "Garbage is . . . sort of private, don't you think?"

Brody looked at his watch. It was after nine. Before he left the office he called the Coast Guard station at Montauk and told the duty officer about Ben Gardner. The officer said he would dispatch a patrol boat at first light to search for the body.

"Thanks," said Brody. "I hope you find it before it washes up." He was suddenly appalled at himself. "It" was Ben Gardner, a friend.

"We'll try," said the officer. "Boy, I feel for you guys. You're having some summer."

"I only hope it isn't our last," said Brody. He hung up, turned out the light in his office and walked out to his car.

AS HE TURNED INTO his driveway Brody saw the familiar blue-gray light of television shining from the windows. He walked through the front door and poked his head into the living room. His oldest boy, Bill, fourteen, lay on the couch. Martin, the middle son, age twelve, lounged in an easy chair, his shoeless feet propped up on the coffee table. Nine-year-old Sean sat on the floor, his back against the couch. "How goes it?" said Brody.

"Good, Dad," said Bill, without shifting his gaze from the set.

"Where's your mom?"

"Upstairs. She said to tell you your dinner's in the kitchen."

"O.K. Not too late, Sean, huh? It's almost nine-thirty."

Brody went into the kitchen, and got a beer from the refrigerator. The remains of a pot roast sat on the table in a roasting pan. He sliced a thick slab of meat and made himself a sandwich. He put it on a plate, picked up his beer and climbed the stairs to his bedroom.

Ellen was sitting up in bed, reading a magazine. "Hello," she said. "A tough day?"

"You heard about Ben Gardner?" He put the plate and the beer on the dresser and sat down to remove his shoes.

"Yes. I got a call from Grace Finley asking if I knew where Dr. Craig was. She wanted to give Sally a sedative."

"Did you find him?"

"No. But I had one of the boys take some Seconal over to her."

"I didn't know you were taking sleeping pills."

"I don't often. Just every now and then."

"Where did you get them?"

"From Dr. Craig, when I went to him last time about my nerves. I told you."

"Oh." Brody began to eat his sandwich.

Ellen said, "It's so horrible about Ben. What do you think Sally will do?"

"I don't know," said Brody. "Have you ever talked money with her?"

"There can't be much. She's always saying she'd give anything to be able to afford meat more than once a week, instead of having to eat the fish Ben catches. Will she get Social Security?"

"I'd think so, but it won't amount to much. There may be something the town can do. I'll talk to Vaughan about it."

"Have you made any progress?"

"You mean about catching that damn thing? No. Meadows called that friend of his down from Woods Hole, so he's here."

"What's he like?"

"He's all right, I guess. He seems to know the area pretty well. As a kid he spent his summers in Southampton."

"Working?"

"I don't know, living with his parents probably." He finished his sandwich in silence, as Ellen aimlessly turned the pages of her magazine.

"You know," she said, "I think we should give the boys tennis lessons."

"What for? Have they said they want to play?" Brody rose, took off his shirt and trousers, and began to get ready for bed.

"No. Not in so many words. But it's a good sport for them to know. It will help them when they're grown up."

"Where are they going to get lessons?"

"I was thinking of the Field Club. I think we could get in. I still know a few members."

"Forget it."

"Why?"

"Number one, we can't afford it. I bet it costs a thousand bucks to join, and then it's at least a few hundred a year."

"We have savings."

"Not for tennis lessons! Come on, let's drop it." He walked to thc dresser to turn out the light.

"It would be good for the boys."

Brody let his hand fall to the top of the dresser. "Look, we're not tennis people. We wouldn't feel right there. *I* wouldn't feel right there." He switched off the light, walked over to the bed and slid in next to Ellen. "Besides," he said, nuzzling her neck, "there's another sport I'm better at."

Ellen yawned. "I'm so sleepy," she said. "I took a pill before you came home."

"What for?" Brody asked.

"I didn't sleep well last night, and I didn't want to wake up if you came home late."

"I'm going to throw those pills away." Brody turned onto his back and lay staring at the ceiling.

In a moment Ellen said, "What's Harry's friend's name?"

"Hooper."

"Not David Hooper?"

"No. I think his name is Matt."

"Oh. I went out with a David Hooper a long, long time ago. I remember. . . ." Before she could finish the sentence her eyes shut, and soon she slipped into the deep breathing of sleep.

Part Two

5

On her way home on Friday, after a morning of volunteer work at Southampton Hospital, Ellen stopped at the post office to get some stamps from Minnie Eldridge.

It was generally assumed that Minnie Eldridge was in her early seventies and that she had somehow convinced the authorities that she was well under compulsory retirement age. She was small and frail-looking, but able to hustle packages and cartons nearly as quickly as the two young men who worked with her. Ellen sensed that Minnie didn't like her, and she was right. Minnie felt uneasy with Ellen because she was neither summer folk nor winter folk.

Minnie was sorting mail when Ellen arrived.

"Morning, Minnie," Ellen said.

Minnie looked up at the clock and said, "Afternoon."

"Could I have a roll of eights, please?" Ellen put a five-dollar bill and three ones on the counter.

Minnie gave Ellen a roll of stamps and dropped the bills into a drawer.

"What's Martin going to do about that shark?" she said.

"I don't know. I guess they'll try to catch it."

"*Canst thou draw out leviathan with an hook?*"

"I beg your pardon?"

"Book of Job," said Minnie. "No mortal man's going to catch that fish."

"Why do you say that?"

"We're not meant to catch it, that's why. We're being readied."

"For what?"

"We'll know when the time comes."

"I see." Ellen put the stamps in her purse. "Well, maybe you're right. Thanks, Minnie."

Ellen walked to Main Street and turned right, past a boutique and an antique shop. She stopped at Amity Hardware and went inside. There was no immediate response to the tinkle of the bell as she opened the door.

She walked to the back of the store, to an open door that led to the basement. She heard two men talking below.

"I'll be right up," called the voice of Albert Morris. "Here's a whole box of them," Morris said to the other man. "Look through and see if you find what you want."

"Cleats," Morris said as he climbed to the top of the stairs.

"What?" said Ellen.

"Cleats. Fella wants cleats for a boat. Size he's looking for, he must be captain of a battleship. What can I do for you?"

"I want a rubber nozzle for my kitchen sink."

"They're up this way." Morris led Ellen to a cabinet in the middle of the store. "This what you had in mind?" He held up a rubber nozzle.

"Perfect."

As he rang up the sale Morris said, "Lots of people upset about this shark thing. Maybe this fish expert can help us out."

"Oh, yes. I heard he was in town."

"He's down cellar. He's the one wants the cleats."

Just then Ellen heard footsteps on the stairs. She saw Hooper coming through the door and felt a surge of girlish nervousness, as if she were seeing a beau she hadn't seen in years.

"I found them," said Hooper, holding up two large stainless-steel cleats. He walked over to the counter, smiled politely at Ellen and said to Morris, "These'll do fine." He handed Morris a twenty-dollar bill.

Ellen hoped Albert Morris would introduce them, but he seemed to have no intention of doing so. "Excuse me," she said to Hooper, "but I have to ask you something."

Hooper looked at her and smiled again—a pleasant, friendly smile.

"Sure," he said. "Ask away."

"You aren't by any chance related to David Hooper, are you?"

"He's my older brother. Do you know David?"

"Yes," said Ellen. "Or rather, I used to. I went out with him a long time ago. I'm Ellen Brody. I used to be Ellen Shepherd."

"Oh, sure. I remember you."

"You don't."

"I do. No kidding. Let me see. . . . You wore your hair shorter then, sort of a pageboy. You always wore a charm bracelet. I remember that because it had a big charm that looked like the Eiffel Tower, right?"

Ellen laughed. "My heavens, you have quite a memory."

"It's screwy the things that impress kids. You went out with David for what—two years?"

"Two summers," Ellen said. "They were fun."

"Do you remember me?"

"Vaguely. You must have been about nine or ten then."

"About that; David's ten years older than I am. Another thing I remember: everybody called me Matt, but you called me Matthew. You said it sounded more dignified. I was probably in love with you."

"Oh?" Ellen reddened, and Albert Morris laughed.

Morris handed Hooper his change, and Hooper said to Ellen, "I'm going down to the dock. Can I drop you anywhere?"

"Thank you. I have a car. So now you're a scientist," she said as they walked out together.

"Kind of by accident. I once took a course in marine biology, and —bingo!—I got hooked on sharks."

Ellen laughed. "It's like having a passion for rats."

"That's what most people think," said Hooper. "But they're wrong. Sharks are beautiful. They're like an impossibly perfect piece of machinery. They're as graceful as any bird. They're as mysterious as any animal on earth. No one knows for sure how long they live or what impulses—except for hunger—they respond to." He stopped, looked at Ellen, and smiled. "I'm sorry. I don't mean to lecture."

"You must be the world's greatest living shark expert."

"Hardly," Hooper said with a laugh. "But after graduate school I spent a couple of years chasing sharks around the world. I tagged them in the Red Sea and dove with them off Australia."

"You dove with them?"

Hooper nodded. "In a cage mostly, but sometimes not. If you know what you're doing, you can reduce the danger to almost nil. The one trip I missed out on, the one I would have given anything to go on, was Peter Gimbel's trip. It was made into a movie. I dream about that trip. They were in the water with two great whites, the same kind of shark that's here now."

"I'm just as glad you didn't go on that trip," said Ellen. "But tell me about David. How is he?"

"He's O.K., all things considered. He's a broker in San Francisco."

"What do you mean, 'all things considered'?"

"Well, he's been married twice. His first wife was—maybe you know this—Patty Fremont."

"Sure. I used to play tennis with her. She sort of inherited David from me. That's a nice way of putting it."

"That lasted three years, until she latched onto someone else. So David found himself a girl whose father owns most of an oil company. She's nice, but she's got the IQ of an artichoke. If David had had any sense he would have held on to you."

Ellen blushed and said softly, "You're nice to say it."

"I'm serious. That's what I'd have done."

"What did you do? What lucky girl finally got you?"

"None, so far. I guess there are girls around who just don't know how lucky they could be." Hooper laughed. "Tell me about yourself. No, don't. Let me guess. Three children. Right?"

"Right. I didn't realize it showed that much."

"No, no. I don't mean that. It doesn't show at all. Not at all. Your husband is—let's see—a lawyer. You have an apartment in town and a house on the beach in Amity."

Ellen shook her head, smiling. "Not quite. My husband is the police chief in Amity."

Hooper let his surprise show for only an instant. Then he said, "Of course—Brody. I never made the connection. Your husband seems like quite a guy."

Ellen thought she detected a flicker of irony in Hooper's voice, but then she told herself, Don't be stupid, you're making things up.

"Do you live in Woods Hole?" she said.

"No. In Hyannis Port. In a little house on the water. I have a thing about being near the water. Say, do you still dance?"

"Dance?"

"Yeah. You and David won a contest, didn't you?"

The past—like a bird long locked in a cage and suddenly released—was suddenly swirling around in her head, showering her with longing. "A samba contest," she said. "At the Beach Club. I'd forgotten. No, I don't dance anymore. Martin doesn't, and even if he did, I don't think anyone plays that kind of music now."

"That's too bad. David said you were terrific. Well, I should get down to the dock. You're sure I can't drop you anywhere?"

"Positive, thank you. My car's just across the street."

"O.K." Hooper held out his hand. "I don't suppose I could get you out on a tennis court late some afternoon."

Ellen laughed. "Oh, my. I haven't held a tennis racquet in my hand since I can't remember when. But thanks for asking."

"O.K. Well, see you." Hooper hurried off to his car. As he pulled out into the street and drove past her she raised her hand and waved, tentatively, shyly. Hooper struck a hand out of the car window and waved back. Then he turned the corner and was gone.

A terrible sadness clutched at Ellen. More than ever before she felt that her life—the best part of it, at least—was behind her. Recognizing the sensation made her feel guilty, for she read it as proof that she was an unsatisfactory mother, an unsatisfied wife. She thought of a line from a song Billy played on the record player: "I'd trade all my tomorrows for a single yesterday." Would she make a deal like that? She wondered.

A vision of Hooper's smiling face flashed across her mind. Forget it, she told herself.

WITH THE BEACHES closed and with police patrolling them, Amity was practically deserted on the weekend. Hooper cruised up and down the shore in Ben Gardner's boat, but the only signs of life he saw in the water were a few schools of baitfish. By Sunday night he told Brody he was ready to conclude that the shark had gone back to the deep.

"What makes you think so?" Brody had asked.

"There's not a sign of him," said Hooper. "And there are other fish. If there was a big white in the neighborhood, everything else would vanish."

"I'm not convinced," said Brody. "At least not enough to open the beaches. Not yet." He almost wished Hooper had seen the fish. To his policeman's mind negative evidence was not enough.

On Monday afternoon, Brody was sitting in his office when Ellen called.

"I'm sorry to bother you," she said. "But what would you think about giving a dinner party? I can't even remember when our last one was."

"Neither can I," said Brody. But it was a lie. He remembered all too well their last dinner party: three years ago, when Ellen was in the midst of a crusade to re-establish her ties with the summer community. She had asked three summer couples. They were nice enough people, Brody recalled, but the conversation had been stiff and uncomfortable. Brody and the guests had few common interests, and after a while the guests had fallen back on talking among themselves. When they had left, after Ellen had done the dishes and said twice to Brody, "*Wasn't* that a nice evening!" she had shut herself in the bathroom and wept.

"Well, what do you think?" said Ellen.

"I guess it's all right. Who are you going to invite?"

"First of all, I think we should have Matthew Hooper."

"What for? He eats over at the Abelard, doesn't he? It's all included in the price of the room."

"That's not the point. He's alone in town, and he's nice."

"I didn't think you knew him."

"I ran into him in Morris's on Friday. I'm *sure* I mentioned it to you. It turns out he's the brother of the Hooper I used to know."

"Uh-huh. When are you planning this shindig for?"

"I was thinking about tomorrow night. And it's not going to be a shindig. I simply thought we could have a nice, small party with a few couples. What about the Baxters? Would they be fun?"

"I don't think I know them."

"Yes, you do. Clem and Cici Baxter. She was Cici Davenport. They live out on Scotch Road. He's taking some vacation now."

"O.K. Try them if you want. How about the Meadowses?"

"But Matthew Hooper already knows Harry."

"He doesn't know Dorothy."

"All right," said Ellen. "I guess a little local color won't hurt."

"I wasn't thinking about local color," Brody said sharply. "They're our friends."

"I know. I didn't mean anything."

"If you want local color, all you have to do is look on the other side of your bed."

"I *know*. I said I was sorry."

"What about a girl?" said Brody. "I think you should try to find some nice young thing for Hooper."

There was a pause before Ellen said, "All right. I'll see if I can think of somebody who'd be fun for him."

WHEN BRODY arrived home the next evening Ellen was setting the dinner table. He kissed her and said, "It's been a long time since I've seen that silver." It was Ellen's wedding silver, a gift from her parents.

"I know. It took me hours to polish it."

"And will you look at this?" Brody picked up a tulip wine glass. "Where did you get these?"

"I bought them at 'The Lure'."

"How much?" Brody set the glass down on the table.

"Twenty dollars. But that was for a whole dozen."

"You don't kid around when you throw a party."

"We didn't have any decent wine glasses," she said defensively.

Brody counted the places set. "Only six?" he said.

"The Baxters couldn't make it. Clem had to go into town on business, and Cici thought she'd go with him. They're spending the night." There was a fragile lilt to her voice, a false insouciance.

"Oh," said Brody. "Too bad." He dared not show that he was pleased. "Who'd you get for Hooper, some nice young chick?"

"Daisy Wicker. She works for Gibby at 'The Bibelot'."

"What time are people coming?"

"The Meadowses and Daisy at seven-thirty. I asked Matthew for seven. I wanted him to come early so the kids could get to know him. I think they'll be fascinated."

Brody looked at his watch. "If people aren't coming till seven-thirty, we won't be eating till eight-thirty or nine. I'll starve to death before then. I think I'll grab a sandwich." He started for the kitchen.

"Don't stuff yourself. I've a delicious dinner planned."

Brody sniffed the kitchen aromas, eyed the clutter of pots and packages and said, "What are you cooking?"

"It's called butterfly lamb. I hope I don't botch it."

"Smells good," said Brody. "What's this stuff in the pot by the sink? Should I throw it out?"

Ellen hurried into the kitchen. "Don't you dare—" She saw the smile on Brody's face. "Oh, you rat." She slapped him on the rear. "That's gazpacho. Soup."

Brody shook his head. "Old Hooper's going to wish he ate at the Abelard," he said.

"You're a beast," she said. "Wait till you taste it."

At 7:05 the doorbell rang, and Brody answered it. He was wearing blue uniform slacks and black shoes. He felt crisp and clean. But when he opened the door for Hooper, he felt outclassed. Hooper wore bell-bottom blue jeans and loafers with no socks. It was the uniform of the young and rich in Amity.

"Hi," said Brody. "Come in."

"Hi," said Hooper. He extended his hand, and Brody shook it.

Ellen came from the kitchen in a long batik skirt and a silk blouse. She wore the cultured pearls Brody had given her as a wedding present.

"Matthew," she said. "I'm glad you could come."

"I'm glad you asked me," Hooper said, shaking Ellen's hand. Then he dug into the pocket of his jeans and handed Ellen a small package wrapped in tissue. "For the hostess," he said.

Ellen tittered and carefully unwrapped the paper. Inside was what seemed to be a pendant, an inch or so across.

"It's a tiger-shark tooth," said Hooper. "The casing's silver."

"It's lovely. Where did you get it?"

"In Macao. There's a superstition that if you keep it with you, you'll be safe from shark bite. Under the present circumstances, I thought it would be appropriate."

"Completely," said Ellen. "Do you have one?"

"I have one," said Hooper, "but I don't know how to carry it. I don't like to wear things around my neck, and if you carry a shark tooth in your pants pocket, you end up with a gash in your pants."

Ellen laughed and said to Brody, "Martin, could I ask a favor? Would you run upstairs and get that silver chain out of my jewelry box? I'll put Matthew's shark tooth on right now."

Brody started up the stairs, and Ellen said, "Oh, and Martin, tell the boys to come down."

As he rounded the corner at the top of the stairs Brody heard Ellen say, "It *is* such fun to see you again."

Brody walked into the bedroom and sat down on the edge of the bed, clenching and unclenching his right fist. He felt as if an intruder had come into his home, possessing subtle weapons he could not cope with: looks and youth and sophistication and, above all, a communion with Ellen born in a time which, Brody knew, Ellen wished had never ended. He felt that Ellen was trying to impress Hooper. He didn't know why. It demeaned her, Brody thought; and it demeaned Brody that she should try, by posturing, to deny her life with him.

"To hell with it," he said aloud. He stood up, opened a drawer and took out Ellen's silver chain. Before going downstairs he poked his head into the boys' rooms and said, "Let's go, troops."

Ellen and Hooper were sitting on the couch, and as Brody walked into the room he heard Ellen say, "Would you rather that I not call you Matthew?"

Hooper laughed. "I don't mind. It sort of brings back memories."

"Here," Brody said to Ellen, handing her the chain.

"Thank you." She unclasped the pearls and tossed them onto the coffee table. "Now, Matthew, show me how this should go."

Brody went into the kitchen to make drinks. Ellen had asked for vermouth on the rocks, Hooper for a gin and tonic. The liquor was kept in a cabinet over the sink. He tugged at the metal door handle, and it came off in his hand. Without thinking, he pegged it into the garbage pail. From a drawer he took a screwdriver and prised open the cabinet door.

He poured Ellen's vermouth and mixed Hooper's drink, then started to make a rye and ginger for himself. By habit he began to measure the rye with a shot glass, but then he changed his mind and poured until the glass was a third full. He topped it off with ginger ale, dropped in a few ice cubes and reached for the two

other glasses. The only convenient way to carry them in one hand involved sticking his index finger down inside one glass.

The boys, neatly dressed in sport shirts and slacks, had joined Ellen and Hooper in the living room. Billy and Martin were crowded onto the couch with them and Sean was sitting on the floor. Brody heard Hooper say something about a pig, and Martin said, "Wow!"

"Here," said Brody, handing Ellen the glass with his finger in it.

"No tip for you, my man," she said. "It's a good thing you decided against a career as a waiter."

Brody looked at her, considered a rude remark and settled for, "Forgive me, Duchess." He handed the other glass to Hooper.

"Matt was just telling us about a shark he caught," said Ellen. "It had almost a whole pig in it."

"No kidding," said Brody. He took a long swallow of his drink.

"And a human bone," said Sean.

"I said it looked like a human bone," said Hooper. "There was no way to be sure at the time."

"Hey, Dad," said Billy. "You know how a porpoise kills a shark?"

"With a gun?"

"No, man. It butts him to death. That's what Mr. Hooper says."

"Terrific," said Brody, and he drained his glass. "I'm going to have another drink. Anybody else ready?"

"On a week night?" said Ellen. "My!"

"Why not? It's not every night we throw a no-kidding, go-to-hell dinner party." Brody started for the kitchen but was stopped by the doorbell. He opened the door and saw Dorothy Meadows, dressed in a dark blue dress. Behind her was a girl Brody assumed was Daisy Wicker—a tall, slim girl with long, straight hair. She wore slacks and sandals and no makeup. Behind her was the unmistakable bulk of Harry Meadows.

"Hello, there," said Brody. "Come on in."

"Good evening, Martin," said Dorothy Meadows. "We met Miss Wicker as we came into the driveway."

"I walked," said Daisy Wicker. "It was nice."

"Good, good. Come on in."

Brody led them into the living room and turned them over to Ellen for introduction to Hooper. He took drink orders, but before he fixed them he made a fresh one for himself, and he sipped it as he prepared the others. By the time they were ready he had finished about half his drink, so he poured in a generous splash of rye and a dash more ginger ale.

He took the women's drinks first, and returned to the kitchen for Meadows's and his own. He was taking one last swallow before rejoining the company when Ellen came into the kitchen.

"Don't you think you better slow down?" she said.

"I'm fine," he said. "Don't worry about me." As he spoke he realized she was right: he had better slow down. He walked into the living room.

The children had gone upstairs. Dorothy Meadows was chatting with Hooper about his work, while Harry listened. Daisy Wicker was standing alone, on the other side of the room, gazing about with a subdued smile on her face. Brody strolled over to her.

"You're smiling," he said.

"Am I? I guess I was just interested. I've never been in a policeman's house before."

"And what have you decided? It looks just like a normal person's house, doesn't it?"

"I guess so." She took a sip of her drink and said, "Do you like being a policeman?"

Brody couldn't tell whether or not there was hostility in the question. "Yes. It's a good job, and it has a purpose to it."

"Don't you feel alienated?"

"Why the hell should I feel alienated? Alienated from what?"

"From the people. I mean, the only thing that justifies your existence is telling people what not to do. Doesn't that make you feel freaky?"

For a moment Brody thought he was being put on, but the girl never smiled or shifted her eyes from his. "No, I don't," he said. "I don't see why I should feel any more freaky than you do, working at the whatcha-ma-call-it. What do you sell there anyway?"

"We sell people their past. It gives them comfort."

"What do you mean, their past?"

"Antiques. They're bought by people who need the security of their past. I bet that's important to you, too."

"What, the past?"

"No, security. Isn't that supposed to be one of the heavy things about being a cop?"

Brody glanced across the room and noticed that Harry Meadows's glass was empty. "Excuse me," he said. "I have to tend to the other guests."

Brody took Meadows's glass and his own into the kitchen. Ellen was checking the meat in the broiler.

"Where the hell did you find that girl?" he said. "Under a rock?"

"Who? Daisy?"

"She's a spook. She's just like some of the kids we bust who start smart-mouthing us in the station." He made a drink for Meadows, then poured another for himself. He saw Ellen staring at him.

"What's the matter with you?" she said.

"I guess I don't like people coming into my house and insulting me."

He picked up the two drinks and started for the door.

Ellen said, "Martin . . ." and he stopped. "For my sake . . . please."

"Calm *down*," he said. "Everything'll be fine."

He refilled Hooper's drink and Daisy Wicker's. Then he sat down and nursed his drink through a long story by Meadows. Brody felt all right—pretty good, in fact—and he knew that if he didn't have anything more to drink before dinner, he'd be fine.

At 8:30 Ellen brought the soup plates out from the kitchen and set them around the table. "Martin," she said, "would you open the wine for me while I get everyone seated? There's a bottle of white in the icebox and there are two reds on the counter. You may as well open them all. The red will need time to breathe."

"Of course it will," Brody said as he stood up. "Who doesn't?"

He found the corkscrew and went to work on the two bottles of red wine. He pulled one cork cleanly, but the other crumbled, and pieces slipped into the bottle. He took the bottle of white out of the refrigerator, uncorked it and took it into the dining room.

Ellen was seated at the end of the table nearest the kitchen. Hooper was at her left, Meadows at her right. Next to Meadows, Daisy Wicker, then an empty space for Brody at the far end of the table, and, opposite Daisy, Dorothy Meadows.

When he had poured the wine Brody sat down and took a spoonful of the soup in front of him. It was cold, and it didn't taste anything like soup, but it wasn't bad.

"I love gazpacho," said Daisy, "but it's such a pain to make that I don't have it very often."

"Mmmm," said Brody, spooning another mouthful.

"Have you ever tried a G and G?"

"Can't say as I have. What is it?"

"Grass and gazpacho. Instead of herbs, you sprinkle a little grass over the top. It's really wild."

Brody didn't answer right away. He scooped out the last little bit of his soup, drained his wine glass in one draft and looked at Daisy, who was smiling sweetly at him. "You know," he said, "I don't find—"

"I bet Matt's tried one." Daisy raised her voice and said, "Matt, excuse me." The conversation at the other end of the table stopped. "I was just curious. Have you ever tried a G and G? By the way, Mrs. Brody, this is terrific gazpacho."

"Thank you," said Ellen. "But what's a G and G?"

"I tried one once," said Hooper. "But I was never really into that."

"Matt'll tell you," said Daisy to Ellen, and she turned to talk to Meadows.

Brody cleared away the soup bowls and Ellen followed him into the kitchen.

"I'll need some help carving," she said.

"Okeydoke," said Brody, and Ellen hefted the lamb onto the carving board.

Brody searched through a drawer for a carving knife and fork. That Wicker dame was right about one thing, he thought as he slashed the meat: I sure feel alienated right now. A slab of meat fell away and he said, "Hey, it isn't done." He held up the piece he had sliced. It was pink and, toward the middle, almost red.

"That's the way it's supposed to be."

"Not if it's lamb, it isn't. I'm not gonna eat raw lamb!"

"Martin, believe me. It's all right to cook butterfly lamb sort of medium. If you don't want to eat it, don't eat it, but that's the way I'm going to serve it."

"Then cut it yourself." He dropped the knife and fork on the board, picked up the two bottles of red wine and left the kitchen.

"There'll be a short delay," he said as he approached the table, "while the cook kills our dinner. She tried to serve it as it was, but it bit her on the leg."

Brody filled the wine glasses and sat down. He took a sip of his wine, said, "Good," then took another.

Ellen came in with the lamb. She returned to the kitchen and came back carrying two vegetable dishes. "I hope it's good," she said. "I haven't tried it before."

"What is it?" asked Dorothy Meadows. "It smells delicious."

"Butterfly lamb. Marinated."

"Really? What's in the marinade?"

"Ginger, soy sauce, a whole bunch of things."

When everyone had been served and Ellen had sat down, Hooper raised his glass and said, "A toast to the chef."

The others lifted their glasses, and Brody said, "Good luck."

Meadows took a bite of meat and said, "Fantastic. It's like the tenderest of sirloins, only better. What a splendid flavor."

"Coming from you, Harry," said Ellen, "that's a special compliment."

"It's delicious," said Dorothy. "Will you promise to give me the recipe? Harry will never forgive me if I don't give this to him at least once a week."

"He better rob a bank," said Brody.

"But it is delicious, Martin, don't you think?"

Brody didn't answer. He had started to chew a piece of meat when a wave of nausea hit him. He felt detached, as if his body was controlled by someone else. His fork felt heavy, and for a moment he feared it might slip from his fingers. It was the wine. It had to be. With exaggerated precision he reached forward to push his wine glass away from him. He sat back and took a deep breath. His vision blurred. He tried to focus his eyes on a painting above Ellen's head, but he was distracted by the image of Ellen talking to Hooper. Every time she spoke she touched Hooper's arm—lightly, but, Brody thought, intimately, as if they were sharing secrets. He didn't hear what anyone was saying. The last thing he remembered hearing was, "Don't you think?" Who had said it? He looked at Meadows, who was talking to Daisy. Then he looked at Dorothy and said thickly, "Yes."

She looked up at him. "What did you say, Martin?"

He couldn't speak. He wanted to stand and walk out to the kitchen, but he didn't trust his legs. Just sit still, he told himself. It'll pass.

And it did. His head began to clear, and by the time dessert was served he was feeling well. He had two helpings of the ice cream in crème de cacao and chatted amiably with Dorothy.

They had coffee in the living room, and Brody offered drinks, but only Meadows accepted. "A tiny brandy, if you have it," he said.

Brody poured Meadows's drink and thought briefly of having one, too. But he resisted, telling himself: don't press your luck.

At a little after ten Meadows yawned and said, "Dorothy, I think we had best take our leave."

"I should go, too," said Daisy. "I have to be at work at eight. Not that we're selling very much these days."

Meadows stood up. "Well, let's hope the worst is over," he said. "From what I gather from our expert here, there's a good chance the leviathan has left."

"A chance," said Hooper. "I hope so." He rose to go. "I should be on my way, too."

"Oh, don't go!" Ellen said to Hooper. The words came out much stronger than she had intended, and she added quickly, "I mean, the night is young. It's only ten."

"I know," said Hooper. "But if the weather's good, I want to get out on the water early. I can drop Daisy off on my way home."

Daisy said, "That would be fun."

"The Meadowses can drop her," Ellen said.

"True," said Hooper, "but I really should go so I can get up early. But thanks for the thought."

They said their good-byes at the front door. When Hooper extended his hand to Ellen she took it in both of hers and said, "Thank you *so* much for my shark tooth."

"You're welcome. I'm glad you like it."

"We'll see you again before you go?"

"Count on it."

"Wonderful." She released his hand. He said a quick good night to Brody and walked to his car.

Ellen waited at the door until both cars had pulled out of the driveway, then she turned off the outside light. Without a word she began to pick up the glasses, cups and ashtrays.

Brody carried a stack of dessert dishes into the kitchen, set them on the sink and said, "Well, that was all right."

"No thanks to you," said Ellen. "You were awful."

"I was?" He was surprised at the ferocity of her attack.

"All evening, from start to finish, you were awful."

"What are you talking about?"

"I don't want to talk about it."

"Just like that. You don't want to talk about it. Look . . . O.K., I was wrong about the damn meat. I'm sorry. Now—"

"I said I don't want to talk about it!"

Brody was ready for a fight, but he backed off, sober enough to realize that Ellen was close to tears. So he said only. "Well, I'm sorry about that," and walked out of the kitchen.

As he was undressing, the thought occurred to him that the cause of all the unpleasantness was a fish: a mindless beast that he had never seen. The ludicrousness of it made him smile.

He crawled into bed and fell into a dreamless sleep.

6

Brody awoke with a start; something was displaced from the normal pattern of his awakening. He threw his arm across the bed to touch Ellen. She wasn't there.

He sat up and saw her sitting in a chair by the window. Rain splashed against the panes, and he heard the wind whipping through the trees.

"Lousy day, huh?" he said. She didn't answer, continuing to stare fixedly at the drops sliding down the glass. "How come you're up so early?"

"I couldn't sleep." She seemed subdued, sad.

"What's the matter?"

"Nothing."

"Whatever you say." Brody got out of bed.

When he had dressed he went down to the kitchen. The boys were finishing their breakfast, and Ellen was frying his egg. "What are you guys gonna do on this crummy day?" he said.

"Clean lawnmowers," said Billy, who worked during the summer for a local gardener. "Boy, do I hate rainy days."

"And what about you two?" Brody said to Martin and Sean.

"Sean and Martin are going to the Boy's Club," Ellen said. "Can you drop them off on the way to work?"

"No problem. And you?"

"I've got a full day at the hospital. Which reminds me. I won't be home for lunch. Can you get something downtown?"

"Sure. I didn't know you worked a full day Wednesdays."

"I don't, usually. But one of the girls is sick. I said I'd fill in."

After Brody and the boys had left, Ellen looked at the clock on the kitchen wall. It was a few minutes to eight. Too early? Maybe. But better to catch him now, before he went off somewhere. She held out her right hand and tried to steady the fingers, but they quivered uncontrollably. She went upstairs to the bedroom, found the number for the Abelard, hesitated for a moment, then dialed.

"Abelard Arms."

"Mr. Hooper's room, please."

Ellen heard the phone ring once, then again. She could hear her heart beating, and she saw the pulse throb in her right wrist. Hang up, she told herself. Hang up. There's time.

"Hello?" said Hooper's voice.

Ellen swallowed and said, "Hi. It's me . . . I mean it's Ellen."

"Oh, hi."

"I hope I didn't wake you."

"No. I was just going for breakfast."

"Good. It's not a very nice day. Will you be able to work?"

"I don't know. I was trying to figure that out."

"Oh." She paused, fighting the dizziness that was creeping up on her. Do it, she said to herself. The words spilled from her mouth. "I was wondering, if you can't work today . . . if there was any chance you'd like to . . . if you're free for lunch."

"Lunch?"

"Yes. You know, if you have nothing else to do."

"You mean you and the chief and I?"

"No, just you and I. Martin usually has lunch at his desk. I don't want to interfere with your plans or anything. . . ."

"No, no. That's O.K. What did you have in mind?"

"There's a wonderful place up in Sag Harbor. Banner's. Do you know it?" She hoped he didn't. She didn't know it, but she had heard that it was good and quiet and dark.

"Sag Harbor," said Hooper. "That's quite a hike for lunch."

"It's only about twenty-five minutes. I could meet you there whenever you like."

"Any time's all right with me."

"Around twelve-thirty, then?"

"Twelve-thirty it is. See you then."

Ellen hung up the phone. Her hands were still shaking, but she felt elated, excited. Her senses seemed alive and incredibly keen. She felt more intensely feminine than she had in years.

She took a shower. Then she stood before the full-length mirror examining herself. Would the offering be accepted? She had worked to keep in shape, to preserve the smoothness and sinuousness of youth. She could not bear the thought of rejection.

She dressed in her hospital clothes. From the back of her closet she took a plastic shopping bag, into which she put fresh underthings, a lavender summer dress and a pair of low-heeled pumps. She carried the bag to the garage, tossed it into her Volkswagen, and drove to Southampton Hospital.

She didn't know exactly when she had decided on this rash, dangerous plan. She had been thinking about it—and trying not to think about it—since the day she first met Hooper. She had now weighed the risks and calculated that they were worth taking. She wanted to be reassured that she was desirable—not just to her husband, but to the people she saw as her real peers, the people among whom she still numbered herself. The thought of love never entered her mind. She sought only to be restored.

She was grateful that her work at the hospital demanded concentration, for it prevented her from thinking. At 11.45 Ellen told the supervisor of volunteers that she didn't feel well. She thought she'd probably go home and lie down.

SHE DROVE MOST OF THE WAY to Sag Harbor, then stopped at a gas station. When the tank was full and the gas paid for, she used the ladies' room to change her clothes.

It was 12:25 when she arrived at Banner's, a small steak-and-seafood restaurant on the water. The parking lot was concealed from the street, for which she was grateful; there was just a chance that someone she knew might drive by, and she didn't want her car in plain view.

The restaurant was dark, with a bar on the right as she walked in, and tables in the center. The bartender, a young man with a Vandyke beard and a button-down shirt, sat by the cash register reading a paper, and a waitress stood at the bar, folding napkins. They were the only people in the room. Ellen looked at her watch. Almost 12:30.

The waitress saw Ellen and said, "Hello. May I help you?"

"Yes. I'd like a table for two, please. For lunch."

"Fine," said the waitress. She walked Ellen to a table in the middle of the room. "Is this all right?"

"I'd like to have that corner booth, if you don't mind."

"Sure," said the waitress, "Anywhere you like." She led Ellen to the booth, and Ellen slipped in with her back to the door. Hooper would be able to find her. "Can I get you a drink?"

"Yes. A gin and tonic, please." It was the first time since her wedding that Ellen had had a drink during the day.

The waitress brought the drink, and Ellen drank half of it immediately, eager to feel the relaxing warmth of alcohol. Every few seconds she checked the door and looked at her watch. It was almost 12:45. He's not going to come, she thought.

"Hello." Hooper slid into the seat opposite her and said, "I'm sorry I'm late. I had to stop for gas, and the station was jammed." He looked into her eyes and smiled.

Ellen looked down at her glass. "You don't have to apologize. I was late myself."

The waitress came over, and Hooper, noticing Ellen's glass, ordered a gin and tonic.

The waitress left. "I don't normally drink at lunch," said Hooper. "After about three drinks I say stupid things."

Ellen nodded. "I know the feeling. I tend to get sort of . . ."

"Impetuous? So do I."

"Really? I thought scientists weren't ever impetuous."

Hooper smiled. "Beneath our icy exteriors," he said, "we are some of the raunchiest people in the world."

They chatted about old times, about people they had known, about Hooper's ambitions in ichthyology. They never mentioned the shark or Brody or Ellen's children. It was an easy, rambling conversation, which suited Ellen. Her second drink loosened her up, and she felt happy and in command of herself.

She wanted Hooper to have another drink, and she knew he was not likely to take the initiative and order one. She picked up a menu and said, "Let me see. What looks good?"

Hooper picked up the other menu, and after a minute the waitress strolled over to the table. "Are you ready to order?"

"Not quite yet," said Ellen. "Why don't we have one more drink while we're looking?"

Hooper pondered for a moment. Then he nodded his head and said, "Sure. A special occasion."

The waitress brought their drinks and said, "Ready?"

"Yes," said Ellen. "I'll have the shrimp cocktail and the chicken."

"I'll have the scallops," said Hooper.

"Anything to start?"

"No," said Hooper, raising his glass. "This'll be fine."

In a few minutes the waitress brought Ellen's shrimp cocktail. When she had left, Ellen said, "Do you know what I'd love? Some wine."

"That's a very good idea," Hooper said, looking at her. "But remember what I said. I may become irresponsible."

"I'm not worried." As Ellen spoke, she felt a blush crawl up her cheeks.

"O.K.," Hooper said, "but first I better check the treasury." He reached in his back pocket for his wallet.

"Oh, no. This is my treat."

"Don't be silly," he said. "I'd like to take *you* to lunch."

She toyed with one shrimp left on her plate. "Well . . . ."

"I know you're only being thoughtful," Hooper said, "but don't be. Didn't David ever tell you about our grandfather?"

"Not that I remember. What about him?"

"Old Matt was known—and not very affectionately—as the Bandit. At one point he owned most of Denver. So all I've ever had to worry about was whether to keep the bundle of money he left me or give it away."

"What did your grandfather do?"

"Railroads and mining. Technically, that is. Basically he was the landlord of the red-light district." Hooper laughed. "And from what I hear, he liked to collect his rent in trade."

"That's supposed to be every schoolgirl's fantasy," Ellen ventured playfully.

"What is?"

"To be a . . . you know, a prostitute."

"Was it yours?"

Ellen laughed to cover her blush. "I don't remember if it was exactly that," she said. "But I guess we all have fantasies of one kind or another."

Hooper smiled and called the waitress. "Bring us a bottle of cold chablis, would you, please?"

Something's happened, Ellen thought. She wondered if he could sense the invitation she had extended. Whatever it was, he had taken the offensive.

The food came, followed a moment later by the wine. Hooper poured Ellen a glass of wine, then filled his own and raised it for a toast. "To fantasies," he said. He leaned forward until his face was only a foot from hers. His eyes were bright, liquid blue and his lips were parted in a half-smile.

Impulsively, Ellen said, "Let's make our own fantasy."

"O.K. How do you want to start?"

"What would we do if we were going to . . . you know."

"That's a very interesting question," he said with mock gravity. "Before considering the what, however, we'd have to consider the where. I suppose there's always my room."

"Too dangerous. Everybody knows me at the Abelard. Anywhere in Amity would be too dangerous."

"There must be motels between here and Montauk."

"All right. That's settled."

ELLEN ARRIVED HOME a little before 4:30. She went upstairs, into the bathroom, and turned on the water in the tub. After her bath, she put on a nightgown and climbed into bed. She closed her eyes and gave in to her fatigue.

Almost instantly, it seemed, she was awakened by Brody saying, "Hey, there, are you O.K.?"

She yawned. "What time is it?"

"Almost six."

"Oh-oh. I've got to pick up the boys."

"I got them," said Brody. "I figured I'd better, once I couldn't reach you."

"You tried to reach me?"

"A couple of times. I tried you at the hospital at around two. They thought you'd come home. Then I tried to reach you here."

"My, it must have been important."

"No. If you must know, I was calling to apologize for whatever I did that got you upset last night."

A twinge of shame struck Ellen, and she said, "You're sweet, but don't worry. I'd already forgotten about it."

"Oh," said Brody. "So where were you?"

"I came home and went to bed. My thyroid pills aren't doing what they should."

"And you didn't hear the phone? It's right there." Brody pointed to the table near the other side of the bed.

"No, I . . . I took a sleeping pill. The moaning of the damned won't wake me after I've taken one of them."

Brody shook his head. "I really am going to throw those things down the john. You're turning into a junkie." He went into the bathroom. "Have you heard from Hooper?" he called to her.

Ellen thought for a moment about her response, then said, "He called this morning to say thank you. Why?"

"I tried to get hold of him today. The hotel said they didn't know where he was. Did he say what he was going to be doing?"

"He said . . . he said he might try to work on the boat, I think. I really don't remember."

"Oh. That's funny."

"What is?"

"I stopped by the dock on my way home. The harbormaster said he hadn't seen Hooper all day."

ON THURSDAY MORNING Brody got a call summoning him to Vaughan's office for a noon meeting of the Board of Selectmen. He knew what the subject of the meeting was: opening the beaches for the weekend—the Fourth of July weekend.

The town hall was an imposing, pseudo-Georgian affair—red brick with white trim and two white columns framing the entrance. The rooms inside were as preposterously grandiose as the exterior. They were huge and high-ceilinged, each with its own elaborate chandelier. Mayor Vaughan's office was on the southeast corner of the second floor, overlooking the town.

Vaughan's secretary, a wholesome, pretty woman named Janet Sumner, sat at a desk outside his office. Brody was paternally fond of Janet, and he was idly mystified that—aged about twenty-six—she was still unmarried. He usually made a point of inquiring about her love life, but today he said simply, "Are they all inside?"

"All that's coming." Brody started into the office, and Janet said, "Don't you want to know who I'm going out with?"

He stopped, smiled and said, "Who is it?"

"Nobody. I'm in temporary retirement. But I'll tell you one thing." She lowered her voice and leaned forward. "I wouldn't mind playing footsie with that Mr. Hooper."

"Is he in there?" Janet nodded. "I wonder when he was elected selectman."

"I don't know," she said. "But he sure is cute."

As soon as he was inside the office Brody knew he would be fighting alone. The only selectmen present were long-time allies of Vaughan's: Tony Catsoulis, a contractor who was built like a fire hydrant; Ned Thatcher, a frail old man whose family owned the Abelard Arms Inn; Paul Conover, owner of Amity Liquors; and Rafe Lopez, a dark-skinned Portuguese elected to the board by the town's black community.

The selectmen sat around a coffee table at one end of the room. Hooper stood at a southerly window, staring out at the sea.

"Where's Albert Morris?" Brody said to Vaughan after greeting the others.

"He couldn't make it," said Vaughan. "I don't think he felt well."

"And Fred Potter?"

"Same thing. There must be a bug going around." Vaughan stood up. "Well, I guess we're all here. Grab a chair and pull it over by the coffee table."

He looks awful, Brody thought as he watched Vaughan drag a straight-backed chair across the room. Vaughan's eyes were sunken and dark. His skin looked like mayonnaise.

When everyone was seated Vaughan said, "You all know why we're here. And I guess it's safe to say that there's only one of us that needs convincing about what we should do."

"You mean me," said Brody.

Vaughan nodded. "Look at it from our point of view, Martin. The town is dying. Every day we keep the beaches closed, we drive another nail into our own coffin."

"Suppose you do open the beaches for the Fourth, Larry," said Brody. "And suppose someone gets killed."

"It's a calculated risk, but I think—we think—it's worth taking."

"Why?"

Vaughan said, "Mr. Hooper?"

"Several reasons," said Hooper. "First of all, nobody's seen the fish in a week."

"Nobody's been in the water, either."

"That's true. But I've been on the boat looking for him every day—every day but one."

"I meant to ask you about that. Where were you yesterday?"

"It rained," said Hooper. "Remember?"

"So what did you do?"

"I just . . ." He paused, then said, "I studied some water samples. And read."

"Where? Your hotel said you were out all afternoon."

"So I was out!" Hooper said angrily. "I don't have to report in every five minutes, do I? You're not even paying me!"

Vaughan broke in. "Come on. This isn't getting us anywhere?"

"Anyway," said Hooper, "I haven't seen a trace of that fish. Not a sign. And the water's getting warmer every day. It's almost seventy now. As a rule great whites prefer cooler water."

"So you think he's gone farther north?"

"Or out deeper, into colder water. He could even have gone south. You can't predict what these things are going to do."

"That's my point," said Brody. "You can't predict it. So all you're doing is guessing."

Vaughan said, "You can't ask for a guarantee, Martin."

"Tell that to Christine Watkins. Or the Kintner boy's mother."

"I know, I know," Vaughan said impatiently. "But we have to do something. God isn't going to scribble across the sky, 'The shark is gone'."

"And when someone else gets killed? Who's taking the blame? Who's going to talk to the husband or the mother or the wife and tell them, 'We were just playing the odds, and we lost'?"

"Wait a minute, Martin."

"If you want the authority for opening the beaches, then you take the responsibility, too."

"What are you saying?"

"I'm saying that as long as I'm chief of police in this town those beaches will not be open."

"I'll tell you this, Martin," said Vaughan. "If those beaches stay closed over Fourth of July weekend, you won't have your job very long. Twenty minutes after they hear you won't open the beaches the people of this town will impeach you, or find a rail and run you out on it. Do you agree, gentlemen?"

"I'll give 'em the rail myself," said Catsoulis.

"My people got no work," said Lopez. "You don't let them work, you're not gonna work."

Brody said flatly, "You can have my job any time you want it."

A buzzer sounded on Vaughan's desk. He stood up angrily and picked up the phone. There was a moment's silence, and he said to Brody, "There's a call for you. Janet says it's urgent. You can take it here or outside."

"I'll take it outside," Brody said, wondering what could be urgent enough to call him out of a meeting with the selectmen. Another attack? He left the room and closed the door behind him. Janet handed him the phone on her desk, but before she could release the "hold" button Brody said, "Tell me, did Larry call Albert Morris and Fred Potter this morning?"

Janet looked away from him. "I was told not to say anything."

"Thank you, Janet. Push the button." Janet pushed the button, and Brody said, "Brody."

Inside his office Vaughan saw the light stop flashing and he gently eased his finger off the receiver hook and placed his hand over the mouthpiece. He looked around the room, searching each face for a challenge. No one returned his gaze.

"It's Harry, Martin," said Meadows. "I know you're in a meeting so I'll be brief. Larry Vaughan is up to his tail in hock."

"I don't believe it."

"A long time ago, maybe twenty-five years, before Larry had any money, his wife got sick. It was serious. And expensive. My memory's a little hazy on this, but I remember him saying afterward that he had gotten a loan to pull him through. Larry told me the man's name. It was Tino Russo."

"Get to the point, Harry."

"I am. Now jump to the present. A couple of months ago, before this shark thing ever began, a company was formed called Caskata Estates. It's a holding company. When the summer didn't shape up well, Caskata began to buy properties at low prices. It was all perfectly legitimate. But then—as soon as the first newspaper reports about the shark thing came out—Caskata really started buying. The lower the real estate prices fell, the more they bought—with very little money down. All short-term promissory notes. Signed by Larry Vaughan, who is listed as the president of Caskata. The executive vice-president is Tino Russo, whom the *Times* has been naming for years as a second-echelon crumb in one of the five Mafia families in New York."

Brody whistled through his teeth. "And Vaughan has been moaning about how nobody's been buying anything from him. I still don't understand why he's being pressured to open the beaches."

"I'm not sure. I imagine he's way over-extended. The only way he can get out without being ruined is if the market turns around and the prices go up. Then he can sell what he's bought and get the profit. Or Russo can get the profit, however the deal's worked out. If prices keep going down he can't possibly meet his notes when they come due. He'll lose his cash, and the properties will revert to the original owners. My guess is that Russo still has hopes of big profits, but the only way he has a chance of getting them is if Vaughan forces the beaches open. It's all—"

"You're a God-damned liar, Meadows!" Vaughan's voice shrieked into the phone. "You print one word of that and I'll sue you to death!" There was a click as he slammed down the phone.

"So much for the integrity of our elected officials," said Meadows.

"What do you think I ought to do, Harry? I offered them my job before I came out to talk to you."

"Don't quit, Martin. We need you. If you quit, Russo will get together with Vaughan and hand-pick your successor. If I were you, I'd open the beaches."

"And let the mob take their money and run."

"What else *can* you do? You keep them closed, and Vaughan'll get rid of you and open them himself. Then you'll be no use to anybody. This way, if you open the beaches and nothing happens, the town might have a chance. Then, maybe later, we can find a way to pin something on Vaughan."

"All right, Harry, I'll think about it," said Brody. "But if I open them, I'm gonna do it my way."

When Brody went back into Vaughan's office Vaughan said, "The meeting's over."

"What do you mean, over?" said Catsoulis. "We ain't decided anything."

Vaughan said, "Don't give me any trouble, Tony! It'll work out all right. Just let me have a little chat with the chief. O.K.? Now everybody out."

Hooper and the four selectmen left the office. Vaughan shut the door, walked over to the couch and sat down heavily. He rested his elbows on his knees and rubbed his temples with his fingertips. He said, "I swear to you, Martin, if I had any idea how far this would go, I'd never have gotten into it."

"How much are you into him for?"

"The original amount was ten thousand. I've tried to pay it back, but I could never get them to cash my checks. Then they came to me a couple of months ago. They didn't want the money. They wanted me to make a few investments. Everybody'd be a winner, they said."

"And how much are you out now?"

"Every cent I have. More than every cent. Probably close to a million dollars." Vaughan took a deep breath. "Can you help me, Martin?"

"The only thing I can do for you is put you in touch with the DA. If you'd testify, you might be able to slap a loan-sharking rap on these guys."

"I'd be dead before I got home from the DA's office, and Eleanor would be left without anything. That's not the kind of help I meant."

Brody looked down at Vaughan, a huddled, wounded animal, and felt compassion. He began to doubt his own opposition to opening the beaches. How much was self-protection, and how much was concern for the town?

"I'll tell you what, Larry. I'll open the beaches. Not to help you, because I'm sure if I didn't open them you'd find a way to get rid of me and open them yourself. I'll do it because I'm not sure I'm right anymore."

"Thanks, Martin. I appreciate that."

"I'm not finished. Like I said, I'll open them. But I'm going to post men on the beaches. And I'm going to have Hooper patrol in the boat. And I'm going to make sure every person who comes down there knows the danger."

"You can't do that!" Vaughan said. "You might as well leave the damn things closed. Nobody's going to the beach if it's crawling with cops."

"I can do it, Larry, and I will. I'm not going to make believe nothing ever happened."

"All right, Martin." Vaughan rose. "You don't leave me much choice. If I got rid of you, you'd probably go down to the beach as a private citizen and run up and down yelling '*Shark!*' So all right. But be subtle—if not for my sake, for the town's."

Brody arrived home at 5:10. As he pulled into the driveway the back door to the house opened and Ellen ran toward him. She had been crying, and she was still visibly upset.

"Thank God you're home!" she said. "Come here. Quick!" She led him to the shed where they kept the garbage cans. "In there." She pointed to a can. "Look."

Lying in a twisted heap atop a bag of garbage was Sean's cat—a big, husky tom named Frisky. The cat's head had been twisted completely around, and the yellow eyes overlooked its back.

"How the hell did that happen?" said Brody. "A car?"

"No, a man." Ellen's breath came in sobs. "Sean was right there when it happened. A man got out of a car, picked up the cat and broke its neck. Then he dropped it on the lawn, got back in his car and drove away."

"Did he say anything?"

"I don't know. Sean's inside. He's hysterical, and I don't blame him. Martin, what's *happening?*"

Brody slammed the top back on the can. "Son of a *bitch!*" he said. His throat felt tight, and he clenched his teeth. "Let's go inside."

Five minutes later Brody marched out of the back door. He tore the lid off the garbage can, and pulled out the cat's corpse. He took it to his car, pitched it through the open window and climbed in. He backed out of the driveway and screeched away.

It took him only a couple of minutes to reach Vaughan's Tudor-style mansion just off Scotch Road. He got out of the car, dragging the dead cat by one of its hind legs, mounted the front steps and rang the bell.

The door opened, and Vaughan said, "Hello, Martin. I—"

Brody raised the cat and pushed it toward Vaughan's face. "What about this, you bastard? One of your friends did this. Right in front of my kid. They murdered my cat! Did you tell them to do that?"

"Don't be crazy, Martin." Vaughan seemed genuinely shocked. "I'd never do anything like that. Never."

Brody lowered the cat and said, "Did you call your friends after I left?"

"Well . . . yes. But just to say that the beaches would be open tomorrow."

"That's all you said?"

"Yes. Why?"

"You damned liar!" Brody hit Vaughan in the chest with the cat and let it fall to the floor. "You know what the guy said after he strangled my cat? You know what he told my nine-year-old boy? He said the same thing you did. He said, 'Tell your old man this—be subtle.'"

Brody turned and walked down the steps, leaving Vaughan standing over the gnarled bundle of bone and fur.

7

Friday was cloudy, with scattered light showers, and the only people who swam were a young couple who took a quick dip early in the morning just as Brody's man arrived at the beach. Hooper patrolled for six hours and saw nothing. On Friday night Brody called the Coast Guard for a weather report. He wasn't sure what he hoped to hear. He knew he should wish for beautiful weather for the holiday weekend, but privately he would have welcomed a three-day blow that would keep the beaches empty. The report was for clear and sunny skies with light southwest winds. Well, Brody thought, maybe that's for the best. If we have a good weekend and nobody gets hurt, maybe I can believe the shark is gone. And Hooper's sure to leave.

He wanted Hooper to go back to Woods Hole. It was not just that Hooper was always there, the expert voice to contradict his caution. Brody sensed that somehow Hooper had come into his home. He knew Ellen had talked to Hooper since the party: young Martin had mentioned something about the possibility of Hooper taking them on a beach picnic to look for shells. Then there was that business on Wednesday. Ellen had said she was sick, and she certainly had looked worn out when he came home. But where had Hooper been that day? Why had he been so evasive when Brody had asked him about it? For the first time in his married life Brody was wondering.

He went to the kitchen phone to call Hooper at the Abelard Arms. Ellen was washing the supper dishes. Brody saw the phone book buried beneath a pile of bills and comic books on the kitchen counter. He started to reach for it, then stopped. "I have to call Hooper," he said. "You know where the phone book is?"

"The number is six five four three," said Ellen.

"How do you know?"

"I have a memory for phone numbers. You know that."

He did know it, and he cursed himself for playing stupid tricks. He dialed the number.

"This is Brody," he said, once Hooper answered.

"Yeah. Hi."

"I guess we're on for tomorrow," Brody said. "The weather report is good."

"Yeah, I know."

"Then I'll see you down at the dock at nine-thirty."

"O.K. Nine-thirty."

"By the way," Brody said, "Did things work out with Daisy Wicker?"

"Well . . . yeah, now that you mention it. Is that part of your job, to check up on people's sex life?"

"Forget it. Forget I ever mentioned it." He hung up the phone and turned to Ellen. "I meant to ask you. Martin said something about a beach picnic. When's that?"

"No special time," she said. "It was just a thought."

"Oh." He looked at her, but she didn't return the glance. "I think it's time you got some sleep."

"Why do you say that?"

"You haven't been feeling well. And that's the second time you've washed that glass."

ON SATURDAY AT NOON, Brody stood on a dune overlooking the private beach at Scotch Road, feeling half secret agent, half fool. He was wearing a polo shirt and swim trunks. In a beach bag by his side were binoculars, a walkie-talkie, two beers and a sandwich. Offshore, between a quarter and half a mile, the *Flicka* moved slowly eastward. Brody watched the boat and said to himself: At least I know where *he* is today.

The Coast Guard had been right: the day was splendid—cloudless and warm, with a light onshore breeze. The beach was not crowded. A dozen or so teenagers were scattered about in their ritual rows. A few couples lay dozing—motionless as corpses, as if to move would disrupt the cosmic rhythms that generated a tan. A family was gathered around a charcoal fire in the sand, and the scent of grilling hamburger drifted into Brody's nose.

Brody reached into his beach bag and took out the walkie-talkie. He pushed a button and said, "You there, Leonard?"

In a moment the reply came back, rasping through the speaker. "I read you, Chief. Over." Hendricks had volunteered to spend the weekend on the public beach, as the third point in the triangle of watch.

"Anything going on?" said Brody.

"Nothing we can't handle, but there is a little problem. People keep coming up to me and trying to give me tickets to get onto the beach. I got one right here. It says, 'Shark Beach. Admit One. Two fifty.' Some sharpie on Main Street is apparently making a killing selling tickets people don't need. Over."

"Go to the phone and call headquarters. I want a man to go down to Main Street and arrest whoever it is. If he comes from out of town, run him out of town. If he lives here, lock him up."

"O.K., Chief. Another thing; there are some TV guys here interviewing people. Over."

"How long have they been there?"

"Most of the morning. I don't know how long they'll hang around, specially since no one's going in the water. Over."

"As long as they're not causing any trouble."

"Nope. Over."

"O.K. Hey, Leonard, you don't have to say 'over' all the time. I can tell when you're finished speaking."

"Just procedure, Chief. Keeps things clear. Over and out."

Brody waited a moment, then pushed the button again and said, "Hooper, this is Brody. Anything out there?" There was no answer. "This is Brody calling Hooper. Can you hear me?" He was about to call a third time when he heard Hooper's voice.

"Sorry. I was out on the stern. I thought I saw something."

"What did you think you saw?"

"I can't really describe it. A shadow, maybe. Nothing more."

"You haven't seen anything else?"

"Not a thing. All morning."

"Let's keep it that way. I'll check with you later."

"Fine. I'll be near the public beach in a minute or two."

Brody put the walkie-talkie back in the bag, sat down and unwrapped his sandwich.

By 2:30, the beach was almost empty. People had gone to play tennis, to sail, to have their hair done. The only ones on the beach were half a dozen teenagers.

Brody's legs had begun to sunburn, so he covered them with his towel. He took the walkie-talkie out of the bag and called Hendricks. "Anything happening, Leonard?"

"Not a thing, Chief. Over."

"Anybody go swimming?"

"Nope. Wading, but that's about it. Over."

"Same here. What about the TV people?"

"They're gone. They left a few minutes ago. They wanted to know where you were. Over."

"Did you tell them?"

"Sure. I didn't see why not. Over."

"O.K. I'll talk to you later." Hearing a car engine, Brody stood up, wrapped his towel around his waist to keep the sun from his legs, and walked to the top of the dune. A white panel truck was parked on Scotch Road. The lettering on its side said, "WNBC-TV News." The driver's door opened, and a man got out and trudged through the sand toward Brody. He was young, with long hair and a handlebar mustache.

"Chief Brody?" he said when he was a few steps away.

"That's right."

"I'm Bob Middleton, Channel 4 News. I'd like an interview."

"About what?"

"The whole shark business. How you decided to open the beaches."

Brody thought, What the hell; a little publicity can't hurt the town, now that the chances of anything happening—today, at least—are pretty slim. "All right," he said. "Where do you want it?"

"Down on the beach. It'll take a few minutes to set up, so I'll give a yell when we're ready." He went back to the truck.

Brody walked down toward the water. As he passed the group of teenagers he heard a boy say, "What about it? Anybody got the guts? Ten bucks is ten bucks."

A girl said, "Come on, Limbo, lay off."

Brody stopped, feigning interest in something offshore.

Another boy said, "If you're such hot stuff, why don't *you* go?"

"I'm the one making the offer," said the first boy. "Well, what do you say?"

There was a moment's silence, and then the other boy said, "How far out do I have to go?"

"Let's see. A hundred yards. O.K.?"

"You've got a deal." The boy stood up.

The girl said, "You're crazy, Jimmy. Why do you want to go in the water? You don't need ten dollars."

"You think I'm scared?"

The boy turned and began to jog toward the water. Brody said, "Hey!" The boy stopped. Brody walked over to the boy, and showed his badge. "What are you doing?" he said.

"Going swimming. It's legal, isn't it?"

Brody nodded. Then he lowered his voice and said, "Do you want me to order you not to?"

The boy looked past him at his friends. He hesitated, then shook his head. "No, man. I can use the ten bucks."

"Don't stay in too long," said Brody.

"I won't." The boy scampered into the water. He flung himself over a small wave and began to swim.

Brody heard footsteps running behind him. Bob Middleton dashed past him and called out to the boy, "Hey! Come back!"

The boy stopped swimming and stood up. "What's the matter?"

"I want some shots of you going into the water. O.K.?"

"I guess so," said the boy. He began to wade back.

Two men came up beside Brody. One was carrying a 16-millimeter camera and a tripod. The other carried a box covered with dials and knobs. Around his neck was a pair of earphones.

"Right there's O.K., Walter," said Middleton. He took a notebook from his pocket and asked the boy his name.

The sound man handed Middleton a microphone, then backed up to the cameraman, feeding wire off a coil in his hand. "I gotta get a level on the kid," he said.

"Say something." Middleton held the microphone a few inches from the boy's mouth.

"What do you want me to say?"

"That's good," said the man with the earphones.

"O.K.," said Middleton. He looked at the camera and said, "We have been here on the Amity beach since early morning, and no one has yet ventured into the water, although there has been no sign of the shark. I'm standing here with Jim Prescott, a young man who has just decided to take a swim. Tell me, Jim, do you have any worries about what might be swimming out there with you?"

"No," said the boy. "I don't think there's anything out there."

"So you're not scared."

"No."

Middleton held out his hand. "Well, good luck, Jim. Thanks for talking to us."

The boy ran into the water and began to swim.

"How much do you want of this?" said the cameraman, tracking the boy as he swam.

"A hundred feet or so," said Middleton. "But let's stay here till he comes out. Be ready, just in case."

Brody had become so accustomed to the far-off, barely audible hum of the *Flicka*'s engine that his mind no longer registered it as a sound. But suddenly the engine's pitch changed from a low murmur to an urgent growl. Brody looked beyond the swimming boy and saw the boat in a tight, fast turn, nothing like the normal slow, ambling sweeps it had been making. He put the walkie-talkie to his mouth and said, "You see something, Hooper?" The boat slowed, then stopped.

"Yes," said Hooper's voice. "It was that shadow again. But I can't see it now. Maybe my eyes are getting tired."

Middleton called to the cameraman, "Get this, Walter." He walked to Brody and said, "Something going on, Chief?"

"I don't know," said Brody. "I'm trying to find out." He said into the walkie-talkie, "There's a kid swimming out there."

"Where?" said Hooper.

Middleton shoved the microphone at Brody, sliding it between his mouth and the walkie-talkie. Brody brushed it aside, but Middleton quickly jammed it back.

"Thirty, maybe forty yards out. I better tell him to come in." Brody tucked the walkie-talkie into the towel at his waist, cupped his hands around his mouth and called, "Hey, come on in!"

The boy did not hear the call. He was swimming straight away from the beach.

The boy who had offered the ten dollars heard Brody's call and came to the water's edge. "What's the trouble?" he said.

"Nothing," said Brody. "I just think he'd better come in."

"Who are you?"

Middleton stood between Brody and the boy, flipping the microphone back and forth from one to the other.

"I'm the police chief, kid," Brody said. He turned to Middleton. "And you keep that microphone out of my face, will you?" He spoke into the walkie-talkie. "Hooper, he doesn't hear me. You want to toot in here and tell him to come ashore?"

"Sure," said Hooper. "I'll be there in a minute." And Brody saw the boat, which had been heading west, swing toward shore and kick up a shower of spray from the bouncing bow.

Eighty feet below the *Flicka* the fish sensed the change in the noise. For hours its sensory system had been tracking the strange sound above. It had not felt compelled either to attack the "creature" passing overhead or to move away. But now it turned, banking as smoothly as an airplane, and followed the sound toward the beach.

The boy stopped swimming and looked toward shore, treading water. Brody waved his arms and yelled, "Come in!" The boy waved back and started swimming. He swam well, rolling his head to catch a breath, kicking in rhythm with his arm strokes. Brody guessed he was sixty yards away and that it would still take him a minute or more to reach shore.

It took Hooper only thirty seconds to cover the couple of hundred yards and draw near the boy. He stopped just beyond the surf line, letting the engine idle. He didn't dare go closer for fear of being caught in the waves.

The boy heard the engine and raised his head. "What's the matter?" he called to Hooper.

"Nothing," Hooper answered. "Keep swimming."

The boy lowered his head and swam. A swell moved him faster, and with two or three more strokes he was able to stand. The water was up to his shoulders, and he began to plod toward shore.

"Come on!" said Brody.

Middleton spoke into the microphone: "Something is going on, ladies and gentlemen, but we don't know exactly what. All we know for sure is that Jim Prescott went swimming, and then suddenly a man on a boat out there saw something. Now Police Chief Brody is trying to get Jim to come ashore. It could be the shark; we just don't know."

Hooper put the boat in reverse, to back away from the surf. As he looked off the stern he saw a silver streak moving in the gray-blue water. For a second Hooper did not realize what he was seeing. When the realization struck he cried, "Look out!"

"What is it?" yelled Brody.

"The fish! Get the kid out! Quick!"

The boy heard Hooper, and he tried to run. But in the chest-deep water his movements were slow and labored. He stumbled, then stood and leaned forward.

Brody ran into the water and reached out. A wave hit him in the knees and pushed him back.

Middleton said into the microphone, "The man on the boat just said something about a fish. I don't know if he means a shark."

The boy was pushing through the water faster now. He did not see the fin rise behind him, a sharp blade of brownish gray.

"There it is, Walter!" said Middleton. "See it?"

"I'm zooming," said the cameraman. "Yeah, I've got it."

"Hurry!" said Brody. He reached for the boy. The boy's eyes were wide and panicked. Brody's hand touched the boy's, and he pulled. He grabbed the boy around the chest, and together they staggered out of the water.

The fin dropped beneath the surface, and, following the slope of the ocean floor, the fish moved into the deep.

Brody stood in the sand with his arm around the boy. "Are you O.K.?" he said.

"I want to go home." The boy shivered.

"I bet you do," Brody said.

Middleton came up. "Can you repeat that for me?"

"Repeat what?"

"Whatever you said to the boy. Can we do that again?"

"Get out of my way!" Brody snapped. He took the boy to his friends, and said to the one who had offered the money, "Take him home. And give him his ten dollars." The other boy nodded, pale and scared.

Brody pushed the "talk" button on his walkie-talkie. "Leonard, can you hear me?"

"I read you, Chief. Over."

"The fish has been here. If anybody's in the water down there, get them out. Right away. The beach is officially closed."

As Brody went to pick up his beach bag Middleton called to him, "Hey, Chief, can we do that interview now?"

Brody sighed and returned to where Middleton stood with his camera crew. "All right," he said. "Go ahead."

"Well, Chief Brody," said Middleton, "that was a lucky break, wouldn't you say?"

"It was very lucky. The boy might have died."

"So where do you go from here?"

"The beaches are closed. For the time being that's all I can do."

"What does that mean for Amity?"

"Trouble, Mr. Middleton. We are in big trouble."

"In retrospect, Chief, how do you feel about having opened the beaches today?"

"How do I *feel?* What kind of question is that? Angry, annoyed, confused. Thankful that nobody got hurt. Is that enough?"

"That's just fine, Chief," Middleton said with a smile. "Thank you, Chief Brody." He paused, then said, "O.K., Walter, that'll wrap it. Let's get home and start editing this mess."

AT SIX O'CLOCK Brody sat in his office with Hooper and Meadows. He had already talked to Larry Vaughan, who had called—drunk and in tears—and muttered about the ruination of his life.

"Well," said Hooper, "what are you going to do now, Chief? I mean, beyond closing the beaches."

"I'd be happy to hear any suggestions. Personally, I think we're going to be lucky if there's a town left after this summer."

"Isn't that a bit of an exaggeration?"

"I don't think so. Do you, Harry?"

"Not really," said Meadows. "The town survives on its summer people. Martin, I have been thinking about that fellow Quint over in Montauk. The one who bills himself as a 'monster' fisherman."

"I've heard the name," said Brody. "A couple of years ago he got in trouble for harpooning porpoises. But we've got a monster that *needs* to be caught."

"You're joking," said Hooper. "How do we know the guy isn't a phony or a drunk or something?"

"You got any better ideas?" Brody took a phone book from his desk and opened it to the Qs. He ran his finger down the page. "Here it is. Quint's Monster Fishing." He dialed the number.

"Quint," said a voice.

"Mr. Quint, this is Martin Brody. I'm the chief of police in Amity. We have a problem."

"I've heard. I figured you'd call sooner or later."

"Can you help us?"

"That depends."

"On what?"

"On how much you're willing to spend, for one thing."

"We'll pay whatever you charge by the day."

"I don't think so," said Quint. "My usual rate's two hundred a day. But I think you'll pay double."

"Not a chance."

"Good-by."

"Wait a minute! Come on, man. Why are you holding me up?"

"You got no place else to go."

"There are other fishermen."

Brody heard Quint laugh—a short, derisive bark. "Sure there are," said Quint. "You already sent one. Send another one. Send half a dozen more. Then when you come back to me again, maybe you'll even pay triple. I got nothing to lose by waiting."

"I'm not asking for any favors," Brody said. "But can't you at least treat me the way you treat regular clients?"

"You're breaking my heart," said Quint. "You got a fish needs killing, I'll try to kill it for you. No guarantees, but I'll do my best. And my best is worth four hundred dollars a day. Take it or leave it."

Brody sighed. "I don't know that the selectmen will give me the money."

"You'll find it somewhere."

Brody paused. "O.K.," he said. "Can you start tomorrow?"

"Nope. Monday's the earliest. I got a charter party tomorrow."

"Can't you cancel them?" Brody asked.

"Nope. They're regular customers. You're just a one-shot deal. And there's one more thing," said Quint. "I'm gonna need a man with me. My mate quit, and I wouldn't feel comfortable taking on that big fish without an extra pair of hands."

"Why did your mate quit?"

"Nerves. Happens to most people after a while in this work."

"But it doesn't happen to you."

"No. I know I'm smarter'n the fish."

"And that's enough, just being smarter?"

"Has been so far. What about it? You got a man for me?"

Brody said casually, "I'll be there." He was shocked by the words as soon as he said them.

"You? Ha!"

Brody smarted under Quint's derision. "I can handle myself," he said.

"Maybe. But I still need a man who knows something about fishing. Or at least about boats."

Brody looked across his desk at Hooper. The last thing he wanted was to spend days on a boat with Hooper, especially in a situation in which Hooper would outrank him in knowledge, if not authority. He could send Hooper alone and stay ashore himself. But that, he felt, would be admitting his inability to conquer the strange enemy that was waging war on his town. He knew he would have no peace until he had proven himself.

Besides, maybe—over the course of a long day on a boat—Hooper might make a slip that would reveal what he had been doing last Wednesday. Brody was becoming obsessed with finding out where Hooper was that day it rained. He wanted to *know* that Hooper was at the movies, or playing backgammon at the Field Club, or smoking pot with some hippie. He didn't care what it was, as long as he could know that Hooper had not been with Ellen.

He cupped his hand over the mouthpiece and said to Hooper, "Do you want to come along? He needs a mate."

"Yes," said Hooper. "I'll probably live to regret it, but I want to see that fish, and I guess this is my only chance."

Brody said to Quint, "O.K., I've got your man."

"Monday, then, six a.m. at Freeman's Dock in Montauk."

"How will I know your boat?"

"You can't miss it. The *Orca*. It's right under my sign."

"All right. See you Monday."

"One more thing," said Quint. "Cash. Every day. In advance."

"All right," said Brody. "You'll have it." He hung up and said to Hooper, "Monday, six a.m., O.K.?"

"O.K. What's the name of his boat?"

"I think he said *Orca*," said Brody. "I don't know what it means."

"It doesn't *mean* anything. It *is* something. It's a killer whale."

Meadows and Hooper rose to go. At the door Hooper turned and said, "Thinking of orca reminds me of something. You know what Australians call great white sharks?"

"No," said Brody, not really interested. "What?"

"White Death."

"You had to tell me, didn't you?" Brody said as he closed the door behind them.

Part Three

8

The sea was as flat as gelatin. There was no whisper of wind to ripple the surface. The boat sat still in the water, drifting imperceptibly in the tide. Two fishing rods, in rod holders at the stern, trailed wire lines baited with squid into the oily slick that spread westward behind the boat. Hooper sat at the stern, a twenty-gallon garbage pail at his side. Every few seconds he dipped a ladle into the pail and spilled the chum overboard.

Forward, in two rows that peaked at the bow, lay ten wooden barrels the size of quarter kegs of beer. Each was wrapped in several thicknesses of three-quarter-inch hemp, which continued in a hundred-foot coil beside the barrel. Tied to the end of each rope was the dart-shaped steel head of a harpoon.

Brody sat in the swiveled fighting chair bolted to the deck, trying to stay awake. He was hot and sticky. They had been sitting and waiting for six hours, and the back of his neck was badly sunburned.

He looked up at the figure on the flying bridge. Quint was dressed entirely in khaki, save for a pair of graying sneakers. Brody guessed Quint was about fifty. He was six feet tall and weighed about thirteen stone. His hair, crew-cut in a sharp V, was black—a shade or two darker than his eyes, which were the darkest eyes Brody had ever seen. His skin was browned and creased by wind and salt and sun. When he gazed off the stern he seemed to sight down his long, straight nose as if it were a rifle barrel. His eyes, fixed on the slick, rarely blinked.

Brody tried to stare at the slick, but the reflection of the sun on the water hurt his eyes, and he turned away. "I don't see how you do it, Quint," he said. "Don't you ever wear sunglasses?"

"Never." Quint's tone did not invite conversation.

Brody looked at his watch. It was a little after two; three or four more hours before they would give up for the day and go home. "Do you have a lot of days like this, when you just sit and nothing happens?"

"Some."

"And people pay you even though they never get a bite?"

Quint nodded. "That doesn't happen too often. There's generally something that'll take a bait. Or something we can stick."

"Stick?"

"With an iron." Quint pointed to the harpoons on the bow.

Hooper said, "What kind of things?"

Quint cut him off. "Something's taking one of the baits."

Shading his eyes, Brody looked off the stern, but as far as he could see, the slick was undisturbed, the water flat and calm. "Where?" he said.

"Wait a second," said Quint. "You'll see."

The wire on the starboard fishing rod began to feed overboard with a soft metallic hiss.

"Take the rod," Quint said to Brody. "And when I tell you, throw the brake and hit him."

"Is it the shark?" said Brody.

The possibility that at last he was going to confront the beast, the monster, the nightmare, made his heart pound. He wiped his hands on his trousers and took the rod out of the holder and stuck it in the swivel between his legs.

Quint laughed—a short, sour yip. "That thing? No. That's just a little fella. Give you some practice for when your fish finds us." Quint watched the line for a few seconds, then said, "Hit it!"

Brody pushed the small lever on the reel forward, then pulled back. The tip of the rod bent into an arc. Brody began to turn the crank to reel in the fish, leaning forward and cranking quickly as he picked up slack, then hauling backward. "What the hell have I got here?" he said.

"A blue shark," said Quint.

"He must weigh half a ton."

Quint laughed. "Maybe a hundred 'n' fifty pounds."

Brody hauled and leaned, hauled and leaned, until finally Quint said, "You're getting there. Hold it." Brody stopped reeling.

With a smooth, unhurried motion Quint swung down the ladder from the flying bridge. He had a rifle in his hand, an army carbine. He stood at the gunwale and looked down. "You want to see the fish?" he said. "Come look."

In the dark water the shark was acrylic blue. It was about eight feet long, slender, with long pectoral fins. It swam slowly from side to side, no longer struggling.

"He's beautiful, isn't he?" said Hooper.

Quint flicked the rifle's safety to Off, and when the shark came within a few inches of the surface, he squeezed off three quick shots. The bullets made clean round holes in the shark's head, drawing no blood. The shark shuddered and stopped moving.

"He's dead," said Brody.

"He's stunned, maybe, but that's all," said Quint. He took a glove from one of his hip pockets, slipped his hand into it, and grabbed the wire line. From a sheath at his belt he took a knife. He lifted the shark's head clear of the water and bent over the gunwale. The shark's mouth was open two or three inches wide. Quint jammed the knife into the shark's mouth and tried to extract the hook, but the shark bit down, holding the blade in its small triangular teeth. Quint pulled and twisted until the knife came free.

"I guess you're paying me enough so I can afford to lose a hook." He slit the shark's belly, then cut the leader with a pair of wire cutters, and the shark slid overboard.

"Now watch," said Quint. "If we're lucky, in a minute other blues'll come around, and there'll be a real feeding frenzy. That's quite a show. The folks like that."

Brody saw a flash of blue rise from below. A small shark—no more than four feet long—snapped at the body of the disemboweled fish. Its jaws closed on a bit of flesh, and its head shook violently from side to side. Soon another shark appeared, and another, and the water began to roil. Fins crisscrossed on the surface, tails whipped the water. Amid the sounds of splashes came an occasional grunt as fish slammed into fish.

The frenzy continued for several minutes, until only three large sharks remained, cruising back and forth beneath the surface.

"My God!" said Hooper.

"You don't approve," said Quint.

"I don't like to see things die for people's amusement. Do you?"

"It isn't a question of liking it or not," said Quint. "It's what feeds me." He reached into an ice chest and took out a baited hook and another leader. Using pliers, he attached the leader to the end of the wire line, then dropped the bait overboard.

Hooper resumed his routine of ladling the chum into the water. Brody said, "Anybody want a beer?" Both Quint and Hooper nodded, so he went below and got three cans from a cooler. As he left the cabin, Brody noticed an old cracked and curling photograph nailed to the bulkhead. It showed a dead shark lying on a beach. There was nothing else in the photograph to compare the shark to, so Brody couldn't determine its size.

Brody left the cabin, gave the others their beers, and sat down in the fighting chair. "I saw your picture down there," he said to Quint. "What is that fish? Just a shark?"

"Well, not *just* a shark. It was a big white—about fourteen, fifteen feet. Weighed over three thousand pounds."

"How did you catch it?"

"Ironed it. But I tell you," Quint chuckled, "it almost caught us."

"What do you mean?"

"Damn thing attacked the boat. No provocation, no nothing. We were sitting out here minding our own business, when wham! It felt like we was hit by a freight train. Knocked my mate right on his ass, and the customer started screaming bloody murder that we were sinking. Then the bastard hit us again. I put an iron in him and we chased him—seemed like halfway across the Atlantic."

"Why didn't he go deep?" asked Brody.

"Couldn't. Not with those barrels following him. They float. A fish that big can drag one or two of them down with him and keep them there for a while. But before too long the strain gets to him, and he'll come to the surface. So you just keep looking for the barrels to pop up, and you follow them. Anyway, it took us five hours and seven irons to get him calmed down enough so I could throw a tow rope round his tail."

"You wouldn't try to catch the fish we're after on a hook and line, would you?" asked Brody.

"Hell, no. From what I hear, the fish that's been bothering you makes the one we got look like a pup."

"Then how come the lines are out?"

"Two reasons. First, a big white might just take a little squid bait like that. It'd cut the line pretty quick, but at least we'd know he was around. The other reason is, we might run into something else that'll take the bait. If you're paying four hundred bucks, you might as well have some fun for your money."

"Suppose the big white did come around," said Brody. "What would be the first thing you'd do?"

"Try to keep him interested enough so he'd stick around till we could start pumping irons into him. And that's where we'll have a little trouble. The squid isn't enough to keep him interested. Fish that size'll suck a squid right down and not even know he's ate it. So we'll have to give him something special that he can't turn down, something with a big ol' hook on it that'll hold him at least until we can stick him once or twice."

From the stern, Hooper said, "What's something special, Quint?"

Quint pointed to a green plastic garbage can nestled in a corner amidships. "Take a look for yourself. It's in that can."

Hooper walked over to the can, flipped the metal clasps and lifted the top. He gasped at what he saw. Floating in the can full of water was a tiny bottle-nosed dolphin, no more than two feet long. Sticking out from a puncture on the underside of the jaw was the eye of a huge shark hook, and from a hole in the belly the barbed hook itself curled forward. Hooper clutched the sides of the can and said, "A baby."

"Even better," Quint said with a grin. "Unborn. I cut it from the mother myself. Did you ever see anything so tender in your whole life?"

Hooper gazed into the can for another few seconds, then slammed the top back on and said, "Where did you get the mother?"

"Oh, I guess about six miles from here, due east. Why?"

"You killed her."

"No." Quint laughed. "She jumped into the boat and swallowed a bunch of sleeping pills." He paused, waiting for a laugh, and when none came he said, "Sure I killed her. You can't rightly buy them, you know."

Hooper stared at Quint. He was furious, outraged. "You know they're protected."

"When I fish, son, I catch what I want."

"But what about laws? Don't—"

"What's your line of work, Hooper?"

"I'm an ichthyologist. I study fish. That's why I'm here."

"O.K., you study fish for a living. If you had to work for a living—I mean the kind of work where the amount of money you make depends on the amount of sweat you put in—you'd know more about what laws really mean. That law wasn't put in to stop Quint from taking one or two porpoise for bait. It was meant to stop big-time fishing for them, to stop nuts from shooting them for sport. So you can moan all you want, Hooper, but don't tell Quint he can't catch a few fish to help him make a living."

"I get your message," said Hooper. "Take it while you can, and if after a while there's nothing left, why, we'll just start taking something else. It's so stupid!"

"Don't overstep, son." Quint's voice was flat, toneless, and he looked directly into Hooper's eyes. "Don't go calling me stupid."

"I didn't mean that, for God's sake. I just meant—"

On his perch midway between the two men Brody decided it was time to stop the argument. "Let it drop, Hooper, O.K.?" he said. "We're not out here to have a debate on ecology."

"I bet all you know about ecology is someone telling you you can't burn leaves in your backyard."

"Listen, damn you! We're out here to stop a fish from killing people, and if using one porpoise will help us save God-knows-how-many lives, that seems to me a pretty good bargain."

Hooper smirked and said to Brody, "So now you're an expert on saving lives, are you? Let's see. How many could have been saved if you'd closed the beaches after the—"

Brody was on his feet moving at Hooper before he consciously knew he had left his chair. "You shut your mouth!" he said. Reflexively he dropped his right hand to his hip. He stopped short when he felt no holster at his side, scared by the sudden realization that if he had had a pistol he might have used it.

A quick, sharp laugh from Quint broke the tension. "I seen that coming since you came aboard this morning," he said.

THE SECOND DAY of the hunt was as still as the first. The boat lay motionless on the glassy sea, like a paper cup in a puddle.

Brody had brought a book along to pass the time, a sex mystery borrowed from Hendricks, called *The Deadly Virgin*. He did not want to have to fill time with conversation, which might lead to a repeat of yesterday's scene with Hooper. It had embarrassed him—Hooper, too, he thought.

Today they seldom spoke to one another, directing most of their comments at Quint. Brody sat reading in the fighting chair, a hat protecting his face; Hooper was at the stern, ladling chum and occasionally shaking his head to keep awake, and Quint on the flying bridge, watching the slick.

Suddenly Quint said, his voice soft, "We've got a visitor."

Brody snapped awake. Hooper stood up. The starboard line was running out, smoothly and very fast.

"Take the rod," Quint said.

Brody took the rod, fitted it into the swivel and held on.

"When I tell you," said Quint, "you throw that brake and hit him." The line stopped running. "Wait. He's turning. He'll start again." But the line lay dead in the water, limp and unmoving. After several moments Quint said, "Reel it in."

The line came clear of the water and hung at the tip of the rod. There was no hook, no bait, no leader. The wire had been neatly severed. Quint hopped down from the bridge and looked at it. "I think we've just met your friend," he said. "This wire's been bit clean through. The fish probably didn't even know he had it in his mouth. He just sucked the bait in and closed his mouth and that did it."

"So what do we do now?" said Brody.

"We wait and see if he takes the other one, or if he surfaces."

"What about using the porpoise?"

"When I know it's him," said Quint, "then I'll give him the porpoise. I don't want to waste a prize bait on some little runt."

They waited. The only sound was the liquid plop of the chum Hooper ladled overboard. Then the port line began to run.

Brody was both excited and afraid, awed by the thought of what was swimming below them, a creature whose power he could not imagine. Hooper stood at the port gunwale, transfixed by the running line.

The line stopped and went limp.

"He's done it again," said Quint. He took the rod out of the holder and began to reel. The severed line came aboard exactly as the other one had. "We'll give him one more chance," said Quint, "and I'll put on a tougher leader. Not that that'll stop him, if it's the fish I think it is."

From a drawer in the cockpit he took a four-foot length of three-eighth-inch chain.

"That looks like a dog's leash," said Brody.

"Used to be," said Quint.

"What's next if this doesn't work?"

"Don't know yet. I could take a four-inch shark hook and a length of chain and drop it overboard with a bunch of bait on it. But if he took it, I wouldn't know what to do with him. He'd tear out any cleat I've got on board." Quint flipped the baited hook overboard and fed out a few yards of line. "Come on, you bastard," he said. "Let's have a look at you."

The three men watched the port line. Hooper bent down, filled his ladle with chum and tossed it into the slick. Something caught his eye and made him turn to the left. What he saw sucked from him a throaty grunt that made the others turn to look.

"My God!" said Brody.

No more than ten feet off the stern, slightly to the starboard, was the conical snout of the fish. It stuck out of the water perhaps two feet. The top of the head was sooty gray, pocked with two black eyes. The mouth was open not quite halfway, a dim cavern guarded by huge, triangular teeth.

Fish and men confronted each other for ten seconds that seemed frozen in time. Then Quint yelled, "Get an iron!" and, obeying himself, he dashed forward for a harpoon. Just then the fish slid quietly backward into the water. The long, scythed tail flicked once, and the fish disappeared.

"He's gone," said Brody.

"Fantastic!" said Hooper. "That fish is everything I thought. And more. He's fantastic! That head must have been four feet across."

"Could be," said Quint, walking aft to deposit in the stern two harpoon heads and two barrels with their coils of rope.

"Have you ever seen a fish like that?" Hooper asked.

"Not quite," said Quint.

"How long was he, would you say?"

"Twenty feet. Maybe more. With them things, it don't make

much difference over six feet. Once they get to six feet, they're trouble."

Brody felt a chill. "He looked like he was grinning," he said.

"Don't make him out to be more than he is," said Quint. "He's just a stupid garbage bucket."

"How can you say that?" said Hooper. "That fish is a beauty. It's the kind of thing that makes you believe in a god."

A noise behind Hooper made him turn. It was a swishing noise, a liquid hiss. Knifing the water thirty feet away was a triangular dorsal fin more than a foot high. It was followed by a towering tail that swatted left and right in tight cadence.

"It's attacking the boat!" cried Brody. Involuntarily, he backed into the seat of the fighting chair.

"Hand me that iron," said Quint.

The fish was almost upon the boat. It raised its head, gazed vacantly at Hooper with one of its black eyes, and passed under the boat. Quint raised the harpoon and turned back to the port side. The throwing pole struck the fighting chair, and the dart dislodged and fell to the deck.

"Damn!" shouted Quint. "Is he still there?" He reached down, grabbed the dart and stuck it back on the end of the pole.

"Your side!" yelled Hooper. "He's passed this side already."

Quint turned as the gray-brown shape of the fish pulled away from the boat and began to dive. He dropped the harpoon, snatched up the carbine and emptied the clip into the water behind the fish. "Bastard!" he said. "Give me some warning next time." Then he put the carbine down and laughed. "At least he didn't attack the boat," he said. He looked at Brody. "Gave you a bit of a start."

"More'n a bit," said Brody. He shook his head, as if to reassemble his thoughts. "I'm still not sure I believe it." His mind was full of images of a torpedo shape streaking upward in the blackness and tearing Christine Watkins to pieces; of the boy on the raft, unknowing, unsuspecting, until suddenly seized by a nightmare creature. "You can't tell me that thing's a fish," he said. "It's more like one of those monsters they make movies about."

"It's a fish, all right," said Hooper. "And what a fish!"

"You think he'll come back?" said Brody.

"I don't know," said Quint. "You never know what they're going to do." From a pocket he took a notepad and a pencil. He extended his left arm and pointed it toward shore. He closed his right eye and sighted down the index finger of his left hand, then scribbled on the pad. He moved his hand a couple of inches to the left, sighted again and made another note. Anticipating a question from Brody, Quint said, "Taking bearings so if he doesn't show up for the rest of today, I'll know where to come tomorrow."

Brody looked toward shore. "What are you taking them on?"

"Lighthouse on the point and the water tower in Montauk. They line up different ways depending where you are."

"You can see them?" Brody strained his eyes, but all he could make out was a dim gray line of land.

"Sure. You could too, if you'd been out here for thirty years."

Hooper smiled. "Do you really think he'll stay in one place?"

"He sure as hell stayed around Amity," said Brody.

"That's because he had food," said Hooper. There was no irony in his voice, no taunt. But the remark was like a needle stabbing into Brody's brain.

They waited, but the fish never returned. At a little after five, Quint said, "We might as well go in."

"You don't think we should spend the night, to keep the slick going?" said Brody.

Quint thought for a moment. "Nope. First, the slick would be big and confusing, and that would screw us up for the next day. Second, I like to get this boat in at night."

"I guess I can't blame you," said Brody. "Your wife must like it better, too."

Quint said flatly. "Got no wife."

"Oh. I'm sorry."

"Don't be. I never saw the need for one." Quint turned and climbed the ladder to the flying bridge.

ELLEN WAS FIXING the children's supper when the doorbell rang. She heard the door open, heard Billy's voice, and a moment later saw Larry Vaughan standing in the kitchen door. It had been less than two weeks since she had last seen him, yet the change in his appearance was startling. As always he was dressed perfectly, but he had lost weight, and the loss showed in his face.

Embarrassed when she found herself staring, Ellen lowered her eyes and said, "Larry. Hello."

"Hello, Ellen. I stopped by to say farewell."

Ellen said, "You're going away? For how long?"

"I don't know. Perhaps for good. There's nothing here for me anymore. What few assets there are will belong to my . . . partners." He spat the word and then he said, "Has Martin told you about . . . ?"

"Yes." Ellen looked down at the chicken she was cooking.

"I imagine you don't think very highly of me anymore."

"It's not up to me to judge you, Larry. How much does Eleanor know?"

"Nothing, poor dear. I want to spare her, if I can. That's one reason I want to move away." Vaughan leaned against the sink. "You know something? Sometimes I've thought that you and I would have made a wonderful couple."

Ellen reddened. "What do you mean?"

"You're from a good family. You know all the people I had to fight to get to know. We would have fitted in in Amity. You're lovely and good and strong. You would have been a real asset to me. And I think I could have given you a life you would have loved."

Ellen smiled. "I'm not as strong as you think, Larry."

"Don't belittle yourself. I only hope Martin appreciates the treasure he has. Anyway, no point in dreaming." He walked across the kitchen and kissed the top of Ellen's head. "Good-by, dear," he said. "Think of me once in a while."

Ellen looked at him. "I will." She kissed his cheek. "Where are you going?"

"I don't know, Vermont, maybe, or New Hampshire. I might sell land to the skiing crowd."

"Send us a card so we'll know where you are."

"I will. Good-by." Vaughan left the room, and Ellen heard the screen door close behind him.

When she had served the children their supper Ellen went upstairs and sat on her bed. "A life you would have loved," Vaughan had said. What would it have been like? There would have been money and acceptance. She would never have missed the life she led as a girl, for it would never have ended. There would have been no craving for renewal and self-confidence and confirmation of her femininity, no need for a fling with someone like Hooper. But it would have been a life without challenge, a life of cheap satisfactions.

As she pondered what Vaughan had said she began to recognize the richness of her relationship with Brody. It was more rewarding than any Larry Vaughan would ever experience, an amalgam of minor trials and tiny triumphs that added up to something akin to joy. And as her recognition grew so did a regret that it had taken her so long to see the waste of time and emotion in trying to cling to her past. Suddenly she felt fear—fear that she was growing up too late, that something might happen to Brody before she could savor her awareness. She looked at her watch: 6:20. He should have been home by now.

She heard the front door open. She ran down the stairs, wrapped her arms around Brody and kissed him hard on the mouth.

"My God," he said when she let him go. "That's some welcome."

9

"You're not putting that thing on my boat," said Quint.

They stood on the dock in the brightening light. The sun had cleared the horizon, but it lay behind a low bank of clouds that touched the eastern sea. The boat was ready to go. The engine chugged quietly, sputtering bubbles as tiny waves washed against the exhaust pipe.

Quint stood with his back to the boat, facing Brody and Hooper, who stood on either side of an aluminium cage. The cage was slightly over six feet tall, six feet wide and four feet deep. Inside it were a scuba tank, a regulator, a face mask and a neoprene wet suit.

"What the hell is it anyway?" said Quint.

"It's a shark cage," said Hooper. "Divers use them to protect themselves when they're swimming in the open ocean. I phoned last night and my friends brought it down from Woods Hole."

"And what do you plan to do with it?"

"When we find the fish I want to go down in the cage and take some pictures."

"Not a chance," said Quint. "A fish that big could eat that cage for breakfast."

"But *would* he? I think he might bump it, might even mouth it, but I don't think he'd seriously try to eat it."

"Well, forget it."

"Look, Quint, this is a chance of a lifetime. I wouldn't have thought of doing it until I saw the fish yesterday. No one's ever filmed a twenty-foot white swimming in the open ocean. Never."

"He said forget it," said Brody. "So forget it. We're out here to kill that fish, not make a home movie about it."

Hooper said to Quint, "I'll pay you."

Quint smiled. "Oh, yeah? How much?"

"A hundred dollars. Cash. In advance, the way you like it." He reached into his back pocket for his wallet.

"I said no!" said Brody.

"I don't know," said Quint. Then he said, "Hell, I don't guess it's my business to keep a man from killing himself if he wants to."

"You put that cage on the boat," Brody said to Quint, "and you don't get your four hundred." If Hooper wants to kill himself, Brody thought, let him do it on his own time.

"And if the cage doesn't go," said Hooper, "I don't go."

"We'll find another man," said Brody.

"Can't do it," said Quint. "Not on this short notice."

"Then the hell with it!" said Brody. "We'll go tomorrow. Hooper can go back to Woods Hole and play with his fish."

Hooper was angry—angrier, in fact, than he knew, for before he could stop himself, he had said, "That's not all I might. . . . Oh, forget it."

A leaden silence fell over the three men. Brody stared at Hooper, unwilling to believe what he had heard. Then suddenly he was overcome by rage. He reached Hooper in two steps, grabbed both sides of his collar and rammed his fists alongside Hooper's neck. "What was that?" he said. "What did you say?"

Hooper clawed at Brody's fingers. "Nothing!" he said, choking. "Nothing!"

"Where were you last Wednesday afternoon?"

"Nowhere!" Hooper's temples were throbbing. "Let me go!"

"Where were you?" Brody twisted his fists tighter.

"In a motel! Now let me go!"

Brody eased his grip. "With who?" he said.

"Daisy Wicker." Hooper knew it was a weak lie. Brody could check it out with no trouble. But it was all he could think of. He could stop on the way home and phone Daisy Wicker, beg her to corroborate his story.

"I'll check," said Brody. "You can count on it."

Behind him Brody heard Quint laugh sharply. "Are you two going today or not?" he asked. "Either way, Brody, it'll cost you."

Brody was tempted to cancel the trip, to return to Amity and discover the truth. But he said to Quint, "We'll go."

"With the cage?"

"With the cage. If this bastard wants to kill himself, let him."

"O.K. by me," said Quint. "Let's get this circus on the road."

They slid the cage across the wooden dock, and down into the cockpit. Brody was surprised at how light it was. Even with the diving gear inside it couldn't have weighed more than two hundred pounds. Then Quint pushed the throttle forward and headed the boat toward the open sea.

Gradually, as the *Orca* cruised through the long ocean swells, Brody's fury dulled. Maybe Hooper was telling the truth. He was sure Ellen had never cheated on him before. But, he told himself, there's always a first time. And once again the thought made his throat tighten. He climbed up to the flying bridge and sat on the bench next to Quint.

Quint chuckled. "What is it, you think Hooper's been fooling around with your wife?"

"None of your damn business," Brody said.

"Whatever you say. But if you ask me, he ain't got it in him."

"Nobody asked you." Anxious to change the subject, Brody said, "Are we going back to the same place?"

"Same place. Won't be too long now."

"What are the chances the fish will still be there?"

"Who knows? But it's the only thing we can do."

"You said something the other day about being smarter than the fish. Is that all there is to it?"

"That's all there is. You just got to outguess 'em. It's no trick. They're stupid as sin."

"But there are fish you can't catch, aren't there?"

"Oh sure, but that only means they're not hungry, or they're too fast for you, or you're using the wrong bait."

Quint fell silent for a moment, then spoke again. "Once," he said, "a shark almost caught *me*. It was twenty years ago, I gaffed a fair-sized blue, and he gave a big yank and hauled me overboard."

"What did you do?"

"I come up over that transom so fast I don't think my feet touched anything between water and deck."

Quint pulled back on the throttle, and the boat slowed. He took a piece of paper from his pocket, read the notes and, sighting along his outstretched arm, checked his bearings. "O.K., Hooper," he said. "Start chuckin' the stuff overboard."

BY TEN O'CLOCK a breeze had come up—not strong, but fresh enough to ripple the water and cool the men, who sat and watched and said nothing. The only sounds were the idling engine beat and the regular splash as Hooper poured chum off the stern.

Brody sat in the fighting chair, struggling to stay awake. He yawned, then he stood, stretched and went down the three steps into the cabin. "Anybody want a beer?" he called.

"Sure," said Quint.

Brody took out two beers, and had started to climb the stairs when he heard Quint's flat, calm voice say, "There he is."

Hooper jumped off the transom. "Wow! He sure is!"

It took Brody's eyes a moment to adjust, but then, off the stern, he saw the fin slicing through the water. The fish was thirty yards away, Brody guessed.

Quint walked forward and fastened a harpoon head to the wooden shaft. He set a barrel on the transom to the left of Hooper's bucket and arranged the coiled rope beside it. Then he climbed up on the transom and stood, his right arm cocked, holding the harpoon. "Come on, Fish," he said. "Come on in here."

The fish cruised slowly back and forth, but he would come no closer than fifty feet.

"I don't get it," said Quint. "He should come in and take a look at us. Throw some squid bait overboard. And make a big splash. Let him know something's there."

Hooper said, "What about the porpoise?"

"Why, Mr. Hooper," said Quint. "I thought you didn't approve."

"Never mind that," Hooper said, his eyes bright with excitement. "I want to see that fish!"

"We'll see," said Quint. "If I have to use it, I will."

They waited—Hooper ladling, Quint poised on the transom, Brody standing by one of the rods.

"Hell," said Quint. "I guess I got no choice." He set the harpoon down and jumped off the transom. He flipped the top off the garbage can next to Brody, and Brody saw the lifeless eyes of the tiny porpoise as it swayed in the briny water. The sight repelled him, and he turned away.

"Well, little fella," said Quint. "The time has come." He took out a dog-leash chain and snapped one end of it into the hook eye protruding from beneath the porpoise's jaw. To the other end of the chain he tied several yards of three-quarter-inch hemp. Then he made the rope fast to a cleat on the starboard gunwale.

"You said the shark could pull out a cleat," said Brody.

"It might just," said Quint. "But I'm betting I can get an iron in him and cut the rope before he pulls it taut enough to yank the cleat." Quint carried the porpoise over to the transom and cut a series of shallow slashes in its belly before tossing it into the water. He let out six feet of line, then put the rope under his foot on the transom.

"Why are you standing on the rope?" asked Brody.

"To keep the little fella where I can get a shot at the shark. But I don't want to cleat it down too close. If the shark took it and didn't have any running room, he could beat us to pieces."

The shark was still cruising back and forth, but coming closer to the boat with every passage. Then it stopped, twenty feet away. The tail dropped beneath the surface, and the great head reared up, mouth open in a slack, savage grin, eyes black and abysmal. Brody stared in mute horror.

"Hey, Fish!" Quint called. He stood on the transom, legs spread, his hand curled around the shaft of the harpoon that rested on his shoulder. "Come see what we've got for you!"

For another moment the fish hung in the water, watching. Then soundlessly the head slid down and disappeared.

"He'll be coming now," said Quint.

Suddenly the boat lurched violently to the side. Quint's legs skidded out from under him, and he fell backward on the transom. The harpoon dart separated from the shaft and clattered to the deck. Brody tumbled sideways, grabbing the back of the chair as it swiveled around. Hooper slammed into the port gunwale.

The rope attached to the porpoise tautened and shivered. The wood under the cleat began to crack. Then the rope snapped backward, went slack, and curled in the water beside the boat.

"I'll be damned!" said Quint. "I never have seen a fish do that before. He either bit through the chain, or else. . . ." He walked over to the starboard gunwale and grabbed the chain. It was intact, but the hook it was attached to was nearly straight.

"He did that with his mouth?" said Brody.

"Bent it out nice as you please," said Quint. "Probably didn't slow him down for more than a second or two."

Brody felt light-headed. He sat down in the chair and drew several deep breaths, trying to stifle his mounting fear.

"Where do you suppose he's gone?" said Hooper.

"He's around here somewhere," said Quint. "That porpoise wasn't any more to him than an anchovy is to a bluefish. He'll be looking for more food." He reassembled the harpoon and re-coiled the rope. "I'll tie up some more squid and hang 'em overboard."

Brody watched Quint as he wrapped twine around each squid and dropped it overboard. When a dozen squid had been placed around the boat, Quint climbed to the flying bridge and sat down.

Brody looked at his watch: 11:05. At 11:30 he was startled by a sharp, resonant *snap*. Quint leaped down the ladder, sprang across the deck and picked up the harpoon. "He's back," he said. "He took one of the squid." A few inches of limp twine hung from a cleat amidships.

As Brody looked at the remnant he saw another piece of twine—a few feet farther up the gunwale—go limp. "He must be right underneath us," he said.

"Let's put the cage overboard," said Hooper.

"You're kidding," said Brody.

"No, I'm not. It might bring him out."

"You're out of your mind. What are you going to do if he does come out?"

"First I'm going to take some pictures of him. Then I'm going to try to kill him."

"With what, may I ask?"

"This." Hooper held up a stick with a thong at one end.

"Good thinking," Quint said with a derisive cackle. "If that doesn't work, you can tickle him to death."

"What is that?" said Brody.

"It's called a bang stick or a power head. Basically it's an underwater gun." He pulled both ends of the stick, and it came apart in two pieces. "In here," he said, pointing to a chamber, "you put a twelve-gauge shotgun shell." He took one from his pocket and pushed it into the chamber. "Then you jab it at the fish, and the shell goes off. If you hit him right—the brain's the only sure place—you kill him."

"Even a fish that big?"

"I think so. If I hit him right."

"And if you don't? Suppose you miss by just a hair."

"What concerns me is that if I miss, I might drive him off," said Hooper. "He'd probably sound, and we'd never know if he died or not."

"Until he ate someone else," said Brody.

"That's right."

"You're plain crazy," said Quint.

"Am I, Quint? You're not having much success with this fish. I think he's more than you can handle."

"That right, boy? You think you can do better'n Quint? Fine and dandy. You're gonna get your chance."

Brody said, "Come on. We can't let him go in that thing."

"What are *you* bitchin' about?" said Quint. "From what I seen, you'd just as soon he went down there and never come up. At least that'd stop him from—"

"Shut your mouth!" Brody's emotions were jumbled. Could he really wish a man dead? No. Not yet.

"Go on," Quint said to Hooper. "Get in that thing."

"Right away." Hooper removed his shirt, sneakers and trousers, and began to pull the neoprene suit over his legs. "When I'm inside," he said, forcing his arms into the rubber sleeves of the jacket, "stand up here and keep an eye out. Maybe you can use the rifle if he gets close enough to the surface."

When he was dressed Hooper fitted the regulator onto the neck of the air tank and opened the valve. He sucked two breaths from the tank to make sure it was feeding air. "Help me put this on, will you?" he said to Brody.

Brody held the tank while Hooper slipped his arms through the straps and fastened a third strap around his middle. He put the face mask on his head. "I should have brought weights," he said.

Quint said, "You should have brought brains."

Hooper put his right wrist through the thong at the end of the power head, picked up his camera and walked to the gunwale.

"O.K.," he said. "Let's put her over." They lifted the cage overboard and secured it with two lines to cleats on the starboard gunwale. It sank until the ropes stopped it, a few feet beneath the surface. "If you'll each take a rope and pull the cage to the surface, I'll open the hatch and go in through the top," said Hooper.

Quint and Brody pulled on the ropes, and the cage rose in the water. When the hatch broke the surface Hooper said, "O.K., right there." He spat in the face mask, rubbed the saliva around on the glass and fitted the mask over his face. He reached for the regulator tube, put the mouthpiece in his mouth and took a breath. He unlatched the hatch and flipped it open, put a knee on the gunwale, then stopped and took the mouthpiece out of his mouth. "I forgot something." He walked across the deck and rummaged through his trouser pockets. Then he unzipped his wet-suit jacket.

"What's that?" said Brody.

Hooper held up a shark's tooth, a duplicate of the one he had given Ellen. He dropped it inside his wet-suit. "Can't be too careful," he said, smiling. He replaced his mouthpiece, took a final breath and jumped overboard through the open hatch.

Before he hit the bottom of the cage Hooper curled around and pulled the hatch closed. Then he stood, looked up at Brody, and put his thumb and index finger together in the O.K. sign.

Brody and Quint let the cage descend until the top was about four feet beneath the surface.

"Get the rifle," said Quint. He climbed onto the transom and lifted the harpoon to his shoulder.

Brody went below, found the rifle and hurried back on deck.

In the cage Hooper waited for the bubbly froth of his descent to dissipate. He felt serene. He was alone in blue silence speckled with shafts of sunlight that danced through the water. He looked up at the gray hull of the boat. Even with the bright sunlight, the visibility in the murky water was poor—no more than forty feet. Hooper turned slowly around, trying to pierce the edge of gloom and grasp any sliver of color or movement. Nothing.

Carried by the tide, one of the small white squid slipped between the bars and, tethered by twine, fluttered in Hooper's face. He pushed it out of the cage. He glanced downward, started to look away, then snapped his eyes down again. Rising at him from the darkling blue—slowly, smoothly—was the shark.

Hooper stared, impelled to flee but unable to move. As the fish drew nearer he marveled at its colors: the top of the immense body was a hard ferrous gray, bluish where dappled with streaks of sun. Beneath the lateral line all was creamy white. Hooper wanted to raise his camera, but his arm would not obey.

The fish came closer, silent as a shadow, and Hooper drew back. The head was only a few feet from the cage when the fish turned and began to pass before Hooper's eyes, as if in proud display of its mass and power. The snout passed first, then the jaw, slack and smiling. And then the black, fathomless eye, seemingly riveted upon him. The gills rippled—bloodless wounds in the steely skin.

Tentatively, Hooper stuck a hand through the bars and touched the flank. It felt cold and hard, not clammy but smooth as vinyl. He let his fingertips caress the flesh—past the pectoral fins, the pelvic fin, the thick, firm genital claspers—until finally they were slapped away by the sweeping tail.

Hooper heard faint popping noises, and he saw three straight spirals of angry bubbles speed from the surface, then slow and stop, well above the fish. Bullets.

"What the hell is he doing down there?" said Brody. "Why didn't he jab him?"

Quint stood on the transom, harpoon clutched in his fist, peering into the water. "Come up, Fish," he said. "Come to Quint."

The fish had circled off to the limit of Hooper's vision—a spectral blur. Hooper raised his camera and pressed the trigger. He wanted to catch the beast as it emerged from the darkness.

Through the viewfinder he saw the fish turn toward him. It moved fast, tail thrusting vigorously, mouth opening and closing. Hooper changed the focus. Remember to change it again, he told himself, when it turns.

But the fish did not turn. It struck the cage head on, the snout ramming between two bars and spreading them. The snout hit Hooper in the chest and knocked him backward. The camera flew from his hands, and the mouthpiece shot from his mouth. The fish turned on its side, and the pounding tail forced the great body farther into the cage. Hooper groped for his mouthpiece but couldn't find it. His chest was convulsed with the need for air.

"It's attacking!" screamed Brody. He grabbed one of the tether ropes and pulled, desperately trying to raise the cage.

"Damn your soul!" Quint shouted.

"Throw the iron!" Brody yelled. "Throw it!"

"I can't throw it! I gotta get him on the surface! Come up, you devil!"

The fish slid backward out of the cage and turned sharply to the right in a tight circle. Hooper reached behind his head and located the mouthpiece. He put it in his mouth and drew an agonized breath. It was then that he saw the wide gap in the bars, and saw the giant head lunging through it again. He raised his hands above his head, grasping at the escape hatch.

The fish rammed through the space between the bars, spreading them still further. Hooper, flattened against the back of the cage, saw the mouth reaching, straining for him, lips pulled back from serrated teeth in a frenzied grimace. He tried to lower his arm and grab the power head. The fish thrust again, and its jaws closed around his torso. Hooper felt an incredible pain as if his guts were compacted. He jabbed his fist into the black eye. The fish bit down, and the last thing Hooper saw before he died was the eye gazing at him through a cloud of his own blood.

"He's got him," cried Brody. "Do something!"

"The man is dead," Quint said.

"How do you know? We may be able to save him."

"He's dead."

Holding Hooper in its mouth, the fish backed out of the cage. Then, with a thrust of its tail, it drove itself upward.

"He's coming up!" said Brody.

"Grab the rifle!" Quint cocked his hand for the throw.

The fish broke water fifteen feet from the boat, surging upward in a shower of spray. Hooper's body hung from either side of the mouth. For a few seconds Brody thought he saw Hooper's glazed, dead eyes staring through his face mask, while the black eye of the fish rolled backward in contempt and triumph.

Simultaneously, Brody reached for the rifle and Quint cast the harpoon. The target was huge, a field of white belly, and the distance was not too great for a successful throw above water. But as Quint threw, the fish slid downward, and the iron went high.

Brody shot without aiming, and the bullets plopped harmlessly into the swirl.

The fish might never have been there. There was no noise save the whisper of a breeze. From the surface the cage seemed undamaged. The water was calm. The only difference was that Hooper was gone.

"What do we do now?" said Brody. "What in the name of God can we do now? There's nothing left. We might as well go back."

"We'll go back," said Quint. "For now."

"For now? What do you mean? The fish is too much for us. It's not real, not natural. All we can do is wait until God or nature or whatever the hell is doing this to us decides we've had enough. It's out of man's hands."

"Not mine," said Quint. "I am going to kill that thing."

"I'm not sure I can get any more money after what happened today."

"Keep your money. This is no longer a matter of money."

"What do you mean?"

Quint said, "I am going to kill that fish. Come if you want. Stay home if you want. But I am going to kill that fish." His eyes seemed as dark and bottomless as the eye of the fish.

"I'll come," said Brody. "I don't guess I have any choice."

"No," said Quint. "We have no choice."

When the boat was tied up, Brody walked toward his car. At the end of the dock there was a phone booth, and he stopped beside it, prompted by his earlier resolve to call Daisy Wicker. But what's the point? he thought. If there was anything, it's over now.

Still, as he drove toward Amity, Brody wondered what Ellen's reaction had been to the news of Hooper's death. Quint had radioed the Coast Guard before they started in, and Brody had asked the duty officer to phone Ellen.

BY THE TIME BRODY arrived home Ellen had long since finished crying. She had wept angrily, grieving not so much for Hooper as in hopelessness and bitterness at yet another death. Hooper had been her lover in only the most shallow sense of the word. She had not *loved* him, she had used him.

She heard Brody's car pull into the driveway, and she opened the back door. Lord, he looks whipped, she thought. His eyes were red and sunken, and he seemed slightly hunched as he walked toward the house. She kissed him at the door and said, "You look like you could use a drink."

"That I could." He went into the living room and flopped into a chair.

She went into the kitchen, filled a glass with equal portions of vodka and orange juice, and brought it to him. She sat on the arm of his chair and said, "Well, it's over now, isn't it? There's nothing more you can do."

"We're going out tomorrow. Six o'clock."

"Why?" Ellen was stunned. "What do you think you can do?"

"Catch the fish. And kill it."

"Do you believe that?"

"I'm not sure. But Quint believes it. God, how he believes it."

"Then let him go. Let him get killed."

"I can't."

"Why not?"

Brody thought for a moment and said, "I don't think I can explain it. But giving up isn't an answer."

Tears spilled out of Ellen's eyes. "What about me and the children? Do you want to get killed?"

"No, God, no. It's just. . . ."

"You think it's all your fault. You think you're responsible for that little boy and the old man. You think killing the shark will make everything all right again. You want revenge."

Brody sighed. "Maybe I do. I don't know. I feel . . . I believe that the only way this town can be alive again is if we kill that thing."

"And you're willing to get killed trying to—"

"Don't be stupid! I'm not even willing to go out in that goddam boat. I'm so scared every minute I'm out there I want to puke."

"Then *why go?*" She was pleading with him, begging. "Can't you ever think of anybody but yourself?"

Brody was shocked at the suggestion of selfishness. "I love you," he said. "You know that . . . no matter what."

"Sure you do," she said bitterly. "Oh, sure you do."

AROUND MIDNIGHT the wind began to blow hard from the northeast, whistling through the screens and soon bringing a driving rain. Brody got out of bed and shut the window. He tried to go back to sleep, but his mind refused to rest.

At five he got up and dressed quietly. Before he left the bedroom he looked at Ellen, who had a frown on her sleeping face. "I do love you, you know," he whispered, and he kissed her brow. He started down the stairs and then, impulsively, went and looked in the boys' bedrooms. They were all asleep.

10

When he got to the dock Quint was waiting for him—a tall, impassive figure whose yellow oilskins shone under the dark sky. He was sharpening a harpoon dart on a carborundum stone.

"What does the weather mean?" said Brody.

"Nothing," said Quint. "It'll let up after a while. Or even if it doesn't, he'll be there." He hopped aboard the boat.

"Is it just us? I thought you liked an extra pair of hands."

"You know this fish as well as any man, and more hands won't make no difference now. Besides, it's nobody else's business."

Quint walked forward and cast off the bowline. Then he pushed the throttle forward, and the boat eased out of the slip.

The channel was rough, for the wind was at odds with an ebbing tide. The pounding bow cast a mantle of spray.

They had been under way only fifteen minutes when Quint pulled back on the throttle and slowed the engine.

"We're not as far out as usual," Brody said. "We can't be more than a couple of miles offshore."

"Just about."

"So why are you stopping?"

Quint pointed to a cluster of lights farther down the shore. "That's Amity there. I think he'll be somewhere between here and Amity."

"Why?"

"I got a feeling. There's not always a why to these things."

"Two days in a row we found him farther out."

"Or he found us." Quint's tone was sly.

Brody bristled. "What kind of game are you playing?"

"No game. If I'm wrong, I'm wrong."

"And we try somewhere else tomorrow." Brody half hoped Quint would be wrong, that there would be a day's reprieve.

"Or later today. But I don't think we'll have to wait that long." Quint lifted a bucket of chum onto the transom. "Start chummin'," he said, handing Brody the ladle. "O.K.," he said. "Now let's see how long it takes."

The sky had lightened to full, gray daylight, and in ones and twos the lights on the shore flicked off. The stench of the mess Brody was ladling overboard made his stomach turn, and he wished he had eaten before he left home.

Suddenly he saw the monstrous head of the fish—not five feet away, so close he could reach over and touch it with the ladle—black eyes staring at him, silver-gray snout pointing at him, gaping jaw grinning. "Quint!" Brody said. "There he is!"

Quint was down the ladder and at the stern in an instant. As he jumped onto the transom the fish's head slipped back into the water, and a second later it slammed into the transom. The jaws closed on the wood, and the head shook violently from side to side. Brody grabbed a cleat and held on, unable to look away from the eyes. Quint fell to his knees on the transom. The fish let go and dropped beneath the surface, and the boat lay still again.

"He was waiting for us!" yelled Brody.

"I know," said Quint. "We've got him now."

"*We've* got *him?* Did you see what he did to the boat?"

"Give it a mighty good shake, didn't he?"

Brody saw fever in Quint's face—an anticipation that strummed the sinews in his neck and whitened his knuckles.

The boat shuddered again, and there was a dull, hollow thump.

"What's he doing?" said Brody.

"He's chewing a hole in the bottom of the boat, that's what! Look in the bilge." Quint raised high his harpoon. "Come out, you son of a bitch!"

Brody raised the hatch cover over the engine room and peered into the dark, oily hole. There was water in the bilges, but there always was, and he saw no new hole. "Looks O.K. to me," he said. "Thank God."

The dorsal fin and tail surfaced ten yards to the right of the stern and began to move again toward the boat. "There you come," said Quint, cooing. "There you come." He stood, right hand extended to the sky, grasping the harpoon. When the fish was a few feet from the boat, Quint cast his iron.

The harpoon struck the fish near the dorsal fin. Then the fish hit the boat, and Quint tumbled backward. His head struck the fighting chair, and a trickle of blood ran down his neck. He jumped up and cried, "I got you! I got you, you miserable bastard!"

The rope attached to the iron dart snaked overboard as the fish sounded. Then the barrel popped off the transom and vanished.

"He took it down with him!" said Brody.

"Not for long," said Quint. "He'll be back, and we'll throw another into him, and another, and another, until he quits." Quint pulled the string attached to the wooden harpoon shaft and brought it back aboard. He fixed the shaft to a new dart.

His confidence was contagious, and Brody now felt ebullient, gleeful, relieved—free from the mist of death. Then he noticed the blood on Quint's neck, and he said, "Your head's bleeding."

"Get another barrel," said Quint. "And bring it back here."

Brody ran forward, unlashed a barrel, slipped the coiled rope over his arm and carried the gear to Quint.

"There he comes," said Quint, pointing to the left. The barrel had come to the surface and bobbed in the water. Quint raised the harpoon above his head. "He's coming up!"

The fish broke water like a rocket lifting off. Snout, jaw and pectoral fins rose straight up, and Quint leaned into the throw. The second iron hit the fish in the belly, just as the great body began to fall. The belly smacked the water with a thunderous boom, and a blinding spray covered the boat.

The boat lurched once, and again, and there were sounds of banging and splintering.

"Attack me, will you?" said Quint. He ran to push the throttle forward, and the boat moved away from the bobbing barrels.

"Has he done any damage?" said Brody.

"Some. We're riding a little heavy aft. He probably poked a hole in us. But we'll pump her out."

"That's it, then," Brody said happily.

"What's what?"

"The fish is as good as dead."

"Not quite. Look."

Following the boat, keeping pace, were the two red wooden barrels. They did not bob. Dragged by the great force of the fish, each cut through the water, pushing a wave before it.

"He's chasing us?" said Brody. "He can't still think we're food."

"No. He means to make a fight of it."

For the first time Brody saw a shadow of disquiet cross Quint's face. "Hell," Quint said, "if it's a fight he wants, it's a fight he'll get." He throttled down to idling speed, jumped to the deck and up onto the transom. He picked up another harpoon. Excitement had returned to his face. "O.K.," he called. "Come and get it!"

The barrels kept coming. Quint stood waiting, harpoon raised.

The fish hit the boat head-on with a noise like a muffled explosion. Quint cast his iron. It struck the fish atop the head, over the right eye, and it held fast. The rope fed slowly overboard as the fish backed off.

"Perfect!" said Quint. "Got him in the head that time."

There were three barrels in the water now, and they cruised in rough unison on the surface. Then they disappeared.

"*Damn!*" said Quint. "That's no normal fish that can sound with three irons in him and three barrels to hold him up."

The boat trembled, seeming to rise up, then dropped back. The barrels reappeared twenty yards from the boat.

"Go below," Quint told Brody, as he readied another harpoon. "See if he done us any dirt that time."

Brody swung down into the cabin. He pulled back the threadbare carpet and opened a hatch. A river of water was flowing aft. He went topside and said to Quint, "It doesn't look good. There's a lot of water under the cabin floor."

"I better go take a look. Here." Quint handed Brody the harpoon. "If he comes back stick this in him for good measure."

Brody stood near the bow, holding the harpoon. The floating barrels twitched now and then as the fish moved about below. How do you die? Brody said silently to the fish. He heard an electric motor start.

"No sweat," said Quint, walking forward. He took the harpoon from Brody. "The pumps should take care of it. We'll be able to tow him in."

Brody dried his palms on the seat of his pants. "Are you really going to tow him in?"

"I am. When he dies."

"And until then?"

"We wait."

For three hours they waited. At first the barrels would disappear every ten or fifteen minutes, then their submergences grew rarer until, by eleven, they had not gone under for nearly an hour. By 11:30 the barrels were wallowing in the water.

"What do you think?" said Brody. "Is he dead?"

"I doubt it. But he may be close enough to it for us to throw a rope around his tail and drag him till he drowns."

Quint switched on the electric winch to make sure it was working, then turned it off again. He gunned the engine and moved the boat cautiously toward the barrels.

When he came alongside the barrels Quint reached overboard with a gaff, snagged a rope and pulled a barrel aboard. He unsheathed his knife and cut the rope from the barrel. Then he stabbed the knife into the gunwale, freeing both hands to hold the rope and shove the barrel to the deck. He climbed onto the gunwale, ran the rope through a pulley and down to the winch. He

took a few turns around the winch, then flipped the starter switch. As soon as the slack in the rope was taken up, the boat heeled hard to starboard, dragged down by the weight of the fish.

The winch turned slowly. The rope quivered under the strain, scattering drops of water on Quint's shirt.

Suddenly the rope started coming too fast. It fouled on the winch, coiling in snarls. The boat snapped upright.

"Rope break?" said Brody.

"Hell, no!" said Quint, and Brody saw fear in his face. "The son of a bitch is coming up!"

The fish rose vertically beside the boat, with a great rushing whoosh, and Brody gasped at the size of the body. Towering overhead, it blocked out the light. The pectoral fins hovered like wings, stiff and straight, as the fish fell forward.

It landed on the stern with a shattering crash, driving the boat beneath the waves. Water poured in over the transom. In seconds Quint and Brody were standing in water up to their hips.

The fish's jaws were not three feet from Brody's chest. In the black eye, as big as a baseball, Brody thought he saw his own image. "Damn your black soul!" screamed Quint. "You sunk my boat!" A barrel floated into the cockpit, the rope writhing like a worm. Quint grabbed the harpoon dart at the end of the rope and plunged it into the soft white belly of the fish. Blood poured from the wound and bathed Quint's hands.

The boat was sinking. The stern was completely submerged, and the bow was rising. The fish rolled off the stern and slid beneath the waves. The rope, attached to the dart Quint had stuck into the fish, followed.

Suddenly Quint lost his footing and fell into the water. "The knife!" he cried. His left leg lifted above the surface, and Brody saw the rope coiled around Quint's foot.

Brody lunged for the knife stuck in the starboard gunwale, wrenched it free, and turned back, struggling to run in the deepening water. He could not move fast enough. He watched helplessly as Quint, arms reaching toward him, eyes wide and pleading, was pulled slowly down into the dark water.

For a moment there was silence, except for the sucking sound of the boat slipping gradually down. The water was up to Brody's shoulders when a cushion popped to the surface next to him. "They'd hold you up all right," Brody remembered Hendricks saying, "if you were an eight-year-old boy." Brody grabbed the cushion.

He saw the tail and dorsal fin break the surface twenty yards away. The tail waved once left, once right, and the dorsal fin moved closer. "Get away, damn you," Brody yelled.

He tried to swim to the bow of the boat, which was almost vertical now. Before he could reach it, the bow slid beneath the surface. He clutched the cushion, and he found that by putting his forearms across it and kicking constantly he could stay afloat without exhausting himself.

The fish came closer. It was only a few feet away, and Brody screamed and closed his eyes, waiting for an agony he could not imagine.

Nothing happened. He opened his eyes. The fish was only a foot or two away, but it had stopped. And then, as Brody watched, the steel-gray body began to fall downward into the gloom.

Brody put his face into the water and opened his eyes. He saw the fish sink in a graceful spiral, trailing behind it the body of Quint—arms out, head thrown back, mouth open in mute protest.

The fish faded from view. But, kept from sinking further by the bobbing barrels, it stopped somewhere beyond the reach of light, and Quint's body hung suspended, a shadow twirling slowly in the twilight.

Brody raised his head, cleared his eyes, and began to kick toward the shore.

The Writing Benchleys

ALEX GOTFRYD

"My interest in sharks," says Peter Benchley, "began during summers on Nantucket, when my parents and I would charter boats and go shark-fishing." His grandfather, the humourist Robert Benchley, had spent his holidays on that lovely island off Massachusetts in the 1920's; and his parents, the novelist Nathaniel Benchley and his wife, have for some time been year-round residents.

Peter Benchley thus represents the third generation of a writing family. After graduating from Harvard in 1961, he worked as a reporter for *The Washington Post* and then joined the staff of *Newsweek*, where he spent three years as Radio–TV Editor. From March, 1967, until the end of Lyndon Johnson's presidency, Mr. Benchley was a speech-writer in the White House.

Since then he has been free-lancing: as a television commentator and as a contributor to magazines as diverse as *The New Yorker, National Geographic,* and *Vogue*. He has also written the screenplay for *Jaws,* which is due to start shooting this summer.

Mr. Benchley, whose hobbies include scuba diving, tennis, and the guitar, lives with his wife Wendy, their daughter Tracy, six, and son Clayton, four, in Pennington, New Jersey. He is now at work on his second novel, about diving for sunken treasure.

A PALM FOR MRS. POLLIFAX
Dorothy Gilman

MONTBRISON

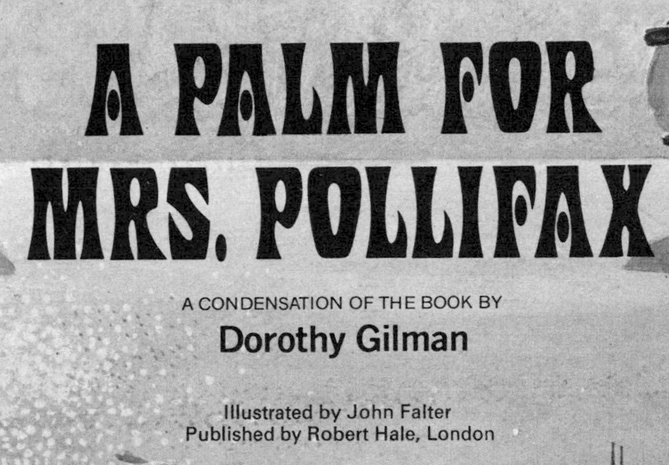

A PALM FOR MRS. POLLIFAX

A CONDENSATION OF THE BOOK BY

Dorothy Gilman

Illustrated by John Falter
Published by Robert Hale, London

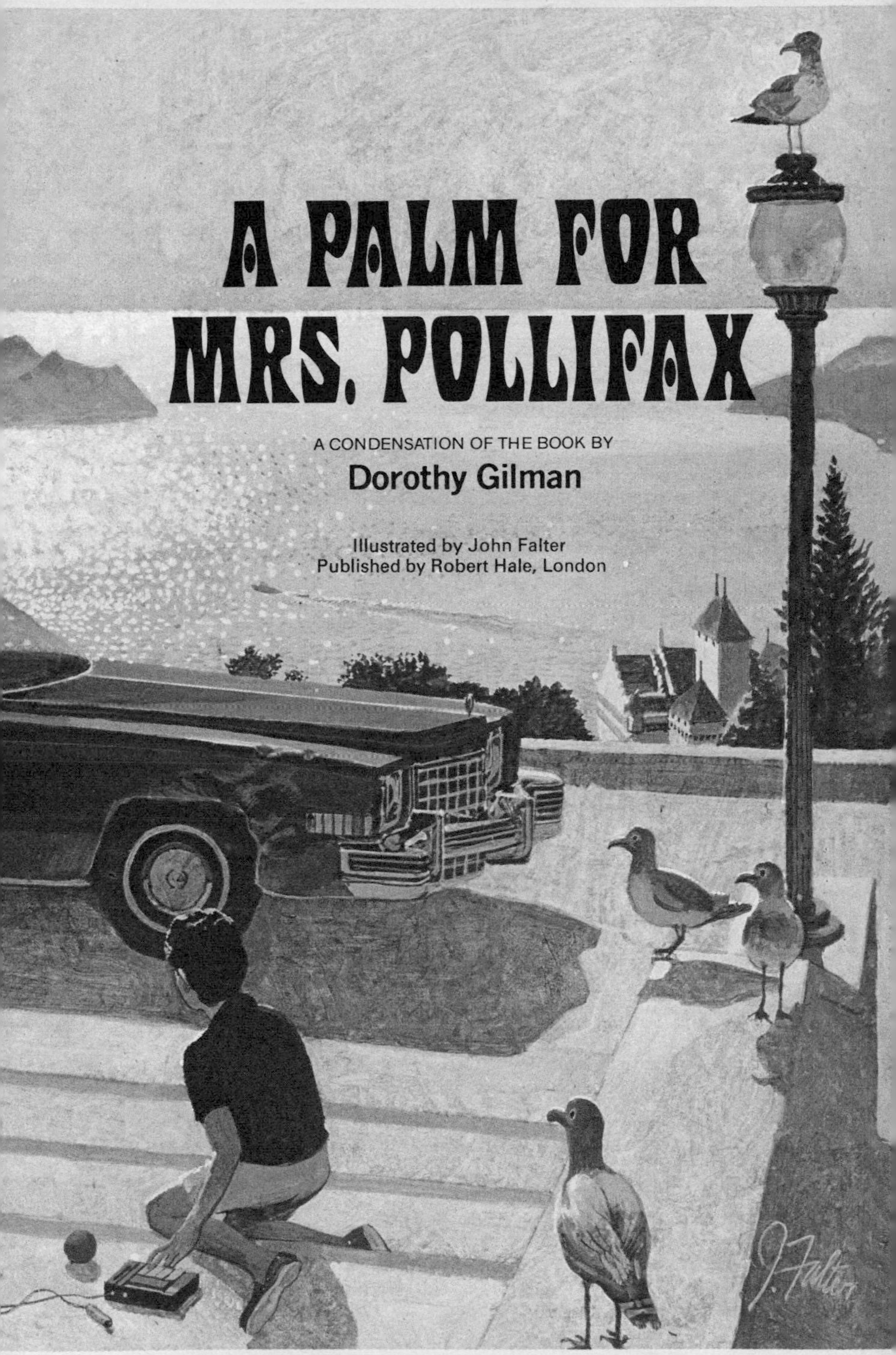

When Mrs. Pollifax checked into a luxurious Swiss clinic with a "case of good old Hong Kong flu", the only germ she *really* carried was the germ of the mission imparted to her by Mr. Carstairs of the CIA. The makings of a deadly bomb and the clinic overlooking Lake Geneva were somehow connected. Emily Pollifax was to make that connection.

An unconscious woman in a bedroom down the hall, a frightened little boy with a tape recorder, the sudden arrival of a flamboyant sheikh—all interested Mrs. Pollifax. The CIA told Interpol that Mrs. Pollifax's "distractions are notorious but never without point." Anything that interested her interested them.

As she blunders along the fine edge of danger, peace in the Middle East hangs in the balance. A beguiling story of mystery mixed with laughter and genuine suspense.

1

IT WAS morning and Mrs. Pollifax was seated on the floor of her living room, legs crossed beneath her as she tried to sustain the lotus position. She had been practicing Yoga for a number of months now. She could almost touch her forehead to her knee, and once—propped up by Miss Hartshorne, her neighbor in 4-C—she had stood dizzyingly on her head. But she could not manage the lotus position for more than a minute, and she had begun to despair of becoming a contemplative.

"I'm too cushiony—I can't fold." She sighed, and rued the more than sixty years in which she had sat on chairs and couches, but never on the floor. Then this moment of disappointment passed. It was, after all, a delightful, sunny day, and at noon there was a meeting of the Save-Our-Environment Committee. As she climbed to her feet she heard Miss Hartshorne calling from the hall, and a moment later a loud knock on the door.

Mrs. Pollifax padded across the room in her leotards. It was only nine fifteen, but the middle of the day for Miss Hartshorne, who took brisk walks at six, and whose energy could be devitalizing. Mrs. Pollifax braced herself. "I was just leaving the building," her neighbor cried breathlessly, "when this special delivery came for you, Emily, and knowing you probably weren't even *dressed* yet"

—her voice wavered between disapproval and tolerance of a friend's eccentricities—"I took the liberty of signing for it."

"Kindness itself," said Mrs. Pollifax, who turned her attention to the letter as Miss Hartshorne hurried away. It was postmarked Baltimore, Maryland, and sent airmail special delivery. It implied a distinct note of urgency. Baltimore . . . urgency . . . Mrs. Pollifax found herself recalling certain small, secret trips she had made in the past for a gentleman named Carstairs. She felt a flutter of excitement as she opened the envelope and drew out a sheet of paper emblazoned with the letterhead of one William H. Carstairs, Attorney-at-law, The Legal Building, Baltimore, Maryland.

"Attorney-at-law indeed!" She sniffed, and sat down. The letter appeared to be a carbon copy of the original, but the address to which it had been sent was carefully deleted. Across the bottom of the page, in red pencil, Carstairs' assistant, Bishop, had scribbled, *We need you; what are you doing on Thursday?*

Mrs. Pollifax began to read the letter: *Dear M. Royan,* it opened. *In reply to our telephone conversation of this morning I am enclosing the suggested deposit of five hundred dollars for the convalescence of my mother-in-law, Mrs. Emily Pollifax . . .*

"Mother-in-law!" Mrs. Pollifax exclaimed. "Convalescence?"

. . . at your Hotel-Clinic Montbrison. It is of the utmost urgency that she be given rest and treatment . . .

The telephone began to ring and Mrs. Pollifax edged toward it, eyes on the letter. Picking up the receiver she said absently, "Yes, yes, I'm here." *. . . and I shall persuade her to place herself entirely in your hands. I am delighted to hear . . .*

"Mrs. Pollifax?"

"Speaking, yes." *. . . that room 113 will be reserved for her, with its private bath and view of the lake . . .*

"Mr. Carstairs' office calling. Will you hold, please?"

"Oh, gladly," she cried, thoroughly alert now because both letter and telephone call meant that her life was about to accelerate again, adjust to that fine edge of danger which—like eating fish riddled with small bones—exacted the most scrupulous awareness.

The next voice on the phone belonged to Carstairs' assistant. "He's already left for the airport," Bishop told her. "He's hoping you can meet him in New York at noon, at the Hotel Taft."

"It's that important?" breathed Mrs. Pollifax.

Bishop sighed. "Isn't it always?"

"I have this letter; it just arrived."

"It should have arrived yesterday,." said Bishop. "I haven't asked how you are yet, Mrs. Pollifax, but I will as soon as I hear whether you can get to New York this morning."

"Let me think. I can catch a train and be there by noon, yes," she said. "*If* I hurry."

"Then I won't ask how you are," Bishop said. "At the Taft you're to go directly to room three twenty-one without stopping at the desk. I hope to hell your telephone isn't tapped."

Mrs. Pollifax's voice was shocked. "Whyever should it be?"

"God knows. Have you joined anything lately?"

"Only the Save-Our-Environment Committee."

"Bad," he said gloomily, and hung up.

Mrs. Pollifax hurried into the bedroom to exchange leotards for a suit. Wrinkled, she noted crossly as she glimpsed herself in the mirror, and she sighed over the multiplying hobbies—environment, karate, garden club, Yoga, a little spying now and then—that left her so little time for grooming. She jammed her newest hat over her flyaway hair and telephoned for a taxi.

AT eleven fifty-eight Mrs. Pollifax stepped out of the elevator at the Hotel Taft and walked down a carpeted hall. The door of room 321 stood open, and for the briefest of moments Mrs. Pollifax entertained thoughts of skulduggery, of Carstairs lying inside in a pool of blood—and then Carstairs stepped into view, tall, lean and very much alive.

"Hello there," he said, shaking hands warmly. "I ordered coffee and sandwiches—it *was* good of you to hurry. Come inside."

"You've grown sideburns!"

"One must move with the times," he said modestly, closing the door behind them. He turned and studied her. "You look splendid. As a matter of fact, much too healthy for what we want. White powder," he mused. "A cane perhaps?" He shook his head at her wild hat. "Sit down and have some coffee." Mrs. Pollifax sat down and he wheeled the serving table toward her, then poured coffee for them. "Bishop says you received a copy of the letter."

"This morning," she acknowledged.

"The sandwiches," he said, "are bacon, lettuce and tomato." He seated himself nearby. "*If* you can do this job for us you'll have to leave day after tomorrow, on Thursday."

"If?" she inquired with a lift of an eyebrow.

"Yes." He hesitated. "I have to warn you this assignment is different from your others. It's not a courier job."

Mrs. Pollifax put down her sandwich. "I'm being promoted!"

He laughed. "Promoted to new hazards is more like it, Mrs. Pollifax, if your sentiments have not changed."

"In my previous trips there were, of course, a number of risks, but they never seemed excessive at the time. I always enjoy myself so much—quite selfishly, I can assure you—and meet the most astonishing people. In any case it's difficult to look ahead, isn't it? No, my sentiments haven't changed, Mr. Carstairs."

"Thank God," he murmured. Then, snapping his fingers, he said, "I forgot Bishop!" He hurried to the telephone and Mrs. Pollifax saw that the receiver had been propped against a lamp. Picking it up, Carstairs said, "You heard, Bishop? Call Schoenbeck in Geneva and set things in motion." He hung up. "Now you know where you're going. Switzerland."

"Oh, how nice! I did hope I wasn't going behind the Iron Curtain again. After escaping from Albania—"

He grinned. "Well, it's not every member of the New Brunswick Garden Club who can escape from Albania, is it? Let's see what you can do with Switzerland. I want to place you in the Hotel-Clinic Montbrison as a patient, but while you're there under medical observation you will in turn please observe the clinic."

"Is it a clinic or a hotel?" asked Mrs. Pollifax, puzzled.

"We're not accustomed to the combination in America," he admitted, "but European habits differ. Montbrison is a clinic to which the wealthy of the world repair for treatment, rest, to lose weight. The hotel concept makes it exceedingly pleasant, and I'm told the food is superb. It has a considerable reputation internationally, drawing people from the Middle East as well as Europe."

Carstairs returned to his chair and pondered her over steepled fingers. "We're in trouble, Mrs. Pollifax," he said at last. "It's classified information, and since it now involves Interpol it's not my story to tell. To wrap it up in one sentence, however, there have lately been two small, very alarming thefts of plutonium, the first one here in America, the more recent in England."

"Plutonium!" echoed Mrs. Pollifax. "But that's used in—"

"Exactly. The stolen pounds add up to a dangerous amount—in fact, almost enough to make a small atom bomb. Plutonium is man-made, you know; it's processed in a nuclear reactor. This has kept it a toy of the moneyed countries and inaccessible to underdeveloped countries. The two thefts took place with uncanny efficiency. And we have reason to believe that at least one of the shipments was sent by mail to the Hotel-Clinic Montbrison."

"Can something like that just be sent through the *mail?*" said Mrs. Pollifax incredulously.

"Oh yes. For one small atom bomb you need only about eleven pounds of plutonium. Which is what terrifies us," he added pointedly. "So far nine pounds are missing. Damnable business, as you can see." He moved to a leather case on the table, opened it and drew out a slide projector. Wheeling the table to the center of the room, he said, "Mind turning off the switch just behind you?"

He turned on the projector and a square of light appeared on the opposite wall. A moment later it was occupied by a close-up of a small wooden crate. "This is how we think the shipment looked," said Carstairs. "With letters stenciled on each side of the box: MEDICAL SUPPLIES—HANDLE WITH CARE."

"That's not the actual box?"

"No—a reconstruction from a description given us. It's believed to have been shipped airmail, special delivery, special handling. It would have reached the clinic nine days ago."

"Would it still be there?" asked Mrs. Pollifax in surprise.

"We can't be sure. With the cooperation of the Swiss police, Interpol put a man in the clinic as a waiter. This man—his name is Marcel—found no shipment or record on the premises. Then British Intelligence sent in a man named Fraser as a patient." He hesitated. "Unfortunately Fraser had an accident, Mrs. Pollifax. Two days ago he fell into a ravine near the clinic. He was dead when they found him."

"Oh dear," said Mrs. Pollifax. "Under the circumstances it sounds suspicious, don't you think?"

He nodded grimly. "I should add that we've not been completely frank with the people at the clinic. They've been told we're investigating hard drugs, and we've not taken them into our confidence about Fraser or Marcel. We won't about your presence, either." He added dryly, "After all, it could be someone inside the clinic who's using the place for these illegal activities. Now Fraser's dead. It could have been a freak accident. Or he could have discovered something. In that case—" He tactfully refrained from completing the sentence and said instead, "You have me to blame, Mrs. Pollifax, for volunteering your services. The Swiss are cooperating. Interpol is of course involved, as well as the United States government—and therefore we in the CIA—and the English have a stake in this, too."

The compliment was unspoken but obvious. Mrs. Pollifax said doubtfully, "But do you really think that I—"

He threw up his hands. "I can think of at least ten agents of mine who are well-trained and experienced, but I have a feeling that this situation needs something more—a rare kind of intuitiveness, a talent for sniffing out what others miss. You're good with people, and you simply don't act like a professional agent." He added abruptly, "What we are looking for—aside from stolen plutonium, Mrs. Pollifax—is evil in its purest form."

"Evil," she mused. "That's an old-fashioned word."

"Positively Biblical," he agreed, "but you have to remember that one of the illicit uses to which plutonium can be put is hideous to contemplate." She nodded. "I think you'd better see what was inside that crate." He leaned over his slides again. "Here we are—exhibit number one."

Mrs. Pollifax studied the innocent-looking object projected on the wall. "*That's* plutonium?"

"Yes, shaped into a metal button weighing about two kilograms. Not very prepossessing, is it?" He switched to another slide. "Each button was individually packed into a plastic bag and then"—he changed slides—"placed in a can filled with inert gas, which in turn was placed inside this odd contraption which looks like a birdcage. If you come across any of these items, don't touch, except with the special gloves you'll be given. Now I'll show you a diagram of the Hotel-Clinic Montbrison before we conclude this.

You recall it's room one thirteen that's been reserved for you."

"Any special reason?"

"Oh yes. From your balcony you'll have a marvelous view of Lake Geneva, and you'll also be able to see, on your left, a primitive dirt road, incredibly steep, that circles the next mountain. From any other floor it's screened by the trees." He flicked on a new slide that showed the terrain surrounding the clinic. Standing up he pointed to a small x. "Every night at ten there'll be a car parked at a point on this road that you can see from your room. You'll signal from your balcony with a flashlight. That will be your contact with the outside world."

She frowned. "Won't anyone else see me signaling?"

He shook his head. "Room one thirteen is quite high. Actually it's on the third floor. The clinic's built into the mountainside, with the treatment rooms on the ground level, the reception and dining rooms on the next level, and the patients' rooms beginning above that. As soon as you've signaled each evening, the car will turn on its lights. You'll flash your light twice if all's well, but if you've something urgent to report you'll blink your light four times. Then you can expect an incoming phone call within the half hour. Since it will come through the clinic's switchboard, we'll work out some kind of simple code for you, based on your health." He unplugged the projector and returned it to its case. "Other than this, your job will be to mingle with the guests, do as much judicious exploring as possible, watch, listen, and don't admire any sunrises at the edge of a one-hundred-foot drop."

"I won't," she promised.

"We've booked you for a six p.m. flight to Geneva day after tomorrow. I'll cable the clinic and ask that you be met at the airport by a limousine—as befits the mother-in-law of a noted Baltimore lawyer," he added with a grin.

"And what am I recovering from?" asked Mrs. Pollifax.

"How about a case of good old Hong Kong flu?"

"All right," she agreed, "but what concerns me if I'm leaving so soon is what I tell people like my son in Chicago, my daughter in Arizona. The garden club. My neighbor Miss Hartshorne, the art association . . ."

"Go on," said Carstairs, looking fascinated.

". . . the hospital auxiliary, the Save-Our-Environment Committee and"—she paused to frown at the expression on his face—"my karate instructor."

"I waited for the last with bated breath. It still carries impact."

"My karate strikes do, too," she told him modestly. "But what is my"—she searched for the proper word—"cover?"

"Well, I suggest you visit Adelaide Carstairs, living in Baltimore." He grinned. "I'll leave it to you to embroider on her. I'm sure you can come up with something dramatic."

He glanced at his watch. "Good lord, one o'clock! Have I covered everything? Now I'll want you at Kennedy International by four o'clock Thursday. You'll be paged over the loudspeaker system and given another briefing, as well as your tickets and the code that we'll establish for you." He held out his hand. "Well, Mrs. Pollifax," he said ruefully, "here we go again."

"Yes," she said, rising and shaking his hand.

"*Bon voyage.* Finish your bacon, tomato and lettuce and leave the key at the desk." At the door he stopped with one hand on the knob. "And damn it, don't disappoint me by getting your head bashed in."

She was really quite touched by the emotion in his voice. She returned to her sandwich wondering whether Adelaide Carstairs should be an elderly aunt who had broken her hip—rather dull; a niece who had eloped with a scoundrel, or a friend who had just been swindled and needed comfort and advice. In the end Mrs. Pollifax turned Adelaide Carstairs into a plain old school friend, recently widowed.

I'm sure you remember my speaking of her, Mrs. Pollifax wrote her daughter in Arizona that evening. *I'll just go down to Baltimore for a week or two and cheer her up*, she added.

THE next morning, feeling more cheerful, she went downtown shopping, but with no intention of buying either a dowdy hat or a cane; she had in mind a dinner dress. For a long time Mrs. Pollifax had secretly yearned for something more contemporary than the offerings of the third-floor matrons' department. She headed for the Psychedelic Den and spent an interesting hour chatting with a young clerk in minidress and boots who thought that Mrs.

Pollifax must be going to a masquerade party. Which, in a way, was quite true.

She brought home a long purple print gown and an assortment of prayer beads. The gown made her look rather like the high priestess of a religious cult, but it was a satisfying change. It was also drip-dry, she reminded herself virtuously.

Next she must explain her departure to Miss Hartshorne. "She's feeling lonely," Mrs. Pollifax told her neighbor over a cup of tea. "Period of adjustment, you know." By this time Adelaide had taken on shape and substance and almost did exist. "She and her husband were very close," she added.

Miss Hartshorne's mouth tightened. "I've been your friend long enough to say what I think, Emily. You let people take advantage of you. I've tried for years to persuade you to do some traveling with me, but no, you simply won't travel at all. What you lead, Emily, is an unhealthily dull life. You never go anywhere interesting; you never meet new people. It's no vacation at all, cheering up an old friend. Your essential problem, Emily, is that you have no sense of adventure."

"None at all," said Mrs. Pollifax, beaming at her friend, "but won't you have another cup of tea, anyway, Grace?"

"YOUR attention, please. . . . Your attention, please. . . . Will Mrs. Emily Pollifax go to the information desk."

Mrs. Pollifax picked up her suitcase and carried it to the airport information desk. Almost at once a man hurried toward her carrying a suitcase in one hand and a bouquet of violets in the other. She peered at him in astonishment. "Bishop!"

He leaned over to kiss her lightly on the cheek, then thrust the flowers into her hand. "Beware the Greeks bearing gifts. How are you? I'm delighted to see you."

"And I you," she said. "It never occurred to me they'd—"

"*Ssh*, Mrs. Pollifax," he said conspiratorially, and picked up her suitcase. "Follow me." He led her around the corner to a door marked PRIVATE. PERSONNEL ONLY. Opening it, he ushered her in and locked it behind them. "We're being loaned this office for ten minutes." He placed his suitcase on the desk. "You realize you're giving me a disastrous time by taking on this job, don't you? Carstairs can't make up his mind whether he's sending you up a blind alley or into a lion's den. He's in a dither."

"Oh, really, everything sounds very simple, and it will be such a pleasant change for me."

"I see. Well, then, let's get on with it." He opened his suitcase. "I have here one flashlight of unparalleled quality. Plus a supply of batteries—we can't risk a communications breakdown."

"Flashlight and batteries," repeated Mrs. Pollifax, opening her own suitcase and tucking both inside.

"One code in a sealed envelope that also contains Swiss francs. The code you will kindly memorize en route and then destroy. One pack of matches with which to destroy said code. And—oh, you are going to have a fun time—one Geiger counter."

"Geiger counter! Carstairs didn't mention a Geiger counter."

"Actually a scintillation counter," he amended, pulling out a handsome leather jewel case. "He left it for me to mention, because when he saw you we were still working out how to conceal it. You can't go poking about for radioactive stuff without help, can you? You'll also need these gloves I've included. Now take a look at this." He opened the box.

"Are they real?" she gasped, staring at an emerald pendant, an enormous diamond pin and two glittering ruby necklaces.

"They're absolutely fake," he said, "but damn expensive fakes. Aren't they gorgeous?" He bent over the box. "See this tiny gold button on the hinge? Give it a good push and you'll have released the lock and can pull out the tray." He removed it and displayed a dial and two knobs set into a smooth metallic surface. He turned one of the knobs and they listened to a faint humming sound. "That's normal," he said. "Proves it's working. The needle on the dial zooms when it sniffs out anything interesting. And here are your tickets." He tapped a list with one finger. "Tickets, jewel case, flashlight, batteries—"

"And violets," she reminded him. "Very handsome of you, too. I adore violets."

"So I see." He glanced in amusement at her hat, which looked like a bathing cap overgrown with violets and pansies. "Oh yes—

there's one more item. The waiter Marcel." Bishop took a photograph from his wallet and showed her a dark-haired, high-cheekboned, gloomy face. "About five feet five. Broad-shouldered. But avoid him, let him be the one to find you."

"Right," said Mrs. Pollifax efficiently.

"And that's about it," he concluded sadly, "so I daresay you'd better leave." He unlocked the door, opened it, then closed it again and said sternly. "You *will* take care? Just try to find the you-know-what and be well-behaved?"

"I shall feel I've behaved very well if I find the you-know-what," she told him.

He sighed. "Yes, but I want to point out that any crook who takes on this sort of game is very tough. Strictly jungle type."

Mrs. Pollifax looked at him. "What's wrong, Bishop?"

He scowled. "Hang it all, Carstairs didn't want you shaken up, but I think you ought to know. The autopsy report on Fraser came in this noon. The chap was dead before he fell into the ravine."

"Before he fell," she repeated automatically.

"Yes. The blow that killed him couldn't have come from any of the rocks he—uh—his body hit on the way down."

"I see," she said quietly. "You mean he was very definitely murdered. Thank you for mentioning it, Bishop, I'll keep it in mind. You'll let me go now?"

"Reluctantly," he said, opening the door. "*Very* reluctantly."

THE code, when Mrs. Pollifax opened it in the plane's lavatory, struck her as being really very funny. It read like Dick-and-Jane.

All is quiet—"I am getting rested."
I am worried—"I have a cough."
I feel I may be in danger—"I believe I am running a temperature."

Below these simple sentences were the code names:

Marcel—"Cousin Matthew"
Plutonium—"Uncle Bill"
Police—"Peter"
Carstairs—"Adelaide"

After reading the code several times, she burned it in an ashtray and returned to the cabin to watch a Western film. As for Bishop's parting words, she preferred not to think about them for the moment. Fraser's death meant there *was* something worth murdering for at Montbrison.

Long before the film ended, the sky beyond her window had turned silver and she watched horizon-long bands of orange and pink dissolve into sunshine. It was only midnight in New York, but they had crossed a time zone to meet Europe's dawn.

Mrs. Pollifax now attempted to enter her new role. "I'm a mother-in-law recovering from the flu," she repeated to herself, and tried out a small cough. "My son-in-law, William Carstairs, lives in Baltimore." There would be a limousine waiting for her, delightful thought, and she would be whisked off to the clinic—about an eighty-minute drive—and there she must look suitably tired.

Mrs. Pollifax coughed again, very delicately, and practiced looking tired.

2

THE limousine chauffeur drove silently and skillfully, and Mrs. Pollifax stared out of the window at gentle mountains, red-tiled roofs and brief glimpses of a pale and shining Lake Geneva. They passed terraced vineyards, villages waking up, and after an hour of driving they began to climb.

Mrs. Pollifax leaned forward eagerly. The road zigzagged breathtakingly high above the lake. Slowing somewhat, they entered a village laid out at a seventy-degree angle on the slopes of the mountain. Shops edged the slanting street, among them a café with umbrellas blossoming over rows of bright tables. The car turned down a narrow paved road, they passed a stone church clinging to the mountainside, then entered a shaded wood with a ravine far below. Ahead Mrs. Pollifax saw a discreet sign: PRIVATE. HOTEL-CLINIC MONTBRISON.

The driver pointed to a large, rambling building almost suffocated by trees and shrubbery. They turned into a steep, narrow drive between two laurel bushes, rode past a greenhouse and arrived at the main door of the clinic.

At the entrance a stocky young man in a green apron was sweeping the steps, while a small boy of ten or eleven sat on the top stair, watching. Both looked up curiously.

Mrs. Pollifax stepped out of the car and glanced through the open door into the gloomy, dark-paneled reception hall, and then the boy got up and called out shrilly, "*Bonjour, madame!*" This was followed by a torrent of French.

Mrs. Pollifax smiled. "I'm sorry, I speak only English."

"But madame, I speak English, too," he told her, jumping up and down. "Are you to be a patient here? Are you English? Have you arrived by air? Will you stay long?"

A man in a black uniform appeared, said something quieting to the boy in French and smiled at Mrs. Pollifax. "I am the head porter, madame. Welcome to the clinic. You are Madame Pollifax?" She nodded. "This way." He gave brisk orders to the man in the green apron, who dropped his broom and picked up Mrs. Pollifax's suitcase. "Please, you will come in and register. Then you will wish breakfast, of course. It will be sent to your room at once."

Inside, she signed the register and handed over her passport. "This will be returned to you within the hour," he said pleasantly. "May you enjoy your visit here, madame."

As she moved slowly upward in the elevator cage she looked down and saw the boy standing just inside the entrance staring after her. His brief excitement had collapsed; his eyes were huge and filled with sadness. She was glad when the ascent cut her off from his view.

Mrs. Pollifax crossed her room to open the balcony door. "Oh, *lovely*," she whispered, moving to the railing. From the third floor she looked across the tops of high trees stirring in a breeze. Beyond, and almost straight down, a steamer on the lake was leaving behind it a tiny v. Lake Geneva spread almost to the horizon, like a pale blue, upside-down sky. Quiet morning sounds rose to her balcony: the rise and fall of traffic far away, birds calling, a muffled toot from the steamer, a church bell—all muted by distance and height.

She looked down in search of the garden and saw a broad ledge that ran in front of her balcony, connecting it with the next and continuing to the end of the building. The ledge cut off much of the view, but she could see the well-kept grass, bright flowers, a graveled path overhung with pink roses, and a gazebo.

She looked for and found her road, off to the left, just where Carstairs had said it would be, a narrow scar on the next hillside, unpaved and climbing at a precipitous angle. A flock of swallows encircling a tall Lombardy poplar interrupted her gaze, but they were the only sign of life at Montbrison.

A knock sounded on the door. Reluctantly she left the balcony and walked inside, calling, "Come in."

A waiter entered, tray in hand. With a flourish he placed it on a table. "Madame wishes it here or on the balcony?"

"I think I'd fall asleep if I breakfasted on the balcony," she told him, and they exchanged a long, interested look. He was a stocky young man, quite swarthy, with bright blue eyes, and black hair parted in the center like a Victorian bartender. In Bishop's photograph he'd looked gloomy. He still looked gloomy, but it was the sourness of a comedian who could fire off a string of ribald witticisms without a muscle quivering in his face. Marcel was something of a clown, she thought.

"I'll sit here," she said, and promptly sat down.

"Madame has been sent the European *petit déjeuner*—very small," he explained ruefully. "If madame wishes more she may dial the room service. I may pour your coffee?" He leaned over and said in a low voice, "There is one particular counterfeit among the guests, madame; an Englishman, Robin Burke-Jones, usually in the garden afternoons. None of his credentials check out; all data he gave upon registering is false."

"Thank you," said Mrs. Pollifax, smiling at him and nodding. "I think I have everything I need."

"One hopes!" he said. "If not"— he shrugged—"the menu for service is on the desk. *Jambon ou lard, oeufs sur le plat, oeuf poché sur toast . . .*" His eyes were positively dancing. "My name is Marcel, madame. *Bon appétit!*" He bowed and walked out.

My confederate, she thought gratefully. A night without sleep had left her feeling jaded and a little disoriented. Ravenous also, she began to spread marmalade on her croissants. Over coffee she gazed around the room, which was cool and high-ceilinged, all white with touches of blue, and a deep red Oriental rug on the floor. Tonight she would begin exploring with the scintillation counter; for now, a brief morning nap would not be decadent.

As she moved to the bed she saw that Marcel had left the door ajar, and that it was slowly opening. "Who's there?" she called.

"*Bonjour, madame.*" The small boy who had been at the entrance looked even more forlorn standing there, his arms slack at his sides. "Would you be my friend, madame?"

She stared down at him in astonishment. "Are you a patient here?" she asked. He was very brown, thin and leggy, with jet-black hair.

He shook his head. "Grandmama is a patient and I am here with her. Have you grandchildren, madame?"

"Yes, three," she told him.

From somewhere down the hall a voice called, "Hafez? Hafez!"

The boy turned with a sigh. "Here, Serafina."

A sallow-faced woman in black joined him, took his hand, bent over and admonished him in a language new to Mrs. Pollifax.

Hafez pushed out his underlip, and there were tears in his eyes. "But this is my friend—one *must* have friends!"

The woman pulled him away, and Mrs. Pollifax peered after them. At the far end of the hall a man in a wheelchair watched the boy and the woman approach. Seeing Mrs. Pollifax, he pushed his way back into the room behind him. Hafez and the woman went into the room opposite, and the two doors closed.

A curious child, thought Mrs. Pollifax. She walked to the bed, lay down and fell asleep.

THREE times she was awakened by knocks on the door—the first time by a young woman in white who said she was a nurse and would return, the second by a woman in white who said she was a dietician and would return. Then came the secretary of the clinic, a pigeon-breasted woman who explained that lunch was from noon to one o'clock, dinner from six to eight. Mrs. Pollifax would be examined by a doctor tomorrow morning.

"Doctor? I'm only tired," pointed out Mrs. Pollifax.

"Ah, but everyone is examined; it is the rule of the clinic. I understand also that you have not been weighed by the nurse yet, nor given menu instructions to the dietician." She shook her head reproachfully and went out.

It occurred to Mrs. Pollifax that at such a pace the quietness of the clinic might be an illusion. She changed from her traveling suit to a dress and went downstairs to do a little reconnoitering before lunch.

She found two solariums on the reception floor—also a pair of television rooms side by side. The dining rooms lay at the far end of the corridor—Mrs. Pollifax could see waiters moving behind glass-paneled doors. She paused at what looked to be the library and glanced in at heavy furniture and rich oak paneling.

One piece of dark furniture was occupied by a deeply tanned young man who lifted a blond eyebrow and said, *"Bonjour, madame,* but that's the limit of my French."

"It's just about the limit of mine, too," she admitted, and decided this was an opportunity to meet her first adult guest. She sank into an overstuffed chair and wondered if she could ever get out of it. "You're waiting for lunch, too?"

"I am waiting," he said gloomily, "for something to happen in this place. After eight days here I would consider the dropping of a spoon almost intolerable excitement."

Mrs. Pollifax looked at him with amusement. With sleepy green eyes and white teeth, he just missed being impossibly handsome by a nose that had been broken and still looked a little stepped on; it gave humor to his face. "You do look as if you're accustomed to more excitement."

"You're staring at my purple slacks and red shirt," he accused. "I thought Montbrison might have a touch of the casino about it. After all, it's patronized by many of the same people, except when they come here it's to repair their livers. How was I to know that repairing the liver is almost a religion?"

"I had no idea," said Mrs. Pollifax, fascinated. "Is it?"

"My dear lady"—he sighed—"when I saw the Count Ferrari at Monaco in April, he had a blonde in one hand and a pile of chips in the other. The count," he added, "is seventy-five if he's a day. Here at Montbrison he is suddenly mortal and positively devout about it. He comes into the dining room with a plastic bag of pills—red, green, blue, pink."

Mrs. Pollifax laughed. "If you're so bored—and since you look so extremely healthy—why do you stay?"

"Because my doctor sent me." He hesitated, then added crisply, "I'm recovering from the Hong Kong flu, you see. And you?"

Mrs. Pollifax hesitated. She said without expression, "Actually I'm recovering from the Hong Kong flu, too." This produced a curiously awkward silence. "I hear it was a particularly virulent strain last winter," she ventured.

"Uh—yes," he agreed. At that moment the dining-room doors swung open. "Lunch!" he cried, springing to his feet. He helped her up. "You have to watch these chairs," he said sternly. "You can disappear forever in one."

"I'll remember that. By the way, I'm Mrs. Pollifax."

He bowed elegantly. "How do you do. And I'm— *Bonjour,* General d'Estaing," he called to an old man leaning heavily on a cane as he negotiated the hall to the dining room. "May I help you?" He was off like an Olympic runner to aid the general.

Mrs. Pollifax's table was in a corner of the first dining room, the number 113 discreetly displayed on the shining damask cloth between a vase of wild flowers and the oil-and-vinegar tray. She had a strategic glimpse of those sharing her ell but no view at all of the other two rooms.

The general was helped to a single place in the center of the room and then her tanned young friend wandered off to his own table. A subdued Hafez and the sallow woman in black occupied the long table for six by the window. He had mentioned a grandmother, but the woman with him gave every evidence of being a maid or companion. Mrs. Pollifax wondered who the others in their party could be, and where they were.

Only one other guest looked familiar and that was the man in the wheelchair whom she'd seen in the hall opposite Hafez' door. He wheeled himself to a solitary table facing the window, so she could see only his profile. His skin was dark. He wore glasses, and a black mustache decorated his lip. His shoulders were massive under his wrinkled business suit. He looked out of place but indifferent to it; he ate quickly, and wheeled himself out before Mrs. Pollifax reached her dessert.

I must learn something about all of them, she reminded herself. Marcel had mentioned the garden; she would spend the afternoon there.

THE garden was bright with sun and flowers. Mrs. Pollifax inspected the beds of begonias with a professional eye, then headed for a chaise longue. Just to be certain that she wouldn't fall asleep, she attempted to elevate it to a sitting position.

"You're pushing all the wrong things," said a voice behind her, and a young woman in a bikini, body glistening with sun oil, put down her towel and books and leaned over the chair. It sprang upright immediately.

Mrs. Pollifax smiled. "How efficient you are! You're British?"

The girl shook her head. "Belgian."

"I saw you in the dining room. I'm Mrs. Pollifax."

"How do you do. I'm Court van Roelen." Her face was all cheekbones and angles, with a pair of eyes that blazed like blue jewels—it was a breathtaking combination.

Over the girl's head Mrs. Pollifax saw her nameless friend of the library in the center of the lawn staring openmouthed at the girl. He was now wearing yellow slacks, an orange shirt and a polka-dot cravat. He strolled toward Mrs. Pollifax. "I think a spoon just dropped," he said.

"I could hear the reverberations," she told him.

He grinned. "Don't let me interrupt anybody's sunbath. I'll just pull up another chair and we can turn this into a cozy threesome. Numerologically, you know, three is a number of great strength." With a lift of his brow he asked Mrs. Pollifax, "You were about to introduce us?"

"I will if you'll tell me your name."

"Burke-Jones. Robin Burke-Jones."

Mrs. Pollifax gave him a quick glance; she had made a better choice than she'd realized in her first adult encounter.

"I haven't seen you before," Burke-Jones told the girl. "You've just arrived?"

"I've been here for ten days," she said coolly, "but I've been on the mountain every day hiking."

"Hiking?" he echoed. "There's nothing restful about hiking."

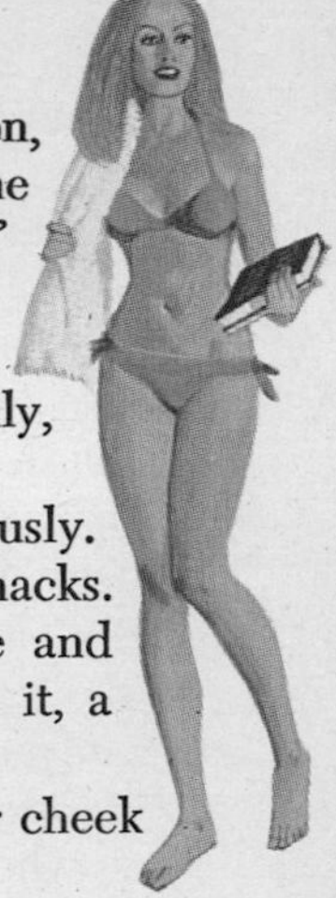

"I don't come here to rest," she said. "It's my vacation, and I prefer to avoid resorts; they're always so full of"—she glanced at his exquisitely arranged cravat—"playboys."

"Well." He beamed. "We must discuss this further."

"I don't see why," she said, turning to tan her back.

"Speaking of playboys," Mrs. Pollifax said wickedly, "what do you do, Mr. Burke-Jones?"

"Spend my time envying playboys," he said virtuously. "Actually, I'm in the import business. Curios and knickknacks. A shop in Brighton, another in Dover, branches here and there. And you, Miss van Roelen? You are not, I take it, a playgirl?"

Her voice was muffled against the towel on which her cheek rested. "Administrative assistant, UNESCO."

"Oh, very worthy," he murmured, and lifted a brow at Mrs. Pollifax. "Wouldn't you say so, too?"

He was really impossible, she thought, and also rather nice, but he was going to have a problem with Miss van Roelen. "Extremely so," she told him, and wondered what he really did.

The glass doors opened and Hafez appeared, dressed in fresh shorts and white shirt and carrying a small black box. The servant followed like a shadow and took a chair under a tree. Hafez set the box on the grass and began fiddling with knobs and a tiny microphone. It looked like a tape recorder.

Abruptly Court sat up and called to a woman strolling down the graveled path. "Oh, Lady Palisbury . . ."

Mrs. Pollifax watched the woman's face brighten at the sight of Court. "Hello, there," she called, cutting across the lawn toward them. "I've been walking in the ravine." From under a huge sun hat a pair of deep-set eyes regarded them warmly.

"I just wanted to ask, did you find your missing diamond?"

Lady Palisbury shook her head. "No, my dear, but it will turn up, I'm sure."

"Lady Palisbury, this is Mrs. Pollifax and Mr. Burke-Jones."

She nodded pleasantly. "I'm not going to join you, no matter how comfortable you look. I'm on my way in to wake up my husband. He has a massage at four."

Lady Palisbury strolled away. As she passed Hafez he held up the microphone to her while he cradled the tape recorder under his arm. She smiled graciously and spoke into it before she disappeared inside.

Mrs. Pollifax watched as Hafez suddenly streaked across the garden and shouted to a waiter, "*Monsieur, un* Coca-Cola?"

"Does his grandmother ever keep him company?" she asked.

"Didn't know he had one," said Burke-Jones.

"It must be terribly dull for him here," Court said, hugging her knees. "I suspect he's rather brilliant. I don't know when he sleeps—he's all nerves. He's one guest I meet consistently at six in the morning when I leave for my walks. He told me yesterday about pulsars. Stars, you know, or planets—I forget which."

"Mmm," said Mrs. Pollifax, watching the boy approach the general, whom a nurse was helping into a chair under a tree.

The general, too, spoke into the microphone. Court laughed. "He has persuaded the general to say, '*Ici la police. Sortez, les mains en l'air!*' which means 'This is the police. Come out with your hands up.' The general," she added, "was once head of the Sûreté."

Robin looked startled. "I thought he was an army general."

"He was. He went to the Sûreté after World War Two."

"So he's a French police chief," murmured Mrs. Pollifax, watching Robin's face speculatively.

He said crossly, "How do you happen to know so much about everybody, Miss van Roelen?"

Court smiled. "I met the general here last summer. He's very old and alone and hasn't much longer to live."

But it was now their turn with Hafez, who was suddenly in front of them shrilly demanding that they say something.

"I'll volunteer, Hafez," said Mrs. Pollifax, and he came eagerly to her side. She took the microphone, thought a moment, and then recited an old nursery rhyme. It delighted Court, who volunteered a verse about an old man with a beard.

"I prefer the general's announcements to your frivolous limericks," said Robin, and grasping the microphone, he called, "Come out with your hands high—the jig is up!"

But Mrs. Pollifax's glance had returned to Hafez. His eyes were far too bright, his gestures nervous and curiously without meaning. He doesn't really know what he's doing, she thought; he doesn't care, either; he acts for the sake of being in motion. As he returned the mike to the tape recorder, she saw that his hands were trembling. She realized that the boy was living under an intolerable tension.

"Tiresome brat," said Robin when the boy had dashed off.

"Overactive thyroid?" suggested Court, lying down again.

"No," said Mrs. Pollifax slowly, "it's more than that." She was remembering when her own son, Roger, was six and booked for a tonsillectomy, and a playmate had told him the doctor would smother him with a pillow in the operating room. Roger had lived with that terror for two days before he had entrusted it to her, but even now she did not care to remember those two days. "I think he's frightened," she said.

"Frightened?" echoed Court doubtfully. "What could possibly frighten a child here?"

Mrs. Pollifax shook her head. The boy was not just frightened, he was desperately, nightmarishly afraid.

DINNER that evening was *sauté de veau marengo,* which turned out to be veal, and Mrs. Pollifax began to think of buying a French dictionary. In her youth she had studied Latin, but she had forgotten every scrap with the exception of *Fortuna audaces iuvat*—Fortune favors the bold. The phrase contained a certain amount of comfort for her now, as she considered when she should begin her nocturnal prowlings.

"You come all the way from America?" said Lady Palisbury as the two of them sat in the library, Mrs. Pollifax with her demitasse, Lady Palisbury knitting as she waited for her husband to join her for dinner.

"This morning, yes. I have an internationally minded son-in-law," Mrs. Pollifax told her with a smile.

Lady Palisbury brightened. "Oh, how nice. We have four, all darlings. They're so soothing after a household of daughters, all of whom are darlings, too, but given to shrieks and squeals and quarrels." She glanced up anxiously. "I do wish John would come before we get involved with the yodelers."

"Yodelers?" said Mrs. Pollifax, startled.

"The clinic arranges"—her mouth curved—"little weekend entertainments for us. Tonight there are yodelers from the village."

"How neighborly," said Mrs. Pollifax. Her attention sharpened as she saw Hafez and his companion leaving the dining room.

"You're curious about the boy," said Lady Palisbury.

"He looks as if he'd been crying," explained Mrs. Pollifax. "Do you know anything about him?"

"They're from Zabya, one of the Arabian oil countries, and the king was in the news recently—something about a birthday party and giving away all the royal land to his people."

Mrs. Pollifax nodded. "I remember that. A nice little man."

The yodelers had arrived. A group of plump, beaming villagers, the women in brightly embroidered dirndls and the men in high socks, shorts, and hats with feathers, had surrounded Lady Palisbury's husband. He separated himself from them and approached his wife. "My dear, who *are* they?" he whispered.

"Yodelers, darling," said Lady Palisbury, putting away her knitting. "This is Mrs. Pollifax, John."

"Splendid," he said absently, and they moved into the dining room, followed by the group of performers.

Strident yodels filled the air. "Good God, have we been invaded?" asked Burke-Jones, strolling in from the solarium.

"Only by folk culture," Mrs. Pollifax told him. "I think it's rather endearing."

He shuddered. "Not to me. Look, I'm driving down to the village for cigarettes. Would you care to come?" He added casually, "I thought I'd ask Court, too."

Mrs. Pollifax smiled faintly. "I'm getting sleepy after a night on the plane. I think she's in the dining room." Barely smothering a yawn, she bid him good-night and went upstairs.

She had left the doors to her room closed; there were two—a thick one soundproofed with quilted fabric and an inner conventional door that could be locked, but she had neglected to do so. Both stood ajar now and Mrs. Pollifax quickened her step. It might be the chambermaid, or it could be Marcel.

It was neither. It was the boy Hafez, sitting in front of the glass-topped desk, hunched over something in his lap.

His hands moved quickly, and the object he'd been holding clicked against the glass top of the desk before he jumped up to face her. "*Bon soir, madame,*" he said. "I have been waiting for you. You did not say if you decided to be my friend."

"I would be delighted to be your friend," she told him, "but you simply mustn't walk into rooms when people aren't there."

"But madame, I knocked and I received no answer. Where else could I have waited?" he asked, a desperate note creeping into his voice. "Serafina would have been very angry and taken me off to bed if she saw me in the hall."

"Do you like Serafina?"

The child shrugged. "Must you tell her I came inside?"

"No, but we can't be friends if you come in uninvited."

He nodded. "Thank you," he said, and walked out, closing both doors behind him.

Mrs. Pollifax stood looking after him, then sat down at the desk. On its top were a hairbrush, a jar of cold cream, a small bottle of aspirin, an address book, a lipstick. Which of the objects had clicked against the glass as he put it back?

She examined the lipstick but it appeared untouched. Then she held the aspirin up to the light. She had bought it before leaving, a small supply of twenty-five tablets in case of emergency. The bottle looked only half filled now. As she returned the bottle to the desk it clicked. Of course—glass against glass.

In a clinic where any nurse could supply aspirin, why did Hafez feel compelled to steal the tablets? Mrs. Pollifax sat and frowned at the bottle, bewildered; she realized that she would have to make a point of meeting Hafez' grandmother soon. Possibly the woman had no idea the child was disturbed.

I wonder, she thought idly, and glanced at her watch. It lacked a few minutes to nine and she did not have to signal with her flashlight until ten. I'll just pay a neighborly call, she thought. I'll make no judgments; I'll just *see*.

Resolutely she left her room and walked down the hall to the door that Hafez had entered that morning. Hafez opened at her knock. "Madame?" he said, looking alarmed.

"Since we're friends, I thought I'd pay a brief call on your grandmother," she told him cheerfully, and walked past him. "I trust she's well enough to receive visitors." She saw an open door on the left, then another on her right.

"But madame—" Hafez' glance leaped anxiously to the left, and Mrs. Pollifax followed it.

A man's voice called out sharply in another language, and Hafez replied. There was an oath, followed by movement. Mrs. Pollifax reached the threshold of the adjoining bedroom and stopped. She had time to meet the shocked glance of Serafina, and time to glimpse the occupant of the bed in the darkened corner, and then she was seized from behind. A man grabbed her left elbow, another her right elbow, and lifting her off the floor, carried her, still erect, to the door. It happened so quickly that her breath was literally taken away.

"Ukhrujee," said one burly attendant. *"Mahsalamah!"*

She was shoved roughly outside. The man across the hall had come to his door. He sat in the wheelchair and watched with narrowed eyes. Then he muttered something and retreated inside.

Mrs. Pollifax sank down into one of the chairs lining the corridor, shaken by the experience. After a few minutes she made her way to her room, not knowing whether to feel shocked, angry or penitent. This isn't New Brunswick, New Jersey, she reminded herself, and then, fiercely, What could you expect, Emily? Obviously the woman isn't well and those attendants were outraged to find a stranger bursting in.

The woman had lain in bed, pale and fragile in her sleep: long braided gray hair, a slightly curved nose, a good jaw. Serafina had been sitting near her. The two attendants apparently stayed in the farther room. The grandmother had not even known of Mrs. Pollifax's arrival, but the man in the wheelchair across the hall had known. Could he possibly be a member of their party?

And Hafez . . . He had been alarmed to see her, but he had made no move to stop her, and as she had been carried out he had looked pleased. Pleased by her coming to pay a call, or by her ejection?

Mrs. Pollifax had expected a vain old woman, doting on a grandson she could neither entertain nor supervise. Instead she had found a still white face lying on a white pillow, and two angry attendants. She must ask Marcel; perhaps he could explain.

She glanced at her watch and walked out to her balcony into a velvety stillness. Far below the lighted garden the lake was black and silent, except for a lone steamer trailing ribbons of gold. The curving shores twinkled with the lights of casinos and villas. On her left the hillside was a brooding silhouette.

At precisely ten o'clock she switched on her flashlight, counted to three, turned it off, then on, then off, and was startled and pleased to see a pair of headlights spring into life. Whoever you are, she thought, it *is* nice to know you're there.

In the garden, someone was turning off the spotlights one by one. The clinic was being put to bed.

It was time for her to get to work.

3

IN Langley, Virginia, it was late afternoon. Carstairs' work had been interrupted in midmorning by an urgent request from the State Department for a report on one of the smaller oil countries in the Middle East. The king of Zabya was celebrating his fortieth birthday on Tuesday, and many heads of state would attend the daylong festivities. Was the country stable enough for the United States to send its vice-president? Carstairs' comments on this during the day had become increasingly unprintable, but the report had been completed and delivered: the vice-president could be sent, but he would have to expect boiled sheep's eyes on the menu.

Bishop wandered into the office. "Schoenbeck's outside. He's flying back to Geneva in two hours and wants to wrap things up."

Schoenbeck was Interpol, a rather pedantic little man with a lined face. He came in, murmered a thousand apologies for the intrusion, and sat down.

"Anything changed?"

"My friend, everything changes" said Schoenbeck. "It is the law of life. I have just learned that Dunlap committed suicide this morning in England."

Carstairs swore gently. "How could he commit suicide in a prison cell? Wasn't he being watched?"

Schoenbeck shrugged. "It does not take long. He hung himself with a bed sheet. A frightened man, obviously. Suddenly more frightened of life than of death."

They were both silent, contemplating this. "No," said Carstairs, shaking his head, "more frightened of *them* than of us. Two ordinary men, one in England, one in America, and nothing in common except that each happened to work in a nuclear-reactor plant —and each succumbed to stealing two buttons of plutonium."

"There is another thing they had in common, my friend," said the man from Interpol. "Both have killed themselves without revealing any other links to this chain."

Carstairs nodded gloomily. "Anything yet on the money?"

"Not a thing, except that—*voila!*—each man had a bank account that was magically bulging. It must have been a cash deal."

Carstairs sighed. "A dead end. Well-organized."

"Indeed yes. It pains me, my friend, that we know so little, and that based on scraps. We know that in each case the plutonium was tossed over the wall during working hours by a workman. We learn that in England a green sedan was seen by a farmer parked beside that wall about the right time, and the same green sedan was seen twenty minutes after the theft parked in front of the post office in Stokely-on-the-Merden. The postal clerk recalls a stranger mailing a crate to Switzerland that day, to the Montbrison clinic. But everything we have is based on the word of a farmer plowing his fields, two housewives gossiping in front of a post office, and the vulnerable memory of a postal clerk."

Carstairs smiled encouragingly. "Monsieur Schoenbeck, what do we ever work with but scraps? Yet the world lurches on."

"Yes, but I am concerned over its continuing to lurch. There is too much hate in the world for plutonium to be drifting about loose. Your agent is now joining ours at Montbrison?"

Carstairs glanced at his watch. "Yes. As a matter of fact she would have been there for some hours now."

"Good," Schoenbeck said. "And we will, of course, continue to follow every possibility concerning the two men who stole the plutonium. The dead can no longer speak, but their friends can. What I want from you, my friend, is an alert transmitted to all your agents. It troubles me deeply that we hear no hints of this in the marketplaces of the world. In Beirut, Marseilles and New York—not a whisper. This is most exceptional—a group this organized turning to this type of crime and no informants, no leaks, no tips. The plutonium has to find a market eventually. And we *must* know who is buying it."

"Do you still believe it's one of the international crime syndicates forsaking drugs for plu—" The telephone interrupted Carstairs. "Yes, he's here."

He handed the telephone to Schoenbeck, who listened, replied in rapid French, listened again, and seemed visibly to sag in his chair as he hung up. "That was Geneva calling. There has been a third theft of plutonium."

"What?" thundered Carstairs.

"Yes. In France. Two metal buttons of plutonium, each weighing a kilogram. Six kilograms are now missing."

Carstairs whistled. "That makes thirteen pounds and two ounces altogether."

Schoenbeck nodded. "They now have their atom bomb. I leave you, my friend, but I think you will find me in France, not Geneva. In the meantime—*c'est la guerre*. Literally."

DURING dinner Mrs. Pollifax had mentally compiled a list of pockets of activity to avoid on her night prowl: the elevator, of course, with its vibrations and whispering cables; the reception desk and telephone switchboard, and whatever medical personnel must be available for restless patients.

She changed into pajamas and robe and checked the jewel case, leaving the tray inside but tucking the jewels in her pocket. Fortune favors the bold, she reminded herself as she walked down the dimly lighted, deserted hall. She took the broad, carpeted stairs to the reception floor. The switchboard was unmanned and the desk empty. She heard a murmur from the television room and concluded that the night porter must be watching a program. Quietly she followed the stairs to the ground floor. This was a rabbit warren of therapy and equipment rooms, offices, and the kitchen. It was also, she had a feeling, the most likely place to hide anything.

Down here the lights had not been dimmed, so, before doing anything else, she looked for a hiding place. An unmarked door concealed a utility room that was mercifully dark, and she slipped inside. Her flashlight moved across pails, brooms, mops and a wall filled with fuse boxes and circuit breakers. From this vantage point she opened the door slightly and listened.

To her right, far down the hall, behind the frosted glass doors to the kitchen, someone whistled monotonously through his teeth. A pastry chef, she decided, baking for the next day. Turning on the scintillation counter, she tiptoed to the wide swinging doors at the opposite end labeled HYDROTHERAPIES.

Hydrotherapies was a gymnasium-sized room occupied by two round tile pools filled with water that gleamed under her flashlight. Whirlpool baths, she guessed as she moved slowly around the sides. A glance at the luminous dial of the counter showed the needle quiet. She opened doors and spent several minutes investigating two offices. The next room was marked UNTERWASSER MASSAGE. With some curiosity she entered and found a large, rectangular green tub on a platform in the center of the room. Pipes and formidable-looking tubes surrounded it, and over the faucets a series of dials added to the impression that she had stumbled into a medieval torture chamber. Water stood in the tub. It is strange how alive and sinister water can look at night, she thought, and with relief opened the door to the hall.

She had now completed her tour of this wing of the ground floor, which was separated from the opposite wing by the lobby containing the staircase, elevator and doors to the garden. She peered into the lobby, then hastily drew back. Barely six feet away someone was trying to break in from the garden. Mrs. Pollifax turned off her scintillation counter and waited while the intruder picked the lock. There was a click and the door swung open.

"Marcel!" she gasped in relief.

He jumped and crossed himself before he saw her standing in the shadows. "You scare the devil from me, madame!"

"Sorry—you frightened me, too. Why are you picking the lock?"

His face turned wry. "Waiters are not allowed keys, madame—and it makes for much difficulty, especially when I am off duty." He joined her in the darkness. "I have spent the last hour in the garden, watching. Have you seen or heard anyone?"

"Only the person working in the kitchen. Why?"

"I swear to you I saw someone on the roofs a few minutes ago." He shook his head. "I do not like it."

"And you want to look around," she said. "But first—really it's providential, meeting you, Marcel. You know Hafez?"

"*Mon Dieu,* who does not?" He lifted his eyes heavenward.

"He seems very frightened. I tried to pay a call on his grandmother less than an hour ago, to speak to her about it." She shivered. "I was carried bodily out of the room by two men."

He whistled faintly. "The Zabyan party," he said thoughtfully. "They occupy rooms one fifty, one fifty-two, one fifty-four. Their meals are served in their rooms, with the exception of the boy and the maid. I have myself delivered some of the meals, and a man in white jacket accepts the trays. Their names are Madame Parviz and grandson Hafez, Serafina Fahmy, Fouad Murad and Munir Hassan. They were not investigated further because they were not here when Fraser was killed."

Mrs. Pollifax frowned. "You're sure of that?"

"Quite, madame. They arrived that same day, shortly after. I will, of course, make inquiries further."

"Oh, please do," she told him. "And there's one other thing: when can I get into the kitchen?"

His glance fell to the jewel case. "Ah, yes I see. Saturday, tomorrow, there will be no one here." He glanced toward the stairs. "I must go. Technically I have been off duty four hours, and should be in my room in the village." He moved to the stairs, listened a moment and then, with a wave of his hand, vanished.

She turned on her scintillation counter and crossed to the door marked SUPPLIES. Inside, small rooms opened off from a narrow hall, with a large storage room at the end. Her flashlight roamed past crates of peaches, spices, chocolate and coffee. Another row contained crates from various drug laboratories in Europe, none of them causing any change on her counter.

She began to have pleasant thoughts of bed, and returning to the lobby she ascended the stairs to the reception floor. The night porter stood by the switchboard leafing through a magazine. "Madame!" he gasped, and rattled off a string of words in French.

She said firmly, "I've been looking for someone to take care of my emeralds." She removed the pendant from her pocket and placed it on the counter. "I saw a sign in my bathroom while I was brushing my teeth that said all valuables should be placed in your safe. How could I possibly sleep after reading that?"

He had trouble removing his eyes from the play of light across the emeralds. "But madame, I have no key. Only the head porter can open the safe. I am sadly sorry. At seven he is on duty."

"Oh well," she said, and put away the pendant with regret. "*Bon soir*, then." She continued up the stairs. As she opened her door she saw Hafez standing silently outside his room, watching her. Then he turned and disappeared. It was five after twelve. The clinic, thought Mrs. Pollifax, seemed to have a night life of its own.

Locking her door, she climbed into bed, reflected that she had at least made a beginning, and on that note fell asleep. She dreamed that she wandered through a labyrinth of rooms, each of them colder, until she reached a hall thick with white frost. In her sleep Mrs. Pollifax shivered.

She opened her eyes to find that a cold wind was blowing through the balcony door. As she lay rebelliously considering the alternatives of getting up and closing the door or getting up to look for a blanket, a curious thought occurred to her: she had not left the balcony door open, she had closed and locked it.

A moment later she realized that someone was in her room.

IF SHE could only reach the lamp on the night table before her unknown guest heard her rustling the covers . . .

Over by the desk a thin beam of light appeared near the floor. Caution vanished. Mrs. Pollifax swept back the sheets, switched on the lamp and stared in astonishment. "You!" she cried.

Robin Burke-Jones slowly rose to his feet. "Damn it, yes," he said, looking shaken.

As she groped for her slippers she wondered exactly how he fitted into this. Though Marcel had warned her, she still admitted a deep sense of disappointment because she had liked this young man. "Kindly tell me just what you're doing in my room at"—she glanced at the clock—"at half past one in the morning."

"I'll be damned if I'm going to tell you," he retorted.

"And you'll be damned if you don't," she reminded him.

"Look here, I don't suppose if I promised to leave the clinic first thing in the morning, ever so discreetly . . ."

She saw her jewel case open on the desk. "Have you a gun?"

He looked offended. "Of course not."

"I'd rather see for myself. Do you mind putting your hands up?"

"Of course I mind," he said snappishly. "But have I any choice?"

"None." She approached him gingerly, noticing for the first time his clothes, a startling contrast to his daytime costumes: black pullover, black slacks and black rubber-soled shoes. Patting him she found no gun, but there was a bulge in his left pocket. "Out," she said sternly. "Empty it."

He sighed. From his pocket he drew a small object that looked like a truncated binocular. "One jeweler's glass," he said resignedly; then he brought out her emerald pendant and the necklaces. "The diamond pin dropped over there. I suppose you know that every one of these pieces—for which you can send me to prison for years—is a blasted fake?"

Mrs. Pollifax stared at him. "But you're only a jewel thief! Why didn't you say so at once! I can't tell you how relieved I am."

He backed away. "Relieved? You said *relieved?*"

"Yes, terribly. It makes *such* a difference." She crossed to the balcony, closed the door and drew the curtains, pleased that her instincts had been sound after all. "But why were you going to steal my jewels if you knew they were fakes?"

"There's a market for good fakes. Look here, are you going to call the police?"

"On the whole, I think not—provided, of course, that you return Lady Palisbury's diamond."

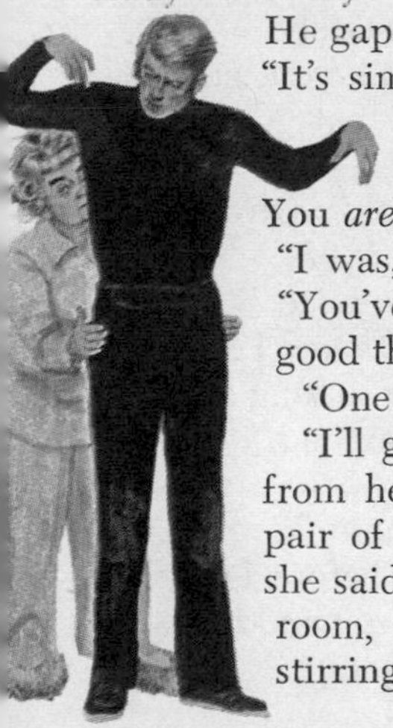

He gaped at her. "Good God, you're clairvoyant!"

"It's simply a matter of putting things together. Lady Palisbury had lost her diamond. Now I find a professional second-story man on the premises. You *are* a professional, aren't you?"

"I was," he said bleakly. "Until tonight."

"You've never been caught before! You must be very good then?"

"One of the best. Oh, how I wish I had a drink."

"I'll get you one." She patted his arm, then removed from her suitcase two envelopes of instant mix and a pair of paper cups. "I always like to travel prepared," she said. "Excuse me a minute." She went into the bathroom, filled the cups with hot water, and returned, stirring them with the handle of a toothbrush.

"*Cocoa?*" he said disbelievingly.

"It helps settle the nerves." She pulled up a chair. "You do realize, of course, that stealing jewelry is dishonest." He managed a smile. "Have you tried more conventional work?"

He shrugged. "On occasion, but never with zest. I like the danger, and I especially enjoy working alone."

She could appreciate his point. "It's been remunerative?"

"Rather. I've managed to salt away some choice real estate. But clothes are a huge expense, and I drive a Mercedes convertible." He sighed. "It takes a damnable lot of money to be rich."

"And I don't suppose Robin Burke-Jones is your real name?"

"Actually, it's plain Robert Jones." He sighed. "I really wish you'd tell me what you're going to do about me."

"I'm thinking about that myself," she admitted. "Tell me, how did you arrive at my balcony, and without any noise?"

"With proper equipment—in this case a rope and rubber-soled shoes—it's no bother. But look here. You ought to be in hysterics over finding a burglar in your room, not plying me with cocoa and inquiring about my techniques."

"I am always interested in people who do things well," she said with dignity.

He put down his cup. "I say, those jewels being fake . . . You're not in desperate straits, are you? I mean, I could lend you a hundred pounds . . . Or give you them," he added politely.

She laughed. "I'm really very touched but thank you, no."

"You're not going to blackmail me, and you're not going to inform—"

Mrs. Pollifax put down her cup and said crisply, "On the contrary, I said nothing about not blackmailing you."

He drew in his breath sharply. "Of course. Yes, I see."

"I propose an agreement—terms, shall we call them? I shall say nothing of tonight's events, or of your—uh—career so long as I hear tomorrow that Lady Palisbury has found her diamond."

"Those are your only terms?"

"Almost. Have you robbed any other people here?"

"No. My technique is never to do it until just before I'm ready to leave a place. By then I know precisely who to rob and how. I've spent the last three nights out on the roofs rehearsing."

"Roofs!" she exclaimed.

"Yes, testing exits and entrances and generally getting the lay of the land. If you must know," he went on, "I overheard you telling the night porter that you had emeralds to put in the safe. I was in the solarium. I decided I'd better pay a visit ahead of schedule and see what you have."

"And Lady Palisbury?"

"No sense of property, that woman. She left her diamond ring on her balcony table two nights ago." He shook his head disapprovingly. "What was a man to do?"

"Yes, I can see the temptation," said Mrs. Pollifax, "to a man with your rather over specialized but invaluable talents. Like police and detectives on the other side of the law, you live by extraordinary wit and deduction."

"Which I'd jolly well better put to work if I'm going to get Lady Palisbury's diamond back before dawn. You're really not going to call the police, and you'll let me—just walk out of this room?"

"You may consider yourself a free man."

He held out his hand and grinned at her. "I say, this has really been awfully pleasant. Strange, but pleasant."

"Actually, it's been delightful," said Mrs. Pollifax, getting to her feet. "Which door will you leave by?"

"I'll feel more secure leaving the way I came. And look, if I can ever do anything for you in return—my room's directly above yours, number two thirteen."

"Two thirteen," she repeated as he vanished onto the dark balcony. Although she listened closely she could hear nothing of his exit. A fantastic performance, she thought, and as she turned off her light she reflected that Robin could prove to be something of a jewel himself.

4

IN THE morning there was a large, hearty doctor named Lichtenstein. While he poked and prodded they made polite conversation about America. He prescribed a metabolism test, a lung X ray, three blood tests and an electrocardiogram.

"All this for Hong Kong flu?" Mrs. Pollifax protested.

"At your age," he hinted delicately, and then, shrugging, "Why else are you here?" She sensibly did not reply. "In the meantime," he concluded, "enjoy Montbrison. Walk in the gardens. Feel free to visit St. Gingolph, and over at Montreux there is the Castle Chillon, where Byron visited." Dr. Lichtenstein stood up, saying to the nurse, "You will please schedule the tests?"

Mrs. Pollifax also stood. "By the way," she said casually, "can you tell me how Madame Parviz is today? She wasn't well enough last night to see me."

The doctor looked blank for a moment. "Oh, the Zabyan group. I know nothing about it. They bring with them their own doctor."

"And you allow that?"

"Of this I do not approve, but"—he shrugged—"it happens sometimes. It is handled entirely by the board of directors."

"You don't know why they're here, then?"

He turned at the door. "I understand the woman is very old, very tired; she wishes to see Switzerland again but with no wish to be examined by foreign doctors. Good day, madame."

Mrs. Pollifax was scarcely aware of his departure. His statement threw new light on the situation. If no one ever saw Madame Parviz— She *must* talk to Marcel. Picking up the phone, she ordered breakfast. But it was brought by another waiter, who said Marcel would not be on duty today until after lunch. There was nothing to do but wait.

After breakfast she was sitting in the garden when a conversation caught her attention. "I was utterly taken aback," said Lady Palisbury, speaking to Court. "We breakfasted on the balcony as usual, and John had no sooner sat down when he jumped up again. And there was my diamond, buried where the two chair cushions met. It had been there all the time!"

"Oh, Lady Palisbury, I'm so glad for you."

"My dear, you have no idea how glad I am for myself. John gave me that ring in 1940."

A few feet away, ensconced in the sun, Robin turned to Mrs. Pollifax and murmured, "I'm actually blushing. It's embarrassing being such a benefactor."

Mrs. Pollifax smiled. "A good deed shining in a dark world—" She followed his gaze to Court, whose long, straight hair gleamed in the sun. She looked wholesome and healthy, her bright pink dress emphasizing her sun-tanned face, and Robin's eyes were fixed upon her.

Beyond Court the doors swung open and a nurse pushed out the man in the wheelchair. Mrs. Pollifax thought idly that his face was a cruel one. She turned her attention back to Robin. "I notice that you didn't pack up and bolt this morning," she teased.

"I decided to stay on a few days." He succeeded in wresting his gaze from Court and flashed a wicked grin at Mrs. Pollifax. "Besides, if I outstay you—"

"Mine was a particularly virulent strain of flu," she assured him.

"I am sorry to hear that! By the way, after I left you last night I began thinking. That jewel case of yours, for instance. I've never known a jewel case to weigh so much. About ten pounds, I'd say."

"Perhaps that's where I keep my genuine jewelry, too."

Court was moving toward them, and Robin jumped to his feet. "Miss van Roelen, I was wondering if you'd care to join me in a walk to the village before lunch."

Court looked at him with steady blue eyes. She turned to Mrs. Pollifax. "I'd like to very much. The three of us?"

Mrs. Pollifax shook her head. "I'm having tests this morning."

Court glanced helplessly at Robin, and Mrs. Pollifax realized that she was actually very shy. She wondered, too, if the girl hadn't sustained a few inner wounds that left her frightened of men. "But I'd certainly appreciate your bringing me four postcards," she said briskly. "It would be terribly kind."

"Of course I will," Court said warmly.

Robin positively glowed with chivalry as he led her across the lawn, and Mrs. Pollifax, who had no need at all of the postcards, watched with a sense of satisfaction. She glanced around the garden and caught the eye of the general sitting nearby, leaning on his cane. He bowed courteously.

"Good morning," she called, but his reply was too low to hear, and she left her chair for the empty one beside him. "Mrs. Pollifax," she told him, extending her hand.

"General d'Estaing, madame." His hand was dry and warm.

"A beautiful morning. You are feeling well today?"

He had surprisingly lively eyes. They twinkled shrewdly in his pale, lined face. "I have survived another day, madame, that is all. I am, after all, eighty-nine."

"Eighty-nine!" exclaimed Mrs. Pollifax.

"The particular problem of being eighty-nine," he continued, "is that one has time to reflect upon a well-lived life but no friends with whom to share the sweep of perspective." He looked out upon the garden. "These young people, I find it strange that they are learning how to live while I am learning how to die."

"Do you wish you could tell them how to live?"

He chuckled. "One cannot tell the young anything, madame."

She laughed. "Very true. General, in your work—I hear that you were head of the Sûreté—you learned a great deal about human nature?"

"Too much," he said dryly.

She hesitated. "You have met, perhaps, with real evil?"

"Evil," he mused. "Yes, but it is not usually in the face or in the words but in the heart. In my experience I have found only one form of evil to leave its visible mark."

"And what is that?"

"That of the professional killer who murders habitually, and in cold blood. It is a curious fact that it shows in the eyes, madame, which poets call the windows of the soul. I have found the eyes of the habitual murderer to be completely empty. The soul can be annihilated, you see—one must not trifle with it."

A nurse entered the garden bearing a tray of medicines. Her eyes fell on Mrs. Pollifax. "Oh, but madame," she cried, "you are the one they search for; it is time for the tests."

Mrs. Pollifax bid the general good-morning and left.

After lunch Mrs. Pollifax stationed herself in the gazebo to wait for Marcel. It was secluded and discouraged company, and she fortified herself with a paperback novel and a discarded *International Herald Tribune* that she had found in the library. The sun grew hotter and the shadows longer. It was a long time before Marcel appeared. When she saw him she stood up and waved.

Marcel made his way to her. He unfurled an order pad and held a pencil poised. "Now, madame, I shall smile, you shall smile, and we can speak."

"It's Madame Parviz again. Have you any information yet?"

"The information will have to come from Zabya. There should be something by tomorrow morning."

She nodded. "There's more, Marcel. Dr. Lichtenstein said that Madame Parviz is very old and wants no foreign doctors examining her. The board of directors complied, but she isn't that old, Marcel; I saw her."

He looked doubtful. "Madame, I do not wish to be tactless, but are you forgetting what we are here for? An invalid woman and a child, it seems most unlikely that they are involved—"

"Of course they're not," she said impatiently, "but there is something very peculiar there. Can you get me a list of the board of directors?"

He shrugged. "I have this already in my files, of course."

"I'm also curious, Marcel, about the man in room one fifty-three, across the hall from Madame Parviz. He's in a wheelchair. I'm wondering if he isn't a member of their party, too."

Marcel sighed. "I can assure you that he is not, madame. He did not arrive with them; he has been here for some time. Nor is he Zabyan. However, I will do very thorough detective work on this man and by tonight I will have more information. But I would prefer to hear something of Robin Burke-Jones, of whom I am most suspicious."

"And rightly so," she said. "Actually, I can tell you a great deal about him, almost all of it reassuring. He's—" Over Marcel's shoulder she saw Robin making his way across the lawn to her. "So if you'll make it crumpets with tea," she said.

He leaned forward. "I go off duty at midnight, madame. Can you meet me on the ground floor at that hour, by the elevator?"

"I'll be there. And lemon with the tea," she added, lifting her voice.

"And you can bring me a Scotch and soda," said Robin, collapsing into the chair beside her. "Walking is strictly for the birds."

"Are you just getting back from the village?" asked Mrs. Pollifax.

He nodded. "We had lunch. Court is still there, playing the organ in that old Anglican church by the café." He shuddered. "The organ, for heaven's sake."

"But how charming," said Mrs. Pollifax, smiling at him. "What a gifted person she must be. What bothers you about that?"

"She doesn't even know I left. We stopped in the church on the way back, and the rector made conversation with us about its flying buttresses and then about music, and Court said she plays, and he begged her to try their new organ. She forgot about me."

"Yes, I thought you might find that a problem. She's quite self-sufficient." In the silence that followed she added tranquilly, "I've heard it makes for the very best marriages, actually."

"Look, I'm not planning to marry anyone. In my profession can you imagine the complication of a wife? All I ask is a decent show of interest. I've got money, I'm not bad looking, I've been around."

Mrs. Pollifax nodded. "You're quite accustomed to having your own way with women, I imagine. What draws you to Court?"

He hesitated as Marcel brought their drinks and withdrew. "She's little," Robin said, scowling. "And cool, but warm underneath. She needs caring for, you can see that at once. She doesn't realize it but there's a vulnerability about her—" He caught himself. "Of course she's impossible. Do you realize that she leaves her bed regularly at five thirty in the morning to *walk*? The girl's obsessed, it's unnatural."

Mrs. Pollifax considered him with sympathy. "I think people like that arouse guilt feelings in the rest of us. My neighbor at home, Miss Hartshorne, is one. Miss Hartshorne's not very popular, but," she added loyally, "she's ever so healthy."

"Exactly," said Robin. "And you called her Miss Hartshorne. She never married?" Mrs. Pollifax shook her head. "Well then, you see? That's just what will happen to Court. She's breathtakingly lovely, but she'll never marry."

Mrs. Pollifax beamed. "Then you needn't worry about falling in love with her, need you? She's no threat at all."

Robin glanced at her accusingly. "You're not paying the slightest attention. You're watching something."

"I'm watching Hafez up on his balcony," she told him. "I wonder why he hasn't been around today." She hesitated and then—it scarcely betrayed any secrets—added, "I tried to pay a call on his grandmother last evening to look over the situation."

"Breathing fire, I suppose, and she told you it was none of your business?"

Mrs. Pollifax put down her cup of tea. "No. I caught only a glimpse of her in bed and then I was literally carried out of the room by two men of the party. And I intend to find out why."

He grinned. "I'll bet you will, too."

"Hello!" called Court, approaching them and looking radiant. "I've been playing the organ all this time; it's been delightful."

Mrs. Pollifax arose. "And now I'm going to excuse myself before I become welded to this chair."

"Oh, but I was looking forward to talking to you!" Court protested. "I have your postcards, too."

They exchanged postcards and centimes but Mrs. Pollifax could not be dissuaded. As she entered the lobby she passed Marcel carrying a tray. "Madame dropped this," he said, handing her a slip of paper. On it he had written: *Room 153, Ibrahim Sabry. Egyptian passport, age 51. Owner small munitions factory. Religion, Islam. Destroy. More later.*

THERE was a film after dinner that evening, and Mrs. Pollifax was reassured to see that Hafez was allowed to attend it. "Oh, madame," he cried in rapture, meeting her in the hall. "Madame, a *film!*" His eyes shone. He tucked his hand into hers and led her into the dining room, where a screen had been erected and chairs rearranged in a half circle. "It is all in French, but I shall explain every word to you," he told her passionately.

"I looked for you all day," she said. "I'm terribly sorry if I upset things by trying to pay a call on your grandmother."

He turned to her with huge eyes. "But madame, I think it was very kind of you. I know that you are a true friend."

"But you were in your room all day?"

"Oh, that is nothing *now*. Look, madame, the picture is going to begin. I will interpret."

He did indeed, reading aloud even the credits, and as the story began, faithfully translating every word. It did not make him popular with the others present. And since it was nearing her Flashlight Hour, anyway, Mrs. Pollifax decided to leave. "You can tell me the plot tomorrow," she whispered to him.

At ten o'clock, feeling rather like Paul Revere, she went to her balcony to signal that she had survived a second day at Montbrison. Again the car lights flicked on in reply. Still she lingered; there was a feel of rain in the warm evening air. The lights along the shore of Lake Geneva were gauzy, like smudged yellow fingerprints on a dark canvas.

At eleven fifty-five, after practicing her Yoga for half an hour, she checked the scintillation counter, tested her flashlight and prepared to learn what Marcel might have discovered. Wearing the slippers that Miss Hartshorne had given her for Christmas, she moved noiselessly down the stairs. Again the reception desk was abandoned, the elevator idle there. She continued to the ground floor. Marcel had not arrived yet, but it still lacked a minute to the hour.

Mrs. Pollifax felt extremely conspicuous waiting here in the brightly lighted hall. The ground floor was quiet except for the sound of water running in the massage room. She checked her watch; it was precisely midnight. The running water was disquieting because someone would no doubt be coming back to turn it off. There was no sign of Marcel.

In the massage room something dropped to the floor. Mrs. Pollifax stopped pacing and became still; objects do not drop to the floor by themselves. She placed the jewel case in the shadow of the stairway and crossed to the door. She hesitated, listening, and then turned the knob. The room was in darkness; she switched on her flashlight as she entered. Across from her the door that led to Hydrotherapies was just closing. Its latch clicked softly and the knob was released from the other side. As she stepped forward the beam of her flashlight dropped and she gasped in horror.

Marcel lay in the pale green tub, his eyes turned vacantly to the ceiling. Blood spattered the sides of the tub and his white jacket. His throat had been cut from ear to ear.

"Oh dear God!" Mrs. Pollifax groped for a chair and gulped in deep breaths of air. He could not have been dead for long, perhaps only seconds before she had descended the stairs.

The water still gurgled into the tub. After a moment—driven by a stern sense of duty—she crept back to Marcel. One trembling hand moved to his bloody jacket but there was no heartbeat. She rinsed the blood from her hand under the faucet, found the handle and stilled the water.

At once she knew that had been a dangerous mistake.

She switched off the flashlight and stood up, in the darkness, in the silence. Somewhere in the offices between her and Hydrotherapies was Marcel's murderer, who knew he wasn't alone: she had just told him so by turning off the water.

There was the faintest stirring in the next room. She shivered. He was coming back to learn who was here. *She must not be found.*

Quietly Mrs. Pollifax backed to the door by which she had entered, opened it, and assessed the distance to the staircase. Impossible. In such a bright light he would clearly see her before she gained the stairs. Across the room she heard the knob turning slowly. She rushed headlong to the utility room, flung herself inside and ran her flashlight over the fuse boxes: they were labeled in French and English. She tugged at the circuit breakers for the ground floor and a second later the light under the closed door vanished.

Footsteps approached the room. Mrs. Pollifax held her breath. He would be waiting for some small sound. He was going to stalk her like prey in an attempt to flush her out of hiding. Then he walked past and down the hall. When she heard the doors to Hydrotherapies open and shut, she slipped out of the room and raced to the stairs, snatching up the scintillation counter from the floor where she had left it.

When Mrs. Pollifax reached the reception level her heart was thudding ominously. She felt almost sick with horror. She stopped to catch her breath and saw the elevator still idle. She entered it and punched the button for the floor above her own. *He must not learn which floor was hers.*

As she ascended, feet pounded up the stairs below her. She realized he was racing to cut her off. With frustrating slowness the elevator rose to the fourth floor and slowly the doors opened. Mrs. Pollifax stepped out. Another moment and she would be trapped—

Robin, she thought. She ran down the hall, found room 213, discovered the door unlocked and skidded inside. Robin was sitting up in bed with a book on his knees. "My dear Mrs. Pollifax," he said, then seeing her face he gasped, "My God, what on earth?"

She placed a finger to her lips and retreated into the darkness of his bathroom. There were advantages in appealing to a cat burglar;

Robin responded at once by reaching for his bedside lamp and plunging the room into darkness. In silence they listened to footsteps walking down the hall. Softly the steps returned. After a short interval the elevator doors slid closed and the elevator hummed as it descended.

Slowly Mrs. Pollifax expelled her breath. Robin opened the door, looked outside, then closed and locked it. He walked across the room to draw the curtains. Turning on a light, he said pleasantly, "We're having a party in my room tonight?"

She left the darkness of his bathroom and found him rummaging in the wardrobe. "There's a bottle of Napoleon brandy here somewhere," he said. "I have never felt that cocoa measures up to brandy in a crisis. Ah, here we are." He poured an inch into a glass. "Drink it down; you look like hell." She sat down and nodded gratefully. "And while you're thawing out," he continued pleasantly, "you'll no doubt think up some outrageous lie to explain why you've been playing hide-and-seek with someone in the halls; but don't try, because I won't believe you. When you stumble into a man's room in the middle of the night, looking as if you'd just seen a corpse, and carrying, of all things, that jewel case—"

"Robin!" she cried sharply.

He picked up the box and carried it to the light. "Sorry, milady," he said. "Obviously you're not what you appear to be." She sat mute as he opened the case. "Let's see, if I designed this—oh, it's very well done—I'd put the lock on one of these hinges, I think, and—" He triumphantly pressed the hinge and removed the tray.

There was silence as he peered down. "Good God—surely not a *Geiger* counter?" He stared at her disbelievingly.

She sighed and put down the emptied glass. "As a matter of fact, it's a scintillation counter."

"What on earth are you after? Uranium?" he joked.

Mrs. Pollifax hesitated and then made a decision. "Plutonium, actually." Robin had saved her from possibly being killed. For this she owed him something, even truth, but Marcel's murder was too dangerous to share. At the moment plutonium seemed much less dangerous. "Interpol is in this," she told him gravely, "and my government, and yours, too."

"Stolen plutonium! Damn clever to send it *here*." He began to look interested. "Not a bad drop-off point at all. Your authorities aren't going to relish your telling me this. Why did you?"

"I find no evil in you, although you do have a somewhat distorted sense of morality in one area. But we're after someone with no morality at all. Someone"—she shivered—"completely amoral, without scruples or fear or compassion or decency."

"Here?" he said in astonishment. "Among the patients?"

"Perhaps."

He looked at her. "So that's why you were relieved to find me only a thief. And tonight? Who was it out there?"

"I wish I'd had the cunning to find out. I was downstairs when I found myself playing cat and mouse with someone in the dark. I reached the reception floor and slipped inside the elevator, planning to walk down a floor to my room, but I was cut off and—"

"And popped in here." He studied her shrewdly. "If that's your story, I won't do any more prying, but it doesn't begin to match your look of terror when you burst into my room. Do you think someone is still out there waiting for you?" He had caught her off guard; she realized that she'd not thought of this yet. Robin shook his head. "I frightened you with that question. All right, let's proceed as if you've stolen the queen's jewels and the police are lurking. Can you manage an eight-foot drop on a rope?"

She brightened. "Over the balcony?"

He seemed amused. "Yes, my dear Mrs. Pollifax, but don't look so eager. Have you ever gone up or down a rope?"

"Yes, once in Albania—" She stopped. "Oh dear, I *am* tired; I should never have said that."

He looked her up and down, taking in her height, her weight, the voluminous robe and fuzzy slippers, and grinned. "I didn't hear you say it. I wouldn't believe it if I did." He removed a flashlight and a coil of efficient-looking rope from his suitcase. "Mountain-climbing rope, the very best." He patted it lovingly. "By the way, there's no ledge on this floor but a perfectly splendid one on yours below, so there will be something under you all the way. I'll go first and check you out." He frowned. "It terrifies me to think your superiors may have sent you here alone and unprotected. I daresay it's the most absolute effrontery to offer my services, but I am indebted to you, and if you should need a gentleman burglar—"

"I can't tell you how much I appreciate that," she said warmly.

"By the way, is your balcony door locked?" She nodded, and he added a circle of keys to his belt. "Full speed ahead then." On the balcony he tied the rope to the railing and tested the knots. "All set? Give me your jewel case. Once over the railing lean out a bit, rope in hand, and then slide down and *in.*"

"In," Mrs. Pollifax repeated. He disappeared. Then she climbed over the railing and grasped the rope. Closing her eyes, she murmured a brief prayer and inched her way down hand over hand.

"Good girl," said Robin, catching the rope and guiding her to the lower balcony. "With a little training you'd make a splendid burglar." He turned his pencil-thin flashlight on the door and a moment later it stood open. "I trust you locked the hall door?"

"No. I thought I might have to retreat in a hurry."

"Then I'd better take a look around." While she put away the scintillation counter he glanced under her bed, into her closet, and then disappeared into the bathroom. "What the devil?"

She heard him sputter angrily and turned questioningly as he reappeared pushing a frightened Hafez in front of him.

"Behind your bathtub curtain," Robin said grimly. "*Hiding.*"

Hafez stood in front of her, taut with anxiety. His eyes were red-rimmed and his cheeks were damp.

"Where have you been?" he cried despairingly. "I waited for you so long."

"Behind the shower curtain?" inquired Robin dryly.

"No, monsieur, in that chair over there—but then I heard voices on the balcony and I was afraid."

"But why aren't you in bed asleep?" Mrs. Pollifax asked softly.

He hesitated, looking at Robin.

"I think you can regard him as a friend," Mrs. Pollifax said. Hafez looked doubtful. "Try," she begged.

"If you say so, madame. I have come to take you to my grandmama. She is awake now. Quickly. Please?" he urged.

"At two o'clock in the morning!" exclaimed Mrs. Pollifax.

Robin said flatly, "Nonsense, lad, Mrs. Pollifax isn't going anywhere except to bed."

Hafez' face literally turned white, as if his whole world depended upon her coming with him. Mrs. Pollifax was touched and astonished. Rallying, she said, "It needn't take long."

Robin said angrily, "Are you mad?"

"Probably."

He sat down in the chair by the desk and mutinously folded his arms. "Well, I'm staying right here until you're settled for the night. If you're not back soon, I'll turn the whole clinic upside down. What's the room number?"

"One fifty, monsieur." Hafez regarded him with awe.

Robin's attitude struck Mrs. Pollifax as exaggerated, considering how little he knew about the events of her evening, and she wondered what caused it. "Let's go, Hafez," she said quietly.

Hafez tiptoed ahead of her down the hall. He drew a key from his pocket, unlocked the door and beckoned her inside the dimly-lit room. Somewhat nervously she stepped across the threshold.

The normality of the scene reassured her. There was no Serafina, and the door to the adjoining rooms was closed. A small lamp on the night table threw shadows against the wall and a circle of light across the bed in which Madame Parviz sat propped against pillows. She wore a rough white homespun robe with a hood that shaded her face, but Mrs. Pollifax could see an uncanny resemblance to Hafez. Brilliant dark eyes under deeply set lids watched her approach; as Mrs. Pollifax drew closer she was shocked to see shadows under the eyes, like bruises. It was a ravaged face, once exotic, but drained of all vitality now. Only the essence of strong character remained.

"Grandmama," said Hafez quietly, "here is my friend Madame Pollifax."

"*Enchanté,*" murmured the woman in a low voice, and one hand lifted to indicate the chair next to the bed. She spoke as if she were making a great effort. "I understand you . . . paid me . . . a call yesterday. When I was . . . asleep."

"Yes. Hafez and I have become friends," said Mrs. Pollifax, smiling. "You've a very charming grandson, Madame Parviz. I've been enjoying him."

Madame Parviz' eyes were fixed intently upon her. "May I . . . ask a favor, then, Mrs. Pollifax?"

Mrs. Pollifax saw that Hafez, standing at the foot of the bed, was watching her with the same intentness. "But of course," she said, suddenly very still and alert.

"If I may ask . . . one thing Hafez . . . cannot do. A cable . . . sent from the village?"

"A cable," repeated Mrs. Pollifax.

"*Not* from the clinic."

"I see," said Mrs. Pollifax. Turning practical, she reached for her purse. "I've pencil and paper. If you'll dictate—"

Hafez said quickly, "It is already prepared, madame."

From beneath her blanket Madame Parviz drew a sheet of clinic stationery. "Please . . . you will read it?"

Mrs. Pollifax read in a conspiratorial whisper: *"To General Mustapha Parviz, Villa Jasmine, Sharja, Zabya: Hafez and I safe and well. Love, Zizi."* Mrs. Pollifax was struck by its normalcy and curious at its necessity. "But it's *not* to be telephoned from the clinic?"

"Please, no."

From the adjoining room there came an abrupt snore, and Hafez and his grandmother exchanged a warning glance.

"She is tired," Hafez said in a low voice.

The audience had ended. "Yes," agreed Mrs. Pollifax, and moved with him to the door. There she looked at him thoughtfully. "You and your grandmother are very close, Hafez." He nodded. His eyes were wary. On impulse she leaned over and kissed the top of his head. "I like you very much, Hafez, and I think you're a very ingenious young man. Good night, I'll go now."

She walked down the hall and entered the sanctuary of her room with relief. Robin still sat in the chair by the desk, arms folded. "Well?" he said glowering at her. "You finally met the vampire grandmother?"

"Yes," she said absently. "It's Sunday. Where does one go to send a cable personally?"

"You'd have to go to Montreux, to a PTT building. The telegraph is open on Sunday mornings—eight thirty, I think. I'll drive you down if you'd like. Suppose you meet me at eight at my car, which is parked near the main entrance. It's a dark blue Mercedes convertible."

"That's very kind of you," she said, surprised.

"Not at all." He walked to the balcony door. "It's certainly been interesting seeing how the other half lives—the respectable half. Oh, by the way, I'd advise your taking a close look at that robe of yours before you wear it again. There's rather a lot of blood around the hem, as if you'd knelt in a puddle of the stuff." She stared at him in astonishment. "When I noticed it I had a fair idea of what frightened you tonight, and frankly it scares the hell out of me. See you at eight." He went out, carefully closing the door behind him.

Mrs. Pollifax moved to the door and locked it. His remark explained the reason for his sudden protectiveness—he *knew*. She took off the offending robe. There was suddenly a great deal to do, a great deal to think about, but she was exhausted. Setting her alarm for seven she fell across her bed and sank into sleep.

5

THE next morning Mrs. Pollifax breakfasted alone in the dining room at seven fifteen. The waiter who served her gave no indication that one of his colleagues had met with violent death during the night. When she had finished her coffee she descended to the ground floor, ostensibly for a stroll in the garden.

The halls were deserted. She moved cautiously toward the open door to the massage room. Inside, the pale green tub gleamed spotlessly. Sunlight from the frosted windows brightened the silver faucets and dials and the immaculate, freshly polished floor. There was not a hint that only hours ago a murder had taken place here. For a moment Mrs. Pollifax wondered if she had dreamed it. Odd, she thought, that no police were on duty. Certainly the discovery of a body would be an embarrassment to the clinic, but its discretion seemed excessive and inhuman.

At eight o'clock she went out to meet Robin in the turnaround. Nothing was said as he drove through the narrow entrance and along the ravine. Emerging from the shadowy woods, he maneuvered his dark blue Mercedes through the sunlit village streets and headed down the mountain toward Villeneuve.

"This is extremely kind of you," Mrs. Pollifax said at last.

"All right," he said harshly, "whose blood was it?"

She had been expecting the question ever since she had stepped into the car. "The waiter Marcel's," she told him.

Looking appalled, Robin drew to a stop by the side of the road. "Hurt or dead?"

"Dead."

"Do you mean murdered?"

She studied his face and nodded. "Yes, in the massage room, in the tub. Did you know him, Robin?"

"We had a bet on today's French bicycle race." He sat staring at her incredulously. "But why a perfectly innocent waiter?" His eyes narrowed. "Or wasn't he that?"

"Actually, he wasn't. He was an Interpol man looking for the same thing I am."

Robin whistled through his teeth. "Well, at least they didn't send you here alone, which lifts my respect for your superiors a notch. Look here, if there's anything I can do to help—"

"You're helping now, Robin, and I appreciate it."

He nodded and eased the car out into traffic again. "This cable you're sending is for Hafez' grandmother, of course?"

She smiled. "How wasted you are on petty crime, Robin. Yes, it's for Madame Parviz. Would it be against your scruples to help me do some balcony spying on room one fifty tonight?"

He laughed. They were now threading through the quiet streets of Montreux. "My dear Mrs. P, I'd be delighted to do some spying with you. What exactly did you find in room one fifty last night?"

"On the surface, nothing," she said soberly. "Madame Parviz looked very ill, and she asked me to send a cable for her announcing their safe arrival, to a General Parviz in Zabya."

"That sounds normal enough."

"Yes, except that she and Hafez have been here for a week, and she insisted the cable *not* be sent from the clinic. There was a kind of hushed urgency about our meeting. Ever since I met him, Hafez has seemed frightened. He's an unusually intelligent child, and I've not wanted to be melodramatic, but I've felt he's been trying desperately to cope with something quite beyond him, and to tell me something. I've been getting little unspoken messages consistently." She hesitated, feeling for words. "Of course children sometimes exaggerate, too, so I had to be sure. Now I'm beginning to understand."

He parked the car opposite a large building that bore the sign PTT. "It's just eight thirty," he told Mrs. Pollifax. She crossed the street, and at the telegraph window copied out the message, hesitating only at the space for the sender's name. Secrecy seemed to matter very much to Madame Parviz. She reflected, then, feeling quite resourceful, wrote: *William Carstairs, The Legal Building, Baltimore, Maryland.*

"You were beginning to understand something," said Robin when she rejoined him. "I hope you'll not leave me hanging."

"I'm beginning to understand why it's been impossible for Hafez to tell me anything. He *can't.* I'm also beginning to understand to what lengths he went to arrange my visit last night with his grandmother. It wasn't easy."

Robin looked startled. "You're implying there's a great deal wrong indeed."

"Yes, I am. Can we go back now? I want to sit in the garden and think, preferably over a pot of very hot coffee."

He started the car. "Think about what?"

"About a half-filled bottle of aspirin, what I report at ten o'clock tonight when I make my contact with Interpol, and about Marcel's death."

"Which explains everything and nothing. I think I'm going to keep a very close eye on you today, if you don't mind."

"No, I don't mind at all," said Mrs. Pollifax.

AT THE clinic there still were no police. After Robin had gone upstairs, she lingered in the lobby by the reception desk. "Madame is looking for someone?" asked the porter. She shook her head. "Perhaps Madame would like a copy of yesterday's *Herald Tribune*?"

She thanked him, tucked it under her arm and went upstairs. As she changed into a lighter dress she scanned the paper. Turning a page, she saw a photograph of King Jarroud of Zabya, and because this was Hafez' king, she ran her eyes down the column. On Tuesday the king was celebrating his fortieth birthday and his tenth year in power. . . . A parade, lunch in the palace beside the beautiful Arabian Nights pool, the vice-president of the United

States among the long list of invited luminaries . . . Jarroud, a monarch popular with the people but not with the upper class, who distrusted his sweeping reforms.

Fifteen minutes later she went out to the garden, pulled a chaise longue into the sun and lay down, recalling Marcel's dancing blue eyes and his comic gestures. Why had it been necessary to kill him?

The general was being helped into a chair by the nurse. The Palisburys, Mrs. Pollifax noticed, had established themselves under the poplar tree. The man in the wheelchair, Ibrahim Sabry, was reading a newspaper at a table with a pink umbrella. The tableau was repeating itself but Marcel was missing.

She went back in her mind to yesterday. Marcel had not thought important her anxieties about Madame Parviz but he had agreed to look into them. And he had told her that he would have information for her at midnight.

He had been safe yesterday afternoon, she was sure of it.

She thought, Whatever Marcel did after I saw him must have taken him in a new and forbidden direction. Whatever Marcel had discovered between half past three in the afternoon and midnight, she must discover, too.

"I hate to disturb your thinking," said Robin, pulling up a chair, "but shouldn't there be an air of repressed alarm here today, a few damp eyes, a policeman or two? I can't help noticing that business is very much as usual– Oops!" he said, ducking.

Mrs. Pollifax looked around. Walking across the lawn toward Ibrahim Sabry was one of the handsomest men she had ever seen. Sabry was looking up, and everyone in the garden was watching as well. The stranger was a figure out of an epic: tall, lean, proud, a beak of a nose, eyes gleaming under straight quizzical brows, his smile a flash of white in his swarthy face. "Who," said Mrs. Pollifax with feeling, "is *that?*"

Robin, looking sheepish, turned his back on the newcomer, who was now shaking hands with Sabry. "Reflex action," he confessed. "I forget that people I've lifted jewels from have no idea I'm the culprit. That's Yazdan Kashan."

"He looks extremely difficult to take anything from," said Mrs. Pollifax. "Should I know who he is?"

"Well, don't faint, but he's a real bona fide sheikh."

"Ah," she said with pleasure, "they really do exist then! But no longer, I take it, on the desert?"

Robin grinned. "Not when they belong to one of the world's richest families. It was Kashan's grandfather who rode camels with the wind. Kashan's father discovered he had pitched his tents on some of the world's richest oil fields, in the Middle East, and Yazdan's the new breed. Went to Oxford, then became a playboy and left jewels lying around carelessly—at least he was damn careless in Paris when I ran into him in '65. He was my first major job; I had to remind myself for months afterward that he could afford the loss." He added indignantly, "I hope you don't think I became a criminal *easily*."

"He apparently has come to Montbrison to visit Mr. Sabry," said Mrs. Pollifax. "What country is Mr. Kashan from?"

"Frankly I haven't the foggiest."

Hafez walked slowly across the lawn, twined one arm around Mrs. Pollifax's chair, and hung on it. "There's going to be Wiener schnitzel for lunch," he confided. But his gaze rested on the two men under the pink lawn umbrella.

"Do you know Mr. Sabry, the man in the wheelchair, Hafez?" she asked, watching his face.

"Yes, madame, he has the room across the hall from me."

"But did you know him before you came to the clinic?"

He shook his head. "No, madame."

"And Mr. Kashan, the man visiting him, do you know him?"

Hafez' eyes blazed before he dropped his gaze to the ground. "I know him," he said tonelessly.

"Is he from Zabya then?"

"Yes, madame." He lifted expressionless eyes and added, "I will go to lunch now. *Bonjour*."

Robin watched him leave, then raised an eyebrow. "I must say you sounded rather like an inquisitor."

"And Hafez like a robot," she said thoughtfully. "Which means, I think, we've just had an important conversation."

The sheikh lunched with Ibrahim Sabry in the dining room, their heads close together as they engaged in conversation, frequently with gestures, but all of it too muted for Mrs. Pollifax to overhear. Court arrived a few minutes after Mrs. Pollifax, calling across the tables, "Will you be in the garden this afternoon?" Mrs. Pollifax nodded; she had no intention of being anywhere else.

Later, in the garden, Court came striding across the lawn. "I have to talk to you," she said. "Do you mind awfully?"

Mrs. Pollifax had been watching Sheikh Kashan wheel Sabry into the gazebo; the wheelchair barely fitted through the narrow arch. Now Sabry was safely within, and the sheikh, seated at a round table, was pulling papers from an attaché case.

She turned her attention to Court as the girl slipped into a chair beside her. "I'm available," she told her, smiling.

Court looked close to tears. "I packed my suitcase this morning," she said, her voice trembling, "and then after lunch I went up and unpacked it again." She pulled a handkerchief from her purse and blew her nose. "I simply don't know what to do."

Mrs. Pollifax said gently, "Perhaps if you'd tell me what seems to be the matter—"

"Oh," said the girl angrily, "I don't want to fall in love again; that's what's the matter. And of all people with *him*. He's so much like Eric. I can't bear that."

"You haven't told me who Eric is," Mrs. Pollifax reminded her.

"My husband," said Court, wiping her eyes. "I married him when I was eighteen and we were divorced when I was twenty, and that's eight years ago."

Mrs. Pollifax nodded. "So you were married very young, and it wasn't a happy marriage, and now Robin reminds you of Eric?"

Court shivered. "The pattern's terrifyingly similar. Robin's so *attractive*, and he doesn't work for a living, which means no character at all. He's been everywhere, done everything—and that's just how it was with Eric. They're both playboys. I hate love," she announced. "It *hurts*."

Mrs. Pollifax smiled. "Really, love has nothing to do with hurt, you know; it's we who supply the wounds. I wonder if you can be sure Robin is just like Eric? When you find out more about him there may be a few—well, surprises." Mrs. Pollifax patted her affectionately on the arm. "What you need, I think, is a little Zen. Tremendously refreshing. There's a great deal to be said for letting life just happen."

"Without *control?* But that's *frightening!*" cried Court.

Mrs. Pollifax laughed. "On the contrary, it's much less painful than fighting every step of the way, and so much more delightful than trying to arrange life like a table setting. It's quite exciting to see what will happen along next."

"At your age," said Court cautiously, "there are still surprises?"

Mrs. Pollifax beamed at her forgivingly. "Frequently, I can assure you. Some pleasant and some not."

"So there you are!" Robin called from the path. "I thought my two favorite ladies had vanished into thin air." He sat down and smiled at Court. "Where have you been all day?"

Mrs. Pollifax let Court reply while she glanced casually across to the gazebo. The sheikh had returned his papers to the attaché case and was standing, delivering what looked to be some final instruction. Sabry listened intently. Yet how empty his eyes are, she thought idly; and suddenly the general's words slipped into her mind: "I have found the eyes of the habitual murderer to be completely empty." Sabry's eyes were like stones. She sat upright in amazement. If Sabry were not in a wheelchair . . . But what a diabolically clever disguise! It's possible, she thought, terribly possible. He was even here when Fraser was. Marcel said so.

Court and Robin were staring at her. "What on earth are you thinking?" demanded Robin.

"I was wondering what keeps Mr. Sabry in a wheelchair."

Court looked taken aback, but Robin's glance was thoughtful.

"I heard it was multiple sclerosis," volunteered Court. "I know he takes whirlpool baths."

"Strokes and broken limbs leave marks for doctors to see," mused Mrs. Pollifax, "but multiple sclerosis is a very slow disease, isn't it?" It made a good cover. She was remembering Marcel's words: "I will do very thorough detective work on this man," and a picture came to her mind of Marcel entering Sabry's room. Her eyes returned to the gazebo.

The sheikh was pushing Sabry's wheelchair through the arch. They moved to the shade of the poplar and a formal exchange of farewells took place. As he walked away the sheikh turned and called over his shoulder, "I'll be back tomorrow." He strode quickly through the glass doors and vanished, leaving Sabry with a sheaf of papers in his lap. He began to sort and then to read them.

She stood up. "Court, may I borrow Robin for a few minutes?"

"Of course," Court said, looking baffled.

Robin followed Mrs. Pollifax to the ground-floor entrance. Inside she turned to face him. "I want to search Ibrahim Sabry's room. Can you unlock his door for me?"

"That's a damn fool idea."

"There may not be another chance, Robin; it's nearing teatime and Sabry looks settled. I want to find out if he's really an invalid. There has to be something—a pair of shoes with worn heels, a snapshot. Robin, do hurry!"

"All right. Take the elevator. I'll meet you." He ran up the stairs two at a time and Mrs. Pollifax entered the elevator. At her floor she stepped out to wait, and after several minutes he rejoined her. "I insist upon going in with you," he said firmly.

"Absolutely not. If anything happens, you're the only one who knows what I've been up to."

His mouth tightened. "I'll stand on his balcony until you've left, then. Woman, you're only an amateur at this!"

She looked at him with exasperation but it was his skill that would unlock the door. "All right," she said, "the balcony then," and led the way down the hall. Robin bent over the lock of number 153, the door opened and they entered Sabry's room.

"Now please—out of sight," she urged.

He moved across the room, stopping only to unlock the two doors of the huge wardrobe. Blowing her a kiss, he slipped through the balcony door and was gone.

Mrs. Pollifax looked around. This room was darker than hers because it faced the mountain that hung over the clinic, but otherwise it was identical. Going first to the desk, she unearthed a number of papers written in Arabic. She turned to the right-hand side of the wardrobe that Robin had so thoughtfully unlocked for her and went through Sabry's clothes, but she found no traces of blood on them, nor were there any shoes. There was a suitcase, however, and Mrs. Pollifax carried it to the bed. It was relatively small, weighing roughly twenty pounds. An identification tag dangled from its handle and she saw to her surprise that it belonged to the sheikh, who must have brought it with him. A temporary address had been scribbled on the tag in pencil: *Suite 1-A, Hotel Montreux-Palace, Montreux, Suisse.* That must be where the sheikh was spending the night. Then why leave a suitcase with Sabry? For safekeeping, perhaps? She leaned over the catch but it had been doubly secured by two small padlocks. Leaving the suitcase on the bed, she returned to the wardrobe to search the left side. She turned the knob, tugged and drew the door open.

Marcel's body, wrapped in glistening transparent plastic, was doubled into the entire half of the wardrobe, his head turned toward her, his vacant eyes staring.

Mrs. Pollifax screamed.

She could not remember screaming before in her life. It was an involuntary outraged protest. In the charged silence that followed she heard the handle to the balcony door turn and then the sound of running feet in the hall. The door to the hall was thrown open and Sabry stood gaping at her. There was no wheelchair.

He glanced from the suitcase on the bed to the opened doors of the wardrobe. With three strides he crossed the room and struck her on the cheek. "Fool!" he gasped. "Imbecile, who are you?" He drew a gun from his pocket, stalked across the hall and knocked at room 154. One of Madame Parviz' white-jacketed attendants answered, and Sabry gestured at Mrs. Pollifax, still standing in his room. The man's eyes widened and he sucked in his breath with a hiss. Behind him appeared Hafez and the second attendant.

Mrs. Pollifax had started to edge slowly toward the hall when Hafez saw her. "Madame!" he cried in a shocked voice. "Oh, madame!" Darting under Sabry's arm, he ran across the hall and flung his arms around her protectively. "She is my friend Madame Pollifax. Don't you dare touch her!"

Sabry viciously slapped him. "You told her!"

"I did not," Hafez gasped. "I did *not.* Monsieur, I beg of you! You think I risk Grandmama's life?"

Mrs. Pollifax listened in fascinated horror. A knot had just been untied and an unraveling of the mystery had begun.

Sabry went to the wardrobe and locked both doors. He told the attendants, who had hurried into the room, "She has seen what is inside. We must get her out of here." To one attendant he said,

"Get the wheelchair"; to the second man he said, "Get the car, Munir." To Munir's question in Arabic he said, "We do nothing until we speak with Yazdan."

"What does he mean?" whispered Mrs. Pollifax to Hafez.

His hand tightened convulsively in hers. "They are going to take you to the sheikh in Montreux. They will ask him what to do about you. Madame, you are in great trouble."

Munir had gone for the car. The other attendant emerged from Hafez' room wearing a sport jacket and pushing the wheelchair. Sabry sat down in the chair. "Bring the suitcase, Fouad—place it on my lap with a blanket to cover it. Quickly! It's not to be left here again." To Mrs. Pollifax he said, "You will be leaving the clinic now for a pleasant little Sunday drive. The boy will go, too. You will walk quietly beside my wheelchair. If you make a move or try to signal anyone, the boy will pay with his life, do you understand?" His look raked her face with hatred.

"I understand," she said quietly. There was no need to speculate any longer about evil: she had just met it, and it shook her.

"And you, Hafez," he continued softly, "you will recall your own situation and see that you behave. Serafina will remain with your grandmother. It needs only a telephone call—"

"I know," Hafez said in a strangled voice.

"Show them your gun, Fouad." Fouad brought out a pistol, displayed it and returned it to his pocket.

"Good. We will go." Sabry's voice was contemptuous.

And so began their exodus down the long carpeted hall: a man in a wheelchair, with a woman on one side, a boy on the other and an attendant behind. Mrs. Pollifax realized that for the moment nothing could be done.

When the elevator reached the reception floor and the doors slid open, Sabry nodded to the porter at the desk. At the entrance Fouad neatly maneuvered the wheelchair down the steps. Off to one side Munir stood at the door of a long black limousine with the motor running. After a swift glance around, Sabry climbed out of the wheelchair to take his place at the wheel while Fouad folded the chair and put it in the trunk. Munir pushed Mrs. Pollifax and Hafez into the rear, where Fouad joined them on a jump seat, his gun out of his pocket now and leveled at Hafez.

With Munir beside Sabry in front, the car slowly moved up the drive and entered the road to the village. Mrs. Pollifax tried to give Hafez a reassuring smile and failed. She was wondering what Robin could do. The most obvious course, calling the police, could involve complications and delays, and neither she nor Hafez had time. She began instead to think of what *she* could do. When they reached the Hotel Montreux-Palace someone would be sent to summon the sheikh. None of their captors realized that she knew karate. She and Hafez together might overpower the remaining two men and escape. But not without the suitcase, thought Mrs. Pollifax; she was growing very interested in a suitcase with two locks that could not be left behind.

Two quick karate chops to disable them, she thought. Hafez opens the car doors and I snatch the suitcase— She fastened her gaze on the back of Sabry's neck and plotted the precise route of her karate strike while she tried not to think what would happen if she failed.

They reached Villeneuve and turned to the right along the waterfront, heading for Montreux. Her glance fell to the mirror attached to the side of the car. In it, to her astonishment, she saw a dark blue Mercedes convertible. Her heart beat faster. There must be thousands of dark blue Mercedes in Switzerland, but this one was allowing other cars to pass while it remained at exactly the same distance behind them.

It was a wide road, with increasing traffic. Looking past Sabry she saw a castle ahead on the opposite side of the road. She was staring at its turrets and ancient stone walls when Fouad suddenly cried, "*Ha-sib! Ookuff!*"

Mrs. Pollifax saw a flash of dark blue and a familiar profile on their left as Robin surged ahead of the limousine. What followed happened all at once: the Mercedes cleared their car and slowed; Sabry leaned on his horn and cursed; the Mercedes jerked to a stop and Sabry's car rammed it from behind with a crash and grinding of metal. Furiously Sabry tried to start the limousine but there were only rattling noises. "Out!" he shouted.

Doors opened and Mrs. Pollifax and Hafez were hustled outside to stand under the rock wall that rose almost perpendicular to the road. Fouad's gun prodded her in the back. Mrs. Pollifax saw that the accident had blocked the lane to Montreux, and cars were coming to a standstill behind them. On the opposite side traffic was slowing to watch. Beyond stood the castle, a modest sign identifying it as Chillon, open for tourists from nine to six.

Turning to Fouad, Sabry snarled, "Take them into the castle. Hurry! Take this, too." He thrust the suitcase at Fouad. "Come back in forty-five minutes."

Mrs. Pollifax considered running, but Fouad held Hafez tightly by the arm. Out in the road Robin and Sabry were confronting each other in fury. "You're damn right I cut you off!" she heard Robin shout. "How could I do anything else when you swerved and accelerated at the same time? And what's a cripple doing at the wheel? By God, you'll pay for this! Somebody call the police!" he shouted. *"Gendarmes! Polizie!"*

Good thinking, she commented silently.

Fouad hurried Mrs. Pollifax and Hafez across the highway and over a bridge to the ticket booth. He shoved coins across the counter and held up three fingers. As a police siren sounded they walked through the huge ancient gate and into an open, cobbled courtyard.

"CHILLON was built around the thirteenth century," said the guide, "to guard the narrow defile between the lake and the mountains and to collect taxes on all merchandise that was carried along the ancient road to Italy over the Great St. Bernard Pass."

"I hope there are dungeons," said Hafez.

They stood in the courtyard at the edge of a tour group. Mrs. Pollifax looked at Fouad. He seemed cross and bored, gripping the suitcase with his left hand while his right remained on the gun in his pocket.

"*Are* there dungeons?" Hafez asked Fouad.

With a martyred air Fouad handed each of them the map and leaflet that had been distributed at the gate. She could sympathize with his predicament; he had hoped they might sit somewhere for forty-five minutes, but the few benches in the courtyard were filled with Sunday visitors. Fouad had decided to remain just behind a tour group, and gave his prisoners instructions to speak to no one.

"There *are* dungeons"—Hafez consulted the diagram—"but not

until we pass the underground vaults." He lifted innocent eyes to Mrs. Pollifax. "Isn't it tremendous that there are dungeons?"

"Tremendous," she said gravely, and wondered if he was receiving signals from her as clearly as she was receiving them from him.

They entered the basement chamber, a dim, medieval world of vaulted ceilings, ancient pillars and a floor of earth worn smooth by centuries. Through the loopholes in the walls Mrs. Pollifax could look out, almost at water level, and see Lake Geneva stretching to the horizon, its waters gently lapping against the walls. "The dungeons are next," Hafez read aloud from his leaflet.

"Bonivard's prison," said the guide in English after completing his first recitation in French. "It was here, in the sixteenth century, that Bonivard, prior of St. Victor's, near Geneva, remained chained to this fifth pillar for four years."

A murmur of incredulity swept through the group. As Mrs. Pollifax leaned nearer to hear the guide, Fouad gave her a level, expressionless stare. "Bonivard, who had favored the Reformation, was freed in 1536, and was immortalized in the nineteenth century by the English poet Byron, whose name is scrawled on this third pillar."

Hafez started toward the third pillar. Fouad reached out and pulled him back. "*La!*" he said flatly.

Certainly this was a grim place to spend four years. Recalling the equally grim circumstances that might await her and Hafez, Mrs. Pollifax glanced at her watch: it was five twenty-five. Fouad would return them to the highway—and Sabry—at six, which was Chillon's closing hour, she remembered. If they could separate themselves from the group, Hafez could outrun Fouad, but Mrs. Pollifax knew she could not. Fouad held all the cards—and a gun. She glanced at Hafez, who was beginning to look disappointed in her. She, on the other hand, had begun to feel hopeful. Waiting did not bother her; it would give Fouad more time in which to grow bored. So, having a gift for enjoying the moment, she gave herself over to medieval history and the enchantment of the castle. And it was enchanting. They moved up a narrow wooden staircase to the next level, through the Grand Hall of the High Bailiff, the Coat-of-Arms Hall, the Duke's Chamber, and then a chapel, where they lingered before they filed through a passageway up and into the Grand Hall of the Count.

"In the Middle Ages used for receptions and banquets," recited Hafez from the leaflet.

What impressed Mrs. Pollifax more than the history of the hall was its immediacy to the lake. Casement windows stood open to the sun and the breeze from the water, and seats had been built at each one. The high-ceilinged room was empty except for ancient tapestries on the walls and huge, carved wooden chests placed here and there.

Chests . . . Mrs. Pollifax felt a quickening of interest. Pausing beside one, she ran her hand over its carving and then casually tried the lid and discovered that it opened without resistance. It was empty except for a coil of thick rope, and she quickly closed it. Hafez had followed her investigation and tactfully glanced away. Turning to Fouad he said, "It's like the old castle at home."

Next came the torture chamber, which Fouad seemed to regard with relish. Then she heard someone up ahead call out in English, "Latrines! Oh, do look!"

Fouad signaled them to follow the group on to the next high-ceilinged room, but Mrs. Pollifax firmly shook her head. "I want to look, too," she told him. "I've never felt that history books satisfactorily explained the hygienic arrangements of the past." With a martyred sigh Fouad led them to the corner and Mrs. Pollifax lifted a wooden cover. She found herself looking down a cobblestoned, chimneylike chute, long since sanitized, to the shallow water of the lake below. "Why—how astonishing," she said. It was dizzying to look from this height at water lapping against the rocks. "And how ingenious," she murmured.

As the tour group moved on to the next room, leaving her and Hafez alone with Fouad, she stood motionless, suddenly alert. It was now or never. She flattened her right hand, waiting.

"We go now," said Fouad, tapping her on the shoulder.

Mrs. Pollifax turned. With the velocity of a coiled spring her hand struck Fouad in the stomach. He gasped, dropping the suitcase. As he doubled over clutching his middle, she stepped back and delivered a karate chop to the base of his skull. He staggered, then slipped to the floor unconscious.

"*Mon Dieu!*" gasped Hafez. "That was karate!"

"I don't think I killed him," Mrs. Pollifax said earnestly. "Quickly, Hafez, there are wooden chests in here, too."

He sprang into action, propping open a chest in the corner and running back to help drag Fouad across the stone floor. Lifting and pushing, they dropped him into the chest.

"His gun." Hafez retrieved it from Fouad's pocket and handed it to her. They closed the lid just as the next tour group entered the adjoining torture chamber, and in no time Mrs. Pollifax and Hafez were sitting on the chest talking amiably, the suitcase between them.

"How long will he be—uh—indisposed, madame?" asked Hafez.

"It's so difficult to remember. It's a matter of pressure points and degrees, and of course no one gets hurt in class. Anyway, let's not wait and see; let's *go*."

They caught up with the original tour group, passed it and hurried to the drawbridge that led to the courtyard. "We left Fouad in Latrinehaus Thirteen," Hafez said, squinting at the diagram.

"May he rest in peace," she added. "Put away your literature, Hafez, and let's see if we can leave without being seen."

From behind a low wall they assessed the main courtyard and the entrance gate. The little souvenir house was being locked for the night by a guard, and a second guard was drawing bars across the small entrance door to the castle proper. Closing time was two minutes away, realized Mrs. Pollifax with a glance at her watch. She looked beyond the gate and ducked back.

"What is it?"

"Munir. He's just outside the gate, watching everyone leave."

"But it's closing time!" cried Hafez. "Where can we go?"

Mrs. Pollifax's eyes searched the courtyard, but a castle that had stood guard against attack for centuries had not been built with a variety of entrances. There was only the one gate. "If we can't go forward we'll have to go back," she said, and grasping his hand, she hurried him across the courtyard and up the stairs to the drawbridge. A guard called out to them. Mrs. Pollifax shouted back, "We've left our raincoats inside!"

"*Imperméables!*" called Hafez blithely, and they plunged ahead through room after room until they reached the Grand Hall of the Count. When they stopped to catch their breath the silence was sudden and disconcerting. A long shaft of late afternoon sun reached the middle of the room.

"The chests," Mrs. Pollifax said. "Climb inside one."

"I really don't want to, but I will. What do we do after this?"

"For encores," she said tartly, "we'll try again to get out when the castle's settled down." She lowered herself into a chest, mildewy and tomblike. She was soon grateful for its protection, however. Some ten minutes later a guard entered, whistling cheerfully. He walked around locking windows, and went on to the next chamber. Mercifully there was no sound from Fouad in the room beyond, and soon both footsteps and whistling died away.

Half an hour later voices drifted up from the level below. "But monsieur, I cannot take you farther; as you can see, the castle is locked for the night. I myself have inspected it. Nobody is here."

It was Sabry who replied, but she could not hear his words. The guard's answer was impatient. "Monsieur, the castle is closed." A door slammed, followed by silence.

The silence deepened. Mrs. Pollifax closed her eyes drowsily. The mildew seemed less potent, the warmth hypnotic. She awoke with a jolt and pushed open the chest. It was still daylight; she saw by her watch that it was seven fifteen. I mustn't do that again, she thought, and climbed out of the chest to rouse Hafez. She lifted the top and saw that he'd been playing ticktacktoe on the lid with a piece of chalk. "What else do you carry in your pockets?" she asked.

He stood up and from the big pocket of his windbreaker drew out a jackknife, his tape recorder, a roll of tape, a pencil, and a slice of Wiener schnitzel in a soggy paper napkin. She smiled. "You might as well add Fouad's gun to your collection. I'll carry the suitcase. Let's take a look around, shall we?"

"Do you really think they are convinced we're not here?"

"No," she said, "but they might go away to consult the sheikh."

Hafez climbed out of the chest and pocketed the gun. Together they tiptoed through the cool, high-ceilinged rooms to the stairs, but now they found them barred by a heavy door with an ancient lock. Mrs. Pollifax rattled the latch but the door did not budge. She felt a sense of foreboding. She wondered how many other doors she had passed without noticing them. They hurried back through the rooms toward the exit by which they had first entered the castle, but here, too, was a stout door, closed and locked.

Hafez's eyes were huge. "We are locked in the castle, madame?"

"Yes," she said, and it seemed to her that her voice reverberated through all the empty rooms. Except the castle wasn't empty. "Fouad!" she gasped.

They ran back to the room where they had left him. Opening the chest Hafez said with relief, "He is still here, madame."

He was still breathing, too, noted Mrs. Pollifax. He lay on his back, knees lifted, and gave no sign of returning consciousness, but she did not enjoy the thought of being locked in the castle with him. "There was rope in one of those rooms," she told Hafez. "We've got to bind his wrists and ankles."

Hafez stared down at Fouad. "If this was war I would shoot him, even if I am only ten years old."

"Don't be bloodthirsty," she chided him. "Come, let's tie him up—and gag him, too—and then we'll have supper."

"*Supper?*"

"Well," she pointed out hopefully, "I was thinking of your Wiener schnitzel. *If* you'd care to share it," she added politely.

6

In Langley, Virginia, it was mid-Sunday afternoon. Carstairs unlocked his office door and entered. Shrugging off his jacket, he sat down at his desk and saw with pleasure that with two hours' work he could clear away last week's minutiae and begin the next seven days with a minimum of encumbrances. His buzzer sounded and he flicked on the switch. "Mr. Carstairs?" said the bright young voice from the office in Baltimore serving as Mrs. Pollifax's cover.

"Afternoon, Betsy. They've stuck you with Sunday?" he said.

"Yes, sir, and I'm so glad you're in. I've a *most* peculiar call on the switchboard, sir. A Mr. Parviz insists on talking with you, but he's not even on our list. He's calling from Zabya. Something about a cable you sent him. His English is either a little primitive or he's very upset, and the connection's dreadful, too."

Carstairs frowned. "How could he have our unlisted number?"

"Apparently he had the address and turned it over to the Zabyan embassy in Washington, and they came through with the telephone number. Is the telephone company bribable, sir?"

"Not to my knowledge, and I can't imagine an embassy going to so much trouble. It'll be a damn nuisance if we have to change the number. Put him on my line so I can find out who he is."

Carstairs leaned over, switched on the tape recorder and sat back. There was a series of pops, followed by a peculiar underwater sound that occasionally accompanies transatlantic calls, and Carstairs heard a harsh, accented voice say, "Mustapha Parviz speaking. I am connected with Mr. William Carstairs, please?"

"You are, sir. What can I do for you?"

"I am calling in reference to the cable I received from you early today. You have just arrived back in America?"

"Just arrived back?" echoed Carstairs.

"Yes. I received the cable you sent me from Europe at noon here by Zabyan time."

"Ah, the cable," said Carstairs craftily.

"Yes. It is most urgent, sir—I must learn the circumstances under which you saw them. Are they safe? Are they in Montreux?"

Carstairs stiffened. "Montreux!" he exclaimed. "Switzerland?"

The man at the other end of the line drew in his breath sharply. "You are playing with me, sir. I implore you—you must know this is a matter of life and death. Where are they?"

Carstairs said swiftly, "I think we might clear this up very quickly, Mr. Parviz, if you'll just read me the cable."

The voice turned cold. "If you sent it, sir, I scarcely need read it."

"But you say that you received a cable from Montreux *today*—"

"You don't know." The voice broke. "You did not, then, after all—" the man said, and hung up.

Carstairs stared at the telephone in astonishment. After a moment he switched on the recording machine and replayed the tape, listening carefully. Mustapha Parviz—the name struck him as vaguely familiar. "Are they safe? Are they in Montreux?" Parviz had lost or misplaced something, documents or people, and it had something to do with Montreux. "A matter of life and death." There was no mistaking the desperation in that voice. It was obvious that Parviz had no idea to whom he was speaking. Nor did he care; he wanted only information. But who would have sent him a cable bearing Carstairs' name?

He picked up the telephone and put through a call to Bishop, finally reaching him at a Georgetown number. "It's Sunday," Bishop reminded Carstairs. "Day of rest and gladness, remember? I'm at a party with a stunning blonde."

"Congratulations," Carstairs said dryly. "Now can you tell me why the name Mustapha Parviz sounds familiar?"

Bishop sighed. "Because he's in the Zabyan report we did for the State Department last week. It's *General* Mustapha Parviz, head of the Zabyan army."

"Good God," said Carstairs.

"Don't you remember? Parviz, son of a tentmaker, educated with Jarroud so that the future king would rub shoulders with the poor. After military school he saved Jarroud's life by taking a bullet in his shoulder intended for Jarroud. Now Mustapha's general of the whole shebang."

"A fact he neglected to mention," mused Carstairs. "One more question, Bishop. If someone sent a cable from Montreux giving the sender as William Carstairs, Baltimore—"

"That could be only one person, sir—Mrs. Pollifax. We've just two agents in Switzerland this week and the other one has no knowledge of the Baltimore covering address."

"It is just the sort of thing she'd do."

"Do you think Mrs. Pollifax is into something, sir?"

Carstairs said testily, "For heaven's sake, Bishop, she's been there only three days."

"Do you want me at the office, sir?"

"No. But stay available while I contact Schoenbeck in Geneva."

He hung up and had a call put through to Schoenbeck's office. While he waited he ordered a pot of coffee and drew out the Zabyan file. He was studying it when his call to Geneva reached

Schoenbeck's assistant, who explained in a formal voice that Schoenbeck had left Geneva several hours ago to confer with Monsieur Gervard, his agent in charge of the Lake Geneva area.

Carstairs said abruptly, "Look here, we've an agent at Montbrison, too, and I've had a peculiar telephone call—"

The voice was soothing. "No, monsieur, it has nothing to do with your agent, Mrs. Pollifax. It is our agent, Marcel, who has disappeared for the moment."

"When did you last hear from Marcel?" demanded Carstairs. "And what was on his mind?"

"His last report was yesterday—Saturday—at the usual hour of five o'clock, monsieur. As to what was on his mind"—the voice hesitated, then turned silky—"he mainly expressed some doubts about your agent, sir."

Carstairs' voice became even silkier. "May I ask why?"

"But of course, monsieur. He had requested her to make the acquaintance of a man named Burke-Jones, about whom serious suspicions have been aroused, and she did this. But she became distracted by a small child staying at the clinic. Marcel had begun to feel that maternal instincts had blunted her—uh—shall we say perceptions?"

Carstairs said curtly, "You may tell Schoenbeck that Mrs. Pollifax is distracted by everything that comes her way but never to the detriment of the job. Her distractions are notorious but never without point. When was Marcel's next contact to be made?"

"He should have telephoned at seven this morning, monsieur, before going to work."

"That's nearly fifteen hours ago! It's nine p.m. your time."

"Yes, monsieur. Naturally we have made discreet inquiries. He did not return to his room in the village last night."

"Has my agent been told about this?"

"A call was attempted, sir. Unfortunately your agent had just left for a drive with friends."

"What friends?"

The voice was disapproving. "I'm sure I cannot tell you, sir, but I'll ask Monsieur Schoenbeck to contact you upon his return."

"Do that," said Carstairs. "I'll wait for his call." He hung up swearing and put through a call to Montbrison. The porter on night duty said in disjointed English that there was no answer from Mrs. Pollifax's room.

This was worrisome. If it was nearly ten o'clock there, she ought to be getting ready to signal from her balcony! "Who was on duty this afternoon, and how can I reach him?" Carstairs asked. He wrote down the name and home telephone number of the head porter. Then, consulting the code given Mrs. Pollifax, he picked up the phone and dictated a cable to be sent to her: "Urgently request explanation cable sent in my name Sunday. Uncle Bill on the loose again in France. Where is Cousin Matthew? Are you running a temperature? Love, Adelaide. Got that?"

"Yes, sir."

"Now get me Switzerland again—a Monsieur Piers Grundig, in St. Gingolph."

At that moment Bishop walked in. "You sounded upset. Something's up, isn't it? What do you think it is?"

Carstairs shrugged helplessly. "I wish I knew. Marcel disappeared between five o'clock Saturday and seven o'clock this morning their time, and in midafternoon today Mrs. Pollifax went for a drive—with friends, I'm told—and she doesn't seem to have returned yet. I'm beginning to think Mrs. Pollifax is missing, too. And I had that damned mysterious call from Parviz. Hello?" he barked into the phone. "Is this Piers Grundig, head porter at the Hotel-Clinic Montbrison?" He waved Bishop to sit down.

His questions to the man were concise. He had seen Madame Pollifax leave for a drive with people from the clinic? At what hour? And the names of the friends? He reached for a pad. "Monsieur Sabry, yes," he wrote. "Two gentlemen not familiar to you, and the boy Hafez. Hafez what? . . . Parviz," he echoed in a hollow voice. "I see. Thank you very much, Monsieur Grundig."

He hung up, and seeing his face Bishop said, "Trouble?"

"Trouble or a very remarkable coincidence," growled Carstairs. "And nothing from Schoenbeck yet. I gave Mrs. Pollifax to Interpol like a gift and they show every evidence of having discarded her like a boring Christmas tie."

"Well, you know she doesn't look like a gift at first glance, sir. She confuses people by looking the cozy grandmother type."

"This time I'm beginning to have the feeling that the wrong

people have discovered she's dangerous. And Interpol could be the last to guess. Bishop, it's time someone explains Mrs. Pollifax to Interpol. Is your passport available?"

Bishop brightened. "In my desk, sir."

Carstairs nodded. "Take along the tape of Parviz' call and give it to Schoenbeck, but first you're to find out where the hell Mrs. Pollifax is." He glanced at his watch. "It's half past four. You've just time to catch the six o'clock plane to Geneva. It will get you there —given the time differences—by seven thirty tomorrow morning."

"On my way, sir," said Bishop, snatching up the tape.

"Oh, and Bishop—"

He turned at the door. "Yes, sir?"

"Keep me posted!"

It was nearing midnight and it seemed to Mrs. Pollifax that it had been dark forever. Around eight o'clock they had divided Hafez' Wiener schnitzel, but that, too, felt a long time ago. Mrs. Pollifax and Hafez sat on the floor in the Grand Hall of the Count, their backs against a wooden chest. Odd little noises punctuated the silence: the scurrying of mice, the explosive creak of wood as the temperature dropped. From time to time she lighted a match from the pack that Bishop had given her to look at her watch, the flare of light picking out the suitcase beside her and the small arsenal in her lap: Hafez' jackknife, Fouad's gun, a segment of rope. At the moment Mrs. Pollifax would gladly have traded them all for a warm coat and some food. "What are you doing now?" she called softly to Hafez.

"I am at the window, madame, looking at the stars. I can see the head of Ursa Major, and also the Chair of Cassiopeia. Oh, madame, they shine so clear, so bright." He came back to sit beside her. "I shall be an astronomer when I grow up," he said firmly.

"I am sure you will. But go on with your story, Hafez," she said. "I want to know everything."

"Where was I?" he asked. "Oh yes. After finding me in the bazaar, Munir drove me to the Zabya airport, but my father was not there. Fouad kept saying, 'He is inside the plane; they're giving him oxygen until the doctor comes.' So I ran up the steps and Grandmama lay stretched out on three seats, quite unconscious."

"Drugged," said Mrs. Pollifax.

"Yes. And as I went to her they closed the door, and that's when I understood they had tricked me and nothing at all had happened to my father. The plane took off at once. There were two pilots, and there was Serafina, who seems to be a nurse. There was Fouad and Munir, and a steward who served food. We had one meal and I think it was drugged because I fell asleep afterward. When we landed I could scarcely believe we had flown all the way to Switzerland. That was when Mr. Sabry came on board to explain."

"That you were hostages," said Mrs. Pollifax.

"Yes, madame. He said we were going to a very nice place, a clinic, and I would be free to walk around and enjoy myself but my grandmother would be kept prisoner in her room. If I confided in anyone, my grandmother would be given an injection that would kill her at once. He said Fouad and Munir would always be with her, and that whether she lived or died would be up to me."

"An intolerable tension," Mrs. Pollifax murmured. They really were ruthless. "And so your grandmother was kept drugged until you stole the aspirin from me, Hafez?"

"You saw that, madame?" He looked up at her, his face a pale oval in the darkness. "It was all I could think to do." His voice was trembling. "In the bottle next to Grandmama's bed there were pills that they used to keep her drugged. I replaced them with the aspirin. I thought if she could wake up, we could talk of what to do. And she did," he added proudly. "She said we must be very brave, and cable my father that we are safe—even if we are not safe—and then place our lives in the hands of Allah. Madame, do you think Allah sent you?"

"The CIA sent me," she said dryly.

"Madame, I am very worried about her."

Mrs. Pollifax groped for his hand and squeezed it. "I think she'll be all right while they look for you, Hafez. Two hostages are better than one. But do you know what's behind all this?"

"No. But I am sure it has something to do with my father being general of the Zabyan army. No one could ever use the army to overthrow the government as long as my father is general. Because he is very loyal to King Jarroud."

"They have found a way to divide his loyalties now," she pointed out softly. They're probably planning a coup, she thought. The blackmailed General Parviz could save his family or his king, but it was unlikely that he could do both. A diabolical trap, and very well planned; Parviz wouldn't think of looking for his family in a quiet clinic in Switzerland.

A coup d'etat in Zabya remained abstract for Mrs. Pollifax. What mattered more to her was keeping Hafez and Madame Parviz alive while the actors played out their intrigues on a stage elsewhere. "When your father receives the cable sent this morning, Hafez, what do you think he will do?"

"I do not know, madame. If he thinks me safe, and if they promise not to kill the king—then, to save bloodshed, he *might* do as they ask—turn over his army to them. But only to avoid a great bloodletting."

"What influence has your mother?"

"Oh, she is dead, madame, since when I was a child."

"You're the whole family then?" She was startled. "You, your grandmother and your father. Now tell me about the sheikh. He's involved in this somewhere?"

"Oh yes, madame. It was his private plane that brought us to Switzerland. His plane has been pointed out to me many times."

So the remaining pieces of the puzzle had slipped into place. Mrs. Pollifax was remembering King Jarroud's birthday party on Tuesday— Oh, perfect, she reflected. The army would be out in force, yet attention would be diverted to the festival and the visiting heads of state. Given careful planning, the day would end with the king deposed or dead and the government taken over by—

By the sheikh, of course. She remembered the flashing smile, the dark handsome face of the man whom Robin had called one of the richest men in the world. She thought, what does one do with so much money? He's already explored the world of the senses—of women, cars, jewels. What next? He would want power. It was the ultimate toy, the deepest psychological lust of all. Her hand moved to the sheikh's suitcase. I have Hafez and I have this, she thought, and wondered what they would do to get them back.

In the nearby room Fouad moaned, and Mrs. Pollifax nudged Hafez. "We'd better look at Fouad," she told him, and led the way. They bent over the chest with a lighted match. In a half hour or so he would begin to remember why he was in the chest.

She groped for a place to sit. It must be one o'clock by now, already Monday morning. The caretaker of the castle would be asleep in his apartment by the gate, and the highway would be nearly empty of cars, but *someone* would be outside—waiting.

Hafez tapped her on the arm. "Madame, don't you prefer a chest? You are seated on the latrine."

She was startled, and one hand moved to the splintery surface to discover that she was indeed sitting on the wooden cover that concealed the latrine, while below— "Hafez!" She began to smile in the darkness. "*Think*, Hafez! What's below me?"

"Lake Geneva," he said doubtfully. "And rocks."

"A way out of the castle. Hafez. A way *out*."

"Down that chute?" he said incredulously. "But madame—how? It is two floors high, surely."

"I'm thinking of the rope," she told him eagerly. "I managed a rope once, over Robin's balcony. It will all depend on the strength of the rope. We must be resourceful, Hafez."

Hafez' voice quickened. "Oh *yes*, madame!" He ran for the rope. "Here, try it. Do you think—"

"Let's tie it to the suitcase, drop it down and see what happens," she urged. "Light a match."

Matches flared briefly, one after the other. They secured one end of the rope to the iron bolt of the window shutter on the wall nearby and the other end to the suitcase handle. Gently they lowered the weight down the chute; it bumped softly against the stones and hung, swaying back and forth.

"How far down do you think it went?" whispered Hafez.

"Twenty feet, possibly thirty." She was assessing the twenty-pound suitcase against Hafez' weight and her own, and she was not sure of the odds. To entrust their lives to a rope that had lain in a damp chest perhaps for years—

Hafez touched her arm. He said in a low voice, "Madame." She heard it, too, and stiffened with a chill of terror. Not far away a voice had lifted in momentary anger. "Munir," whispered Hafez. "Madame, they're *inside the castle.*"

How *could* they be inside? A ladder? There was no magic about it; they had brought equipment and were coming in. If they had a ladder they could scale the outside wall and reach one of the barless windows on the stairs.

She quickly placed the rope in Hafez' hand. "Go hand over hand," she told him sternly, "not too fast. If I can't make it, take the suitcase to Robin. Tug the rope twice when you land. The walls will be near enough to touch with your feet if you panic."

"I do not panic," Hafez whispered scornfully, and she saw his shadowy form step over the side and vanish. The shutter creaked as it felt his weight, but the rope remained steady.

In the chest across the room Fouad groaned. In the corridor beyond, a beam of light flashed across the stones and vanished. "Fool! Keep the light away from the window!" It was Sabry's voice. When she felt two tugs on the rope Mrs. Pollifax climbed over the side. She thought, Madness! But she didn't hesitate.

It was dark and cold in the chute. The rope strained at her weight. Her hands burned from the coarse hemp. Down—down. Something brushed past her, wings fluttering, and then she reached the suitcase and dangled there. "Jump, madame," whispered Hafez excitedly. "It's not far."

She let go, slid across wet rocks and promptly sat down in the water, head spinning dizzily. "Please, madame—do hurry," gasped Hafez, cutting away the suitcase with his knife.

Mrs. Pollifax stumbled to her feet. Hafez handed her the gun and the knife and lifted the suitcase. She followed him. The water was up to her knees. The rocks underfoot were slippery with lichen. As they waded slowly around the castle, she slipped and fell again. She was drenched when they reached the cobbled shore, and as she waded out of the water she stopped and looked up at the dark turrets. Suddenly a thin beam of light impaled her and vanished. A familiar voice said, "So, it's really you?"

It was a voice from another world. "Robin?"

"Over here—in a rowboat," came his stage whisper, and she heard the creak of oarlocks and a muted splash of water. "Climb in," he said. "Whatever kept you so long?"

"And now let's get the hell out of here," Robin said, steadying her as she fell into the boat. As he began to row, the darkness was thinning and she could see the silhouette of the rocks through which he threaded the boat as he headed toward a distant cove. He spoke only once, "Are those *teeth* I hear chattering?"

Hafez giggled, and Mrs. Pollifax said "Yes" with dignity.

The boat hit the graveled shore at a point where the castle was hidden by trees. "I rented a car," Robin said. "It's straight ahead."

"You're a miracle, Robin," she said. "It's the greatest piece of luck, your being on the lake."

"Luck! It was getting a bit too crowded at the front of the castle. The lake was the only place left. There's a blanket on the back seat. Get moving while I tie up the boat."

When he joined them, Mrs. Pollifax and Hafez were huddled under the blanket. Climbing in behind the wheel, he spoke sternly. "Look here, I've spent the whole night debating whether to go to the police, then postponing it because I didn't want to upset your applecart, but don't you think it's time I drive like hell now to a police station?"

Hafez said desperately, "Madame, my grandmother . . ."

Mrs. Pollifax nodded. "Hafez is right. We *must* get back to the clinic, Robin; it's where Sabry will head as soon as he discovers we've gotten away. There isn't time to go to the police and then spend the next fifteen minutes explaining."

He angrily started the car. "Then you'd better explain why it's so important you go back. What *did* happen in Sabry's room?"

"Everything, and all of it ominous," she said grimly. "Hafez and his grandmother are hostages, and Sabry's a murderer, and your old friend the sheikh is heavily involved, and Serafina is guarding Madame Parviz, who's been kept drugged, and just one telephone call from Sabry could end her life—"

"Yazdan! But this is incredible," protested Robin.

"And Marcel"—her voice broke—"Marcel's body is in Sabry's closet. That's why I screamed."

Robin groaned and increased their speed; they were already entering Villeneuve.

"Oh, and we left Fouad tied up in a chest inside the castle," she continued, "but he was already beginning to stir, and once they find him they need only telephone the clinic, you see."

"But what are these demented people up to?" Robin asked as he drove at top speed toward the mountains.

"I think a coup d'etat in Zabya," said Mrs. Pollifax. "The king is celebrating his birthday on Tuesday."

"But that's tomorrow."

"Yes," she said. Sabry and Munir were obviously running out of time if they planned a triumphant entry into Zabya tomorrow. Perhaps they had thought to bury Marcel somewhere on the mountainside. And it certainly did not appear that Interpol even knew that Marcel was dead. She tried to think what she would do if she were Interpol, for they knew at least that she had not signaled last night from her balcony. But she was too tired, and she suspected that Interpol did not expect a great deal of her.

"And Robin, there's also this suitcase. It has two padlocks and I'm hoping you'll unlock them for me. It belongs to the sheikh and obviously has something to do with whatever they're planning."

"I can hardly wait." Robin said lightly.

They had entered the mountain village, turned a corner at high speed, and now drove down the road along the ravine to the clinic. The rising sun was dusting the mountain peaks with gold. The lake below was wrapped in a drifting mist.

Hafez said in an anguished voice, "Serafina will be waiting for Mr. Sabry, and if she sees us without him— You understand, monsieur, they kill so easily."

"That," said Robin grimly, "I'm beginning to understand." He turned off the engine and coasted down the incline past the greenhouse, halting abreast of the main entrance. "Tiptoe around to the garden door," he whispered.

A few minutes later they were inside on the ground floor next to the massage room. "Now," said Robin, "we'll go boldly up in the elevator, each of us pressed against the wall. With luck the porter will think the elevator's going up empty."

Mrs. Pollifax offered him the gun. "Would you like this?"

"No, but I daresay it talks louder than I do." He shoved it in his pocket. He reached out and ruffled Hafez' jet-black hair. "Your father must be proud of you. You're quite a lad, Hafez."

The elevator carried them past the night porter and up to the third floor. They tiptoed down the hall to room 150 and Robin tapped on the door. There were muted footsteps and then Serafina asked, "Who's there?"

In a thick voice Robin grunted, "Sabry."

The door opened a crack and Serafina peered out. Quickly Robin placed his foot inside and leaned against the door. Serafina gaped in horror, then turned to flee. Robin seized her, placed a hand across her mouth and dragged her to a chair. "Someone bring me a curtain cord and a gag. Hurry, she's slippery as an eel."

Hafez produced both. Robin gagged her and then wound the cord round and round her and under the chair. "Now what?"

"I think we move Madame Parviz to my room while I telephone the police," decided Mrs. Pollifax. "This room is not safe."

Robin said, "I couldn't agree with you more." He joined Hafez by the bed, where his grandmother was lying unconscious. He lifted her slight body easily, carried her down the hall to Mrs. Pollifax's room and placed her on the bed.

Mrs. Pollifax put down the suitcase. "Open it," she said.

Robin brought out his keys. Carrying the suitcase to the desk, he set to work. "Look, can't you be calling the police while I do this?" The first padlock was quickly removed. The second, a combination lock, was then removed, and with a grunt of triumph he opened the suitcase. Sandlike grains of filler spilled across the desk. The suitcase was lined with small plastic sacks of the stuff, which had split during the jolts of the night. Puzzled, Mrs. Pollifax pushed them aside to discover a layer of shredded newspapers. She peeled this away and suddenly stepped back in horror.

"But what is it?" whispered Hafez.

Mrs. Pollifax was staring at two innocent-looking drab cans suspended in birdcagelike contraptions and placed in a nest of cotton. She had seen a picture of similar cans before, projected on the wall of a room in the Hotel Taft. She said in a shaken voice, "It's plutonium—I've found the plutonium."

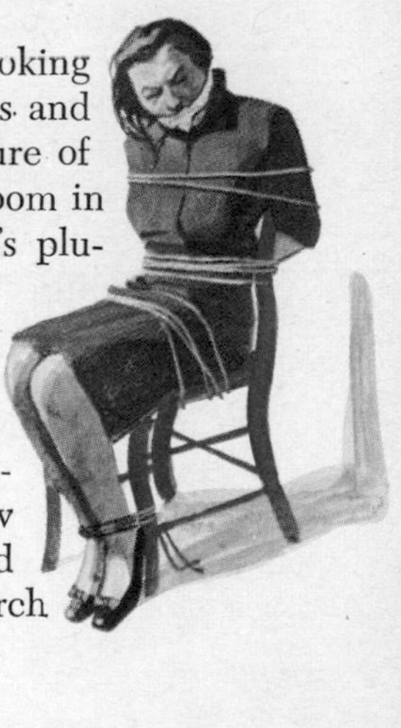

The intrigues of Sabry and the sheikh took a dark and more ominous turn. She was breathless and frightened, for she had not connected the internal affairs of their country with her own mission at Montbrison. She was remembering how Marcel had insisted that the old grandmother and the boy couldn't possibly be involved in the search for plutonium, and she recalled, too, her reply: "Of course they're not, but there is something very peculiar there." The two puzzles had always been just one.

She had taken time out to catch a minnow and had unexpectedly reeled in a whale.

"I MUST telephone," she said. Hafez, awed, leaned over the suitcase. "Don't touch it!" she said. "Not without gloves."

She replaced the packing. "I'm going downstairs and call the police and then Mr. Carstairs in America. I shall never make the night porter understand unless I'm face to face with him."

Mrs. Pollifax, with the suitcase, Hafez' pocketknife and the special gloves Bishop had provided, hurried down the stairs to the reception floor with Robin and Hafez in her wake. The porter rose, apparently startled at such an early exodus. "Madame?"

"I want you to put through two telephone calls for me," she said. "First to the police." He looked alarmed, then shrugged. Dropping a colored envelope on the desk in front of her, he moved to the switchboard and plugged in a line. Mrs. Pollifax checked her watch—it was nearly six thirty—then opened the envelope and read Carstairs' cablegram, which had arrived during the night.

Her immediate reaction was one of intense gratitude—at least *someone* guessed that something was wrong—but Carstairs was several thousand miles away. Where were Marcel's people? She glanced at the porter, who was swearing in Italian into the mouthpiece. "Did you reach the police?" she asked.

He shook his head. With a bewildered look he removed the headpiece and moved to the rear of the board, checking knobs and outlets. "The line—she is dead," he announced.

A chill crawled up Mrs. Pollifax's spine. Robin, equally startled, tried the lights. Nothing happened. They, too, were dead.

They're coming, she thought, and drew a deep breath to calm her skidding heart. She found herself remembering the aerial view of Montbrison that Carstairs had projected on the wall of the Hotel Taft. The clinic was isolated in seventy acres of forest and ravine, with only one road entering the property from the village a mile away. It would be very easy to lay siege to it. "But there are only three of them," she said aloud.

"Four if you count the sheikh," said Robin grimly. "And don't say 'only' four. It's like saying there are 'only' four copperheads loose in a small room."

She pulled a memo pad from her purse and began writing. Handing Robin the slip of paper, she said, "One person ought to be able to get away. Don't take your car. Go by the path down the mountain, and after you've called the police, telephone this number in Baltimore."

"And leave you here alone? They've already succeeded in cutting the wires. Next they'll put up a roadblock and walk in the front door and—"

"Making it all the more important that you get help. Have you forgotten Madame Parviz—and Hafez—and the suitcase?"

He sighed. "All right." He pocketed the memo and gave Hafez a tap on the shoulder. "Take over, friend," he said, and ran down the stairs to the exit into the garden.

Mrs. Pollifax turned to Hafez. "Go to my room and stay with your grandmother. Lock everything and let no one in. Do you understand?"

"Very clearly, madame." He turned and raced up the stairs.

Mrs. Pollifax took the suitcase, knife and gloves and walked downstairs to the basement. She entered the storage room and closed the door. With Hafez' pocketknife she ripped a corner off a carton labeled peaches. Then she opened the suitcase.

Drawing on her gloves, she cautiously lifted the two cages from the suitcase, removed the cans of plutonium and carried them carefully to the darkest corner of the room. Then she dragged a sack of charcoal in front of them to conceal them and returned to the case of fruit. Clearly the cans of peaches were the proper size, but each was adorned with a garish paper label. She began to peel away the labels with the pocketknife. Scraping and cutting, she removed all but the smallest fragments from two cans. She rubbed down their shining exteriors with charcoal, inserted them into the cages, packed both in the suitcase and replaced the filler and newspapers. She disposed of the gloves in a wastebasket and hurried upstairs with the suitcase to her floor. She turned the corner and abruptly stopped, one hand at her throat. The door to her room stood open. She forgot caution and rushed toward it.

The room was empty, and the door to the balcony stood wide. There was no sign of Madame Parviz or Hafez. Moving to the balcony, Mrs. Pollifax leaned over the railing and looked down into the garden. "Hafez?" she called.

She hurried down the hall to room 150 and opened the door. Serafina remained bound to the chair, her eyes screaming silent hatred. Mrs. Pollifax absently patted her shoulder as she passed. The other two rooms were empty. What had happened while she was in the clinic basement? She ran back to the staircase.

"Good morning," said Court cheerfully, descending from the floor above. "There's something wrong with the elevator."

But Mrs. Pollifax was already hurrying down the stairs. The head porter came to meet her. "Madame," he said, "there are two policemen inquiring for you."

"Thank heaven," she said.

"They would like for you to go with them to the headquarters. A small passport misunderstanding, I am sure."

"Passport misunderstanding?" She stopped, her eyes on the backs of the two uniformed men standing in the hall. One of the policemen slowly turned. It was Fouad, looking very Continental in uniform. "Good morning, madame," he said pleasantly.

"Good morning," said Munir, walking swiftly to her side.

It was already too late; each of them held her by an arm. "These aren't policemen!" she cried to the porter. "They came with Madame Parviz; they belong in room one fifty-four!"

He looked startled. "Madame?"

"Help me!" she called to Court, who stood on the staircase, transfixed, watching.

Gently but firmly Fouad and Munir were pushing her to the main door. "Help—help!" cried Mrs. Pollifax as the pressure on her arms mounted. The head porter gaped at her blankly. When they reached the door she turned and shouted to Court, "They're *not* the police—get help!" Then Fouad and Munir lifted her over the threshold and carried her up the driveway toward two cars blocking the entrance.

The sheikh jumped out of the nearer car, a red Volkswagen. They carried her, still struggling, past it, and Mrs. Pollifax glanced inside and with a sinking heart recognized the figure collapsed on the rear seat: it was Madame Parviz. She was hurried along to a black Rolls-Royce. Her hands were roped together and she was shoved inside so roughly that she fell across the trousered legs of the man already occupying the back seat. Those trousers—they were purple, she saw in dismay—and as she was plucked from the floor and hurled into the seat, Robin said grimly, "They caught me, too—in the garden. A bloody rout, I'd say."

7

AFTER leaving Mrs. Pollifax, Hafez had gone up to her room and locked himself inside with his grandmother. When he heard footsteps in the hall he was sitting quietly beside the bed. He stood up, expecting to hear Mrs. Pollifax call, "Hafez?"

But Mrs. Pollifax did not call. The knob of the locked door turned slowly. His heart hammering, he moved back to stand beside his grandmother. He heard a low, sibilant whisper. "It's locked. Hand over the skeleton key." It was Fouad at the door.

Hafez' heart thudded so violently that he thought it must surely burst through his shirt. "Grandmama," he whispered, but his grandmother did not stir. He began to search for a weapon—scissors, a paperweight—but there was nothing. He thought of the contents of his pockets: his tape recorder, spare tape, a pencil.

He backed farther and farther from the bed until he reached the balcony door. He realized with acute grief that he must abandon his grandmother. If he were taken by these men, there might be no hope for either of them.

He slipped behind the curtains and stepped out on the balcony just as the door to the room opened. As the two men walked inside, he climbed over the railing onto the ledge and crouched there, out of sight, trying to think of a way to keep an eye on Fouad and Munir without being seen himself.

In his eight days at the clinic Hafez had explored all the corners and unmarked rooms. Now he recalled the dumbwaiter in the utility closet next to room 148. He cautiously made his way along the ledge, reached the balcony of room 154 and climbed over the railing. The door stood open and he walked through the room to the hall door and peered out. The corridor was empty.

Taking a deep breath he raced down the hall and ducked into the utility closet. Opening the door of the dumbwaiter, he tugged at the ropes and brought the box up to the third floor, climbed inside and began to lower himself.

There were voices in the kitchen, waiters grumbling over the loss of electricity and the tediousness of a wood-burning stove. The dumbwaiter reached the bottom of the shaft and Hafez pushed open the door, stared at three startled faces and climbed out. "*Bonjour,*" he said brightly, and walked past them to the door and outside into the maze of trellises that concealed the exit. He dodged around the greenhouse, climbed the bank to the road and took refuge in a clump of bushes from which he could see the front door. He hoped it was the correct door to watch.

Thinking of all the people inside asleep made him feel lonely. Even if they were awake, he thought, they wouldn't *believe* what was happening. It was the first time he had understood that most people wall out what is disturbing. It took very special people like Mrs. Pollifax and Robin to understand. He felt a wave of infinite gratitude toward them and decided he would be like them when he grew up.

A movement at Sabry's window caught his eye. He saw Fouad walk out on the balcony and wave toward the road. A moment later Sheikh Yazdan Kashan strolled down the driveway and entered the clinic. Several minutes later Fouad and Munir hurried out of the front door carrying his grandmother.

Where are the police? wondered Hafez impatiently.

The two men carried their burden up the driveway. As they came abreast of Hafez in his hiding place he ducked his head and moved parallel to them through the bushes. At the top of the incline the clinic's entrance was blocked by a small red Volkswagen and a long black Rolls-Royce. Sabry emerged from the latter and helped the two men place Madame Parviz inside the Volkswagen. The three then stood beside the car, talking.

Hafez had no paper but he drew out his pencil and on the inside of his jacket he carefully copied down the license numbers. He had scarcely finished when the sheikh came out of the clinic. He and the three men began arguing, and Hafez heard his name spoken. Then Fouad and Munir stripped off their jackets and stepped behind the cars. When they reappeared Hafez saw that they wore police uniforms. The sheikh opened the trunk of the Rolls and tossed their other clothes inside.

Hafez watched Fouad and Munir walk down the driveway and he guessed they were going into the clinic to find Madame Pollifax. If they captured her, too, then he would be the only one left who knew what had happened—and all he would have would be the license numbers of two cars that probably would vanish before the police came. It was not enough.

Now the sheikh had climbed inside the car and he and Sabry sat talking. It was very quiet except for the low murmur of their voices and birds chattering in the tall trees.

"We must be resourceful," Madame Pollifax had said.

Hafez moved swiftly. He crawled to the back of the Rolls and ever so gently tried the lid to the trunk. It opened with a creak—the sheikh had not slammed it tight! The murmur of voices continued as he climbed inside, lowered it softly behind him and stuffed a corner of Fouad's jacket into the opening to leave a crack for fresh air.

When the Rolls reached the village it turned and began a precipitous climb up the mountain. Mrs. Pollifax looked at the sheikh, facing her from the jump seat. "Where are we going?"

He smiled. "I go far, but you and the others will go no farther than I wish you to go. You have been a very naughty lady."

She told him that sounded patronizing.

His eyebrows lifted. "How so? You and your friend Burke-Jones have been only a minor inconvenience, no more than a buzzing gnat. Can one give to a gnat importance?"

"I can't speak for Mrs. Pollifax," said Robin, "but I resent being called a gnat, damn it."

The sheikh laughed. "Well said, Burke-Jones. Your face is familiar, by the way. Have we met?"

"Paris—'65," Robin said shortly. "The Comte de Reuffe's week-end party. Gabrielle's ball."

"Ah yes. A gay year, '65. It lingers in my mind like vintage wine on the palate. I hear that Jackie has married twice since then."

Robin nodded, but Mrs. Pollifax only half listened. She was

looking around her as the road narrowed. They were moving through dark woods; they rounded a curve and suddenly they were at the top of a mountain. But this peak was no more than a stepping-stone to what lay beyond—higher peaks that merged into other, taller mountains stretching ahead like an endless cyclorama. It was a patchwork quilt of forest, with seams of green on the lower slopes broken up by small villages and chalets.

"I can't believe it," Robin was saying. "Gabrielle a nun?"

It was too civilized for Mrs. Pollifax. "Where are we going?" she asked again. She recalled that only Madame Parviz had been in the back of the Volkswagen . . . but if they had found her they must have found Hafez, too. "Where is Hafez?" she demanded.

The sheikh shrugged. "I don't think we need worry about Hafez. He is—shall we say, expendable?" Over his shoulder he called, "Ibrahim, are we nearly there?"

"Nearly there, Sayyid."

Expendable, thought Mrs. Pollifax, and felt a little sick.

They had reached a bald, windswept plateau. Mrs. Pollifax looked out of the car window and caught a glimpse of Lake Geneva far below. The car slowed, turned off the paved road and jolted over a winding cart track, the Volkswagen following.

They approached a knoll littered with boulders and pebbles. We must be too high for trees, decided Mrs. Pollifax, and began to feel the hopelessness of their situation. She told herself that it would be better to take each moment as it came, and acknowledged for the first time that not many moments might lie ahead.

The car cleared the knoll and in the distance Mrs. Pollifax saw a weather-beaten Alpine chalet perched absurdly among the rocks, its shuttered windows overlooking what must be a spectacular view of the country miles below. A single stunted tree was its only companion.

When the car reached the chalet, Robin peered out. "I say, this doesn't seem up to your standards as a *pied-à-terre.*"

"Oh my dear fellow," said the sheikh, "this was rented only last evening, when it became apparent that you and your friend were nuisances. A pity, too, for it amused me to use the clinic. I happen to be a member of the board of directors, you see."

I don't think we're going to get out of this, thought Mrs. Pollifax bleakly as the Volkswagen pulled up beside them. Fouad opened the car door and went up the steps to unlock the chalet. The sheikh stepped out. Sabry raised his gun. "You will go inside the chalet," he told the captives without expression.

Robin got out next, and as he turned to face her she saw that the right side of his face was scratched and torn, his right eye swollen almost closed. "Oh Robin," she said sadly.

"I've obviously lived much too sedentary a life," he said lightly. "A fact that I intend to rectify if I ever get out of this." His hands were also tied, but as Mrs. Pollifax climbed out he succeeded in lifting them to touch her arm reassuringly. At the moment it only made her want to cry.

Inside the chalet every window was shuttered and barred. As Fouad lit an oil lamp he looked at Mrs. Pollifax briefly, and she saw the hate in his eyes. Then he carried the lamp to a table in the middle of the room, his face impassive.

"Cheerless place," said Robin behind her. "Rather like a cottage at Brighton in the off-season."

Munir carried in Madame Parviz and lowered her, none too gently, to the couch in front of the fireplace. The sheikh counted an enormous number of Swiss francs into Sabry's palm and wished him well. Then Sabry left.

"I wish I knew where he's going," Mrs. Pollifax said to Robin in a low voice.

The sheikh heard her. "But I have no secrets from you. Ibrahim has gone to bring back a helicopter. This terrain is quite suitable for its landing. I've no intention of lingering here, and since I've no idea what hints you may have left at the clinic, I shall proceed as if all of Switzerland were looking for me."

Mrs. Pollifax lowered herself into a straight chair near the fireplace, her tied wrists extended awkwardly in front of her. "What do you plan to do with us?" she asked.

The sheikh walked to the fireplace and rested a hand on the mantel. "We have a proverb that says, 'If you are a peg, endure the knocking; if you are a mallet, strike.' I hope that you will endure with fortitude the consequences of your meddling. However, to answer your question: The helicopter will have no room for you and Mr. Burke-Jones. There will be space only for Fouad,

Munir, Ibrahim, myself, and Madame Parviz, who is still of some importance as a hostage. Now please, let us say no more. There are always a few who have to be sacrificed for the greater good. We also have a saying, 'What is brought by the wind will be carried away by the wind.'"

Munir came in carrying wood and lighted a fire. He spread a rug on the floor in front of it—a gorgeous Persian rug, Mrs. Pollifax noted. Incense was placed on the mantel, a match applied, and the scent of sandalwood met her nostrils. Then Munir retired to the kitchen and the rattle of cups could be heard. Mrs. Pollifax walked to the fire to warm herself, but she was uncomfortable so near the sheikh. She retreated to the end of the couch and sat down near Madame Parviz' feet. The poor woman was still unconscious, her eyes closed, but a second later Mrs. Pollifax was not so sure. She thought a gleam of light showed between the fringe of her lashes and the bone of her cheek.

Munir returned carrying a tray with tiny cups and a large, beak-nosed brass coffeepot which exuded a spicy fragrance and a cloud of steam. Firelight flickered across the rug, picking out its jewellike colors and the patina of brass; the chalet was rapidly turning into an Arab tent.

Mrs. Pollifax had noticed Fouad squatting in the shadows at the door with his gun. "These plans you have," she said to the sheikh, looking at him steadily. "You're responsible for the death of Marcel and the death of a man named Fraser, and now you would kill us as well. Why?"

He shrugged. "In war many people are killed. But how is it that you know about Fraser?"

Robin was watching her with curiosity. "You can't possibly mean the English chap who was injured at the clinic last week! Do you mean he was murdered?"

The sheikh smiled. "He was a professional British agent, my dear Burke-Jones, who had worked in the Middle East and had met Sabry. But so long as Ibrahim convalesced quietly there was no harm in sharing the clinic. But of course once the Parvizes arrived Fraser would have guessed something was up. He had to be removed."

Robin thought a moment, then said, "I happen to be a British agent, too, you know, and since Mrs. Pollifax has absolutely nothing to do with this I insist that you let her go at once."

Before Mrs. Pollifax could protest this wasted act of gallantry the sheikh laughed. "I don't believe you for a moment, Burke-Jones, and I couldn't possibly allow her to go free. She knows too much. Munir, bring the food, and then you may cut their ropes so that they can eat. It is better anyway that there be no marks on their wrists."

No marks on the bodies, thought Mrs. Pollifax, and as a second tray was brought in bearing pastries and dates she experienced an almost hysterical urge to laugh. A Persian rug, tiny cups of Arabian coffee, incense, and a sheikh—it was too much. Then, abruptly, she felt like bursting into tears. "You travel with originality," she managed to say.

The sheikh flashed his white smile at her. "Anything is possible with money."

"Including the buying of armies and lives?" she said tartly. She held up her wrists to Munir, who severed the bonds, and when he had done this she rubbed them, wincing.

The sheikh paused with his cup halfway to his lips. "Constructive means to a good end. It is of considerable benefit to myself and to Zabya for me to become its ruler."

"A new toy for you?" she suggested, and looking into his eyes she saw how lightly civilization sat upon him.

He forgave her with a smile. "I intend to rule Zabya. It will be a quick bloodletting. I have a well-trained cadre of followers waiting in the desert. I have munitions hidden away, and I have acquired several well-paid physicists for the making of certain sophisticated instruments of power. As you see, when one has money one can buy anyone."

"You couldn't buy King Jarroud," pointed out Mrs. Pollifax.

"True, but I have undermined him. General Parviz will be no trouble to me; the road to the throne is open."

"And when you have completed your coup d'etat?"

"I shall have Zabya—and oil. Oil is power. Jarroud is a fool, he threatens to turn over Zabyan oil to the rabble. Oil is too precious for such waste, for whoever has oil can dictate his terms to the entire world."

"Zabya isn't the only Middle Eastern country with oil," pointed out Robin.

The sheikh laughed. "No, but I shall be able, as its ruler, to impose my terms upon all the oil of the Middle East."

Mrs. Pollifax, guessing the answer, asked softly, "How?"

He shrugged. "Certain threats made. I might point out that one judiciously placed bomb of the proper magnitude would interrupt the world's supply of oil for years. I can assure you that attention will be paid. The key to it all—the key to the masterstroke—lies in that suitcase on the table. You broke open the locks but you couldn't possibly understand what you saw."

This cheered Mrs. Pollifax's flagging spirits because she was the only one in the room who knew that he was referring to two cans of peaches instead of several kilograms of plutonium.

The sheikh rinsed his fingers in a bowl of water and dried them on a towel that Munir held out to him. Then he rose. "Join me, Munir, it's time." To Fouad he said, "Remain attentive and shoot if they move."

He and Munir disappeared into another room and she exchanged glances with Robin across the Persian rug. Some fifteen feet away Fouad leaned against the door, his eyes bored as he watched them. There was silence except for the crackling of the fire. From the next room the sheikh intoned in a powerful voice, *"La illaha illa llah, Muhammad rasul allah."*

"He's praying," Robin whispered. "I daresay we should be praying, too. It does begin to look a bit final, the three of them against two of us. And when Sabry gets back there'll be four."

From the couch a low voice said, "Not two against four. Three." Lips barely moving, eyes closed, Madame Parviz said, "There is a poker on the hearth."

"We'd better not look at her," Mrs. Pollifax advised Robin.

"A bit of luck having her conscious," he said in a low voice. "I'm not sure I can reach the poker without Fouad seeing me. Have you noticed how carefully they keep their distance from us?"

"They're aware I know some karate," explained Mrs. Pollifax.

"So that's it!" said Robin. "I must say that until meeting you I seem to have led the most commonplace life. If you know karate, Madame Parviz can be armed with the poker, and all we need are some brass knuckles for me. Stay with us, Madame Parviz!"

"It's a break not having our hands tied," Mrs. Pollifax pointed out. "How long do you suppose we have?"

"Until Sabry brings back the helicopter. It's not hopeless, you know. If we can stall, catch them off-balance . . ."

Stall, mused Mrs. Pollifax. "There's one thing I could do that might give us time. I can tell the sheikh I replaced the two cans in the suitcase with two cans of peaches from the clinic."

The glance Robin gave her was withering. "That's a singularly uninspired idea and not at all up to your usual standards. Do you take him for a fool?"

"But that's exactly–" She stopped as the sheikh returned. At that moment they heard a helicopter's blades beating the air some distance away. Fouad opened the door and looked out.

"Allah be praised," said the sheikh, "he's early. Munir"–he gestured toward the rug–"pack up our things. Let Sabry take care of them."

The sound of the helicopter filled the room; a gust of air blew in through the open door, scattering ashes from the fireplace. The noise abruptly stilled, and Mrs. Pollifax heard the crunch of shoes outside. Her heart began to hammer sickeningly against her ribs. As Sabry entered the room, she stood up and addressed the sheikh in a clear loud voice, "I have something to say to you."

THE sheikh glanced at his watch. "Say it, but be quick."

She said steadily, "There are only cans of peaches in your suitcase."

"I beg your pardon!" he said in astonishment.

"Good grief," groaned Robin.

Her head went higher. "Just before you brought me here I substituted two cans of fruit for the two original cans. The real ones are back at the clinic."

The sheikh looked amused. "Which means that we should not kill you yet, is this correct? Instead we should drive back to the clinic and play hide-and-seek again?"

"Whatever you feel necessary," she said calmly. "But I wanted to stress that if you kill me now you won't know how to find the original two cans."

"Munir, bring us a can opener," he said, watching her face. Munir brought one from the kitchen. "Give it to her," ordered the sheikh.

Munir handed Mrs. Pollifax the can opener. Opening the suitcase she slowly removed the plastic bags of filler and then the layers of shredded newspaper. Detaching one of the cans from its cage, she set it on the table, gripped the handle of the can opener and bent over it.

Abruptly a hand was placed over hers and she looked up into the cold dark eyes of the sheikh. "That will be enough," he said curtly. "You are a very good actress and it's a clever trick, but do you really believe I would allow you to injure the contents of this can?" With a bored sigh, he moved to the fireplace.

"But it's only a can of peaches. How can I persuade you unless I open it?"

"Shoot her, Ibrahim," he said. "She grows tiresome."

"You dastardly coward," cried Robin, stepping forward.

"Back!" snarled Ibrahim Sabry, lifting his gun.

His sharp command was echoed by one from outside the chalet and Mrs. Pollifax saw Robin stop in midstride. Everyone stopped—it was like a game of statues, Robin with one foot off the floor, the sheikh with arm lifted, Fouad by the door with his mouth open, Sabry four feet away with his gun leveled at her head. And when the scene unfroze, she thought, Robin would place his foot on the floor, the sheikh would lower his hand, Sabry's finger would squeeze the trigger and she would die. The moment seemed endless; she wanted to scream, "Get it over with!" and then she realized that what had turned them to stone was the voice from outside.

"Ici la police. Sortez, les mains en l'air!" called the voice.

No one moved. The moment stretched out interminably. A picture flashed into her mind of a sunny morning in a garden and an old man leaning on a cane, and then she understood that it was the voice of General d'Estaing. She thought incredulously, The general *here?*

Then a second voice called, "Come out with your hands high—the jig is up!"

Robin's voice. *Robin's voice on a tape recorder.*

"Hafez," she whispered. He was alive.

"What the devil!" cried the sheikh, and at once the spell was broken. Mrs. Pollifax threw herself at Sabry and knocked the gun out of his hand. As it clattered to the floor she slashed at him with her other hand and he staggered and fell. She saw that Robin had hurled himself upon Fouad and was struggling for his gun. As Munir ran across the room to pluck Sabry's gun from the floor, she kicked him. He grasped her leg and brought her down to the rug and they rolled over. The gun went off and sent a searing flame up her left arm. Just as Munir reached for her throat with both hands a figure in a long white robe made a dash for the poker, then rushed across the room and hit him over the head with it.

Mrs. Pollifax sat up. Her head was spinning and she felt a little sick. Madame Parviz was standing over Fouad, and Robin was sitting on the floor brushing dust from his trousers. The sheikh and his suitcase were nowhere to be seen. Mrs. Pollifax stumbled to her feet, swayed a little and made her way to the door.

The sheikh was in the helicopter, and as it lifted from the ground she exchanged a look with him through the plexiglass window. The helicopter turned and soared away over the hill, and as its noise diminished she heard the tape recorder repeat over and over, "the jig is up the jig is up the jig. . . ."

She sat down weakly on the top step. The droning mechanical words seemed to come from the solitary tree on the hillside. "Hafez?" she called.

Hafez emerged from behind the tree and came bounding over the rocks. "Madame!" he cried. "Oh, madame, it worked!"

"Hafez," she said with feeling, "you've just saved our lives. However did you find us!"

"But madame, I never left you! I hid in the trunk of the limousine. Don't you remember you said we must be resourceful?" Then he saw her arm and his eyes widened in horror. She heard him shout, "Grandmama! Robin! She has been shot!" and then, "Monsieur, she is fainting!"

Someone leaned over her, she was lifted and carried to the car, while over and over the tape recorder called out, "the jig is up the jig is up. . . ." In the darkness that followed she heard voices—Bishop's first of all, but that was impossible because Bishop was in

America, and then she thought she heard General d'Estaing speaking, and Court's reply, and then Dr. Lichtenstein commanding them to be quiet and there was silence. A long black silence.

8

MRS. POLLIFAX opened her eyes to find that she was lying in bed in her room at Montbrison. She stared at the ceiling, and then her eyes moved slowly down the wall, which an evening sun had striped with gold, and when they focused on the face of the man seated beside her bed she said, "What are you doing here!"

Bishop looked up from a magazine and grinned. "Carstairs sent me. He had a strong hunch things were going wrong."

She said dreamily, "They went wrong for me in the right way. Or right for me in the wrong way." She frowned. "Why do I feel so peculiar, Bishop?"

"You've just had a bullet removed from your arm. You were bleeding so badly that Dr. Lichtenstein didn't want to move you. He gave you a whiff of something and did it in his office. They don't have an operating room here."

"Oh," she said, trying to make sense of this. She peered at her arm and discovered it swathed in gauze and bound to a splint.

"It's still Monday—only seven o'clock in the evening," he assured her. "Interpol has been here all day putting the pieces together and worrying like hell about you. They found a woman tied to a chair in room one fifty, and Marcel's body in the closet of room one fifty-three. I take it you've had a rather busy weekend?"

"Yes," she said, looking back on it from a vast distance, and she struggled to sit up. "The sheikh?"

Bishop shook his head. "He got away in his private plane."

"But the coup d'etat?"

"Firmly squashed—we *think*—but here's Schoenbeck," Bishop said, rising. "He can tell you about it. Mrs. Pollifax, it's high time you meet Henri Schoenbeck of Interpol."

Monsieur Schoenbeck advanced into the room looking a little shy, but his eyes warm as they encountered hers. "And I, madame, am in your debt. It is my loss that we meet only now, madame."

"Are you the person to whom I signaled?" she asked.

"No, no, that was our agent Gervard." His lips curved in a faint smile. "It may amuse you, madame, to learn that we had planned to pay a call upon you today and set up a more suitable contact. We had wanted," he explained, "to give you the weekend to become oriented. A plan, I might add, that has nearly cost you your life. It may console you somewhat to learn that at this moment the sheikh's three men are entering a nearby prison."

"It consoles me," she admitted, "but the sheikh has flown away, I hear, with his peaches?"

Schoenbeck and Bishop exchanged glances, then Schoenbeck said, "There is no need to pretend any longer, madame. I have been told that you tried to persuade the sheikh that he did not have the plutonium but you are quite safe now, you know."

Mrs. Pollifax sighed. "I suppose there *is* something absurd about peaches, Monsieur Schoenbeck, but I can assure you that what I said was true. The plutonium never left the clinic. It's here."

"I think I believe her," said Bishop in an astonished voice.

"Never left the clinic!" echoed Schoenbeck. "Then the French plutonium is no longer in the hands of the sheikh? Madame, if you would tell me precisely where it is . . . ?"

Mrs. Pollifax ignored the question and instead smiled at him dazzlingly. "What do you think of Robin, Monsieur Schoenbeck?"

"Robin? He has surprised me; that much I will say."

"If you mean Burke-Jones, isn't he the chap you all suspected of killing Fraser?" asked Bishop.

Schoenbeck looked pained. "Unfortunately, yes. It appears that the man is nothing but a jewel thief."

Mrs. Pollifax said, "Yes, and a very *good* jewel thief. I'm delighted he's told you about himself, but you must see that by being honest with you he's absolutely ruined his career." She looked at Schoenbeck sternly. "Is there anything you care to do about that, Mr. Schoenbeck?"

"Yes, madame, there is, but I am wondering how you guessed it."

"Frankly it occurred to me several days ago. He's tremendously efficient at picking locks and he enjoys working alone. He's surprisingly clever in emergencies and he has gorgeous clothes."

Schoenbeck said dryly, "I am not such a fool, madame, as to allow his talents to slip through my fingers. I have already made approaches and he appears most interested." He added, "I can only wish that young Hafez could work for Interpol, too."

"I think he prefers to become an astronomer," put in Mrs. Pollifax. "Where is he?"

"He and his grandmother are still talking on the telephone to Zabya, but he is anxious to see you."

She shook her head in wonder. "If it hadn't been for Hafez—"

"Please," said Schoenbeck firmly. "It is better that you rest. Allow me instead to brood over how near the sheikh came to completing his matched set of plutonium." Schoenbeck smiled faintly. "It's much too small a world these days for anyone like the sheikh to vanish for long, Mrs. Pollifax. I foresee no *large* problems in recapturing the plutonium that is still missing, madame. We can promise to—how do you say—hush up the story if he quietly returns the missing pounds and promises to retire from politics. If his machinations became known he would, after all, be blackballed by his social clubs and his people."

"You really think he'd mind?" asked Bishop curiously.

"Yes, he would," said Mrs. Pollifax. "He's a snob. And what he'd mind people knowing most of all was that he *failed*. He was," she shivered, "a thoroughly fascinating, horrid sort of man."

Schoenbeck rose. "And now if you'll excuse me I shall begin the process of looking for him." He bowed and strolled to the door.

"Monsieur Schoenbeck," Mrs. Pollifax called after him softly, "the plutonium is in the basement storage room, in the farthest corner, hidden behind a sack of charcoal."

He smiled. "Thank you, madame."

Bishop rose, too. "Well, Mrs. Pollifax," he said, walking over to kiss her lightly on the cheek, "it's time for me to fly away again. You've orders to stay through the week until you've thoroughly convalesced. If you don't, Carstairs will have my head."

"But I'm delighted to stay," said Mrs. Pollifax. "Can you imagine Miss Hartshorne's reaction if I should go back to New Brunswick with my arm like this? She'll say it's exactly what I deserve for spending a dull week in Baltimore visiting an old friend." With a small twinkle she added, "Miss Hartshorne feels I lack a sense of adventure."

"Good God," said Bishop with a shudder. "And if your arm is still in a sling when you go home, what will you tell her?"

"That I tripped over Adelaide's cat, I think, and broke my arm."

Bishop grinned. "Then I needn't worry about you anymore. By the way, I think you'll find yourself in good company this week. Hafez and his grandmother will be staying a few days until Madame Parviz feels better. General Parviz will fly over on Friday to take them home."

From the doorway Hafez said, "Please, may we come in?"

"She's all yours," Bishop said, and blew Mrs. Pollifax a kiss.

Hafez, Robin and Court tiptoed in and stood at the foot of the bed beaming at her. She saw that Robin and Court were holding hands and she guessed that Robin, having unburdened himself to Interpol, had unburdened himself to Court as well. Mrs. Pollifax said mischieviously, *"Ici la police. Sortez, les mains en l'air!"*

Hafez laughed and ran around the bed to sit beside her, his face shining with happiness. "Madame," he said, "we are all alive."

"Isn't it surprising?" she said.

"And madame," he continued eagerly, "I have been speaking to my father on the telephone and you will meet him on Friday. He wishes to thank you in person and—"

"Hafez is back to normal," pointed out Robin, grinning.

"—and he is bringing from King Jarroud the Palm of Isa, the highest award which is given in my country. It is named after the shepherd who saved our country from invasion in 1236. He threw himself from a cliff to warn the people in the valley that the enemy was in the hills, and when they saw him fall, with the enemy's arrow piercing his heart, they knew their country was in danger. And my father says on Friday we will have a small party here to present to you this medal. Isn't that magnificent, madame?"

"And you didn't even have to throw yourself off a cliff," pointed out Robin.

Court shivered. "You have all—the three of you—been in such danger and I didn't even *know.*"

Robin turned and looked at her. "If I'm going to work for Interpol, now that Mrs. Pollifax has succeeded in making an honest man of me, you'll have to grow accustomed to a spot or two of danger. That is, if you're going to marry me."

Court said softly, "*Am* I going to marry you, Robin? Well . . ." She glanced at Mrs. Pollifax and laughed. "Yes, I believe I am!"

"Bravo," said Mrs. Pollifax.

Robin kissed the top of Court's head. "The wisest decision you've ever made, my dear, and it gives me a perfectly brilliant idea. If Hafez' party is Friday, there is just time to get a special license. We can be married here at the clinic."

"And Mrs. Pollifax can be the matron of honor," cried Court. "Oh, Mrs. Pollifax, you will, won't you?"

Mrs. Pollifax considered this with pleasure. "I can't think of anything I'd enjoy more. Why I can wear my drip-dry purple print gown and my prayer beads."

"That I can't wait to see," Robin said fervently.

"But who could be the best man?"

"Oh, no problem there." Robin placed a hand on Hafez' shoulder. "There's only one person who could possibly qualify."

Hafez looked up at Robin and grinned.

With a blissful sigh Mrs. Pollifax leaned back against her pillows and watched them. She acknowledged that her arm was hot and uncomfortable, and that ahead of her lay the greatest ordeal of all—Miss Hartshorne—but what is brought by the wind, she remembered, will be carried away by the wind. With this she dismissed all thoughts of the sheikh and settled down to enjoy a genuine convalescence.

Dorothy Gilman

Condensed Book readers first met the redoubtable old lady who is probably America's most unconventional secret emissary in Dorothy Gilman's *The Unexpected Mrs. Pollifax.* Now Mrs. Pollifax's attractive creator has done it again, and with such cheerful enthusiasm that working on these books is obviously for Miss Gilman a pure labour of love. After all, as she herself has said, "Mrs. Pollifax is a woman who has happen to her everything that I want to happen to me." It's not surprising, then, that these stories have in them a happy quality of dreams come true.

Although Miss Gilman's life seems to have been lacking in quite all the excitements she would have wished, certainly her recent great literary success has enabled her to travel widely about the world. No matter how light-hearted Mrs. Pollifax's adventures may be, Miss Gilman believes in researching them thoroughly. She has been to Lake Geneva, and even to the real-life prototype of her Hotel-Clinic Montbrison. She may not have gone so far as to study karate, which her heroine uses so effectively in this latest adventure, but she did attend one judo class, "was thrown around all night", and did not return for the balance of the course. She has studied Yoga, and thinks it helps in acquiring a sense of peace with oneself and with the world around. Just like Emily Pollifax, she has trouble with the lotus position.

Miss Gilman's enthusiasms, however, are not wholly connected with her writing. Just recently she has set out on a quite new adventure: at her recently acquired seafront house in Nova Scotia she plans to harvest and dry seaweed from her own beach for fertilizing ten acres of land, and to pursue her hobby of growing medicinal herbs. Or so she tells us. It's just possible, of course, that Mrs. Pollifax's next mission will involve unmasking a fiendish seaside herbalist with plans to poison the entire American continent.

THE FEARFUL VOID
Geoffrey Moorhouse

The Fearful Void

a condensation of the book by

Geoffrey Moorhouse

Published by Hodder and Stoughton, London

Out in the parched, murderous wastelands of the desert fear waits. To some men it may even beckon: to Geoffrey Moorhouse such fearful desolation presented a challenge that had to be met. There was challenge also in a journey no man had made before—3,600 miles by camel across the Sahara from the Atlantic Ocean in the west to the River Nile in the east.

He was to come very close to death. The heat of the day, the cold of the night, thirst, hunger, disease, bone-weariness, even the downright dishonesty of his Arab companions, these were to bring him to despair and beyond. But he would find loyalty in the desert also, and beauty, and life-saving compassion.

Moorhouse writes vividly of his Arab guides, fascinating individuals, people with their full share of human strengths and weaknesses. He came to terms with these men, as he did with their alien food, with the difficulties of their language, even with the recalcitrance of their camels. And he came to terms with his own fear.

Geoffrey Moorhouse is a remarkable man. In this book he relives with total honesty his five months of journeying across some of the most barren and merciless terrain in the world.

Chapter One

It was a child, screaming in nightmare, which awoke me. As I rose from the depths of my sleep, sluggishly, like a diver surfacing from the seabed, the corridors of the hotel echoed with terrified cries. They poured over the balcony beyond my room and filled the courtyard beneath, they streamed out into a town ankle-deep in sand under a new moon, and were lost, plaintively, among the low dunes scattered to the south and east. I reached consciousness to the dimmer sound of a father's voice gentling the infant terrors away, and the night became stealthy with silence again. But the spell of tranquillity had been broken.

For a while I lay blankly and widely awake, knowing that in a day or two I must leave this room's security and move off into those dunes, and that a man called Mohamed was even now travelling from his encampment in the desert, to be my companion on a fearful journey into the awful emptiness that stretched for three thousand miles and more to the east.

I, too, in the past few months had experienced childish nightmares, and now again, the images shaped themselves over my bed. I saw myself asleep somewhere out in the nothingness, then wakening suddenly at some sound. Appalled, I saw that Mohamed was carefully leading our camels away. I was unable to move or call out, so transfixed was I by the pains he took not to disturb me. By the time I'd struggled up, he'd vanished, with the camels, our water and our food. I had nothing but a sleeping-bag and the dying embers of our camp fire.

The sequence ended abruptly there. I shifted uneasily, switched on the light and began to read myself into torpor.

But my body had become clammy, though the night was cool.

I was afraid.

IT WAS IN THE SPRING of 1971 that I had decided to attempt a crossing of the great Sahara desert by camel, from west to east—and I did so quite simply because I was afraid.

I was flying home over the Sahara at the time, at the end of some field work for a book on missionaries. The earth beneath was hidden under a vivid orange fog. Whether it was a sandstorm or merely the colour of the desert reflected on cloud, I had no means of knowing. But this orange pall covered the desert as far as the eye could see, and it was the first time that the terrible immensity of that wilderness had registered: three and a half million square miles of desert at once became a staggering reality, instead of a mere statistic.

I was aware that it had not been crossed the long way by one man using the desert's traditional form of transport, though for ages before Europeans ventured into the interior, there were well-defined routes south to north from Black Africa below the Sahara to White Africa fringing the Mediterranean. Slaves were regularly herded from the markets of Tombouctou and Chad up to Fez, Tripoli and elsewhere on the northern littoral. But there had never been any logic to a journey made from the Atlantic to the Nile, or vice versa. The intervening space had gradually become known from the time of Herodotus to consist of nothing but sand, rock and diminishing savannah.

Instantly, impulsively, I wanted to grapple with the void down there, I wanted to stretch myself out to its limits. Instantly too, my heart and my body recoiled from the prospect. The palms of my hands became damp with sweat as another part of me seriously wondered whether I could possibly commit myself to the biggest desert on earth.

One of my weaknesses is a deep need to justify my actions; I have always found it very difficult to do something simply for the hell of it. Certainly, the possibility of a giddy and unique success was not enough by itself to set me on my way. But I did not need to look far for a justification of this journey. It was there in my instant recoil from commitment, in the fearful sweat that sprang out of my palms. I would use this journey to examine the bases of my fear, to observe in the closest possible proximity how a human being copes with his most fundamental funk.

I was a man who had lived with fear for nearly forty years. To say this is not to suggest that I had lived in a permanent sweat of terror. To live one's life in fear is something much less spectacular: it is to act, for a great deal of the time, from negative rather than positive motives. We hesitate to speak to strangers, for instance, for fear of a rebuff. We are loth to act generously because we fear more may be taken from us than we really wish to give. We are reduced in our ability to go forward and warmly embrace Life itself and all who share it with us. Fear can thus be seen as the most corrosive element attacking the goodness of the human spirit. And the most insidious form of fear is certainly the fear of being afraid.

In my own case, I recognized that my deepest fears were those of annihilation, of being surrounded by what is hostile, of being unwanted, of being lost. And while I had come to know a great deal of my fearful self, there were still extremities that I hadn't been able to examine. To do this it would be necessary to place myself in a completely unknown context, in which imagination might find the most fearful possibilities.

The Sahara fulfilled the required conditions perfectly. Not only did the hazards of the desert represent ultimate forms of my fears, I was also almost totally a stranger to it. I had never in my life touched a camel, let alone ridden what was said to be the most intractable of beasts. I was not even capable of communicating with the desert inhabitants, for I spoke not a word of Arabic. My only obvious asset for such a venture was a fair degree of physical fitness.

Friends were later to say my idea seemed so preposterous that they assumed I would soon drop it. But long before I had finished writing about nineteenth-century missionaries, I was quite certain where my nagging wish to know would next take me. And though it might well be that I should be drawn across the desert by the prospect of an explorer's crown, I also knew that, more powerfully still, I would in truth be propelled by my own fears.

BY THE END OF MARCH 1972, I was free to begin my preparations for the journey. It was obvious that I must take the fullest possible advantage of the desert winter. The Sahara is no place for a traveller in summer, when the air temperature can rise to 134°F, and the sand temperature to 168°F. I must therefore be in a position to move away from the Atlantic coast by the beginning of November at the latest; so I must leave England early in October, to allow time for acclimatization. I had six months in which to ready myself, and there was much to be done.

The first priority was clearly to start learning Arabic. I have never been a linguist. Though I had travelled widely as a journalist, I had never managed to pick up more than a smattering of any tongue other than French; and the prospect of tackling one of the notoriously difficult languages at the age of forty both deterred and excited me. I enrolled as a pupil in a small school hemmed in by *kebab* cafés off the Tottenham Court Road. It was run by a Mr. Beheit, late of Cairo and points adjacent, who assured me that after three months of his special treatment I would speak Arabic fluently. Whereupon he drew from his desk a postcard which an old pupil had sent him from somewhere in the Middle East, reporting the astonishment of local Arabs that he could converse with them like a native. It was written in English.

My own tutor was named Ahmed, and for a couple of hours every day we would face each other across a small table, while I would inquire the way to some oasis, anxiously demand fodder and water for my camels, wonder politely whether the sheikh was prepared to grant me audience. It was hard going. The problem was increased by the need to assimilate a vocabulary that would vary from place to place across five Arab countries that each practised vernaculars of their own. By the end of June I was approximately in the position of a fifteen-year-old who, equipped with a modicum of schoolroom French, nervously awaits his first trip to Paris.

I arranged at this time to find out something about camels.

Armed with a temporary employee's permit, I began to visit the London Zoo in the mornings, before the public was allowed in. I had hoped that perhaps it might be possible for me to learn the elements of camel riding there, but the only saddlery in London was designed for the use of small children on the backs of two-humped Bactrian camels, shaggy creatures from Asia, which are unknown in the Sahara. What I could learn, however, was to become used to having camels about me. It was a small but important step.

They had three Arabian camels at the Zoo, and one of them was a heavily-built bull named Fred. As we walked towards his pen for the first time, his keeper told me about the perversity of bulls. They were liable to attack without provocation, he said, and they always went for a man's belly with their teeth. Fred was sitting down when we arrived at his pen. As we entered, he shambled to his feet and padded over towards us. I stood my ground, manfully. A single pace away and his neck arched high in the air. Then there gradually emerged from the side of his mouth a large pink bubble. Fred's keeper grinned at me, and explained that thus the bull camel betrays his excitement when confronted with a cow. "He fancies you," he said.

The feeling never became mutual, but I eventually overcame my initial timidity to such an extent that, wondering just how strong the camel's neck was, the keeper and I swung from it together, like a pair of children, legs in the air. The bull stood patiently showing no sign at all that he noticed the sudden weight.

After these early morning excursions to the Zoo, I went home to grapple with Arabic, or else I spent afternoons in the library of the Royal Geographical Society, reading the reports of various expeditions into the Sahara. The evenings were increasingly spent in star-gazing. It was vital that I should become a proficient navigator, which meant a great deal more than an ability to use a map and compass. One needed in addition a bubble sextant, a nautical almanac, a set of sight reduction tables and a handbook of instruction in what appeared to be a witheringly mathematical art.

Night after night I trudged across Hampstead Heath, trying to distinguish Aldebaran or Capella in the great orange glow that dimmed all but the brightest stars above London. Having reached certainty in picking out half a dozen stars, I could begin to obtain fixes from them. Unfortunately, when I actually came to use the sextant the fixes I got were distinctly at variance with what I knew my position to be. I assumed that my feeble mathematics were failing me, so I persisted through many cold and semi-obscure nights to plot myself west of Bristol, east of Tolpuddle and at a number of points right in the middle of the English Channel—anywhere, in fact, except in North London. Finally I conceded that perhaps the sextant, newly calibrated though it was, might be at fault. An acquaintance in the R.A.F. arranged for it to be tested. A few days later I was informed that there was an error of 2° 17 mins. built into the wretched thing. It was returned to me "rectified beyond the theoretical limits of accuracy". Next day I worked out a fix to within five miles. I would need to do better than this in the desert: there would be waterholes to find, literally no more than holes in the ground, easily missed unless one arrived within a mile or so by navigation. But at least I had only the errors of inexperience to overcome from now on.

As my beginning, I chose the Mauritanian capital of Nouakchott, a place virtually on the seashore of the Atlantic, where I might expect to obtain camels. From there I would ride in a southeasterly curve across Mauritania and into Mali, to reach Tombouctou. There I could probably rest a little and replenish my stores before heading northeast, towards the Algerian oasis of Tamanrasset, almost exactly in the centre of the Sahara. This would be my halfway point, before moving out across the Libyan desert, by way of Murzuk, to reach the Nile at Luxor. I would then have ridden about 3,600 miles. Assuming that I could cover about twenty miles a day, which all expert opinion seemed to agree upon as a reasonable rate of progress by camel, this would have meant about six months of riding. But it was quite impracticable to suppose that there would be no delays: camels would have to be replaced and there was always the possibility of falling ill and having to stay put until the sickness passed. To be caught in the Libyan desert in summer was probably to perish; so it seemed that I would have to spend the summer in Murzuk, before continuing the journey in October. With luck, I might reach the Nile by Christmas 1973.

There was one man whose advice I had to have—Theodore Monod, one of the polymaths of our time: an ichthyologist, geologist,

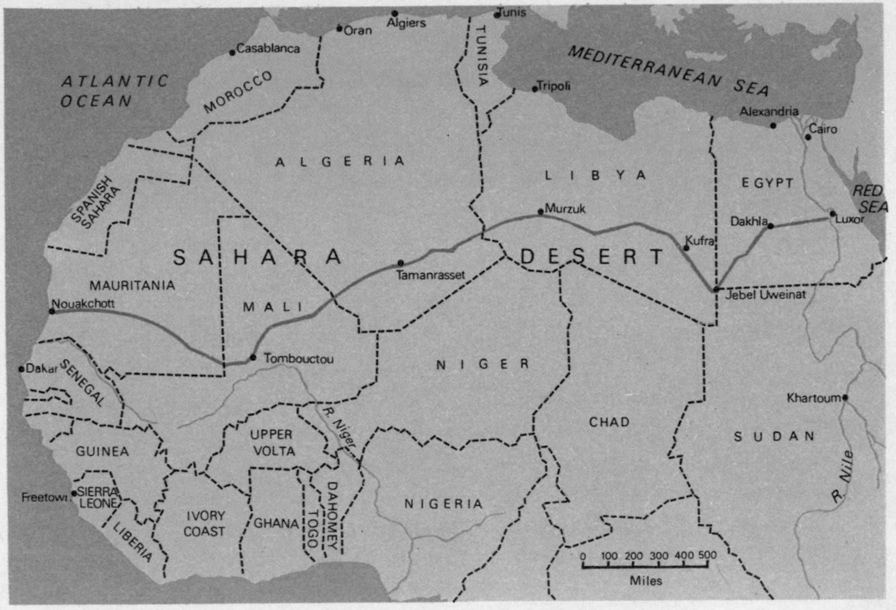

Author's intended 3,600-mile route across the Sahara Desert.

orientalist, linguist and also France's chief connoisseur of English doggerel verse. A formidable explorer, for nearly half a century he crossed and recrossed the Western Sahara by camel. Now seventy, he has the physique of forty-five, the mental attack and verve of thirty. He drives his battered Mercedes saloon with all the dash of a playboy. He has enthusiasm, and he shares it.

For two or three months we corresponded about my plans, Monod offering a variety of suggestions seeded with quotations from Edward Lear. In August, I went over to France, to the Monod country home near Sens. In his library, a converted barn which probably contains everything that has ever been printed about deserts, he was able to provide much practical guidance. You must never, he said, place a goatskin on the ground overnight or you may find that by morning most of the water inside it has disappeared into the sand, by the process of osmosis. You must always allow your beasts to browse wherever they can, however impatiently you may be delayed, for in the next few hundred miles there may be nothing at all for them to eat.

Even more important to me than such wisdom was Monod's

assumption that I was not on a fool's errand, and that my journey most certainly could be accomplished with reasonable luck, and competent guides, provided one set about it intelligently.

By the time I returned from France, there was little more than a month left before I must be away. I collected a variety of inoculations, put together a small kit of medicines, and listened to what the School of Tropical Medicine had to say about salt intakes and minimal water requirements. I assembled my pieces of equipment and stowed them in two kit-bags. Almost everything was severely practical, but if I was to spend a year or more in the Sahara I would need some books to prevent my mind from vegetating. In the end, I settled for Dawood's translation of the Koran, into which I had only dipped so far, Solzhenitsyn's *August 1914*, and Archibald Wavell's classic anthology of verse, *Other Men's Flowers*, an old stand-by. I also carried my Arabic dictionary.

On the brink of departure my vision had foreshortened sharply. At the start of my preparations I had seen the journey as a sweeping movement from Atlantic to Nile, but it slowly became impossible to contemplate the whole vast project. After all, my primary aim was not to establish a record, but to explore an extremity of human experience. The Nile was simply a physical object to be aimed for.

I had reached a point of tension where I could relax only when I was with my three children. Andrew and I walked across Dartmoor one weekend, ostensibly so that Dad could practise compass work on a Saharan Training Exercise and Andrew could feel he had a hand in all this, but really so that I could watch him grow for forty-eight hours and leave another small mark on him. Conceivably it might be the last one. I had no real sense of doom, but I recognized that at the bottom of all the fear lurked the real possibility of catastrophe. This brought much tenderness to the last weeks in England, and my wife J. and I discovered, in spite of our separation, that we could hug each other once again.

I left London early in October for Paris before flying on to Africa. I had to lobby the Mali Embassy there for permission merely to set foot in their country with a camel. After a prolonged negotiation, I was told that it would be necessary to visit Bamako, deep in the African bush, before I could set any kind of course across the Sahara for Tombouctou. If I failed on that mission—and I was given the impression that my chances of success were no more than even—then my expedition to the Nile might founder before it properly began. After leaving the Embassy with a letter of recommendation to the Director-General of the Security Services in Bamako, on a sudden whim I took a photocopy of it. This was an act of foresight I was to be very glad of.

I had one more appointment, and I kept it a few hours before catching the plane to Dakar. I went to the Russian Orthodox Church for the Sunday morning Mass, as I had got into the habit of doing whenever I could, over a number of years. Originally drawn there by the quality of its choir, I was more and more impelled by a presence in the place. I had long since rejected most of Christianity's codified faith, but here, in the spell cast by those rumbling basses and skirling Slav sopranos, by the drift of incense and by the operatic movements of the priests and acolytes, I had increasingly come to feel that I was close to some aspect of truth that had hitherto eluded me. I never left that place without feeling calmer and stronger, surer of goodness and rightness in mankind, than when I entered. Indeed, without awareness of God, without a sense of common relationship with God and with each other through God, we are quite lost; people spinning helplessly and hopelessly through a fearful void of the spirit . . . .

As I walked out along the Rue Daru, where the autumn leaves were starting to untidy the pavements, the fortifying influence of the Mass was with me. I would never be more prepared for a journey across the wilderness.

I STAYED IN DAKAR only long enough to be plundered by the most rapacious taxi-drivers in creation, and flew on to the southeast, over the arid bush of sub-Saharan Mali, to present myself and my letter of recommendation to the Director-General of the Security Services in Bamako. This M. Bagayoko, I had been told, was a man more powerful even than the President of the Republic himself. All the corridors of power radiated from his office, and no foreigner could remain in the country for more than seven days without personal supplication at his headquarters. As my passage across Mali by camel was liable to take anything up to a couple of months, it was imperative that I get this matter settled before I set off. I had no doubt that imprisonment in Mali might last a long time and be excessively unpleasant.

I never, in fact, set eyes on M. Bagayoko. For almost a week I marched and countermarched across the dusty little capital, bearing indecipherable pieces of paper from one office to another. I spent many hours in a dilapidated ante-room at security HQ, and many more hours in my room at the Grand Hotel, relic of French colonialism. In between, I began my programme of acclimatization, working my body hard, pouring in as much liquid as I could and proportionately increasing my intake of salt, as prescribed by the School of Tropical Medicine in London. At last, with only a few hours remaining before my seven-day visa expired, I emerged with a passport much stamped upon, which I hoped would be sufficient to convince any of the security forces in the Sahara that I had M. Bagayoko's approval.

A weekend in Dakar, and I took plane to Nouakchott. A dozen years before, there had been nothing at this point in the wilderness except a huddle of fishermen's huts a mile or two from the beach. But now there was an artificial capital, created when Mauritania gained her independence from the French; sprawling blocks of low concrete buildings, almost encircled by a wide perimeter of tents. It was unlike any town I had ever visited before. The shops were ranged in lines shaded by verandahs, but instead of pavements, one trod upon fraying linoleum tiles. There was a single main street laid with tarmac, ceremonially wide, with a strip bearing neon lights down the middle. The sand had drifted so thickly that even here vehicles moved with no more than soft crunching sounds, as they would in Europe just after a heavy fall of snow. Grey and fine was the sand, fine enough to trickle through an hour-glass, containing in each handful a million fragments of pulverized seashell.

It would have been a very drab place had it not been for the bright sky-blue of the Mauritanian national dress, the great billowing robe which they call the *boubou*. Practically every man wore it, unless he was in uniform, in superior government service, or in the employment of the Western oil companies. As I stood outside my hotel that night, disappointed that the stars seemed quite as obscure as they had been on Hampstead Heath, a couple came along the road, their feet skidding gently backwards in the yielding sand. The woman was singing in a high, childish voice the verses of some tantalizing Arab chant whose words I could not pick up. Between the verses, the man broke into a nasal snatch of chorus, a roundabout tune with only sound to it . . . *la-la li-larra-li-la*. . . . Until that moment I believed I had come to some bastard place, made mostly at the insistence of Europe. But on hearing that duet, I felt the old thrill of the strange and the faintly intimidating come creeping up my spine. I knew I was on the track of what I was after.

By extreme good luck, there was an Englishwoman highly placed in the government service here, who now introduced me to the head of her secretariat, Ahmed ould Die. He was a boyish, slim man with an engaging habit of laughter, and for all his youth, a very powerful man in Mauritania, hereditary chief of an upcountry tribe as well as head of the Republic's tiny tourist department. Within a day or two of my arrival, Ahmed had planned to obtain one of his tribesmen to accompany me on the first stage of my journey into the desert, but he warned me that almost certainly I would have to begin my journey elsewhere, for in Nouakchott there were very few camels to be had, and they of extremely poor quality. Mauritania was now entering its fourth year of drought, the desert was littered with carcasses, and beasts strong enough for a long passage into the interior were more likely to be found farther north, at Akjoujt, where there was still good grazing. Moreover, I should not expect to get away before the middle of November, for Islam had just entered the month-long fast of Ramadan, and Ahmed's tribesman would not wish to leave his encampment until it was over. In the meantime, it might be an advantage if I spent a few days out of town, in camp with some nomads, where I could learn how to ride camels and began to pick up a little Hassaniya, the local dialect, of which I so far knew nothing.

It was an excellent proposition and within a week I found myself moving south in a Land-Rover packed with provisions and great drums of water, which my host for the next few days was taking home to his camp. This Mafud was a trader, who divided his time between Nouakchott and the tent where his family now awaited him. It was one of a dozen or so spread out over a couple of square miles, some distance inland. The landscape here undulated in great rolling waves of sand, but there were many trees in it, some of them in leaf. There were clumps of grasses, all of them brown and dry, and almost all of them an absolute plague upon human beings. Most widespread was the cram-cram, which cast into the wind fluffy seedlings equipped with tiny sharp hooks that attached themselves to clothing and flesh alike, pricking intolerably. Another variety dropped hard spiky shells upon the ground and these, slipping easily between the soles of the sandal and the feet, would penetrate excruciatingly up to half an inch in depth. Even the trees were armed with long lancet thorns. Here in this wilderness these people would remain, until their small flocks had eaten what little edible vegetation there was. Then they would move on, in the endless, timeless, enervating rhythm of the nomad existence.

As we drove up to Mafud's tent, a gang of children came scampering out. A handful of men emerged more steadily, murmuring "*Marhaba;* welcome". Mafud's wife lingered dutifully behind, spreading cane mats and putting down cushions to ease the homecoming of her lord and the stranger he had brought with him. The men threw themselves down in a circle, full of gossip as they started the long conversational process of making tea. As I was to discover interminably over the next few months, this was paramount in the life of the desert, an operation that could easily be made to extend over an hour or more, with repeated infusions progressively sweetened in one small pot, poured deftly from some height into tiny glasses. "*Bismellahi!* In the Name of Allah!" the drinker would cry, as he tipped back his glass, just like a boozer shouting "Cheers!" Then the pot would be refilled with water, a larger chunk of sugar would be added, and the talk would continue for another space while the mixture bubbled quietly upon the glowing embers of charcoal.

I had already bought some clothes for the journey: a *boubou* and a *serwal*, which was a pair of baggy silk trousers reaching down to the calves, and a *howli*, which was simply four metres of black cloth to be wound round the head as protection from the sun. I had no great taste for fancy dress, but these things had been evolved out of the environment into which I was consigning myself, and it made sense to adapt as much as possible to local conditions. Apart from any other consideration, I had little wish to be conspicuous. Now Mafud urged me to change into these clothes, and this I did awkwardly, while the children shrieked with laughter, the men shouted encouragement, and even Mafud's wife grinned discreetly behind her hand. Having shown me how to wind the howli round my head into a compact turban, so that it would not disintegrate into swathes of cloth upon my shoulders, my host proceeded to conduct me on a small tour of the encampment. If I felt thirsty, I should draw water from the goatskin *guerba* hanging from the thorn tree over there. If I needed a torch in the night, I would find it in the corner of the tent, just there. Then he led me a little distance away, just over a rise in the ground, and proceeded to instruct me in the art of what he fastidiously called *le cabinet.* You dropped your serwal thus, under cover of the encircling boubou, you squatted thus and, having attended to your affairs, concealed all traces with sand.

An hour or two later, unable to delay the operation any longer, I stole out of the tent, torch in hand. As I rose from the ground I realized I had made a cardinal error by removing my serwal entirely. It was an enormously baggy garment, with very tiny holes for the legs, lost somewhere in the many folds of silk at the bottom. I shuffled to one side, to get onto clean sand, while I began to struggle to find the leg holes, totally enveloped in the tent-like structure of the boubou. For a moment or two I hopped round on one foot, desperately trying to find the second leg hole in my serwal, trying just as hard not to step on the hem of my boubou and bring myself crashing to the ground. Suddenly, I heard a rustling sound nearby. I froze, for might this not be a snake? Then I realized that the entire family had rushed up to behold the *Nasrani* (Westerner) dancing one-legged, in some eccentric ritual ablution of his own, upon their sand dune. There and then I decided that these were probably the most inconvenient clothes ever devised by man.

There was further merriment around the tent next morning at the prospect of my initiation as a camel-rider. An old man named Gul Mahomed arrived with a great grey bull already saddled for my use, but first there was tea-making and an hour of desultory talk before he indicated that he was ready to begin instruction. It would have been unthinkable otherwise. The beast was couched on the ground, a folded blanket was placed as a pad inside the saddle and I was motioned forward to mount. I managed to gain my seat to great applause.

With Gul Mahomed leading the beast by its head-rope, we lolloped off across the sandy scrub, in a rocking motion that could easily, I guessed, become soporific once your body became accustomed to the hard wooden edges of the saddle. I began to learn things. You carried a long riding stick, and with this you tapped the camel on the right side of his neck if you wanted to veer left. To make him trot you cut him smartly on the rump. To stop him, you hauled hard on the head-rope. To make him couch so that you could dismount, you tapped him on the back of the head and hissed at him until he went down on his knees. After a couple of hours, it seemed to me that the discomforts of camel-riding had been greatly exaggerated. True, it was tricky work rising from the ground, when you were flung heavily backwards, then forwards, then backwards again, as the animal came up onto its knees, then to the full extent of its hind legs and finally all-standing on its front feet too; and vice versa when coming to ground. Otherwise, it seemed largely a matter of allowing the body to sway back and forth with the beast's motion without straining to sit tight.

Thus I acquired my beginner's confidence, and a pattern of days developed, in which Gul Mahomed would take me riding for a couple of hours before mid-morning, when the sun began to grill the earth and sap the life out of a man. Then I could feel the sand burning through the soles of my sandals; my lips dry, the spittle become bitter on my tongue, thick and gummy at the corners of my mouth, and I could see how men might die in the heat of the desert. Away from the shelter of the tent, men would come and go only on the briefest of errands, refreshing themselves at great lengths with tea in between. The household's religious tutor would sit with the children and begin the day's instruction in the Koran. Large curved boards, beautifully smooth from generations of use, were brought out of the tin trunk which contained the most precious family possessions. On these *loakh* he would inscribe in black ink the texts which each child had to learn by heart. The children would sit in corners, peeping at the loakh and murmuring to themselves until they thought they had the verses memorized; then they would step forward to be tested. Meanwhile, for Mafud's wife and sister there seemed always to be grain or rice to be prepared, or tattered garments to be stitched.

On the days when Mafud's return to the tent was expected, his wife would spend hours daubing the palms of her hands and the soles of her feet with henna, staining them a deep arterial red. Then Mafud would arrive like a warrior prince, leap down from his Land-Rover with a rifle in his hand and stride to the back of his tent, where a mattress had been laid for him. There he would sit, bolt upright and cross-legged, with his newly-hennaed wife sitting at his right side, and the rifle placed carefully on the ground at his left. In front of him everyone else would sit in a half-circle, like a court exchanging obedient simplicities with its monarch. Not till Mafud had given a sign, would someone move out of place to start making the first ritual round of tea.

Awkwardly I had clothed myself before these people; awkwardly I fell as best I could into their ways, and I could see little to romanticize in their life. I discovered what it was to be pinched with cold night after night, then withered with heat day after day. The differences in temperature were astonishing. One morning at seven o'clock there was frost upon the windscreen of Mafud's Land-Rover. Yet a little after noon when I stuck the thermometer into the sand outside, the mercury climbed to 131°F. The food disgusted me, though I have never been a delicate eater. We ate mounds of boiled rice or *couscous*, totally without spices or seasoning, and extremely dull, while the meat arrived tepidly raw after the briefest contact with the camp fire. Most trying of all was the lack of privacy. Apart from the delicate matter of *le cabinet*, everything one did was with half a dozen onlookers sitting within a few feet, scrutinizing, commenting, implicitly participating. A new tension was thus added to the ones I had brought with me, and to release it I would walk off into the dunes, whenever I decently could, to be alone.

I returned to Nouakchott a few days before the end of Ramadan. I had learned as much as I was likely to about camels at the hands of Gul Mahomed. Although he seemed content to walk miles each day, with me riding near him, he refused to let me out of his sight. There was no arguing him out of his obstinacy. The bull was very strong, he said, and if I rode off alone it would gallop away with me: and his gestures towards the horizon suggested that I might well end up in Tombouctou far ahead of schedule.

In the town once more, I busied myself with the sextant each day, gradually refining my sighting errors until I was consistently getting latitude sights to within a mile. I walked to the Atlantic one afternoon, a four-mile hike across the municipal refuse ground and then into some high dunes which hid the ocean from the town. There were people on the beach, but I found an empty spot well away from them, and they left me alone to enjoy the green swell creaming in out of a smoky horizon. Next time I looked upon such waters, I thought, I'd be flying over them, on my way home.

The following night a *marabout*, a holy man, somewhere in the north of Mauritania, spotted the first trace of a new moon. Ramadan was over. In the morning I followed crowds to the mosque on the outskirts of the town. Thousands of people were drawn up in a huge circle around a dais where the Imam stood in front of three microphones. Closest to him was a multitude of men, all clad in robes which were new and stiff with starch, not just Mauritanian blue, but white and black and yellow as well. Outside this great circle stood a thin line of women, at a respectful distance from the rites. Slowly the Imam chanted and the multitude, with slippers off and prayer mats on the ground, knelt and bowed heads in unison, till each brow was smeared with dust. When it was over, they drifted back into town, full of gentle pleasure, with smiles at the prospect of the feast that marked this day. Up the road, in the courtyard of some tenements, a man was preparing the carcass of a sheep, studiously disembowelling it onto a sheet of linoleum laid upon the sand. At the gate of my hotel, there was a puddle of dried blood where another animal had been slaughtered in full view. These people concealed so little from each other. My people concealed so much.

My time on this fringe of civilization was running out. A few nights later I returned from star-gazing to find a message. Would I report to the Presidency in the morning to meet Mohamed? We could be away next day. I was suddenly panic-stricken. My hands began to tremble and I felt a little sick. Before, there had always been at least a theoretical chance to withdraw. Now I was completely committed. My head whirled with trembling thoughts. I hadn't managed to find in Nouakchott a drug I'd been advised to obtain as an extra precaution against malaria. One of my sandals was becoming unstitched. They said boil all water, but how could you insist on it when camping with nomads, how could you even slip a purifying tablet into a common drinking vessel? Please God help me . . . I sweated coldly in the night.

I heard the child scream in the next room to mine.

Chapter Two

By next morning, luckily, the nausea had left my stomach. I was tense, but the panic had died down. What was more, I liked the look of Mohamed ould Moctar ould Hmeida as soon as I saw him in Ahmed's office. He was a small wiry man from the Tagannt plateau, country through which we must pass in the next week or two. He was about my own age, an ex-soldier who had served with the French Camel Corps. He sat motionless while Ahmed recited the details of the agreement to be made between us. Mohamed would accompany me as far as Oualata, an oasis close to the border with Mali, possibly as far as Tombouctou itself, and he would discharge his duties at my convenience. For this I would pay him the equivalent of £2 a day, plus his food and equipment, and I would find the fare back to his encampment, by the swiftest means available.

As Ahmed ran through each item, Mohamed signified assent with a series of affirmative clicks: he scarcely uttered a word from start to finish. Most of the time he looked at the floor, not subserviently, but like a footballer being harangued by the referee. Just occasionally he lifted his eyes to take me in; and when he did, it was a very level look. The sergeant, I thought, weighing up the green new officer who doesn't know one end of a rifle from the other. At Mafud's camp I had met no one with whom I would have cared to commit myself to the desert; they had all become softened by their proximity to the capital. This man was different. He exuded toughness, and I was much comforted by his presence. We gathered our baggage and found a battered Peugeot station wagon that would take us to the camel market in Akjoujt.

Only a handful of beasts were hobbled there next morning, and not one of them looked as strong as the animal I had been riding the week before. I was not sorry when Mohamed suggested that we should move on to Atar. Akjoujt was a depressing place, built in the shadow of the great steelworks which produced almost the whole of Mauritania's national income. The town seemed to consist of nothing but dust—dust blowing, dust mixed with garbage, dust packed into blocks and constructed into habitations.

It was night again before we reached Atar and went stiffly in search of lodgings. We found them in the house of the local baker. Atar was a substantial town, celebrated throughout the land for the quality of its date groves, and Sidi Ahmed the baker was known throughout Atar for his generosity to strangers, whom he would lodge in his own bedroom rather than see turned away.

We lingered in Atar for two days. The camels here looked in much better shape than at Akjoujt. Mohamed, however, stressed that at Tidjikdja, the oasis nearest his encampment, the very strongest camels could be bought for £60. The prices in Atar were outrageously higher than that.

We bought no camels in Atar, but we assembled much equipment and food. We wandered in and out of tiny workshops, fingering saddlebags, testing the strength of ropes, rummaging among guerbas. We prodded dates sewn up into skins, carefully weighed great cones of solid sugar, sniffed suspiciously at boxes of green China tea. Buying these things was a cumbersome process, involving much idle conversation before a sale was arranged and some urchin was recruited to carry the goods to the increasing pile of our possessions heaped in Sidi Ahmed's courtyard. That good and open-handed man never once complained of imposition. Instead he busied himself on our behalf, finding a metal-worker who would make the complicated lock for the *tassoufra*, the great leather bag in which we would carry our foodstuffs behind the saddle.

Once more we moved on by vehicle. Our stores were pitched into a high-sided truck, our two saddles were lashed to the backboard, and we climbed up to join a score or so of people spread-eagled in confusion above an already heavy load of boxes, tin trunks, sacks and bedding rolls. With many a cry of "*Bismellahi!*" we lurched out of the market place and rumbled across the town. Then we stopped. A man with a rifle climbed up, hauling a wife and five children after him. Many household possessions followed. So did half a dozen sheep, bleating with anguish.

The mood of the passengers progressed from carnival gaiety, through subdued endurance, to silent exhaustion. By the time the truck drew up in moonlight at the oasis of Chinguetti, we had been buffeted together for nearly ten hours, though we had covered no more than eighty miles. Mohamed and I bedded down for the night in a corridor of the old French fort at the invitation of the man with the rifle, who had turned out to be the incoming commandant of the military outpost there.

Chinguetti was where Monod had started his long traverse of Mauritania forty years before, on the very edge of the Western Sahara. I was to do the same. It fulfilled exactly the conventional image of a desert oasis, as did no place that I had so far visited. Here, set amid date palms, was a village of mud houses and tents made of hide stretched domelike over latticeworks of palm branches. Facing the village across a great open space was the old fort. Once the French tricolour had fluttered above its low, crenellated walls. Now, however, under the green and gold flag of Mauritania, the fort had an unbusinesslike air. Its handful of troops seemed to spend most of their time lying in the sand by the front gate, playing interminable games with little balls of camel dung versus rows of tiny sticks. They were, as often as not, competing with their new garrison commander, a simple man who wondered whether England was to be found next door to Guinea.

For three days we camped in the fort, while Mohamed made desultory forays round the village to inquire about beasts. Uneasily, I began to wonder whether my first assessment of him had been premature. The farther we travelled from Ahmed ould Die's office in Nouakchott, the less helpful he became. It was now past the middle of November. I had impressed upon him the urgency of getting under way, but still he seemed to prefer idling his time in the company of distant relatives, to any great show of activity. Moreover, he insisted on my keeping pace with his own insatiable appetite for food, becoming truculent when neither my stomach nor my emotions could absorb another mouthful of half-cooked meat, or millet made sloppy and revolting with the addition of rancid fat. He would lecture me upon the necessity of following the customs of Mauritania, not of Europe: while his friends silently watched this small humiliation of a Nasrani by one of their own.

Now he announced that we must wait until we reached Tidjikdja before purchasing camels, but that a couple of beasts could be procured instantly for hire, to take us on the first stage of our journey. A young man would travel with us, in order to take the hired camels back to Chinguetti, but after that we would be on our own. This was not the beginning I had intended, but it was one I would have to accept, for I could not now afford to lose a day more than necessary of the relatively cool winter weather.

We set off early in the morning of November 23, with the shadows still long and wide on the sand. As we plodded up a long hill of sand out of Chinguetti I experienced, for the first time in weeks, the sheer contentment of fruitful physical exertion. At last my journey had begun. I moved buoyantly ahead of our tiny caravan, Mohamed and the lad walking together, leading the two camels by their head-ropes. I could hear them gossiping behind me and was glad that I did not have to take part in their conversation, for even after weeks of talking French and Arabic, communication still exhausted me and I was grateful for silence.

At the top of the hill I could appreciate as never before the awful proposition of crossing endless sand dunes, sculptured by the wind into overwhelming cliffs and sensuous crescent curves. At a distance, they had the beauty of abstract patterns. Close to, they had beauty of texture: there were edges to these dunes so clean and sharp that you wanted to run your finger along them, and the very finest sand was skimmed whitely off the edges like spindrift by the gentlest of winds. Yet all this beauty was deceptive. Each dune had a hard side, packed tight by ages of prevailing winds, and it was important to keep to this, where even a loaded camel would leave no more than a footprint. Move onto the soft side of a dune, and an unburdened man would sink through the surface sometimes up to his knees in the scalding surface sand.

All day we laboured up and down these dunes, eyes screwed up against the flaring white light. In the middle of the morning one of my sandals broke and I walked barefoot until we rested at noon and I could repair it. By then, I found that I had a large blister on the ball of my foot, containing a tight packing of sand. Also the

Saddling up: November 1972.

early exhilaration had already been replaced by tiredness and a thirst that made the throat sore and produced a number of recurring, liquid images. One was of Andrew and me at the end of our Dartmoor walk, stuffing ourselves with grapes and ice cream before catching a bus into Plymouth. Oddly, these images were a comfort and not a torment in this desperately arid place. But as I surveyed my blistered foot and poured a canteen full of water down my drying gullet, I wondered what shape I would be in after walking all the way to the oasis of Tidjikdja, well over a week away.

The rule of the road with camels was that you walked with them for the first hour or so of a day's journey, while it was still cool. You mounted and rode until noon. You rested through the worst heat of the day, then rode again until you made camp. Mohamed had invited me to mount after a couple of hours but I had refused. There were only two beasts for three men; as it was impossible for all of us to ride, then all of us must march. I was disinclined to accept special treatment because I was unaccustomed to desert travel and was also acutely aware that a battle for authority had developed between Mohamed and me. The more points I could score now, the better the relationship might be in the long run.

So we marched steadily all day. Once or twice we had to stop to adjust a load, when a beast began to roar with the discomfort of a rope or a cooking pot digging into its bones. This was a laborious business, for each time we had to unhitch kitbags and tassoufra, guerbas and oddments, then heave them all up into place again. I was very ready to call a halt when the evening's cool began to drift over the sand. Spotting a stunted tree at the foot of a huge dune, we agreed to rest there for the night. There was some dead wood for a fire and a scattering of grass for the animals.

As the coolness turned to cold, we squatted around our small fire to drink tea, to eat dates and stodgy uncooked pudding made of grubby flour mixed with water and rancid dripping. This diet would only be varied by plain rice, and by meat whenever we could obtain it. I didn't quite see how it was expected to hold body and soul together, but I approached it with an appetite, for the walk had made me hungry. The moment we had finished, we rolled into our blankets, behind a windbreak of saddles and baggage, for the cold was starting to bite into our limbs.

By seven in the morning we were on the march again, after shivering over tea and the remains of the pudding. By the middle of the day a different kind of desert stretched ahead, a plain of black dusty gravel with occasional heaps of sand, no more than the height of a house, and every few miles a thorn bush or two. The camels seemed to move with little effort here, their legs going down with metronomic regularity. But this firm ground was cruelly hard on our own feet. Mine were in a painful state by evening and those of the other two, although hardened by permanent exposure since birth, seemed to be in much the same condition. Both men were as eager as I to anoint their soles with a salve that I had brought.

Tidjikdja lay almost due south of Chinguetti, but scarcely ever were we to march on that line. We proceeded instead from one point of water to another, in a series of dog-legs. For the moment I was happy to leave direction-finding to my companions, who presumably knew this local landscape well enough not to lose their way. Later in my journey I would have to assume the whole responsibility for navigation.

We reached our first objective, the well of Chig, on the fourth day. For five hours we had slogged wearily up and down mounds of sand scattered thinly above a bedding of hard rock. A wind had arisen, blowing grit into our faces, to add to the misery. But then we topped a rise and beheld a sandy valley, studded with bushes, with a dark blur of many trees at the far end. I had become so accustomed to the loneliness of our march that I was startled to observe two familiar shapes in a patch of shade ahead. A camel was couched under a great thorn tree and, alongside him, another lay full length in the sand. "There must be somebody at the well already," I called to Mohamed.

"No," he replied, "there won't be anybody."

It was then I noticed that both these camels were motionless. We had drawn level with the sitting animal before he showed the slightest sign of life, and even then he barely turned his head in our direction. The other was dead. Its companion, said Mohamed, would soon be dead, too. He explained that they had become fatally exhausted, travelling too far on too little food, until their legs started to give way under them. In this condition, camels would fall down, once, twice, three times maybe, and each time their owners would manage to get them up and moving again, in the hope of reaching pasture before it was too late. But then they would go down once more, and this time nothing that a man could do would get them to their feet again. They would be left to die even when, as here, with the bitterest irony, their final collapse came as they reached the salvation they were seeking.

"*Inshallah,*" said Mohamed. "It is the will of God." What a very desolate phrase that could be.

The well was only a few hundred yards farther on, a hole in the sand, perhaps four feet wide and twenty deep. It seemed to me that if such a well were situated among sand dunes or even on an open plain, one might easily pass within half a mile and never see it, and that was not a comforting thought. The only clues here were a criss-cross of tracks and an area sprinkled with small dark balls of camel dung, which would be blown away by the next sandstorm. We sloshed water into the cooking pots for our beasts to drink from.

After sucking noisily at three or four gallons, the animals appeared to be satisfied, so we turned to filling our guerbas. We had left Chinguetti with four of these goatskins bulging with water and two of them were now more than half empty. I was drinking five or six pints a day, the others a little less, quite apart from the liquid we were taking with tea and cooking.

We pressed on into a series of days that became blurred by a thickening haze of weariness, consistently penetrated by the consciousness of pain in various parts of the anatomy. My lips had started to crack, and I had perversely started a heavy bronchial cold which made my chest jagged and tight inside. The most eagerly-awaited moments were those at midday and evening when we put back the first glass of syrupy tea, knowing that there were two more to come, each loaded with properties that would restore energy to our wilting bodies. I began to wonder if I could keep this march up as far as Tidjikdja, let alone journey on to Tombouctou; and the idea of reaching the Nile seemed a monstrous piece of fantasy.

Mohamed was at his best now. When our pace showed signs of slackening, he took the head-rope of the leading camel and all but hauled the beast along. When it was his turn to march at the back of our small column, he would clap his hands and make yipping noises to encourage both beasts to longer strides. When I lay feebly in a heap at a midday camp, he stoned my share of the dates and handed them to me one by one; then he fell back exhausted himself.

The days were punctuated by their small incidents. One day it had been necessary to set off at three in the morning in order to reach the well of Mrechet by the next evening. As we walked across a gravel plain which glowed like a snowfield in the moonlight, the young man started to sing. "He's asking Allah to keep the moon alight," Mohamed told me. And Allah did.

Once or twice, a day was to be remembered because I was able to take in some moment of natural beauty. Sometimes this would be early in the morning, when the earth glowed with a golden light and shadows lay long upon the ground. Or else the moment came during darkness, when everything was still and I was rested, and I could follow the slow movement of the stars. But between dawn and dusk the senses were too dulled to be aware of much more than discomfort. Thus we marched across vistas of shattered rock, with howling hot winds in our faces, across empty expanses of gravel upon which the sun hammered as upon an anvil.

The morning of my forty-first birthday, we had been marching for half an hour or so when the young man, immediately ahead of me, suddenly swivelled to his left, hauling the camels after him to get them away from a clump of dried grass, pointing with excitement as he did so. A horned viper was coiled there beautifully camouflaged, its skin matching exactly the colour of the sand and grass. I would never have noticed it. Mohamed came up and stoned it to bits with large rocks, in a savage reflex of elemental fear. He had already, a day or two before, killed a scorpion I had found between my sleeping bag and ground blanket, when I shook my things out one morning. It was a delicate shade of jade green, almost translucent. But as I bent down to look, its sting arched over with menace; and when I touched its back lightly with my stick, it struck wickedly at the wood.

We came down into the Wadi Rachid across great boiler plates of sun-blackened rock, leading the camels with care, for the surface of these huge boulders was treacherous, the crevices between them very deep. At the bottom of our descent was a new world of living vegetation, the greenest place I had so far seen in Mauritania, with grasses and trees growing thickly, and even a small cultivated patch. That afternoon we reached Mohamed's tent. It was pitched with two others on a small plateau above the wadi, a rather bleak place compared with what we had just seen. Nevertheless, efforts at cultivation had been made here, too, though the melons were pitifully small and the maize was dry and stunted. As we approached the tents the little man's walk became that of a commander swaggering back to base with booty after a successful skirmish. He did, indeed, bring some loot, for back in Atar I had given him an advance of money with which to buy things for his family. After reaching the Wadi Rachid, he had also hinted strongly that it was the custom in his country for a traveller to present a sheep to the family of his companions. I bought one from the first people we met. As soon as we had unloaded our gear and disposed ourselves round the tent, Mohamed slaughtered the animal, while women made up a fire and started preparations for cooking.

Mohamed's wife was a buck-toothed girl, perhaps five months

gone in pregnancy, already the mother of two small children. He was exceedingly brisk in his dealings with her, but he fondled his small son with great tenderness, gazing at him with the only expression of real softness I ever saw relaxing those hard features. I knew well by now his attitude to females, for he had spelt it out one night under the stars after he had been questioning me about England. Was it true, he asked, that my people were ruled by a queen? When I said that it *was* true, he snorted with contempt. "Me," he said, "I never take orders from a woman. Never. Never." Then he spat in the sand for emphasis.

The next few hours passed in almost continuous gorging. Mohamed seemed to contain a bottomless pit, though his belly was as neat and hard as ropework. He tore at the legs of lamb greedily, savagely, the fat trickling down his chin and into his beard. Then he smashed the bones and sucked at the marrow. It was a wild, animal performance. When I had first seen its like at Mafud's tent, I had been sickened by it. Now I could watch it with more equanimity. The surrender of myself to this environment had begun.

In the morning Mohamed completed a very elaborate toilet by dabbing scent upon his face. Then he announced breezily, "Well, we'll get moving again tonight." No we wouldn't, I said, we'd get moving straight away. It was a mean response, but I was anxious to be in Tidjikdja to equip us properly with our own camels, and I was, above all, paying him back for having chided me patronizingly a few nights before when I had confessed to missing my children. "Look at me," he had said. "When we pass my camp, I shall not linger with my family, though it will be weeks before I see them again. You must be the same kind of man." Now he muttered something crossly to himself; but within an hour he was ready for departure.

Next day, just before noon, ten days and two hundred miles from Chinguetti, we made camp on a hillside above a valley that was thick with palms. They streamed away towards the distant horizon in two files, and Tidjikdja was somewhere at the far end, hidden behind another hill. We rested in the shade of some thorn bushes till mid-afternoon, for Mohamed said one should never arrive at an oasis until darkness had fallen, otherwise the camels wouldn't settle down for the night. He slept most of his time away, while I wrote my notes. So by the time we reached Tidjikdja it was pitch black, but I was fully aware of a powerful sensation that had been creeping upon me ever since our first sight of the palm trees. I felt safe again.

ON THE RARE OCCASIONS when the wadi at Tidjikdja flowed with water there would be a river two hundred yards wide, dividing the humpbacked tents pitched among palm trees on the south bank from the rows of mud houses standing on the north bank. Even in the fourth year of the drought, the north bank, with its fringe of tiny shops on whose doorsteps men always lounged aimlessly, still felt much like a waterfront, but the steps now dropped deeply into sand and formed a kind of wharf running the length of a non-existent water's edge.

We lodged there in a room shared by five others. The room had once been whitewashed, but now its walls were filthy and flaked, its floor a rubble of dust and date stones. In Europe one would have described it as a cowshed, but here it was a welcome shelter from heat and cold alike. Droves of children came to peer through the doorway at the Nasrani.

We had been there for twenty-four hours when the camel boy rose to his feet, wrapped his howli round his head and announced "I'm off." We went to help him load the camels in the lane outside and then, with a handshake and a big grin, he set out on the lonely way back to Chinguetti – out into the wilderness as casually as though he were strolling down the Tottenham Court Road.

Mohamed showed no such anxiety to be on his way again, but the following day he said he'd found someone who would sell us two camels for £150. When I reminded him that in Atar he had vowed that the very finest beast could be obtained here for a maximum of £60, he said the majority of camels had left only the week before for sale in Atar. Next day he invited me to take a look at one of the bulls. What about the other one, I asked. Ah, that one, he said, was to be found back at the Wadi Rachid and he, Mohamed, would ride this one there to collect it. Why the hell, I demanded, had he not taken steps to buy the beast three days before, when we had passed Rachid on the way to his own tent? Ah, he didn't know then that the camel would be there. For a man on whose doorstep all these animals were variously deployed, this seemed to me a very thin story indeed and I told him so, suspecting that he was now paying me back for my failure to allow him a day longer with his family. Hurt by my bluntness, he accused me of not trusting him. We parted coolly, he taking the remainder of the £150 to complete the transaction.

The next few days were a miserable trial of waiting for him to return. One morning I heard an aircraft descending, and watched a small monoplane land on the oasis airstrip half a mile away. Instantly I longed to take flight on it back to Nouakchott, back to Europe, back home. I wanted to be away from the appalling filth of these surroundings, from the awfulness of this food, from the loneliness of spirit and the increasing alienation I felt. I wanted to fly from children who shouted "Nasrani!" mockingly at every corner, from adults who slithered deviously from one fiction to another as it suited their purpose.

I lurked around the village until the plane took off again for the West, then I strolled up to the airstrip and sat upon a boulder. A half gale was beginning to drum up out of the desert and plumes of dust were streaming down the gravel of the runway. The first week of December was over and in London the Christmas shopping crowds would have started to plunder the length of Oxford Street. At my present rate of progress it would be nearly the end of January before I reached Tombouctou, when I had assumed I would complete my first stage soon after New Year's Day.

After almost a week in Tidjikdja I was pacing down the airstrip at sunset when I saw a rider leading a second camel at the trot round the edge of the oasis. Mohamed had returned, and so great was my relief at the prospect of moving on again that I told him to keep the change from the camel-buying. Swollen thus with 6,000 francs and the memory, I assumed, of two nights in his tent, he promised we would leave next afternoon, after he had attended to one or two small matters of his own. However, at last I had my own beasts, and it was with a mixture of excitement and nervousness that next day I led my two camels up the lane and into open scrub, while Mohamed exchanged farewells with three women who had appeared as we were about to depart. However, we had been walking for little more than an hour when Mohamed indicated

The author—a picture taken by his guide

Mohamed ould Moctar ould Hmeida

some succulent trees about a mile off our course and said that we must stop there for the night, because the camels needed feeding. It was only four o'clock, but I remembered Monod's advice about grazing and did not demur.

As the sun began to dip over the horizon, I noticed a couple of men walking in our direction, though on a course that would not run through our camp. One of them carried a very ancient-looking rifle, but otherwise there was nothing unusual about them. The men, deep in conversation and taking not the slightest notice of us, were never within three hundred yards of us before they disappeared into the dune behind. Mohamed, however, suddenly became very excited. There was, he said, something odd about the men. We must get back to Tidjikdja at once. They were going to encircle us behind the dunes and would surely attack us the moment darkness fell. This seemed to me patent nonsense. No one intending attack, I said, would have allowed us to see him. The men were plainly going to some encampment. Not so, said Mohamed; no encampment lay in that direction. "You are a Nasrani," Mohamed said contemptuously. "I am a Moslem. You do not understand these people as I do. We must go, quickly, I am not afraid for myself, but I cannot have your blood on my hands."

I had to concede my ignorance and he knew it. Hastily he started to pick up a few possessions. We must leave everything else, including the camels, which had wandered off in the gathering gloom, hobbled to browse out of sight. This was a man who appeared to be very badly shaken by fear while I, stumbling irritably in his wake, felt oddly detached about the whole affair. It was too much like a caricature for me to take it seriously.

Mohamed had recovered his composure by the time we returned to our cowshed. In the morning, he told me, we must go to the *préfet* and inform him of what had happened; the matter would then be his responsibility. Meanwhile, he, Mohamed, would now go out and watch carefully who entered and left the oasis during the next few hours.

Mohamed did not return until we were making the first round of tea in the morning, his face still stupid with sleep. Where had he been all night, I asked. There was no reply. I repeated my question sharply. Thickly, he murmured something about spending the night with a cousin. What cousin? The one who had seen us off the previous afternoon, the woman with her two friends. "Right," I said. "We're going to the préfet now." I was vicious with resentment, for it had been dawning on me slowly that I had been the victim of a confidence trick, the whole object of which had been to let him bed a woman he fancied.

The préfet told me he couldn't believe that there had been any danger, but he'd get a couple of trackers from the barracks and go out to look at the ground.

We drove out to our abortive camp by Land-Rover. Not a thing had been touched in our absence. The préfet and his trackers scrutinized the ground for only a few moments before the official drew me apart from the others. "It's a nonsense," he said. "Everybody passes this way from the village to the encampment. The men were simply returning home last night."

My anger was now stoked heavily with a variety of grudges against Mohamed. I even thought I had the reason why we had not bought camels in either Akjoujt, Atar or Chinguetti: it was because he had arranged before he left for Nouakchott to deal with kinsmen in Tidjikdja and Rachid, presumably on the understanding that he would get a cut. I was also quite certain he had unloaded much of our foodstuffs at his camp: what we had bought in Atar had been supposed to last us a month and we had been obliged to replace it in Tidjikdja within a fortnight.

Although the best solution by far would be to dispense with his services forthwith, he had wheedled advances out of me and now owed me something like forty days of work. I really couldn't afford to let him go. But what were the chances, I asked the préfet, of getting a good man to accompany us to the next oasis, starting without delay? It was easy, the préfet replied; he knew just the man.

Chapter Three

The activity of the next hour was little short of the miraculous. We drove back into Tidjikdja, stopped there by a tent and hailed a lanky, aquiline fellow who sat on a blanket, surrounded by women and children. The préfet explained my needs to him and the money

I was offering. At once the man nodded and, without pausing to do more than fill a tassoufra with some things and pick up a saddle, joined us in the vehicle. By eleven o'clock I was on the march again, striding ahead with the camels while Sidi Mahmoud ould Sheddadi loped beside me on long, spindly legs. Mohamed had to bustle like a spaniel in order to keep up the pace. The following day we would reach the camp where Sidi Mahmoud's camel was grazing, and he could ride from there.

It was clear that I would have to use all the tact I could muster in my dealings with Mohamed over the next few days. He had much to resent; above all, his exposure as a coward in front of the préfet. I must jolly him out of this as gently as possible, while making it plain that I was no longer the gullible novice he had picked up in Nouakchott.

By evening we were talking to each other again, and it was not worry about our relationship that gave me a disturbed sleep that night. The room in Tidjikdja, I now discovered, had been filthier than I supposed. I was crawling with lice.

Next day started badly with a freezing wind, and I was forging ahead of the other two in an effort to warm myself up when I heard a commotion behind me. Turning, I saw the younger of the two bulls bucking, its baggage falling off around it onto stony ground. Mohamed and Sidi Mahmoud quietened the beast down. I started to collect the things that had been pitched off . . . then stopped and swore violently. There, lying against a rock, was the sextant. A few feet away was its case, the fastenings burst open, one of the wooden sides partially stove in. The instrument itself appeared to be undamaged, but heaven knew what delicate balance of the interior mechanism had been upset by the violence of such a fall. I felt a little sick at the implications. Sidi Mahmoud was familiar with the route to the next oasis of Tichit, but I did not care to dwell on the navigational problems that might lie beyond. Grimly I banged the box back into shape and repacked the sextant before we continued. There was little point in trying to check its accuracy here, with only an approximate position to go by; that must wait till Tichit.

I was explaining my fears about the sextant when Mohamed showed open hostility for the first time. It was of no importance if the sextant were broken, he told me, as it was a useless toy anyway.

Maps, too, were rubbish, constructed by Europeans who knew nothing at all about the region. I held tightly on to my patience and questioned him in detail, as I had not done before, about his knowledge of the country that lay between us and Tombouctou. I discovered now that he had never been outside Mauritania, as I had been led to understand. Then he dropped his bombshell: he didn't have an identity card, anyway. I knew this meant that he would be unable to travel out of Mauritania to Tombouctou, that he had quite deliberately deceived me in Nouakchott.

There was nothing to be done about it, and I was not at all downcast at the prospect of losing Mohamed earlier than I had first anticipated. But I felt badly cheated. From now on, I resolved, everyone in this blasted country would have to demonstrate his honesty before I treated him as anything but a rogue. And from now on, the pace and the manner of this journey would be regulated by my wishes, and not by any sauntering indolence of my companions.

After spending the night at Sidi Mahmoud's camp, we rode steadily, though I scarcely fitted the commanding role that my resolution decreed, as I had trouble keeping my mount at the trot and trailed badly behind the other two. From time to time they glanced back at me, then turned away, grinning to each other. They were, I noticed, with little relish, becoming very matey indeed. Then I discovered that if I gave my bull a great belt with the riding stick he would, after a protesting snarl, actually start to gallop and recover the lost ground. What was more, I found that by crossing my feet over his neck, gripping the pommel of the saddle between my thighs, and raising my arms in a balancing movement, I could ride at the gallop without feeling that I was about to fall overboard. The result was that we made exhilarating progress till five o'clock, when we spotted a tent about a mile away to our right. Sidi Mahmoud turned to me. "Camp?" he asked. Mohamed said nothing, but watched me carefully. "No," I replied firmly, "we go on for another hour." They both looked exceedingly put out, but I was much concerned to impose my own will upon the party this night, and we trotted on.

There were many nomads in the desert between Tidjikdja and Tichit, and we spent almost as many nights in the company of others as we did in solitude. The undulating sands which we crossed were desolate though broken by occasional trees and clumps of withered grass and it was not until much later in my travels that I realized how comparatively rich this area was in pasture for animals. Here there was at least some substance on which they could feed; elsewhere there would be none at all.

Everything in these nomadic lives was bent towards a preoccupation with food. There is a word, *ghudda*, which is an omnibus expression for food of any kind. Whenever men talked together in this undernourished land, you could be sure that the word "ghudda" would be uttered by one person or another every few sentences. If they were not arguing about the absence of "ghudda" for their animals they were deploring the high cost of "ghudda" for human beings. Food of every kind was their obsession, in a way that no Westerner had known it for a long time.

For myself, I was happiest when we spent our nights alone, for my nerves became frayed by the uncongenial atmosphere of the camps. The perpetual cadging wore me down, not so much because it was a constant drain upon our provisions, as by the manner in which it was conducted. People rarely asked me for something directly and simply: almost always a request was served with a hint of collusion by my two companions, or with some devious moral pressure. One night we stayed with an engaging fellow who spoke Arabic as I had learned it and with whom I could talk more easily than ever I managed to in Hassaniya. We got on well together and, when he asked me for a tin of coffee I was pleased to give it to him in gratitude for his friendship. Next morning I heard him whispering in the ear of Mohamed, who then turned to me with the following advice. "This man is a great chief. All the Nasrani who meet him give him something. He wishes you to give him tea and sugar." And I did; but this time it was not such a willing gift.

I was, of course, succumbing to the persecution complex that has visited every lone traveller who finds himself in a totally alien environment. I was still in the grip of my chest-racking cold and the lice were tormenting me abominably. Also the riding was beginning to produce a crop of sores to compensate for the loss of those that were easing from my feet. In the company of Mohamed and Sidi Mahmoud, self-pity was augmented by the suspicion that they were ganging up against me. They had also developed a nasty habit of ridiculing me in front of other people.

On our ninth evening since leaving Tidjikdja, we came to the oasis of Tichit. All afternoon we had ridden across glaring sand beside an escarpment, then over a range of steep dunes which the wind had carved into fantastic shapes I associated with alpine snowfields, full of enormous overhangs. The beasts grunted with the effort of uphill struggle, which they made in jerky bursts, each rider leaning as far forward as possible to put his weight over the camel's shoulders. Riding downhill was even harder, for the camels, moaning now, ran stiffly in long strides to avoid losing control while we, leaning backwards, our arms braced against the sides of the saddles, had our spines and shoulders jolted heavily.

Tichit is a very ancient village, founded in the eighth century, celebrated for its buildings, which were constructed of uncemented stone. But centuries of warfare and neglect have transformed the oasis into a ruin, with dilapidated walls which look as though they have undergone systematic bombing. The most substantial dwelling by far, apart from the house occupied by the préfet, was that of the village headman, Sharif Ahmedu, to which we made our way at once. People in Nouakchott had assured me that he would be very glad to offer me shelter. In this, they were a little misleading. The Sharif did indeed allow us to sleep and feed in the corridor of his courtyard, and I would wake in the mornings to find him, a picturesque figure clad in a gorgeous russet cloak and hood, regarding us enigmatically from behind a pillar. But when I came to pay him for our lodgings, offering him 5,000 francs (£10) for the two nights of our stay, which was somewhat more than I had paid before, he refused to accept my money. The price, he said, was 9,000 francs. Even Mohamed and Sidi Mahmoud sucked their teeth with disapproval when I told them how much I had been obliged to pay. Yet within half an hour, the Sharif had sidled up to Mohamed and bade him ask me for some medicine to cure a pain in his head. I decided the old ruffian should be served in kind. Handing him a couple of codeine tablets, I announced that they would cost him 200 francs apiece.

The avarice of Sharif Ahmedu, however, was the least of my worries in Tichit. The first morning I climbed onto the roof of his house and tested the sextant. The result was hopelessly inaccurate. Possibly the alignment of the sextant's mirror had been crucially shifted by the fall from the camel's back. I wasn't at all sure what the long-term implications of this blow to my navigation might be, but I had already made up my mind to go on from Tichit towards Tombouctou, even if the sextant should prove to be finished. Since reaching the escarpment I was confident that, if the worse came to the worst, I could myself lead the way to the border oasis of Oualata at least, for the map showed that these rocks now continued distinctly in a curve across the desert, Oualata itself being perched on top of them. As for finding wells, I could probably fix my positions by compass. Such considerations apart, my pride would not allow me to quit at this stage. I was set upon a journey 3,600 miles long and I had not yet travelled 500 of them. Although at Tichit, more than ever before, I yearned to go home, failure at this point would have been abject.

I made an effort to shed Sidi Mahmoud in Tichit, but I was now virtually without money, in no position to hire anybody else. I had reached Tichit with a note that should have enabled me to recover cash from the post office there, but the postal chief had been flown to hospital and, without his authority, the postal note was uncashable. Once more a Mauritanian préfet came to my aid. If I cared to address some travellers' cheques to Ahmed ould Die in Nouakchott, he would see that they went by the next week's plane. Ahmed could then arrange to have cash waiting for me before I reached the Mali border. But it would be necessary for me to travel not to Oualata but to Nema, where there was an airstrip. This would put maybe a hundred miles on my journey, but now I had no choice.

WE WERE MARCHING our beasts out of the village, when Mohamed asked me to carry on for a little while alone: he and Sidi Mahmoud had some business in one of the houses, they would catch me up soon. I walked on placidly, enjoying the solitude of the moment. I would give much, I thought, to be able to go on like this. But I wondered whether I would have the courage to do so. This was something quite apart from the practical considerations of travelling alone, the length of time it took, for instance, even with two men, to find the camels each morning. Though their forelegs were always tightly hobbled together, they could move extraordinary distances in their search for food, proceeding with a determined shuffle or in a series of comical bunny hops. A solitary rider's energy could be dangerously dissipated by bringing them in, just as it would be heavily taxed by the need to load or unload the baggage four times each day. But even if I could find the energy for these tasks over a matter of weeks and months, could I also muster the plain gut courage to go on alone in the desert? I had begun to doubt it. I could see very well what people meant when they had told me that I would most certainly be crushed by the immensity of the desert if I found myself in it alone. As I walked between the hard outline of the escarpment and the blank anonymity of the endless dunes, I was a caterpillar wriggling across an apparently eternal nothingness.

Sidi Mahmoud ould Sheddadi.

I turned to see my companions about half a mile behind, a third figure with them. I slackened my pace and they joined me. The newcomer was a gap-toothed young man who paid no attention to me at all.

"Where's the boy going?" I asked.

"Just down there," said Mohamed, nodding straight ahead. "He's joining some friends in an encampment."

It wasn't until three days later, in the middle of nowhere, that I decided this encampment was a long time in appearing, and broached the subject again. Calmly, Mohamed announced that the lad's destination was near the oasis of Nema. A week before, I would have blown up in his face. As it was, I simply turned away wearily. I couldn't abandon the youth where we were. At the same time, I seriously wondered whether our supplies would see four of us through the next ten days or so. The only solution was to push on as hard as possible and get this nightmare of a passage over.

We plodded on through bitterly cold mornings and the scorching torrents of noontide winds that flushed the bare skin even where it had tanned deeply after weeks of exposure. We came to the well of Touijinit, and paused to water our camels.

A mob of perhaps twenty beasts was there before us, brought down from the pastures above the escarpment by two herdsmen, and we exchanged news with them. There was, they said, a little ghudda for beasts up there. But down here there was nothing, nothing at all, for as far as a man might ride strongly in a week. A few yards from the well lay the withered carcass of a camel, bearing witness to the desperate aridity of this area,

We climbed the escarpment so that our camels might find their precious ghudda. Between the sands and the rocks, a narrow strip of ground bore a scattering of yellowed grasses and even, from time to time, a tree on which the animals could browse. This was the setting for my Christmas. By the half-light of dawn I attempted to de-louse my garments: lice were secreted within the gathering at the waist of my serwal and they infested the sweater which I had started to pull on at night and during the early cold of the day. The string vest which I habitually wore provided an excellent refuge for them in its many joints. It was so cold, this morning, that I had difficulty in getting the others on the move before 9.30. They seemed to be even wearier than I was, inquiring more than once during the morning whether we might not ride now. There was no question of doing so, for we were in dunes again, all of them steep and soft enough to have the camels in trouble without the added burden of riders.

Periodically during the day, I took flight to J. and the children. In spite of my resolve to banish all thoughts of home, I had for days past followed the rising Christmas tide of tree decorating, cooking and hubbub. It was strangely a comfort rather than a sadness: some presents I had left behind me. I wondered whether it had been wise or upsetting to leave for the family my tape-recorded reading of "A Child's Christmas in Wales"; for my elder daughter, Jane, I knew, had gone through spasms of worrying whether I would safely return. But I had wanted to share their Christmas and it had seemed gentlest to do it by way of Dylan Thomas.

At sunset I managed to heat on our evening fire the small Christmas pudding I had brought from England. The four of us enjoyed a mouthful apiece, the other three expressing great satisfaction after their initial suspicions were allayed.

As we worked our way slowly towards the eastern limit of the escarpment, before turning south, I came to realize why Erbah, the young man, had become attached to my party. He had been recruited by the other two simply to take much of the drudgery off their hands, in exchange for our food and company. Whenever we camped it was Erbah who was told off by Mohamed to start looking for wood and camel dung for the evening fire; in the mornings it was he who went searching for the camels.

I found it curious that Mohamed and Sidi Mahmoud seemed to be tiring much more than I was. Mentally I often felt played out, but my body seemed now to have taken a second wind, so that for the first two hours of our daily march I would stride on ahead while they trailed behind. It occurred to me that I had much greater reserves of energy than they, doubtless the result of forty years' consistently high nourishment. And they felt the cold cruelly, wrapping their headcloths tightly around their faces, so that only their eyes were visible between the swathes. One night I awoke to see Mohamed stoking up the embers of our fire, then scraping the warm sand under his blanket before lying down again. Even in a sleeping bag, the cold continually wakened me at night. If it were not the cold it would be the lice, or the moon shining into my face. I doubt whether I had enjoyed more than two hours' unbroken repose since Tidjikdja.

We came out of the dunes and started to move across a flat pancake of gravel, maybe a mile and a half in diameter, encircled by sandy scrub. In the middle of it was a circle of stones and in the centre of the circle, again made with stones, the words "Bou Zib". It was an old French airfield, abandoned for some twenty years, with not the slightest trace left of any buildings. As we tramped across its surface, I wondered what colonial strategy had been responsible for its appearance; and whether, in due course, another might find some use for it. And this was, for a moment, the justi-

"There was nothing . . . as far as a man might ride strongly in a week."

fication of Bou Zib's existence: to provide me with a tiny mental exercise in the tedium of my journey; that and a navigational beacon from which I might plot my further course.

I went back to take my turn on the camel ropes. As Mohamed handed them over, he announced that in two days we should pass the end of the wadi which eventually led to Oualata. What were we going to do about Sidi Mahmoud? He, I said, should return home as planned. As for Mohamed himself, when we reached Nema I would give him some travellers' cheques, along with a plane ticket to Tidjikdja via Nouakchott.

When I told him my decision, he broke into an aggrieved bickering. I should give him a camel instead of buying him a plane ticket. It would take him a long time to get home by flying this roundabout way, he shouted, and his wife was pregnant. I don't think I managed to avoid a grin when I pointed out that it would take a lot longer to ride home by camel. Then something in his tone—"You have decided, then?"—wiped the grin from my face.

We started riding a little later and Mohamed began officiously to correct my mannerisms. I should place my foot thus, when mounting, and hold the head-rope so when in the saddle. I was in no mood for his patronage now, and irritably waved him away. We jogged on slowly, with a great space between us. Then he drifted over to me, one arm arrogantly resting on his hip. He looked up at me, with a wicked half-grin on his face. "Why won't you buy me a camel, then?" he demanded and there was no mistaking the truculence of his manner. It was a challenge, and in a fury I rose to it. My riding stick came up and I levelled it at his head menacingly: had he been a foot or so nearer, I believe I might have slugged him with it on the spot. "Listen", I shouted, "and listen well, little corporal. The subject is closed. Do you understand? It's finished!" And I brought the stick down with a thump on his saddle. I was shaking with rage. He glared at me for an instant, open-mouthed with shock. Then he uttered something between a grunt and a sneer, and dragged his camel away from mine, to resume his moody passage across the sands. He did not mention the subject again.

Our food situation was, as I had expected, becoming poor, and by December 30 it was serious. Our flour had been finished three or four days ago and there was little left of either dates, rice or meat. The entrance of the wadi leading to Oualata now stretched wide open to the east of us, and Sidi Mahmoud announced that he was going home. I handed him 1,000 francs to buy food in Oualata and wished him well. Then Mohamed turned to the tassoufra and began to divide the contents. It appeared that Sidi Mahmoud had decided to return home direct, instead of making a detour to the oasis. I was beyond arguing about the small deception which had winkled more money out of me; I was too content to be rid of Sidi Mahmoud. After the first few days, he had been essentially a weak yes-man to Mohamed's various ploys, and thus some threat to my security. But as he turned away and mounted his camel without a word to any of us, without a backward glance, I could not help being moved by the bravery of his going back alone. It would be three weeks before he regained his own tent across some of the most awful travelling country in the world. I recognized that I could not have done what he was undertaking.

His departure left us with little to eat before Nema, which was still three days away. We had enough rice for two meals, and thirty three dates—all of them withered, some of them so dessicated as to be virtually inedible. Had one felt fit and well, the landscape would have been exciting here, for the plain now and then erupted into huge rocky hills, gaunt and stratified and lonely, with half a day's journey in between each. I took scant notice of such things, however, for hunger was beginning to deaden all the senses. I had long since become accustomed to its daily advance, to those tentacles of discomfort that slowly crawled up the belly and into the mind. But now I noted less the perpetually bitter taste in the mouth, than the increasing stupor of giddiness. I began to weave uncertainly when I was walking; and riding I rolled around the saddle as inertly as a sack of potatoes.

At noon on New Year's Day 1973, we drank water, ate nothing, and collapsed into sleep. I was astonished that such a transformation had overtaken me in such a short time; only a few days before, I had been surging ahead of my party on the march. Now a curious detachment had set in. Lying there on the ground, I wanted nothing but the peace that would let me sink into sleep and forget.

We dragged ourselves on, taking turns to share the two camels. Though we exchanged no words on the subject, it was implicit in our situation when dusk came that we would not stop to make camp, but would continue our sluggish movement through the darkness. Nema was not too far off now, and there were always nomads camped in country immediately around an oasis.

It was young Erbah who spotted the faint flicker of a camp fire burning in the distance. It took us half an hour to draw close enough to see that here were the mud walls of houses. We got down drunkenly beside the nearest dwelling and began to unhitch our gear. Faces appeared, but no one helped us until Mohamed burst out angrily at them. Grudgingly they moved to our assistance, grudgingly they put down mats in the lee of a wall. "*Ma marhaba;*

not welcome," I said to Mohamed wearily. He did not reply, and for once I warmed to the man. He was, I realized, ashamed of these people. For an hour we lay slumped upon the mats, before a woman brought a bowl of milk, which we sucked noisily in turn. That was all we received from this settlement.

Little though it was, the bowl of milk kept us going through a hot and windless morning, until we came to a small encampment of tents among trees. There, with the last few coins in my possession, we bought sugar and some tea, the leaves being carefully measured out and handed over in a small drinking glass. This blessed infusion revived us enough to face the last few miles to Nema in good heart.

We overtook a small family, a man, his wife and their son, and they were the most attractive nomads I had seen. The parents laughed together, amiably and affectionately, and looked as if they cared to be in each other's company. There was not a hint of dominance in him, or of subservience in her. I had not before seen a nomad man and woman who appeared to be living together on the basis of what I could recognize as friendship and equality. They shared some food with us and we pottered on comfortably together towards the oasis, across a plain now fertile with maize.

It was long after nightfall when we came to Nema and found lodgings with some kinsmen of young Erbah. Next morning, disconsolately, I discovered at the post office that there had been no word from Nouakchott. Once more I turned to the official residence for help, and I secured an interview with a formidable-looking man whose headcloth concealed much of his face. He questioned me sharply about the purpose of my arrival in Nema, and about my journey as a whole, all the time doodling on a pad in front of him. Then, without looking up, he uttered a sigh and said in impeccable English, "Well, you've a long way still to go, haven't you?"

I gaped with amazement, for they were the first words I had heard in my own language for the best part of two months. He put his head back, and laughed marvellously at my surprise. We swung our hands into a delighted clasp of greeting.

This man, Abdellahi ould Erebih, was to offer me much comfort as well as kindness over the next few days. He had been his country's ambassador in Cairo and Bonn, and I found it very odd indeed that someone of his intelligence should now be dumped in an insignificant township on the edge of the Sahara desert. Yet I did not once detect in him a trace of bitterness at this apparent waste of his considerable talents. He had much natural dignity, a piety that he wore very lightly, and he seemed totally at peace with himself in this environment.

Abdellahi did three things at once to raise my spirits. He promised to telegraph Nouakchott about my money, he asked an assistant to find someone to travel to Tombouctou with me, and he suggested that I move into what was euphemistically called the Government rest house. It was rather ramshackle and grubby, he said, but at least it would give me peace and quiet. After a rusty water tank had been laboriously filled from the well outside, it enabled me to wash for the first time since Nouakchott. I found a mirror and was dismayed at my appearance. My face was scorched and windblasted, the nose cracked open along the bone, the lips badly swollen and blistered. The bloodshot eyes were staring, strained, the eyes of someone on the run.

Next day I returned from some errand to find Mohamed sharing tea on the floor of our room with a newcomer. He was introduced as Sid' Ahmed ould Eli ould Simmad, and the man who would travel with me beyond Nema. He was of much the same build as Mohamed, and he tipped his head on one side when requesting something, rather like a cocker spaniel attending to master's whistle. I was not at all pleased that the two had struck up an acquaintance, for I could imagine that Mohamed would conceive it as at least a tribal loyalty to inform his successor of every weakness in the Nasrani. I was very sharp with both, in my attempt to convey the message that the easy meat Mohamed had discovered in Nouakchott was no longer being served up on a platter in Nema.

Meanwhile, Abdellahi, impatient for a reply from Nouakchott, had privately arranged for a wealthy trader to give me cash in exchange for some travellers' cheques. No sooner had this transaction been completed than a man came running from the post office to announce that Ahmed's money also had arrived. In this glow of affluence I explained to Mohamed that I was now in a position to hand him, in addition to his outstanding wages, 20,000 francs in cash, and he could either buy himself an air ticket or a place in a truck that would go down the dirt road linking Mauritania's villages below the desert. I had no doubt at all which course he would fancy most.

That night I awoke to see him doing something secretively by the shaded light of a torch. He had his back turned to both Erbah and me and he was murmuring quietly to himself, over and over again, "*Ilhamdu Lillah;* in the name of God." He was counting out the 56,000 francs I had given him. He could never have handled so much money in his life before. If he was careful, he might just be able to buy two camels with it. Even though I disliked the man intensely by now, I could not begrudge him this fortune. He was, after all, very poor and I was very rich.

Next morning we parted, and it was a shame that two men who had travelled so far together did so with so much relief. "Well," I said, "buy a good camel, Mohamed." He barely touched my outstretched hand, muttered a tight-lipped "good luck," and turned quickly away, scurrying down the street with Erbah like a small boy excitedly heading for the sweet shop with his new spending money.

Chapter Four

In better spirits than I could remember for a long time, I led the way up the steep hill behind Nema. In this dusty little town lying doped with heat between the throbbing gravel plain to the north and the parched scrublands to the south, I had been conscious of more concerted warmth flowing towards me than ever before in Africa. A youth in the shop where I re-provisioned, informed me cheerfully that he had heard about my coming on the radio. Men in the streets wished me good luck and safe journey. All this, and solvency again, set me on the stage to Tombouctou eagerly and in good heart. The one setback I had received in Nema was that for the first time I was in the throes of chronic diarrhoea and acute stomach cramps whenever I took food. However, I was, if anything, merely astonished that I had not been attacked by such a tummy bug much earlier.

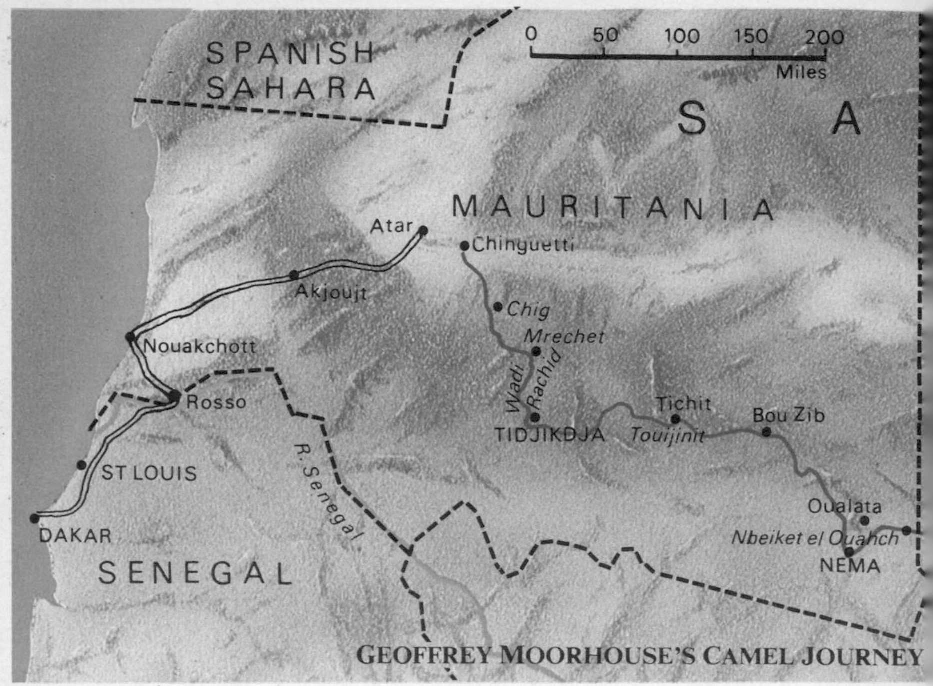

GEOFFREY MOORHOUSE'S CAMEL JOURNEY

I was also coming to the conclusion that in Sid' Ahmed I might have a companion more suited to my temperament and needs. After our contract had been made, he had asked what exactly I required of him on this journey. My reply was that essentially I wanted him to do the heavy physical work, for I had become worn out by the hard journey across Mauritania, whereas he would be fresh. The route-finding, I said, I was prepared to tackle myself. "Ah, good," said Sid' Ahmed, "for I can lead you to Nbeiket el Ouahch"—a well almost on the border with Mali—"but after that I don't know the way to Tombouctou." If the man could be as open as that before we set off, I thought, he had something that I prized.

Moreover, he showed eagerness in everything he did. We were now heading for his tent, where he could deposit his advanced wages and collect his own camel for the return journey, and the moment we stopped at midday, he scrambled like a monkey up the nearest tree with an axe, to chop down the tastiest high branches for the camels. He was anxious to get going again after the break; it was the shortest halt for food I could remember. In the evening,

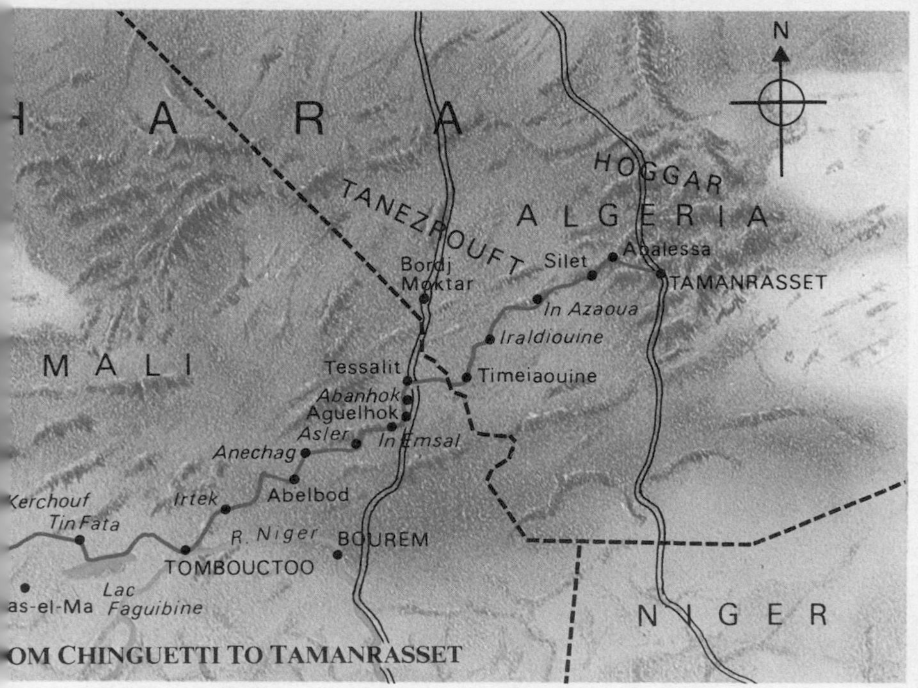

OM CHINGUETTI TO TAMANRASSET

before we slept, he asked me if my charts marked all the wells he knew in the region. I reeled off the names one by one, and he, concentrating as my finger traced the place of each, replied, "Yes, yes—no, don't know that one—yes—no, ah yes, but we call it. . . ." This was an excellent beginning. If we continued together like this, it should be a good journey.

We rode hard and fast again next day, and reached Sid' Ahmed's tent as the heat was going out of the afternoon. There, in the lambent glow that followed sunset, the people of the encampment said prayers together outside their tents, the men shoulder to shoulder, with the small boys behind them, the women and girls standing a little to one side. In that brief space when the lingering blue of the desert sky was swiftly overtaken by shadow, lending every shape a softness that it never knew by the harsh light of day, the people bowed deeply, knelt and submitted their heads to the dust; then they rose before kneeling again and kissing the earth. All this time the senior man at each tent intoned the words of adoration. But when these people knelt for the last time it was in silence, their faces turned to the eastern darkness. I had watched this same expression on the faces of Italian peasants kneeling before statues of the Virgin Mary, and upon Mongolian comrades as they stood contemplating the marble blockhouse that shelters Lenin's corpse in Moscow.

In the desert I never knew any of my companions miss a prayer time, in the morning, at midday, in late afternoon or at nightfall. I would wait on such occasions, quietly on one side until they had done, and I had never failed to be moved by their devotion. However repugnant some of Islam's philosophies might seem, the devotion itself was clearly central to the life of these people and fortifying in circumstances that were otherwise almost wholly bleak. These Moslem nomads were sharing the proximity to vitality, to truth, to holiness, which I had fleetingly experienced in the Russian Orthodox church in Paris.

At the end of the family worship, with the light now almost vanished from the sky, Sid' Ahmed laid a hand upon the outermost pole of his tent and fairly bellowed into the night that prayers had just been said in this household, in the name of Allah, the compassionate and merciful. I liked this man. He had gusto.

In the morning, he despatched his two sons to find his camel out in the pastures. While they were gone he rubbed his face with the contents of a tin labelled Tarzan's Mustard Ointment (Made in Ghana) and then disappeared to gossip with the other men.

By the time the boys returned it was past noon and, a lamb having been slaughtered for our journey, everyone gobbled at the carcass. I picked cautiously at a small piece of liver and wondered how long it would be before my ailment cleared up.

We got away at three o'clock, and I had not known such warmth in a desert farewell. At Mafud's camp and throughout my time with Mohamed, I had often reflected how curious it was that, although people fairly flocked to greet someone arriving, they paid scarcely any attention when he departed. It was not so here, however. As I led the camels away from the tents, Sid' Ahmed walked some distance behind, surrounded by his kinsmen and their women. The men pressed their hands upon his and put their arms round him. A woman, walking alongside, carefully made signs across the palm of his hand with her rosary. Children danced and waved, shouting his name, and Sid' Ahmed himself responded to all this affection with wide-eyed pleasure.

The next day was unpleasant. I had never really shaken off my bronchial cold, and we now found ourselves riding directly into a strong wind from the east, which seemed to set my nostrils aflame. My inability to eat much was beginning to take the stuffing out of me, so that I was riding like a sack of potatoes again, barely able to sit straight in the saddle. Walking, too, was a penance, for the cram-cram was thick upon the ground. We had one mishap after another. First, a tin mug disappeared, which I had inadequately secured. Then a bag, tied on by Sid' Ahmed, plunged to the ground, smashing cigarettes and leaving an awful mess of bits and pieces inside its battered canvas. Finally, and much worse, there was a sudden gusher below the left flank of my camel and, as I struggled to control the startled beast, I looked down to see water pouring out of a guerba. It was the only skin we had jointly heaved up into place, and we exchanged looks without a word. With three others still well-filled, the loss was not serious, but I made a mental note that such a thing must never happen again.

We camped that night with nomads, and I was glad to crawl into someone's tent, without the need to set up our own refuge. That evening and night was one of intermittent sleep and haphazard thoughts. I emerged from a doze to perceive people eating food which I had refused, to avoid the scalding pains which would instantly have followed. In my hunger, I dwelt much on my stomach, my imagination floundering towards oases of gooseberry pie, rich stews, then I began seriously to consider the respective merits of bread and cheese and sticky Danish pastries.

By the time we reached the well of Nbeiket el Ouahch, however, the drugs I was now taking seemed to be having some effect. Still, I was feeling so wasted that an hour or two of riding had me reeling in the saddle, and I almost fell when I dismounted.

The well itself was much more sophisticated than any I had seen so far. Not only had it a deep concrete shaft, with four outlying troughs for watering many beasts, but it was equipped with a wooden pulley at the angle of each trough. A camel was hitched to the rope running over each pulley and driven away from the well to haul the bucket up. As we came up to it, half a dozen men were drawing water for a herd of camels, the ones standing by the shaft shouting loudly to those leading the haulage beasts as the buckets surfaced, squirting jets in all directions. As much as warning their mates to turn back again, they seemed to be enjoying the shrieking echoes they were producing from deep inside the shaft.

We made camp with these men and once more I found myself warming to Sid' Ahmed. Far from inflicting the petty humiliations that I had occasionally experienced before, he seemed actually to be proud of his relationship with me. "When this Nasrani," he told them, "flew from England to Africa, he was sitting in the sky for six hours!" And they all shook their heads and clicked their tongues: aeroplanes they seemed to understand, but to stay in the sky for six whole hours was obviously regarded as some unconnected form of the miraculous. I then heard my companion extolling my excellence as a navigator, which at that stage was more than a large assumption on his part, for I had done nothing but keep a compass check over ground that he knew well enough by heart. "Tell them," he said with massive confidence, "tell them which way it is to Tombouctou." I drew the chart from its case, fiddled with the protractor, found the bearing with my compass and flung an arm out decisively across the sand and scrub that surrounded us monotonously. "Eeehhh!" they all said, with definite approval. Sid' Ahmed beamed. I seemed, Allah be praised, to have got it right. I noticed, nonetheless, that before we moved away, Sid' Ahmed was careful to inquire about the route to the next well.

We probably crossed the frontier sometime during the next morning, January 12, two men and three camels simply moving from one arbitrary longitude to another with an uncertainty that mocked territorial possessions and international politics. There was nothing to tell us at any given hour whether we were still in Mauritania's share of the wilderness or Mali's.

The days now telescoped into a sequence of pain, hunger and blinding exhaustion. Only thirst was missing from the perpetual agonies of travel, for there were never more than a couple of days between wells, and I never suffered more than the bitter and gummy dryness of the mouth that began within half an hour or so of drinking. Otherwise, I was rapidly sinking into something close to a physical wreck. There were raw patches of flesh spreading everywhere from my ribs to my thighs. A network of sores had broken out on my face. Curious blisters had started to appear upon my hands. Resentfully I scrutinized this damage, contemplating myself with growing distaste. Not only were precious possessions slowly falling to bits—the kitbags worn into holes, the books badly tattered—but my body, cared for so much over the years, was becoming unrecognizable. Oh, yes, one feared these things very much; the loss of possessions and the loss of beauty.

The drugs no longer seemed capable of holding my sickness in check. Nothing that I ate remained in the body for more than a quarter of an hour or so. I was existing on liquids alone and the emotional comfort of masticating a few dates, a handful of rice or a fragment of meat. I could only guess what my condition would have been without the invigorating refreshment of highly sweetened tea and coffee. By the time we were halfway to Tombouctou, I knew that I was in deep trouble.

A succession of brief but vivid cameos lodged in my consciousness during these days. There was a night when we camped with nomads in a deep basin of sand. A great fire had been built up, and every time I woke, it was to see a group of sheep huddled motionless around this fire, their glass-eyed, slightly anxious faces glowing in the yellow light.

There was another evening when some friendly people put up a small tent for our benefit, and then produced a great stream of children and old men, all suffering from eye infections, the first stage on the road to trachoma. I was squeezing tetracycline across the lids of the prettiest child I had seen for months, a slim and delicate girl with pigtails hanging to her waist, when I suddenly fell over, half-swooning away, my body drenched with sweat.

Then, with Tombouctou still five days away, my camel, the twelve-year-old bull I had ridden down from Tidjikdja, started to founder. Once or twice before, after being unloaded, he had seemed reluctant to rise again. Now he fell down, his forelegs giving way beneath him. With Sid' Ahmed hauling on his head-rope and with me kicking him hard behind, we got him up, and put him between the other two camels. We fastened head-ropes to saddles, and led them in line ahead for half an hour. Then the rope which Sid' Ahmed was hauling pulled taut with sudden strain, the rope behind broke in two, and the bull was down on his knees again. We got him up once more, spliced the head-rope and started off. Almost immediately, the same thing happened again. Again we got him moving, and this time he kept going until we made camp for the night.

I was badly spent myself by now. I had drunk a mug of coffee before starting the day's march, I had eaten a boiled potato at noon, which had gone straight through me, and I had sipped a round of tea. On Sid' Ahmed's orders, I lay like a log while this splendid fellow arranged our camp, collected wood, made up a fire, brewed tea, did everything himself. I raised myself on an elbow as he offered me the first glass. "You're a good man, Sid' Ahmed," I said. His head tilted to one side in that mannerism I had associated with wheedling. I realized now that essentially it betrayed embarrassment. "You're a good man yourself, *sayyid*," he replied. Quickly, I turned my head away from him. I could feel the tears springing into my eyes, starting to roll down my scarecrow cheeks.

The next day we marched for much longer than usual, having some vague intention of sparing the sick bull. After a mile or so I stumbled and fell. For a fraction of a moment, as I collected my breath on hands and knees, I was in two minds whether to get to my feet again or lie down and rest. Then I hauled myself up and carried on walking. Sometime later I fell again. Finally Sid' Ahmed insisted that I mount his own bull, while he walked with the other two.

I clutched the pommel, as I had not done since my 'prentice days, in an effort to reduce the pain from my body sores, and tried to think of my children setting off to school. Normally, the vacuum hours of a day's journey were much relieved by such thoughts. They were my lifeline, a promise that what I cared for most deeply went on without me and would be there awaiting me at the end of this journey. But now I had neither the strength nor the will to hold those images. They seemed to have no meaning in this blinding struggle. They were irrelevant. Even food was irrelevant now. I could no longer identify my stomach-empty pain. Body was pain; it had no separate parts.

On January 17 we marched again. I fell down once, the sick bull twice. At some stage in the day we reached the well of Tin Fata and I, sitting dazed under a tree, could hear Sid' Ahmed asking three men if they had a camel they could sell. But he returned from the wellhead without a word and we marched on.

Next day, we had walked for three hours when the sick bull fell again. This time we couldn't get him up. Sid' Ahmed turned away and began to cast around for wood. I supposed he had decided that we should make camp, but when he returned with an armful of firewood, he dumped it alongside the sitting beast. He said that sometimes a fire would make an exhausted animal rise when everything else had failed. I shook my head. "No", I said, "we're not going to do that." Sid' Ahmed gestured impatiently. "Then we must leave him," he said. And I remembered—how long ago it seemed—the two camels I had seen abandoned near the well of Chig.

Sid' Ahmed removed the animal's head-rope and the few small things it had been carrying. We mounted the other two camels and slowly rode away. I did not look back. I was blank about this, too.

We were now heading for Lac Faguibine, a sheet of water, about fifty miles long and ten miles across. It seemed a pretty implausible thing to find in the Sahara desert, but almost as soon as we left the dying bull, we entered a region quite unlike anything I had seen before. The ground became thickly forested with thorn trees, pitifully poor in green leaves but set so close together that the place was eerie with a blessed gloom which protected us from the sun's burning. I was but dimly aware of gratitude, for my mind was clamped on the twenty yards immediately ahead and the need to hang onto my seat. We rode on, the trees' thorny branches scratching our arms and plucking at our garments.

Sid' Ahmed ould Eli ould Simmad.

Then it lay before us, this miracle of water, surrounded by a flat, white, sandy shore. Here and there were tiny islands, covered in green vegetation. Two dugouts were fishing a few hundred yards offshore. To the east, a few miles away, was a ridge of low rocky hills, and the lake at that end so much reminded me of a Scottish loch that I wanted to embrace everything I could see. Slowly our camels walked up the shore towards those hills, past a tiny bay marvellously fringed with green trees and rushes. Children were bathing, scuttering the water up into each other's faces and squealing with laughter. A heron was standing up to his knees, peering steadily at the surface. An egret stood quietly some way off, on the edge of the rushes.

I suspected that Lac Faguibine might breed the flukes of Bilharzia, otherwise I too would have stripped off and bathed. So we sat there for a little while, while the camels drank deeply, and then we walked quietly on past the hills to make our camp for the night.

Next morning we were crossing the desolate plain beyond the lake in a high wind that was laced with dust from the open desert, when the flaming agony of my saddle sores and the jolting of my camel's gait was such that I couched the beast and dismounted. I had walked no more than a few hundred yards when I pitched forward and lay there, without the energy to rise again. I raised my head. Sid' Ahmed was some distance away, riding slowly, waiting for me to catch up. Foolish man, he didn't know that I wasn't going to this time. My head went down on my arms.

I heard Sid' Ahmed hissing his camel to couch, and a voice somewhere above me curtly saying that I must move on. Murderously my head came up. How dare this little bastard take it upon himself to disturb me when I wished to be left alone. He had a grin of superiority on his rotten wheedling face, he was waving his arms forward imperiously and shouting "Come on, advance, advance!" as though he were talking to a dog. Hurling obscenities at him in English, I dragged myself up so that I could mount and pursue this appalling little tick to tell him what I really thought of him.

At midday, camped beside some bushes, I wondered whether I would have lain in the sand for good if I had been travelling alone. Sid' Ahmed, who had conceivably just saved my life, paused before downing the third glass of tea. "Tomorrow night, Inshallah, Tombouctou." Then he grinned at me.

We left the plain behind and continued across shallow sand dunes well-covered in scrub. At first we walked for a while, Sid' Ahmed soon outstripping my meander, which had become so slow that the camel I was supposed to be leading was close behind me, his neck looming over my head. In an effort to jerk some vitality into my tired body, I began to hum "The British Grenadiers"

It was exactly the wrong choice of music. It had been the regimental march of the old Lancashire Fusiliers, in which my grandfather had been an undistinguished but very proud lance-corporal in the Boer War. When I was a child and the tune had been played on the radio, I could remember how Grandad would stiffen at the sound and announce, with a gleam in his damp old eyes, "I've marched thousands of miles across the desert to that tune." As I hummed the first few bars, I remembered all this again, and burst into tears, thankful for once that Sid' Ahmed was so far ahead that he couldn't possibly see what was going on. I was crying for so many things. For my present abysmal state, for my loneliness, for the memory of that gentle old man. I was crying, too, I think, from a sense of shame: for he had come home from two wars to support a blind wife, a divorced daughter and a small grandson, and had not failed one of them at any time; while I, who had not been to any war, had failed so many people. I wished that Grandad were still alive to know that I too was slogging through the desert: I wanted to be told that he might have been proud of me.

We made camp that night in the sandy scrub, and we cooked our last piece of meat in the embers of the fire, such a gritty, dried-up lump of gristle as I would not have thrown to a pet animal in England. But I needed anything that would nourish, and I wolfed it down greedily.

Next day, after the midday camp, in thorn trees once again, we came upon the first wheel tracks since Nema, and began to watch eagerly for a sign of habitation. Uncharacteristically, I was the first to spot it. A pale flash above the treeline caught my eye and I realized I was looking at a tall cylinder of corrugated iron, possibly a water tower. Then gradually the trees around us parted and in the diminishing light of late afternoon the grey buildings of fabulous Tombouctou came slowly into full view.

We reined in our camels and paused a moment before dismounting. I looked at my companion. "Well," I said, "we got there."

"Inshallah," said Sid' Ahmed, looking to his front. He tilted his head. "Ilhamdu Lillah! Allah be praised!"

MONOD HAD DESCRIBED Tombouctou to me as "a dreadful place", but I could not see why. Given my condition when I arrived, no town could possibly have seemed other than a welcome refuge, yet I found something more in Tombouctou, a tantalizing mixture of styles, something between a small French provincial town, any town in Black Africa and a rather grand desert oasis.

The French strain was represented by the basketball court in front of the *lycée,* and by the methodical placing of traffic signs in a community that didn't have much traffic. Black Africa was in the market place, with mammies sitting by piles of vegetables, and in the great pit behind the solitary hotel, into whose muddy water day-long processions of people climbed with buckets and plastic jerrycans, with laughter too and merriment, something that never happened at a well in the desert, where people drew water deliberately and, having done so, would sit and talk quietly as though afraid to challenge the gaping silence that surrounds them.

The rest of Tombouctou was of the desert, which had drifted into every street, so that the sound of everything was muted into crunching sibilants. It was a town without an echo, a town more colourfully of the desert than any place I had visited, with the billowing robes of the camel men running from deep royal blues, through lime and avocado greens, to gorgeous oranges and yellows. The trappings of the camels here were ornate, the halters tricked out with tiny bells and brass work, the beasts themselves more splendid than any I had seen before. Most were white, woolier than the brown camels of Mauritania, bigger-boned and firmer-humped and, such was the combination of their breeding and the spirit of the Tuareg tribes, that they seemed always to be ridden at a roistering gallop.

The medley of tourists in the one hotel seemed to find the sanitation unspeakable, the catering inadequate and the service slatternly bad. To me the hotel was a luxurious haven, although I had almost been thrown out before I even got to the reception desk. A policeman observing two filthy Arabs approaching the terrace, one of them insolently marching towards the door, got up to fling the fellow off the premises, and realized only just in time that this intruder was, in fact, a European and therefore entitled to enter the hotel, however disgusting his appearance.

I changed much of that appearance very quickly. I shed my desert clothes and sent them to be deloused and washed, donning jeans and shirt instead. The effect on morale of this alone was enormously uplifting. As soon as I was clean I reached for antibiotics, smearing ointment upon my wounds, digesting pills for my sickness. Somehow, I must eat well in Tombouctou and keep the food inside me, if I was to continue this journey. I must also rest, and restore some of the wastage that had already taken place. For three or four days I did little else, lying on my bed for hours, drifting between consciousness and sleep, rising only at meal-times to shovel in the most welcome food I had ever tasted; bread, pasta, fish, decently-stewed mutton, crème caramel and more bread. After a day or two I began to retain all this nourishment.

The finest thing in Tombouctou, however, was the mail awaiting me there. Andrew had carefully copied out the leading positions in the English football leagues, and Jane told how at Christmas they had listened to my reading of Dylan Thomas, surprised that I had managed some sort of Welsh accent. A Benedictine monk I had known for years had dragooned half a dozen convents into praying for me, and the sisters were wondering about the theological niceties of praying for my camels too.

Now that I had achieved the first objective, I rose to a subdued form of elation and began to plot the way ahead. One thing was already settled in my mind: if I were to reach the Nile, it would now have to be the result of a continous movement. I simply did not have the resources, spiritual much more than physical, to spend seven months in a Libyan oasis. The question remained whether it would be possible to drive 2,500 miles straight through to Luxor. The odds seemed much against it, but it might be done if I could keep my present pace at its highest level—I had ridden something over 1,100 miles in two months, and I could risk riding into the edge of summer. Meanwhile, I contented myself with simply laying the best course to Tamanrasset.

I had by now been lulled into complacency about official territorial prohibitions. At Bamako in October, I had been made well

Tombouctou

aware of the political hazards of travelling across Mali. But, with that visa in my passport, I had been able to settle in Tombouctou without difficulty.

A few days later, however, when I felt well enough to take a look at the town, I was out walking when a Jeep drew up beside me. Two policemen ordered me to get in. I was driven to the police bureau and led into a dusty room full of filing cabinets and a desk. I found myself facing a very smart and slicked individual, with a thin moustache and a skin which was several shades lighter than that of any other policeman on the premises, wearing a red turtleneck sweater under a khaki drill shirt and dangling a fly whisk from his fingers. He looked as though interrogation was his bread and butter. He was very hostile to start with, in a controlled way that hinted at the coiled power of a snake. Where was my Mauritanian companion? he asked. Why was I travelling by camel? I heard a sergeant outside ordering the Jeep driver to "go and collect this man's effects," and I tried to answer the questions calmly. Then I played my trump card, the photostat I still had of the letter of recommendation from the Mali Embassy to the Director-General of the Security Services in Bamako. Handing this over to the commissioner now, I artfully dropped the name of M. Bagayoko, as though he had personally guaranteed my safe-conduct across the republic. Maybe he had, though I had never met the gentleman.

At once the hostility was replaced by level correctness. I offered cigarettes. The commissioner wasn't a smoker, but his lieutenant accepted politely. The commissioner, still twitching his fly whisk, gave me what he called advice. I was absolutely forbidden to go anywhere near the oases of Kidal and Tin Zouatan, which were areas of the highest military security. I must not even travel across the desert outside Tombouctou. Instead, I must take the dirt road east to the village of Bourem; there I must switch to the trans-Saharan highway running north into Algeria. As long as I understood all this clearly, I was free to leave Tombouctou.

By this time, Sid' Ahmed had made arrangements for his return home. Within a week, a small caravan would be leaving for the border, and he proposed to ride with it. But, mindful of my interests, he had found someone prepared to sell me a new camel, so that I should be able to continue with a pair of beasts. It was a handsome, white seven-year-old, very solidly built. Fancying it on sight, I bought it there and then.

I had asked Sid' Ahmed if he could find someone to go with me as far as the Algerian border. A few days later he introduced me to a man he identified as his "cousin", though I knew that the word did not express the relationship understood in the West. It is possible, indeed, that the title was bestowed simply because the two had the same given names, the newcomer being called Sid' Ahmed ould Mohammed.

He was a good deal older than anyone I had travelled with before, probably nearer sixty than the forty-five he claimed, though I was not to see his bald head until we were well away from Tombouctou. But he seemed amiable; he spoke a little French as well as Hassaniya, and he, like Mohamed, had done time in the colonial camel corps many years before.

In the courtyard outside my hotel room, provisions slowly mounted. For a journey that should in theory take us no more than three weeks before we were in a position to replenish our stores, we amassed 15 kilos of dates, 10 of rice, 1½ of tea, 3 of potatoes, 3 of onions, 8 packets of lump sugar, 2 pieces of rock salt, 1 kilo of peanuts, 5 tins of Nescafé, 4 tins of evaporated milk and 4 cartons of cigarettes. I was thus much better provisioned than before, appreciating by now the need to feed well. I was also allowing for the undoubted fact that a proportion of our stores would find its way into stomachs other than our own.

After six days in Tombouctou I felt well enough to go on. Indeed, I must go on without more delay if I was to have an outside chance of reaching the Nile. I was still walking slowly, but it seemed to me that I could manage again, even though I had really very little relish for committing myself once more to the wilderness beyond these comforting walls. I spent a restless last night in my room, my nerves jangling me awake every hour or two.

On January 26, I said farewell to Sid' Ahmed, feeling sad to see the last of such a good and decent companion. I wished he were still riding with me, especially as ould Mohammed seemed exceedingly wooden. As we led the two camels through the back lanes of Tombouctou towards open country, I only hoped that I would not have to check up on every commonplace thing he did.

Chapter Five

We left the town by its northeastern edge. Ould Mohammed's young son was with us, and the two camels were much overloaded. Besides the baggage and provisions for our journey, they were carrying foodstuffs to be deposited, with the boy, at the family's tent. Ould Mohammed had told me that this was "only an hour" outside the town. In the event, it was almost noon the next day before we reached the tent, and I in a filthy temper. Although ould Mohammed had vowed that, after taking a meal, we would continue our journey without delay, by the time we arrived I was being nagged to linger until the following day, on a variety of pretexts. Why was it, I asked myself, that a man in ould Mohammed's position could not straightforwardly say, "Look, I haven't seen my family for a fortnight; do you mind if we stay a day with them before going on?" It would have been impossible to resist such a plea. As it was, the devious methods of these people only made me cantankerous and sometimes unreasonable.

On this occasion, however, I gave in without much argument. The long walk in the heat had tired me. I was, moreover, beginning to feel ill again. My sores had almost healed, but the churning within said that my intestinal sickness was on the way back. As long as I took drugs, all was tolerably well; the moment I came to the end of the prescribed dosage, food dropped from one end of my body to the other almost as soon as it had been shovelled in. This was a pattern that would now stay with me until the end of the journey.

As I lounged away the afternoon in the shade of a thorn tree, I had much on my mind. Ould Mohammed was evidently much more sophisticated than anyone I had travelled with before. He had bought several packets of Gauloises in Tombouctou, which he smoked with a flourish. At our first meal he had brought from his tassoufra a spoon, and eaten his rice with that. Yet it was already clear that he was abysmally deficient as a camel handler. He had stood around uttering words of command while I and his small son together loaded the beasts, until I had curtly ordered him to join in. We had been obliged to stop every hour or so to readjust the loads, and on each occasion it was because ould Mohammed had failed to secure something properly. I had come to the conclusion that it must have been years since he had travelled with camels, possibly not since his days with the French Army nearly a couple of decades before.

My other worries concerned ould Mohammed's gloomy prognostications about the tendencies of the local tribes of Tuareg. I carried no gun, not having fired a rifle since my days in the school cadet corps and taking the view that an armed man is much more likely to provoke hostility than not. Ould Mohammed seemed to think that this was a grievous error. In the past few months, he said, he knew of half a dozen instances where travellers had been set upon and murdered for food because people were going hungry as a result of the drought.

Another worry was that our prolonged march to ould Mohammed's tent had taken us almost exactly along my original chosen route, and put me in peril of imprisonment by being where I was. I scrutinised the charts again, and concluded that if I crossed the desert and struck the trans-Saharan highway below the border oasis of Tessalit, I could avoid the two sternly proscribed oases of Kidal and Tin Zouatan, which it would obviously be folly to visit. I could then trot up the highway to Tessalit for a couple of days as though I had been following the police commissioner's orders from the start. With care, our provisions might just see us through. I decided therefore to continue across the desert and risk being found by a military patrol.

Sid' Ahmed ould Mohammed.

We made an early start, with

ould Mohammed in excellent spirits. As soon as we were riding he broke into song. He was quite the best singer I had yet heard, skirling a wild, warlike chant with great nasal verve, plunging through interminable verses that challenged any enemies to come and do their worst, but warning them to take care for we, we of the righteous, had Allah on our side.

For all his jauntiness, though, he was still quite hopelessly inept when it came to loading camels, and at one stage in the afternoon he fell asleep in the saddle, his head lolling tipsily on his chest. For good measure, that night I awoke to watch him stealthily raiding the tassoufra for a handful of dates. He was the only man I had known to break the great unwritten rule of desert travel, that companions share everything and do not steal from the common store.

Then, next day, as we trotted down a low dune, I saw wheel tracks running along the level ground at right angles to our course. Instinctively, I cut my beast into a gallop to get over them and out of sight across the dune opposite. Having put them well behind me, I paused and waited for ould Mohammed to catch up. I asked him about the military camp in the desert, and he gave me the reply that it was far away, nowhere near where we were heading. A little later, I heard a growing hum and saw a Land-Rover, about a mile away, driving along the tracks we had just crossed. I had scarcely got over the shock of it, thanking my lucky stars for a narrow escape, when I topped another dune; and there, no more than half a mile away, was the military camp itself.

My heart thumped as I took it all in—the long range of mud buildings, the Land-Rover which was now speeding towards the gateway, the sentry boxes, the soldiers moving inside the fortified square. Then I swivelled my camel below the concealing edge of the dune and beat it into a gallop to get us away from this place as fast as possible. For three days I had been warning ould Mohammed against this danger and yet the imbecile had allowed us to ride almost up to the front door. I roared at him to follow me and, when he had drawn alongside, I blazed at him furiously with anger fuelled by fear.

For an hour I kept us at this gallop, my heart thumping erratically as I visualized all sorts of undesirable happenings if the military found me here, against the express orders of the security forces, equipped as I was with a compass and navigational manuals that could be mistaken for code books by any illiterate. We had to get away from this area rapidly, which meant much hard riding in the next couple of days.

We spent that night near a couple of tents pitched among a group of thorns. I saw danger in the possibility of someone mentioning to the military that a Nasrani had been seen in the district, but we needed to beg a little water. I had not yet accustomed myself to the idea that everything about this expedition was now my responsibility, and had thus left the filling of our guerbas to ould Mohammed. We consequently had run out of water.

The next day, after filling our guerbas at the well of Irtek, we had put something like twenty miles between us and the military camp, before we halted.

It now seemed unlikely that the soldiers would happen upon us, and that evening was one of the most beautiful I had known in the desert. As I lay inert, while the water boiled for tea, the sun slid

The Well of Irtek.

down out of a paling sky, its edges trembling for a moment, as though liquid, before it disappeared. The camels, browsing among a bit of scrub, were outlined darkly against its glow. We had set up camp beside the only tree for miles, and a cricket was singing somewhere deep within its thorny branches. Apart from that noise and the sputtering of the flames, the world was soundless, without even a wisp of wind. In this stillness, I could see the fruitfulness of the desert that mystics had found. Lying there at peace, one felt so close to a brink of revelation that it seemed almost within will-power. But not quite. Not on this journey. One could never rest long enough. Always there must be movement, the anxious transit from one water-hole to another.

Next day, I spotted a movement ahead of us, a tiny disturbance against the dazzling glare of the sand, that was translated into a spreading pattern almost at once. Half a dozen gazelles were leaping off to avoid our coming, flying as fast as the desert hares we sprang from time to time, bounding and galloping in springing arcs, their white rumps flicking with motions of fear.

That afternoon also we passed a small area of thorn bushes and around each was a palpitating cloud of white butterflies, such an astonishing display of fragile beauty that for the next mile or so I kept turning my head to mark the place where they had been. For the rest of the day my curiosity fed on ecological balances. What on earth was it about those bushes that attracted the first butterflies I could recall seeing on this journey?

January turned into February and, in spite of the intermittent sickness and lousy sores that had broken out again on my body, I was buoyant. The danger from the military was now past and I would have been well content had it not been that the days had become much hotter, a month earlier than I had been led to expect. It was still bitterly cold at night, but it was now warm before eight o'clock, and gaspingly hot by nine. By 10.30 the back of my throat was beginning to thicken, my tongue was almost completely dry, and I could sink half the contents of my water bottle, about one pint, almost in a single gulp. The increase in temperature I could only measure crudely by the amount of water I was consuming each day. Before, I had scarcely ever needed six pints. Now I was taking eight pints, and still could not shake off the thirst.

Navigation too was becoming more of a strain, the landscape being almost without features. It was easy enough to keep a compass bearing when there was a tree, or a prominent outcrop of rock somewhere on the horizon. In the absence of natural features, however, the trick was to hold the shadows of men and beasts in the same quarter for long periods, but I didn't trust my own judgment of this enough yet, preferring to stop every twenty minutes or so to check my course by the instrument.

On February 5 we made our midday camp at the well of Abelbod below a long reef of rocks which were at times obscured by a haze of scudding grit. All morning the wind had been rising, driving clouds of dust into the sky so that, by noon, the sun glowed indistinctly in a leaden atmosphere. We were cooking our rice when there was a movement nearby. Two women had appeared halfway round a large thorn bush. My presence evidently deterred them, for they would not come any nearer and when I looked in their direction they drew up the hoods of their black dresses to obstruct my view. But ould Mohammed crawled over to them and they talked intently for some time. Then he gave them some tea and sugar, and they disappeared as mysteriously as they had come.

He looked severe when he returned to my side. "They say the country behind here, towards Anechag, is bad," he said. "There've been some killings lately." Anechag was the next well and we needed to use it, for there was only one other before the trans-Saharan highway, about a week away. The women had asked ould Mohammed whether he carried a gun and the wily old fox had told them that of course he did; it was stowed away inside his tassoufra. He evidently treated this encounter with the women seriously, so we did not linger to rest after we had eaten. As soon as the rice was consumed, we packed up and made off again.

We climbed the reef and began to cross a table of bare, black gravel. After an hour or so, the wind died and by mid-afternoon the sun blazed down on us unhindered once more. As we descended into a wide and sandy wadi crammed with scrub, there was a flash of blue to our right, and my senses pricked at the prospect of danger. But then a shepherd wandered into view and greeted us amiably. After a few moments' conversation, he was persuaded to part with a lamb, taking a little tobacco in return.

It was butchered on the spot, and I watched with only the faintest stirring of emotion. I was much changed by the desert. The Englishman in me dimly acknowledged something called cruelty to animals, but the savage much more aggressively relished the prospect of meat for the first time in ten days or more.

We rode on, like a pair of buccaneers, with the corpse lashed to ould Mohammed's saddle as our booty. We struggled up and across a range of rock, perhaps five hundred feet in height, walking our camels down the steep sides of the wadi, and made our camp among a thicket of trees close under the line of cliffs. Any fearful undercurrents had now gone. We had slaughtered, we were triumphant, we were men of the desert. I slept uneasily that night, but it was more from anxiety that someone would ride up and share our precious lamb than from fear of being attacked.

It was noon next day when we arrived at Anechag and men were already busy hauling water from the deep shaft for a great mob of beasts. Here, as never before, I was aware of suspicion. Ould Mohammed clearly felt it too, for he was unusually silent as we waited our turn to draw water. Nor did the half dozen men gathered there seem eager to make conversation. They stared wordlessly at me and at our baggage. After we had filled two of our guerbas, ould Mohammed motioned me towards our camels, and together we hitched the guerbas into place and mounted. We were both in a hurry to leave, and we should have enough water to see us to the well of Asler, which was only three or four days ahead.

We set off down the valley at a brisk trot. As we began riding, some of the men at the well hastily mounted their camels and came fast in pursuit. When they had pulled their beasts into step alongside ours, I saw that one of the men was almost completely blind. His right eye was white with trachoma, his left becoming milky, too. In order to bring me into some kind of focus, he held his hands as though they were binoculars, presumably to shut out dazzling and painful light. But as he did this only when looking at me, it made me feel I was being singled out for some particularly keen and malevolent examination. It was a forlorn hope that the men would swerve off in some direction other than ours; they were clearly intent on sticking to us, and questioned us persistently about our purpose in these parts. I left most of the talking to ould

Mohammed, who glibly recited some cock-and-bull story about a mission for the Government.

Inevitably, the men unloaded their camels near ours when we camped among a clump of trees late in the afternoon. We had given them a haunch of the lamb, but no sooner had we started our fire than three of them rose from behind a bush and walked over to squat beside us. One announced without introduction that we were in the presence of a famous marabout, who desired some tea and sugar. I handed over the goods very grudgingly indeed. I had already noticed that morning that we had only enough sugar left for another couple of days at the most, with something like five days before we could hope to obtain more. But I was in no position to deny anything to anyone in these parts; the stories I had heard of men killing for food were too vividly on my mind. When the "marabout"—who had not spoken a word—and his two companions left us, two more men appeared, and each of them demanded tea and sugar to take away. Beneath the superficial talk it seemed that all these visitors were essentially watching, weighing up, quietly waiting . . . for what?

Lately I had been sleeping naked in my bag, to be less troubled by lice. But this night I kept my clothes on. I also stuck my knife into the sand by my side, where I could grab it in an emergency. As I lay down, there was a small rustling by the tassoufra, and a tiny brown head popped up for a moment before disappearing again among the baggage. It was the first jerboa I had seen in the desert. Two or three hours must have passed before I slept, and ould Mohammed didn't even seem inclined to lie down. He sat swathed in his blanket by the fire, nodding off occasionally. Next morning a corpse lay in the sand beyond my feet. Ould Mohammed had killed the jerboa, a creature as inoffensive as a mouse, when he saw it coming out of the tassoufra in the middle of the night. But there had been no other visitors.

We got away soon after dawn, eating a few nuts with our tea to avoid delay. We rode almost due east, holding closer to the towering side of the sand sea than to the cliffs, for there the going was easier for my camel. His normal gait was the shuffle of an old man making for the bathroom in his bedroom slippers, and on rougher going he had a tendency to trip. All day we plodded steadily on, while a hot wind drove across the wide valley until it was spent against the cliffs, which sent the heat back at us in great dehydrating waves. Yet the cliffs were a comfort, for I could follow each turn and each opening in them on the chart. Riding that day was much like running down a coastline after a long time in the open sea. If it had not been for the terrible heat it would have been an enjoyable passage, for we saw no one after breaking camp; danger seemed past once more. But by mid-afternoon all energy had suddenly drained from my body, and I rode slumped in the saddle until we made our evening camp.

Thursday, February 8, began inauspiciously. We finished the sugar with our first round of tea. All our stores were at a low ebb, particularly the dates, our other chief source of energy. The cliffs dropped away to our right, slowly slipping over the southern horizon. The sand sea which we now entered had flattened into a white plain without a single reference point, frightening in its loneliness. I knew that at our present pace we would be lucky if we got to the well of Asler before Saturday. We must keep our beasts at a decent trot and not linger too long over our midday camp.

We had only just started to ride when a strong headwind blew up, turning the blue sky muddy, a white spindrift of sand steaming along the surface of the plain towards us. Visibility was reduced with incredible speed. By 11.30 this dust storm had so intensified that, when we saw a solitary tree looming out of the haze to our right, we made for it and unloaded the camels. We drank water and ate a few dates, spitting out sand along with the stones. Then we wrapped ourselves tightly in our robes and lay under the lee of the baggage and saddles.

At three o'clock, the storm slackened. All but our largest possessions were smothered in sand. The blankets on which we were lying had disappeared except where our bodies covered them. There were three or four inches of sand in the cooking pot. We stood in the middle of a thick fog and I wondered how on earth we were going to make our way through it to the well of Asler.

Never before had I been forced to concentrate on a compass needle as I did when we started riding again. With the visibility never more than a quarter of a mile, and sometimes down to 250 yards, I found myself checking the instrument every ten minutes, reining in my camel for stillness each time I did so. There was not even shadow by which one might gauge the consistency of direction, for the sun had vanished from the sky.

Then the worst possible thing happened. Ould Mohammed, who had been trailing behind for some time, came riding alongside me and my eye caught something hanging from his saddle. It was one of the guerbas, dangling nose down, the lashing which should have supported it swinging uselessly. It had been well over half-full of water when we started. There was now not a drop left.

I was so stunned that I could only point to it. Ould Mohammed looked down and made a gesture of astonishment. Then he recovered his poise, swept the emptiness ahead of us imperiously with his arm, and announced that the loss didn't matter because we would be at Asler by nightfall. I knew very well that there was not the slightest possibility of this happening. I also knew that we were now facing a crisis.

By six o'clock, fatigue had hit me again like a crippling blow and, with darkness imminent, we stopped for the night. As there was nothing but bare sand as far as the eye could see, the camels went without food and we did little better, munching a little raw potato and onion because they contained moisture. We had two pints of water left, which was not going to last very long in the heat of the next day. Having taken no more than three or four pints in the previous twenty-four hours, I was beginning to dehydrate badly. It was this, as much as the lack of sugar, that made me so blindingly weary. I dropped off to sleep still sitting up in my bag. Sometime later I awoke, cut through with cold, and heard a movement a few yards away. Ould Mohammed was squatting by the tassoufra, munching the last of our dates. Resentfully, I tried to curse him roundly for his greed, but the voice I heard sounded more like a reproachful whine.

We drank half our water neat before facing Friday and ate more raw potato and onion. It was a beautifully clear morning when we set off, but by 9.30 the sandstorm had blown up again. Visibility dropped to a quarter of a mile but we could not afford to stop. We had to move fast to Asler or we might perish. The chart showed that it was set between two reefs and, if only the storm lifted, we would have something to look for.

By 4.30 the storm had died again, and slowly the sun reappeared, the visibility increased and we could see for several miles around. There was not a rock or a tree in sight; nothing but empty sand again. We went on.

The light was almost gone when I called a halt. We climbed from our camels like old men, very slowly easing ourselves down on anxious arms. We couched the beasts by our sides. We would have no energy to bring them to us in the morning and there was nothing on which they might browse. The effort of unloading the baggage was enough to prostrate us mutely for a long time before we could muster the strength for more movement.

I had to face the fact that we were lost. The well of Asler was somewhere in the vicinity, but whether it was to the north, to the south or somewhere behind us, I had no idea at all. Nor did there seem much point in trying to find it now, from such a totally uncertain position. The only sensible course lay to the east. The trans-Saharan highway could not be much more than thirty miles from where we were, and as it ran directly from north to south we were bound to strike it by riding east. If we reached the highway we would presumably meet a vehicle before long, and that would be our salvation. The question was whether we could get there before we both died of thirst. Thirty miles would normally be one and a half day's journey, but half a day had already passed since we finished the last of our liquid, and I recalled reading that twenty-four hours without any water in these temperatures was the limit of human endurance. I had brought several packets of emergency blocks of highly concentrated glucose and other foods from England. From the way my throat had already swollen, I guessed that it would soon be so blocked that nothing solid would get past my mouth. I explained what the package contained to ould Mohammed, and started to chew some. The process was so painful that tears came to my eyes and, wiping them away on the back of my hand, I licked them up with a clumsy tongue.

Ould Mohammed had said almost nothing since we made our camp for the night, except to murmur prayers where he sat, over and over again. He ate a little but sat so quietly with a blanket round his shoulders, that it occurred to me he might be resigning himself to death. I crawled over to him and took his limp hand in mine. "We're not going to die, ould Mohammed," I said quietly. "We're going to find water tomorrow. We are." He didn't even look up into my face. "Inshallah," he replied, nodding very slowly. "Inshallah." After that I lay down. It was past eleven o'clock and I didn't wake up again until after four. This was the longest unbroken sleep I'd had for ages.

In the hour or so before dawn I lay still, enjoying the warmth of my sleeping bag and trying not to swallow. Ould Mohammed was huddled by the side of his saddle, completely muffled by his blanket. Light seeped over the horizon, grey-blue surmounted by orange. Gradually, the stars were doused one by one. I shook ould Mohammed and then tried to eat some more rations, but the pain was so great that I gave up and spat them out.

We were on the move not long after six o'clock. Urgently I tapped my camel's shoulder to keep him at a good trot. Everything in me was totally concentrated upon holding our course, that I was anaesthetized from the pain in my throat, in my skull and in the lousy saddle-rubbed sores of my body. Occasionally I looked back, to see ould Mohammed riding farther and farther behind. For nearly five hours I continued thus, more a robot than a man, my eyes screwed upon that next dip in the sandy ground ahead, then the one which followed it, after that another and another and another.

I had overrun the marks in the sand before I realized what they were. I turned the bull and walked him back. Groggily I dismounted to look at them more closely. They were a broad set of tracks made by a number of camels, moving from the south slightly to the west of north.

Slowly ould Mohammed shortened the distance between us, but when he saw the tracks his reaction was electrified. He brought his camel to earth with a rusty shout, and almost went full-length in his haste to dismount. "Look, look," he shouted, pointing with outstretched arm. "They passed one hour ago. Only one hour. We must follow them. Hurry, hurry!" He turned to snatch at his camel's head-rope again, preparing to mount. I stood still, wondering what to do. I had no faith left in my companion's judgment of anything, but after a moment's hesitation I took a deep breath and nodded. O.K., we would follow the tracks.

As my beast came up on his feet I clouted him to get moving fast but felt myself about to topple from the saddle within a few lunging strides. I hauled him down to a trot. Ould Mohammed, however, was thrashing his beast to a frantic pace, himself bouncing dangerously in the saddle like a pebble on a drum. Before long he was a speck in the far distance. Then he disappeared beyond a great leisurely roll of the sand sea.

I had been trotting for a long time when something dark appeared against the skyline. My heart started thumping: this must be ould Mohammed, he must have stopped, he must have found them . . . but in a little while I saw that the dark shape was just an outcrop of rock.

Things were becoming blurred. I was struggling to fix my attention on the object of this ride. I was alone. I had lost ould Mohammed. Where had he gone? Why had he left me? It was now two hours since we had turned off our course. Other shapes became rocks as I came near to them. The world was camel tracks and me. We would go together till the end of time.

There was nothing else.

Another dark speck on the skyline didn't fool me. But this time it *was* ould Mohammed. He had dismounted and there was a group of people near him. I started to gallop. A quarter of a mile away now, and unmistakably I could see men carrying something towards ould Mohammed's camel. I could hear a small boy babbling, "Thank you God, Thank you God," over and over again, and it was me, trying not to cry, my face twisting like a child's, wanting to be brave.

Four men were there, besides ould Mohammed. As I rode up to them, they walked towards me, their hands raised in greeting. Cumbersomely my camel came down and very awkwardly, like a puppet, I lowered my body from the saddle. When I put the weight on my feet I reeled forward. Then I recovered and saluted them. A man thrust into my hands our cooking pot, half full of water.

I shall never forget the look on his face as he held the vessel to me. There was something about it, wide-eyed and anxious. "*Shrabt, shrabt,*" he said, very gently. "Drink!" and held the pot while I tilted it to my mouth. There was all manner of filth floating on top of that water; morsels of rice from the dirty pot, strands of hair from the guerba, fragments of dung from the bottom of some well. But the water itself was clear and I could sense the coolness of it even as its level tipped in the cooking pot. It was the most wonderful thing that had happened to me, just seeing it tip, knowing that it was all mine. I sucked at it greedily, and almost passed out with the pain. One of the other men quickly put his arm round my shoulders. I tried again, more carefully, and it oozed down my throat in a fiery trickle. I stood there a long time, drinking in this invalid fashion, until I felt myself swooning and lay down on the ground.

We had been unbelievably lucky. These men were the rearguard of an encampment whose people had set out from the south two or three days before, hoping to find more pasture to the north. Most of them has passed this way before the sandstorm and their tracks were obliterated by the wind. These four had been delayed by the need to round up camels which had strayed over a wide area. They had ridden over the ground where we first saw their tracks some four hours or so before we got there. If they had not been herding a dozen camels, and therefore proceeding more slowly than usual, we would never have caught them.

We made a fire of dung and brewed unsweetened tea, and they talked with ould Mohammed while I lay prostrate in a daze. My companion's capacity for revival seemed far greater than mine. He was sitting up, gesturing grandly, recounting our adventures. I got up and walked away from him, suddenly wanting to be alone. How very, very fortunate I was and how very beautiful living was. What were all my people doing this Saturday afternoon in February? I stood with them there for quite a long time, until calm returned and I was just gazing at the shadows of cloud across sand.

After a while the men left us, having transferred half a skinful of their own precious water to one of our guerbas. We would have to be careful with it, but it should see us through to safety. They had suggested that our best course was to make for the well of In Emsal, only a mile or two outside the oasis of Aguelhok on the highway. Still having no exact idea of our position, I had got one of them to point the direction to me, while I took a bearing along his outstretched arm. We therefore started riding at 55° but, after an hour or so, ould Mohammed announced that we must go due north.

I was prepared to concede his superiority as a tracker, but nothing more, and I very roughly told him to shut up and keep moving. At once we flamed up into a raging argument. We were both badly overstrung by what had happened to us and needed to work out our pent-up emotions on the other. Our shoutings died down and we plodded on in disagreeable silence.

I knew what I was looking for. The chart showed that there was a ridge of rocks running alongside the highway. As soon as that appeared on the horizon, sanctuary would not be far away. The men had said we ought to reach In Emsal sometime the next morning, but I warily accepted the prospect of not refilling our guerbas until late the next day.

The sun was beginning to set when we rode out of the sand sea and onto a gravel plain. At the far side of it there were many trees, and as soon as we reached them we camped for the night. It was an eerie place after the barren emptiness of the sand. It represented life, for many of the trees were in leaf, and our camels would eat well for the first time in several days. But it was deserted, nothing at all stirred in it, as though all life had fled. That night I knew that I wanted more than anything else to go home, to get away from all this. It would be very easy to pick up a truck going north along the highway and I would be in Algiers a few days later, back in London within the week. But that would be too chicken for words. I *must* get to Tamanrasset, even if I could manage nothing more. Maybe I would go on from there. Maybe I wouldn't.

We set off early on Sunday, ould Mohammed cocky again, myself cautious. I judged that we would probably reach the well or Aguelhok itself within four or five hours, but he was confident that we would be there in two. In little more than an hour I saw the low range of hills I had been seeking. We reached the top of the rocky ridge and there, below us, was a broad swathe of vehicle tracks. It didn't look like a highway to me and it seemed probable that the main route ran parallel to it, on the other side of more trees which grew beyond. But there could be no doubt at all that we were not far from our goal.

I explained to ould Mohammed what our position seemed to be and he agreed that we would do well to follow the vehicle tracks to the north. We had been riding along them for no more than twenty minutes when he pointed to the ridge on our left, said he had seen a man up there, and started off in that direction. I followed him and caught him up on the ridge. There was no one in sight. Suddenly ould Mohammed hit his beast into a gallop and raced off down the hill, heading back into the open desert. I raced after him and only halted him by barging my camel across the path of his. We had another raging argument.

It struck me that ould Mohammed had perhaps gone crazy. He had, after all, eaten little for two or three days and he was badly dehydrated. I handed him the last of our water and he drank it thirstily. I tried to reason with him gently, as though he were a child. For a moment his mad resolution seemed to weaken, then he flung out an arm again. "Look," he shouted, "there's the town." I told him there was nothing to be seen but the trees through which we had ridden that morning, and once more he raged at me. I knew I was very near the end of my tether. There was no anger or resentment left. It was without any feeling at all that I told ould Mohammed, "You go that way if you want, but I'm going to the road." He was silent for a moment. Then he told me to stay in the shadow of a tree for half an hour, no more. If he hadn't found the well by then, he would come back with me to the highway. Then he galloped off.

I sat with my back against the trunk of a thorn tree and watched his figure dwindle in the distance. He started by riding to the west, but then swerved to the north. After that I lost him among the vegetation. My mind whirled with anxiety. I ought to have prevented him riding back suicidally into the desert, but I couldn't see how. I began to work out a plan, in case he didn't return. I would stay put until late afternoon, for another two and a half hours, by which time the day would be cooling off. I would then ride east until I struck the highway, and there I would rest until first light.

The time passed very slowly. My white bull was restless, refusing to couch for more than a few minutes, so that I had to get up at intervals and bring him back to my tree. I was consciously holding down a lid on my fear. Suddenly, I heard an old familiar sound which had been missing from my life for the past three months, the roaring whistle of a jet aircraft. I looked up as it passed overhead. Ironically, it was a comfort more than a distress to visualize the super-civilized ease of the people sitting up there, at a moment when I was weighing up my chances of utterly basic survival.

It was three o'clock, and ould Mohammed had been away for nearly two hours, when I saw his figure galloping back. He must have been less than a hundred yards away, and I still motionless against my tree trunk, when I realized that there was a guerba, a full guerba, behind him athwart the saddle. The bloody man had found the well.

He leaped down, gabbling triumphant phrases that I couldn't take in. I got myself up and staggered over to where he was untying the waterskin. I hugged him. "Sorry, sorry," I said. "You were right and I was wrong." He looked embarrassed and made a great fuss of urging me to drink. In the next few minutes, I gulped about four pints, and the pain of drinking didn't matter any more. After that we made a fire and brewed some tea, while he told me about In Emsal. It was not far, he said, and some Tuareg were camped there. He had dumped the baggage, watered himself and his camel, filled the guerba and come racing back.

We rode very slowly the way he had come, into trees that became fuller and thicker with leaves than any I had seen for a long time. A couple of men rose to greet us as we arrived in the clearing where the wellhead was. Here was life again. Some goats were foraging among the trees, standing with their forelegs high up the trunks, while they snatched and nibbled at the lowest leaves. Birds were skimming through the air and strutting over the ground; a kind of guinea fowl and something like a large blackbird, with a dark green body and a ruddy underside. Water, probably enough water to last me to the end of my days, was being sloshed extravagantly from buckets into troughs for the camels. I emptied another canteen-full down my throat. Then I collapsed in a heap.

OULD MOHAMMED'S recuperation was much swifter than mine. After resting for an hour or so, he suggested riding into Aguelhok to buy badly needed provisions. He would, he said, be back before nightfall. Meanwhile, I lay for a long time flowing in and out of sleep, not thinking very clearly about anything, not even conscious of any vast relief that I was safe. My only movements were to reach for my water bottle and pour the contents down. Each time, within half an hour, I was conscious of raging thirst again. I was dehydrated and the tissues of my body, gradually shrunken since Anechag, had to be slaked. Gradually the sun disappeared and the night settled down. I was half-asleep wondering vaguely whether my companion had run into trouble, when I started at the sound of an engine. Sitting up, I could see two beams of light fingering the sky, dipping and rising, coming towards us. Slowly I rose to my feet, my guts tightening with anticipation.

The vehicle stopped about fifty yards away and I could hear voices talking loudly above the rumble of the engine. Its headlights still glared so powerfully into my face that I could see nothing of the men in the vehicle, whose outline suggested a Jeep. And then, from the blinding light, four soldiers slowly emerged. Each carried an automatic rifle. They stopped about five yards away. I stood perfectly still, waiting for the next move.

An officer appeared, a Negro from the south, with three deep tribal scars cut on each cheek. I greeted him and asked him what the trouble was. There was no trouble, he said, very shortly. Were all these things mine, he asked, indicating the baggage strewn round the tree. They were, I said.

He gave an order and three of the soldiers stepped forward and started to gather my things together. I bent down to pick up my money belt and one rushed forward and jabbed the muzzle of his gun into my side. I gasped with pain and all but overbalanced. The officer asked me what was in the belt and, when I told him, he picked it up and held on to it. My other possessions were pitched into the open Jeep. It was only then that I saw ould Mohammed sitting on the vehicle's floor. He said not a word as I climbed in. The soldiers sat balancing on the sides of the Jeep as we drove off. After what I had recently been through, I was now tense more at the prospect of something awful happening accidentally than anything else.

At a settlement of mud buildings we headed for a gateway lit by a solitary arc lamp. The Commandant of Aguelhok, tall and elegant in khaki drills and sweater, stood there waiting for us, an Alsatian dog at his side. I was marched in close order behind him to his office. I got a push in the back as I crossed the threshold, but the Commandant himself was very correct. He indicated a seat opposite him. The officer who had captured me made his report and the Commandant asked me what I was doing in the desert. I told him, then suggested he should look at my passport and, most particularly, at the photostat of the letter from Paris to M. Bagayoko. It was extracted from my money belt and the Commandant read it carefully. The soldiers, all this time, had been gathered close around me, as though ready to pounce. But now the Commandant made a dismissive gesture and their bodies relaxed with—was I imagining it?—a suggestion of disappointment.

The Commandant apologized to me for the trouble I had been caused. If there was anything he could do for me, he was at my disposal. Evidently ould Mohammed had been hauled into the barracks after being seen to spend much money in the store. When questioned by the military, the ass had spun a story about my being a wealthy Arab. It was small wonder that the troops had been sent to bring in such a suspicious-sounding prisoner, especially as there was clearly great hostility between the Black African government and the Tuareg tribes. There was, I said, one thing the Commandant could do for me. He could write a letter to his colleague commanding the Tessalit garrison, explaining the position, so that I might avoid a repetition of this misunderstanding. He did this at once, then ordered his man to take my baggage down to a house where my companion and I might lodge for the night.

My camel was brought in to Anguelhok at first light the following day, but we did not leave until the afternoon. Ould Mohammed kept disappearing to drink tea with different people, and I sat for hours against the wall of the store, somewhere between a dazed lethargy and the old tension of wanting to be on my way. A truck was being loaded ready to start the journey to Algeria. Three young French students were waiting to go with it. They expected to be in Marseilles in four days, home in Paris within six. I so much wanted to travel with them, but I knew that I wouldn't. I had to go back into the desert on a camel, or waste everything I had so far done. I now knew precisely what the most fearful thing consisted of: it was fear of encounter with a person, with a task, with anything at all intimidating that might cross my path. If I could go into the desert again to face what I knew to be there, I could walk forward for the rest of my life into all the deserts of my mind.

My determination faltered once or twice again during the three-day journey up the highway to Tessalit, as ould Mohammed was still incorrigibly negligent. When we came to move on after a midday camp, I found that a guerba which had been left hanging almost full in a tree was more than half-empty because he had failed to secure the neck properly. Then my white bull went lame, his left forepad cut by a stone. Ould Mohammed said that the beast could still carry me, but the animal limped so badly under my weight that I decided to walk instead. He continued to ride the brown, berating me loftily for my slowness on foot.

I was in no great shape myself. At the first camp we made after the oasis, I was violently sick in the night, with abdominal pains. It was several days before my intestines recovered their old equilibrium, which was based upon a dosage of drugs that would have dismayed any general practitioner. The heat, too, seemed to have reached new heights. Where the skin was exposed to the direct rays of the sun, it felt as though a burning glass were being held over it. I was drinking more copiously than ever before, but at least, for the present, there was no danger of going dry again, and our progress was soothed by the healthiest sound in the world, the swish-slosh of filled guerbas swinging on either side of the saddles.

Thus we came to the last outpost of Mali. The highway curved into a gully lined with palms. Beyond was a spread of mud buildings. The Commandant of Tessalit received me cautiously, but after reading the letter from Aguelhok treated me as though I were a kinsman of M. Bagayoko himself.

Next day, two white bulls were mustered for my approval, to replace those I had brought, but they were miserable beasts. Their bones jutted sharply, one of them had broken teeth, and both looked worn by the effects of the drought. The Commandant apologized that there was nothing better to be found and suggested that, tired as my own beasts were, it would be safest if I continued to Tamanrasset with them, together with these new specimens. With four camels I should be able to spread loads thinly. There seemed no alternative to this plan, so I accepted it.

The arrangement provoked a final contretemps with ould

Mohammed. I had made the mistake of telling him that I would give him one of my old camels in addition to his outstanding wages. Now I had to inform him that the camel would be continuing with me. He did not fly into a rage when I broke the unwelcome news. Much worse, he became a cringing beggar, who laid his hand upon my arm and told me pitifully that I had dealt him a grievous blow. I hardly thought so, for he had just collected 70,000 francs from me, which represented wages plus a bonus in place of the camel.

For all my gratitude at his finding the well the previous Sunday, I was profoundly relieved to see the last of him. When he asked me to write him a letter of recommendation to any other Nasrani who might seek his employment, I carefully issued a warning to whomsoever the letter might concern, that they travelled with ould Mohammed entirely at their own risk. I would have liked to believe I was writing without malice; but I doubted it.

Chapter Six

Ibrahim Ag Sowanaki had been found for me by the Commandant with the same sense of urgency that had produced the two camels. At twenty-seven he was much younger than most of those I had travelled with. He had a wife and three children, four camels of his own, and a small garden in which he grew vegetables for the garrison. He was a tall, handsome man with aquiline features, the steadiest pair of eyes I had seen and a mouth that might curl in scorn but never, I guessed, shift at opportunity. I was immediately taken by him, although he was a Tuareg and communication with him would be difficult, for his own language was Tamachek, of which I knew nothing. At the outset, we had no more than a couple of hundred words in common, a dash of Arabic seasoned with a pinch of French. Yet I had no doubt that we would get on well together. On this journey, my first impressions had often been unsound: my first snap judgment of Ibrahim Ag Sowanaki, however, turned out to be faultlessly accurate.

Apart from new camels and fresh provisions, it was also

necessary to obtain more equipment in Tessalit. With luck, we might reach Tamanrasset in three weeks, and in the last few days before getting there we would pass through two small oases. Up to that point, however, there were but three wells available and one of these was rumoured to be dry. This time, therefore, I would travel with six guerbas, instead of four, and I also obtained a special pack saddle on which one camel could bear water and baggage, but no rider. My companion introduced a novel item of his own, a great broadsword which he strapped to his belt.

We set off on February 16, late in the afternoon. As our tiny caravan padded away between the buildings, a raggle-taggle of soldiery bobbed alongside, advising and joking and wishing us well. We were heading for the miniature mountains, a mixture of black rocky ridges and piles of shale, which I could now see crammed close together away to the northeast. For a day or two there would be no problem with navigation, because a dusty track led through these rocks as far as the Algerian border camp of Timeiaouine, and Ibrahim had traversed it once or twice. Beyond that he had never been, but I foresaw far less difficulty in finding our way than I had experienced in riding from Tombouctou. The charts showed a great deal of high ground between here and Tamanrasset, the bulk of it inclined on almost exactly the bearing we needed to follow ourselves. The one over-riding need for absolute precision would be, as always, in the location of those precious wells.

We made our camp a couple of hours after leaving the oasis. I was again very ill that night. When Ibrahim returned from hobbling the camels he looked gloomy. Three of them, he said, were so feeble that he did not believe they would reach Tamanrasset. If we were to have a reasonable chance of getting through we would have to walk.

Riding would, in any case, have been out of the question next morning, for we were threading our way through a very narrow passage between enormous black boulders. We negotiated gulleys without number, some of them so strewn with rubble that we had to unhitch the camels and lead them one by one up or down these obstacles. It was punishing work in the great heat that flared out of those rocks. They emitted a metallic smell much like that of a clean oven which has been burning for hours. After the midday camp we came out onto a gravel plain. I was badly spent by nightfall and my feet had become very sore. The sand here was coarse and easily worked inside the rotting canvas of my plimsolls. The white bull from Tombouctou, on the other hand, was by then limping much less severely. Ibrahim had relieved its cut pad by rubbing in rock salt as an antiseptic and then packing the wound with fragments of its own wool, which he had chewed up into a dressing. Throughout the day he had been watchfully checking each camel in turn, to see that ropes did not chafe, that loads were evenly balanced; and twice during the midday camp he had got up to examine the guerbas, to see whether any had sprung a leak. Not even Sid' Ahmed had shown such care over detail.

Our second full day out of Tessalit saw us start with fingers numbed by cold, yet within two hours I was trailing a good hundred yards behind the train, my energy draining fast again in the overpowering heat. Wryly I compared myself with the man who three months before had been impatiently driving Mohamed and Sidi Mahmoud out of their lethargy. I was now very thankful indeed to rest at any excuse. The worst moment in every day came after the midday camp when, already dog-tired, one faced the effort of loading up, with nothing to look forward to but four hours of slog. That afternoon, I began to trip and fall down again, so that when Ibrahim suggested I ride for a little while, I gratefully mounted the stronger of the two Tessalit beasts. I rode for an hour, but had to dismount three times to squat. After dark that day, when I had recovered some strength, I weighed up my chances of getting through to Murzuk before the weather made further progress impossible. I no longer thought of reaching the Nile.

We marched into Timeiaouine next morning. There were watchtowers manned by sentries above its gateway, there was a military bustle of soldiers inside the square, while outside the walls twenty or thirty army camels, magnificent beasts, were crouched in lines upon the sand. At our coming, a squad of troops emerged and crowded round us, but I had no cause for alarm here.

Armed with a letter of introduction from the Algerian Ambassador in London, I was given a royal meal by the commander of the fort, who seemed even more sceptical than I was about my chances of reaching Libya. He told me that within a week or two it would be far too hot to travel. "You'll see," he said. "March is a killer in the desert."

We walked on. We walked through a series of bitterly cold starts to each day which were swiftly overtaken by heat that did not cease to scorch the flesh until the sun was sliding out of the sky to the west. Each day I was tottering badly towards the end, far behind Ibrahim so that he had the camels half-unloaded by the time I caught him up at the place where we would camp for the night.

On the evening of the sixth day out of Tessalit, we descended a ridge into the first area of grazing we had seen apart from Timeiaouine. Ibrahim had taken to leaving his broadsword lashed to a saddle, and he now stopped to buckle it to his belt. I wondered whether he expected hostility, but was told that a Tuareg must be properly dressed when he met strangers, the sword being regarded as a symbol of manhood more than a potential weapon. We had made our camp under a high dune when three men appeared, bringing to our fire small bundles of kindling, which they offered like posies, as a gesture of friendship. Ibrahim said they had a few sheep and were willing to sell one if we wished. He slaughtered the lamb they fetched, with the Bowie-knife I had brought from England. As he cleaned it in the sand afterwards, he examined its blade with approval. "It's a fine knife, this," he said. That was the only time he came anywhere near asking for anything beyond his wages.

Ibrahim Ag Sowanaki.

We awoke next morning with grit lashing our faces and a screaming wind driving sand in sheets all around. It was patently hopeless to move in such conditions, for we could see no farther than the nearest bush. We munched a few dates and then covered ourselves in blankets.

I fell into a kind of coma, conscious of nothing but the battering, abrasive elements. About noon, Ibrahim, bending over me, shouted that the storm was beginning to slacken.

Laboriously we extracted baggage that had almost vanished under the drifted sand. We roused the camels, all couched nearby with their rumps turned towards the wind, and began to haul them along a track deeply worn by the nomads from whom we had bought the sheep. At the well of Iraldiouine, we carefully filled the six guerbas to their fullest extent. We needed every drop we could carry away with us, for there was but one more well before the small oasis of Silet, and that was the one which by all accounts might now be dry. Then we pressed on for perhaps a couple of miles, until a tree appeared in the thickening haze ahead. The storm was blowing as fiercely as in the morning, so we couched the beasts and started to unload again. We rolled into our blankets once more, and passed more hours sheltering blindly from the blasting of the sand.

Next day dawned cold and clear and a new world lay endlessly ahead. We had thus far been marching close to the rocky massif. But now it curved away to the right, off our direct course, and we were confronted with what looked like an eternal plain. The scale of the panorama reduced two men and four camels to insects creeping forward to a rim of the world that might never be reached. It was appalling: but, at the same time, it was exciting, spellbinding. For over three months I had laboured across the Sahara and there had been few moments when I had experienced its magnetism to which so many men before me had succumbed. But now I began at last to understand its attraction. It was the awful scale of the thing, the fusion of pure elements from the heavens above and the earth beneath, untrammelled by anything contrived by man.

As well as the white bull from Tombouctou, the brown had also now sustained a cut. He was, moreover, perpetually foaming at the mouth. Still, thrice in one day, when we passed solitary clumps of grass, we almost rammed them down the throats of these two animals and the stronger of the Tessalit bulls. The broken-toothed creature we ignored; it had barely bothered to eat even when we came across pasture, and we could not waste sustenance on a camel whose death seemed imminent. We had faced the fact that we would lose camels and we now carefully, brutally planned for their loss. My old riding camel with the cut pad now carried nothing at all on its back, while the broken-toothed bull bore the pack saddle and all the water. As soon as he died, this load would be transferred to the unburdened animal. We were applying the law of the desert. It was a shameful code but only in this fashion would two men survive.

I never doubted that I would survive, although I was fully aware that physically my plight was almost as great as on that awful day when Sid' Ahmed had bullied me into going on. My feet were swelling rapidly, and I was retaining food only by consuming twice the prescribed dose of drugs each day. Perpetually my mouth burned and my throat ached with dryness. I barely noticed the lice that were feasting in abundance upon my scraggy flesh.

One made what mental shifts one could to relieve the staggering tedium of these hours. On this plain lay stones with colours that swirled across the spectrum. Some were translucent white, others a dazzling green, and alongside either you might see a pebble dyed a gaudy red, or stones whose darker patterns had a ceramic quality fired by the terrible heat of the Sahara's summer. These multi-coloured stones helped to fix attention when the head drooped with exhaustion. Many times my mind floundered obsessively around some utterly trivial thing which seemed immensely important. I spent the whole of an afternoon contemplating the cheese and onions that I would cook for myself as soon as I regained my own kitchen. For thirty-six hours I ransacked my head for the name of an undistinguished Australian who had played at fullback for an unexceptional Rugby League club some twenty-five years before.

On February 25, we reached the well of In Azaoua. It was not, in fact, dry; but there was very little water in it. Ibrahim scooped up enough muddy liquid to fill one guerba. The other five were each rather less than half-full. We should have little water left by the time we reached Silet. As we tied the guerba to the pack saddle, a small caravan came into sight: eight camels, heavily loaded, and a small flock of goats, all in the custody of a man, a youth and a tiny boy. They were, they said, travelling from Kidal to Tamanrasset to sell the goats and a cargo of dried meat. We exchanged greetings before Ibrahim and I moved off, leaving the newcomers to extract what water they could from the pitiful well.

Late that afternoon the plain ended at a great barrier of sand. Painfully we toiled up its slope, then across a plateau so soft that the feet submerged ankle deep at every step. Both men and beasts were almost done with exhaustion by the time we came to a hazardous descent on the far side of the plateau. Below stretched a vast basin of sand, with a group of trees in the middle, bounded on the far side by range after range of dunes. It took us half an hour to get ourselves down, but we managed it without accident.

The light was beginning to fade from the sky, and we were camped by the trees, when we saw the caravan descending the plateau in our tracks. The man and the youth led each camel in turn, one on either side of its head, down the slope. The tiny boy scrambled down alone with the goats. He could not have been more than five or six years old, yet he was required to live as a man in conditions from which I, half the time, shrank with faint heart.

The three brought their animals towards our trees, made their camp at a little distance, then came over to share our meal. When

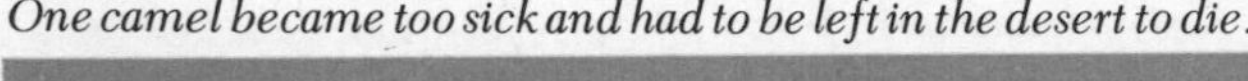

One camel became too sick and had to be left in the desert to die.

they had returned to their blankets, Ibrahim suggested that we start marching again before dawn. The camels, he said, were failing fast, and the stage was not far off when at any camp we made one or more of the camels might not be induced to rise from the ground again. We must therefore extend the distances between our camps.

At a little after three o'clock we prepared to start. Never in my life had I seen the moon looming as large as when it topped the horizon. It seemed to fill a quarter of the heavens, a full circle which itself was encircled by a colossal golden penumbra, a moon from a children's picture book, with the colour of a Gloucester cheese. There was a sleepy farewell salute from the bundle of blankets nearby as we set off. There was not a breath of wind, though it was excessively cold. Had I been snowballing in an English winter, I could scarcely have felt colder. In this condition we attacked the dunes and it was heavy work, the brown bull and the broken-toothed white frequently falling to their knees. Dawn found us on gravel again and all day we plodded on, blistered now as fiercely by the sun as we had been frozen under the moon. My old white was the first camel in line, the two beasts from Tessalit in the middle, the brown bull behind them. I was belabouring them from behind with my riding stick in an effort to keep them going, offering them a pain that might be worse than the awful dragging of their bodies. There was nothing but pain in this desert, for human beings and animals alike. Only in death was there relief.

It was the next day that the brown went down. He had begun to move at an angle to the other three, his head still tethered to the saddle ahead, his rump swinging out to the right, going forward in little rushes each time I clouted his haunch. Then he went down with a thump, breaking the head-rope. Ibrahim stopped the train at my shout and came back to help me get the bull to his feet again. We refastened the broken rope and continued, but almost at once the beast went down again. We raised him once more and something very curious happened. Before we could attach the severed ends of rope, he cantered forward, past the two Tessalit camels, to the beast which had shared the long journey from Tombouctou with him. He rubbed his shoulder against that of the white. Then he turned at a right angle, facing it, and sat down again.

Ibrahim shrugged. "He's finished," he said.

I had been unmoved when one of my camels foundered before. This time I felt sadness hanging like a weight on my throat. The brown bull had been such a gallant animal. He had travelled an intolerable distance to serve my purpose. Now I was abandoning him in the middle of the most barren wilderness we had crossed together, just as the day's heat was beginning to burn. He would be dead by nightfall. As we moved off, the brown bull turned his head slowly to watch our going. Then he turned away again, his back to the sun, his head pointing to the west.

We marched on and by that day's end I wondered how much further I could continue myself. Waves of nausea flowed through my stomach and there was a heavy ache around my kidneys. My left leg had started to drag, so that I was consciously trying to bring it forward with each step. By the time the sun was setting, we had been walking for more than twelve hours. Ibrahim wanted to continue for another two, but I couldn't take any more.

Ibrahim's strength was draining, too. His face was now strained and his lips were grey. Yet not once had he faltered in anything, never had he responded to cross words of mine with anything but his usual calm and careful attention to whatever he was doing.

We started the next day's march in the night again. When dawn came, there were three or four great mountains ahead, all but hull down on the horizon. It was late in the afternoon before we were hard against them, barring our way, perhaps 1,500 feet high. As we made for a gap between them, we saw that the mountain shoulders consisted of colossal black boulders piled on top of each other, some so finely balanced that they looked as if a fingertip would send them crashing down. We could also see that the gap was very narrow indeed, a rubble of boulders which would have offered a decent scramble for an unhindered man.

The camels made it plain that they were unwilling to try it. I hauled hard on the head-rope of the Tombouctou white, while Ibrahim thrashed it from behind with his stick. Weary as the beast was, it kicked viciously, narrowly missing Ibrahim's head. It was otherwise immovable. I tried another tack. Still pulling firmly on the rope, I began to murmur to the camel, as though it were a child. Slowly it started to come forward, roaring and grunting with fear. Then it had to rush down a rock to avoid slipping. Committed, now it came forward in more rushes and careful pauses while it felt nervously for a foothold with a foreleg. Within half an hour I had it through the gap. The broken-toothed beast from Tessalit was persuaded to follow the same way. Only the strongest of the camels refused to budge in response either to beating or gentling. Ibrahim said he would lead it back round the mountain and meet me somewhere on the other side.

A couple of hours later, with the sun almost gone, I saw him emerge far behind me, from the shelter of the hillside. He was not alone. The youth we had first met at In Azaoua was with him, with most of the beasts in the caravan. There was no sign of the man or the small boy. They, he said, were following him somewhere behind, with one camel and the goats. We pressed on in twilight, into rising stony ground. We had been moving for an hour in darkness before we found a clump of trees and stopped. It was only then that Ibrahim told me we had no water left. Nor had the youth, his supplies were on the camel accompanying the father and the child. But they never appeared.

Ibrahim and I set off at dawn. The youth said he would wait for the others to catch up. Presumably they had camped when night fell, not wishing to lose our tracks in the darkness. Our camels were twitching and shaking as we loaded them up, the broken-toothed beast swaying on his feet. God knows how he had got this far, for neither of us had expected it. By the middle of the morning we were beginning to stagger as badly as the beasts and there was no tension on any of the head-ropes, for neither of us had the strength to pull them from the front. We were just managing to walk, and that was all. When Ibrahim said we must ride, I did not even nod. We rode for perhaps an hour, the relief tremendous, towards a full-blooded range of mountains, with Silet somewhere on this side.

We walked again, casually, incapable of anything more as the creeping paralysis of dehydration spread through our limbs. A hot wind flared murderously at us from the west. It was the first day of March now, and the wind already had me within its range.

I became aware of trees somewhere ahead. Then there was a tent. Ibrahim was squatting by it, drinking from a brass bowl. Then a small boy was running towards me, trying not to spill what was in the bowl. The water in it was the colour of diluted blood. This was the most beautiful thing in the world. There was nothing in the world as beautiful as this bowl.

It was a little before two, and for the next three hours we lay inert beneath bushes, drinking water and eating dates. We had been there some time when a blur in the haze behind us was transformed into a group of camels proceeding along our tracks. The youth was mounted on the leading beast, but of the father, the child and the goats there was still no sign. After speaking with the young fellow for a while, Ibrahim told me the others were coming and I relaxed into semi-coma again. As the heat wore out of the day, we thanked the people of the tent for their kindness and moved on, the youth and his camels with us. Within the hour we were in the oasis itself, a sprawling settlement of tents with only a small collection of buildings in the middle. We refilled our guerbas at a watercourse that did service as the well of Silet. In England it would have been called a ditch, a sluggish thing half-choked with weed; but the water itself was clean and sweet. Kneeling by it that evening, as the camels sucked at the surface and shook their jowls around me, it seemed the greatest bounty I had known for a long time. When the beasts were done, we ambled on a little way to make our camp on the far side of the settlement.

Only then did I really begin to worry about the missing pair. Reason told me that the man and the child had water, as well as goats that could give them milk and meat. Our tracks were vivid enough to follow and there had been no wind strong enough to wipe them out. Yet the fact was that they had not now been seen for a day and a half. They could quite easily have had some accident, the father falling from his camel and breaking his leg or worse. That tiny boy, younger than my son Michael, might still be out there alone in that emptiness. Guilt suddenly engulfed me. I should have insisted on staying put this morning, until the others appeared; or I should have insisted that we turn back to look for them.

I tried to sleep. When I awoke, it was long past dawn and the youth had gone, said Ibrahim, to look for the others. I told him to wait until I returned. Then I walked back to the oasis. I remembered seeing a Land-Rover parked outside the buildings in the centre. I found two people in Western dress, agriculturists down from Algiers to advise the local people on planting crops. They watched me keenly as I explained, as best I could, what had happened and where the youth had parted company with the missing pair. A foreman, one of the locals, was summoned and went off to fetch the Land-Rover. I paused, wondering whether I should go with him. One of the officials said, "Thank you. We'll find them." As I shifted, still half-undecided whether to leave, he added, "They're very tough, these people, even the little boys. Tougher than you. . . ." He grinned, disarmingly. "Tougher than me, too."

It was mid-morning when Ibrahim and I set off again, slogging towards the foothills of the Hoggar mountains. By mid-afternoon we were amongst them, creeping up a long hill of slaggy rock whose summit was littered with cairns and grave slabs. How very symbolic, I thought, of what this journey had become. Behind me lay the corpses of two camels that had died on my behalf. Somewhere out there too, in the place whence we came, that small boy might even now be dying in a heap of dust. I was haunted by the chance of tragedy and my own part in its making. I was suddenly, furiously, abysmally certain that I could go no further than Tamanrasset. Under the dreadful, drilling heat of this appalling sun I had become an automaton that marched. I was scarcely recognizable as a human being with the responses that alone distinguished us from the animals. I wondered whether I had forfeited a little of my soul to the desert; maybe the greater part of it.

We camped that night in a grove of trees before one of the most breathtaking views I could remember in many years of roaming the world. Far ahead was the full flourish of the Hoggar, an enormous mountain range of jagged peaks that radiated the light of the setting sun, glowing white against the deep blue sky, formidable in their presence and operatic in their grandeur. I would not reach the Nile now. The Hoggar would be my prize.

We walked down to Abalessa next morning. I had known no oasis more fruitful than this. There were small fields on the outskirts, head-high in crops that were thick and ripening and vividly green. The place was superbly irrigated, with a stream that wound around and between the houses. When we had watered the camels, two of them began to snatch at the abundant leaves. The broken-toothed

The final stage: Ibrahim led the depleted camel train.

bull meandered slowly to the shade of the thickest branches and settled down without a sound. We never got him up again. He could go no further, and we knew it. Ibrahim thought that, sitting in the shade, the bull might last a couple of days. No more.

We rearranged the baggage, discarding some things that were heavy and no longer of importance to us. Then we set out to walk the two-day journey to Tamanrasset.

On Monday, March 5, we came to the most sophisticated thing I had seen since Dakar, the perimeter of Tamanrasset airport. We ignored the warning notices and plodded straight across it. A line of electricity pylons began at the other side and we followed them. The town itself was all but concealed, even at this distance, in a small forest of trees, heavy with leaves.

We walked through the trees and suddenly, I found myself leading two camels and a companion in torn and dusty desert clothes down a surfaced street lined with trees, whitewashed half-way up their trunks. Inside the lines of trees were pavements. There were tables set out at intervals along these pavements and people were sitting at them, drinking coffee. I walked on, not daring to speak to any of them, not at all sure where I was going, or what I was seeking. Towards the end of the street, I noticed a long low building with a courtyard and a crude sign which called it an hotel. In a reflex from a world apart from the one I had just crossed, I stopped and couched the camels.

It was not the ending I had wished.

I SPENT MOST of the next ten days lying on a bed in the Tin-Hinan Hotel, trying to gather enough strength to face the journey home to England. At first I could do little but raise myself from my bed to eat meals. I walked unsteadily to the post office, crowded with tourists, and after half an hour there I was reeling with faintness. I wrote out a cable to tell everybody at home of my presence here and my failure to go further. I was reluctant to go back as a defeated man, and I was nervous of the world to which I must return, even though the memory and the promise of this had strengthened me more than anything else in the previous four months. I had no wish at all, for the moment, to speak with people who shared my own natural ways. They would ask questions about the desert and I did not want to talk of it just yet. So I shut myself in my room and, instead of drinking coffee upon the shaded pavements, I opened the tassoufra and ate a few nuts and dates alone.

Listlessly, I worked out the navigational details of my journey. I measured the distance between the places where I had camped each night. They totalled 1,857 miles and, allowing for the fact that my companions and I had not often moved in straight lines, it meant that I had probably travelled some 2,000 miles. Since Tessalit, Ibrahim and I had come 373 miles and, apart from two brief periods of riding, we had walked every inch of the way. At least, I thought, I had not given up too easily.

The Tin-Hinan Hotel was a refuge well appointed by whoever had built it, though its comforts were somewhat reduced by the time I got there. Tamanrasset was suffering a water shortage, and it was two days before I was able to wash. Then it was only possible in the municipal steam baths, where a black man and I hove

buckets of warm water over each other with childish abandon. The only other occupants of that moist and sombre cavern were lean and straggle-haired youths from Europe and America, the itinerant residue of what was once identified as the hippie culture.

Ibrahim, suspicious of the Tin-Hinan, had preferred to seek lodgings with a distant kinsman of his in town. He came to my room each day to see how I was faring and to report his progress in selling the two camels. He obtained a very decent price for them in the end, considering their condition. I told him to keep the money. It was his by right. From the beginning he had attended to the animals with the care of a mother for her children and it was no fault of his that two had died. I owed him a great deal more than anything I could give him.

I kept my own saddle, the tassoufra, the satchel in which were stored the tea things, a couple of the guerbas and the bucket. The rest of our equipment and what remained of our stores I handed over to him. When I put my Sheffield Bowie into his hands his eyes widened with pleasure. He reached for his belt and loosened his short Tuareg knife. I must, he said, take that in exchange; my son might like it. He incised his own name upon the blade, and we were very pleased together.

Ibrahim would make his way home with a military patrol which was crossing the desert in vehicles, travelling to the Algerian border post of Bordj Moktar on the other Saharan highway where he would have no difficulty in finding a truck to carry him the last miles down to Tessalit. He would be home within a few days. If I ever came back to the desert and wanted to continue my journey, he said, I must seek him out and we would travel much farther next time. We would, I agreed; we would do that. Then we hugged each other farewell. It was the first time we had touched, and there was much warmth in our embrace.

There was one more thing I wished to do before I took flight to Algiers and then to England. I wanted to see the two camels that had been mine, and their new owners. Next day, I walked down to the place where camels were bought and sold. But there was no sign of mine.

5 March 1973. Journey's End.

As I went back up the main street, I saw a familiar figure sitting at a table. It was the agriculturist from Silet, whose assistance I had sought for the missing man and child. He had almost forgotten about that matter, he said. But, yes, the two were safe. The Land-Rover hadn't found them, but they had walked into Silet the day after I left, having spent the previous two nights with some nomads they had met. They should be in Tamanrasset in a few more days.

He chatted on, affably, but I was not really listening. My mind was absent with relief. At least I could go home without a conscience haunted by the spectre of betrayal.

I said good-bye to him, feeling empty as I paused for a moment, and took a last look round. I knew I could not go on. I must return to my own people. Only with them could I replenish what had been poured out of me in the ride across Mauritania, in the collapse before Tombouctou, in the sandstorms near the well of Asler, and in the long march with Ibrahim.

I started down the street again to begin my journey home. I had made a kind of peace with myself. The rest of it would have to come slowly, in whatever lay ahead.

Geoffrey Moorhouse

For six months after his return to civilization Geoffrey Moorhouse wrote nothing. Not only was he emotionally stunned by his experiences in the desert but he was also desperately ill – suffering from amoebic dysentery. And also from a sense of shame that afflicts him even now – the feeling that, if only he had pushed himself a little harder, he could have gone farther. That he would almost certainly have died had he done so is beside the point: his sense of shame remains.

And this perhaps provides a significant clue to the man himself – half starry-eyed romantic, half stern realist. A man whose childhood heroes were adventurers like Lawrence of Arabia and the great Victorian writer-explorer, Sir Richard Burton, a man who himself set forth on one of the great romantic enterprises of recent times. And at the same time a man who returns to write of his remarkable exploits strictly in terms of discomfort, unheroic endurance, and ultimately even a personal sense of failure.

Geoffrey Moorhouse is now forty-one years old, a much-travelled journalist, his reputation as an author firmly established. People are important to him – though his marriage has failed, his close involvement with his family remains of prime importance. He sets himself exacting standards. He wonders now if Burton, in his private diaries, ever descended to "the trivia that adorn my own notebooks" Yet Burton was a fallible human being; one can be sure that his diaries were a true reflection of that humanity, just as Moorhouse's are. One can also be sure that the courageous man who first opened the dark continent of Africa to Western eyes would recognize in Moorhouse a kindred spirit, someone very like himself, driven to explore the farthest limits of man's capacity to endure.

PIED PIPER
Nevil Shute

A CLASSIC OF OUR TIME

PIED PIPER

ondensation of the book by

Nevil Shute

strated by Jim Russell
blished by Heinemann, London

PIED PIPER———

First there were Ronald and Sheila: British children, at least they were obedient and well brought-up. Then there was Rose: well, she was peasant-French and capable, old for her ten years. Later there would be Pierre, and later still the Dutch boy called Willem. By the time the Polish boy, Marjan, had joined his group the old man was almost past counting.

Possibly he'd been foolish. Possibly the May of that particular year—1940—had been an unwise time to take a fishing holiday in France. It wasn't even as if he was particularly good with children: his own son's childhood was far in the past and that was anyway a time it pained him now to think about.

Still, there he was and there the children were, in a country ravaged by an invading army. And though he might be old he was by no means doddering. Possibly the chance to be of use again was just what he needed. . . .

Chapter One

His name was John Sidney Howard, a retired country solicitor, and he was a member of my club in London.

I came in for dinner that night at about eight o'clock, slung my gas-mask onto a peg, unbuckled my revolver-belt and hung it up, and crowned the lot with my naval cap. I strolled over to the tape and studied the latest news. It was neither good nor bad, much as it had been for three months, since France was overrun.

When I had finished dinner, I went upstairs to the smoking-room and ordered coffee. In a few minutes there was a step beside me and Howard, a tall, emaciated man of about seventy, lowered himself into a chair near me. A boy, unasked, brought him coffee and brandy.

Presently he spoke. "It really is a most extraordinary thing that you can't get a decent cup of coffee in this country."

I said: "A chap who deals in coffee once told me that ground coffee won't keep in our climate. It's the humidity, or something."

"Ground coffee goes off in any climate," he said dogmatically.

He went on talking about coffee and things like that for a time. Then we talked about fishing. It was a perfect godsend to find someone who could talk of other things beside the war. He was an ardent fisherman, and I have fished a little.

When he spoke of fishing and of France, it put me in mind of an experience of my own. "I saw some chaps in France doing a damn funny sort of fly-fishing," I said. "They had a great bamboo pole about twenty-five feet long with the line tied on the end of it—no reel. They used wet flies, and trailed them about in rough water."

He smiled. "Where did you see them fishing like that?"

"In the Jura," I said. "Practically in Switzerland."

He smiled reflectively. "I know that country very well—very well indeed," he said. He was silent for a few moments. Presently he said: "I wanted to try that wet fly-fishing in those streams this summer. It's not bad fun, you know."

"It'll be some time before we can go fishing out there again," I said. So it was I who turned the conversation to the war.

He said: "Yes—it's a very great pity. I had to come away before the water was fit to fish. It's not much good out there before the very end of May."

I turned my head. "You went out there this year?" Because the end of May that he had spoken of so casually was the time when the Germans had been pouring into France through Holland and Belgium, when we had been retreating on Dunkirk and when the French were being driven back to Paris and beyond.

He said: "I went out there in April. I meant to stay for the whole of the summer, but I had to come away."

I stared at him, smiling a little. "Have any difficulty in getting home?"

"No," he said. "Not really."

"When did you leave the Jura, then?" I asked.

He thought for a minute. "June the eleventh, I think," he said.

I wrinkled my brows in perplexity. "Were the trains all right?"

He smiled. "They weren't very good," he said reflectively.

"How did you get along then?"

He said: "I walked a good deal of the way."

As he spoke, there was a measured *crump . . . crump . . . crump . . .* as a stick of bombs fell, possibly a mile away. Then came the wail of the sirens.

"Damn and blast," I said. "What do we do now?"

The old man smiled patiently: "I'm going to stay where I am."

There was good sense in that. It's silly to be a hero to evade discomfort, but there were three very solid floors above us.

It was about half-past ten. Howard asked me: "How long do you suppose we shall have to sit here?"

"Till it's over, I suppose. The last raid went on for four hours."

Howard lifted up his glass and held it to the light, then remarked: "Well, there are less comfortable ways of passing a raid."

"True enough. You said you were in France when all this started up. Did you come in for many air raids there?"

"Not real raids. There was some bombing and machine-gunning of the roads, but nothing very terrible."

He spoke so quietly about it that it took a little time for me to realize what he had said. But then I ventured: "It was a bit optimistic to go to France for a quiet fishing holiday in April of this year."

"Well, I suppose it was," he replied thoughtfully.

HE SAID HE HAD BEEN very restless, that he had suffered from an urge to get away and to go and do something different. He was a little hesitant about his reasons, but then he told me that he hadn't been able to get a job to do in the war.

He was living in the country when the war broke out. His married daughter had come back from America to stay with him, bringing her little boy. She was married to a New York insurance man called Costello, vice-president of his corporation and very comfortably off.

Then war broke out, and Costello cabled for them to go back to Long Island. They went, and Howard was left to live alone with occasional visits from his son John, a Squadron-Leader in Bomber Command.

It was lonely for the old man, of course. Then, at the beginning of March, something happened that made a great change in his life. He didn't tell me what it was.

After that, he shut up his country house and came to London, living mostly at the club. For two or three weeks he was busy enough, but after that time started to lie heavy on his hands. And still he could get nothing to do in the war.

It was spring by then. Each day he went for a walk in Hyde Park and Kensington Gardens, and watched the crocuses as they came out, and the daffodils. As the sun grew stronger, the urge came on him to get away from England altogether for a while. There didn't seem to be any great reason why he should remain in England. It was then that he began to think about the Jura. Matters in France were quite normal, as there seemed to be a stalemate on the Western Front.

If he went out there he would be just in time to see the flowers come thrusting through the snow; if he stayed on for a month or two he would come in for the fishing. He looked forward very much to fishing in those mountain streams.

He wanted to see as much of the spring as he could. He wanted to see all that new life coming on, replacing what was past, because of what had happened.

He had much less difficulty in getting to France than he had expected. He left London on the morning of April 10th. He got on the crowded steamer in Folkestone harbour at about eleven in the morning, and there they sat till the late afternoon. Nobody could tell them what they were stopping for, although it was a pretty safe guess that it was a submarine.

At about four o'clock there were a number of explosions out at sea, and soon after that they cast off and got away.

It was after one o'clock when they finally got to Paris. Howard went to the Hotel Girodet, just off the Champs Elysées, that he had stayed at before, and went on next day towards the Jura. He was feeling a little shaky after the fatigue of the crossing, so that day he only went as far as Dijon. Next day, he felt very well and took the afternoon train on into the Jura. The train got to Saint-Claude at dusk. He had sent a telegram from Dijon to the hotel at Cidoton asking them to meet him, and the hotel car was waiting, a ten-year-old Chrysler driven by the *concierge*. He took the old man's bags and they started off for Cidoton.

It was dark when they drew up at the hotel. Howard went slowly up the stone steps, pushed open the heavy oak door and went into the hall. The side door leading into the *estaminet* flew open, and there was Madame Lucard, buxom and cheerful as ever, with the children round her and the maids grinning at him.

They gave him a vociferous French welcome, chattering at him nineteen to the dozen. He would take a little glass of Pernod?

And then, Monsieur his son, he was well too?

Well, they had to know. He turned away blindly. "Madame," he said, "my son John is dead. He crashed in his aeroplane, over the Heligoland Bight."

Chapter Two

Cidoton is a tiny hamlet—fifteen or twenty cottages, no more. The hotel is the only house of any size in the place. It has about fifteen bedrooms, and in the season it's a ski-ing centre. The hills sweep down to it all round, fine slopes of pasture dotted here and there with pinewoods.

Howard settled down at Cidoton. The mountain air did him a world of good; reviving his appetite and bringing him restful sleep at night. But he was not happy. While the snow lasted, the slopes were haunted for him by the memory of seeing John come hurtling over the brow. Sometimes the fair-haired French girl, Nicole, who came from Chartres, seemed to be with him, flying along with him in the same flurry of snow.

Presently as the sun grew stronger, the snow went away. Then flowers began to appear and his walks had a new interest. He grew much more settled as the spring drew on.

Mrs. Cavanagh helped him, too, though at first he had been worried and annoyed to find an Englishwoman staying in the hotel, so far from the tourist track. He had not come to France to speak English or to think in English. For the first week he sedulously avoided her, together with her two children.

Cavanagh was an official in the League of Nations at Geneva. He was fearful of an invasion of Switzerland by the Germans, and had sent his wife and children into Allied France. Each weekend he motored across the border to visit them, a sandy-haired, worried-looking man of forty-five or so.

The second weekend he came, Howard had a talk with him. He appeared to be oddly unpractical. He was devoted to the League of Nations even in this time of war.

"A lot of people say that the League has been a failure," he explained. "Now, I think that is very unfair. If you look at the record of that last twenty years. . . ." And so on.

Howard came to the conclusion that Mr. Cavanagh was a tedious fellow. The extent of his sincerity was not made plain to Howard till the day he met Mrs. Cavanagh in the woods, and walked back to the hotel with her.

He found her a devoted echo of her man. "Eustace would never leave the League," she said. "Even if the Germans were to enter Switzerland, he'd never leave Geneva. There's still such great work to be done." She paused, and then she said: "That's why he sent me and the children into France. It's only just for a few weeks, until the situation clears a little," she said placidly. "Then we shall be able to go back."

After that they often passed a word or two together, and he fell into the habit of drinking coffee with her each evening after dinner. He got to know the children too. Ronald was a dark-haired little boy of eight. He was mechanical, and his toy train littered the floor of the salon with its tin lines. Sheila was just five. For the moment her life was filled with a passion for coloured chalks, and once Howard drew for her the little pig that went to market.

He would have liked to have got to know the children better, but he was shy, with the diffidence of age. One day he watched them while they played among the pine trees. It seemed that they wanted to play a game they called *attention* which demanded a whistle, and they had no whistle.

The little boy said: "I can whistle with my mouth," and proceeded to demonstrate. His sister pursed up her lips and produced only a wet splutter. From his deck-chair the old man spoke suddenly.

"I'll make you a whistle, if you like," he said.

They were silent, staring at him doubtfully.

"I'll make you one out of a bit of that hazel bush."

They stared at him, incredulous. He got up from his chair and cut a twig from the bush. "Like this."

He sat down again, and began to fashion a whistle with his penknife. The children watched his slow, wrinkled fingers, as he stripped the bark from the twig, cut deftly with the knife, and bound the bark back into place. He put it to his lips, and it gave out a shrill note. He gave it to the little girl. "You can whistle with your mouth," he said to Ronald, "but she can't."

"Will you make me one tomorrow?"

"All right, I'll make you one tomorrow." They went off together, and whistled all over the hotel till the bark crushed beneath the grip of a hot hand. But the whistle was still good for taking to bed.

"It was so very kind of you to make that whistle for the children," Mrs. Cavanagh said that evening. "They were simply thrilled."

"Children always like a whistle, especially if they see it made," the old man said. "I promised Ronald that I'd make him one tomorrow."

Tomorrow was May 10th. As the old man sat in his deck-chair beneath the trees carving a whistle for Ronald, German troops were pouring into Holland. The Dutch Air Force was flinging its full strength of forty fighting planes against the Luftwaffe. In Cidoton the only radio happened to be switched off, and so Howard whittled at his hazel twig in peace.

It did not break his peace much when they switched it on. In Cidoton the war seemed very far away. He listened to the news from time to time in a detached manner. He got his first great shock when Leopold, King of the Belgians, laid down his arms on May 29th.

But on that day nothing could upset him for very long. He was going fishing for the first time next morning, and the evening was occupied in sorting out his gear, soaking his casts and selecting flies. He walked six miles next day and caught three blue trout. He got back tired and happy at about six o'clock, had dinner and went up immediately to bed. In that way he missed the first news of the evacuation of Dunkirk.

Next day he was jerked finally from his complacence. He sat by the radio in the *estaminet* for most of the day, distressed and worried. The retreat from the beaches stirred him as nothing had for months; for the first time he began to feel a desire to return to England. He wanted to be in the thick of things again.

By June 4th the last forces had left Dunkirk, and Howard had made up his mind. He admitted as much that night to Mrs. Cavanagh. "I don't like the look of things at all," he said. "I think I shall go home. I should be in my own country."

She looked at him, startled. "But surely, you're not afraid that the Germans will come here, Mr. Howard?"

"No," he said, "they won't get much farther than they are now. But at the same time, I think I shall go home."

She knitted on quietly. "I shall miss having you to talk to in the evenings," she said. "The children will miss you, too."

"I shall miss them," he said.

He gave a week's notice to Madame Lucard that night and planned to leave on the eleventh. On June 9th Cavanagh appeared unexpectedly from Geneva. He seemed more distrait than usual, and vanished into the bedroom with his wife.

An hour later he tapped upon the door of Howard's bedroom. "May I come in?" he said.

"By all means. Won't you sit down?"

The other sat down diffidently. "I hear you're going home?" he said.

"Yes. I feel that at a time like this my place is in England."

There was a short silence. Then Cavanagh said: "In Geneva we think that Switzerland will be invaded."

Howard looked at him with interest. "Do you now! If that happened, what would you do?"

Cavanagh got up and walked over to the window, looking out over the meadows and pinewoods. Then he turned. "I should have to stay in Geneva," he said. "I've my work to do."

"Would that be very—wise?"

"No," said Cavanagh frankly. "But it's what I have made up my mind to do."

He came back and sat down again. "I've been talking it over with Felicity," he said. "I've got to stay here. Even in German occupation there would still be work for us to do."

"Would the Germans allow the League to function at all?"

"We have positive assurances that they will."

"What does your wife think about it?" asked Howard.

"She thinks that it's the proper thing to do. She wants to come back to Geneva with me. . . . It's about that that I looked in to see you. If we do that, things may go hard with us before the war is over. If the Allies win they'll win by the blockade. There won't be much to eat in any German territory."

Howard stared at the little man in wonder. "I suppose not." He had not credited Cavanagh with such courage.

"It's the children," the other said apologetically. "We were thinking—Felicity was wondering . . . if you could possibly take them back to England with you, when you go."

He went on hurriedly, before Howard could speak: "It's only just to take them to my sister's house in Oxford. It's asking an awful lot, I'm afraid. If you feel you couldn't manage it . . . we'll understand."

Howard stared at him. "My dear chap," he said, "I should be only too glad to do anything I can to help. But I must tell you, that at my age I don't stand travel very well. I'm nearly seventy, you know. It would be safer if you put your children in the care of somebody a little more robust."

"That may be so, but there *is* nobody. The alternative would be for Felicity to take the children back to England herself." He added, a little pitifully, "We want to be together. It may be for years."

The old man thought for a moment. "Well, I've been going seventy years and I've not died yet. I suppose I may last a few weeks longer. I'll take them, if that's what you want me to do."

Cavanagh went away to tell his wife, leaving the old man in a flutter. Possibly he should engage a village girl from Cidoton to travel with them as far as Calais to act as a *bonne*. Perhaps Madame Lucard would know somebody. . . .

It was only later that he realized that Calais was in German hands, and that his best route would be by way of St. Malo to Southampton.

He came down presently, and met Felicity Cavanagh in the salon. She caught his hand. "It's so very, very kind of you to do this for us," she said.

"Not in the least," he said. "I shall enjoy having them as travelling companions."

He broached the matter of a girl to her, and they went together to see Madame Lucard. But Cidoton proved to be incapable of producing anybody willing to go with them. "It doesn't matter in the least," said Howard. "After all, we shall be home in twenty-four hours. Just tell me about their clothes and what they say when . . . er . . . they want to retire."

He went up with her that evening to see them in bed. "So you're coming back to England with me, eh, to stay with your auntie?"

Ronald looked up at him with shining eyes. "Are we going in a train?"

Howard said: "Yes, we'll be a long time in the train."

Sheila piped up: "Will we have dinner in the train?"

"Yes," he said. "I expect you'll have your tea and your breakfast in it too."

Presently their mother got them settled down to sleep, and followed Howard downstairs. "I've asked Madame Lucard to pack you a hamper of food," she said. "It'll be easier to give them their meals in the *wagon-lit* than bother with the restaurant car."

That night he went to bed early. He slept very well, and woke early, as he usually did. He lay in bed considering all he had to attend to. Finally, he got up feeling uncommonly well. It did not occur to him that this was because he had a real job to do.

The next day was spent in a flutter of business. The children were taking little with them; one small portmanteau held their clothes. From their mother the old man learned about their garments, how they went to bed, and what they had to eat.

Cavanagh took Howard aside that night and gave him the money for their journey. "I can't tell you how terribly grateful we are to you," he muttered. "It just makes all the difference to know that the kids will be in England."

The old man said: "Don't worry about them any more. I've had children of my own to look after, you know."

He went up to his room. Everything was packed; his portmanteaux, his rods in the long tubular travelling-case. It was bright moonlight, and he stood for a while at his window looking towards the mountains. It was very quiet and still.

He turned away uneasily. It had no right to be so peaceful, here in the Jura. Two or three hundred miles to the north the French were fighting desperately along the Somme; the peace in Cidoton was suddenly unpleasant to him, ominous. It had helped him over a bad time, but it was time that he moved on.

Next morning all was bustle. He and the Cavanaghs were down early, and had their breakfast together in the dining-room. Then the old Chrysler was at the door to take them to Saint-Claude.

The leave-taking was short and awkward. The children were

eager to climb into the car. Their father and mother kissed them, awkward and red-faced, but the children's minds were filled with the delicious prospect of a day and night in a train.

Howard bundled them into the back of the car. Then he turned back to their mother. "They're very happy," he said gently. "That's the main thing, after all."

Half an hour later the car drew up at the station of Saint-Claude, and their luggage was carried to a first-class compartment. The little train puffed out up the valley, and Saint-Claude was left behind. That was the morning on which Italy declared war on the Allies, and the Germans crossed the Seine to the north of Paris.

Chapter Three

By the time they got to Andelot, three hours later, they had had their lunch. Sheila had fallen asleep, curled up by old Howard with her head resting on his lap; Ronnie had stood looking out of the window most of the way, singing a French nursery rhyme.

As they drew into the little country station where they had to change, Howard roused Sheila. She woke up hot and fretful and began to cry a little. The old man wiped her eyes, got out of the carriage, lifted the children down onto the platform, and then got the hand luggage.

He walked along the platform with the children beside him, found the stationmaster, and inquired if the *Rapide* from Switzerland to Paris was likely to be late. The man said that no trains from Switzerland would arrive. However, a train would run from the frontier at Vallorbes to Dijon. It had been expected for two hours.

Howard was annoyed and worried. By the time he got to Dijon it would be evening, and there was no knowing how long he would have to wait there for a train to Paris.

He set himself to amuse the children. Ronnie was interested in the railway trucks and the shunting engine; he was very little trouble. Sheila however was peevish and fretful, quite unlike the child he had known in Cidoton.

An hour and forty minutes later, the train for Dijon pulled into the station. He managed to find one seat and took Sheila on his knee, where she soon fell asleep. Ronnie stood by the door looking out of the window, chattering in French to a fat old woman in a corner.

Presently this woman leaned forward to Howard. She said: "Your little one has fever, is it not so?"

Startled, he said in French: "But no. She is a little tired."

She fixed him with beady black eyes. "She has a fever. It is not right to bring a child with fever in the train. It is not hygienic. I do not like to travel with a child that has a fever."

There was a grunt from one of the other occupants.

Howard turned to the woman. "Madame," he said, "you have children of your own, I think?"

She snorted at him. "Five," she said. "But never have I travelled with a child in that condition. It is not right, that."

He said: "Madame, I ask for your help. These children are not my own, but I am taking them to England for a friend. I did not know the little one was feverish. Tell me, what would you do?"

The little beady eyes of the old peasant woman fixed him. "Has she got spots?"

"I—I don't think so. I don't know."

She snorted. "Give her to me." She took Sheila from him. With quick fingers she undid the child's clothes and had a good look at her back and front. "She has no spots," she said, replacing her garments. "But fever—poor little one, she is as hot as fire. She should be in bed."

Howard reached out for Sheila and took her back; he thanked the Frenchwoman for her help. The whole carriage discussed infant welfare till the train got to Dijon.

The station at Dijon was a seething mass of soldiers. With the utmost difficulty Howard got the children and his bags out of the train. He had an attaché case and a suitcase and his rods with him in the carriage; the rest of his luggage with the children's portmanteau was registered through to Paris. Carrying Sheila and leading Ronnie by the hand, he could not carry any of his luggage; he left everything in a corner of the platform and thrust his way towards the exit.

At the hotel where he had stayed before, he was told that all the rooms were taken by the military.

"But mademoiselle, I have a sick child to look after," he explained to the girl at the desk. "Go and fetch Madame, perhaps it will be possible for us to arrange something."

Twenty minutes later he was in possession of a room, and apologizing to an indignant French subaltern whose captain had ordered him to double up with another officer.

The chambermaid, a stout, untidy woman bulging out of her clothes, bustled about. "The poor little one," she said. "She is ill—yes? Be tranquil, monsieur. Without doubt, she has a little chill. All will be well in two days, three days, perhaps."

She watched Howard as he began to undress Sheila; at the disturbance she began to cry again. The chambermaid began a stream of motherly French chatter to the child, who gradually stopped crying. Howard surrendered Sheila to her. "Go and look for a doctor, monsieur, if you wish," she said. "I will stay with them for a little."

He left them, went down to the desk in the hall, and asked where he could find a doctor. The girl paused for a moment. "I do not know, m'sieur . . . yes. One of the officers in the restaurant—he is a *médecin major*."

After some inquiry he found the *médecin major* just finishing his meal, and explained the position to him. The man followed him upstairs.

Ten minutes later he said: "Be easy, monsieur. She must stay warm in bed tomorrow, and perhaps longer. But tomorrow I think that there will be no fever any more."

Howard asked: "What has she got?"

The man shrugged his shoulders indifferently. "Who knows? She is not infectious. Keep her in bed, monsieur. And light food only; I will tell Madame below. No wine."

"No," said Howard. He took out his note-case. "Without doubt," he said, "there is a fee."

A note passed. The Frenchman folded it and put it in the breast pocket of his tunic. He paused for a moment. "If you go to England," he said, "It may be necessary that you should go via Brest. Always, there will be boats for England at Brest."

The old man stared at him. "But there is a service from St. Malo."

The doctor shrugged. "It is very near the Front. Perhaps there will be only military traffic there." He hesitated. "It seems that the *sales Boches* have crossed the Seine, near Rheims."

Howard said quietly: "That is bad news."

The officer turned and went downstairs. Howard followed him, and got from the restaurant a jug of cold milk and a few little plain cakes for the children and a couple of feet of bread for his own supper. He carried these things to his own room, afraid to leave the children very long.

He gave them their supper. Sheila seemed cooler, and drank her milk with very little coaxing. Then it was time to put Ronnie to bed. The children had no nightclothes, but he made a game of it with them, and tucked them up carefully. "Now you be good," he said. "I'm just going to get the luggage. I'll leave the light on."

He found the station yard thronged with lorries and guns, with a few light tanks. In the station itself troops covered all the platforms, smoking, squatting on the dirty asphalt, resting their backs against anything that offered. Howard searched painstakingly for his luggage. Eventually he found his rods and the small attaché case; the suitcase had vanished, nor could he discover any trace of the registered luggage, though that he expected to find when they reached Paris.

The loss of the suitcase was a serious matter. It had either been stolen, or placed in safe-keeping by some zealous railway official. He would look for it in the morning. He made his way back to the hotel. He bought a small bottle of brandy, and went up to the bedroom to dine off brandy and water and his length of bread.

Presently he stretched himself to sleep uneasily in the armchair, desperately worried over what the next day would bring. One fact consoled him; he had his rods, quite safe.

Dawn came at five and found him still dozing uneasily. The children woke soon after that and began chattering; the old man stirred and sat up stiffly. He rubbed a hand over his face; he was feeling very ill.

In the station yard outside his window, lorries, tanks and guns were on the move. He turned back to the children; Sheila was better, but still obviously unwell. He washed her face and arms; then combed her hair with a small pocket comb.

He got Ronnie up, washed him, and set him to dress himself;

then he sponged his own face and rang the bell for the chambermaid. He was unshaven, but that could wait.

She came, and he ordered coffee and rolls and jam; when she came back with a loaded tray, he ventured: "I must go out this morning to look for my luggage, and to buy a few things. I will take the little boy with me. Would you listen for the little girl, in case she cries?"

The woman beamed at him. "Assuredly. I will bring *la petite* Rose, and she can play with the little sick one."

Howard said: "Rose?"

Little Rose, it appeared, was ten years old, the daughter of the woman's brother, who was a wine waiter at a hotel in London. He was a widower, so his sister made a home for *la petite* Rose.

Howard had to exercise a good deal of tact to get rid of her before his coffee cooled.

An hour later, spruce and shaved and leading Ronnie by the hand, he went out into the street. The little boy, dressed in beret, overcoat, and socks, looked typically French; by contrast Howard in his old tweed suit looked very English. For ten minutes he let the child have his fill of the *camions*, guns, and tanks in the market square. Then they passed on into the station.

For half an hour they searched the platforms, but found no sign of the lost suitcase. Nor could the overworked officials give any help. At the end of that time Howard gave it up.

They left the station and walked towards the centre of the town to buy pyjamas for the children. They bought some sweets to take back for Sheila, and a large green picture-book called *Babar the Elephant*. From the newspaper he learned of Italy's declaration of war and of the German Army's advance across the Marne. The situation was even more serious than he had imagined. It was in his mind to hire a car, if possible, to take them all the way from Dijon to St. Malo and the boat. The emergency seemed to justify the expense.

Up in the bedroom things were very happy. *La petite* Rose was there, a shy little girl with long black hair and an advanced maternal instinct. Already Sheila was devoted to her. *La petite* Rose had made a rabbit from two of Howard's handkerchiefs and three little bits of string, and this rabbit had a burrow in the bedclothes;

when you said "Boo" he dived back into his burrow, manipulated by *la petite* Rose. In the middle of their chatter three aeroplanes passed very low over the station and the hotel.

Howard gave Sheila the picture-book. Babar the Elephant was an old friend of *la petite* Rose; she drew Ronnie to the bed, and began to read the story. The little boy soon tired of it; he went and leaned out of the window hoping to see more aeroplanes go by.

Howard left them there, and went down to the restaurant to order lunch to be sent up to the bedroom.

It came presently, brought by the chambermaid. There was much excited chatter about the pictures of Babar, and about the handkerchief rabbit. The woman beamed all over.

Sheila said: "I want Rose to come back after lunch, Monsieur Howard."

He said slowly: "You'd better go to sleep after lunch." He turned to the woman. "If she could come back at four o'clock?" To Rose: "Would you like to come and have English tea with us?"

She said shyly: "*Oui, Monsieur.*"

After lunch, Howard made Ronnie lie down on the bed with his sister, then stretched out in the armchair, and read to them from a book given to him by their mother. Before very long the children were asleep: Howard slept for an hour himself.

Tea was a happy time. *La petite* Rose, it seemed, knew a game which involved the imitation of animals in endless repetition—

My great-aunt lives in Tours,
In a house with a cherry-tree
With a little mouse (squeak, squeak)
And a big lion (roar, roar)
And a wood pigeon (coo, coo) . . .

and so on. It was a game that made no great demand on the intelligence, and Sheila wanted nothing better. It was a very merry tea-party, so merry that the grinding of caterpillar tracks and the roaring of exhausts outside the window passed unnoticed.

Though Sheila was obviously better, it would not be right, Howard decided, to travel on the next day. But on the day after that, he thought, it should be possible to get away. He would see about the car that night.

After both children were in bed, he went down to the lobby, and said to the girl at the desk: "I want to hire a car the day after tomorrow—for a journey to St. Malo in Normandy. The little girl is still not very well. I think it will be easier to take her home by car. Can you tell me which garage would be the best?"

She said doubtfully: "The Garage Citroën would be the best. But it will not be easy, monsieur—the cars have all been taken for the army. It would be easier to go by train."

He shook his head. "I'd rather go by car."

She shrugged. "Monsieur could go to see Monsieur Duval perhaps, at the garage. If anybody in Dijon could produce a car for such a journey it would be he."

She gave him directions for finding the garage; ten minutes later he was in the Frenchman's office. The garage owner was quite positive. "A car, yes," he declared. "I could find the car. But petrol—not a litre that has not been taken by the army. And then, the roads. It is not possible to make one's way along the road to Paris. Also I could not find a driver for a journey such as that. The Germans are across the Seine, monsieur; they are across the Marne. Who knows where they will be the day after tomorrow?"

The old man was silent.

The Frenchman said: "If monsieur wishes to get back to England he should go by train, and he should go very soon."

Howard thanked him for the advice, and went out into the street. Dusk was falling; he stopped by a café, went in, and ordered a Pernod. He took the drink and sat down at a table, staring at the garish advertisements on the walls.

Things had grown serious. If he left at once, it might be possible to win through to St. Malo and to England; if he delayed another thirty-six hours it might very well be that St. Malo would be overwhelmed, as Calais had been, and Boulogne. It seemed incredible that the Germans could still be coming on so fast. Surely, surely they would be checked before they got to Paris?

He got up and went back to the hotel. In the lobby the girl said to him. "Monsieur has found a car?"

He shook his head. "I shall stay here till the day after tomorrow. Then, we will go on by train." He paused. "One thing, mademoiselle. I will only be able to take one little bag for the three of us. If I leave my fishing-rods, would you look after them for me for a time?"

"But certainly, monsieur. They will be quite safe."

After he had had dinner, he went up to the bedroom. The chambermaid met him in the corridor. He had the impression that she was near to tears. "Is anything the matter?" he asked gently.

She lifted the corner of her apron to her eyes. "I am dismissed," she muttered. "I am to go tomorrow. After five years continuously."

The old man said: "But why has Madame done this?"

"The hotel is closing tomorrow. It is to be an office for the railway." She raised her tear-stained face. "All of us are dismissed, monsieur, everyone. All the hotels are closing, and what family can now afford a servant? I do not know what will happen to me, and *la petite* Rose."

He was dumbfounded, not knowing what to say.

"You will be all right," he said at last. "You have some relations that you can go to, no doubt?"

"There is nobody, monsieur. Only Rose's father, in England."

Howard remembered the wine-waiter in London. He said a word or two of meagre comfort to the woman; but it was impossible for him to give her any help in her great trouble.

In the bedroom, the children were sleeping very deeply. He sat for a little reading in the armchair, but he soon grew tired and went to sleep.

When he awoke the dawn was bright; the children were awake and playing in the bed; Sheila was cool and apparently quite well.

It was a worrying sort of a day. The news from the north was uniformly bad; in the town people stood about in little groups talking in low tones. He went to the station after breakfast with Ronnie, to inquire about the trains to Paris, leaving Sheila in the devoted care of *la petite* Rose. They told him at the station that the service to Paris was much disorganized, but trains were leaving every three hours. So far as they knew, the services from Paris to St. Malo were normal.

While in the town he bought a couple of woollen jerseys for the children and a grey, fleecy blanket. Of all difficulties, the one he dreaded most was that the children would get ill again.

Back at the hotel the hall was already thronged with seedy-looking French officials, querulous from their journey and disputing over offices. Upstairs *la petite* Rose was reading to Sheila, who looked up at Howard, bright and vivacious, as he remembered her at Cidoton.

"*Regardez*," she said, "*voici* Jacko climbing right up the *queue de* Babar onto his back!" She wriggled in exquisite amusement. "Isn't he *naughty*!"

He looked at the picture with them. "He is a naughty monkey isn't he?" he said.

Rose asked very softly: "*Qu'est-ce que monsieur a dit?*"

Ronnie explained to her in French what the monsieur had said, and the bilingual children went on in the language of the country. To Howard they always spoke in English, but French came naturally to them when playing with other children.

They were quite happy by themselves. Howard got out the attaché case; it was very small to hold necessities for three of them. He decided that Ronnie might carry that one, and he would get a rather larger case to carry himself, to supplement it. Fired by this idea, he went out to buy a cheap fibre case.

On the landing he met the chambermaid. She hesitated, then stopped him. "Monsieur is leaving tomorrow?" she said.

"I think the little girl is well enough to travel," he replied.

She hesitated again, and then she said: "Monsieur is travelling direct to England?"

He nodded. "I shall not stay in Paris. I shall take the first train to St. Malo."

She turned her face, lined and prematurely old, up to him beseechingly. "Monsieur—it is terrible to ask. Would you take *la petite* Rose with you, to England?"

He was silent; he did not quite know what to say. She went hurriedly on. "I have the money for the fare, monsieur. And Rose is a good little girl. She would not trouble monsieur."

He stared down at the tear-stained face. "But why do you want to send her to England?" he asked. "She will be quite safe here."

The woman said. "I have no money, monsieur. Her father is in England, but he cannot send money to us here. It is better that she should go to England, now. Besides, we are afraid of what is coming here, all of us. . . ." She began to cry again.

He patted her awkwardly upon the shoulder. "There," he said. "I will think about it this afternoon. It's not a thing to be decided in a hurry."

He made his escape from her, and walked towards the centre of the town, wondering how he could evade the charge of another child. Presently, he sat down in a café and ordered himself a *bock*.

It was not that he had anything against *la petite* Rose. On the contrary, he liked the child; she was a quiet, motherly little thing. But she would be another drag on him. He knew himself to be in danger. If he delayed more than was necessary, he would be engulfed by the invading army. For an Englishman that meant a concentration camp, for a man of his age that probably meant death. Even for French children, if France were beaten, it would be a terrible time.

It was a pity he could not take little Rose with him. . . . Was it impossible to take her? It seemed desperately cruel to leave her behind.

He sat irresolute for half an hour, then got up and walked slowly back to the hotel. He found the chambermaid. "I have made up my mind," he said heavily. "*La petite* Rose may come with us to England; I will take her to her father. She must be ready to start tomorrow morning, at seven o'clock."

Chapter Four

Early next morning there was a tap on the door, and the chambermaid was there with breakfast. Behind her came *la petite* Rose, dressed in her Sunday best, with a large black straw hat, a tight black overcoat, and white socks. She carried a little attaché case.

Howard said kindly in French: "Good morning, Rose. Are you coming with us to England?"

She said: "*Oui, monsieur.*"

"That's fine," he said. He turned to the chambermaid. "Sit down and have a cup of coffee with us."

The woman said: "*Merci, monsieur.* But I have the sandwiches to prepare, and I have had my coffee."

She left Rose with them and went out. In the bedroom Howard sat the children down, each with a buttered roll and a cup full of weak coffee. There was a roar above the hotel, and a twin-engined, low-wing monoplane, dark green in colour, flew directly in a line with their window. In the distance there was a little, desultory rattling, like musketry fire upon a distant range.

The old man sat on the bed, staring at the plane as it receded in the distance. They'd never have the nerve to fly so low as that. It must have been a French one.

Rose's aunt returned with several parcels of food for the journey, and a large wine bottle full of milk. There was nothing now to wait for, and the old man was anxious to get to the station. He picked up their bags and shepherded them all down the stairs.

At the door of the hotel he turned to the chambermaid. "If there is any difficulty I shall come back here," he said. "Otherwise I will send a telegram when we reach England, and Rose is with her father. *Au revoir, mademoiselle.*"

"*Au revoir, monsieur. Bonne chance.*" She stood and watched as he guided the three children across the road in the thin morning sunlight, the tears running unheeded down her face.

In the station there was great confusion. It was quite impossible to find out the times or likelihood of trains. The most that he could learn was that trains for Paris came in at *Quai* 4 and that there had been two since midnight. He led the children through the crowd. *Quai* 4 was practically deserted, rather to his surprise; all the traffic seemed to be the other way. He walked along to a seat, and settled the children to wait until a train should come.

After about an hour and a half, a train came. It steamed in, towering above them; there were two soldiers on the footplate of the engine with the train crew.

He found a first-class compartment.

To his delight, it was not a crowded train. It went slowly, stopping at every station and occasionally in between. From Dijon to Tonnerre is seventy miles; they pulled out of that station at about half-past eleven, three hours after leaving Dijon. The children had stood the journey pretty well so far; for the last hour they had been running up and down the corridor shouting, while the old man dozed uneasily.

He roused after Tonnerre, and fetched them all back into the carriage for sandwiches. Eventually the children were full. He gave them each a cup of milk, and laid Sheila down to rest upon the seat, covered with the blanket he had bought in Dijon. He made Rose and Ronnie sit quietly and look at Babar; then he was able to rest himself.

From Tonnerre to Joigny is thirty miles. The train was going slower than ever, stopping for long periods for no apparent reason. It pulled into Joigny soon after one o'clock. It stood there in the hot sunlight, interminably. Presently a man came down the corridor.

"*Descendez, monsieur,*" he said. "This train goes no farther."

Howard stared up at him dumbfounded. "But—this is the Paris train?"

"It is necessary to change here. One must descend."

"When will the next train leave for Paris?"

"I do not know, monsieur. That is a military affair."

He got the children into their coats, gathered his things together, and presently was on the platform, burdened with his luggage, with the three children trailing after him. He went straight to the station-master's office. There was an officer there, a *capitaine des transports*. The old man asked a few straight questions, and got straight answers.

"There will be no more trains for Paris, monsieur. I cannot tell you why, but no more trains will run north from Joigny."

There was a finality in his tone that brooked no argument. The old man said: "I am travelling to St. Malo, for England, with these children. How would you advise me to get there?"

The young officer stared at him. "St. Malo? That is not the easiest journey now, monsieur." He thought for a moment. "There would be trains from Chartres . . . And in one hour, at half-past two, there is an autobus for Montargis . . . You must go by autobus via Montargis, monsieur, then on to Chartres. From Chartres you will be able to go by train to St. Malo."

Howard retired to the platform, where he got out his little map and traced the recommended course across country to Chartres. It skirted round Paris, sixty miles farther west. So long as there were buses one could get to Chartres that way, but Heaven alone knew how long it would take.

He went and found the bus out in the station yard, and sat in it with the children. Worried and distracted by their chatter, he tried to plan his course. Montargis was within sixty miles of Chartres and the railway to St. Malo; provided he could get a bus to carry him that sixty miles he would be all right. If all went well he would reach Chartres that night, and St. Malo the next morning.

The bus filled with a hot, sweating crowd of French country people. All were agitated and upset, and all bore enormous packages with them. Howard took Sheila on his knee to make more room and squeezed Ronnie standing up between his legs. Rose pressed up against him, and an enormous woman with a very small infant shared the seat with them. From the conversation in the bus Howard learned that the Germans were still pouring on, but that Paris would be defended to the last. Nobody knew how far the Germans had advanced. It was wise to move, to go and stay with relations farther to the west.

It was stifling in the bus. Howard, looking down, saw that Rose had gone very white. He bent towards her.

"Are you tired?" he said kindly. She shook her head mutely. He struggled with the window at his side, opened it a little and let in a current of warm, fresh air.

Eventually the driver climbed into his seat, and the grossly overloaded vehicle lumbered from the square. They left the town after a couple of stops, carrying an additional load of people on the roof.

Presently, Rose made a little wailing cry. Her face was greenish; before Howard could do anything to help her she had vomited on the floor.

For a moment he was startled and disgusted. Then patience came back to him; children couldn't help that sort of thing. She was coughing and weeping; he pulled out his handkerchief and wiped her face and comforted her.

"*Pauvre petite chou,*" he said awkwardly. "You will be better now. It is the heat."

With some struggling he moved Sheila over and lifted Rose up on his knee, so that she could have more air.

The road was full of traffic, all heading west. Battered cars, lorries, wagons, donkey-carts, all were loaded with people making for Montargis. These wound in and out among crowds pushing hand-carts, perambulators, wheelbarrows even, all loaded with their goods. It was incredible to Howard; it seemed as though the whole countryside was in flight before the armies.

Halfway to Montargis the bus heeled slowly to the near side. The driver wrestled with the steering; a clattering bump, rhythmic, came from the back wheel. The vehicle drew slowly to a stop beside the road.

The driver got down from his seat to have a look. Then he walked slowly back to the entrance to the bus. "*Un pneu,*" he said succinctly. "*Il faut descendre—tout le monde.* We must change the wheel."

Howard got down with relief. They had been sitting in the bus for nearly two hours. He took the children one by one behind a little bush in decent manner; a proceeding which did not escape the little crowd of passengers collected by the bus. They nudged each other. "*C'est un Anglais . . .*"

The driver, helped by a couple of the passengers, wrestled to jack up the bus and get the wheel off. Howard watched them working for a little time; then it occurred to him that this was a good opportunity to give the children tea. He sat down upon the grass verge in the shade of a tree, and gave them sandwiches and milk.

Presently Rose said she heard an aeroplane.

"Lots of aeroplanes," Ronnie said.

Howard strained his ears to hear them. "Can you see where they are?" he asked. A cold fear lurked in the back of his mind.

The children scanned the sky. "*V'là,*" said Rose, pointing suddenly. "*Trois avions—là.*"

Ronnie twisted round in excitement to Howard. "They're coming down towards us! Do you think we'll see them close?"

They watched the three aircraft losing height towards the road, about two miles away. Howard expected to see them land among the fields beside the road, but they did not land. They flattened out and flew along just above the treetops, one on each side of the road and one behind flying down the middle. A little crackling rattle sounded from them as they came.

From the bus a woman shrieked: "*Les Allemands!*" and pandemonium broke loose. The driver of a little Peugeot car looked back over his shoulder, and drove straight into the back of a mule-cart, smashing one of its wheels and cascading the occupants and load onto the road. The French around the bus dashed madly for the door, hoping for shelter in the glass and plywood body, and jammed in the entrance. The machines flew on towards them, their machine-guns spitting.

Howard caught Sheila and Ronnie and pulled them close to him. He shouted to Rose to lie down, quickly.

Then the machines were on them, low-winged monoplanes with curious bent wings, dark green in colour. A burst of fire poured into the bus, and a few bullets spattered in the ground a few yards behind Howard and his children.

Then the two flanking aircraft had passed, and the centre one was very near. Looking up, the old man could see the bombs slung in their racks beneath the wing: he watched in agony for them to fall. The machine passed by them, not a hundred feet away. He saw the bombs leave the machine three hundred yards up the road, and watched as the debris flew upwards.

He released the children, and sat up. Ronnie was flushed and excited. "Weren't they *close*!" he said. "I did see them well. Did you hear them firing guns?"

He was ecstatically pleased. Sheila was quite unaffected.

Howard found Rose inclined to tears. He moved to her. "Don't cry," he said in French. "Come and drink your milk."

"Are they coming back? I don't like the noise they make."

He patted her on the shoulder. "Never mind. The noise won't hurt you. I don't think they're coming back."

Ronnie said: "I wasn't frightened, was I?"

Sheila echoed: "I wasn't frightened, was I?"

The old man said patiently: "Nobody was frightened. Rose doesn't like that sort of noise, but that's not being frightened." He stared over to the little crowd around the bus. He must go and see what happened there. "You can have an orange," he said. "One-third each. Will you peel it, Rose?"

He left the children happy in the prospect of more food, and went slowly to the bus. There was a violent and distracted clamour from the crowd, but to his astonishment, there were no casualties. From the right a dozen bullets had entered the body of the bus

towards the rear; from the left the front wheels, bonnet and radiator had been badly shot about. His attention was attracted by a gloomy little knot of men who had lifted the bonnet and were staring despondently at the engine. A great pool of water lay beneath it from holes in the radiator and cylinder.

It took a moment or two for the full meaning of this to come home to Howard. "What does one do?" he asked the driver. "Will there be another bus?"

"Not unless they find a madman for a driver." There was a strained silence. Howard realized, appalled, that he and the children would have to walk, very likely the whole of the way to Montargis. Perhaps as much as fifteen miles.

He went into the wrecked body of the bus and collected their belongings. He took his burdens back to the children and laid them down upon the grass. It was impossible to take the suitcase with them; he packed it with the things that they could spare most easily and left it in the bus. That left the two bulging little cases and the parcels of food. He could carry those himself.

"We are going to walk to Montargis," he explained to the children. "The bus won't go. There's something the matter with the engine."

"May I go and see?" asked Ronnie.

Howard said firmly: "Not now."

They started out to walk. The heat of the day was passing; it was not yet cool, but it was bearable for walking. They went at Sheila's rate which was very slow. Presently they came to the place where the bombs had dropped.

There were two craters in the road, and a little crowd of people busy at the side of the road; too late, he thought to make a detour from what he feared to let the children see.

Ronnie said clearly and with interest: "Are those dead people, Mr. Howard? May I go and see?"

He steered them over to the other side of the road. "No," he said. "You mustn't go and look at people when they're dead. They want to be left alone."

He herded them past in silence. Sheila was singing a little song and showed no interest; Rose crossed herself and walked by with averted eyes.

Slowly they approached a place where two motor-cars were jammed in the middle of the road. One of the cars was wrecked beyond redemption. A bomb had burst immediately ahead of it, and then a tree had fallen on top of it, crushing the roof. There was much blood upon the road.

Four men were struggling to lift the tree aside to clear the road for their own car to pass. On the grass verge a quiet heap was roughly covered by a rug.

Pulling and heaving at the tree, the men rolled it from the car and dragged it back, clearing a narrow passage with great difficulty. Then they clambered back into their old de Dion. The car moved slowly forward round the tree and up the road ahead.

Fifty yards up the road it stopped. One of the men leaned back and shouted at Howard. "You—with the children. You! Look after the little boy!"

They let the clutch in and drove on. Howard looked around in bewilderment. At the far side of the road, twenty yards beyond the tree, a little boy of five or six, dressed in grey, was standing utterly motionless, staring down the road towards them. His face was a dead, greyish white.

Howard caught his breath at the sight of him. He had never seen a child looking like that, in all his seventy years.

He crossed quickly over to him, the children following. The old man said: "Are you hurt at all?"

There was no answer. The child did not appear to have heard.

"Don't be afraid," Howard said. Awkwardly he dropped down on one knee. "What is your name?"

There was no answer.

He got to his feet again, desperately perplexed. He could not stay a moment longer than was necessary in that appalling place. Equally, it seemed impossible to leave this child. In Montargis there would be a convent; he would take him to the nuns.

He crossed to the other side of the road, telling the children to stay where they were. He lifted up a corner of the rug. They were a well-dressed couple, not more than thirty years old, terribly mutilated. He nerved himself and opened the man's coat. There was a wallet in the inside pocket, with an identity-card. Jean Duchot, Rue de la Victoire, Lille.

He went back to the children. Sheila came running to him, laughing. "He is a funny little boy," she said. "He won't say anything at all!"

Howard took Sheila by the hand. "Don't bother him," he said. "I don't suppose he wants to play just now."

He said to Rose and Ronnie: "You take one of the cases each for a little bit." He went up to the little boy and said to him: "Will you come with us? We're all going to Montargis."

There was no answer, no sign that he had heard.

Howard stooped and took his hand. "*Allons, mon vieux*," he said, with gentle firmness "we're going to Montargis." He turned to the road; the boy trotted docilely beside him. Leading one child with either hand, the old man strolled down the long road, the other children following.

More traffic overtook them, and now there was noticeably a greater proportion of military lorries mingled with the cars. The dust they made was very trying to the children. With the heat and the long road they soon began to flag. Howard did what he could to cheer them on, but they were obviously tiring. There was a farm not very far ahead; he turned into it, and asked the haggard old woman at the door if she would sell some milk. She said there was none, but led them to the well in the courtyard, and pulled up a bucket of water for them.

They rested a little by the well. In a barn, open to the courtyard, was an old perambulator. Howard strolled across to look more closely, the old woman watching him, hawk-eyed. It was covered in filth, and with one broken spring. He went back to the old lady and commenced to haggle.

Ten minutes later it was his, for a hundred and fifty francs. She threw in a frayed piece of old rope with which he lashed the broken spring. It was a filthy object, and grossly expensive, but it solved a great many of his problems.

He bought a little bread from the old woman and put it with the cases in the pram. Rather to his surprise nobody wanted to ride, but they all wanted to push it; he found it necessary to arrange turns.

"The youngest first," he said. "Sheila can push it first."

Rose said: "May I take off my shoes? They hurt my feet."

He was uncertain. "I don't think that's a good idea," he said. "The road will not be nice to walk on."

She said: "But monsieur, one does not wear shoes at all, except in Dijon."

It seemed that she was genuinely used to going without shoes. After some hesitation he let her try it, and found that she moved easily over the roughest parts of the road. He spent the next quarter of an hour refusing urgent applications from the English children to copy her example.

Presently Sheila tired of pushing. Rose said: "Now it is the turn of Pierre."

Howard said to her. "How do you know his name is Pierre?"

She stared at him. "He said so—at the farm." The old man had not heard a word from the little boy; indeed he had been secretly afraid that he had lost the power of speech. Rose chatted to Pierre as they pushed the pram together, having fun with him in childish, baby French. When she trotted with the pram he trotted with her; when she walked he walked, but otherwise he seemed completely unresponsive. The blank look never left his face.

Ronnie said: "Why doesn't he say anything, Mr. Howard?"

Howard said: "He's been very unhappy. You must be as nice and kind to him as ever you can."

They digested this in silence for a minute. Then Sheila said in French: "Then why don't you make him a whistle, like you did for us?"

Rose looked up. "*Un sifflet?*"

Ronnie said in French: "He can make whistles ever so well out of a bit of wood. He made some for us at Cidoton."

She jumped up and down with pleasure, telling Pierre that the monsieur was going to make him a whistle.

"I don't mind making him a whistle," Howard said placidly. He doubted if it would be any good to Pierre, but it would please the other children. "We'll have to find a hazel bush."

They strolled along the road in the warm evening and presently Howard saw a hazel bush. They had walked for three-quarters of an hour since leaving the farm, and it was time the children had a rest; he cut a straight twig with his pocket-knife. Then he took the children into a field and made them sit down with an orange to eat between them. They sat watching him entranced, except for the little boy in grey; he did not seem capable of concentrating upon anything. Even the sections of orange had to be put into his mouth.

The old man finished cutting, bound the bark back into place and lifted the whistle to his lips. It blew a little low note, pure and clear.

"There you are," he said. "That's for Pierre."

Rose took it. She blew a note on it. Then, gently, she put it to Pierre's lips. "*Siffle*, Pierre," she said.

There was a little woody note above the rumble of the lorries on the road.

Chapter Five

Presently they got back to the road. Evening was coming upon them; out of a cloudless sky the sun was dropping down to the horizon. The old man heard in the distance the hum of aëroplanes, the crack of gunfire and some heavier explosions. Upon the road the lorries of French troops, all making for the west, were thicker than ever.

Clearly it was impossible for them to reach Montargis. By his reckoning they had walked about five miles. There were still ten miles or so ahead of them. It was time for them to find a lodging. There was a farm on the right of the road. He turned into it and asked for a bed for the children.

The gnarled old woman said: "There are no beds here. Do you take this for a hotel?"

A younger woman behind her said: "They could sleep in the barn, *ma mère*."

"Eh? The barn?" The old dame looked Howard up and down. "Have you any money?"

He said: "I have enough to pay for a good bed for these children."

"Ten francs."

"I have ten francs. May I see the barn?"

They led him to the barn. Empty and comfortless. He shook his head. "I am desolated, madame, but the children must have a bed. I must look somewhere else."

He heard the younger woman whisper something about the hayloft. The women turned aside and conferred.

The hayloft proved to be quite possible. He made a bargain for them to sleep there for fifteen francs. He found that the women had milk for them, but little food, so he gave half his bread to the younger woman to make bread and milk for the children.

Half an hour later he was doing what he could to make the children comfortable upon the hay. The younger woman came in with two blankets. "Do not tell *ma mère*," she said gruffly.

He thanked her, and busied himself making a bed for the children. She stood there watching him silently. Presently the children were comfortable and settled for the night. He left them and walked to the door of the barn and stood looking out.

The woman by him said: "You are tired yourself, monsieur."

He was deadly tired. Now that his responsibilities were over for a while, he had suddenly become slack and faint. "A little tired," he said. "I shall have supper and then I shall sleep with the children. *Bonne nuit*, madame."

She went back to the farmhouse, and he turned to the pram, to find the rest of the bread. The old woman called sharply from the house. "You can come and have soup with us, if you like."

He went into the kitchen gratefully. The old woman helped him to a large bowl of steaming broth, then said suddenly: "Are you from Alsace? You speak like a German."

He shook his head. "I'm an Englishman."

"Ah—an Englishman!" They looked at him with renewed interest. "But the children, they are not English."

The younger woman said: "The bigger boy and the smaller girl are English. They were not talking French."

With some difficulty he explained the position to them. They listened to him in silence, only half-believing what he said.

He felt much better after the soup. He thanked them courteously and went out into the yard. On the road the lorries still rumbled past, but firing seemed to have ceased altogether.

The old woman followed him to the door. "They do not stop tonight," she said, indicating the road. "The night before last the barn was full. Twenty-two francs for sleeping soldiers—all in one night." She turned and went indoors again.

He went up to the loft. The children were all asleep, curled up together in odd attitudes; the little boy Pierre still had the whistle clutched in one hand. Howard withdrew it gently and put it on the chopping machine, then he trod down a little of the hay and lay down himself, pulling his jacket round him.

He did not sleep well. At about six he got up and went down the ladder and sluiced his face under the pump. The women were already busy about the work of the farm. He spoke to the older one, and asked if she would make some coffee for the children. Three francs, for the four of them, she said. He agreed and went to get the children up.

He found them already running about. He sent them down to wash their faces at the pump. The little boy in grey hung back. From the ladder Rose called to him, but he would not go.

Howard, folding up the blankets, glanced at him. "Go on and wash your face," he said in French. "Rose is calling you."

The little boy put his right hand on his stomach and bowed to him. "Monsieur," he whispered.

The old man stood looking at him non-plussed. It was the first time he had heard him speak. The child stood looking up at him imploringly.

"What's the matter, old boy?" Howard said in French.

He whispered that he had lost his whistle.

The old man gave it to him. "Here it is," he said. "Quite safe. Now go on down and let Rose wash your face." He watched him thoughtfully as he clambered down the steps.

He gave the children their coffee in the kitchen of the farm with the remainder of the bread. At about quarter past seven he led them out onto the road again, pushing the pram before him.

High overhead a few aeroplanes passed on a pale blue, cloudless sky; he could not tell if they were French or German. On the road the military lorries were thicker than ever, and once a team of guns passed by them, drawn by tired horses.

They went very slowly, not making more than a mile and a half in each hour. It was no good hurrying the children, Howard thought. They would reach Montargis by evening, but only if the children took their own pace.

They reached a hamlet called La Croix at about ten o'clock,

where there was one small *estaminet* which sold a few poor groceries. The children had been walking for three hours and were beginning to tire. He led them in and bought them orange drinks.

There were other refugees there, sitting glum and silent. One old man said presently: "They say the Germans have taken Paris."

The wizened old woman of the house said that it was true. It had said so on the radio. A soldier had told her.

Howard listened, shaken to the core. It was incredible that such a thing could happen. Silence fell upon the room again; it seemed that no one had any more to say.

Howard had hoped to buy oranges, but no oranges were left and no fresh bread. He bought half a dozen large thick biscuits, some butter and a long, brown, doubtful-looking sausage. For his own weariness he bought a bottle of cheap brandy. That, with four bottles of the orange drink and a dozen chocolate bars, completed his purchases.

Their rest finished, he led them out upon the road again. It was full of refugees. Farm carts, drawn by great Flemish horses, lumbered down the middle of the road. Around them seethed the motor traffic; cars, occasional ambulances and motor-cyclists and long trails of people pushing hand-carts and perambulators.

The heat was intense. At about a quarter to twelve they came to a place where a little stream ran beside the road, and here Howard decided to make a halt; he pushed the perambulator a little way over the field away from the road to where a little sandy spit ran out into the stream beneath the trees.

"We'll stop here to eat," he said to the children. "Go and wash you hands and faces in the water." He took the food and sat down in the shade; he was very tired, but there was still five miles or more to Montargis.

Ronnie said: "May I paddle, Mr. Howard?"

He roused himself. "Bathe if you want to," he said. "It's hot enough. Take your things off and have a bathe before *déjeuner*, if you want to."

The English children needed no further encouragement. They were out of their clothes and splashing in the water in a few seconds. Howard watched them for a minute, amused. Then he turned to Rose. "Would you like to go in, too?" he said in French.

She shook her head in scandalized amazement. "It is not nice, that, monsieur. Not at all."

He glanced at the little naked bodies gleaming in the sun. "No," he said reflectively, "I suppose it's not." He turned to Pierre. "Would you like to bathe, Pierre?"

The little boy in grey shook his head.

Howard said: "Wouldn't you like to take your shoes off and have a paddle, then?" He turned to Rose. "Help him, Rose."

She took the little boy's shoes and socks off and they went down and paddled. Howard sat down again in the shade of the trees where he could see the children. Presently Sheila splashed a little water at the paddlers; he heard *la petite* Rose scolding. He saw the little boy in grey, standing in an inch of water, splash a little back. And then he heard a sound that was quite new to him. Pierre was laughing.

Behind his back he heard a man say: "God love a duck! Look at them bleeding kids—just like Brighton."

Another said: "Never mind about the kids. Look at the mud they've stirred up. We can't put that stuff in the radiator. Better go on upstream a bit. And get a move on or we'll be here all night."

Howard swung round and there, in British Royal Air Force uniform, were two men. One was a corporal and one a driver.

"I'm English," he burst out. "Have you got a car?"

The corporal stared at him. "And who the hell might you be?"

"I'm English. These children are English, two of them. We're trying to get through to Chartres. Have you got a car?"

"Workshop lorry," said the corporal. He swung round on the driver. "Get the water and start filling up, Bert." The driver went off upstream swinging his can.

The old man said: "Can you give us a lift?"

"I dunno about that, mate. How far do you want to go?"

"I'm trying to get back to England. Where are you making for?"

The corporal said: "Place called Brest. Officer said to go there if we got cut off, and we'd get the lorry shipped back home from there."

Howard said: "Take us with you."

The other looked uncertainly at the children. "I dunno what to say. I ain't got room for all of you."

Howard said slowly: "I see . . . If it's a matter of room, will you take the four children through to Brest with you?"

"Leaving you here?"

"I'll be all right. In fact, I'll get along quicker without them."

"Don't talk so bloody soft. What'd I do with four kids and only Bert along with me?" He swung round on his heel. "Come on then, get them kids dressed toot and sweet."

He swung off back towards his lorry. Howard hurried down to the children. "Come on and get your clothes on, quickly," he said. "We're going in a motor-lorry."

Ronnie faced him, stark naked. "What sort is it? May I sit by the driver?"

Sheila, similarly nude, echoed: "May I sit by the driver too?"

"Come on and get your clothes on," he repeated.

He hurried the children all he could, but they were wet and the clothes stuck to them; he had no towel. Before he was finished the two Air Force men were waiting to start. "Will you be able to take my perambulator?" he asked, a little timidly.

The corporal said: "We can't take that thing, mate. It's not worth a dollar."

The old man said: "I know it's not. But if we have to walk again, it's all I've got to put the little ones in."

The driver chipped in: "Let 'im take it on the roof, corp. We'll all be walking if we don't get hold of juice."

"Call this a workshop lorry!" the corporal said. "Perishing Christmas tree, I call it. All right, stick it on the roof."

He hustled them towards the road. The lorry stood gigantic by the roadside, the traffic eddying round it. Inside it was stuffed full of machinery, an enormous lathe standing in the middle. The men's kitbags occupied what little room there was.

Howard hastily removed their lunch and watched the pram heaved up on the roof. Then he helped the children up among the machinery. The corporal refused point-blank to let them ride beside the driver. "I got the Bren there, see?" he said. "I don't want no perishing kids around if we runs into Jerries."

Howard consoled Ronnie, and himself climbed into the lorry. The corporal got up by the driver, and with a low purr and a lurch the lorry moved off.

They settled down to the journey. The old man got out their *déjeuner* and gave them a little food. Very soon they came to Montargis. Through a little trap-door in the partition between the workshop and the driver's seat the corporal said to Howard: "Ever been here before, mate? You don't know where the petrol pump would be? We got to get some juice from somewhere. . . ."

Howard shook his head. "I'm afraid I don't. I'll ask someone for you, if you like."

"Do you speak French that good?"

The driver said: "They all speak it, corp. Even the kids."

They pulled up at the crossroads in the middle of Montargis. The old man asked the way to the military petrol pump. A baker directed him and they found the French transport park. Howard went with the corporal to speak to the officer in charge. They got a brusque refusal. The town was being evacuated.

The corporal swore. "I got to get this lot to Brest," he said. He turned to Howard, suddenly earnest. "Look, mate," he said. "Maybe you better beat it with the kids. You don't want to get mixed up with the bloody Jerries."

The old man said: "If there's no petrol, you may as well come with us."

The Air Force man said: "You don't savvy, mate. I *got* to get this lot to Brest. That big lathe. Machine tools is wanted back home. I *got* to get it home—I *got* to."

He ran his eye around the park. It was filled with decrepit dirty French lorries; rapidly the few remaining soldiers were leaving. The officer who had refused them drove out in a Citroën. "I bet there's juice somewhere about," the corporal muttered.

He swung round and hailed the driver. "Hey, Bert," he said: "Come on along."

The men went ferreting about among the cars. They found no store of petrol, but presently Howard saw them working at the deserted lorries, emptying the tanks into a can. They collected about eight gallons and transferred it to the enormous tank of the Leyland. "It ain't much," said the corporal. "Forty miles, maybe. Still, that's better'n a sock in the jaw. Let's see the bloody map, Bert." The map showed them Pithiviers, twenty-five miles farther on. "Let's get goin'."

The road was ominously clear and they made good speed. From time to time an aeroplane flew low above the road, and once there was a sharp burst of machine-gun fire very near at hand.

In an hour they were near Pithiviers, and drew up by the roadside for a consultation. The town seemed to be deserted in the blazing afternoon sunlight.

They stared at it, irresolute. "I dunno as I fancy it," the corporal said. "It doesn't look right to me."

The driver said "Bloody funny nobody's about. You don't think it's full of Jerries, corp? Hiding, like?"

"I don't mind walking in ahead to have a look," Howard said.

"Walk in ahead of us?"

"I don't see that there'd be much risk in that with all these refugees about. I'd rather do that than drive in with you if there's any chance of being fired on."

"O.K.," the corporal said at last. "Nip in and have a look, mate. Wave something if it's all right to come on."

The old man said: "I'll have to take the children with me. You see, they're in my charge. Just like your lathe."

The driver burst out laughing. "That's a good one, corp! Just like your lathe," he said.

The corporal said: "Well, put a jerk in it, anyway."

The old man got down from the lorry and lifted the children down one by one onto the deserted road. He started off towards the town, leading the little ones by the hand. He made all speed possible, but it was twenty minutes before he reached the town.

There were no Germans to be seen. The town was virtually deserted; only one or two very old women peered at him from behind curtains or around the half-closed doors of shops. In the gutter a tattered, dirty child was chewing something horrible.

It was a beastly, sordid little town, the old man felt. He caught one of the old women at a door. "Are the Germans here?" he said.

"They are coming from the north," she quavered. "They will ravish everyone, and shoot us."

The old man felt this was nonsense. "Have you seen any Germans in the town yet?"

"There is one there."

He looked round, startled. "Where?"

"There." She pointed a trembling, withered hand at the child in the gutter. "It speaks only German. It is the child of spies." She caught his arm with senile urgency. "Throw a stone and chase it away. It will bring the Germans to this house if it stays there."

She shouted imprecations at the child in the gutter. The child lifted his head and looked at her with disdain.

There was nothing more to be learned from the old hag. He turned away; as he did so there was a sharp crack, and a fair-sized stone rolled down the pavement near the German spy. The child slunk off fifty yards and squatted down again upon the kerb.

The old man was very angry, but he had other things to do. He said to Rose: "Look after the children for a minute, Rose, don't let them go away or speak to anyone."

He hurried back along the road till he came in sight of the lorry, half a mile away. He waved his hat at it, and saw it move towards him; then he turned and walked back to the children. As the lorry overtook him, the corporal leaned down from the cab. "Any petrol here, do you think, mate?"

"I don't know. I wouldn't hang about here very long."

"That's right," the driver muttered. "It don't look so good."

"We got to get juice."

"We got close on five gallons left. Get us to Angerville."

"O.K.," the corporal said to Howard. "Get the kids into the back and we'll 'op it."

Howard looked round for his children. They were not where he had left them; they were up the road with the German spy, who was crying miserably.

"Rose," he shouted. "Come on. Bring the children."

Rose faced the old man, her little face crimson with anger. "Somebody threw a stone and hit him. I saw them do it."

A stream of blood was running down the back of the child's neck. A sudden loathing for the town enveloped the old man. He took his handkerchief and mopped at the wound.

La petite Rose said: "It is not right to throw a stone at him, and a big woman, too, m'sieur. This is a bad, dirty place."

Ronnie said: "He's coming with us, Mr. Howard. He can sit on the other end of Bert's kitbag by the 'lectric motor."

The old man said: "He belongs here. We can't take him away with us."

"He doesn't belong here," said Rose. "Two days only he has been here. The woman said so."

There was a hurried, heavy step behind them. "For Christ's sake," said the corporal.

Howard turned to him. "They're throwing stones at this child," he said, showing the man the cut.

"Who's throwing stones?"

"The people in the village. They think he's a German spy."

"Who—'im?" The corporal stared. "He ain't more'n seven years old! Anyway, we got to beat it."

"I know." The old man hesitated. "What'll we do? Leave him here in this disgusting place? Or bring him along with us?"

"Bring him along, mate, if you feel like it. I ain't worried over the amount of spying that he'll do."

The old man bent and spoke to the child. "Would you like to come with us?" he said in French.

The little boy said something in another language.

Howard said: "*Sprechen Sie deutsch?*" It drew no response.

He straightened up. "We'll take him with us," he said quietly. He picked up the spy and they hurried to the lorry.

In the van, crouched down beside the lathe with the children huddled round him, the old man pulled out his sticky chocolate. He broke off five pieces for the children; as soon as the German spy realized what it was he stretched out a filthy paw and said something unintelligible. He ate it greedily and stretched out his hand for more.

"You wait a bit." The old man gave the chocolate to the other children. Pierre whispered: "*Merci, monsieur.*"

La petite Rose leaned down to him. "After supper, Pierre?" she said. "Shall monsieur keep it for you to have after supper?"

The little boy whispered: "Only on Sunday. On Sunday I may have chocolate after supper. Is today Sunday?"

The old man said: "I'm not quite sure what day it is. But I don't think your mother will mind if you have chocolate after supper tonight. I'll put it away and you can have it then."

He rummaged round and produced one of the hard biscuits he

had bought in the morning, and with some difficulty broke it in two; he offered one half to the dirty little boy in the smock. The child took it and ate it ravenously.

Rose scolded in French: "Have you not been taught how to behave? You should say like this"—she swung round and bowed to Howard—"*Je vous remercie, monsieur.*"

Her words passed him by, but the pantomime was evident. He looked confused. "*Dank, Mijnheer,*" he said awkwardly. "*Dank u wel.*"

Howard stared at him, perplexed. It was a northern language, but not German. It might, he thought, be Flemish or Walloon, or even Dutch. In any case, it mattered very little; he himself knew no word of any of those languages.

They drove on at a good pace through the hot afternoon. The hatch to the driver's compartment was open; from time to time the old man leaned forward and looked through at the road ahead. It was suspiciously clear. The whole countryside seemed empty.

Three miles from Angerville the corporal spoke to Howard through the hatch. "Getting near that next town now," he said. "We got to get some juice there, or we're done."

The old man said: "If you see anybody likely on the road I'll ask them where the depot is."

In a few minutes they came to a farm. A man was carrying sacks from a car into it. "Stop here," the old man said, "I'll ask that chap."

They drew up by the roadside. "Only about a gallon left now," said the driver. "We run it bloody fine, an' no mistake."

Howard got down and walked back to the man. "We want petrol," said Howard. "There is, without doubt, a depot for military transport in Angerville?"

The man stared at him. "There are Germans in Angerville."

There was a momentary silence. Howard stared across the farmyard at the lean pig rooting on the midden, at the scraggy fowls scratching in the dust. So the trap was closing on him.

"How long have they been there?" he asked quietly.

"Since early morning. A regiment came from the north."

"Have you any petrol? I will buy any that you have, at your own price."

The peasant's eyes glowed. "A hundred francs a litre."

"How much have you got?"

The man looked at the gauge upon the battered dashboard of his car. "Seven litres. Seven hundred francs."

Less than a gallon and a half. Howard went back to the corporal.

"Not very good news, I'm afraid," he said. "The Germans are in Angerville."

There was a pause. "Bloody 'ell," the corporal said at last. "How many are there there?"

"A regiment, he said."

The old man told them about the petrol. "That's not much good," the corporal said. "With what we've got, that wouldn't take us more'n ten miles." He turned to the driver. "Let's 'ave the map."

Together they pored over the sheet; there was no side road between them and the town; behind them there was no road leading to the south for nearly seven miles.

The corporal said: "Got a fag?"

The driver produced a cigarette; the corporal lit it and blew a long cloud. "Well," he said presently, "this puts the lid on it. I wanted to get home with that big lathe. I wanted to do that as much as I ever wanted anything in all my life. Straight, I did. But I ain't going to."

The old man said gently: "I am very sorry."

The other shook himself. "You can't always do them things you want to most."

He got down on to the ground. "What are you going to do?" asked Howard.

"I'll show you." He led the old man to the side of the great lorry. About halfway down its length there was a little handle sticking out, painted bright red. "I'm going to pull that, and run like bloody 'ell."

"Demolition," said the driver at his elbow. "Pull that out an' up she goes."

The corporal said: "Come on, get them kids out. I'm sorry we can't take you any farther, mate, but that's the way it is."

Howard said: "What will you do, yourselves?"

The corporal said: "Push off cross-country to the south an'

hope to keep in front of the Jerries." He hesitated. "You'll be all right," he said, a little awkwardly. "They won't do nothin' to you, not with all them kids."

The old man said: "We'll be all right. Don't worry about us."

Together they got the children down onto the road; then they lifted down the pram.

"So long, mate," said the corporal.

The old man said: "So long."

He gathered the children round him and set off with them down the road in the direction of Angerville. From time to time Howard glanced over his shoulder; the men by the lorry were sorting out their belongings. Then one of them, the driver, started off across the field towards the south, carrying a small bundle. The other bent to some task at the lorry.

Then he was up and running. When he had gone about two hundred yards there was a sharp, crackling explosion. Parts of the lorry sailed up into the air and fell upon the road and fields. A little tongue of fire appeared, and it was in flames.

Ronnie said: "Coo, Mr. Howard. Did it blow itself up?"

"Yes," he said heavily. A column of thick black smoke rose from it on the road. "Don't bother about it any more."

Two miles ahead of him he saw the roofs of Angerville. With a heavy heart he led the children down the road towards the town, and the German army.

Chapter Six

They were about half a mile from the town when Ronnie said: "Listen to the band."

"Eh?" said Howard. "What's that?"

Ronnie said: "There's a band playing in the town. May we go and listen to it?" But his ears were keener than the old man's, and Howard could hear nothing.

On the way into the town they passed some dirty lorries at a garage, filling their tanks at the pump. The men moving around them were German soldiers. They had sad, tired, expressionless faces; they moved about their work like so many machines.

Sheila said: "Are those Swiss soldiers, Mr. Howard?"

"No," he said, and gathered the children around him. "Look," he said in French, "you mustn't be afraid. They are German, but they won't hurt you."

They were passing a little group of them. From the crowd an *Unterfeldwebel* came up to them; he wore long black boots and breeches stained with oil. "That is the proper spirit," he said in harsh, guttural French. "We Germans are your friends. Very soon you will be able to go home again."

The children stared at him, as if they did not understand what he had said.

Howard said in French: "It will be good when we have peace again." There was no point in giving up before he was found out.

The man smiled, a set, expressionless grin. "How far have you come?"

"From Pithiviers."

"Have you walked so far?"

"No. We got a lift in a lorry which broke down a few miles back."

The German said: "So. Then you will want supper. In the *Place* there is a soup-kitchen which you may go to."

Howard said: "*Je vous remercie.*"

The man was pleased. He ran his eyes over them and frowned at the little boy in the smock. He stepped up and took him by the head, not ungently, and examined the wound on his neck.

"So!" he said. "By the church there is a field hospital. Take him to the *Sanitätsunteroffizier*." He dismissed them curtly and turned back to his men.

They went on to the centre of the town. At the crossroads in the middle there was a market square before a large grey church. In the centre of the square the band was playing.

It was a band of about twenty German soldiers, playing doggedly, doing their duty for their Führer. They wore soft field caps and silver tassels on their shoulders. Behind the band a row of tanks and armoured cars were parked. Ronnie said in English. "May we listen to the band, Mr. Howard?"

The old man looked quickly round. Nobody seemed to have heard him. "Not now," he said in French. "We must go with this little boy to have his neck dressed."

He led the children away from the crowd. "Try not to speak English while we're here," he said quietly to Ronnie.

"Why not, Mr. Howard?"

Sheila said: "May I speak English, Mr. Howard?"

"No," he said. "The Germans don't like to hear people speaking English." He said in French: "If you speak English I'll find a little frog to put in your mouth."

Rose said: "Oo—to hear what monsieur has said! A little frog! It would be horrible, that."

The field hospital was on the far side of the church. It consisted of a large marquee extending from a lorry. At the entrance a lance-corporal of the medical service stood picking his teeth.

Howard said to Rose: "Stay here and keep the children with you." He led the little boy up to the tent. He said to the man in French: "The little boy is wounded. A little piece of plaster or a bandage, perhaps?"

The man smiled, a fixed, mirthless grin. He examined the child deftly. "*So!*" he said. "*Kommen Sie—entrez.*"

The old man followed with the child into the tent. A dresser was tending a German soldier with a burnt hand; the only other occupant was a doctor wearing a white overall. The orderly led the child to him and showed him the wound.

The doctor nodded briefly. He turned the child's head to the light and looked at it. He opened the child's soiled clothes and looked at his chest. Then, rather ostentatiously, he rinsed his hands.

He crossed the tent to Howard. "You will come again," he said in thick French. "In one hour," he held up one finger. "One hour."

"*Bien compris,*" said the old man. "*A six heures.*" He left the tent. Surely it could not take an hour to dress a little cut?

Still there was nothing he could do. He did not dare enter into any long conversation with the German; sooner or later his British accent must betray him.

He went back to the children.

Earlier in the day at the sand spit—how long ago it seemed!—Sheila had lost her knickers. It weighed on Howard's mind and now was the time to rectify that omission. He led them to a draper's shop, pushed open the door, and a German soldier, the orderly from the hospital, was at the counter. It was too late to draw back, to do so would have raised suspicion.

A little bundle of clothes lay upon the counter. A yellow jersey, a pair of brown shorts, socks and a vest. "*Cinquante quatre, quatre vingt dix.*" said the old woman behind the counter.

The German pushed a little pad of paper towards her, and she wrote the sum upon the pad for him. He wrote his own name and the unit carefully beneath. He tore off the sheet and gave it to her. "You will be paid later," he said, in difficult French. He gathered up the garments.

She protested. "I cannot let you take away the clothes unless I have the money. My husband—he would be furious. Truly, monsieur—that is not possible at all."

The German said stolidly: "That is money, good German money. If you do not believe it, I will call the Military Police."

The woman stared at him, dumb. There was a momentary silence in the shop; then the hospital orderly gathered up his purchases and swaggered out. The woman remained staring after him, uncertainly fingering the piece of paper.

Howard went forward. She roused herself and showed him children's pants. He chose a pair for Sheila and put them on her.

He left the shop and went a little way up the Paris road, hoping to avoid the people. German soldiers were still pouring into the town. He walked for a time in the increasing crowd, tense and fearful. At last it was six o'clock; he left the children by the church in the *Place* and went back to the hospital.

The orderly saw him coming. "Wait here," he said. "I will tell the Herr Oberstabsarzt."

The man vanished into the tent. The old man stood waiting at the entrance patiently. The warm sun was pleasant now, in the cool of the evening. But he was tired now, very, very tired. If only he could see the children right, then he could rest.

There was a movement in the tent, and the doctor was there, leading a boy by the hand; a strange, new child, sucking a sweet, spotlessly clean, hair trimmed. He had a clean white dressing on his neck. He wore a yellow jersey and a pair of brown shorts, socks and new shoes. The clothes were all brand new, and seemed vaguely familiar to the old man. The little boy smiled at Howard.

The old man stared at him, dumbfounded. The doctor said genially. "So! My orderly has given him a bath. That is better?"

The old man said: "It is wonderful, Herr Doktor. And the dressing on his neck. I do not know how to thank you."

The doctor swelled visibly. "It is not me that you must thank, my friend. It is Germany! We Germans have come to bring you peace, and cleanliness, and the ordered life that is true happiness. We Germans are your friends."

"Indeed," the old man said faintly, "we realize that, Herr Doktor."

"So," said the man, "what Germany has done for this little Dutchman, she will do for all Europe. A new order has begun."

There was an awkward silence.

The doctor gave the child a little push. "Take him away," he said. "You are his father?"

Fear lent speed to the old man's thoughts. The truth was best. "He is not mine," he said. "He was lost and quite alone in Pithiviers. I shall take him to the convent."

The man nodded, satisfied with that. "I thought you might be Dutch yourself," he said. "You do not speak like these French."

"I am from the south," he said. "From Toulouse. But I am staying with my son in Montmirail. Then we got separated in Montargis; I do not know what has become of him. The children I was with are my grandchildren. They are now in the *Place*. They have been very good children, m'sieur, but it will be good when we can go home."

He rambled on, getting into the stride of his tale. The doctor turned away rudely. "Well, take your brat," he said. "You can go home now. There will be no more fighting."

He went back into the tent. The old man took the little boy by the hand. He found Rose standing more or less where he had left her, with Sheila and Pierre. There was no sign of Ronnie.

He said anxiously to her: "Rose, where is Ronnie?"

She said: "M'sieur, he has been so naughty. He wanted to see the tanks. I told him it was wrong. I told him you would be very cross with him. But he ran off, all alone."

Sheila piped up, loud and clear, in English: "May I go and see the tanks, too, Mr. Howard?"

Mechanically, he said in French: "Not this evening. I told you that you were all to stay here."

He looked around, irresolute. He must go and look for Ronnie. If he left the children there they might get into further trouble. He took hold of the pram and pushed it ahead of him. "Come this way," he said.

Pierre edged up to him and whispered: "May I push?"

It was the first time that the old man had heard the child volunteer a remark. "Of course," he said. "Rose, help him."

He walked beside them towards the parked tanks and lorries, anxiously scanning the crowd. There were German soldiers all about the transport, grey, weary men, consciously endeavouring to fraternize with a suspicious population. Some had little phrase books in their hands. Sheila said suddenly: "There's Ronnie, over there! Right inside the tank, with the soldiers!"

The old man thought quickly. He knew that Ronnie would most probably be speaking French; but he knew also that he himself must not go near the little boy nor must his sister; in his excited state he would at once break into English. Yet, he must be got away immediately, while he was still thinking of nothing but the tank. Within five minutes of him losing interest in the tank the Germans would be told that he was English, that an old Englishman was strolling round the town.

Sheila plucked his sleeve. "I want my supper," she said. "May I have my supper now? Please, Mr. Howard?"

"In a minute," he said absently. But that was an idea. If Sheila was hungry, Ronnie would be hungry too. There was a soup kitchen nearby in the *Place*. He showed it to Rose. "I am taking the little children down there, where the smoke is, for our supper," he said casually. "Go and fetch Ronnie, and bring him to us there. I will walk on with the little ones."

He sent her off, and watched her running through the crowd. He saw her come to the tank, and speak urgently to the Germans; then she was lost to sight. The old man sent up an urgent personal prayer for success. Their future lay in the hands of two children, and in the hands of God.

There was a trestle table, with benches. He parked the pram and sat Pierre and Sheila and the little Dutch boy at the table. Soup was dispensed in thick bowls, with a hunk of bread; he drew four bowls for the lot of them and brought them to the table.

He turned and Rose was at his elbow with Ronnie. The little boy was still flushed and ecstatic. "They took me right inside!" he said in English.

The old man said gently in French. "If you tell us in French, then Pierre can understand too!" He did not think that anyone had noticed. But the town was terribly dangerous for them.

Ronnie said in French: "There was a great big gun, and two little guns, m'sieur, and you steer with two handles."

Howard said: "Come and eat your supper." He gave him a bowl of soup and a piece of bread.

Sheila said enviously. "Did you go for a ride, Ronnie?"

The adventurer hesitated. "Not exactly," he said. "But they said I might go with them for a ride tomorrow. They speak funnily. I could hardly understand what they wanted to say."

Rose said suddenly: "They are dirty Germans, who come here to murder people."

The old man coughed loudly. "Eat your supper," he said. "That's enough talking for the present." More than enough, he thought; if the German dishing out the soup had overheard they would be in trouble.

At all costs he must get the children out of Angerville. There were still some hours of daylight. The children were tired, he knew, yet it would be better to move on.

When the children had finished eating he thanked the German cook politely, and led them out onto the road to Chartres. The sun was still warm, though it was dropping towards the horizon; manifestly, they could not go very far. Yet he kept them at it, anxious to get as far as possible from the town.

The problem of the little Dutch boy engaged his attention. He had not left him or Pierre with the Sisters as he had planned; it had not seemed practical when he was in the town to search out a convent. Pierre was no trouble, but this new little boy was quite a serious responsibility. He could not speak one word of any language that they spoke. Howard did not even know his name. Perhaps it would be marked upon his clothes.

Then, with a shock of dismay, the old man realized that the

clothes were gone for ever. The only link with his past now lay in the fact that he had been found abandoned in Pithiviers upon a certain day in June—lay in the evidence which Howard alone could give. Without that evidence, it would never be possible to find his parents or his relatives.

They walked on down the dusty road.

Sheila said fretfully: "My feet hurt."

He picked her up and put her in the pram, and Pierre with her. He pushed the pram wearily ahead. It was essential that they should stop soon for the night.

At the next farm he went in to see if it was possible for them to find a bed. There was a strange stillness in the place. He called out, but no one answered. He tried the door to the farmhouse, and it was locked. There was no sign of life.

As on the previous night, they slept in the hay loft. He had expected excitement and fretfulness, but the children were too tired. In a short time they were all asleep under a canvas rick cover.

Howard lay resting on the hay near them, tired to death. In the last hour he had taken several nips of brandy; now he lay upon the hay and fatigue soaked out of him. They were in a desperate position. There could be no hope now of getting through to England. The German front by now might have reached to Brittany itself. All France was overrun.

Exposure might come at any time. His French, though good enough, was spoken with an English accent. If he was to get out of France he would need the help of some French citizen. But he knew no one in this part of France.

He lay musing bitterly on the future, only half-awake. It was not quite correct to say that he knew nobody. He did know, very slightly, one family at Chartres. They were people called Rouget, no Rougeron. He had met them at Cidoton eighteen months before, when he had been there with John for the ski-ing. The father was a colonel in the army; the mother had been typically fat and French, pleasant enough in a very quiet way. The daughter Nicole had skied well.

He had seen a good deal of the father. He began to consider Rougeron seriously. If by some chance he should be in Chartres, there might yet be hope for them. At any rate, they would get good advice from him. Howard became aware at this point of how much he wanted to discuss his difficulties with some adult.

Presently he slept. He woke several times in the night, gasping and breathless. Each time he sat upright for half an hour and drank a little brandy. At five o'clock he woke for good, and sitting up against a heap of hay, resigned himself to wait till it was time to wake the children.

He would go to Chartres, and look up Rougeron. It was not much more than twenty-five miles. The bad night that he had suffered was a warning; it might well be that his strength was giving out. If that should happen, he must find the children someone else. With Rougeron, if he were there, the children would be safe.

At seven o'clock Sheila woke up, and climbed out of her bed. Her movements woke the others. Howard got up stiffly and herded them all before him down the ladder to the farmyard, and made them sluice their faces beneath the pump.

There was a step behind him, and he turned to meet a formidable woman, who was the farmer's wife. She demanded crossly what he was doing there.

He said mildly: "I have slept in your hay, madame, with these children. A thousand pardons, but there was no other place where we could go."

"Who are you? You are not a Frenchman. No doubt, you are English, and these children also?"

He said: "These children are of all nationalities, madame. Two are French and two are Swiss, from Geneva. One is Dutch." He smiled: "I assure you, we are a little mixed."

She eyed him keenly. "But you," she said, "you are English."

He said: "If I were English, madame, what of that?"

"They are saying in Angerville that the English have betrayed us, that they have run away, from Dunkirk."

He felt himself to be in peril. This woman was quite capable of giving them all up to the Germans.

He faced her boldly and looked her in the eyes. "Do you believe that England has abandoned France?" he asked. "Or do you think that is a German lie?"

"These filthy politics," she said at last. "I know only that this farm is ruined. I do not know how we shall live."

He said simply: "By the Grace of God, madame."

She was silent for a minute. Then she said: "You *are* English, aren't you?"

He nodded without speaking.

She said: "You had better go away, before anybody sees you."

He turned and called the children. Then, pushing the pram in front of him, he went towards the gate.

She called after him: "Where are you going to?"

"To Chartres."

She said: "By the tram?"

He repeated uncertainly: "The tram?"

"It passes at ten minutes past eight. There is still half an hour."

He had forgotten the light railway, running by the road. "Is it still running, madame?"

"Why not? These Germans say that they have brought us peace. Well then, the tram will run."

He thanked her and went out onto the road. He waited where the track crossed the road, and fed the children on biscuits and chocolate. Presently, a little puff of steam announced the little narrow-gauge train, the so-called tram.

Three hours later they walked out into the streets of Chartres, still pushing the pram. It was as easy as that; a completely uneventful journey.

Chartres, like Angerville, was full of Germans. They swarmed everywhere. The troops were clean and well disciplined; Howard saw nothing in their behaviour to complain of. In a telephone directory he found the name of Rougeron; they lived in the Rue Vaugiraud. He did not ring up. Instead, he asked the way, and walked there, the children trailing after him.

Rue Vaugiraud was a narrow street of tall, grey-shuttered houses. He found the house, and went upstairs slowly, for he was short of breath, the children following him. Rougeron lived on the second floor. He rang the bell of the apartment.

There was the sound of women's voices from behind the door. There was a step and the door opened before him. It was the daughter, the one that he remembered at Cidoton.

She said: "What is it?"

In the passage it was a little dark. "Mademoiselle," he said, "I have come to see your father, *monsieur le colonel.* I do not know if you will remember me; we have met before. At Cidoton."

She did not answer for a moment. She wore a grey cloth skirt and a dark blue jumper, with a black scarf at the neck.

She said at last. "My father is away from home. I—I remember you very well, monsieur."

He said easily in French: "It is very charming of you to say so, mademoiselle. My name is Howard."

"I know that."

"Will *monsieur le colonel* be back today?"

She said: "He has been gone for three months, Monsieur Howard. He was near Metz. That is the last that we have heard."

He had feared as much. He hesitated and then drew back.

"I am so sorry," he said. "I had hoped to see *monsieur le colonel*, as I was in Chartres. You have my sympathy, mademoiselle. I will not intrude any further upon your anxiety."

She said: "Is it—is it anything that I could discuss with you, Monsieur Howard?" He got a queer impression from her manner that she was pleading, trying to detain him at the door.

He could not burden the girl and her mother with his troubles; they had troubles of their own to face. "It is nothing, mademoiselle," he said. "Merely a little personal matter."

She drew herself up and faced him, looking him in the eyes. "I understand that you wish to see my father, Monsieur Howard," she said quietly. "But I know very well what you have come to talk about. We can talk of this together, you and I." She drew back from the door. "Will you not come in and sit down?" she said.

Chapter Seven

He turned and motioned to the children. Then he glanced at the girl, and caught an expression of bewilderment. "There are rather a lot of us, I'm afraid," he said.

She said: "But . . . I do not understand, Monsieur Howard. Are these your children?"

He smiled. "I'm looking after them. They aren't really mine. I am in a position of some difficulty, mademoiselle."

She swung round and called: "Maman! Come quickly: here is Monsieur Howard, from Cidoton!"

The little woman that Howard remembered came bustling out. He stood with the children pressed close round him in the small salon, trying to make the two women understand his presence with them. It was not an easy task.

The mother gave it up. "Well, here they are," she said. "Have they had lunch? Are they hungry?"

The children smiled shyly. Howard said: "Madame, they are always hungry. But do not derange yourself: we can get lunch in the town, perhaps?"

She said that that was not to be thought of. "Nicole, stay with m'sieur for a little, while I make arrangements." She bustled off into the kitchen.

"Will you sit down and rest a little," the girl said. "You seem to be very tired." She turned to the children. "And you, too, you sit down and stay quiet; lunch will be ready soon."

The old man looked down at his hands, grimed with dirt. He had not washed properly, or shaved, since leaving Dijon. "I am desolated that I should appear so dirty," he said.

"It is not easy to keep clean in times like these." She smiled at him. "Tell me from the beginning, monsieur—how did you come to be in France at all?"

He lay back in the chair. It would be better to tell her the whole thing; indeed, he was aching to tell somebody, to talk over his position. "You must understand, mademoiselle," he began, "that I was in great trouble early in the year. My only son was killed. He was in the Royal Air Force, you know. He was killed on a bombing raid."

She said: "I know, monsieur. I have the deepest sympathy for you."

He hesitated, not quite sure if he had understood her correctly. Some idiom had probably misled him. He plunged into his story. In the end she turned to him in wonder.

"So really, monsieur, none of these little ones have anything to do with you at all?"

"I suppose not," he said.

She pressed the point. "But you could have left the two in Dijon for their parents to fetch them from Geneva? You would have been able then to have reached England in good time."

He smiled slowly. "I suppose so."

She got to her feet. "You will wish to wash," she said. "Come, I will show you. I will also see that the little ones wash."

She led him to an untidy bathroom. He looked around for a razor, but the colonel had been away too long.

For lunch, Madame Rougeron had produced a *risotto*; they sat down round the table in the salon and had the first civilized meal that Howard had eaten since Dijon.

After lunch he discussed his future with them, while the children played together in a corner of the salon.

"I wanted to get back to England, of course," he said. "I still want to. But at the moment it seems difficult."

Madame Rougeron said: "There are no boats to England now, m'sieur. The Germans have stopped everything."

There was a silence.

Sheila, bored with playing on the floor, came up and pulled his sleeve, distracting him. "I want to go out for a walk. May we go out for a walk and see some tanks?"

He put his arm around her absently. "Not just now," he said. "Stay quiet for a little. We'll go out presently." He turned to Madame Rougeron. "I don't see that I can leave the children, unless with their relations," he said. "I have been thinking about this a good deal. It might be very difficult to find their relations at this time. And practically impossible to find the little Dutchman's parents. We don't even know his name."

Beneath his arm, Sheila said. "I know his name. It's Willem."

Howard said: "Has he got another name?"

Ronnie looked up from the floor. "He's called Eybe. Just like I'm called Ronnie Cavanagh, so he's called Willem Eybe."

Madame said: "But if he can't speak any French or English, how did you find that out?"

The children stared at her, a little impatient of adult density. "He *told* us," they explained.

Howard said: "Did he tell you anything more about himself?" There was a silence. "Suppose you ask him who his daddy and mummy are, or where he comes from?"

Sheila said: "But we can't understand what he *says*."

Howard said: "Never mind, then." He turned to the two women. "They'll probably know all about him in a day or two," he said. "It takes a little time."

The girl nodded. Her mother turned to Howard. "So, monsieur," she said, "it is clear that you are in difficulty. What is it that you want to do?"

"If I could get them to England," he said. "I think I'd send Pierre and the Dutch boy to America. They would be quite safe there." He explained. "My daughter has a big house on Long Island. She would make a home for them till the war ends, and then we could try to find their relations." He smiled slowly. "So all I want is to get to England with these children, madame." He thought for a minute. "Also," he said gently, "I do not wish to get my friends into trouble." He rose from his chair. "It has been most kind of you to give us lunch."

The girl sprang up. "You must not go." She swung round on her mother. "We must devise something, Mother."

The older woman shrugged her shoulders. "It is impossible. The Germans are everywhere."

The girl said: "If father were here, he would devise something."

There was a silence, broken only by Ronnie and Rose chanting their little song about the animals. Howard said: "You must not put yourselves to inconvenience on our account. I assure you, we can get along very well."

The girl said: "But monsieur—your clothes alone—they are not in the French fashion. One would say at once that you are an Englishman, to look at you."

He glanced down ruefully; it was very true. "I suppose so," he said. "It would be better if I got some French clothes."

She said: "My father would be glad to lend you an old suit, if he were here." She turned to her mother. "The brown suit."

Madame shook her head. "The grey is better. It is less conspicuous." She turned to the old man. "Sit down again," she said quietly. "Nicole is right. We must devise something. Perhaps it will be better if you stay here for the night."

He sat down again. "That would be too much trouble for you," he said. "But I should be grateful for the clothes."

Sheila came up to him again, fretful. "Can't we go out now and look at the tanks, Mr. Howard?"

"Presently," he said. He turned to the two women, speaking in French. "They want to go out."

The girl got to her feet. "I will take them for a walk," she said. "You stay here and rest."

After a little demur he agreed to this; he was very tired. "One thing," he said. "Perhaps while you are out it would be possible for me to borrow an old razor?"

The girl led him to the bathroom and produced all that he needed. "Have no fear for the little ones," she said. "I will not let them get into trouble."

"You must be very careful not to speak English, mademoiselle," he said. "The two English children understand and speak French very well. Sometimes they speak English, but that is dangerous."

She laughed up at him. "Have no fear, *cher* Monsieur Howard," she said. "I do not know any English. Only a phrase or two. The children will be safe with me."

He helped her to get the children ready to go out, and saw them off together down the stairs. Then he went back into the little flat; madame had disappeared, and he resorted to the bathroom for his shave. Then, in the corner of the settee in the salon he fell asleep.

The children woke him as they came back into the flat. Ronnie rushed up to him. "We saw bombers," he said ecstatically. "Real German ones, ever so big, and they showed me the bombs and they let me go and touch them, too!"

Sheila said: "I went and touched them, too!"

Ronnie said: "And we saw the bombers going off to bomb the ships upon the sea! It was *fun*, Mr. Howard."

He said, mildly: "I hope you said 'Thank you' very nicely to Mademoiselle Rougeron for taking you for such a lovely walk."

They rushed up to her. "Thank you *ever* so much, Mademoiselle Rougeron," they said.

He turned to her. "You've given them a very happy afternoon," he said. "Where did you take them?"

She said: "To the aerodrome, monsieur." She hesitated. "I would not have gone there if I had realized . . . But they do not understand, the little ones."

"No," he said. "It's all great fun to them."

Madame appeared again at six o'clock. She had made soup for the children's supper and prepared a bed in her own room for the two little girls. She had made up a bed in the corridor for the three boys; Howard had a room to himself. He thanked her.

"One must first get the little ones to bed," she said. "Then we will talk, and devise something."

When the children were settled for the night, Howard sat down with the two women to a supper of thick meat broth and bread and cheese, with a little red wine mixed with water. He helped them to clear the table, and accepted a curious, thin, dry, black cigar from a box left by his absent host.

Presently he said: "I have been thinking quietly this afternoon, madame. I think it would be better to try to get into Spain."

The woman said: "It is a very long way to go." They discussed the difficulties: even if he made the journey there was no sort of guarantee that he could ever get across the frontier.

The girl said: "I also have been thinking, but in quite the opposite direction." She turned to her mother. "Jean Henri Guinevec," she said.

Howard said: "Who is he?"

The girl said: "He is a fisherman, of Le Conquet. In Finisterre. He is a great friend of my father. He would help us," she said confidently. "He has a fine big boat that could cross easily to England."

Howard gave this serious attention; certainly it seemed more hopeful than any attempt to get back through Spain. They discussed it in all aspects. Obviously, it was impossible to find out how Guinevec was placed; the only thing to do would be to go there and find out. "But if Jean Henri should have gone away," the mother said, "there are the other fishermen. One or other of them will help you, when they know you are friendly with my husband." She spoke with simple faith.

The old man said: "It really is most kind of you to suggest this. If you would give me a few addresses, then we will go tomorrow." He hesitated. "It will be better to go soon," he said. "Later, the Germans may become more vigilant."

"That we can do," said madame.

Presently, as it was getting late, she got up and went out of the room. After a few minutes the girl followed her; Howard could hear the mutter of their voices in the kitchen.

Nicole came back alone from the kitchen. "Maman has gone to bed," she said. "She gets up so early in the morning. She has asked me to wish you a very good night on her behalf."

He said something conventionally polite. Nicole hesitated and then went on: "My mother and I think that it would be better that I should come with you to Brittany, Monsieur Howard."

There was a momentary silence; the old man was taken by surprise. "That is a very kind offer," he said. "Most generous of you, mademoiselle. But I do not think I should accept it." He smiled at her. "You must understand, I may get into trouble with the Germans. I should not like to think that I had involved you in my difficulties."

She said: "I assure you, monsieur, I have discussed the matter with Maman, and it is better that I should go with you." In the dusk it seemed to him that her eyes were very bright, and that she was blinking a little. "Do not refuse me, Monsieur Howard," she said at last. "I want so very much to help you."

He was touched. "I was only thinking of your safety, mademoiselle," he said gently. "You have done a very great deal for me already. Why should you do any more?"

She said: "Perhaps you did not know, monsieur. Your son and I . . . John . . . we were good friends." There was an awkward pause. "So it is quite decided," she said, turning away. "Now, monsieur, I will show you your room."

Her mother had been before her, and had laid out upon the bed a long, linen nightgown, the slumber-wear of *monsieur le colonel.* The girl looked round. "I think that there is everything you will want," she said. "You will call if there is anything we have forgotten?"

He said: "Mademoiselle, I shall be most comfortable."

"In the morning," she said, "do not hurry. Before we can start for Brittany, one must make inquiries—on the quiet, you will understand, monsieur. That we can best do alone, my mother and I. So I will bring coffee to you at about eight o'clock."

She went out and closed the door behind her; he remained for a time staring thoughtfully after her. He could not understand her at all. At Cidoton, as he remembered her, she had been very shy and reserved, as most middle-class French girls were. She had changed very much, it seemed to him. It had been nice of her to tell him in her queer, French way that she had been good friends with John; his heart warmed to her for that. To have her help might make the whole difference to his success in getting the children to England.

He put on the long nightgown and got into bed; the soft mattress and the smooth sheets were infinitely soothing. He had not slept properly in a bed since leaving Cidoton.

He thought again of the change in the girl. She still had the carefully-tended curly head; the trimmed eyebrows and the manicured hands were just the same. But her expression was different. And the black scarf she wore about her neck made her look like a widow. He wondered if she had lost a fiancé in the war. He must ask her mother, delicately, before he left the flat; it would be as well to know in order that he might avoid any topic that was painful.

He was still sleeping when she came in with his coffee and roll. He woke easily and sat up in bed, and thanked her.

She told him that her mother was already out marketing in the town, and making certain inquiries. She would be back in half an hour or so; then they would make their plans.

The girl brought him the grey suit of her father's, rather worn and shabby, with a pair of old brown canvas shoes, a horrible violet shirt, a celluloid collar rather yellow with age, and an unpleasant tie. "These clothes are not very chic," she said apologetically. "But it will be better for you to wear them, Monsieur Howard, because then you will appear like one of the *petit bourgeoisie*. I assure you, we will keep your own clothes for you very carefully."

Three-quarters of an hour later he was up and dressed, and standing in the salon while the girl viewed him critically. "You should not have shaved again so soon," she said. "It makes the wrong effect, that."

He said that he was sorry. She herself wore a very plain, black dress to her ankles. On her feet she wore low-heeled, clumsy shoes and coarse black stockings.

Madame Rougeron came in and put down her basket on the table in the salon. "There is a train for Rennes at noon," she said unemotionally. "There is a German soldier at the *guichet* who asks why you must travel, but they do not look at papers. They are very courteous and correct." She paused. "But there is another thing."

She took from the pocket of her gown a folded handbill. "A German soldier left this paper with the *concierge* this morning. There was one for each apartment."

It was in French, and it read:

CITIZENS OF THE REPUBLIC!

The treacherous English, who have forced this unnecessary war upon us, have been driven into disorderly flight from our country. Now is the time to root out these warmongers whereever they may be hiding.

These scoundrels who are living in secret in our homes like disgusting parasites, will make trouble for all of us with the Germans, who are only anxious to build up a peaceful regime in our country. If these fugitives should commit sabotage or espionage, the Germans will keep our fathers, our husbands, and our sons in long captivity. Help us drive out these pests!

It is your duty if you know of an Englishman in hiding to tell the police, or the nearest German soldier. This is a simple thing that anyone can do, which will bring peace and freedom to our land.

Severe penalties await those who shield these rats.

VIVE LA FRANCE!

Howard read it through quietly twice. Then he said: "It seems that I am one of the rats, madame. After this, I think it would be better that I should go alone, with the children."

She said that it was not to be thought of.

Nicole said: "It would be impossible for you to go alone, as things are now. I do not think you would get very far before the Germans found that you were not a Frenchman, even in those clothes." She flipped the paper with disgust. "This is a German thing," she said. "You must not think that French people talk like this, Monsieur Howard."

She went out of the room. The old man, grasping the opportunity, turned to her mother. "Your daughter has changed greatly since we were at Cidoton, madame," he said.

She stared at him. "You do not know, then?"

"How should I know anything about her madame?" he said gently.

She hesitated for a minute. Then she said: "She was in love with a young man. She tells me nothing . . . and now he is dead."

Nicole came bursting into the room, a little fibre case in her hand. "This we will carry in your perambulator," she said. "Now, monsieur, I am ready to go."

There was no time for any more conversation with Madame Rougeron. It was hard on the girl, terribly hard; perhaps this journey, dangerous though it might be, would not be altogether a bad thing for her. It might distract her mind.

There was a great bustle of getting under way. They all went downstairs; Madame Rougeron had many bundles of food, which they put in the perambulator.

Ronnie said: "Will we be going where there are tanks, Mr. Howard?" He spoke in English.

Howard said, in French: "Not today. Try to speak French while Mademoiselle Rougeron is with us, Ronnie; it is not very nice to say what other people cannot understand."

Nicole said: "Now we are quite ready." She turned and kissed her mother. "Do not fret," she said. "Five days—perhaps a week, and I will be home again. Be happy for me, Maman."

The old woman stood trembling, suddenly aged. "Take great care," she said. "These Germans—they are wicked, cruel people."

The girl said gently: "Be tranquil. I shall come to no harm." She turned to Howard. "It is time for us to go, monsieur."

They left the apartment and started slowly down the street, Howard pushing the loaded pram and Nicole shepherding the children. She had produced a rather shabby black Homburg hat for the old man, and this, with his grey suit and brown canvas shoes, made him look very French.

Presently she said: "Give me the pram, monsieur. That is more fitting for a woman to push, in the class we represent."

He surrendered it to her: they must play up to their disguise.

"When we come to the station," she said, "say nothing at all. I will do all the talking. Do you think you could behave as a much older man? As one who could hardly talk at all?"

"I will do my best."

"We have come from Arras," she went on. "You are my uncle, you understand? Our house in Arras was destroyed by the British. You have a brother who lives in Landerneau. It is a little country town forty kilometres inland from the sea. I think they may allow us to go there, when it would be impossible for us to travel directly to the coast. From there we can then walk to the coast."

They approached the station. "Stay with the children," she said quietly. "If anyone asks you anything, be very stupid."

The approach to the station was crowded with German transport lorries. It was clear that a considerable detachment of troops had just arrived by train; apart from them the station was crowded with refugees. Nicole pushed the pram through into the booking-hall, followed by Howard and the children. The old man, mindful of his part, walked with a shambling tread; his mouth hung open a little, and his head shook rhythmically.

Nicole shot a glance at him. "It is good, that," she said.

She left the pram with him and pressed forward to the booking-office. Howard, peering through the throng with sagging head and half-closed eyes, saw a German *Feldwebel*, smart and efficient in his grey-green uniform, stop her and ask a question. She motioned towards him and the children. The *Feldwebel* glanced over them, shabby and inoffensive, their only luggage in an ancient pram. He motioned her to the booking-office. Another woman claimed his attention.

Nicole came back to Howard and the children with the tickets: "Only as far as Rennes," she said, in coarse peasant tones. "That is as far as this train goes."

The old man said: "Eh?" and wagged his sagging head.

She shouted in his ear. "Only to Rennes."

He mumbled thickly: "We do not want to go to Rennes."

She made a gesture of irritation and pushed him ahead of her to the barrier. A German soldier stood by the ticket-puncher; the old man checked and turned back to the girl in senile bewilderment. She said something cross and pushed him through. Then she apologized to the ticket-puncher. "He is my uncle," she said. "He is a good old man, but he is more trouble to me than all these children."

The man said: "Rennes. On the right," and passed them through. The German stared at them indifferently; one set of refugees was very like another. So they passed through onto the platform and climbed into a very old compartment with hard wooden seats.

Ronnie said: "Is this the train we're going to sleep in, M'sieur Howard?" He spoke in French, however.

Howard said: "Not tonight. We shan't be in this train for long."

But he was wrong. From Chartres to Rennes is about two hundred and sixty kilometres; it took them six hours. In the hot summer afternoon the train stopped at every station, and many times between. The body of the train was full of German soldiers travelling to the west; three coaches at the end were reserved for French civilians.

It was an anxious journey. When there were other people with them in the carriage the old man lapsed into senility. The children ran up and down the corridor, singing "My great-aunt lives in Tours", with all its animal repetitions.

At long last they pulled into Rennes. There everyone got out; the German soldiers fell into two ranks in orderly array upon the platform and were marched away. There was a German officer by the ticket-collector. Howard put on his most senile air, and Nicole went straight up to the collector to consult him about trains to Landerneau.

Through half-closed eyes Howard watched her, the children clustered round him, dirty and fretful from their journey. He waited in an agony of apprehension; at any moment the officer might ask for papers. Then it would all be over. But finally he gave her a little pasteboard slip, and dismissed her.

She came back to Howard. "Mother of God!" she said crossly and rather loudly. "Where is now the pram? Do I have to do everything?"

The pram was still in the baggage-car. The old man shambled towards it, but she pushed him aside and got into the car and pulled it down onto the ground herself. Then, in a little confused huddle, she shepherded them to the barrier.

"It is not five children that I have," she said bitterly to the ticket-collector. "It is six." The man laughed, and the German officer smiled faintly. So they passed out into Rennes.

She said quietly to him as they walked along: "You are not angry, Monsieur Howard? It is better that I should pretend that I am cross. It is more natural so."

He said: "My dear, you have done wonderfully well."

She said: "Well, we have got halfway without suspicion. Tomorrow, at eight in the morning, a train leaves for Brest. We can go on that as far as Landerneau."

She told him that the German officer had given them permission to go there. She produced the ticket he had given to her. "We must sleep tonight at the refugee hostel, in the Cinéma du Monde," she said. "This ticket admits us.

They gave up their cards at the entrance and pushed their pram inside. The seats had all been removed. An old Frenchwoman issued them with a straw palliasse and a blanket each and showed them a corner where they could make a little camp apart from the others. "The little ones will sleep quiet there," she said.

There was an issue of free soup at a table at the end of the hall, dispensed by a German cook, who showed a fixed, beaming smile of professional good humour.

An hour later the children were laid down to rest. Howard did not dare to leave them, and sat with his back against the wall, tired to death, but not yet ready for sleep. Nicole went out and came back presently with a packet of Caporal cigarettes. "I bought these for you," she said.

He was not a great smoker, but touched by her kindness he took one gratefully. She poured him out a little brandy in a mug and fetched a little water from the drinking fountain for him; the drink refreshed him and the cigarette was a comfort. She came and sat beside him leaning up against the wall.

He asked about her father. She had little more to tell him. He had been commandant of a fort in the Maginot Line; they had heard nothing of him since May.

The old man said: "I know what that sort of anxiety means. It blackens everything for a long time afterwards."

She said quietly: "Yes. Day after day you wait, and wait. And

then the letter comes, or it may be a telegram, and you are afraid to open it to see what it says." She was silent for a minute. "And then at last you do open it."

He nodded. He felt very close to her; they had shared the same experience. He had waited just like that when John had been missing. For three days he had waited; then the telegram had come. He was immensely sorry for her.

Quite suddenly, he felt that he would like to talk to her about John. They had been friends. He blew out a long cloud of smoke. "I lost my son, you know," he said with difficulty, staring straight ahead of him. "He was shot down by three Messerschmitts on his way back from a bombing raid. Over Heligoland."

There was a pause.

She turned towards him. "I know that," she said gently. "They wrote to me from the squadron."

Chapter Eight

In the cinema people were moving about, laying down their palliasses for the night. The air was full of the fumes of the cooking-stove at the far end, and the smoke of French cigarettes.

Howard glanced towards the girl. "You knew my son as well as that, mademoiselle?" he said. "I did not know."

In turn, she felt the urge to talk. "We used to write," she said. "Ever since Cidoton we used to write, almost each week. And we met once, in Paris—just before the war. In June."

The old man said: "My dear, I never knew anything about this."

"No," she said. "Nor did I tell my parents."

There was a silence while he tried to readjust his outlook. "You said they wrote to you," he said at last. "But how did they know your address?"

She shrugged her shoulders. "He would have made arrangements," she said.

He stared ahead of him awkwardly. "Your mother told me that you had had trouble, that there had been a young man—who was dead. No doubt, that was somebody else?"

"There was nobody else," she said quietly. "Nobody but John."

He looked at her. "May I ask one more question?"

"Yes, monsieur."

"You have been very good to me," he said quietly. "I think I understand now. That was because of John?"

There was a long silence. She sat looking out across the room, motionless. "No," she said at last. "That was because of the children."

He said nothing, not quite understanding what she meant.

"One loses faith," she said quietly. "One thinks that everything is false and bad." He was still puzzled. "I did not think there could be anyone so kind and brave as John," she said. "But I was wrong, monsieur. There was another one. There was his father." She turned away. "So," she said, "We must sleep." She did not want to talk any more.

He lay down on the palliasse, shifted the rough, straw-filled pillow and pulled the blanket round him. The girl settled down upon her own bed on the other side of the children.

Howard lay awake, his mind in a tumult. He felt that he had known that there had been something between this girl and John, yet that knowledge had not reached the surface of his mind. How close had their friendship been, then? Perhaps she would tell him as time went on.

He lay awake for several hours, turning these matters over in his mind. After a long time, he slept.

He woke in the middle of the night, to the sound of wailing. He sat up, but Nicole was before him. She was crouching down by Willem, who was crying as if his heart would break. The girl put her arm around him and spoke to him in soft, baby French. The old man rolled out of his blanket, got up stiffly and moved over to them.

"What is it?" he inquired. "What is the matter?"

The girl said: "I think he has had a nightmare—that is all. Presently he will sleep again." She turned again to comfort him.

Howard knelt down clumsily beside them. "Do you think he is unwell?" he asked.

She shook her head; already the sobs were dying down. "I do not think so," she said softly. "Last night he did this, twice. It is bad dreams, I think. Only bad dreams."

The old man's mind drifted back to the unpleasant town of Pithiviers; it would be natural, he thought, for bad dreams to haunt the child.

"He is almost asleep again now," she said softly. "In a minute I will lay him down." She paused, and then she said, "Go back to bed, Monsieur Howard. I shall not be long."

Presently, the little boy was sound asleep, Nicole laid him gently down upon his pillow and pulled the blanket round him. Then she got up. "Now," she said quietly, "one can sleep again, until next time."

He did not wake again in the two or three hours that was left of the night. By six o'clock the place was all astir; there was no chance of any further sleep. Howard got up and straightened out his clothes as well as he could; he felt dirty and unshaven. The girl got the children up and, with Howard, helped them to dress. She, too, was dirty and unkempt.

Ronnie said: "I don't like this place. May we sleep in a farm tonight?"

Howard said: "I'm not quite sure where we shall sleep tonight. We'll see when the time comes."

Sheila, wriggling her shoulders, said: "I do *itch*."

There was nothing to be done about that. Howard left the children at a trestle table and went to get bread and coffee for them. The bread was hard and tasteless and the coffee bitter, with little milk. The children did not like it, and were querulous; it needed all the tact of the old man and Nicole to prevent their grumbles calling the attention of the German cook. There was some chocolate left, he shared this out among them and this made a little relish to the meal.

They left the cinema and made their way towards the railway station. The town was full of Germans. They tried to get chocolate for the children at several shops, but the soldiers had swept the town clean of sweets of every kind. They bought a couple of long rolls of bread, a brown sausage and some lettuces for their journey.

At the station they passed the barrier without difficulty, surrendering their billeting pass to the German officer. They put the pram into the baggage-wagon on the train for Brest, and climbed up into a third-class carriage.

All day the train ground slowly on in the hot sun. It was not crowded, and they seldom had anybody in the carriage with them. The German troops travelling were confined strictly to their own part of the train, but on all the station platforms they were much in evidence. At towns such as St. Brieuc, the exit from the station appeared to be picketed by a couple of German soldiers; at the wayside halts they did not seem to worry.

Nicole drew Howard's attention to this feature. "It is good, that," she said. "At Landerneau it may be possible to go through without questioning. But if we are stopped we have still a good story to tell."

He said: "Where are we going to tonight, mademoiselle?"

She said: "There is a farm about five miles from Landerneau. It was the home of Jean Henri's wife, before she married. I have been there at the time of the horse fair. Her father, Monsieur Arvers, breeds horses for our army."

The train rolled on in the hot sunlight. They gave the children lunch which kept them amused and occupied for a time, but they were restless and bored.

It was four o'clock when the train pulled into the little station of Landerneau. They tumbled out of the carriage with relief, and fetched the pram from the baggage-car. There was no guard at the *guichet* and they passed through into the town.

Landerneau was a sleepy little town upon a tidal river running to the Rade de Brest. It was built of grey stone, set in a rolling country dotted round with little woods; it reminded Howard of the Yorkshire wolds. The air was now fresh and sweet, with a faint savour suggesting that the sea was not so very far away.

The town was sparsely held by Germans. Their lorries were parked in the square beneath the plane-trees by the river, but there were few of them to be seen. Their behaviour was most studiously correct.

Unchallenged, Howard and Nicole walked through the town and out into the country beyond. They went slowly for the sake of the children. Rose and Willem were allowed to take their shoes off and go barefoot, rather to the disapproval of Nicole. "The class which we represent would not do that," she said.

The old man said: "There's nobody to see."

They went sauntering on, Willem pushing the pram with Pierre. Ahead of them three aircraft crossed the sky in steady purposeful flight towards the west, flying at about two thousand feet. Nicole stared at the three pencil-like shapes in the far distance. "It was marvellous when aeroplanes were things of pleasure," she said.

He nodded. "Have you ever flown?" he asked.

She said: "I flew with John over Paris. It was wonderful . . ."

He was interested. "You went with a pilot, I suppose. Or did he pilot the machine himself?"

"He flew it himself, of course, m'sieur. It was just him and me."

He said: "I have never flown over Paris. Is it beautiful?"

She shrugged. "I do not think that anything is beautiful seen from the air, except the clouds. But that day was marvellous, because there were those big, fleecy clouds. For more than an hour we played in them, flying around and over the top. And every now and then, far down below, one would see Paris, the Concorde or perhaps the Etoile. Never shall I forget that day."

They walked on in silence for a time, until Nicole pointed ahead of them. "That is the house—amongst those trees."

The farm that she pointed to lay about a mile ahead. It seemed to be fairly large and prosperous; there were horses in the nearby paddocks. About it rolled the open pasture of the wold.

In half an hour they were close to it. They went up to the lodge that stood beside the entrance; here Nicole inquired for Monsieur Arvers. They were directed to the stables; leaving the children with the pram at the gate, they went forward together, and met Aristide Arvers halfway. He was a small man of fifty-five or so, thin, with sharp features and a shrewd look. He wore a shapeless black suit with a soiled scarf wrapped around his neck, and a black hat.

Nicole said: "Monsieur Arvers, do you remember me? You were so kind as to invite me here three years ago, with my father, Colonel Rougeron. You showed my father round your stables. After that you entertained us in your house."

He nodded. "I remember, mademoiselle. Monsieur le colonel was very interested in my horses for the army." He hesitated. "I hope you have good news of Monsieur le colonel?"

She said: "We have had no news for three months, when he was at Metz." She went on quickly. "If my father had been at home he would no doubt have come to see you himself. As he is not, I have come instead."

His brows wrinkled slightly, but he bowed. "That is an added pleasure," he said perfunctorily.

"May we, perhaps, go to your office?"

"But certainly." He turned and led them to the house, into a littered office. He closed the door and gave them chairs; there being no other seats, he leaned backwards against the edge of the desk.

"First," said the girl, "I wish to introduce you to Monsieur Howard. He is an Englishman."

The horse-breeder raised his eyebrows a little, but bowed ceremoniously. "*Enchanté*," he said.

Nicole said: "I will come directly to the point, Monsieur Arvers. He is travelling with several children, and he is trying to return to England. My mother and I have talked about this, and it seemed to us that Jean Henri could help perhaps with one of his boats. Or Jean Henri might know of some friend who would help. There is money enough to pay for any services."

The man said nothing for a time. At last: "The Germans are not to be trifled with," he said.

Howard said: "We appreciate that, monsieur. We do not wish that anyone should run into trouble upon our behalf. That is why mademoiselle has come to talk to you first."

It took nearly twenty minutes to elucidate the full story. At last the Frenchman said: "It is impossible. If Jean Henri should put his hand to this he would be in great danger. The Germans would shoot him, beyond all doubt. You have no right to suggest such a thing." He paused, and then he said: "I have my daughter to consider."

There was a long pause. At last the old man turned to Nicole. "That's the end of that," he said. He smiled at Arvers. "I understand perfectly," he said. "In your place, thinking of my daughter, I should say the same."

The Frenchman turned to the girl. "I regret very much that I cannot help you in the way you want," he said.

She shrugged her shoulders. He looked uncomfortable. "These children," he said, "where are they now?"

They told him that they were waiting in the road, and he walked with them to the gate. The children were playing at the edge of a pond, muddy and rather fractious.

Arvers said awkwardly: "Would it help you to stay here for the night?"

Nicole said warmly: "You are very kind, monsieur."

They called the children and introduced them one by one to the horse-dealer; then they went towards the house. The man called his wife as they approached the door. He told her that the party was to stay with them for the night, introduced her formally to them. Nicole shepherded the children after her into the kitchen. Arvers turned to Howard.

"You will take a little glass of Pernod, perhaps?" he said.

A little glass of Pernod seemed a very good idea. They went into the salon. Arvers brought the Pernod, with glasses and water, and the two men settled down. They talked about horses and about country matters, chatting pleasantly for a quarter of an hour.

Then the Frenchman sat silent, staring into his glass.

"This is a bad time for children, this filthy war," he said at last. "And now that France is defeated, it is going to be worse. You English now will starve us, as we starved Germany in 1918."

Howard was silent.

"I shall not blame your country if you do that. But it will be bad for children here."

"I am afraid it may be," said the old man. "That is why I want to get these children out of it. One must do what one can."

Arvers shrugged his shoulders. "There are no children in this house, thank God. Or—only one." He paused. "That is a hard case, if you like."

Howard looked at him inquiringly. "A friend in Paris asked me if I had work for a Pole," Arvers said. "In December, that was—just at Christmas time. A Polish Jew who knew horses, who had escaped into Roumania and so by sea to Marseilles."

"You took him on?"

"Assuredly. Simon Estreicher was his name, and he arrived one day with his son, Marjan, a boy of ten. There had been a wife, but I will not distress you with that story. She had not escaped the Boche, you understand."

The old man nodded.

"Well, Estreicher worked here till last week, and he worked well. Then last week the Germans came here and took him away. Some filthy swine in town had told them about him."

"Did they take the son as well?"

"They never asked for him. He was in the paddock at the time, so I said nothing. But it was very hard on that boy."

Howard agreed with him. "He is with you still, then?"

"Where else could he go? He is useful in the stables. But before long I suppose they will find out about him, and come back and take him away also."

Nicole came to them presently, to call them to the kitchen for supper. The children were already asleep on beds improvised upstairs by Madame Arvers. They ate in the kitchen, with two men from the farm and a black-haired boy whom Madame called Marjan and who said very little. After supper Arvers escorted Nicole and Howard back to the salon; he produced a set of dominoes and proposed a game. Presently Arvers returned to the subject that was on his mind. "Are many children going to America, monsieur? I cannot comprehend how you can be so positive that they will be welcomed."

Howard shrugged his shoulders. "They are a generous people. These children will be quite all right if I can get them there, because my daughter will look after them. But even without her, there would be many people in America willing to provide for them. Americans are like that."

The other stared at him incredulously. "It would cost a great deal of money to provide for a child, perhaps for years. One does not do that lightly."

"It's just the sort of thing they *do* do," said the old man.

The horse-dealer stared at him keenly. "Would they provide for Marjan Estreicher?" he inquired at last. "No doubt they would not do that for a Jew."

"I don't think it would make the slightest difference. It certainly would make no difference to my daughter," Howard said steadily. "I would take him with me, if that is what you want, and send him to the United States. But before that, I should want help to get them all away."

"Jean Henri?"

"Assuredly, monsieur."

The other got up. "The risk is enormous," he said. "Think what it would mean to my daughter if you should be caught."

"Think what it would mean to that boy, if he should be caught," the old man said.

Nicole said suddenly: "Does Marjan want to go? You cannot make him if he does not want to. He is old, that one."

"He is only ten," said Arvers.

"Nevertheless," she said, "he is quite grown up."

Arvers went out of the room; in a few minutes he returned, followed by the boy. He said to him: "This is the matter, Marjan. This monsieur here is going to England if he can escape the Germans, and from England the children with him are going to America. In America they will be safe. There are no Germans there. Would you like to go with them?"

The boy stood silent. At last he said in almost unintelligible French: "In America, what should I work at?"

Howard said: "For a time you would have to go to school, to learn English and the American way of living. At school they would teach you to earn your living in some trade. What do you want to do when you grow up?"

Without any hesitation the boy said: "I want to kill Germans."

There was a momentary silence. Arvers said: "That is enough about the Germans. Tell monsieur here what trade you wish to learn in America, if he should be so kind as to take you there."

The boy looked up at him. "I want to learn to shoot with a rifle," he said. "I want to learn to throw a knife hard and straight. That is best in the darkness, in the narrow streets, because it does not make a noise."

Arvers smiled a little ruefully. "I am sorry, monsieur," he said. "I am afraid he is not making a very good impression."

The old man said nothing.

Marjan said: "When do we start?"

Howard hesitated, irresolute. This lad might be a great embarrassment to them. On the other hand he felt deep pity for the child.

"If you come with us," he said, "you will have to forget all this about the Germans. You will have to go to school and learn your lessons, and play baseball, and go fishing like other boys."

The lad said gravely: "I could not kill a German yet because I am not strong enough. In America I can learn everything, and come back when I am big and strong."

"That is enough," said Arvers sharply. "Go back to the kitchen and stay there till I call you."

The boy left the room. The horse-dealer said morosely, "I do not know what will become of him."

Howard sat down in the silence which followed. "One of two things will happen to him," he said. "One is, that the Germans will catch him very soon."

"What is the other thing?" the horse-dealer asked.

"He will escape with us to England," said Howard. "He will end up in America, kindly treated and well cared for, and in a year or two these horrors will have faded from his mind."

Arvers eyed him keenly. "Which of those is going to happen?"

"That is in your hands, monsieur. He will never escape the Germans unless you help him."

There was a long, long silence in the falling dusk.

Arvers said at last: "I will see what I can do. Tomorrow I will drive mademoiselle to Le Conquet and we will talk it over with Jean Henri. You must stay here with the children and keep out of sight."

Chapter Nine

Howard spent most of the next day sitting in the paddock in the sun, while the children played around him. His growing, stubbly beard distressed him with a sense of personal uncleanliness, but it was policy to let it grow. Apart from that, he was feeling well; the rest was welcome and refreshing.

From time to time the Polish boy, Marjan, appeared by the paddock gate and stood looking at them, curious, inscrutable. Howard spoke to him and asked him to come and join them, but he muttered something to the effect that he had work to do, and sheered away.

In the middle of the afternoon, suddenly, there was a series of heavy explosions over in the west. These mingled with the sharp crack of gunfire. Then a flight of three single-engined fighters flew over them, heading towards the west.

Ronnie said wisely: "That's bombs, *I* know. They go whee . . . before they fall, and then they go boom. Only it's so far off you can't hear the whee part."

"Whee . . . Boom!" said Sheila. Pierre copied her, and soon all the children were running round wheeing and booming.

The real detonations grew fewer, and presently died in the summer afternoon.

In the later afternoon Nicole came out into the garden, white-faced, with her hand bandaged. She and Arvers had been passing through Brest on the way back from Le Conquet and had been caught there during the air raid. Madame hustled the children into the kitchen for their supper.

Howard asked after her hand. "It is nothing," she said. "When a bomb falls, the glass in all the windows flies about. That is what did it."

"I am so sorry."

She turned to him. "You must not distress yourself on my account, Monsieur Howard. I assure you, I am quite all right, and so is Aristide." She laughed shortly. "At least, I can say that I have seen the Royal Air Force at work. For many months I longed to see that." She took his arm. "Come in the salon and we will drink a Pernod together, and I will tell you about Jean Henri."

They went together into the house. Aristide was not about; in the salon Howard sat down with the girl. Nicole poured Pernod for them and added water.

"About Jean Henri," she said. "He is not to appear in this himself. Aristide will not have that, for the sake of Marie. But in Le Conquet there is a young man called Simon Focquet, and he will take a boat across with you. Many of our young men are slipping away to carry on the battle from England. Focquet is a fishing-boy, and knows boats very well."

"But the Germans will stop that, surely."

She nodded. "Already all traffic has been stopped. But the boats are still allowed to fish around the coast and by Ushant. It will be necessary to devise something."

He said: "Where will he get the boat?"

"Aristide has arranged that for us. Jean Henri will hire one of his boats for fishing to this young man, and Simon then will steal it when he leaves for England. Jean Henri will complain to the *gendarmerie*, and to the Germans, that his boat has been stolen. But Aristide will pay him for it secretly. You should pay Aristide, if you have so much money."

"I have only forty pounds left on my letter of credit. Will that be enough?"

She said: "I think so." Nicole got up from the table. "I must go and see the children in their beds," she said. "Madame Arvers has been very kind, but one should not leave everything to her."

"I will come too," he said.

The children were all sleeping in one room, the two girls in the bed and the three little boys upon a mattress on the floor. Ronnie said: "My blanket smells of horses."

Nothing was more probable, the old man thought. He said: "I expect you'll dream that you're going for a ride all night."

Sheila said: "May I go for a ride, too?"

"If you're very good."

Ronnie said: "But we're all going on a ride to London."

"Not all of you," the old man said. "You and Sheila are going to live with your Aunt Margaret at Oxford."

"Are we? Is Rose going to live with Aunt Margaret, too?"

"No. Rose is going to live with her daddy in London."

Sheila said: "Is Pierre going to live with Aunt Margaret?"

"No," he said. "Pierre and Willem are going to America to live with my daughter. She's got a little boy of her own."

Pierre stared at them. "Won't you be coming with us?"

"I don't think so," Howard said. "I think I shall have work to do in England."

Pierre's lip trembled. "Won't Rose be coming?"

Howard said: "Perhaps Rose's father will want her to go too. Then she would go with you."

After a time they got the children settled down to sleep; they went downstairs again and out into the garden until supper was ready.

The old man said: "I am a little bit worried about Pierre. . . .

Why not go with him yourself, Nicole? That would be best of all."

"Go to America? That is not possible at all, monsieur."

A little fear stole into his heart. "But you are coming to England, Nicole?"

She shook her head. "No, monsieur. I must stay in France."

He was suddenly deeply disappointed. "Do you really think that is the best thing to do?" he said. "This country is overrun with Germans, and there will be great hardship as the war goes on. If you came with us to England you could live with me in my house in Essex, or you could go on to America with the children. That would be much better, Nicole."

She shook her head. "No, monsieur."

"Why not?"

She said: "Are *you* going to America with the children?"

He shook his head. "I would like to, but I don't think I shall be able to. I believe that there'll be work for me to do when I get back."

She said: "Nor would I leave France. Either one is French or one is English, and it is not possible that one should be both at the same time. And in times of great trouble, one must help one's own country."

He said slowly: "I suppose so."

"If John and I—" she hesitated—"if we had married, I should have been English and then it would be different. But now I am not to be English, ever. This is my place that I belong to, and I must stay here. You understand?"

He said: "I understand that, Nicole."

They walked beside each other in silence for the length of the paddock. Presently she said: "Now for the details of the journey. Focquet will take the boat tonight from Le Conquet. Tomorrow night he will put into l'Abervrach to land his fish, or to get bait, or on some pretext such as that. He will sail again at midnight of tomorrow night and you must then be in the boat with him, for he will go direct to England. He must be well away from the French coast before the dawn."

Howard asked: "Is l'Abervrach far from here, mademoiselle?"

"Forty kilometres, no more. There is a little town behind it, four miles inland, called Lannilis. We go there tomorrow."

"Are there many Germans in those parts?"

"I do not know. Aristide is trying to find out."

The boy Marjan passed through the paddock on his way to the house. Howard turned and called to him; he hesitated, and then came to them.

The old man said: "We are leaving here tomorrow, Marjan. Do you still want to come with us?"

The boy said in his awkward French: "If I stay with Monsieur Arvers the Germans will find me and take me away. They will kill me, as they killed my mother and father, because we are Jews. I would like to come with you."

The old man said: "Listen to me, Marjan. We may meet Germans on the way from this place to the coast; we may have to mix with them, eat at their canteens perhaps. If you show that you hate them, they may arrest us all. I do not know if it is safe to take you, if it is fair to Rose and Ronnie and Sheila and Willem and to little Pierre."

The boy said: "I shall not make trouble for you. It will be better for me to go to America now; that is what I want to do. In a few years time I shall be able to kill many hundreds of Germans, secretly, in the dark streets."

Nicole said: "Listen, Marjan. You understand what this means? If you are taken by the Germans all these little boys and girls will also be taken. It would be very wrong of you to bring that trouble on them."

He said: "Have no fear. I shall be good, and obedient, and polite. That way you win their confidence, and you can get them at your mercy in the end."

Howard said: "All right, Marjan. We start in the morning; now go and have your supper and go up to bed."

He stood watching the boy as he made his way towards the house. "God knows what sort of world we shall have when this is all over," he said heavily.

Presently they were called to the kitchen for their supper. Afterwards, in the salon, Arvers talked to them.

"Listen," he said, "and I will tell you what I have arranged." He paused. "Lannilis is full of Germans. But they do not interfere with the traffic of the country, and this is what I have devised for you.

Three miles this side of Lannilis there is a farmer called Quintin, and he is to send a load of manure tomorrow to a fisherman called Loudeac, because Loudeac has a few fields and wants manure. I have arranged all that. The manure will be delivered in a cart with one horse, you understand? You, m'sieur, will drive the cart. Mademoiselle and the children will accompany you for the ride."

Howard said: "That seems sound enough. Nobody would suspect that."

Nicole said: "How do we get into touch with Focquet?"

The horse-dealer said: "Tomorrow night, Focquet will come at nine o'clock to the *estaminet* on the quayside. He will appear to be slightly drunk, and he will ask for Pernod des Anges. There is no such drink. In that way you will know him. The rest I will leave to you."

Howard nodded. "How can we get to Quintin's farm?"

"I will take you myself in the car. That will be safe enough, for it is this side of Lannilis and there will be no questions asked. But there I must leave you." He thought for a minute. "It will be better that you should not start from Quintin's farm much before five o'clock," he said. "That will make it reasonable that you should be in l'Abervrach at nightfall, and even that you should spend the night there, with Loudeac."

Nicole said: "What about Loudeac and Quintin, monsieur? Do they know that Monsieur Howard and the children will escape?"

The man said: "Have no fear, mademoiselle. They know all that they wish to know, and they have been paid."

Howard said: "I must now pay you, monsieur."

They settled down together at the table.

Soon after that they went to bed; refreshed by a restful day, Howard slept well. In the morning he went down for coffee feeling better than he had felt for some time.

Aristide said: "We leave after lunch. That will be soon enough. Now, I have borrowed clothes for m'sieur. You will not like them, but they are necessary." They were very dirty, a coarse, stained flannel shirt, a pair of torn blue cotton trousers, a canvas pullover and a black, floppy Breton cap.

It was now some days since Howard had shaved. When he came down to the kitchen Nicole smiled broadly. "It is very good," she said. "Now, Monsieur Howard, you must again be very deaf and old and stupid. I will talk for you."

Arvers walked round him, studying him critically. "I do not think the Germans will find fault with that," he said.

Arvers made Nicole dirty her black frock a little. With a shawl over her head, he passed her too.

The children needed very little grooming. During the morning they had been playing at the duckpond. Also, Ronnie and Willem were scratching themselves a good deal, which added verisimilitude to the act.

After lunch they all got into Arvers's little van and drove off down the road.

Ronnie said: "Are we going to the train, Mr. Howard?"

"Not just yet," he said. "We shall get out of the car presently and say good-bye to Monsieur Arvers, and then we have a ride in a cart. We shall be among the Germans. They do not like people who speak English, so you must be very careful to speak only in French."

Rose said suddenly: "Marjan says the Germans cut his mother's hands off."

Howard said gently: "No more talk about the Germans now." He turned to Pierre. "What sort of noise does a horse make?" he asked.

Pierre said shyly: "I don't know."

Rose bent over him. "Oh, Pierre, of course you know!"

They played "My great-aunt lives in Tours" all the way through Landerneau. Presently the van slowed, turned off the road, and bumped to a standstill. Arvers swung round to them from the driving-seat. "This is the place," he said. "Get out quickly, it is not wise to linger here."

They were in a very small farmyard, the farmhouse itself little more than a workman's cottage of grey stone. The air was fresh and sweet after the van, with a clear savour of the sea. There was a cart and horse, the cart half-loaded with manure, the old grey horse tied to the gate. Nobody was to be seen.

Arvers said: "Now quickly, monsieur, before a German passes on the road. You have everything quite clear? You take the dung to Loudeac, who lives up on the hill above l'Abervrach. There you unload it; Mademoiselle Rougeron must bring back the cart tomorrow. Focquet will be in the *estaminet* tonight at nine o'clock, and he will be expecting you."

"One thing," the old man said. "This road leads straight to Lannilis?"

"Assuredly." The horse-dealer glanced nervously around.

"How do we find the road out of the town to l'Abervrach?"

Arvers gave them directions. Then he turned away. "That is all that I can do for you. Good luck. In happier days, we may meet again."

The old man said: "I shall look forward to thanking you again for so much kindness."

Arvers swung himself into the seat of the old van, reversed out into the road, and vanished in a white cloud of dust.

Nicole said: "Come, children, up you go."

Howard untied the bridle and led the horse out into the road. He fell into a steady, easy shamble beside the horse, head hanging down.

After about an hour and a half they reached Lannilis, and on the outskirts of the town they were stopped by a sentry. Howard pulled up the horse and stared at him, mumbling something with head hanging and mouth open. An *Unteroffizier* came from the guard-house and looked them over.

He asked in very bad French: "Where are you taking this to?"

The old man raised his head a little and put his hand to one ear. "Eh?"

The German repeated his question in a louder tone.

"Loudeac," the old man said. "Loudeac, outside l'Abervrach."

The *Unteroffizier* looked at Nicole. "And madame goes too?"

Nicole smiled at him and put her hand upon Pierre's shoulder. "It is the little one's birthday," she said. "It is not easy to make a fête these days. But as my uncle has to make this trip this afternoon, we make this little journey for an outing for the children."

The *Unteroffizier* smiled. "Proceed," he said lazily. "Many happy returns of the day."

Howard jerked up the old horse, and they passed up the street. A few houses were evidently requisitioned by the Germans. From one large house the Swastika flag floated lazily from a short staff.

They left the houses behind them. Then, blue and hazy in a dip between two fields, the old man saw the sea.

His heart leaped when he saw it. England seemed very close. By tomorrow evening, perhaps, he would have crossed that blue expanse; he would be safe in England with the children.

Nicole got down from the cart and walked beside him.

They walked in silence for a time. At last he said: "I shall never be able to thank you for what you have done for us."

She said: "I have benefited the most. It was a very bad time when you came. I do not know if I can make you understand." She paused, "I loved John very much," she said. "Above all things, I wanted to be an Englishwoman. Because we meant to marry." She was silent again. Then—"But John was killed. Then the English ran back to their own country, and all the papers, and the radio, began to say that they were treacherous, that they had never really meant to share the battle with us."

"Did you believe them?"

She said: "I was more unhappy than you could know."

"And now? Do you still believe those things?"

She said: "Now I believe that if I had become an Englishwoman, I should have been happy for the remainder of my life. That is a very precious thought, monsieur. For a few weeks it was clouded with doubts and spoilt. Now it is clear once more; I have regained the thing that I had lost."

They breasted a little rise, and there before them lay the river, winding past a little group of houses. The girl said: "That is l'Abervrach. Now you are very near the end of your journey, Monsieur Howard."

They led the horse down the road to the river and along the waterfront. Beside the quay there was a German E-boat apparently in trouble with her engines; men in overalls were busy upon her.

They went out into the country again, then turned up a hill to the little farm of Loudeac. There they tipped the wagon and Howard cleared the manure with a spade. In a quarter of an hour the job was done.

Nicole said: "There is time enough, and to spare. If we go now to the *estaminet*, we can get supper for the little ones."

Howard agreed. They got into the empty cart and moved out of the stable yard towards the village. There was a fishing-boat coming in to the harbour, faintly they heard the putter of an engine.

The old man glanced at the girl. "Focquet," he said.

She nodded.

They went on down to the village. At the *estaminet*, under the incurious glances of the German soldiers, they got out of the cart and went in.

There were a few fishermen standing by the bar, who looked at them narrowly; it seemed to Howard that they had divined his secret. He led the children to a table in a far corner of the room.

Supper came presently, but Nicole and the old man ate uneasily, conscious of glances from the bar, and speaking only to assist the children in their meal.

Their meal finished, the two English children became restless. It was still not nine o'clock, and necessary to spin out time. Ronnie wriggling, said: "May Sheila and I go and look at the sea?"

It was better to have the two of them out of the *estaminet*. Howard said: "Go on. You can go just outside the door and lean over the harbour wall. Don't go any farther than that."

At ten minutes past nine a big, broad-shouldered young man in a fisherman's red poncho and sea boots rolled into the *estaminet*. He took in all the occupants of the *estaminet* in one swift, revolving glance.

"Ha!" he said. "Give me a Pernod des Anges, and to hell with the *sale Boche*."

A man at the bar said: "Quietly. There are Germans outside."

The girl behind the bar wrinkled her brows. "Pernod des Anges? It is a pleasantry, no doubt? Ordinary Pernod for m'sieur."

The man remained silent, holding to the bar with one hand, swaying a little. Howard got up and went to him. "If you would like to join us in a glass of the *rouge*," he said.

"Assuredly." The young man left the bar and crossed with him to the table. "You must be more careful of your French idiom," he said softly. "Leave the talking to me."

He slumped down into a seat beside them. Howard poured him out a glass of the red wine; the young man said quietly: "Here is the matter. My boat lies at the quay, but I cannot take you on board here, because of the Germans. You must wait here till it is dark, and then take the footpath to the Phare des Vaches—that is an automatic lighthouse on the rocks, half a mile towards the sea, that is not now in use. I will meet you there with the boat."

Howard said: "That is clear enough. How do we get onto the footpath from here?"

Focquet told him. Howard was sitting with his back to the *estaminet* door, facing Nicole. As he sat listening to the directions, his eye fell on the girl's face, strained and anxious.

"Monsieur . . ." she said, and stopped.

There was a heavy step behind him, and a few words spoken in German. He swung round in his chair.

There was a German soldier there, with a rifle. Beside him was one of the engineers from the E-boat by the quay in stained blue dungarees.

"Say," he said. "How many of you guys are Britishers?" It was the engineer who spoke in English with a German-American accent.

There was no answer from the group.

He said: "Well, we'll all just get along to the guardroom and have a lil' talk with the *Feldwebel*. And don't let any of you start getting fresh, because that ain't going to do you any good."

He repeated himself in very elementary French.

Chapter Ten

There was a torrent of words from Focquet, poured out with well-simulated alcoholic indignation. The sentry prodded him roughly in the back with the butt of his rifle, and Focquet became suddenly silent. The party were hustled to their feet and herded out of doors.

Two more Germans came hurrying up, bringing with them Ronnie and Sheila. Both were very much alarmed, Sheila in tears.

"Say," the engineer said to Howard, "I guess these belong to you. They talk English pretty fine, finer 'n anyone could learn it."

Howard took their hands. Ronnie said, frightened: "Where are we going to now, Mr. Howard? Have the Germans got us?"

Howard said: "Don't be afraid Ronnie; they won't do anything to hurt us."

The little boy said: "I told Sheila you would be angry if she talked English, but she would do it."

Sheila was still crying bitterly. Howard stooped and wiped her eyes. "Never mind," he said. "You can talk as much English as you like now."

A couple of hundred yards up the road they were marched into the house that was the guardroom. Behind a bare trestle table sat the *Feldwebel*; the guards ranged them in front of him.

He glanced them up and down scornfully. "*Cartes d'identité,*" he said sharply.

Focquet and Nicole produced their French identity-cards; the man studied them in silence. Then he looked up. Howard put down his British passport on the bare table.

The *Feldwebel* smiled faintly, took it up, and studied it with interest. "So!" he said. "*Engländer.* Winston Churchill."

He gave a few orders in German. All the party had was taken away—papers, money, watches, even their handkerchiefs. Then they were taken to another room with a few palliasses laid out on the floor, given a blanket each, and left.

Howard turned to Focquet. "I am very sorry this has happened."

The young man shrugged his shoulders philosophically, threw himself down on one of the palliasses, pulled the blanket round him, and composed himself to sleep.

Howard and Nicole arranged the palliasses for the children, and got them settled down to sleep. Then they sat side by side, staring out of the barred window. It was practically dark within the room; outside the harbour showed faintly in the starlight.

She said: "They will examine us in the morning. What shall we say?"

"Tell them the exact truth."

She considered this for a moment. "We must not bring in Arvers, nor Loudeac or Quintin if we can avoid it."

He agreed. "They will ask where I got these clothes. Can you say that you gave them to me?"

She nodded. "That will do. Also, I will say that I knew Focquet and arranged with him myself."

She crossed to the young man, and spoke earnestly to him. He grunted in agreement; the girl came back to Howard.

"One more thing," he said. "There is Marjan. Shall I say that I picked him up on the road?"

She nodded. "On the road before you came to Chartres. I will see that he understands that."

"Go and lie down now, Nicole," he said. "You must get some sleep."

"I do not want to sleep, monsieur," she said.

He turned to her in the darkness. "I've been thinking about things," he said quietly. "I am so very sorry to have brought you into all this trouble. I did want to avoid that, and I thought that we were going to."

She shrugged her shoulders. "It does not matter." She hesitated. "I also have been thinking. I've been thinking about John."

They sat talking about John for a long time, then fell silent. The girl's breathing grew more regular and the old man knew she was asleep. He covered her with a blanket and then went to stand by the window, looking out over the harbour mouth. The moon had risen; the white plumes of surf upon the rocks showed clearly on the blackness of the sea. It grew colder, so he wrapped himself in a blanket and sat down. Soon, he, too, fell into an uneasy sleep.

At six o'clock next morning a soldier brought them some hunks of bread and a large jug of bitter coffee. They breakfasted, and waited, depressed; even the children sat about in gloomy inactivity.

Eventually, the door was flung open, and the *Feldwebel* appeared. "*Marchez,*" he said. "*Allez, vite!*"

He herded them out, and into a grey, camouflaged motor-lorry. They were taken to Lannilis, and unloaded into the big house, from the window of which floated the Swastika. The *Feldwebel* left them in the corridor with a couple of guards.

They waited for over half an hour. The children became restless. Pierre said, in his small voice: "Please, monsieur, may I go out and play in the square?"

Sheila and Ronnie said in unison: "May I go too?"

Howard said: "You'll have to stay here for a little."

Sheila said mutinously: "I don't want to stay here. I want to go out in the sun and play."

Nicole stooped to her and said: "Do you remember Jacko the Monkey? What did he do?"

Laughter, as at a huge, secret joke. "He climbed up Babar's tail, right up onto his back!"

The stolid, grey-faced Germans looked on. It confused them that their prisoners should be so flippant as to play games with their children outside the very office of the Gestapo.

A door opened, the sentries sprang to attention, clicking their heels. A young officer came out, dressed in a black uniform.

Howard straightened up and Focquet took his hands out of his pockets. The children stopped chattering to stare curiously.

The officer had a notebook and a pencil in his hand. He spoke to Howard first. "*Wie heissen Sie?*" he asked.

Somebody translated into French and the particulars of all the party were written down. Howard declared himself, Sheila and Ronnie to be English; there was no use denying it. He said that Willem and Marjan were of nationality unknown.

The young officer went into the office. In a few minutes the door was flung open again and the party were called to attention. The *Feldwebel* came to the door.

"*Folgen Sie mir! Halt! Rührt Euch!*" They found themselves in the office, facing a long table. Behind this sat the officer who had interrogated them in the passage. By his side was an older man with a square, close-cropped head and a keen, truculent expression. He also wore a black uniform. This man, as Howard subsequently learned, was Major Diessen of the Gestapo.

He looked Howard up and down, noting the clothes he wore. "So," he said harshly, but in quite good English. "We still have English gentlemen travelling in France." He paused. "Nice and Monte Carlo," he said. "I hope that you have had a very nice time."

The old man was silent. There was no point in trying to answer the taunts.

The officer turned to Nicole. "You are French," he said, fiercely. "You have been helping this man in his work against your country. I think you will be shot for this."

The girl stared at him, dumbfounded. Howard said: "There is no need to frighten her. We are quite ready to tell you the truth."

"I know your English truth," the Gestapo officer replied. "I will find my own."

Howard said quietly: "What do you want to know?"

"I want to know what means you used to make her help you."

Howard said: "I will answer your question so far as I can. I have no work in France, but I was trying to get back to England with these children. As for this young lady, she was a great friend of my son, who is now dead. We have known each other for some time."

Nicole said: "Monsieur Howard came to us in Chartres when all travelling to England had been stopped. I have known Focquet here since I was a little girl. We were trying to induce him to take monsieur and the children back to England in his boat, but he was unwilling on account of the regulations."

The old man stood silent, in admiration of the girl. If she got away with that one it let Focquet out completely.

The officer's lips curled. "I have no doubt that Mister Howard wanted to return to England," he said dryly. "It is getting quite too hot here for fellows of his sort."

He said suddenly and sharply: "We captured Charenton. He is to be executed tomorrow, by shooting."

There was a momentary silence while the German eyed the party narrowly.

Howard said at last: "I am afraid I don't quite understand what you mean. I don't know anybody called Charenton."

"No," said the German. "And you do not know your Major Cochrane, nor Room 212 in your War Office in Whitehall."

The old man could feel the scrutiny of everybody in the room upon him. "I have never been in the War Office," he said. "I used to know a Major Cochrane who had a house near Totnes, but he died in 1924. That is the only Cochrane that I ever knew."

The Gestapo officer smiled without mirth. "You expect me to believe that?"

Nicole interposed, speaking in French. "There is a misunderstanding here. Monsieur Howard has come here directly from the Jura, stopping only with us in Chartres."

Howard said: "Would you like to hear how I came to be here?"

The German officer looked ostentatiously at his wristwatch and leaned back in his chair, insolently bored. "I will give you three minutes," he said indifferently.

The old man paused to collect his thoughts. It was impossible for him, at his age, to compress his story into three minutes; his mind moved too slowly. "I came to France from England in April," he said. "I had arranged to go to a place called Cidoton in the Jura, for a little fishing holiday."

The Gestapo officer sat up suddenly. "What sort of fish?" he barked. "Answer me—quick!"

Howard stared at him. "Blue trout," he said. "Sometimes you get a grayling, but they aren't very common."

"And what tackle to catch them with—quickly!"

The old man stared at him, nonplussed, not knowing where to start. "Well," he said, "you need a nine-foot cast. For flies I use a Dark Olive or a large Blue Dun. I got one or two on a thing called a Jungle Cock, but—"

The German interrupted him. "Go on with your story," he said. "I have no time to listen to your fishing exploits."

Howard plunged into his tale. The two German officers listened with growing attention and with growing incredulity. In ten minutes or so the old man had reached the end.

Major Diessen looked at him scornfully. "You must think me stupid to be taken in with such a tale."

Nicole said: "Nevertheless, m'sieur, it is quite true. I knew the son, and I have known the father. The—"

Diessen turned to her. "So," he interrupted, "mademoiselle comes in to support this story. But now for mademoiselle herself. We learn that mademoiselle was a friend of the old English gentleman's son. A very great friend. . . ."

He barked at her suddenly: "His mistress, no doubt?"

She drew herself up. "You may say so if you like," she said quietly. "You can call a sunset by a filthy name, but you do not spoil its beauty, monsieur."

There was a pause. The young officer leaned across and whispered a word or two to the Gestapo officer. Diessen nodded and turned back to the old man.

"By the dates," he said, "you could have returned to England if you had travelled straight through Dijon. But you did not do so. That is where your lies begin in earnest."

Howard was puzzled and distressed. "The little girl," he turned and indicated Sheila, "fell ill in Dijon. I told you so just now. She was too ill to travel."

The German leaned across the table to him, white with anger. "Lies . . . lies . . . lies." Then he leaned back in his chair. "So," he said, "you refuse our kindness and you will not talk. As you wish. Before the evening you will be talking freely, Englishman, but by then you will be in horrible pain. Mademoiselle shall be there to see, and the little children also."

There was a silence in the office.

"Now you will be taken away," the German said. "I shall send for you when my men are ready to begin." He leaned forward. "I will tell you what we want to know. We know you are a spy, operating with Charenton. We know that either you or Charenton sent information to the English of the Führer's visit to the ships in Brest, and that you caused the raid."

He paused. "But what we do not know is how the message was passed through to England, to that Major Cochrane"—he sneered—"that died in 1924. That is what you are going to tell, and as soon as it is told the pain will stop."

He motioned to the *Feldwebel*. "Take them away."

They were thrust out of the room. Howard moved in a daze; it was incredible that this thing should be happening to him.

Focquet was taken from them and hustled off on his own. Howard, Nicole and the children were bundled into a heavily-barred downstairs room, with a heavily-barred window; the door was slammed on them and they were left alone.

Pierre said: "Are we going to have our dinner here, mademoiselle?"

Nicole said dully: "I expect so, Pierre."

Ronnie said: "What are we going to have for dinner?"

She put an arm around his shoulder. "We'll see when we get it. Now, you go and play. I want to talk to Monsieur Howard."

She turned to Howard. "This is very bad," she said. "We are involved in something terrible."

He nodded. "It seems to be that air raid they had on Brest. The one that you were in."

"In the shops that day they were saying that Hitler was in Brest."

Howard stood looking out of the window at the little overgrown garden outside. The situation became clear. In such a case the local Gestapo would have to make a show of energy, to produce the spies who had been instrumental in the raid, or the mutilated bodies of people who were classed as spies.

Presently he said: "I cannot tell them what I do not know, and so things may go badly with me. If I should be killed, you will do your best for the children, Nicole?"

She nodded, making a little gesture of distress.

The long hours dragged past, until at noon they were brought a meal. They waited again. At three o'clock the door was flung open and the *Feldwebel* was there with a guard.

"*Le vieux,*" he said. "*Marchez.*" They marched the old man across the square and into another house. There he was locked into a ground floor room.

There was a table in the middle of the room. At this table a young man was sitting, dark-haired, pale-faced, in civilian clothes. He glanced up as Howard came into the room.

"Who are you?" he asked in French.

The old man stood by the door, beating down his fears. This was something strange and therefore dangerous.

"I am an Englishman," he said. "I was arrested yesterday."

The young man smiled. "Well," he said, and this time in perfect English, "you'd better sit down. I'm English too."

"But . . . what are you doing here?"

The young man said: "I'm waiting to be shot." There was a stunned pause.

Howard drew up a chair, sat down and said at last: "Is your name Charenton?"

The young man nodded. "Yes," he said, "I'm Charenton. I see they told you about me." He sighed. "How did you come to be here?"

Howard rambled into his story. The young man listened quietly. When Howard had finished he got up and walked over to the window. "You'll be all right," he said at last. "They've got no evidence against you—they can't have. Sooner or later you'll get back to England."

Howard said: "What about you?"

Charenton said: "Me? I'm for the high jump. They got the goods on me all right."

Howard said: "If I should get out of this and you should not, is there anything I can do? Any message you would like me to take?"

The young man glanced at him. "Do you know Oxford?"

"Very well," the old man said.

"Then perhaps you know the Trout Inn at Godstow, a pub by a weir pool, a very old grey stone house beside a little bridge. There is the sound of running water all the time, and fish swimming in the clear pool."

"I know it very well indeed. At least, I used to, forty years ago."

"Go there and drink a pint for me," the young man said. "Sitting on the wall and looking at the fish in the pool, on a hot summer day."

Howard said: "If I get back to England, I will do that. But is there no message I can take to anyone?"

Charenton shook his head. "No messages," he said. "There is almost certainly a microphone in this room, and Diessen listening to every word we say. That is why they have put us here together." He raised his voice and said, speaking in German: "You are wasting your time, Major Diessen. This man knows nothing about my affairs." He paused and then continued: "But I will tell you this: one day the English and the Americans will come, and if you kill this old man you will hang one day in public on a gallows."

He turned to Howard. "That ought to fetch him," he said placidly, in English.

The old man was troubled. "I am sorry that you spoke like that," he said. "It will not do you any good with him."

Behind them the door opened. They swung round; there was a German *Gefreiter* there with a private. The private marched into the room and stood by Howard. The *Gefreiter* said roughly: "*Kommen Sie.*"

Charenton smiled as Howard got up. "I told you so," he said. "Good-bye. All the best of luck."

"Good-bye," said the old man. He was hustled out of the room before he had time to say more. As he passed down the corridor to the street he saw through an open door the black uniformed Gestapo officer, his face dark with anger. With a sick heart Howard walked out into the sunlit square between his guards.

They took him back to Nicole and the children. Ronnie rushed up to him. "Marjan has been showing us how to stand on our heads," he said excitedly. "I can do it and so can Pierre. Look, Mr. Howard. Just look!"

Nicole looked anxiously at him. "They did nothing?" she inquired.

The old man shook his head. "They used me to try to make a young man called Charenton talk," he said, and told her briefly what had happened.

Very early the next morning, in the half-light before dawn, the door of their prison opened with a clatter. The *Gefreiter* was there. He shook Howard by the shoulder. "*Auf!*" he said. He indicated to him that he was to get up and dress himself.

Nicole raised herself on one arm, a little frightened. "Do they want me?" she asked in French. The man shook his head.

Howard, putting on his coat, turned to her in the dim light. "This will be another of their inquiries," he said. "Don't worry. I shall be back before long."

She was deeply troubled. "I shall be waiting for you, with the children," she said simply. "They will be safe with me."

"I know they will," he said. "*Au revoir.*"

In the cold dawn they took him out into the square and along to the big house, to an upstairs room at the back. Major Diessen was standing by the window. "Come," he said, "Look out. Nice garden, is it not?"

The old man approached the window. The garden was entirely surrounded by high old red-brick walls covered with fruit trees. It was a well-kept garden, such as he liked to see.

"Yes," he said quietly. "It is a nice garden."

The German said: "Unless you help him, in a few minutes your friend Mr. Charenton will die in it. He is to be shot as a spy."

The old man stared at him. "I met Charenton for the first time yesterday. If you are going to shoot him, you are doing a bad thing. A man like that should be allowed to live, to work for the world when this war is all over."

"A very nice speech," the German said. "I agree with you; he should be allowed to live. He shall live, if you help him." He turned to the window. "Look," he said. "They are bringing him out."

Down the garden path a *Feldwebel* and six German soldiers, armed with rifles, were escorting Charenton. He walked slowly, his hands in his trouser pockets. He did not seem to be particularly distressed.

Howard turned to Diessen. "Why have you brought me to see this?" he asked.

"I have had you brought here," said the German, "to see if you would not help your friend, at a time when he needs help. If you will tell me how he got the information out of France and back to England, to your Major Cochrane, I will stop this execution."

The old man stared at him. "I cannot tell you," he replied. "Quite truthfully, I do not know. I have not been concerned in his affairs at all."

The Gestapo officer stepped back. "I do not believe that," he said harshly. "I am inclined to think you are a spy yourself. You have been wandering round the country in disguise, nobody knows where. You may share his fate."

"Even so," the old man said, "I could not tell you anything of value to you, because I do not know."

Diessen turned to the window again: "You have not got very much time," he said. "Think again before it is too late."

Howard looked out into the garden. They had put the young man with his back to the wall in front of a plum tree. His hands now were bound behind his back, and the *Feldwebel* was blindfolding him with a red cotton handkerchief.

The German said: "Nobody can ever know. There is still time for you to save him."

"I cannot save him in that way," the old man said. "I have not got the information."

The Gestapo officer suddenly thrust his face near to the old man's. "He gave you messages," he said fiercely. "The 'Trout Inn' —beer—water—fish! What does all that mean?"

"Nothing but what he said," Howard replied. "It is a place that he is fond of. That is all."

In the garden the *Feldwebel* had left the young man by the wall. The six soldiers were drawn up in a line in front of him loading their rifles.

"I am not going to delay this matter any longer," said Diessen. "Have you still nothing to say to save his life?"

The old man shook his head.

In the garden the officer glanced up to their window. Diessen lifted his hand and dropped it. The officer gave a sharp word of command. An irregular volley rang out. The old man saw the body by the plum tree crumple and fall, twitch for a little and lie still.

He turned away, rather sick. Diessen moved over to the middle of the room.

"If you are a spy you are at least a clever one," the German said at last.

Howard said: "I am not a spy."

"Why, then, are you wandering round disguised as a French peasant?"

"I have told you that," the old man said wearily, "many times. I have been trying to get these children back to England, to send them to their homes or to America."

The German burst out: "Lies—lies! Always the same lies! You English are the same every time! I do not believe a word of your story."

The old man was very tired. He said, indifferently: "I can't help that. That is what I meant to do with the children."

"You still say that you would have sent them to your married daughter? Where does she live in America?"

"At a place called Coates Harbour, on Long Island."

"Long Island. That is where the wealthy live. Is your daughter very wealthy?"

The old man said: "She is married to an American businessman. Yes, they are quite well off."

The German said incredulously: "You still wish me to believe that a wealthy woman such as that would make a home for all these dirty little children that you have picked up?"

Howard said: "She will do that." He paused, and then he said, "You do not understand. Over there, they want to help us. If they make a home for children, refugees from Europe, they feel that they are doing something worthwhile. And they are."

The German glanced at him curiously. "You have travelled in America?"

"A little."

"Do you know a town called White Falls?"

Howard shook his head. "What state is it in?"

"In Minnesota. Is that far from Long Island?"

"It's right in the middle. I should think it's about a thousand miles." This conversation was becoming very odd, the old man thought. "Let the children go through to England," he said quietly. "Let the young man Focquet sail with them for Plymouth in his boat, and let Mademoiselle Rougeron go to take them to America. Then I will confess to anything you like."

The German got up and walked over to the window. "I do not know what to make of you," he said at last. "I think that you must be a very brave man, to talk as you have done."

Howard smiled faintly. "Not a brave man," he said. "Only a very old one. Nothing you can do can take much from me."

The German did not answer him. He spoke in his own language to the sentry, and they took Howard back to the prison room.

Chapter Eleven

Half an hour later the door of the prison room was thrust open, and two German privates appeared outside. They were carrying a table which they set up in the middle of the room. Then they brought in eight chairs.

Nicole and Howard watched this with surprise. They had eaten all their meals since they had been in captivity from plates balanced in their hands, helped from a bowl that stood upon the floor. This was something different in their treatment, something strange and suspicious.

Presently, the door opened again, and in walked a little French waiter balancing a tray, apparently from some neighbouring café. The man, evidently frightened, spread a cloth upon the table and set out cups and saucers, a large pot of coffee and a jug of hot milk, new rolls, butter, sugar, jam, and a plate of cut rounds of sausage. Then he withdrew quickly, obviously relieved.

The children crowded round the table, eager. Howard and Nicole helped them into their chairs and set to work to feed them. The girl glanced at the old man. "I do not understand why they are doing this," she said quietly.

Howard did not understand it either. Lurking in his mind was the thought that this was a new trick. They had failed with fear; now they would try persuasion.

After the meal one of the sentries came to the door and said: "*Sie können in den Garten gehen.*" With difficulty Howard understood this to mean that they might go into the garden. The children rushed out into it with shrill cries; a day of close confinement had been a grave trial to them. Howard followed with Nicole, wondering.

They spent the whole day in the garden, only going back into their prison room for meals. That night the old man had slept for scarcely an hour when the door was thrust open by a German soldier. He bent and shook the old man by the shoulder. "*Kommen Sie*," he said.

He was hustled away to the room in which they had first been interviewed. The Gestapo officer, Major Diessen, was there sitting at the table. The German soldier who brought Howard in saluted stiffly. The officer spoke a word to him, and he withdrew, closing the door behind him. Howard was left alone in the room with Major Diessen.

Howard glanced at the clock. It was a little after midnight. The windows had been covered with blankets for a blackout.

Presently the German looked up at the old man standing by the wall. "So," he said. "The Englishman again." He opened a drawer beside him and took out a large, black automatic pistol. He slipped out the clip and examined it; then put it back again and pulled the breech to load it. He laid it on the blotting-pad in front of him. "We are alone," he said. "I am not taking any chances, as you see."

The old man smiled. "You have nothing to fear from me."

There was a little silence. Then: "Suppose I were to let you go to England after all so that you could send the children to America? Would you then do me a small service?"

Howard said: "It depends what it was."

The German said: "It is a matter of no difficulty . . ." he paused. His hand strayed to the black automatic on the desk before him, and he picked it up. "There is a certain person to be taken to America," he said deliberately. "I do not want to advertise her journey. It would be very suitable that she should travel with your party of children."

Howard stared at him across the table. "If you mean that you want to use my party as a cover for an agent going to America," he said, "I will not have it."

He saw the forefinger snap round the trigger. He raised his eyes to the German's face and saw it white with anger. For a full half-minute they remained motionless, staring at each other.

The Gestapo officer was the first to relax. "Listen to me," he said, "this is not an agent. This is a little girl of five years old. Anna, the daughter of my brother Karl, who has been killed. At present she is in Paris."

Howard said: "Let me understand this fully. This is a little German girl that you want me to take to America?"

"That is so."

"Where is she going?"

Major Diessen hesitated. "You must understand," he said, "that there were three of us. My oldest brother Rupert fought in the World War, and then went to America. He now has a grocery business in White Falls. He is an American citizen."

"I see," said Howard.

"My brother Karl was *Oberleutnant* in the Second Panzer Division. He was married some years ago. His wife was not wholly Aryan. There was trouble, and she died. Now Karl, too, is dead."

He sat brooding for a minute. Howard said gently: "I am sorry." And he was.

Diessen said: "So there is Anna who must be provided for. I think it will be better if she goes to live with Rupert in America."

Howard said: "Well, I should be very glad to take her."

The German stared at him thoughtfully. "How quickly after you reach England will the children go?"

"I shall hope to send them within a week. That is, if you let us go."

The German nodded. "You must not wait longer. In six weeks we shall be in London. I do not want that you should think I am not confident about the outcome of this war. We shall conquer England, as we have conquered France. But for many years there will be war with your Dominions, and while that is going on there will not be much food for children here or in Germany. It will be better that little Anna should be in a neutral country."

Howard nodded. The Gestapo officer eyed him narrowly. "There must be no trickery. Remember, we shall have Mademoiselle Rougeron. She may return to Chartres and live with her mother, but until I have a cable from my brother Rupert that little Anna is safe with him, we shall have our eye on mademoiselle as a hostage."

Howard thought quickly. "That has another side to it," he said. "If Mademoiselle Rougeron gets into trouble with the Gestapo and I should hear of it in England, this story shall be published in my country and quoted in the German news upon the radio, mentioning you by name."

The German stared at him for a long time. "So," he said at last. "You are clever, Englishman. You have gained all that you want."

"So have you," the old man said.

They settled to the details of the arrangement. A quarter of an hour later the German got up from the table. "No word of this to anyone," he said again. "Tomorrow evening you will be moved from here."

Howard shook his head. "I shall not talk. But I would like you to know one thing. I should have been glad to take your little girl with me in any case. It never entered my head to refuse."

The German nodded. "That is good," he said. "If you had refused I should have shot you. You would have been too dangerous to leave this room alive." He bowed stiffly. "*Auf Wiedersehen*," he said ironically. He pressed a button on his desk; the door opened and the sentry took Howard back to his prison.

Nicole was up, waiting for him. As the door closed she came to him and said: "What happened? Did they hurt you?"

He patted her on the shoulder. "It's all right," he said.

They sat down on the bed together. The moon threw a long shaft of silver light in through the window; faintly, somewhere, they heard the droning of a bomber.

"Listen, Nicole," he said. "I can't tell you what has happened. But I can tell you everything is going to be all right. We shall go to England very soon, and you will go free, back to Chartres to live with your mother, and you will have no trouble from the Gestapo."

She said breathlessly: "But—I do not understand. How has this been arranged?"

He said: "I cannot tell you that."

There was a silence. Then Nicole said: "While you were away I have been thinking, monsieur." In the dim light he could see that she was looking away from him. "Ever since John was killed I have been desolate," she said quietly. "It seemed to me that there was no goodness in the world, that everything had gone mad and foul—that God had died or gone away, and left the world to Hitler."

There was a pause. The old man did not speak.

"But now," she said, "I think I can begin to see the pattern. It was not meant that John and I should be happy together, save for a short time. But now, through John and me, it is intended that these children should escape from Europe to grow up in peace." Her voice dropped. "This may have been what John and I were brought together for," she said. "In thirty years the world may need one of these little ones. It may be Ronnie or it may be Willem, or any one of the others who does great things for the world," she said. "But when that happens, monsieur, it will be because I met your son and we fell in love."

He leaned across and took her hand, and sat there in the dim light holding it for a long time. Presently they lay down upon their beds, and lay awake till dawn.

The next evening after dinner they were taken out and put into a covered van. Two German soldiers got in with them, and they moved off. The van swayed and rolled inland from the coast through the leafy lanes in the warm evening until they came to the outskirts of a town. Nicole peered out. "Brest," she said. "I know this street."

They were taken to the railway station and put into a third-class carriage with their guards.

Ronnie said: "Is this the train we're going to sleep in, Mr. Howard?"

He smiled patiently. "This isn't the one I meant, but we may have to sleep in this one," he said.

Rose said: "I do feel thirsty. May I have an orange?"

There were oranges for sale on the platform. Howard had no money. He explained the requirement to one of the German soldiers, who got out and bought oranges for all of them.

At eight o'clock the train started, and soon it drew up at a little place called Lanissant. Major Diessen, smart and upright in his black field boots, came to the door of their carriage and opened it. The German sentries got up quickly and stood to attention.

"You must get out," he said.

Nicole and Howard got the children out of the carriage onto the platform. Over the hill the sun was setting in a clear sky. The train moved away and they were left standing on the little platform in the middle of the country with the Gestapo officer.

"So," he said. "You will now follow me."

He led the way down the wooden steps that gave onto the road. Outside, in the lane, there was a van with a soldier and a child in it.

Diessen opened the door and made the child get out. "*Komm'*, *Anna,*" he said. "*Hier ist Herr Howard, und mit ihm wirst du zu Onkel Ruprecht gehen.*"

The little girl stared at the old man. Then she stretched out a little skinny arm, and in a shrill voice exclaimed: "*Heil Hitler!*"

The old man said gravely: "*Guten abend, Anna.*" He turned to the Gestapo officer, smiling faintly. "She will have to get out of that habit if she's going to America," he said.

Diessen nodded. "That is so. Now, will you all get into the car. We will not linger in this place."

They all got into the van. Diessen gave a cotton bag tied with a string to Howard, and another to Nicole.

"Your papers and your money," he said briefly. "See that it is all in order."

The old man opened it. Everything that had been taken from his pockets was there, quite intact.

In the gathering dusk they drove through the countryside. At ten o'clock, in the first darkness, they ran softly onto the quay at l'Abervrach.

The Gestapo officer got out and stood for half a minute, staring around. All was quiet and still. There were no guards to be seen. Diessen turned back to the car. "Come," he said. "Get out quickly—and do not let the children talk." He said to Nicole: "There is to be no trickery. You shall stay with me. If you should try to go with them, I shall shoot the lot of you."

She raised her head. "You need not draw your gun," she said. "I shall not try to go."

The German did not answer her, but pulled the big automatic from the holster at his waist. In the dim light he went striding softly down the quay; the others followed.

There was a fishing boat, where the slip ran down into the water, and two men. One was standing on the quay in black uniform, and the other, Simon Focquet, was in the boat, holding her to the quay by a rope rove through a ring.

"In with you, quickly," said Diessen. "I want to see you get away."

He turned to Focquet, speaking in French. "You are not to start your engine till you are past Le Trepied," he said. "I do not want the countryside to be alarmed."

The young man nodded. "There is no need," he said in the soft Breton dialect. "There is sufficient wind to steer by, and the ebb will take us out."

They passed the seven children one by one down into the boat. "You now," the German said to Howard. "Remember to behave yourself in England. I shall send for you in London in a very few weeks' time. In September."

The old man turned to Nicole. "This is good-bye, my dear," he said. He hesitated. "I do not think this war will be over in September. I may be old when it is over, and not able to travel very well. You will come and visit me, Nicole? There is so much that I shall want to say to you."

She said: "I will come and stay with you as soon as we can travel. And you shall talk to me about John."

The German said: "You must go now."

Howard kissed the girl; for a minute she clung to him. Then he got down into the boat among the children.

Focquet was thrusting vigorously with an oar against the quay-side. The old man saw the figure of the girl standing with the Germans by the water's edge. The ebb caught the boat and hurried her quietly out into the stream; Focquet was heaving on a halliard forward and the heavy brown sail crept slowly up the mast. For a moment he lost sight of Nicole as a mist dimmed his eyes; then he saw her again clearly, still standing motionless beside the Germans. Then the gloom shrouded all of them, and all that he could see was the faint outline of the hill against the starry sky.

THE BOAT NOSED into Plymouth Sound late the next afternoon. Ahead of them lay the town, grey and peaceful in the evening sunlight. Howard stared at it and sighed a little. It seemed to him that he had been happier in France than he would be in his own land:

There were other boats before them at the fish quay to which they were directed, boats full of an assortment of nationalities, clambering ashore and into England. They lay off for a quarter of an hour before they could get to the steps, while the gulls screamed around them.

At last they were all stumbling up the steps to join the crowd of refugees in the fish market. Howard was still in the clothes of a Breton labourer, unshaven, and very tired. The children, hungry and exhausted, clustered round him.

A masterful woman, trim and neat in the uniform of the W.V.S. shepherded them to a bench. Howard collapsed half in a coma, utterly exhausted. Half an hour later a young girl brought them cups of tea, which they took gratefully.

Refreshed, the old man took more interest in his surroundings. He heard a cultured Englishwoman's voice. "There's that lot over there, Mrs. Dyson. All those children with the two men."

"What nationality are they?"

"Some of them are English."

There was an exclamation of concern. "I had no idea! But they're in such a *state*!" There was a shocked pause. "That horrible old man—I wonder how he came to be in charge of them."

The old man closed his eyes, smiling a little. This was the England that he knew and understood. This was peace.

Chapter Twelve

The last bomb had fallen, the last gun had fired; over in the east the fires were dying down. Then came the long notes of the "All Clear" from different quarters of the town.

We got up stiffly from our chairs. I went over to the long window at the far end of the room, pulled back the curtains and threw back the shutters. The glass from the window fell in on the carpet with a crash; the wind blew in our faces acrid with the smell of burning.

I turned from the window. "Did you get them over to the States?" I asked.

"Oh yes," he said. "They all went together. I sent a telegram to the Cavanaghs offering to send Sheila and Ronnie, and Tenois asked if he might send Rose. I got a woman that I know to go with them, and take them to Coates Harbour."

"And Anna too?"

He nodded. "Anna went too." We moved towards the door. "I had a letter this week from her uncle in White Falls. He said that he had sent a cable to his brother in Germany, so that ought to be all right."

"Your daughter must have had a bit of a shock when they arrived," I said.

He laughed. "Well, I don't know. I sent a cable asking if she'd have them, and she said she would."

We went downstairs in the grey dawn and parted in the hall. He went out a few steps ahead of me; I paused to ask the night porter about damage to the club. He said that they had had a fire-bomb on the roof.

I yawned. "I spent the night up in the smoking-room talking to Mr. Howard," I said.

The man nodded. "I looked in once or twice and saw you sitting with him," he said. "I said to the steward, I said—quite a good thing you was with him. He's got to look a great deal older recently."

"Yes," I said. "I'm afraid he has."

"He went away for a long holiday a month or two ago," the porter said. "But I don't know as it did him a great deal of good."

I went out, the glass crunching beneath my feet.

Nevil Shute

For a quarter of a century Nevil Shute was almost certainly the most widely-read novelist in the world. Today, fourteen years after his death, his popularity shows little sign of abating. Books like *No Highway*, and *A Town Like Alice* (Condensed Books, 1967 and 1969)—and *Pied Piper*, of course—continue to be read and enjoyed by millions.

Yet, strangely enough, writing success did not come to Shute until his middle years. Indeed, until he was forty he had hardly sought such success, being happily embarked on a career of a very different kind. Following training as an engineer he had joined the De Havilland Aircraft Company in 1921 and risen to be Deputy Chief Engineer. He then moved into airship design and finally founded his own aircraft company. He wrote his first book in 1926, but it was really with the publication of *Pied Piper* in 1942 that he made his name as a novelist. At that time he was scientific adviser to the Royal Navy, and it was not until he had completed his war service that he was able to work full time on his books.

In 1950 he bought a substantial farm near Melbourne in Australia, and emigrated there with his wife and two daughters. A perfectionist in all things, he ran that farm so that, as a friend remembers, "The cattle and pigs he raised always looked as if they had just been washed."

He was a warmhearted man, in his books and in his life. He saw good in the world about him, and chose to write about it. He died in 1960, aged sixty-one. Today he is remembered as a prince among story-tellers.

END PLAY
Russell Braddon

End Play

A CONDENSATION OF THE BOOK BY

RUSSELL BRADDON

ILLUSTRATED BY MICHAEL JOHNSON

PUBLISHED BY MICHAEL JOSEPH, LONDON

". . . We have just been advised of the murder of yet another hitch-hiker. . . . The police say they are confident that she is the fourth victim . . . of the murderer now known as the Motorway Maniac. . . . By now someone must suspect the identity of this dangerous man, and yet be protecting him. . . ."

"Wouldn't you protect me?" Mark asks his brother as they discuss the news bulletin on the murders. But Robbie retorts that it is an absurd question. However, as a deceptively unsubtle Chief Superintendent Cheadle and his apparently dense sergeant take on this peculiar duo as suspects, Mark's question becomes crucial. Robbie, by instinct a winner, treats the inquiry as if it were a game of cards and boldly sets out to take every trick.

Wednesday: Half-Past Two

She had chosen a stretch of road where she could see each oncoming car for a quarter of a mile, to thumb the right car, the right driver.

She wore her brother's faded jeans, scarlet shoes, a voile shirt with the three top buttons undone, its tail knotted across her bare midriff, and a purple, floppy-brimmed hat. Swinging at her side was a shoulder bag. Her thumb sat hitched in the pocket of her jeans; waiting for the right car, the right driver.

Eight passed—six without a glance, two with more than a glance. Both she rejected with a toss of her floppy purple hat. But the ninth, she felt as soon as she saw it at the end of the momentarily deserted road, was the right one; and as the driver's head and shoulders grew more distinct, she knew it.

She swung her insolent thumb twice. And stood motionless as he passed her. Thirty yards on he halted, unlatching the door. And wasn't looking back. She liked that; liked confident men. She strolled to the car, swinging her shoulder bag. With her hip she pushed the door wide and, stooping, thrusting her head inside, asked: "Going far?"

"Far enough"—glancing into the rear-vision mirror, noting the empty road. "Make up your mind."

"Domineering, aren't we?" she jeered. But slid in beside him.

It began to rain, and he switched on the windscreen wipers. Then, turning towards her, placed one arm along the seat top behind her and his other hand on her belly.

"Don't waste time, do you?" she commented, but without rancour.

Not bothering to answer, he withdrew his hand and kissed her. Eyes closed, she failed to notice that his were open and that his hand had gone to the glove box.

Wednesday: Ten Past Three

As perversely as it had started, the rain stopped. Whereupon the sun shone, making the droplets on the windscreen glitter. But Mark Gifford was used to the glare of sun off water. Unblinking, he swung his car out of the narrow country lane and through his brother's gate.

Though the garage at the end of the concrete drive was open, his brother's Morris 1100 stood outside. He pulled onto the lawn beside it and switched off his ignition. Then, reaching behind him, he took a suitcase from the back seat, got out of the car, slammed its door and strode across the soggy lawn.

Sliding open the glass door at the side of the cottage, he stepped inside.

More loudly than he had intended, he called: "Robbie?"

"Who's that?" From the front of the cottage. At which he relaxed.

"Mark, you twit," he replied, dropping his suitcase, tossing his driving gloves on top of it. "Who were you expecting?"

"Oh . . . Elizabeth and Richard, Margaret and Tony. You know, the usual mob."

"You in the bedroom or the head?" A toilet flushed. He glanced around the familiar room. At the far end, the kitchen unit; on either side of the fireplace, chintzy armchairs; leaning against it, a fencer's sabre; in front of it, the sofa; on the chimney piece, the electric clock he had given Robbie for Christmas, a photograph of himself in his officer's uniform, and the transistor radio he had given Robbie for his birthday.

Crossing to the fireplace, Mark switched on the radio. He was twenty-five and he disliked silence. Which the latest chart topper shrilly pierced as Robbie wheeled himself into the room.

If anything, Robbie was better-looking than his brother, his shoulders even broader, his clothes as informally fashionable and his complexion as smooth. Whereas Mark's habitual expression was one of amiablc candour, however, his was bland.

"Vulgar word, head," he rebuked, deftly manoeuvring his chair. "Why can't you say bog like everyone else?" Almost as an afterthought he held out his hand, which Mark shook.

"Hello, Robbie." For all its casualness, Mark's greeting was affectionate. Perhaps too affectionate, because Robbie at once withdrew his hand, looking him up and down.

"God, you're brown," he complained. "And unpunctual! Five, you said"—glancing at the electric clock, which said only a quarter past three. "Or is that stupid machine on the blink again?"

"No," began Mark, glancing at his watch, "it's—" But Robbie, having wheeled himself to the mantelpiece to examine the clock, cut him short.

"Not on the blink. Going. I'll never understand electricity. I mean"—swivelling around to face Mark—"how can the same stuff make clocks tick, kettles boil, fridges freeze, radios talk and television look at you?"

Mark laughed. Always, after each voyage, each time he came home, the same thing. A few minutes of facetious fencing, of parrying any attempt at intimacy. "You really want to know?"

"No. But when all the kettles in Britain suddenly start screaming pop, and the TV sets freeze, don't say I didn't warn you."

"How are you, Robbie?"

"Fine." But reached ostentatiously high to switch off the radio.

"You sound a bit . . ." Mark let the sentence die.

"It's been a long time," Robbie explained with a show of contrition. "I got myself into a state—cleaning."

"Relax, Robbie. My fault for being early. You had a lot to do in the house, and you had to go out—"

"Did the shopping. Steak do for dinner? Have to, 'cos that's what we've got. How was Sydney? And why, for God's sake, don't you sit yourself down?" Even for Robbie it was staccato.

Dumping himself in an armchair, Mark said: "What's wrong?"

At last Robbie smiled. "You know me." He shrugged. "I don't really mind this thing"—slapping the wheels of his chair almost affectionately—"so long as I can kid everyone into *not* wondering how I manage the bog. Anyway"—looking sociable—"how come you're early?"

Hesitating only a second, Mark answered: "Woke up too late to go to the dentist, so I mucked about in the flat and then set off."

Robbie's tenseness had vanished. "Good trip down?"

"Deadly. Sheeting rain and a terrible hitchhiking bird."

"*You* picked up a bird?" Robbie looked both disconcerted and amused; and Mark wished he hadn't mentioned it.

"A raging nympho," he muttered. "But she was lying at the side of the road in this monsoonal rain and I thought it was a hit-and-run job and pulled up; and before I could even open my door, she'd hopped in." Robbie laughed. "Said it always worked and please would I drive her to the Aylesbury post office, where she had to meet her auntie!"

"Sounds reasonable," commented Robbie.

"She was a man-eating blonde, well below the age of consent, with eyes made up like a tart's and an IQ of minus infinity."

"Chance like that, I'm surprised you were early," Robbie said.

"Man-eating birds are not my scene."

"Are any birds your scene?"

Back to the old subject, thought Mark. "I know," he conceded. "I'm twenty-five, unattached and I never talk sex! Well, neither would you if you were at sea with a mob who talked nothing else."

"You mean," corrected Robbie gently, "neither would I if *you* were the one in this chair, virtually a eunuch like me."

Mark met his brother's gaze. "I don't talk that talk to you because you're the brother I've always worshipped," he said simply.

Too simply for Robbie. "Quite right too. I'm extremely worshipful. By the way, did I tell you I'd been picked for the Olympic Games?"

"No!" Mark was delighted. "For archery?"

"Archery, the javelin and fencing." There was a glint of ferocious satisfaction in his eyes that he of all people should represent Britain's paraplegic athletes in three separate sports; satisfaction, Mark realized, not at being best in three sports but at having denied three rivals the places they'd wanted on an Olympic team.

For an instant such ungenerosity made him uneasy. But then he remembered the Robbie of his youth: the superb athlete; the joyous competitor; the medical student in his final year who had been certain of a place on England's squash team, until a mid-court collision had sent him sprawling—and left him a cripple.

But still a competitor. Though Stoke Mandeville Hospital was celebrated for its fighting spirit, it had never produced a more implacable fighter than Robert Gifford. For which one had, Mark acknowledged, to admire him.

He congratulated his brother. "Robbie, that's great. You might have written and told me."

"Didn't I?" Robbie said, ignoring the fact that he never wrote. "If I didn't, I'm sure I meant to. . . . Of course, what the Electricity Board *should* do is invent a machine that takes letters down as you think of them." He waved a hand at the electric outlet beside the fireplace. "Do you reckon you'd get a letter if I plugged myself into that?"

"Yeah. From your solicitor, telling me you'd fried."

They were happy now; playing with words, suspending reality.

"I might just steam," countered Robbie. "Or light up." He headed for the kitchen unit. "Feel like a cuppa? Sorry there's nothing stronger. Got to keep to me budget."

Mark stood up. "I brought some whisky. It's in the car."

Robbie whirled to face him. "Leave it there!" he rapped. Then, visibly controlling himself as he switched the kettle on: "I mean, you've bought me enough. From this elegant chair to my magnificent car and my humble abode that must have cost you a bomb."

"It wasn't my money."

"The old man left the twenty thousand to you."

"For us. He—" About to say, he meant me to look after you, Mark changed his text abruptly. "He knew what a twit you were about money."

"Nonsense," retorted Robbie. "He left you his money because you were his favourite; because he didn't want it frittered away by a second lot of death duties if I predeceased you; and because he knew I'd predecease you by forty years at least."

"Now who's talking nonsense?"

Robbie opened a drawer and carefully took out cups and saucers. "One day my kidneys'll pack it in. The paraplegic's occupational hazard. I know it, you know it, the old man knew it." He took a teapot from a lower drawer. "So, like the sensible solicitor he was, he left everything to you."

He placed the teapot beside the kettle and turned his chair to face his brother. "And very generously you've spent a lot of it on me. But enough's enough. All I want is to see you occasionally—when you can spare the time."

"Robbie, I always look forward to it. Every time I'm home."

Robbie poured hot water into the pot. "I'm surprised you bother," he muttered.

"Oh Robbie!" Mark walked to the wheel chair and, standing behind it, gripped his brother's shoulders. "I look forward to seeing you when I'm home. I like it here."

"Must be the thought of all those blondes thumbing lifts on the way," Robbie bantered. "Though if I were you"—more soberly—"I'd concentrate on brunettes in the future."

"You mean they still haven't caught him?"

Indifferently Robbie shook his head. "The countryside littered with murdered blondes, and apparently they haven't a clue." Opening the refrigerator, he took out a bottle of milk.

"Sure you don't want a whisky?" Mark asked.

"Sure. Take it back to your scruffy mates in your London pad."

Mark hid his disappointment. "They're all bores."

"You could move."

"It's comfortable and cheap, and I'm hardly ever there."

"Well"—pouring tea, somehow indicating disapproval—"it's your life; but a flat with three other blokes is hardly my idea of a love nest."

The old subject. Change it. Not too obviously. "Dirty things, nests."

"Lair, then." Persistent, and testy.

"Lairs are smelly."

Robbie slammed the teapot onto the drainboard. "You're just *not* to be pinned down, are you?"

"As to what?"—defensively, because he'd lied about missing a dentist appointment. What he'd missed was lunch with his girl friend—with whom he'd had a corrosive row about spending three of his six days' leave with Robbie. But that he couldn't tell Robbie. Not the Robbie whom the nurses of his student days had called Dr. Kildare; whom girls no longer even noticed.

"As to what you think, what you hope to do, who you like—"

It had to be stopped. "I think about my job; I hope to become a commodore; and I like you."

Again the tension passed. Smiling wryly, Robbie mused: "The strange thing is, you always did." He passed a cup of tea.

"Nothing strange about it."

"Your parents did adopt me."

"They chose you. Me they made and were stuck with."

"Does that bother you?"

"Never thought about it. Does your being adopted bother you?"

Now it was Robbie's turn to change the subject. "I'm sorry. Been a bastard, haven't I? It's just that after six years you'd think I'd be used to this." He banged the wheel of his chair. "But there are still times—"

"Drink your tea."

They sipped thoughtfully, until the silence became almost tangible, like a wall topped with shards of glass.

"When you're finished," Mark suggested, saying the first thing that came to mind, "I'll set up the target."

A flicker of enthusiasm lightened his brother's grey eyes, then died. "You'll be bored stiff."

"Try me." Mark grinned, picking up the target that leaned against the wall and carrying it to the garden door. "Get your bow and arrows."

So Robbie wheeled himself past the telephone in the hall, past the bathroom on the right and the doorway to the garage on the left, and into his bedroom, while Mark carried the target to the end of the long lawn and set it up against the hedge.

Robbie appeared in the doorway and precisely positioned his chair so that the wheel nearest the target lay along the crack between the second and third floorboards. The target in front of the hedge was exactly fifty yards from this spot; Robbie had once made Mark measure the distance. "O.K. Stand clear."

"I wouldn't insult you"—staying where he was, a few yards to the right of the target.

"Do what you're told. Nowadays my neck gets stiff and my aim can be hairy. What'd people say if I killed you?"

Surprised, because Robbie had never asked him to move before, and perturbed, because Robbie had never before mentioned a stiff neck, he retreated a few yards and watched his brother draw the bow he himself found difficult to draw, hold it steady at full stretch for fifteen seconds, and shoot.

After the last shot Mark plucked six arrows from the target and walked back to Robbie. "Not bad," he said. "You got a bull."

"You're right, it wasn't bad; for someone who's allegedly a master bowman, it was bloody terrible."

"Not if he's got a stiff neck. How long've you had it?"

Ignoring the question, Robbie loosed another round of arrows.

Again Mark collected them. "*Two*. You're getting better."

"Not better enough," grumbled Robbie. "Bring the target in."

Wednesday: Half-Past Three

His bow across the arms of his chair, Robbie watched Mark stroll towards him, the target held single-handed on his head. He's strong, he thought, and good-looking, so why does he keep coming? Hero worship still? Who are you kidding? And why's he smiling? What's there to smile at? On the other hand, if you've got teeth like that, and a tan to show 'em off, why not? Missed the dentist, he'd said.

"How's the toothache?" he asked, as Mark put the target back.

"Just a checkup." Had there been a pause before he answered? "Your neck bothering you?"

"No. It's just that shooting from indoors doesn't *feel* right. I should go to Stoke and practise properly."

"Why not? I could come with you."

"Forget it. You've just arrived," Robbie said, turning away.

"Look," Mark said to him, "you want to practise, don't you? Only you don't want me to come with you?" Looking more perplexed than hurt.

Choose your words, thought Robbie. "Would you believe me"—awkwardly, but with that self-deprecating smile that never failed—"if I said you put me off?"

Mark's face cleared. In a school play Mark had been confident and good, until his eyes had met Robbie's. At which he had dried up and had had to be prompted. "Remember the last school play?"

"You were the best Macbeth I ever saw. Don't tell me *I* put *you* off?"

Mark nodded. "So what time'll you be back?"

"Six," said Robbie. So promptly that Mark realized he'd intended going to Stoke Mandeville all along. Typically, though, he'd manipulated things so that his departure seemed to have been forced upon him.

"I'll put your things in your car." Reaching for Robbie's bow.

"No!" It was uttered with such hostility that Mark recoiled, shocked. Robbie forced himself to sound more reasonable. "I do everything for myself, Mark; you know that."

Yes, Mark had known that since the day he'd first visited Robbie at Stoke Mandeville. "Get the hell out of that chair and *stand!*" a physiotherapist was screaming at Robbie as Mark arrived. He'd wanted to box her ears, screaming like that at a seven-stone wraith. A sick, beautiful child of a man who, after five operations, was a rag doll without his spinal brace; whose once magnificent legs, without their braces, were hopelessly unhinged.

"Stand!" the girl had snarled.

Robbie, groaning, had frantically, unavailingly, struggled to obey, but when Mark had stepped forward to help him, he too had snarled: "Don't you dare! Till the day I bloody die, don't you *ever* dare." And had stood.

Yes, he knew Robbie did everything for himself. "Only being sociable," he apologized. "Like opening a door for somebody."

"I know. Sorry I snapped. But once I let anyone help me with anything, I'll soon let everyone do the lot. Put me to bed, clean the house, get me in and out of the car. . . . *How* I hate getting in and out of that car."

"Ever thought you may be doing too much?"

"The day I can only do less, I'll take those," vowed Robbie, indicating a bottle of phenobarbs that sat on the table beside him.

"Don't say that." It was a subject Mark hated.

"It's my life," said Robbie, who had no dislike of death. "If it stops being interesting, why prolong it?"

"Depends what you call interesting."

"Winning." Robbie grinned. "Preferably gold medals at Olympic and Commonwealth Games! Wonder if they'll go on holding Commonwealth Games when finally they wake up to the fact there's no longer a Commonwealth?"

Mark looked surprised. Since his accident Robbie's interest in politics had been nil. He listened to no news bulletins and read no newspapers. "That's unlike you," Mark commented.

"It's the Games I'd miss, not the Commonwealth." A reference to the emptiness of his life, apart from sport.

"Maybe"—wondering how much a companion would cost—"you shouldn't live alone?" Mark suggested.

"And maybe," scoffed Robbie, "my father shouldn't have broken my back when I was four, so that twenty years later a bump on a squash court'd land me in a wheel chair. But he did. And if he hadn't, I'd never have been put in what the authorities described as 'care'; and then your parents would never have adopted me; and I'd never have been taught to speak properly, or played squash, or grown up with you. So maybe everything turns out for the best in this crummy world—and you should leave well enough alone."

"I didn't know," Mark murmured, "you'd been taught to speak properly."

"First thing the parents did when they got me—sent me to an elocutionist." He laughed. "Don't think they could understand a word I said. Nice of 'em never to have told you, though."

"We could easily get someone to keep you company."

"Actually, kiddo, I prefer it alone. Serious, aren't we? Well, I'd better go. What'll you do?"

"Have a nap."

"Sleep well, then"—wheeling himself to the door. "See you at six."

Glancing restlessly around the room, Mark switched on the radio; picked up Robbie's chest expander and, grimacing, found himself able to stretch it only four times; slashed the air with Robbie's sabre, and felt foolish; opened his suitcase, took out a paperback, and found he had read it already; heard Robbie slam the door of his car and start the engine; listened till he could no longer hear him driving away; then walked out of the front door.

To return, two minutes later, through the garden door, carrying a shoulder bag, a floppy-brimmed purple hat and the body of a blonde in jeans. Depositing the dead girl on the sofa, he stepped back and, still facing her, lowered himself into an armchair.

Wednesday: Ten to Four

His features taut but expressionless, he sat immobile, until he became aware of the dead girl's eyes. Through mascara-ed lashes they were staring at him.

He rose and covered her waxy face with her purple hat. Then unknotted her shirt and, pulling it down, concealed the blood-seeping wound beneath her breastbone. He returned to his chair and sat tensely, marshalling his thoughts.

"First," his housemaster had always admonished him before examinations, "be sure you've read and understood the question." Well, the question here was: *How would you dispose of the corpse of a girl so as to attract no suspicion to yourself while clearly indicating that she is the fourth victim of a murderer-at-large known as the Motorway Maniac?*

In other words, how do you dispose of a body cautiously enough not to be caught, yet recklessly enough for it to be the unmistakable work of a man whose previous victims had all been blatantly dumped in front of police stations?

And what if someone was waiting for her? At this very moment reporting her missing? He leaped to his feet.

"Never flap," his first skipper had admonished him. "Because, if you do, you'll not be able to think straight." So, suppressing the instinct to panic, he made himself think.

If anyone was expecting her, there might be a letter in her shoulder bag. He emptied its contents onto the carpet in front of the sofa. Sunglasses; a steel comb; an Iron Cross on a chain; a long blonde wig; a small purse; a photograph of a wild-haired pop singer inscribed *To Janine Talbot, with thanks and best wishes, Randy*

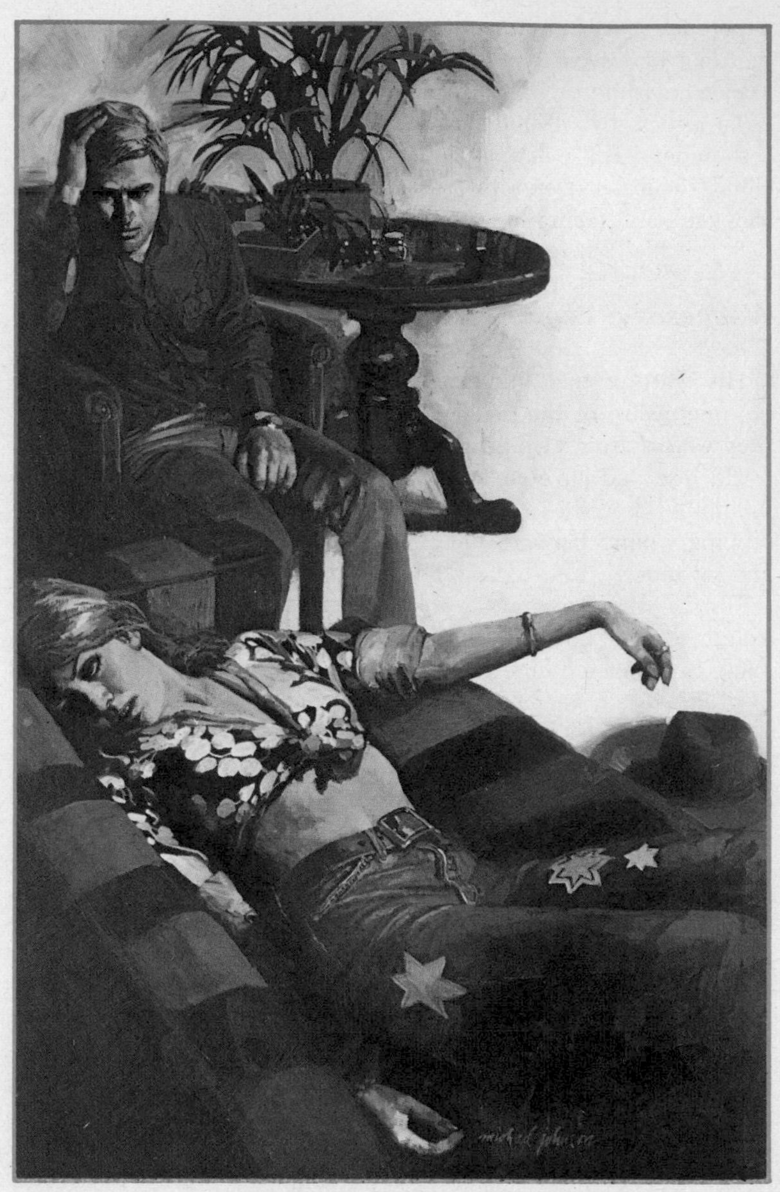

Horn—and on the back of it her name and address; cosmetic items; two keys, and a bottle of perfume.

Hell, the stopper had fallen out and perfume was soaking into the carpet. He ran to the sink, wet the dishcloth, returned to the carpet and, kneeling, rubbed vigorously. In his right hand the cloth, in his left the unstoppered bottle. Which now slopped the last of its contents over his trousers. It'd dry out. Wipe your fingerprints off the bottle and drop it back into the bag. He put the dishcloth back where he'd found it, dried his hands and drew on his driving gloves. No more fingerprints.

No letter, either, so maybe no one was waiting for her. But Robbie would return in an hour and three quarters. And Robbie would *not* be expecting a corpse on his sofa. Robbie. . . . A wheel chair—that was the answer.

Now that he knew what he had to do, Mark moved quickly and coolly. Into the garage for Robbie's old chair; into Robbie's bedroom for a travelling rug. Then, lifting the girl from the sofa, he sat her in the wheel chair, wrapped her fingers around the ends of the armrests and tucked the rug around her legs to bind her flaccid knees together. Her head, however, lolled. Back to Robbie's room for a neck brace. Five minutes later her head was erect, her chin high. He combed her hair and slid on her sunglasses. But even behind tinted lens the eyes remained conspicuously unblinking. He positioned the hat so that the floppy brim shielded them.

Perfect. Now for himself.

Removing his shoes, slacks and shirt, he took a pair of jeans from his suitcase and pulled them on; added a white T-shirt and a pair of plimsolls from Robbie's bedroom; hung the girl's Iron Cross around his neck; adjusted the long blonde wig on his head and, with a rubber band, tied it into a hippie's ponytail. Then he put on Robbie's horn-rimmed Polaroids and examined himself in the bathroom mirror. Horrible, but effective.

He switched off the radio, repacked the girl's shoulder bag, placed it on her lap, slid two pound notes into his pocket, checked the room and wheeled the chair out of the garden door and up the lawn to his car.

He opened the door, lifted the girl with her blanket-swaddled legs onto the front seat, and closed it again. She looked quite comfortable, leaning half against the back of the seat, half against the door.

He folded the wheel chair, dumped it onto the back seat and got in beside the girl. "I'm sorry, love," he told her as he turned into the lane, "but until we get where we're going, I'll have to talk to you so people'll think you're alive."

Thus, talking steadily, rehearsing his plan aloud, he drove her into Aylesbury. It was twenty-five past four.

IT WAS AN HOUR LATER that Robbie laid his bow across his knees and relaxed, pleased with his scores.

He was particularly pleased with his fitness when he surveyed the hospital's recent arrivals, hunched and desperate in their chairs. He shook his head at the thought of the battle that lay ahead of them. Yet none, he knew, would be allowed to even contemplate giving up; because everyone at Stoke helped everyone else. The strong in their chairs dragged the weak. And the staff encouraged them all. Two hundred and fifty maimed bodies propelling themselves into a new way of life.

"How're you doing, Robbie?"

It was the chief physiotherapist. "Fine, thanks, Charlie."

"You looked thoughtful."

"I was thinking about . . ." He surveyed the more athletic of his fellow Stokers. "You work miracles, don't you, Charlie?"

The chief physiotherapist grinned. "Remember the day, about six months after you got here, you said, 'Charlie, I'm sick of all this,' and I slapped you? 'I want to throw something,' you said."

"And you said, 'Right. Be at the field at one forty-five.' And when I got there you handed me a javelin and I threw myself out of my chair! Whereupon you handed me an eight-pound shot and told me to see if I could do any better with that."

"You'd be breaking the world record if you hadn't been so half-witted as to skimp on your training and muck up your neck."

"Not skimping this afternoon. I've left my brother alone at the cottage, though. Not very hospitable of me, was it? Rang him about an hour ago, to apologize, but either the line was out of order or he was so cheesed off he didn't answer."

"He's a big boy now. Oh, dear, look who's coming."

"Charlie!" groaned Robbie. "Stay and protect me."

"Protect yourself," hissed Charlie. "If necessary, shoot"—and abandoned him to his fate. Which took the form of an aging woman and her even older husband.

"Robert!" crowed Mrs. Lipton. "How lovely!" Her lips were too red, her hair too yellow and her figure quite out of control.

"Mrs. Lipton," Robbie greeted her coolly. "Mr. Lipton."

"My dear chap!" said Mr. Lipton, whose tiny hips, sheathed in maroon suede, supported a green-satined paunch.

"You must come to dinner," Mrs. Lipton commanded. "And christen our brand-new pool. What are you doing tonight?"

"My brother's with me."

"Then bring him too. We've always wanted to meet him. Ring him now and ask him," she instructed.

Accompanied by the Liptons, Robbie wheeled himself to the telephone and dialled. He allowed it to ring thirteen times before hanging up. "Line must be out of order," he said. "He doesn't answer."

"Perhaps you got a wrong number?" suggested Mrs. Lipton.

Robbie dialled again, with the same result. "Sorry," he said. "Definitely out of order. Afraid we'll have to postpone that dinner."

Mrs. Lipton pouted. "That's what you always say."

"What's the time?" Robbie asked her.

She examined her diamond-encrusted watch. "Half-past five exactly," she reported.

"Oh Lord," exclaimed Robbie. "I'm late. Thank you for asking me"—and sped towards his car.

AT WHICH MOMENT Mark was re-entering the cottage, carrying a folded wheel chair, a floppy purple hat, a rug and a neck brace—but no longer wearing either the wig or the Iron Cross. "Damn," he muttered looking at the clock. Robbie had said he'd be home at six. And Robbie invariably arrived on the dot. So he had thirty minutes.

Mark spent the first of those minutes planning what had to be done. Then he moved with precision. He took off Robbie's gym shoes and T-shirt and his own jeans. Repacking the jeans, he put on the shirt and slacks in which he had arrived. The rug, glasses, neck brace, T-shirt and shoes he returned to Robbie's bedroom. He wiped the wheel chair with a dishcloth, sprinkled it with dust from the Hoover and carried it into the garage. He vacuumed the dust he had spilled and restored the Hoover to its cupboard. Taking off his gloves, he brushed them clean and tossed them on top of his suitcase. He squirted lighter fluid over the purple hat, carried it into the garden and set fire to it.

He returned at two minutes to six. Switching on the radio, he ruffled his hair and lay face down on the sofa, breathing deeply, as if asleep. As the hands of the clock became vertical, he heard Robbie's car turning out of the lane and into the garage.

Wednesday: Six O'clock

Robbie transferred his twelve stone from driver's seat to wheel chair—a manoeuvre that usually exhausted him; but now so curious was he about Mark's failure to answer the telephone that he accomplished it with ease. Wheeling himself impatiently into the living room, he halted, frowning.

Mark lay flat on his face. The room reeked of perfume and the radio was screeching. Jerking himself to the fireplace, Robbie switched off the radio; then, wheeling about, he amiably demanded, "Little brother, what on earth have you been up to?"

Genuine alarm made it easier for Mark to simulate an abrupt awakening. "Eh?"—sitting up, looking bleary—"what'd you say?"

"I said"—with mock severity—"what on earth have you been up to? The place stinks of perfume." He sniffed. "And petrol."

"Oh, I–I spilled some aftershave on the carpet and tried to rub it off with lighter fluid. I was getting a book out of my case and it dropped."

Robbie peered at the carpet. "You've made a nasty *clean* patch. Why use an aftershave that smells—if you don't mind my saying so—like boarding-school custard?"

"A passenger gave it to me. Surprised you can still smell it, though. I can't."

"I've got a nose like a bloodhound," Robbie told him, staring at the spot on the carpet. "You been out?"

Tyre marks on the sodden lawn, thought Mark. Forgot about them. Had he seen them? Better cover . . . "Engine's been running rough," he explained. "Fiddled about with it and took her out for a run. Worse, if anything. So I thought to hell with it."

"Why?"

"I dunno." Because he couldn't think of a reason. "I guess I wanted a nap." He stood up and switched on the radio. His manner was edgy.

"Take it easy," Robbie urged, wheeling himself to the fireplace to switch the radio off again. "I wasn't prying."

"I want to hear the news," Mark told him sharply.

Robbie grimaced. "Can't imagine why." Referring to the irrelevance, for him, of something that the fit found vital. But he left the radio on.

From which the newscaster's voice announced: "Two Liberian tankers collided this afternoon off the Goodwin Sands, making a total of sixteen collisions this month. Both vessels," advised the newsreader, with evident satisfaction, "are sinking." Then he cleared his throat. "And here is a special news flash. From Aylesbury we have just been advised by the police of the murder of yet another hitchhiker. Thc body of twenty-three-year-old Janine Talbot, of Kings Langley, was found less than an hour ago in the back row of a local cinema."

Robbie wheeled himself to the refrigerator and poured a glass of milk, clearly bored by the violent world of the non-disabled.

"The girl's mother, Mrs. Mavis Talbot, told the police a few minutes ago that Janine left home shortly after two this afternoon to hitchhike to Aston Clinton to see her unemployed boy friend. The police say they are confident that she is the fourth victim, in just over a year, of the murderer now known as the Motorway Maniac. They point out that once again the victim was picked up on the A41, between the M1 turn-off and Aylesbury; that once again the victim is a blonde in her middle twenties; that once again the victim was stabbed under the breastbone and through the heart; that once again the victim was apparently neither robbed nor sexually assaulted; and that once again the murderer has contrived to deposit his victim in a public place without attracting attention.

"'The murderer,' says Detective Chief Superintendent Cheadle, who has headed the squad hunting the Motorway Maniac for fourteen months, 'is a man who hates young women and will murder again unless he is apprehended.' He emphasizes that by now someone must suspect the identity of this dangerous man, and yet be protecting him."

"Must we listen to this drivel?" protested Robbie.

"The police do, however, have a positive lead at last," the newsreader continued. "They are anxious to contact a young man about five feet ten inches tall, who has long fair hair, is wearing dark glasses, jeans, a T-shirt and gym shoes, and who was seen entering the Rex Cinema, Aylesbury, at about four thirty. This man, or anyone knowing his whereabouts, is asked to contact the police. An early arrest, says Chief Superintendent Cheadle, is expected."

Robbie switched off the radio contemptuously. "I'm sorry, Mark, but if you want the rest of your so-called news, get it in your car. An early arrest! What've they got on him now that they didn't have when he dumped the others outside the police stations?"

"According to that"—tapping the silent radio—"someone who can help them with their inquiries."

"Don't they always? And does he ever come forward? Be mad if he did, of course. They'd charge him as soon as they saw him."

"Also"—staring at the radio—"someone's protecting him."

Robbie looked hard at his brother's averted head. "And why," Robbie demanded, "would anyone do that?"

"Wouldn't you protect me?" Mark asked.

"You mean, if I knew *you* were this maniac? It's a hypothetical question, and absurd. Even if you did. . . ." Frowning.

"Did what Robbie?" asked Mark.

Robbie headed for the kitchen. "Time we ate. I'm starving."

"Did *what*?" slapping the mantelpiece with open palm.

"Tell me you picked up a blonde nympho and that the trip was 'deadly'."

Mark collapsed into an armchair. "You know," he confessed, "you had me worried? For a minute I thought you really did suspect me."

"You?" snorted Robbie. "A murderer? You can't even lie, and you're so guileless it's pathetic. If ever you're involved in a murder, it'll be as the victim, not the killer, I promise you."

Mark flushed. "Just as well I was here all afternoon, though, isn't it? Not that I could prove it if I was asked to."

"And why would anyone ask you to?"

"I came by the A41 at the time they say the girl was on it."

"So did a hundred others. But if you *were* asked to prove you'd been here all afternoon, I'd swear I'd spent it with you."

"And you say *I* can't lie," scoffed Mark. "How many people saw you practising at Stoke between four and half-past five?"

"All right. I'd say I telephoned you here at four thirty, and again just before five thirty, and spoke to you both times."

"Why?"

"Because I'm not having you involved in a murder on account of a stupid coincidence."

"I mean, why *would* you have phoned me?"

"To suggest you come to Stoke because I'd decided you wouldn't put me off after all. How's that?"

"Very good. And why'd you ring me the second time?"

"To ask if you'd like to dine with those awful Liptons."

"And how would you convince *them* of that?"

"Wouldn't have to. They invited me and I used you as an excuse. They said bring you, and made me ring you on the spot."

"So you did ring me?"

"Twice. The line was out of order, but I didn't tell the Liptons that. The phone *didn't* ring, did it?"

"Not that I heard." He hesitated. "Then I'm in the clear?"

"Well, of course you are, you half-wit. So long as no one saw you pick up the nympho. You sure no one did?"

"Yes."

"Good!" Robbie seemed to relax, yet almost at once asked: "Anyone see you put her down?"

"Well, I suppose so," Mark answered fretfully. "It *was* in front of the post office. Shouldn't think anyone really noticed, though. I mean, people don't, do they?"

"Who cares anyway? If no one knows you picked a girl up, why should the police want proof that you ever put her down?"

"Must you keep saying 'put her down'? You make her sound like a rabid dog."

Robbie pondered the point. "Makes one think, doesn't it? The most innocent words can be traps. 'Deadly', you said. Sounds innocent enough. Until a blonde's found murdered. 'Anyone see you put her down?' I asked. Sounds innocent enough. Until someone who's picked up a blonde can't prove what he did with her."

"Except," Mark corrected, "you *should* have said *set* her down."

To which Robbie blandly responded: "You know, you're right."

"A Freudian slip?" Mark accused.

"Meaning do I subconsciously think that you, little brother, are the much publicized Motorway Maniac? I've told you"—shaking his head—"you couldn't be. That offer of Scotch still stand?"

"I'll get it."

Placidly Robbie watched him leave, then wheeled himself to the spot on the carpet. He reached down to probe with a suspicious fingertip; straightening, he sniffed, his eyes meantime flickering up and down the sofa. Then he turned to face the garden door, and sat motionless until Mark returned.

"Just a small one," he instructed.

Mark poured deliberately and offered the glass. "That do?"

He had delayed his return long enough to compose himself—and to remind himself of his duty to a disabled brother. A moment ago he had felt close to violence. It must not happen again.

"Perfect," said Robbie. He sipped appreciatively. "Know what I'd like to do tonight?"

"Scrabble?" Mark suggested. "Two-handed bridge?"

Robbie shook his head. "The flicks."

"Anything good on?" The ease and amiability with which he asked the question surprised him.

"Only that Fellini thing at the Rex."

"Seen it," Mark told him, still apparently at ease, but no longer amiable.

"Really?" Robbie looked surprised. "When?"

"Last voyage." And thought, drop it, Robbie, drop it.

"Blast," grumbled Robbie. "The Rex is the only cinema I can get the chair into. Oh well . . ." And Mark knew then that he had to seem willing to visit the scene of the afternoon's crime.

His eyes never leaving Robbie's, he said: "We'll go to the Fellini"—he couldn't bring himself to say "the Rex"—"if you really want to."

Robbie not only wanted to, he was clearly determined to. "Sure you don't mind?" he asked.

"Why should I? It's a super film, and I missed most of it last time." Mark had the feeling they were playing Russian Roulette, except that five words out of every six were loaded. There was only one safe course: to resume the routine of two brothers enjoying a few days together in the country and to avoid all but the most trivial topics of conversation.

"Time to eat," he told Robbie. "Don't argue; just go and wash your grubby face while I vulcanize our steaks"—opening the refrigerator.

"Yes, sir. Oh damn! I forgot to buy vegetables."

"There's a lettuce and some tomatoes. I'll make a salad."

"Dear old Mark." Robbie grinned, heading for the bathroom. "What'd I do without you? Come to that, what'd I do to deserve you?"

Exit Robbie, lobbing a last grenade, thought Mark, beginning to despair.

Wednesday: Seven Thirty

But the meal passed smoothly, Robbie regaling his brother with the latest local gossip. "I feel a bit mean about the Liptons," he confessed as he dried the dishes Mark had washed. "She and Stanley've done a lot for Stokers. She's no kids of her own, so she mothers us. And Stanley bought me my bow. When I got up to eight stone but still wanted to die because Charlie had me exercising with a bow I couldn't draw, Rose oozed alongside one afternoon and said, 'You put on another three stone, Robert, and I'll make my Stanley give you the best bow money can buy.' From that day on I never looked back. And the very day I hit eleven stone, Rose and Stanley arrived with my bow! Same story with dozens of us; and none of us can stand her. That the last?"—putting away a frying pan.

"That's it. How's about we get the cousins tomorrow evening for bridge?"

"Long as I play against you."

"Against?" They usually played together.

"I enjoy squeezing," Robbie said. "Margaret and Andrew haven't a clue about discards, so it's no fun squeezing them. Hey, it's twenty to eight."

They left in Robbie's car, Robbie confidently manipulating the special hand controls, and spent most of the trip into Aylesbury discussing the relative merits of the strong and weak no-trump opening bid.

"Well, you always hold the cards," Mark concluded as they approached the Rex, "so the strong no-trump's all right. But if ever I'm lucky enough to get twelve points, I want to open."

"Better sit quiet and let me get into trouble," Robbie counselled. "Hell"—glancing sideways as they passed the Rex. "Place is swarming with cops!"

"There *has* been a murder."

"Four hours ago," Robbie cavilled, turning into the car park. "What do they think they'll find? The murderer returned to the scene of his crime?"

Mark didn't answer. He got out of the car and waited till Robbie had laboured into his chair, and together they approached the Rex.

A tall, crumple-suited, middle-aged man, his grey hair combed so sleekly back he looked as if he'd been swimming in glycerine, waved them officiously away from the lobby. Into which Robbie promptly wheeled himself.

"Are you blind?" the man snarled.

"Just crippled," retorted Robbie. "How about you?"

"I," the man pronounced, "am a police officer heading a murder investigation."

Chief Superintendent Cheadle, thought Mark, remembering the news bulletin.

"Good for you," said Robbie. "What time's the film start?"

"This cinema, sir, is closed."

"You seem to persist in your assumption that wheel chairs are for the blind. As one of the blessedly sighted, I am, of course, aware that this cinema is closed, but what I asked you was, when will it reopen? In other words, when will this chaos of coppers, this frenzy of fuzz, disperse, so that law-abiding citizens like myself may enjoy the creative art of Mr. Fellini?"

"I've no idea," rasped the chief superintendent.

"In that case, Constable," commanded Robbie, regally downgrading the chief superintendent, "pray take me to someone who has."

"Sergeant!" bellowed the chief superintendent. A blank-faced, fair-haired six-footer in cavalry-twill slacks and the inevitable checked jacket materialized beside him.

"Now," the chief superintendent advised, "you will give Sergeant Robinson your name and address and you will then either move along—where, I don't care—though I would prefer it to be one of the colonies, or I'll arrest you for obstructing the police in the prosecution of their duties."

"Is that what this charade's supposed to be?"

"Your name and address, sir!" roared the chief superintendent.

"Lionel Barrymore, late of Hollywood," Robbie recited.

Mark had had enough.

"Give it to him, Robbie," he said. His brother's almost frenetic flippancy terrified him.

"Robert Stephen Gifford," sighed Robbie. "The Wheel-In—"

"*Wheel*-In?"

"It's a joke," Mark explained, anxious lest Cheadle take further umbrage.

"On the contrary," said Robbie, "It's perfectly serious."

"WHEEL IN," the sergeant printed in his notebook.

"Wheel-In where, sir?" Cheadle inquired with controlled fury.

"Brewers Lane. You go about three miles down this road, turn right just before St. Penelope's and you can't miss it."

"Aylesbury?"

"Aston Clinton," Mark amended.

"*Thank* you, sir," said Cheadle.

Mark squeezed his brother's shoulder, warning him that he had gone far enough.

"I'll pick you up round the corner," he instructed. "Good night, Chief Superintendent."

"Good night, sir."

Mark strode back to the car park while Robbie wheeled himself smoothly away and round the corner into the dim-lit side street flanking the cinema to wait.

A few minutes later Mark drove up and, sliding across the front seat, sat silent as Robbie hauled first himself and then his folding chair into the car, and headed for home in silence. "Bloody fiasco," Robbie said at last.

"A girl *has* been murdered," Mark reminded him once again.

"Girls are murdered, young men become paraplegics—life goes on."

"I'm sorry you didn't get to see your film."

Mark realized he sounded sarcastic, and was relieved that his brother took no offence. Instead Robbie gave him an apologetic grin.

"I'm being childish, aren't I? In a way, though, I am childish. I get excited when you come down. Find myself thinking, Mark's coming. With stories of the big, brave, outside world! And I even think, just like a kid, maybe he'll take me out, to the flicks, anywhere, I don't care, so long as it's out and I'm taken. Ridiculous, isn't it?"

"No," Mark muttered, remembering how often he had forgotten to take Robbie out, glad to sit and talk after his voyages around the world.

Robbie turned into the lane and Mark waited for him to continue. Quite deliberately, though, Robbie digressed. "Can't get over all those coppers. What were they looking for?"

"Clues, I suppose." Mark was wondering just how much damage Robbie had done provoking the chief superintendent.

"One of them," said Robbie, "being *my* name and address?"

"You did rather throw your weight around. And you called the chief superintendent a constable."

"I'll plead insanity!" Robbie decided, coasting into the garage. "Or say I had a blackout"—watching his brother get despondently out of the car. "My Lord, I'll say"—grunting as he dropped his chair by his open door—"I'm sorry"—manoeuvring himself into the chair—"but all I could see was this horrible face leering down at me and shouting, 'When did you last see your brother?' And that's all I remember, my Lord."

As one of his physiotherapists had once remarked, Robbie was almost incorrigibly frivolous: which often made it almost impossible to understand him.

Wednesday: Five Past Nine

Mark had had a shower while Robbie had made a pot of tea. They had just finished their first cup and Mark, clad only in a thigh-length, blue bathrobe, was setting up the camp bed. Robbie's eyes followed his brother's effortless movements.

"You think I went too far with the copper, don't you?" he said at last.

Mark was determined to avoid a clash, and chose his words carefully. "I don't think you exactly endeared yourself."

"Should I have?" Robbie challenged, as if he wanted a clash.

"You made your point—that you don't like coppers—so why didn't you just give them your name and address and leave it at that?"

"I did."

"Lionel Barrymore. Wheel Inn. Near a non-existent church."

"And that mute of a sergeant wrote it down!" crowed Robbie.

The doorbell rang; Mark headed up the hall.

"If it's Margaret or Andrew," Robbie called, "bring 'em in."

"It isn't Margaret or Andrew," Mark reported when he returned.

"Oh, my gawd," Robbie groaned. "They've come for me!"

"Detective Chief Superintendent Cheadle and Detective Sergeant Robinson," Mark announced.

"I trust you found my directions helpful?" Robbie inquired.

"Well, actually, sir, I think my sergeant must have misheard you," Cheadle confessed.

The sergeant looked blank. "*Can* he hear?" asked Robbie.

"Oh yes, sir," said Cheadle, staring at him.

"Superintendent," he advised, "I detest being gawped at."

Cheadle promptly averted his eyes. "I'm sorry, sir."

Deliberately changing his mood, Robbie announced: "Well, whatever I'm supposed to have done, I'm pleading blackouts and the Fifth Amendment. Or does that only work in the U.S.A.?"

Cheadle smiled. "I don't think it'd do you much good at the Old Bailey; but actually, Mr. Gifford, it's nothing *you've* done I've come about." Robbie nodded graciously. "It's something *I* did. I'm afraid I was rather rude to you."

"I cried all the way home."

"Poor Mr. Gifford. All I can say is that I'd just rushed down from the Yard, everything had gone wrong and the press were driving me mad. But when I realized we were passing this way, and saw that your lights were on—"

"You felt you simply had to drop in?" Robbie said sweetly.

Nodding eagerly, Cheadle said: "To apologize, sir. The cinema manager told me you're quite a celebrity."

"So's the Prime Minister," Robbie reminded him in his most cavalier fashion. "But that doesn't mean that when I see the lights on at Number Ten I feel impelled to drop in to apologize for my chronic rudeness about his political ineptitude."

"No, sir; but I need your help. I believe you regularly visit all the disabled in this county who live away from Stoke Mandeville Hospital?"

"I occasionally," Robbie loftily corrected, "visit some of them who aren't doing as well as they should."

Cheadle, who was longing to sit, glanced at the sofa. The request was unmistakable. Just as unmistakably Robbie backed his chair between the sofa and the nearest armchair and blocked access to both.

"You wanted my help," Robbie said, smiling contentedly.

"Ah yes, sir. As someone who occasionally visits some of this county's disabled who aren't doing as well as they should, how would you class a person who allows her wheel chair to be *pushed?*"

In spite of himself, Robbie was interested. "Pushed uphill?"

"No, sir; downhill."

"Definitely not doing as well as she should. Who is she?"

"That's what I came to ask you, sir."

"I have no idea," Robbie said, looking ostentatiously at the clock.

Cheadle ignored the hint. "Her boy friend, or possibly her brother, is good-looking, of medium height, dresses hippie style, has long fair hair—"

"Is in his middle twenties and is wanted by you to help with your inquiries," chanted Robbie. "We heard it on the radio."

Cheadle smiled. "Heard my appeal on the news, did you, sir?"

"Yes."

"Ah. Well, let me give you a description of the girl in the wheel chair. Blonde, slim, rather pretty, wears a floppy purple hat."

"In this county," declared Robbie flatly, "there's no such person."

"But she was *seen*, being wheeled into the Rex by her long-haired boy friend."

"I don't care if she was seen being wheeled into Buckingham Palace by Prince Philip. There's no such *she* in Buckingham*shire*."

"Well, what about the man? Could he be one of Stoke Mandeville Hospital's regular visitors? Does his description ring a bell?"

"He could be; but it doesn't."

"He's a Scot. Does that ring a bell?"

"Wearing tartan jeans, was he?"

Cheadle refused to be provoked. "The girl at the box office remembers his accent."

"Well, hurrah for her," responded Robbie; "but he still doesn't ring a bell." And again looked at the clock.

"Just one thing more, then." Cheadle sighed, apparently taking the hint at last—which he was not. Robbie relaxed. "If you *had* seen the film tonight, how would you personally have left the Rex?"

"By the side door."

"Not through the lobby? The way you'd gone in?"

"The aisle to the side exit slopes downward, Mr. Cheadle, and the street outside that exit is usually deserted. Which I invariably prefer, since getting myself and my chair into my car is quite a performance, and as I've informed you, I detest being gawped at."

"Of course, sir." Cheadle turned to Mark. "And you, sir? How would you have left the Rex?"

"Through the lobby."

"You wouldn't have helped your brother through the side door?"

"My brother wouldn't have let me. Besides, the important thing would have been to get the car to him as quickly as possible, so that he didn't get cold."

"We don't *feel* the cold, Mr. Cheadle," Robbie explained, as if lecturing a half-wit, "but we are susceptible to it."

Cheadle glanced at his sergeant. "Well," he said, "I think that clears *that* up, don't you, Sergeant?" The sergeant had stood motionless throughout. He now looked as animated as a guardsman in a sentry box.

"I don't think," Robbie whispered, "he's entirely with you. Come to that—neither am I. Clears what up?"

"Why no one in the lobby saw the girl being wheeled out by her boy friend. And why the usherette swears she saw a girl in a floppy hat wheeling herself out of the side exit, unaccompanied."

"Then what," exploded Robbie, "were all those stupid questions for? Don't tell me you couldn't have worked it out for yourselves."

"Afraid we couldn't, Mr. Gifford," Cheadle apologized. "But primarily I hoped you could identify the lassie, or the laddie."

"And what good would that have done you?"

"Quite a lot, I suspect. They sat on the aisle in the back row, and when the film ended, shortly after they left, Janine Talbot was found dead in the middle of that row. We think they may have seen her murderer."

"They left before the film *ended?*" Robbie inquired.

"Having entered after it began," Cheadle confirmed.

"Sounds like a terrific film." Robbie jerked his chair around to face his brother. "Thought you said it was super?"

Cheadle turned to Mark. "You've seen this film already, sir?"

Mark nodded. "Part of it. Last voyage. On the *Canberra.* I had to go on duty before the film ended."

"Been on the *Canberra* long? I see from your photograph on the mantelpiece that you're an officer."

"Two years. Second officer."

"I envy you. Well, we mustn't intrude any longer. Thank you for your cooperation, gentlemen. You've been most helpful."

"I'm sorry to hear that," said Robbie.

"I'll show you out," Mark intervened.

For an angry moment the chief superintendent hesitated. Then he nodded curtly. "Thank you. Good night, Mr. Gifford."

The sergeant pocketed his notebook and ball-point pen and Mark ushered the two policemen into the hall.

"Should I have further need of his expert advice," Cheadle murmured apprehensively to Mark, "do you think your brother would mind if I called again?"

"Any time you see the lights on!" shouted Robbie, who had been straining to catch whatever last words the chief superintendent might utter.

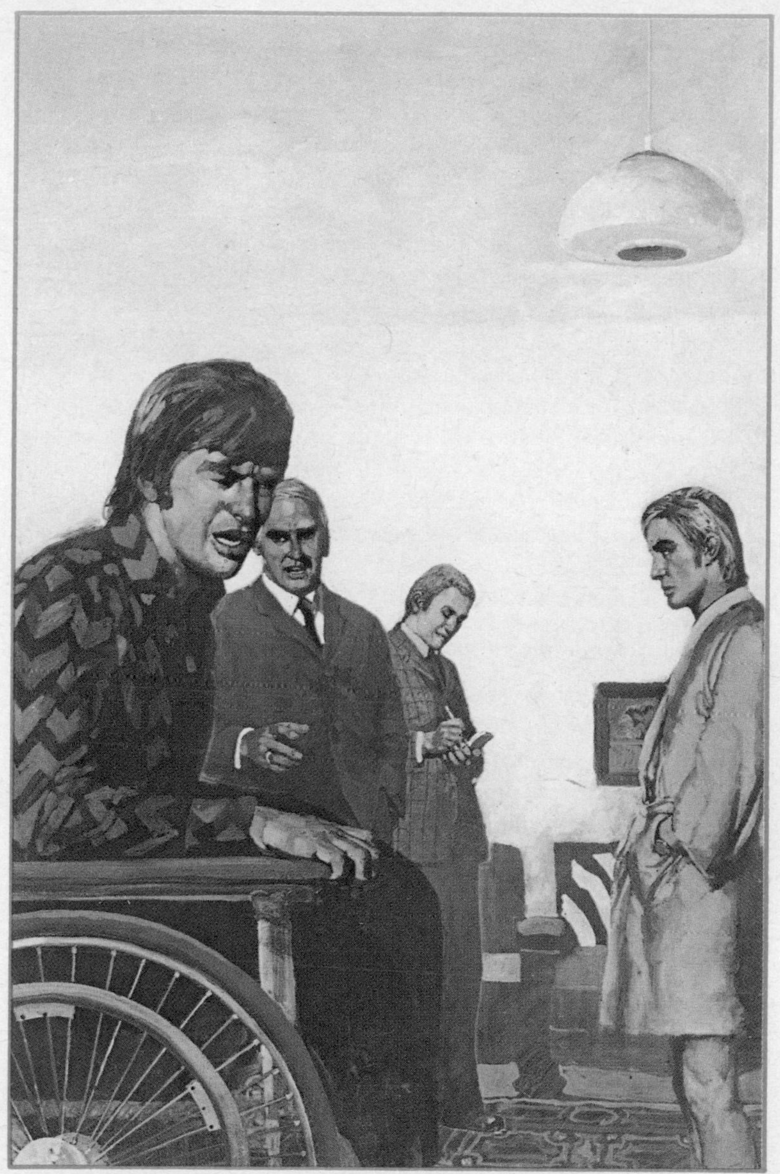

Wednesday: Nine Fifty-five

From the front door Mark watched the policemen's car depart. Then he closed the door and stood thoughtfully a moment in the hall, needing to be alone. But Robbie had to be faced. Barefoot, he padded to the living room.

"You must be tired." Hoping Robbie would go to bed.

"On the contrary, I feel very alert."

Mark made himself smile companionably as he sat sideways in the farther of the two chairs, his legs across its arm. Frowning, Robbie moved his wheel chair forward to confront his brother.

"You look like a sceptical Ironside," Mark forced himself to say.

"I was thinking what an idiot that Cheadle was. *Brilliantine*—in this day and age."

"Does an addiction to brilliantine make him an idiot?"

"Not being able to work out how that dead girl got into the back row of the Rex does."

Mark contrived a bewildered air. "Then I guess I'm an idiot too."

"But you haven't been heading the hunt for the Motorway Maniac for the past year, have you? He has, and he still can't see that the dead girl must be the girl who was wheeled into the cinema by her alleged boy friend."

Mark needed time to answer. Needed also to learn exactly how much Robbie knew. "Cheadle says the usherette saw that girl wheel herself out," he objected.

"Oh Mark. You know the Rex."

Indeed I do, he thought, as aware as Robbie that its usherette never ushed. She simply tore the tickets in half and sat knitting, while the Rex's patrons broke their legs in the dark. The aisle with the side exit was the one farthest from her.

"From where she sits," Robbie continued, "all she'd have seen was the back of a wheel chair and a floppy hat."

"Meaning?"

"Meaning the person in the wheel chair *wasn't* the girl; it was the lad, wearing the girl's hat after he'd ditched the girl—who was dead—in the middle of the back row."

"You're saying he killed her while she sat beside him, carried her along to the middle of the row, then steamed off without anyone hearing or seeing a thing?"

"I'm saying she was dead when he wheeled her in."

"Which no one noticed?"

"No one," Robbie told him with all the dogmatism of experience, "ever notices anything about anyone in a wheel chair."

"No one fails to notice blokes carting bodies up and down the back rows of cinemas, though."

"Not at the Rex. Not on a Wednesday afternoon."

Mark argued no further; to do so was to protest too much. He had chosen the Rex precisely because there were never more than half a dozen old-age pensioners in the audience. "All I'm wondering is why he bothered," Robbie persisted. "Simpler to have dumped her behind a hedgerow."

Mark let that pass; but he had to find out how much Robbie knew. "Shouldn't you wonder what the bloke did with the wheel chair once he got outside?"

"He sat there till there was no one round, stood up, folded his chair and stole away," Robbie explained impatiently. "Got to admire him. He's got guts. *And* he'll get away with it."

So Robbie knew everything. Mark next needed to learn his intentions. "He may, unless you enlighten the police."

"Am I likely to?"

Their eyes met, Mark's calculating.

"Don't you think you should?"

"In my position," Robbie murmured wryly, "one doesn't go volunteering solutions to puzzles like this. It's likely to vex the person involved. Who is then likely to ensure that one vexes him no further."

Mark blinked at the cool logic. "So you'll hold your tongue?"

"Certainly."

"Do you *want* him to get away with it?"

Doubt dulled Robbie's eyes for just a second. Then he wheeled himself to the refrigerator. "To be frank, I don't really care." He poured a glass of milk. "Want some?"

Mark shook his head. "Four girls," he reminded, "have been murdered."

"Ah," said Robbie, "but *why*? Do *you* know why?"

"I wish I did," Mark asserted. "But whatever the reason, it's still murder."

"Four girls," agreed Robbie, "all picked up on the same road. Yet other girls like the one you picked up this afternoon will continue to haunt the A41, and thumb lifts from solitary men as if they were positively anxious to die. And if that's what they want" —smiling brightly—"who's to be blamed if it happens?"

"You can be as dispassionate about it as that?"

"Having long been denied passion, yes. But let me put it another way. If it were sex that obsessed these female hitchhikers, would either of us blame the man who obliged them?"

"That's no analogy, Robbie. This guy doesn't want sex."

"Probably doesn't *want* to murder either."

"He can't avoid obliging blondes with a death wish, you mean?"

"Something like that."

Mark shook his head in frustration. "O.K., one last question. Do you honestly believe this man's more sinned against than sinning?"

"For what it's worth, I do," Robbie answered. "Satisfied?"

"It's food for thought," Mark acknowledged curtly.

"But you're still hungry?" Robbie mocked.

"You always were deep," Mark complained.

"Deep? My father half-murdered me and my mother took his side. *Your* parents were marvellous; but then you came along."

"You weren't *jealous*?"

"I'd have wrung your neck if I'd thought I could get away with it. Until I realized we were getting equal treatment and what a nice kid you were." He shook his head. "Happy days."

"Even then, though, for a while, something went wrong between us, didn't it?"

"You began to grow up," Robbie explained. "Brought friends home from school, got interested in girls. . . ."

Mark frowned. "And you were jealous again?"

"I'd always had your devotion. And when I came home from medical school I'd lost it to your angelic chums, Annabel and—"

"You hadn't lost it."

"Had to share it then—I found I hated it. But," philosophically, "I adjusted."

No, Mark thought, it was the angelic chums you adjusted—Annabel, Deborah, Cousin Margaret. "Why?" he asked.

Instantly Robbie understood. "My natural parents had rejected me, and my new parents merely adopted me. You were the only relative I believed in and I was not about to lose you, little brother, not to anyone."

At which Mark forgave the long-ago betrayals, and felt only remorse that he had never recognized his brother's insatiable need for possessions and security. "You really are deep, aren't you?"

"Almost bottomless at times. Other times"—whimsical suddenly—"weightless. Like an astronaut floating inside his little capsule"—lifting both arms from the rests on his chair—"with nothing to link him to his past except that devoted voice from Houston."

"You feel weightless, sitting like that?"

"Without my arms to register sensation, yes, of course I do."

"God." It was an aspect of paraplegia that had never occurred to Mark, who was so aware of his body.

"Why God? I trust my little capsule, and in my brother Mark I have my devoted voice."

"Oh Robbie."

"I didn't mean to depress you," Robbie disclaimed. "I just meant that you give me the incentive to whirl weightlessly on till splashdown. My strange relationship with you and my ungentlemanly passion for winning are all that keep me going."

"You've explained a lot," Mark told him.

Robbie grinned. "You understand me now, do you?"

"Beginning to." Smiling back, as if they'd somehow averted a disaster.

"Well, don't force it. To understand something as complex as a person, you need intuition as well as logic. Which is why your friend Cheadle will never be able to convict his Motorway Maniac."

"Why?"

Wheeling himself to the fireplace, Robbie picked up his chest expander. "Sit down," he suggested. Mark sat, and Robbie stretched and released the expander without apparent effort half a dozen times. "Cheadle wants to identify the long-haired hippie, right?"

"Right."

"And he has logic, but no intuition, right?"

"If you say so."

"Oh, I say so"—dropping the chest expander with a clatter and taking up his sabre. "If he had intuition, he'd have used it to explain the usherette's statement that she saw a *girl* wheeling herself out of the Rex by the side exit."

He tapped Mark lightly on his thigh with the blade of his sabre. "Mere logic obliges him to accept that what the usherette thought she saw she did in fact see. But I wasn't there either. Yet intuition tells me that actually the girl was slumped dead in the back row and that it was her escort"—tapping Mark's chest—"the usherette saw steaming off in that chair! In other words, Cheadle thinks the Scots hippie's a mere witness; and not even coppers charge witnesses with murder, so—"

"So you don't think this hippie'll be arrested?"

"Not even if they find out who he is," pronounced Robbie.

"Does your intuition identify him?"

Robbie shook his head. "My logic identifies him."

"Tell me more," Mark suggested.

"No. I'll give you the facts and you tell me."

"O.K."

Robbie assumed a cross-examiner's manner, to which his brother responded accordingly. "The lad we're looking for knows the geography and audience habits of the Rex, right?"

"Assuming that he was disposing of a corpse and was not just a witness—yes."

"Let's assume it. And he knows that people deliberately don't look at the face of anyone in a wheel chair, right?"

"Yes."

"He has access to a wheel chair and owns a car, right?"

"Yes."

"He's in his middle twenties, of good physique and medium height, right?"

"Yes."

"He's resourceful. And quite an actor?"

"Why quite an actor?"

"To wheel a dead girl up to a cinema and buy two tickets at the box office, he'd have to be, wouldn't he?"

"I see what you mean."

"And being a resourceful actor, knowing that the woman in the box office is going to remember him anyway, she having sold only half a dozen seats all afternoon, one of 'em for a very conspicuous girl in a wheel chair, what would he do?"

"No idea."

"He'd ensure that she remembered a guy who looked and sounded nothing like his real self."

"How?"

"By dressing uncharacteristically, adopting a Scottish accent, putting on dark glasses and wearing a blond wig. So," and again he tapped Mark on the chest, "who is he?"

"There's no point my trying to work it out," Mark bluffed, "because your basic assumption doesn't make sense. Assuming he had a body to dispose of, why wouldn't he just have dumped it, as you yourself suggested, behind the nearest hedgerow?"

Robbie sighed. "O.K. Let's prove my basic assumption. The Motorway Maniac murdered his fourth blonde today, and she was found in the Rex, right?"

"Yes."

"Daring, like dumping the others outside police stations, right?"

"Yes."

"But each of *them* was dumped at night, when it was dark. At four in the afternoon, where else but in a cinema is there both darkness and a huge element of risk?"

Biting his lip, Mark admitted: "Nowhere."

"And who else but the girl in the wheel chair can be the girl who was subsequently found dead?"

Mark was incapable of further resistance. "No one."

"Then who else but the Scots laddie could've put her there; and why else did he so recklessly put her *there*, except to *prove* that it was the work of the Motorway Maniac?"

In the long silence that followed, Mark found that his brain no longer worked.

"You know everything, don't you?" he said slowly.

"Except"—flicking Mark's scalp with the point of his sabre—"where he got the wig."

"Even why he did it?"

"We both know why he did it," Robbie told him gently.

Mark tried to think. Posed the complex question clearly and told himself there must be an answer. Even told himself that for once there was unlimited time to find the answer. But no answer came; only despair—because now that the truth was out, life could never be the same.

"What should he do next?" he asked dully.

"Nothing," Robbie assured him. "The police'll never work it out, and I'm sure you don't expect me to do it for them?"

"No, but I almost wish you would."

Robbie's head shot up. "*You* won't do anything foolish, will you?" Then harshly: "Like spilling your guts to the law?"

Unable to meet his brother's implacable eyes, Mark abjectly shook his head. Satisfied, Robbie replaced the sabre by the fireplace. But seemed dissatisfied that Mark remained slumped in the chair, head in hands. "Hey," he ordered, demanding his brother's attention. "I know you hate yourself, but you mustn't! For my sake. What's done, kiddo, is done."

Mark flew out of his chair to glower down at Robbie. "And how often," he shouted, "will it be done again?"

Robbie refused to be intimidated. "That's up to you, isn't it? A telephone call to that ape from Scotland Yard and your worries'll be over."

As unexpectedly as he had erupted, Mark wilted. "You know I can't."

"Well, if you change your mind, I shan't try to stop you," Robbie promised. "I'll be having a bath."

HAD MARK BEEN TEMPTED to ring Cheadle, it would have been to no avail. The chief superintendent was in the pub Stoke Mandeville's paraplegics use as their local, talking to people in wheel chairs. But getting nowhere. None of the Stokers remembered an ex-inmate resembling the girl who had wheeled herself out of the Rex. And all of them denied that any friend of a Stoker was a hippie.

Even so, Cheadle felt no compulsion to return to his desk. Every other lead was being explored by his subordinates. The girl's boy friend was being questioned again. The pop singer, Randy Horn, whose autographed picture had been found in the dead girl's bag, had been asked to make himself available for an interview. The evening newspapers had printed an appeal for any girls hitch-hiking on the A41 that afternoon to ring their local police station.

Thanks to Randy Horn and the Maniac's timing (the identity of the body had been established soon after five p.m.), this was the first time Cheadle had been given a break with the media. In each of the Maniac's three previous murders, the victims had been discovered too late for coverage even in the following morning's papers. And by midday—when the evening papers had accorded him hundreds of column inches—the trail had been cold and Cheadle's appeals for cooperation futile.

But this time the victim's body had been discovered and reported to him at a quarter past five. He had also issued a statement to all radio and TV stations in time for their evening news bulletins.

So Cheadle felt entitled to a quiet pint with these nice people from the hospital. He turned to a girl in her twenties. "Long way to come for a drink, isn't it?"

"It's only three-quarters of a mile."

"Don't think I could manage that in a wheel chair."

"Well, actually," she smiled, "*you* couldn't. But after a while one gets the muscles to do it."

When the girl and her friends were ready to leave, Cheadle, concerned for their safety, drove slowly behind them as their crazy convoy of chairs, the weak hooked fore and aft between the strong, rode cheerfully down the road. When the last of them rolled into the hospital grounds, he accelerated towards his Aylesbury hotel, reflecting that if the blonde who'd been seen leaving the Rex *was* in fact an ex-Stoker, she'd be quite capable of having wheeled herself to Edinburgh by now.

Wednesday: Eleven Fifteen

His bath completed, Robbie pulled out the plug and watched the unfelt water subside. When the last of it had gone, he dried himself carefully; and then, just as carefully dried the inside of the bath, because getting out of a slippery bath was risky.

Sitting in the dry, empty bath, he dragged his legs into a yoga position, put a hand on each rim, raised himself, swung so that he could lower his buttocks onto the rim beside his chair (from which he had removed the arm nearest the bath) pulled a nightshirt over his head, pushed himself outward—both hands raised, his lurching trunk momentarily without support—grabbed the far arm of his chair with one hand, the near side of the bath with the other, transferred his rump from the rim to the seat of his chair, lugged his useless legs out of the bath and dropped them onto the footrest, replaced the arm of his chair, unlocked his wheels and rolled himself into the living room.

The effort and concentration had almost exhausted him. Ahead lay the further exertion of getting himself out of his chair and into his bed. And every two hours after that he must wake and turn himself.

Mark watched him fiddle with an alarm clock and, in spite of the horror that now lay between them, felt the familiar tug of compassion. "Your turns?" he asked.

Robbie nodded, smiling resignedly. "Sometimes I think I'd prefer the bedsores."

"Tired?"

"It's been a long day."

"Forget the alarm. I'll turn you tonight."

"Wake every two hours?"

"I doubt I'll be sleeping."

Politely firm, Robbie responded: "Well, that's your business; but turns are mine. And now, if you'll excuse me"—placing the clock on his lap—"it's past my bedtime."

Mark watched him go and, alone again, reverted to the problem of how to control his crippled brother. Or how, most mercifully, to kill him.

Can I control him? he asked himself, and shook his head.

"So you've *got* to kill him," he told himself—to his dismay, aloud. Had Robbie heard? He switched on the radio and began to prowl the room. He picked up the sabre, and rejected it; an arrow, and rejected it; the bottle of phenobarbs, and rejected them. Then reconsidered, remembering Robbie's own remark about those pills. They were, of course, the answer, if Robbie's death was to look like suicide.

But how, mercifully, could one stuff a bottleful of phenobarbs down the throat of a man with two of the most powerful arms in Britain?

You can't, Mark told himself, and flung himself on the camp bed.

The music wasn't loud enough, the bed wasn't long enough and the pillow was too thick. He threw the pillow to the floor and lay face downward. Then propped himself up on his elbows and nodded sickly at the obviousness of it. Babies suffocated in pillows; why not a cripple? Not even suicide. Accidental. But was it a terrifying way to die?

He turned on his back, picked up the pillow and slammed it over his mouth and nose, pressing it tight, counting the seconds. Thirteen, fourteen, fifteen. Must breathe. Air. No air. Red flashes. Roaring. Must breathe. Must—

Appalled, he threw off the pillow, to lie there, gasping "Oh Robbie, Robbie," while Robbie, who had come to complain about the radio and seen instead an instantly recognizable rehearsal of his own execution, wheeled himself silently back to his bedroom.

Switching off the radio and the lights, Mark lay on his back, but did not sleep. And when, two hours later, he heard the clangor of Robbie's alarm clock, he ran to help his brother turn.

But Robbie had locked his door.

Thursday: Ten A.M.

Cheadle had been up since seven and at work since eight.

Janine Talbot's boy friend had been proven guiltless, though unfaithful, by his number two girl friend, with whom he had been in bed the day before between the hours of one-thirty p.m. and two forty-five p.m. The back row of the cinema had revealed to the experts hundreds of fingerprints, none of them in the files.

Three girls had responded to the appeal that anyone who had been hitchhiking on the A41 the afternoon before should come forward. Two of them were locals, who had seen nothing of value; the third was a London typist, who had enjoyed a harmless lift with a lorry driver.

There remained Randy Horn, who had insisted (on the advice

of his public relations adviser) on coming to Aylesbury rather than answer questions in London. He was due at ten fifteen, and already half the photographers in England were waiting outside Cheadle's headquarters.

Cheadle worked on—telephoning, delegating, supervising—and Randy arrived at eleven. Cheadle disliked him on sight.

"Man," exclaimed Randy, "those photographers are really wild. And me stoned out of my mind. Brandy, you know; not hash. Don't want to get busted again, do we?"

But drugs were not Cheadle's business. His business was murder. "Mr. Horn. I take it you know why we asked to see you?"

"Sure, man. The chick with me photo, and where, like, was I yesterday afternoon, right?"

"Just where were you? When your local constable called, you told him you couldn't remember."

"Yeah, well I'd just got up, hadn't I? But I can remember now."

"Doubtless all those photographers cleared your mind?"

"Yeah. I was recording for EMI. They'll tell you."

"I'll ask them," Cheadle promised, angry that anyone should use a murder investigation to drum up publicity. "Good-bye, Mr. Horn."

"That *all?*"

"Unless you want my autograph," Cheadle told him.

Randy left and the photographers and reporters crowded around him. "No comment," he insisted. "Not till I seen my lawyer." Good for a pic and a front-page headline, he reflected.

In his office Cheadle was thinking that it definitely wasn't the boy friend and unfortunately it wasn't Horn. Not that he'd ever thought it was either, but it was best to be sure.

"Sergeant," he called. "Our sailor laddie's had long enough to think things over. Let's visit him this afternoon."

Thursday: Two Thirty

Robbie and Mark passed the morning and their lunch in apparent amiability, each having decided to avoid both the subject of murder and, as far as possible, the other. Mark had polished his car; Robbie had exercized with his weights and chest expander.

Mark had telephoned the cousins to arrange the evening's bridge; Robbie had called Stoke Mandeville to arrange an archery shoot. Outwardly they had not clashed, but their inner reactions, however, were almost irreconcilable. For Mark the destruction of their relationship was shocking. For Robbie it was a fact. Something to be lived with, like his paralysis. He had supported a dead trunk and legs for six years; he and Mark must support the corpse of their fraternal trust for the rest of their lives, relying on courtesy and good humour to make their task tolerable.

After lunch Robbie had said: "I must finish cleaning the house."

"Can I help?" Mark had offered politely.

"No." But in such a tone as to imply no carping reminder of Mark's premature arrival the day before.

"Mind if I go for a spin then? I've been mucking about with the timing again. Best I check it on an open road."

"Whatever your timing may be, you go and check it, kiddo."

So Robbie, towing the Hoover behind him, was cleaning the hall when the telephone rang. "Blast!" he muttered. To answer it, he'd have to get turned around. Hoover still in tow, he yanked open the front door, shot through it, turned on the path outside and sped back to the clamorous phone. Whose receiver he snatched up. "Yes?" he shouted, his vacuum cleaner still whining. "Who?" He switched off the machine. "Sorry; who is it?"

"Richard Fairburn," the receiver told him.

"Oh, hi Doc. What can I do for you?"

"I've been going over my notes. How's your neck?"

"Fine. What made you think—"

"Just checking. My notes say—"

"Yeah, well some of your thicker patients might believe that, but not this one."

"Don't be so touchy. I'm simply making a friendly call."

"Cut it out," Robbie said, alarmed. "You don't make simply friendly calls. Either tell me the truth or—I know: Mark's with you, isn't he?"

Behind him Chief Superintendent Cheadle and the sergeant appeared in the front doorway and halted.

"He is not," Fairburn assured him. "But he telephoned me."

"That's more like it."

"And he tells me you're complaining of stiffness in the neck. Says you told him it's affected your shooting. He suggests—and I'm inclined to agree with him—that you should come back to Stoke for a rest and a checkup."

"Quite unnecessary. I couldn't feel fitter."

"Robbie, you've got lesions in your neck."

"I know I've got lesions in my neck."

"I still can't imagine how anyone as experienced in these things as you could have been mad enough—"

"To lift a television set off a table and onto my lap with the arms of my chair down. I know. Don't tell me. But the bloody thing had gone on the blink for the umpteenth time and the engineer had shown me how to fix it."

"Have you been fixing it again lately?"

"No. Now is there anything else you want to know? You're holding up my housework."

"Nothing else, Robbie."

"Good. And good-bye." And slamming the receiver down, he glowered at the telephone. Until the doorbell rang.

"May I come in?" Cheadle inquired.

Irritably Robbie turned and stared at the men in the doorway.

"I just happened to be passing," Cheadle explained amiably.

"And seeing my door open, thought you'd drop in, again! Well, come in if you're coming." Sourly his grey eyes flickered over the impassive sergeant. "Bring Charlie McCarthy with you."

Closing the door behind them, the two policemen followed him into the living room. "Sorry to hear about your neck, sir," Cheadle said sympathetically.

"Been eavesdropping, have you?"

"You were on the telephone. I couldn't help hearing. All right now, is it?"

"My neck?"

"The TV, sir?"—his inquisitive eyes roaming.

"I got rid of it. More trouble than it was worth."

"Got a good price, I hope?"

"I returned it to the people I *rented* it from," Robbie retorted. "And don't tell me that you came all this way just to discuss my viewing habits."

"No, sir. Actually I came to see your brother. But I gather he's with your doctor?"

"Why don't you ask my doctor?"

Cheadle seemed impervious to sarcasm. "That's a very sensible idea, sir. Er—what's your doctor's name?"

"Fairburn," Robbie said. "Richard Fairburn."

"Lives locally, does he?"

"Yes. At the hospital."

"Then we'll be on our way," lied Cheadle, who made as if to move, then glanced at Robbie's chair. "Remarkable how you can manoeuvre that thing. We saw you speed in and out of the door with your vacuum cleaner behind you. For a moment we wondered whether someone mightn't be trying to do you a mischief, didn't we, Sergeant?"

"The phone rang. If I'm Hoovering the hall beyond the phone, that's the quickest way back to it."

"Most ingenious. Manage everything for yourself, do you?"

He seemed genuinely interested and only vaguely ingratiating, and in spite of himself, Robbie felt his hostility fading. "I do," he said.

"Using only your arms?"

"And my wheels." Smiling modestly.

Cheadle looked apologetic. "I'm being tactless. Forgive me. I didn't mean to embarrass you."

One arm pressed to his stomach, Robbie laughed. "Chief Superintendent," he insisted, "nothing embarrasses me. And if I told you how I did *everything*, you'd be the embarrassed one."

"I don't think I quite understand, sir."

"Not to put it too crudely then, nothing from the chest down works. Except involuntarily, which is *not* what one wants. So when one does want something down here"—gesturing vaguely—"to work, one has to make it do so."

Cheadle looked extremely embarrassed. "You mean—"

"Now, now. Let's just take the diaphragm. It doesn't work, which means I can't laugh or cough."

"But you did," Cheadle contradicted. "A minute ago."

"Know how I did it?" Robbie asked. Cheadle shook his head dubiously. "I placed my right arm across my diaphragm and pressed. Like this." He laughed. "Or again, like this," and coughed.

"Mr. Gifford," said Cheadle respectfully. "I dips me lid to you."

"Just tricks of the trade, Chief Superintendent. Mind you, it's not as easy as it looks. We paraplegics are only a hundred per cent safe with both arms on our armrests, or both hands on our wheels. We tend, you see, to topple."

Cheadle frowned. "You mean if you were to take both arms off your armrests, or both hands off your wheels, you'd be in danger of falling out of your chair?"

"In grave danger. Unless I was perfectly balanced." He demonstrated. "Head high and well back."

"Then I'm not surprised you hurt your neck. Really, sir"—he sounded quite reproachful—"both armrests removed and reaching *forward* to lift a TV off a table onto your lap. In future, if you've got anything heavy to lift, call the police."

For an instant Robbie seemed dumbstruck. Then, one arm pumping at his diaphragm, he shouted with laughter. "Call the police?" He choked, swaying wildly.

"Head back, Mr. Gifford!" Cheadle implored. "And hold *tight*, sir." With difficulty Robbie controlled his mirth and his body. "Ooh, you should be more careful, sir," Cheadle scolded, running a nervous hand over his slicked-back hair. "When I say call the police if you've anything heavy to lift, you mustn't think I'm joking."

"I'm sure you aren't," Robbie acknowledged, furious with Cheadle for having flattered him into dropping his guard.

Cheadle looked at his watch. "Oh dear. Your brother won't be with Dr. Fairburn now, will he? I shouldn't have stood here talking when there's so much to do."

"Busy, are you?" Robbie mocked them.

"Oh yes, Mr. Gifford. Fourteen months we've been at it—"

"And got nowhere." Outside a car door slamming. "If I were in your place, I'd arrest all the hitchhikers."

Mark appeared at the door.

"I don't quite follow you, sir."

"No victims," propounded Robbie, "no murders."

"Ah, but the Maniac'd go unpunished, and we can't have that, can we?"

"Why not, since it looks like we're going to anyway?" Robbie demanded. And before Cheadle could comment on this heresy, called out: "Come in, Mark. I can't stand hoverers."

Mark nodded to the two men. "Chief Superintendent; Sergeant."

"We were talking about poor Mr. Cheadle's painstaking inquiries," Robbie informed him, "and although he has no idea who he's looking for, he's pressing on regardless."

"Oh, on the contrary, Mr. Gifford," murmured Cheadle, all geniality vanished, "we know exactly who we're looking for, and exactly where to find him."

Robbie's head rose slowly and his eyes challenged the chief superintendent's. "Then why no arrest?"

"Because first we must find out how and why he committed all the murders. I'm looking for motive and evidence. No point my arresting the guilty man if I can't get him convicted, is there?"

"Not much, no. Pity you've got no witnesses."

"As it happens, we have our witness. Or rather"—staring vaguely at the target—"we know who that witness is. And we're confident that sooner or later he'll talk, if only out of fear; because he's very close to the murderer, and the murderer knows that *he* knows everything. Talking of which, sir"—turning to Mark—"I wonder could you spare me some of your valuable time?"

"I shouldn't think there's anything I can tell you," Mark objected.

"Well, one never knows; you may have seen something as you drove down from London. No"—holding up his hand—"don't answer now. Just think about it. I've a lot of paperwork to do, so let's make it half-past four. That'll give Sergeant Robinson time for his afternoon cup of tea."

"If four would suit you better," suggested Robbie in an abrupt switch of mood, "I've no doubt you could bully me into making him his cup of tea."

"I think not, thank you, Mr. Gifford. Not when we're on duty. Come on, Charlie!"—and departed.

Mark strode to the open front door and peered at the two policemen. They were examining the lawn by his car. Then they left, and he returned to Robbie.

"They're on to us," he reported.

"Yes," said Robbie calmly, "I believe they are. But this much I promise you, little brother: I'll never let them arrest you."

Cheadle, who had been talking to Dr. Fairburn, sighed as his car turned out of the hospital gates.

"Sorry about the tea break, Sergeant," he apologized. "But he did go on a bit, didn't he?" Sergeant Robinson, driving steadily, said nothing. "I suppose we could take a few minutes off, but we should see those shops. Yes. Aylesbury, as fast as you like. And then we'll hit the Giffords."

As they sped towards Aylesbury he thought over all that Dr. Fairburn had told him in the course of an interview allegedly aimed at establishing the identity of the girl who had been wheeled into the Rex, but very slyly transformed into a chat about Mark, the devoted brother, and Robbie, Stoke Mandeville's star patient and about-to-be quadriplegic.

"Quadriplegic?" Cheadle had asked.

"One who has lost the use of four limbs, as compared with the paraplegic, who has lost the use of only two," Fairburn had explained.

"Does he know that this is what the neck lesions will lead to?"

"Oh yes."

"How soon'll it come?"

"Anytime in the next few months. Most likely at night. He'll just wake up one night and find he can't move a thing."

"And then?"

"Might have a year more. Mark, of course, wants him to come back here at once. Says he does too much; that it's bound to hasten the inevitable, which is true."

"And it all stems from those lesions?"

"That's right."

"Has Mr. Mark told you about his plans for when it happens?"

"Says he'll quit the sea, live with his brother."

"And what sort of life will that be?"

"Hell for Mark. Worse for Robbie."

"Surprised he doesn't kill himself," Cheadle muttered. "He'd just be a head on top of a corpse."

"Some manage marvellously, even happily," Fairburn said.

"I don't doubt that for a second," Cheadle acknowledged. "It's just that Mr. Robert doesn't strike me as the type to be happy though helpless."

"You're right, of course," the doctor admitted.

"An expensive hell for Mr. Mark and a demoralizing one for Mr. Robert. That about it, Doctor?"

"That'll be it."

Suddenly Cheadle wished he'd never met the Giffords.

Thursday: Five Past Five

For the twentieth time Mark looked at the clock. "Half-past four, they said. Where are they?"

"Probably outside waiting for your first shrill cries of hysteria."

He was closer to the truth than he realized. One of Cheadle's experts was, in fact, out on the lawn, kneeling by Mark's car, carefully spooning out plaster of paris.

Mark began to pace the floor. "Oh, for God's sake!" Robbie exploded. "Pull yourself together."

Mark halted. "Keep your contempt for the police, Robbie. You should be admiring me. As you said, I've got guts! And while I'm at it, that chief superintendent's not the fool you think him. He got you talking. When I came in you were relaxed, and *talking*. I wish I knew about what."

Robbie looked sulky. "I know what I'm doing."

"I'm still asking you to treat that man with respect."

"Respect a *copper?* Don't you know what happened when I broke my back?"

"I know your father slung you onto the edge of a table. What's that got to do with coppers?" The doorbell rang.

"I'll tell you later. Meantime I'll tell our chief superintendent absolutely nothing he doesn't already know, so stop worrying. Go on, let them in."

Having admitted the two policemen, Mark led them down the hall, where Cheadle greeted Robbie politely. "Good evening, sir. Sorry we're late."

"Late are you? We hadn't noticed. Sergeant enjoy his tea?"

"There was so much to do, I'm afraid he missed it."

"Ah, how sad," Robbie said, wheeling himself to the kitchen. "And now I suppose we can't offer him one because he's back on duty." He switched the kettle on.

"May we sit,, sir?"

"Do."

Cheadle sat on the sofa sideways, so that he could look back at Robbie. The sergeant sat upright in an armchair, eyes front, so that he could avoid looking at anyone.

"If your boot's on my sofa," Robbie admonished, "remove it!"

Cheadle replaced the offending shoe on the floor and asked: "Been cleaning your carpet, Mr. Gifford?"

Forestalling Robbie, Mark said: "I spilled some aftershave." And took the chair opposite the sergeant.

Cheadle beamed at him. "On yourself as well, I think?"

Mark frowned, wondering whether Robbie had been the chief superintendent's informant.

"My sergeant smelled it yesterday evening when we met at the Rex. Said it smelled like—"

"Custard," chimed in Robbie. "Noticed it as soon as I came in."

"Would that have been before or after you went to Stoke Mandeville to train, Mr. Robert, may I ask?"

Robbie hesitated, transparently debating the wisdom of lying, then answered, with obvious truthfulness: "After." But hastened to add: "Mark was given the stuff by an ungrateful passenger."

Cheadle turned to Mark. "When exactly did you spill it, sir?"

Mark's expression was one of untroubled candour. "Yesterday afternoon."

"Just after you got here?"

"About half an hour after."

"That would have been about . . . three thirty?"

"About three forty."

"So you arrived here at about three?"

"At ten past, exactly."

"And came by the A41?"

"The M1, then the A41, yes." Robbie handed him a cup of tea. "Thanks, Robbie."

"Visit Mr. Robert regularly, do you, sir?"

"Every time he comes home," Robbie intervened, wheeling himself to sit beside his brother, a cup and saucer balanced on his lap. "And all the time he's away he writes. He's a bloody saint."

"And you come straight here from your boat, Mr. Mark?"

"No. I ring Robbie from my London flat first."

"Mind giving me your address?"

"Eleven, Cornwall Crescent, S.W.5."

Cheadle waited till the sergeant had written it down. "So," he continued, "you leave your boat—" Mark frowned. "Something wrong, sir?"

"Ship!"

"Not boat? Now I never knew that. Well, well. So you leave your ship, travel up to London and ring your brother?"

"He's away a lot."

"At his various athletic contests, no doubt. My sergeant tells me"—switching to Robbie with an ingratiating smile—"you hold the world record for the javelin and have won gold medals for fencing and archery."

But Robbie was not to be ingratiated. Not again. "Your sergeant's been busy."

"Can someone in your condition," Cheadle taunted, switching tactics, "really throw a javelin?"

"You bring me your police champion," Robbie retaliated, "put him in a wheel chair, and I bet you a tenner I beat him by twenty feet."

Cheadle shook his head. "I think I'll save my tenner." And reverted to Mark. "So you arrived at about three?"

"At three ten precisely, as I've told you." He began to understand some of Robbie's curtness. Cheadle's apparently ingenuous, apparently inconsequential questions positively invited it.

"So you have," agreed Cheadle, who was beginning to understand the disciplined mind that lay behind Mark's smile. "Where were you between half-past four and six yesterday afternoon?"

More easily than he had thought possible Mark answered the question he had dreaded. "I was having a nap here."

Cheadle watched the sergeant write it down, then resumed his interrogation. "That would be after you'd spilled your lotion?"

"Yes."

"What sort of lotion was it?"

"Bird's, as in Bird's Custard Powder," said Robbie. "Don't tell me you're going to buy some?"

Aware that Robbie had interrupted to give his brother time to think of the name of a lotion, Cheadle contrived not only to conceal his anger but even to look amused.

"My sergeant took a fancy to it, didn't you, Sergeant?"

"Well, it takes all kinds," mused Robbie. "Mark, give him what's left of yours."

Now it was Mark's turn to conceal anger, because Robbie's apparent diversion had turned out to be an ambush.

"I threw it away," he said defiantly.

"Poor Sergeant," mocked Robbie. "No tea and no aftershave."

It was time, Cheadle decided, to put Mr. Robert in his place. "I'm sorry you resent our presence, sir, but this *is* a difficult case."

But Robbie was in no mood for rebukes. "I'm sure it is, you ingratiating twit. I'm also sure that your sergeant's trumped up interest in perfumes advances your inquiries not at all."

"Then perhaps," Cheadle suggested, "we should return to the matter in hand?"

"Undoubtedly," concurred Robbie, "you should."

Cheadle stared thoughtfully at Mark. "You were saying, sir, that between four thirty and six yesterday you were having a nap?"

"I was."

"The entire time?"

Fractionally, Mark hesitated; but not Robbie. "Probably for longer. I left him on that sofa at about half-past three, and later I woke him twice, by telephone. At half-past four, and again at half-past five."

"May I ask what prompted these calls?"

"You may. The first was to suggest he join me at the hospital because—as I explained at the time to our chief physiotherapist—I felt guilty about leaving him here alone. And the second was to ask whether he'd agree to dine with a boring couple called the Liptons who were insisting I invite him."

"That would be Mr. and Mrs. Stanley Lipton, would it?"

"Oh God," groaned Robbie, "don't tell me she's your sister?"

"No, sir, nothing like that. The Liptons live on the A41, and when we questioned them at the time of the third girl's murder they were most helpful."

At which, at last, Robbie looked contrite. "I've been obstreperous, haven't I?"

Heartily Cheadle reassured him. "You've told us a great deal, Mr. Robert. And now, Mr. Mark, can you recall seeing anyone pick up any girl on any of the following dates?" He took a notebook from his pocket. "The afternoon of August the fourth, last year? The evenings of April the twenty-ninth and July the tenth this year? Or yesterday afternoon at about half-past two?"

"I saw no one pick up anyone yesterday," Mark answered firmly. "The other dates, I don't even remember where I was."

"The other dates, sir," Cheadle prompted, "your ship was at Southampton and you were in *this* part of the world. We've checked with the steamship line."

"Then I may well have been on my way down here. But I honestly couldn't say." And could not have looked more honest. Master Mark, Cheadle decided, was the type of officer captains would send to tell passengers there was no need to worry when the ship was sinking, the radio had blown up, the lifeboats had been smashed to pieces and World War III had started.

There was a silence while the sergeant wrote and the chief superintendent pondered. A silence broken by Robbie, cooperative at last. "We can easily find out." He wheeled himself to his desk and took out two diaries. "What date last year did you say?"

"August the fourth," said Cheadle.

Robbie flicked over the pages, found August the fourth, read his entry for that day and demanded the next date. Cheadle obliged.

"April the twenty-ninth this year. And July the tenth."

Robbie frowned at Mark. "You came down on each of those days. *Did* you see anyone picking up anyone else?"

Mark could only shake his head. Though he showed none of it, he felt as lost and close to tears as he had that night in the Pacific when he'd read the cable saying: MOTHER DIED IN HER SLEEP THIS MORNING. OUR THOUGHTS ARE WITH YOU. ROBBIE AND DAD. As he had when he'd seen his father die—and Robbie, from his chair, had extended a compassionate hand.

"May I see those diaries, sir?" he heard Cheadle ask; and, as in a trance, saw Robbie surrender them. Heard Cheadle say—to him—"I see, Mr. Mark, that on the nights of April twenty-ninth and July tenth you left here almost as soon as you arrived. To visit 'the cousins,' as Mr. Robert describes them."

He knew what Cheadle was getting at: on each of those nights a dead girl had been dumped outside a police station. "I usually drop in on them," he admitted wearily. "We grew up together."

"But you, Mr. Robert, never accompany your brother?"

"They visit me twice a week at least," Robbie told him. "And anyway, I'm supposed to avoid late nights."

"Knowing this, Mr. Mark, you wouldn't expect Mr. Robert to accompany you if you proposed visiting, say, after their dinner?"

Mark knew it was pointless to struggle. He nodded passively, and was surprised when Cheadle, instead of arresting him, turned to Robbie. "I gather you're a man of means, Mr. Robert?"

"Now why should you gather that?"

"This house, your specially modified Morris 1100, your clothes, your sporting equipment—"

"Mark bought them. All of them."

"That's very generous of you, Mr. Mark."

Suspecting a snare, Mark answered curtly: "My father left me his money on the understanding that I look after my brother."

"That you've most certainly done. In fact"—glancing around the room—"it seems your brother need only ask and you give."

"My brother," Mark contradicted, sure now that Cheadle was laying a snare, "has never *asked* for a thing. I *give* because he *is* my brother, and because his well-being is important to me."

"Then may I suggest that next time you give him a television you make it a portable?"

"I told you," cut in Robbie furiously, "I rented it. So don't blame Mark. If you must know, I've had the devil's own job stopping him getting me one of those colour jobs."

"Delighted to hear it, sir," said Cheadle, who wasn't, because his snare had been sprung without catching a thing. "Very hypnotic, colour TV. Your javelin throwing would go to pot. Oh—that reminds me. One thing about this last dead girl that's really got us foxed: where did the Scots laddie find the chair he used for wheeling her into the Rex?"

"*Dead* girl? You said she wheeled herself *out* of the Rex!" Robbie looked aggrieved, as if he had been deliberately misled.

"Yes, sir. But now we know she didn't."

"Why?"

"Because she doesn't exist. You told us that! There's no such disabled girl in this county, you said. And the post mortem's confirmed that she died at about two thirty. From which we must further deduce that the Scots laddie somehow laid hands on a wheel chair to transport the body more easily."

"Are you seriously suggesting he spotted her thumbing a lift, offered her one in a wheel chair, bumped her off, pushed her fifteen miles into Aylesbury and deposited her in the Rex?"

"No sir. She was picked up in a car and murdered almost as soon as she entered it. We're suggesting that she was *transferred* to a wheel chair. But where did the laddie get hold of that chair?"

Robbie raised his eyes to heaven. "Hospitals have wheel chairs; airlines have wheel chairs; British Rail has wheel chairs; and plenty of disabled people have *two* wheel chairs."

"Do you have two wheel chairs, Mr. Robert?"

"Have had ever since Mark bought me this new one."

"Then I wonder," Cheadle begged, "if you'd let us borrow your old one?"

"Can't imagine what good it'll do you," Robbie said grudgingly, "but if you want it, it's in the garage." He pointed. "Through that door." The sergeant left to get it. "But you're wrong. A dead girl in a wheel chair—her head'd flop! Be *very* noticeable."

Cheadle nodded. "That's what we thought. But according to the post mortem, the Scots laddie propped her head up with something. I don't suppose you have a neck brace too, have you?"

"Why should I?"

"Your lesion trouble? After you'd lifted your TV off the—"

"All right," Robbie said testily, "so I've got a brace."

"Might we see it?" Cheadle wondered as the sergeant returned with Robbie's old wheel chair.

"In my wardrobe," Robbie advised the sergeant, sighing. "Top shelf. Anything else you want?"

"Just a quick recap, if I may. You, Mr. Mark, arrived here at ten past three yesterday, having come by the M1 and the A41?"

"Yes." Blue eyes watchful, calculating.

"And remained here all afternoon?"

"Except," Mark qualified, his wits returned, "for about five minutes when I drove up and down the lane, testing my engine."

"Ah, I'm glad you remembered that. Explains *two* of the *three* sets of tyre tracks made by your car that we saw on the lawn this afternoon. Perhaps now you could tell me about the third?"

"Testing again today. I'd been mucking about with the timing."

"I see." He seemed satisfied. "And you, Mr. Robert, between four and six were either en route to, at, or on your way back from Stoke Mandeville?"

"I was."

"And at both four thirty and five thirty you telephoned your brother here, and spoke to him on each occasion?"

"That's right."

"Then, for the moment, I shall trouble you no further. Except you won't mind, will you, sir, if we take away your old chair and neck brace? We're planning a little experiment."

"Help yourself."

"Very kind of you, sir. Come along, Sergeant." He turned to Mark. "You'll be here tomorrow, will you, Mr. Gifford?"

"Until seven."

"Excellent. Nice for Mr. Robert to have you so long. I'll return your belongings tomorrow, Mr. Robert, between five and seven."

"As long as it's not tonight. We're playing bridge."

"So your cousin Margaret told me," observed Cheadle brightly. "Enjoy your game. I'll look forward to seeing you both tomorrow."

Thursday: Twenty to Six

Wheeling himself to the sink, washing his teacup, Robbie said: "I thought they'd never go."

"Robbie, what are you playing at? The diaries, the old chair . . ."

"You said, 'Treat him with respect'."

"And you said you'd tell him absolutely nothing—"

"That he didn't already know," qualified Robbie.

"Which included the dates of each of my visits?"

"Do you seriously believe he wouldn't have dug those up for himself? By volunteering them, I've completely disarmed him."

"Having first savagely provoked him? Calling him a twit and drinking gallons of tea right under their two parched noses? And you didn't have to tell him that daft story about talking to me twice on the telephone."

"I suppose you'd rather I'd told him you were out all afternoon disposing of an unwanted corpse?"

Mark's rage gave way to despair. "But Robbie, that's virtually what you did tell him. Now why?"

"Look," said Robbie. "I know you're in a bit of a fix—but one of us had to keep his head. Cheadle wasn't talking idly when he asked me where you'd got hold of a chair, you know."

"Where the *Scots laddie* got hold of a chair."

"If," reminded Robbie, "he was Scots! Anyway, all I did was put into his mind, as possible suspects, hospital porters and airline stewards."

"You put into his mind your chair and me," Mark corrected.

"But he'd told us he knew who the Maniac was and who his witness was. We've got to bluff. Can't you see that?"

"I can't see anything any longer."

"After all you've done for me, do you seriously believe I'd let him pin those murders on you?"

"I try not to."

"That's better." Then, sitting slightly straighter: "I presume you wiped her fingerprints off the chair?"

Mark nodded.

"*Was* it my brace you used?"

"Yes."

"Clean that too?"

Again Mark nodded. "And burned her hat."

"What about the wig?"

"Hers. Before I left the Rex, I put it on her."

"Then they'll never arrest you."

"Well, they won't give me a peerage, that's for sure."

"I never knew you aspired to a peerage!"

"Cut the wisecracks, Robbie."

"Well, snap out of it. The cousins will be here in an hour."

"Cancel it."

"And let Cheadle know we're worried?"

"I *am* worried."

"Mark, he's found no witnesses, no murder weapon and no motive. He'll never be able to arrest you."

Mark's tanned cheeks glistened with sudden tears. Brushing them irritably away, he shouted: "But it can't go on."

"What can't go on?"

"Girls getting killed."

"We've agreed," Robbie reminded him, "that that depends entirely on you."

"Is that *all* you can say?" Frantically beseeching something more.

"What else is there to say?"

"That four girls are dead! And for all you seem to care, it could soon be five, or six . . ."

"Or seven, or eight, or nine," agreed Robbie. "But they'll all of 'em matter less than us." He wheeled himself into the hall.

"Robbie?" Mark called.

"What?"

"Why don't you go to Cheadle? Put an end to it?"

"That's your prerogative," Robbie called back. "Set up the table, will you? And get out the cards and scorers."

Thursday: Half-Past Six

Cheadle sat with the telephone receiver to his ear, waiting for an answer, fingers drumming.

"Ah, Mr. Lipton? Chief Superintendent Cheadle here."

"Hel*lo*, Chief Superintendent. How are you?"

"Busy, I'm afraid, which is why I'm telephoning. We've got a lead. Afraid I can't explain the details . . ."

"I quite understand, Chief Superintendent."

". . . except that the suspect's alibi hangs on whether or not the telephone lines to Aston Clinton on Wednesday evening were, as he alleges, out of order," Cheadle lied glibly.

"Yes?" Mr. Lipton sounded lost.

"You see, no one but the suspect in Aston Clinton seems to have used his phone at exactly that time, so we're having trouble checking his story, and our one hope seems to be a Mr. Robert Gifford—"

"Know him well. Grand chap."

"Indeed he is. Well, Mr. Gifford told us you'd been kind enough to invite him and his brother to dinner on Wednesday evening—"

"That's right, Chief Superintendent. He rang his brother at Aston Clinton at exactly five thirty, and the line *was* out of order."

"Oh no," groaned Cheadle. But he was smiling happily.

"I gave your suspect his alibi?" Mr. Lipton asked anxiously.

"Afraid so. He *did* say 'out of order'—not 'no answer'?"

"I'm sure he said 'out of order', Chief Superintendent."

"Bang goes another lead, then," said Cheadle. "But thank you."

"Not at all, Chief Superintendent. Good-bye."

Cheadle hung up. "Same story as the chief physiotherapist," he told his sergeant. "Line allegedly out of order. Which it may have been; but definitely Master Robert did not disturb our sailor laddie's nap. Not at four thirty. Not at five thirty. Never spoke to him at all. Interesting, but insufficient."

He took an envelope from a trouser pocket and read some notes on the back. "Still, these should do it," he said, and passed the envelope to Sergeant Robinson. "I think you'd better start at the bottom of the list. Get the wheel chair and put our lassie in it. In plain clothes, with a red nose, black teeth and a bow in her hair!"

Nodding, the sergeant left. Cheadle called the weather bureau. "I want to know the rainfall in Aston Clinton yesterday afternoon. . . . Between two forty and three ten? . . . Thank you."

Next he rang a subordinate at Scotland Yard. "By tomorrow midday I want the will of the late Francis Robert Marcus Gifford, of Chichester. I want to know how much he left."

Finally he called Glasgow. "What'd you find out?" he asked, and listened intently. "I see. Where's he now? . . . O.K. Thanks."

He walked then into the next room, where a self-conscious policewoman sat in Robbie's old wheel chair, her nose reddened with lipstick, her front teeth black, in her hair a ludicrous bow.

"What's your first name?" he asked her.

"Iris, sir."

"If I have to talk to you, I'll call you Iris, and you call me Ted.

All right? Keep your head high, Iris; that's it. Now your feet together, forearms along the armrests, fingers wrapped downward. Good! Off we go."

For the next half hour he pushed her around Aylesbury, and observed that oncomers invariably looked at anything but Iris's eye catching face.

"She could've been dead!" he advised his sergeant when they returned. "No one would have noticed."

He picked up a note from his desk. "One-eighth of inch of rain in thirty minutes," he read. "You handle that one, Sergeant." He glanced out the window. "Plenty of light still, and it's only half-past seven."

Thursday: Half-Past Seven

To Margaret and Andrew their Gifford cousins presented a relaxed, united front. "Ho, ho, young Andrew," Robbie greeted him, seizing the initiative. "What mischief have you been up to?"

"Me?" squeaked Andrew, who was twenty-one and interested only in rock climbing.

"You!" accused Robbie. "The police have been here all afternoon trying to break your alibis for when you murdered those three girls but said you were talking with Mark each time."

"They think *I* did it?"

"Don't worry. My diary proved Mark *was* with you."

"But they asked *me* about Mark."

"And they asked Mark about *me*."

"The sods!" Robbie gave his cousin a comforting smile. "Don't worry. They're only doing their job." Which disposed of such disagreeable topics as multi-murder. "How are you, sweet Meg?"

"A bit relieved, actually, " she confessed, blushing. "That Superintendent Cheeseman or whoever he was—"

"Cheadle, my love."

"We thought *he* thought Mark—"

"Mark? Never. No, old Cheadle's just lashing out in every conceivable direction on the principle that he can't go on missing his murderer forever. He even had a go at old Stanley Lipton!

However, enough of that. Andrew, shall we take them on?" And for the next three hours they played bridge—Andrew cautiously, Mark skilfully, Margaret ploddingly, Robbie brilliantly.

"Six diamonds," he opened on the final hand. He held seven winning diamonds, three winning hearts and three spades to the queen; and he knew, by the way Margaret frowned as she arranged her cards, that she had opening points. Margaret always frowned when she had opening points. Which, in this case, could only be the tops in clubs—of which he had none—and spades. So Margaret would double; and he would redouble; and Margaret, who always led her major suit first, would lead her ace of spades; and he would play his queen of spades; and Margaret (thinking, if she had the king, that he had no more spades; if she hadn't the king, that he had it) would lead another suit—and he'd be home and dry.

Margaret doubled; he redoubled; Margaret led her ace of spades; he put up his queen; Margaret hesitated—led the ace of clubs.

He took the trick with a small trump, cleared trumps with his ace and king, led the ace of hearts, and frowned before leading again. Margaret smiled, convinced that his weakness lay in hearts—of which she had four to the knave.

Sighing, as if defeat were inevitable, Robbie led out four diamonds in succession, and watched Margaret discard four spades to the king. Then he led his king and queen of hearts. Which left two small spades in his own hand—both now winners. One small slam, doubled, re-doubled, vulnerable—made.

Laying down his last two cards, he said: "Sorry, Meg"—and thumping his diaphragm, burst out laughing.

"Oh *Robbie*," she protested, "how could you?" Smiling bravely, she left with Andrew ten minutes later.

"She's right, you know," Mark reproached, putting the cards away. "You didn't have to make such a fool of her."

"I squoze her. What's wrong with that?"

"You enjoyed making her look idiotic . . . and you know she's always adored you."

Robbie was unrepentant. "I like winning, and I like squeezing."

"Five diamonds would have given you game and rubber."

"I wouldn't have made five diamonds. I had a string of diamonds and a void in clubs. Margaret had an opening bid, which had to be in spades and clubs. If it was spades, you probably had a void—"

"I had a singleton."

"So, if I'm in five, she risks leading her king of spades after the ace; you discard; she leads another; you trump—and I'm down. The only contract I had a chance of making was a little slam And it was the only contract worth making."

"Because it was a gamble?"

"A challenge! It's all I've got left, the freedom to challenge."

"Is that why you're provoking Cheadle all along the line?"

Robbie grinned. "Against Cheadle I'm playing three-handed bridge, with you the third. I've bid a grand slam; I'm vulnerable and he's got two aces, but I'm going to make him discard them both. That first lead of yours—dumping Miss Talbot at the Rex—has given me my contract."

"And what," demanded Mark, "are his two aces?"

"He knows who the murderer is," whispered Robbie, "and who's protecting him." He glanced at the clock. "Bloody hell, look at the time. Tell you what: while I'm cleaning my teeth, you pour us a nightcap and we'll drink to the success of tomorrow's grand slam."

Mark nodded, but as he watched Robbie wheel himself into the bathroom he knew that he dare not risk tomorrow's game. Whatever Robbie might squeeze Cheadle into discarding, it would not be *both* his aces. So the game must be cancelled.

Pouring two large tots of whisky, he emptied the contents of six phenobarb capsules into the glass he held for Robbie.

Robbie returned from the bathroom and accepted the glass Mark proffered. "To my grand slam," he toasted, peering mischievously at Mark through the whisky. Then hesitated, scowling, and held his glass to the light. "Strange," he announced, "the whisky's full of sediment." He set down his glass on the low table. "You must ask for your money back." He wheeled himself swiftly to his bedroom and promptly shut the door.

Recovering his wits, Mark ran up the hall and turned the knob of the door; but once again it was locked.

"Robbie," he shouted, knocking.

"What?"

"We've *got* to talk."

"Tomorrow," Robbie called back, "when I'll do all the talking."

Friday: Eight A.M.

Cheadle washed the remnants of shaving cream off his face and slicked his grey hair down. He looked fresh, even though he had had no sleep. And he felt pleased with himself. Today, unless he was sadly mistaken, he was going to wrap up the case of the Motorway Maniac. And wrap it up in a way that no police officer had wrapped up a murder inquiry before.

He needed, of course, a few more facts, but he had no doubt they'd arrive before the day was out. Actually, timing was going to matter more than facts. He must enter that cottage at precisely the right moment, and must time perfectly every word and move. One slip and the Gifford boys would have him up a gum tree.

They were a fascinating pair, he reflected as he walked to his headquarters. The sailor so honest he'd only been able to tell two lies, but so resourceful he could brazen his way into a cinema with a corpse in a wheel chair. And the paraplegic so brilliant under interrogation that almost every word had two meanings.

Yet it would be Master Robert who'd make the mistake. No one could go on giving every word two meanings, playing the police at their own game without, in the end, making a mistake. At which precise moment he, Cheadle, would begin the final dialogue.

"Sergeant," he called. Sergeant Robinson appeared instantly. "I know it's almost killing you, sitting dumb while I ask all the questions, but you've got to keep it up. It alarms Master Mark and infuriates Master Robert. Which is just how I want them." He glanced at his notebook. "Now. Before we visit the boys, I want to see Miss Margaret. I'm interested in last night's game of bridge."

Friday: Half-Past Two

For the sixth or seventh time on what had been a grey, drizzly day, Mark knocked at his brother's door; and for the sixth or seventh time there was no answer. "Robbie," he shouted, "for God's sake, you've been in there almost twenty-four hours. At least let me give you something to drink."

"You gave me something to drink last night!" reminded Robbie, breaking his silence at last.

"Robbie, please come out."

"Not till Cheadle arrives."

"That'll be too late and you know it. We've got to talk before he arrives; we can't do it through a locked door."

"I'll come out," Robbie finally agreed, "if you go down to the end of the garden—"

"What the hell for?"

"So you can't jump me. Go down to the garden and shout when you get there. And keep shouting."

"I can't just stand at the bottom of the garden shouting."

"Sing, then, as long as I can hear you and be sure you're not lurking. And take the target with you. I might as well kill *two birds!*"

"I'll shout when I've set it up."

"Do that."

Robbie—a sports jacket over his summer shirt, a rug over his legs—wheeled himself to the locked door and heard his brother's distant shout. Silently laughing, he unlocked his door and pushed himself down the hall.

"*Who*," Mark was singing, "*killed Cock Robin?*"

Robbie put his bow across the arms of his chair, his quivered arrows over his shoulder.

"*I, said the sparrow,*" Mark sang, "*with my bow and arrow . . .*"

"All right," Robbie called from the garden door, sidling his chair and locking the wheels, "you can stop now."

"*. . . When they heard of the death . . .*"

"That's *enough*, Mark!"

"*. . . of poor Cock Robin.*"

An arrow hissed over Mark's shoulder and thudded into the target. "I said," rasped Robbie, "that's enough. Now move aside and whatever it is you want to say, say it from there, while I practise."

"I wanted to say I'm sorry about last night, and to tell you that even if you *had* started to drink that whisky, I'd have stopped you."

A second arrow thudded into the target—a bull.

"Probably you don't believe me," Mark continued. "It doesn't

matter anyway. What matters is Cheadle. Robbie, just do what you said—make sure he hasn't enough to arrest me."

A third arrow hissed and thudded. A second bull. "And if I do?"

"I promise you, you'll be safe."

"Safe maybe"—drawing his bow a fourth time—"but plagued by coppers." His bow at full stretch, quite steady. "They'll never let up." And at last released the arrow. No good. "Blast!"

"But it's the best we can hope for. Isn't it?"

Robbie grinned and shot—a third bull.

"That's better," he commented. "Come inside."

"You've only shot five."

"The sixth I'll keep handy. Now, nice and slow—no, slower than that—come inside. We'll finish our talk in here." And as Mark paced towards him, withdrew, locking his chair so that it was sideways both to the garden door and to the armchair on his left.

As Mark came through the door he raised his bow and drew back the sixth arrow. "Sit," he ordered, nodding at the armchair.

Instead Mark halted, surprised that he felt no fear. He knew that Robbie intended to kill him. Knew that he must either sit and be killed, or at once attempt to escape. Yet he felt only a strangely passive curiosity. Not about death but about Robbie; about whether he could really do it.

"Now turn around." Robbie's voice was gently firm. "You'll not move an inch in any direction before this arrow's through your heart. My arm's strong and my eye's never been better."

Mark about-faced, his back to the arrow's head.

"Reach back with your hand," Robbie ordered.

Mark reached back and felt the armchair. He sidled around it and, turning to face Robbie, found the point not of an arrow but of a sabre touching his chest.

"I switched," said Robbie teasingly, "while your back was turned. You could've got clean away." He prodded a little, the sabre pricking bare tanned skin where the shirt lay open. "Sit."

Mark sat, the sabre an inch from his chest; and running down his chest was a glistening of blood. But still he felt only curiosity.

"Pillows!" Robbie said accusingly. "And phenobarbs! 'I'll turn you tonight'," he mimicked angrily. "You'd have turned me, all right. Straight into my grave."

"What are you planning?" Mark asked.

"You know."

Mark shook his head. "Don't be stupid, Robbie."

"Whatever else I may be," Robbie assured him, dangerously provoked, "I'm never stupid."

"What would be stupider than getting yourself arrested for murdering me?"

"I'm not going to murder you," Robbie protested. "I'm going to kill you accidentally."

"People in chairs don't get accidentally killed with sabres."

"That's why, when you're dead," Robbie countered, "I'll pull you across the arms of my chair, shove this sixth arrow into your chest where the sabre went in, and dump you down by the target. People in front of targets do get accidentally killed by arrows."

"You think the police will think that?"

"No, the police'll think the Motorway Maniac committed suicide. Because he knew his arrest was imminent."

"And how will you, a master bowman, explain shooting someone yards to the left of your target?"

"I'll tell them you set up the target, stood to one side, watched me shoot five, and then, just as I loosed my sixth—to my horror—you stepped straight into the line of flight. 'Why'd he do it?' I'll groan. 'Did he think I'd fired all six?' And then Cheadle'll stand in front of the fireplace and say, 'Now, now, Mr. Robert, you mustn't blame yourself. You did all you could to protect him; but he *was* a murderer and he did know the net was closing'."

Mark nodded, no longer curious, simply wanting it done with.

But Robbie was not to be hurried. "What else can I do? You'll kill me if I don't kill you. And I can't protect myself day and night, can I? What's the alternative? Let Cheadle arrest you?"

"You said the police would *never* arrest me." Mark's passivity had yielded at last to an aggrieved desire to live. "You said they'd never get a conviction because they'd never find a motive."

"I'm afraid I misjudged them. They've established you were near the scene of each crime at the relevant times, and that you had access to the props you needed for your stunt at the Rex. That's opportunity and method, and obviously they're going to rely on them. Purely circumstantial, but they don't seem to care."

"You're forgetting my alibi."

"My phone calls? They'll have broken that by now. Because I told both Charlie and the Liptons at the time that I hadn't got you."

"You have got me, haven't you?"

"Cheadle has."

"Robbie, don't underestimate Cheadle. I know you'll think I'm only saying that because I'm frightened—"

"And you aren't?"

"Terrified, actually. Specially"—nodding at the sabre—"of that."

"You'll feel nothing."

"Make no odds if I do. I'll be dead. But you . . . they'll get you."

"Never. They're not due here for at least two hours; I've got plenty of time, and I've worked it all out."

"They'll still get you. Then it'll be you, in that chair, in prison, for the rest of your life, with nothing to make it bearable. No archery, no javelin throwing, or medals, or cars, or privacy—"

"Stop it!" Robbie shouted, so shaken that the blade of his sabre trembled. He took a deep, shuddering breath, then continued quietly but implacably: "It's no use, kiddo. We've gone too far—you, me, and Cheadle."

"There's an alternative. Let me stay and look after you."

"You'd look after me, all right!"

"Robbie, don't. We could be happy. Plenty of bridge; someone to help you with the chores, go to the flicks with. You'd win every medal at the Olympics."

A mistake! For Robbie there'd be no Olympics, and both of them knew it.

"We've gone too far," Robbie repeated, his face stony.

"Then get it over with."

"In my time, not yours. Yesterday you told me I should respect the police, remember?"

"But Cheadle arrived, so you couldn't tell me why you didn't. Yes, I remember. Go on." Impatient to die.

"Well, it all began," Robbie related, comfortably, "late one night when I was four. I was asleep, when suddenly something—I didn't know what—woke me. I sat up, terrified, and there, on the double bed the other side of that grotty little room, were my dear papa and mama"—gulping—"naked, him forcing her down, and her head thrashing from side to side."

All the colour had gone from his face, and his eyes, inward looking, were blind. Shove the blade aside, Mark thought, transfixed by his brother's eyes. Which suddenly focused, aborting hope.

"That's what woke me," he explained. "My mother screaming 'no' and 'you're hurting me'. I didn't realize what they were doing."

It would have been easy then to disarm him. Instead, the blade forgotten, Mark muttered: "Oh, Robbie."

Robbie nodded. "I thought he was killing her. I shouted, 'Leave her alone!' But he didn't. Didn't even hear me, come to that. And neither did she. So then"—with a shuddering inhalation of breath—"I tried to pull him off her. . . . He stopped just long enough to snarl, 'Get lost' and went back to killing her."

With the thumb and little finger of his free hand Robbie pressed at his temples, as if to obliterate the memory inside his skull. "I was petrified. Not for myself. For her. He looked so huge and pitiless, and I couldn't think what to . . . so I jumped on his back. He didn't miss a beat, just bucked me off. I started yanking his hair then, and he backhanded me onto the floor. So I sank my sharp little teeth into his leg.

"He reared up then, grabbed my neck with one hand, a leg with the other, lifted me over his head, and threw me." Robbie was smiling now. "I flew across the room, bounced off the edge of the table, landed on the floor and was just about to start screaming when my mother shouted, 'And damn well stay there.'

"Which I did, for the simple reason I couldn't move. And I didn't scream because I couldn't feel. I just lay there while they went at it again." He pressed his diaphragm and coughed. "Seemed hours till they stopped and my mother came to look at me. And then all she could say, because I'd started crying, was, 'Stop that bloody snivelling.'

"My father told me to get back to my bed. I couldn't, of course, which got me another hammering. In the end, it got to them that something was wrong, so my father got dressed and went out to phone for an ambulance. While he was out my mother told me,

'You were sneaking out while your father and me was asleep, and you fell down the stairs. You tell the doctor anything else and I promise you, Robbie, I'll murder you.'

"So I told the doctor I'd fallen down the stairs. And I told the NSPCC I'd fallen down the stairs. And the NSPCC told the police it was the most blatant bit of child battering they'd seen in years, only they couldn't prove it unless the police got either my father or my mother to talk.

"And here, little brother, we come to the moral of this pretty tale. Do you know what the police did?" Mark shook his head. "They did nothing. And *you* tell *me* to *respect* them"—jabbing three times with his sabre, drawing a seed pearl of blood each time.

Mark asked simply: "Why've you never told me before?"

Robbie looked surprised. "Never told anyone. At first because I wouldn't admit that my father and mother couldn't stand me; then because I thought I wanted to forget; and finally, when that bump on the squash court finished what my father had begun, because I found that what I really wanted was to keep it all to myself—and feed on it. So I did. And feeding on it has given me the strength to endure this ridiculous life."

"What about me—'your devoted voice from Houston'?"

"I told you, kiddo: you gave my life direction. But my fuel"—his sabre arm tensing—"was hate. And now, I'm afraid"—inching the sabre backward, lining it up—"it's time for splashdown."

"Not yet," Mark murmured. "We've got company."

And Robbie, turning slowly around, saw Cheadle.

"Hel*lo*, Superintendent," he greeted heartily, laying aside his sabre. "You turn up at the most *in*convenient times, don't you?"

Cheadle grinned. He had been standing out of sight in the hall for the past three minutes, and it had not really required that "*Now*" urgently whispered through the miniature receiver he had clamped to his ear to impel him around the corner and into the room. The way Master Robert had said "splashdown" had done that. Yet instantly the same Master Robert had made him laugh.

Quite a boy. No more of a boy, though, than his brother. Because Master Mark, casually rubbing his bare chest, had just risen to greet him with an easy smile.

"Still getting nowhere fast?" Robbie taunted.

"I had to get *here* rather fast. Do you know that one of my men radioed to me on his walkie-talkie that you were about to kill your brother?"

"Now what," Robbie wondered, "could possibly have made him think that? And where is this walking-talking man of yours?"

"Up that tree." Cheadle pointed to an elm. "With a pair of field glasses. Was my man mistaken?"

Robbie turned ironically to Mark. "Was he mistaken?"

"Am I dead?" asked Mark, matching his brother's irony.

"It seems," Robbie pronounced, "your man was mistaken." The sergeant tapped on the glass door. "Come in," Robbie said to him. "I was just telling *Cheadle* here that his man was mistaken. You've come on a fool's errand. Which is nothing if not apt."

We'll see about that, thought Cheadle. It was going to be a dirty battle. He almost wished he could offer quarter. But he was a hunter. Also, Robbie had just called him Cheadle—plain, unadorned Cheadle. He said, smiling submissively, "We meant well, sir. My man couldn't see your face very clearly, but he got a very good view of your *brother* moving backward into that chair. And was sure he looked terrified."

"My brother's an extremely brave man," snapped Robbie. "He'd never have looked terrified."

Cheadle looked at Mark. "Why were you backing round the chair, sir?" he asked.

"A childish habit I can't get out of," Mark assured him, touched by Robbie's loyalty.

"And why were you jabbing Mr. Mark with a sword?" Cheadle asked Robbie.

"I was practising my thrusts," said Robbie. "And it's a sabre."

"And what were you saying as you practised your thrusts?"

"Can't your walking-talking, tree-climbing man read lips?"

"I'm afraid not."

"Then you'll never know the story of my extraordinary life."

"Does one brother tell another the story of his life?"

"If there are parts of it the other doesn't know."

"In your case, I suppose," Cheadle ventured, "that would be the fascinating part before you were adopted?"

"And how," Robbie demanded coldly, "did you find that out?"

"Miss Margaret let it slip when I saw her at lunchtime. She's a nice lass. She thinks you think she's a half-wit."

"Can't imagine why."

"Oh, things like bidding that little slam last night."

Robbie looked both surprised and uncertain. "You play bridge?"

Cheadle nodded. "Rather well, as a matter of fact. You wouldn't have got that slam if the lead had been mine."

All Robbie's uncertainty vanished. "If the lead had been yours, I wouldn't have bid it, you twit. Against you, I'd have waited. Till I could bid a *grand* slam." He winked at Mark.

"Pity we won't have time for a game," said Cheadle regretfully. He knew nothing about bridge except the jargon he'd picked up from Margaret.

"But aren't we playing now?" asked Robbie slyly.

"In a manner of speaking, sir, I suppose we are."

"Let's make the contract seven spades then," Robbie challenged.

"Spades?" queried Cheadle.

"Doesn't the queen of spades mean death?"

"Ah," said Cheadle, accepting the challenge, "of course."

"You realize, don't you, that Mark's your partner; the first lead was his and half the hand's been played?"

"I realize that, sir."

"Did you double? I can't remember."

"No, sir"—recalling Margaret's words. "You're vulnerable and it's a friendly game. I don't care for penalty points."

"How chivalrous of you. You were saying that I was adopted."

"Yes. So one of my men came up with the Glasgow NSPCC's report on the case of a four-year-old called Robert Stephen Thomson—yourself."

"Your interest in my childhood comes a quarter of a century too late. But what else, pray, have your men come up with?"

"The steamship line advised one of them that Mr. Mark was a most resourceful officer. Another got the facts about your television set. Others checked with Stoke Mandeville's chief physiotherapist and the Liptons on the subject of those telephone calls which were your brother's alibi for several rather vital hours on Wednesday."

"Oh dear."

"Yes, you haven't exactly been truthful with us, have you? But may we have the truth now?"

"Try me."

Instead, and with blatant insincerity, Cheadle asked: "Warm enough, are you sir?"

"I told you, we don't *feel* cold. And even if we did, with this on" —tugging at his jacket lapel—"I wouldn't." Tartly. Disconcerted by Cheadle's change of pace.

"Glad to hear it," said Cheadle blandly. Then rapped: "When you made those phone calls here on Wednesday, to whom, in fact, did you speak?"

"To no one." Robbie looked sullen.

"And why was that, would you say?"

"Mark probably didn't hear the phone. Sailors sleep like logs."

Cheadle cocked his head at Mark. "Do you sleep like a log?"

"I do. And I didn't hear the phone."

Cheadle grinned. Mr. Mark, as ever, was sticking to the literal truth. Better to get back to the peddler of tricky half-truths.

"Mr. Robert, on Wednesday afternoon when you left your brother here alone, how exactly did you depart?"

"By helicopter! It had been raining; and I dislike wet roads."

"It had indeed been raining," murmured Cheadle. "But what I meant was, by which door did you leave?"

"That one"—pointing to the garden door, slightly puzzled, because Cheadle wasn't playing the way he'd expected.

"And then to your helicopter, which waited where?"

"On the concrete pad outside its hangar."

"And where was *your* . . . er . . . machine parked, Mr. Mark?"

"On the lawn, beside his helicopter."

"So you wheeled yourself past your brother's car on the lawn, Mr. Robert, and did what?"

"Whirled aloft," Robbie told him airily.

"I see. And as you passed your brother's car, did you notice whether or not it was empty?"

"You mean, apart from the five illegal Pakistani immigrants hiding in the boot?"

"Apart from them."

"As far as I could see, quite empty. But then," he grinned, "from chair level I wouldn't have seen anything anyway. He could've had a couple of corpses laid out on the back seat for all I knew."

Cheadle turned soberly to Mark. "*Did* you have a couple of corpses concealed in your car?"

"Not that I knew of," Mark told him, equally soberly.

"I see. Then let's move on to six o'clock. Mr. Robert. When you returned from Stoke Mandeville, how did you re-enter the house? I mean"—hurriedly—"by which door?"

"The one from the garage."

"And when you came in, where was your brother?"

"On the sofa. Asleep."

"Is that correct, Mr. Mark?"

"I was on the sofa."

Again Cheadle smiled. At what? wondered Robbie.

"And as you entered, I seem to remember you saying, you became aware of an unusual aroma?"

Robbie raised a contemptuous eyebrow. "That wasn't an aroma, Cheadle, it was aftershave."

Cheadle turned to Mark. "You spilled your aftershave, I believe you said, before you . . . er . . . went to sleep?"

"Yes."

"Would it surprise you to know that the murdered girl used the same aftershave? That someone had wiped an empty bottle of it clean of fingerprints?" Mark refused to be provoked. "*You* left her in that cinema, didn't you?" Again no answer. "And having wheeled yourself out in your brother's old chair, you returned here, didn't you?" Silence. "Mr. Gifford, why did you go to such extraordinary lengths to dispose of Miss Talbot's body?"

"Lay off him!" Robbie shouted. "You've no right to indulge in this cat-and-mouse stuff without a warrant."

"Oh, I have a warrant," Cheadle assured them. "But for the moment, nothing you say will be used in evidence against him."

"Then what," demanded Robbie, "are you playing at?"

"I need to *understand* why your brother acted as he did."

"Then you're dimmer even than I thought."

"Why is that, Mr. Gifford?"

"Because any fool—even you—should be able to see that Mark acted as he did because that was his trademark."

For the first time Cheadle saw Mark look shaken.

Robbie saw it too. "I'm telling him nothing he doesn't know, Mark."

"You and your promises." Mark looked suddenly a dangerous man.

"Promises? When he's got a warrant for your arrest? And I'm frightened of you? What do you expect me to do, anyway? Hold these bloodhounds at bay with my little sabre while you make good your escape?"

Glowering, Mark muttered: "I wish you *had* strangled me when you were a kid."

"Did he try, sir?" inquired a tolerant Cheadle.

But it was Robbie who answered. "He was referring to my somewhat ambivalent reaction to his birth."

"You felt like strangling him, did you?"

"Figuratively speaking, frequently. I confessed that to him on Wednesday, which is why, I suppose, he brings it up now, when he's in a spot of trouble."

"Trouble you'd hoped to avert by suppressing evidence that might have led to his arrest, Mr. Robert? You knew who had left the girl at the Rex."

"I'm his brother, aren't I?"

"But you were about to destroy him this afternoon! My walking-talking, tree-climbing man saw you at it."

"To save him from prison. I knew you were coming to make an arrest; and I knew you didn't care that you can't prove motive."

"To be frank, I don't," Cheadle confessed indifferently, but his heart was singing. Master Robert had said too much—without even realizing it. Soon he'd make a mistake. "And you're right: I couldn't even begin to prove your brother's motive."

"Exactly. So I had to save him from arrest."

"And would you have confessed the method whereby you'd saved him?"

"I would not. You'd have found him in front of my target, an arrow through his heart and me in hysterics because I'd accidentally killed him."

"Accidentally?"

"Look at the target." Obediently Cheadle looked. "How many arrows in it?"

"Er . . . five."

"Bowmen shoot six. I'd have told you Mark must've miscounted and stepped into the line of fire just as I shot my last. And you, of course, would have decided it was suicide."

"I wonder."

"Well, at the time you might have wondered; but as time passed, and there were no more motorway murders, you'd have decided it must have been suicide after all."

"Ah yes, of course. How very clever of you, sir," he said, grateful for the long-awaited mistake. He turned amiably to Mark. "Just as well I arrived when I did, then, isn't it? I'd never have been forgiven if I'd let you be killed. Capital punishment that would have been. And that's a relic of our barbarous past, isn't it?"

"Obviously one whose passing you regret," Mark smouldered.

"The passing of judicial homicide, I don't regret, but suicide—" Cheadle gestured to indicate that, in his opinion, in certain cases, there was a lot to be said for a guilty man's judicial suicide. Gestured, but left the thought unspoken.

Understanding perfectly, Mark scowled. "Where do we go from here? To the station? With a blanket wrapped round my head?"

"Talking of heads," responded Cheadle, unhurriedly, "when you entered the Rex were you wearing the dead girl's wig?"

"I was."

"And did you choose the Rex because, as Mr. Robert pointed out, that put the Maniac's mark on Miss Talbot's death?"

"I did."

"And when I asked had you seen anyone on the A41 pick up any girl, and you said no, did you lie?"

It took Mark fully fifteen seconds to reply: "I didn't see *myself* pick up a girl."

"But you did pick one up?"

"Yes."

"At what time?"

"I suppose about five to three."

"Was she alone?"

"Yes."

"Are you married?"

"No."

"Girl friend?"

"Mind your own business."

"When exactly did you work out the details of your plan to deposit Miss Talbot in the Rex?"

"After Robbie had left for Stoke."

"Only then?"

"I could hardly do it while he was here."

"Did you, at any time before you wheeled her into the Rex, remove her from your car?"

"I brought her in here."

"Why?"

"It was too dangerous to leave her in my car. Someone might have called. Anyway, I had to work out a plan."

"In the process of which, you spilled her perfume?"

"Yes."

"Did you bring the others here?"

Again Mark hesitated, almost as if he hadn't understood the question. "You don't really expect me to tell you about them, do you?"

"Not really, no. Except you did tell us about Miss Talbot."

"You knew about her."

"Ever since my sergeant smelled that perfume outside the Rex. On you. In fourteen months that was our first break."

At last he turned to Robbie. "Yours has been a difficult role, hasn't it, sir?"

Robbie bridled. "Don't patronize me, Cheadle."

"No, I genuinely mean it: yours has been a very tricky role. And you've played it superbly, sir."

"I don't know what you're talking about," Robbie disclaimed.

"Well, your various hints to us about your brother's guilt, for one thing. You had to tell us just enough to frighten him, but not enough to let us arrest him, didn't you?"

"I thought if I could stop him killing, and at the same time keep him out of your hands, I was justified."

"But in case we didn't get the message, you told the chief physiotherapist and the Liptons that your brother had just arrived here, but you couldn't raise him by telephone?"

"Yes."

"So that, if worst came to worst, and you had to prove to us that your brother *could* have left Miss Talbot at the Rex, you could refer us to the chief physiotherapist and the Liptons?"

"Yes."

"But at that time, on Wednesday afternoon, when you spoke to the chief physiotherapist and the Liptons, *you didn't even know* that your brother had a dead girl in his car! I asked you. And you said no, all you'd seen was five Pakistanis in the boot."

"Of course I did. For the twentieth time, he's my brother."

"You mean you lied for him about that too?"

"I mean," Robbie sulked, "I saw her body on the front seat of his car as I wheeled past it to get into my own."

"Sitting bolt upright, was she?"

"At first I only saw her hat. And I thought, That's odd. Mark doesn't wear purple hats! So I opened the door. And there she lay, bleeding slightly from a wound in the midriff, but very dead."

"Well, yes, she would have been. The murder weapon entered the body just below the breastbone, travelled upward unimpeded and killed her instantly. Same as the three other girls. Why do you think your brother murdered these four girls?"

"I doubt he knows himself."

"But you were determined he shouldn't stand trial?"

"Yes."

"Do you believe what your brother says, Mr. Mark?"

"He'd never have let me stand trial," Mark agreed.

"Do you know why?"

"Yes."

"Mr. Robert," Cheadle asked rather more deliberately, "were you afraid of your brother simply because *he* knew *you* knew that Janine Talbot's body was in his car on Wednesday afternoon?"

"I became afraid," Robbie answered with equal deliberation, "only when he convinced me he was planning to kill me. On Wednesday night I saw him rehearsing it with a pillow; and last night he offered me a nightcap full of phenobarbs."

"So *he's* tried to kill *you*; and *you*, when I came in this afternoon, were about to kill *him?*"

"We were always"—Robbie smiled—"a close family."

But Cheadle did not smile back. He felt like a juggler with ten balls in the air who knew that to relax for an instant would be to drop them all. Anyway, it was time to catch Mr. Mark again.

"*Did* you try to kill your brother?" he asked Mark.

"I thought about it."

"Why?"

"Isn't motive *your* job?"

"All right," sighed Cheadle, adding a further ball to the ten. "Try this for size. You committed this series of murders close to your brother's home in the confident expectation that suspicion would eventually fall on him?"

Mark stayed silent, waiting for the whole of the question; but Robbie exploded.

"Not even you," he shouted at Cheadle, "are stupid enough to believe a cripple capable of bumping off four able-bodied girls and disposing of their bodies here, there and everywhere."

As if Robbie had never spoken, Cheadle resumed his theorizing, still aiming it at Mark. "You stabbed each girl as she sat beside you in your car—knowing that even a cripple could do that. Later, at times when it could easily be established that Mr. Robert was alone, because you were en route to your cousins, you bundled each of the first three girls out of your car, as it was moving, under cover of darkness, near a police station—knowing that a cripple as strong and determined as your brother could also do that.

"And finally, when we'd failed to identify your brother as the Maniac after three killings, you committed a fourth, disposed of the body in a manner befitting the Maniac, but then, very clumsily, drew our attention to yourself. So clumsily, you hoped to convince us that you were merely an accessory. A devoted accessory ridding his murderous brother of an unwanted corpse, in fact. And that at a time when aforesaid murderous brother, being elsewhere, seemed to have an alibi.

"But it was all too pat, Mr. Mark. I mean, why did you return to the Rex stinking of the dead girl's perfume? Why, if it wasn't to lead us back here to your brother?

"You having led us back, your brother, of course, began to protect himself. By dropping hints to all and sundry. But that didn't worry you, because the more he hinted, the more he appeared to be attempting merely to incriminate you, his accessory.

"Which left you free to kill him and then to tell us, 'I had to do it. I couldn't let you imprison a brother both dear to me and crippled.' Now what do you say to that?"

His discourse concluded, all eleven balls once more safely in hand, Cheadle sat back complacently, demanding applause.

"Clever!" Robbie applauded sarcastically. "Clever Mark, clever copper! You deserve each other."

But Mark, still stolidly appraising the question, said nothing. It would be necessary, Cheadle decided, to rattle him

"How much did your father leave you, sir?" he asked, his tone contemptuous.

Mark frowned. "Leave me? About twenty thousand."

"Actually," Cheadle corrected, "twenty-one thousand pounds and fifty-eight pence. Net. We've checked. And he left it to you on the understanding that you'd provide for your brother?"

"Of course."

"How much has your brother cost you so far?"

"About eight and a half thousand."

"And how much a year do you allow Mr. Robert?"

"Fifteen hundred. After tax."

"After tax, eh? So that, even if your remaining ten thousand is well invested, in seven years time there'll be nothing left?"

"So what?"

"So if you got him out of the way, you'd be ten thousand better off than if you let him live. How's that for a motive?"

"Absurd," Mark told him promptly.

"Why?"

"Because he's only got—"

And, furious with himself for his carelessness and with Cheadle for his deviousness, swallowed the rest of the sentence.

"Exactly," said Cheadle.

Mark challenged: "I don't believe you've got a warrant at all."

"Sorry, sir," said Cheadle, as he withdrew a document from an inside pocket.

Watched intently by Robbie, Cheadle handed across the document, which Mark perused.

"I want to confess," Mark announced, returning the warrant, which Cheadle reluctantly slid back into his pocket.

"Not just now, sir," Cheadle requested. "In any case, not here."

"Now," Mark insisted. "And here. I want my brother to know the facts." Managing a smile which Robbie could not return.

The sergeant, pen poised in air, for once looked uncertain as to how to proceed. "Take it down," Cheadle growled.

"Gawd!" groaned Robbie, and wheeled himself to the garden doorway, his back to them all.

"I, Marcus James Gifford," Mark recited, "of 11, Cornwall Crescent, London, S.W.5, being of sound mind, hereby voluntarily confess to the murders of four girls since August of last year. I also confess to the attempted murder of my brother last night, Thursday the— What's the date?"

Amused, Robbie looked around. "Mark?"

"Yes."

"I *wanted* to die. On Wednesday I as good as told you."

"I know."

"And last night, when I asked you to pour me a nightcap . . ."

"I know that too."

"Only I lost my nerve."

"You don't have to explain."

"To you, perhaps not," Cheadle corrected. "But to me, he does. Why did you want your brother to kill you, Mr. Robert?"

"He was your only witness," Mark intervened. "He wanted to deny you that witness."

"Mark?" Robbie again.

"Yes?"

"I'm sorry I locked my door."

Mark smiled. "I couldn't have done it even if you hadn't."

Robbie laughed, arm on diaphragm. "I couldn't either. Just waved me sword and chattered on about how I'd suffered before you were even born. Strange."

"Forget it, Robbie."

"No. Whatever happens, you remember it." He turned away.

Cheadle decided it was time to start juggling again. "May we now, Mr. Mark, have the rest of your confession? There are a few details outstanding, such as the murder weapon."

"Oh—one of Robbie's old sabres."

"Where is it?"

"In the garage."

"Thank you, sir," said Cheadle courteously. And withdrawing the warrant from his inside pocket, clearing his throat, declaimed: "*Robert Stephen* Gifford, I have here a warrant—"

"But I've confessed!" shouted Mark, leaping from his chair, standing guard between the police and Robbie, his hand on his brother's shoulder.

"To murdering four girls with a sabre?" Cheadle queried.

"Yes."

"That was not the weapon employed," Cheadle told him. "Not that we know exactly what it was, but it wasn't a blade, and whatever it was, we're certain it was your brother who used it."

Robbie turned accusingly around in his chair. "You don't play bridge at all, do you, copper?"

"No, sir. But in my younger days I used to juggle."

"Good God!" exclaimed Robbie. And turning his back on them all once more, he allowed his head to sink on his chest.

Mark moved his hand from his brother's shoulder to his neck, massaging gently, taking no pains to conceal his dislike for Cheadle.

"As we see it, sir," Cheadle told Mark, "your brother hoped we'd suspect you each time a girl was murdered. He picked each of them up about an hour before you'd told him you'd be arriving, and disposed of each of them, except the last, when you were en-route to your cousins. As a cripple he was not a likely suspect—"

"Still isn't," Mark insisted.

"Not a likely one; but not an impossible one. You, however, were."

"Until the Rex I may have been."

"Even the Rex didn't qualify you for the role."

"Why not?"

"The steamship line tells me anatomy is not a subject taught to officers of the merchant marine."

"I don't get the relevance."

"The relevance is that only someone with a thorough grasp of anatomy could have killed all four girls with an identical upward thrust from just below the centre of the rib cage. The Middlesex Medical School tells us your brother was brilliant at anatomy."

"And why," Mark countered, "would anyone so brilliant fumble his fourth murder if he'd succeeded with his first three?"

"Your brother became impatient, sir. He had to trap you this time or not at all, because, as you yourself were about to remark a minute ago, he's less than a year to—"

"Don't!" Mark begged. "Please!"

"He knows, sir," Cheadle insisted. "Dr. Fairburn told us your brother knows those lesions will kill him within the year." He shook his head. "Ironic, isn't it? He claims he got them lifting a rented TV. Only he never did rent a TV. So how *did* he get 'em? Shoving bodies out of his car." Cheadle was gazing at Mark with almost academic pleasure, defying him to disprove what had been so logically demonstrated.

Mark was still massaging Robbie's neck. He was very cool now that he knew the nature of the problem confronting him. "You've got your data wrong," Mark said. "The only body you're sure about was in *my* car, not his."

"Put there by him," agreed Cheadle condescendingly.

"Impossible."

"The wheel marks of his chair prove it. The lawn was soft from the rain. Wherever your brother moved, he left tracks. They're still there, sir. The shallower ones where he wheeled only himself, the deeper ones where he wheeled an extra burden of about a hundred and twenty pounds. We've done tests. And Janine Talbot weighed a hundred and nineteen pounds."

"Someone else could have put her in my car."

"Someone else in a wheel chair? Someone else with a knowledge of anatomy? Someone else who hated you enough to frame you and kill you, and make us believe it was suicide? Someone else who despised policemen so much he incorporated into his plot a gambit that made them a laughing-stock throughout the country?"

"What gambit?"

"Dumping three of his victims outside police stations. The press loved that."

"You can't prove he despises policemen."

"His attitude towards us since Wednesday?"

"The attitude of an innocent citizen whose home you'd invaded."

Cheadle shook his head. "He led us here. He practically thrust that 'aftershave' under our noses, calling it custard."

"Doesn't prove him a murderer."

"He also," Cheadle expatiated, "hates scrubbers."

"Not partial to them myself," Mark retorted.

"You didn't have one for a mother."

"You saying all scrubbers' sons are murderers?"

"Mr. Mark"—Cheadle sighed—"are you still saying that you are the Motorway Maniac?"

"Aren't you forgetting the bird *I* picked up?"

"She came to see us yesterday, and said she'd been picked up at ten to three and dropped off at five past. Gave us a good description of you, sir, as did her aunt, who was waiting for her outside the Aylesbury post office."

It was the alibi Mark had always known he could call upon. Knowing that, he'd been prepared to risk a trial—to give Robbie time. But now that his alibi pointed to Robbie as a murderer, he almost wished he'd never had one. Just as Robbie had wished he hadn't one. Had been so shaken to think that he might have one that he'd asked question after question as to whether anyone outside the post office had seen him "put down" his blonde nympho.

That was the moment, Mark reflected, he'd known for sure what he'd suspected the moment he saw Janine Talbot's body sprawled along the front seat of his car: that his brother was a killer who'd shouted angrily rather than allow Mark to collect the bottle of Scotch from a car parked next to his own, and been downright rude rather than allow Mark to carry his bow and arrows out to his own car, in which lay his latest victim.

Mark allowed his hand to fall from his brother's neck. Everything Cheadle said was true; even that the purpose of all the murders was to incriminate him. Now he too could be murdered. Otherwise, why had Robbie put him in a position where he had to dispose of a body? And not accepted that service with gratitude? And insisted that they return to the Rex?

All along it could only have been Robbie, but he'd been unable to reconcile himself to that, to accept that Robbie should have *wanted* to kill. "He *couldn't* have," he muttered.

"That why you tried to persuade his doctor to recall him to the hospital?" Cheadle inquired. "Because he couldn't have done it? Or because you knew he had, and wanted him somewhere where he couldn't do it again?"

"Sorry"—Mark looked stubborn—"it's all too circumstantial."

"Not at all," Cheadle contradicted. "What if I told you we found traces of Janine Talbot's blood on the seat of his car?"

From Robbie, then, came his only comment on their long dialogue: a sardonic snort of laughter.

Almost sympathetically, Cheadle inquired: "May we dispense with your confession now, Mr. Mark?"

Standing with his back to Robbie's chair, Mark shrugged. "I had to give him time."

"That I understand, sir; but his time has run out and he is a murderer."

"You don't know him."

"Enough to appreciate that he hated his mother for forsaking him, us for not arresting his mother, and you for coming between him and his adoptive parents—an over-simplification, of course. And now, sir"—once again displaying his warrant—"if I may?"

Mark moved around Robbie's chair, to face and comfort his brother, and Cheadle began to intone.

"Robert Stephen Gifford," he charged. But he stopped as he saw Mark's hand dart to Robbie's chest, saw the look on his face, heard him saying: "Save your breath, Chief Superintendent," and saw the weapon embedded beneath Robbie's ribs as the wheel chair was whirled to confront him.

Throwing aside his notebook, the sergeant leaped to the chair.

"Gone?" asked Cheadle, rhetorically, laconically almost.

The sergeant nodded.

"Poor Robbie," Mark muttered, turning his back.

Cheadle peered down at the clothbound haft protruding from Robbie's chest. "So that's the murder weapon. Half an arrow. I suppose we should have guessed." He put the warrant back in his pocket. "Wheel Mr. Gifford to his bedroom, will you, Sergeant? He always hated being gawped at." Mark turned and watched as his brother was wheeled away.

"There are a few things more we must discuss, sir," Cheadle told him. "But first, I think, you should have a cup of tea. May I?" Nodding at the kitchen.

Blindly, Mark waved his assent; and stolidly Cheadle filled the kettle.

Friday: Half-Past Five

Cheadle was looking for the teacups when the sergeant returned from Robbie's bedroom and handed him an envelope. After a moment's thought, Cheadle said to Mark: "A letter for you, sir. From your brother, I suspect. Afraid I'll have to read it too; but if you'd like a few moments alone . . . ?"

Shaking his head, Mark opened the envelope. The first he's ever written me, he thought. And I don't want to read it. But Mark read it while the sergeant phoned for an ambulance.

> Little brother: If you get to read this, I'll be dead instead of you. And if you're not dead, it will be because I've been sitting up all night remembering everything you've ever done for me and doubting my hatred of you for the first time.
>
> I even forgot, for a few hours, that I was never quite sure of the parental love you never doubted.
>
> I even forgot, for a few hours, all those times you called me into the bathroom here to talk to you while you showered; and how, each time I sat impotent in my chair, watching you stretch and stoop and soap yourself, I detested you for your blatant virility.
>
> For a few hours I even doubted the sanity of the end I've planned for you. So, should you read this letter, there are a few things you might like to know.
>
> First, why was I so rattled when you arrived early on Wednesday? Because it was raining when I got back with the girl, and since I can't afford to get wet, I couldn't spend five minutes in the open wiping her grubby prints off the door and anything else she might have touched. I had to leave the car on the drive so that later I could transfer the girl to your car. No room for that in the garage.
>
> So I came inside, but just as the rain stopped, you arrived! I was very put out.
>
> As to how I killed each time. I simply dawdled up and down the A41 till I saw a likely girl, stopped and unlatched the door. If she got in, she had only one chance of staying alive; to resist when I put my hand on her sternum (look it up!) and started kissing her. None of them did. All four closed their eyes and kissed back. I

kept my eye on the place where my hand had been, took a bit of old arrow out of the glove compartment and bashed it home.

Finally, how did I plan to involve you? Simply by telephoning from Stoke and asking you to buy the vegetables I'd "forgotten" to buy for dinner. You'd have gone out to your car, found the girl and either got rid of her, called the police, or waited to ask my advice. Whichever, I'd have contrived to incriminate you enough to make your subsequent suicide feasible.

But when I did phone, you were out already, on your way to the Rex, which has made everything much more exciting since.

That's all I can tell you. I know it doesn't answer the biggest question of all: Did I kill just to implicate you, or for the pleasure of killing as well? I thought I knew. Now I'm not sure. You're banging on my door again. Whichever way this goes, at least, little brother, you'll see no more of

Yours treacherously,
Robbie Thomson

Mark put down the letter and stared into the empty fireplace. Cheadle handed him a cup of tea and left him to his thoughts.

"A bit better now, sir?" he asked when the cup was empty.

Mark nodded. "Do you want this?"—offering the letter.

"Afraid I must, sir"—taking it and lowering himself into an armchair. After reading it Cheadle too stared into the fireplace. Then said: "He was fonder of you than he was prepared to admit."

"What makes you say that?"

"He signs himself Thomson, not Gifford. *Your* name's mentioned nowhere. He refers to you as 'little brother'. Cheer up, sir. You're young and alive."

"I feel old and dead."

"That'll pass."

I wonder, thought Mark. Then he wondered aloud: "Would he have killed me?"

"He had his chance, didn't he?"

Mark remembered the long minutes of his final confrontation with Robbie, felt again the sabre pricking at his chest, saw again the sudden emergence of Cheadle from the hallway.

"Why . . . why did he kill all those girls?"

"I don't know, Mr. Gifford. Our psychiatrist has some theories—

they always do, don't they? Mr. Robert's mother was a blonde and a tart and twenty-three years old when last he saw her. Our psychiatrist suggests he might have been murdering her each time."

"You said it was so he could murder me."

"And our psychiatrist would say that Mr. Robert would convince himself he was plotting to destroy you, with whom there was no blood tie, rather than admit to matricide."

"There's a hell of a gap between plotting and actually killing."

"His father, sir, is XYY," advised Cheadle, as if that explained everything.

"What's that?" asked Mark, to whom it explained nothing.

"A chromosomatic abnormality frequently found in very big, very strong, very violent men. Some, like our psychiatrist, even believe it to be an abnormality which *induces* violence."

"Is Robbie . . . was Robbie XYY?"

"No idea, sir. But his father's at present doing fourteen years for grievous bodily harm—in twenty-seven years he's spent only two *out* of jail—so probably your brother didn't have much of a chance."

Mark thought of the last chance adoption had offered his brother, and muttered: "I wish I'd never been born."

"It was a circumstance over which you had no control," Cheadle said, his tone one of rebuke.

"I needn't have invited him into the bathroom, though. But after boarding school, and life at sea . . . I never thought. . . ."

"I don't think it made a bit of difference, sir. In fact, for once I'm inclined to agree with our psychiatrist: your brother wanted to be caught. Bodies in front of police stations; dragging you back to the Rex. Didn't you *know* you stank of perfume?"

"I couldn't smell it any longer."

"And the way he practically told us how the job at the Rex was done. Is a man who does that trying to get away with it?"

"If it's a challenge he's issuing, maybe he is."

"Well, if that's what he was up to, he was trapped the moment I learned he'd never rented a TV; and when he assured me there'd have been no more motorway murders once you were dead, he gave us his motive for all the killings: to incriminate you."

"And what now?" Mark demanded. "A blaze of publicity about Robert Gifford, the Wheel Chair Murderer?"

Cheadle shook his head. "A coroner's inquiry into the death of a Mr. X who left a suicide letter confessing to the murders."

Mark frowned, both perplexed and suspicious. "Why?"

"The Giffords are blameless. He acknowledged that when he signed himself Thomson. Also, of course, one wants to protect the Stoke Mandeville image. They're remarkable people."

Again Mark frowned. His own efforts to protect Robbie had been less altruistic. "May I stay to see him into the ambulance?"

"Travel with him, if you like. Though if you take my advice, you'll say good-bye to him here."

"Yes." Mark cleared his throat. "When will you be booking me?"

"Sir?" Cheadle looked extravagantly blank.

"I was an accessory," Mark reminded. "To the murder of Janine Talbot. Obstructed you—made a false confession. Remember?"

"No, sir, I don't remember any of that. Sergeant doesn't either, do you, Sergeant? What can you be talking about? The only accessory to murder we remember is that long-haired laddie from Scotland. Who's vanished! Dead by now, quite likely. Heroin, amphetamines; all the same, these hippies." The doorbell rang. "That will be the ambulance, Sergeant. Tell them just to put Mr. Robert on a stretcher in his bedroom and to wait outside, will you?" Though content with his quarry's demise, Cheadle was anxious that the dead should seem peaceful in death, not hunted.

The sergeant departed. Cheadle rinsed the teacups and stacked them on the draining board. The sergeant returned.

"Mr Gifford?" Cheadle said. "If you'd like to see your brother now . . . ?"

"Yes, thank you." He walked slowly to Robbie's room and, entering it, stared down at the stretcher.

Lying on his back, blanket-covered except for his face, Robbie, in death, betrayed none of the horror of his life. His legs could have been the legs of a man who walked. His expression was serene.

So serene that Mark looked again. And discerned not serenity but emptiness. An emptiness that explained nothing, because what he had done was meaningless; that concealed nothing, because behind his eyes was only emotional emptiness.

Looking down at the empty face, Mark whispered: "Good-bye, Robbie"—and returned to Cheadle.

"We'll be on our way, sir." Cheadle hesitated, then held out his hand. "If we meet again, I hope it'll be in happier circumstances."

"Yes." Shaking the hunter's hand.

"Come on, Sergeant."

Mutely the sergeant inclined his head, turned and departed.

About to follow him, Cheadle hesitated again. "Er . . . should the subject of accessories to the murder of Miss Talbot ever arise, sir, you won't forget what I told you, will you?"

"No." Condoning what the hunter had done; ashamed.

"Good-bye, Mr. Gifford."

"Good-bye."

He stood quite still. Heard the front door shut. Heard the ambulance doors shut. Heard the car doors shut. Heard ambulance and police car drive down the lane. And looking slowly around the comfortable, meaningless room—meaningless as Robbie—he wept.

Friday: Five to Six

As they swung right into the road to Aylesbury the sergeant glanced at his superior: a questioning glance, inviting comment. Cheadle caught the question and ignored it. The sergeant coughed. "Sir?" he said.

Cheadle slid low on the seat, tired and reluctant. "What is it, Sergeant?"

"I have the feeling, sir," the sergeant replied—his accent was pure Oxford—"that in the matter of the death of Mr. Robert Gifford, his brother Mark was not alone in his determination to give the deceased, I quote, 'time'."

Cheadle shoved himself upright. "Sergeant, I'm a tired, simple man. Forget your university degrees and speak to me simply."

"Yes, sir. Putting it simply, for two days I think you've been offering Robert Gifford time to make a choice."

"Between what and what?"

"Between life in an institution for the insane, and death by his own hand," said the sergeant with considerable courage.

Cheadle jerked erect. "Pull up!" he ordered. The sergeant brought the car to a halt, his eyes on the road ahead.

"You seriously believe," Cheadle demanded, "that I wanted Robert Thomson to kill himself?"

"Yes, sir." Eyes still front.

"And assuming that I did, would society scream because he obliged me?"

"No, sir. Society'd say nothing; it'd be grateful he was dead."

Cheadle slumped back in his seat. "All hypocrites, aren't we?" He stared moodily through the windscreen. "Want to know something? I *liked* Master Robert. Knew he was a murderer, but liked him. Liked him, but gave him time to kill himself."

"It was a compassionate solution, sir." Aware that he lied; that Cheadle was as much a stranger to compassion as any murderer.

"Hardly compassionate. If I'd arrested him, he'd have got off. He knew that. It's what he meant when he said he was bidding a grand slam in spades. Telling me he was a killer I couldn't convict."

"*Would* he have got off, sir?"

"Certainly. Defence counsel would have accused his brother—dead or alive—of being the real murderer. They'd have shown that the only place Mr. Mark could previously have seen a bit of that Fellini film, for example, was at the Rex. It's never been shown on the *Canberra*. They'd have shown that the only convincing motive was money: Mr. Mark's money that Mr. Robert was spending like water. They'd have tied in knots the girl who gave Mr. Mark his alibi. They'd have shown Mr. Mark had equal opportunity, was a more likely murderer than a cripple and was the only man who could've left the lass at the Rex. They'd have got the jury so confused they'd have been unable to decide that Mr. Robert was guilty beyond all reasonable doubt. Oh—he'd have got off, all right."

"Then why did he kill himself?"

"Because the whole cunning plot fell apart in his hands when he found he couldn't kill his brother. Denied that end, all his murders became not just means to an end but the vicious work of a maniac. He knew it, of course; but it had to be spelled out to him. So I obliged him. You're a sick, murderous maniac, I spelled out to him. Then I gave him time to kill himself."

"Yes, sir." The sergeant's expression was still questioning.

"But?" prompted Cheadle.

"But *I* think he might *not* have killed himself. He could have, of course. When you told him we'd found traces of blood on the seat of his car, and he laughed." The sergeant thumped his diaphragm to indicate how Robbie could have killed himself. "But his brother could've done it just as feasibly. When you started reading the charge, and his hand flashed to Mr. Robert's chest."

"Only to snatch out a bit of arrow, surely?"

"Or plunge it in."

Cheadle nodded fatalistically. "Could've been up the sleeve of either one, of course, waiting. No fingerprints."

"Was it suicide, sir?" the sergeant persisted.

"Suicide, fratricide! Quibbles, Sergeant. It was my kind of judicial homicide."

"Put it like that, sir, society *will* scream."

"But I shan't put it like that. You're the only idealist likely to put it like that."

"Me, sir?"—looking straight at Cheadle.

"You're the one who knows we found no blood on the seat of Master Robert's car. You're the one who knows that my hint that we had was what finally broke Master Robert's will. So when your turn comes to give evidence tomorrow at the coroner's inquiry, how will you put it, my learned friend?"

The sergeant stared blankly through the windscreen, thinking about the cunning with which Cheadle had said: "What *if I told you* we found traces of Janine Talbot's blood on the seat of his car?" And thinking about the fact that it was *he,* not Cheadle, who'd smelled Janine Talbot's perfume on Mark Gifford, and of the promotion that meant so much to him, he intoned:

"I saw the deceased slide something out of his right sleeve and, gripping it firmly with his right hand, drive it upward into his chest. I rushed to his assistance, but he was dead."

Cheadle nodded approval. "Then society'll be happy, won't it?"

"Yes, sir. But just between ourselves, did he do it, or did his brother do it to him?"

"Just between ourselves, Sergeant," rumbled Cheadle, eyes closed, "it no longer matters."

Russell Braddon

Russell Braddon was born in Australia fifty-three years ago. After taking his arts degree at Sydney University, he was catapulted into World War II and a Japanese prison camp in Malaya where he spent four terrible years. "No one," Braddon says, "ever really gets over it." When he emerged from the jungle, his health shaky (malaria, encephalitis, meningitis), he began to study law, loathed it, and had a breakdown instead.

In 1949, recovered, he left Australia for England, determined on a career of writing and public speaking in spite of psychiatrists' tests which "proved" him to have no aptitude for either. On his first day in London he ran into an old friend named Piddington, one half of a little-known mental telepathy act touring music halls, and was promptly hired to write scripts for him. Six months later the Piddingtons had top billing at the London Palladium, and Braddon was writing their biography. *The Piddingtons* launched Braddon on a successful career of his own, to which eight biographies and eleven novels testify. In the spoken word he excels no less; a witty, lively, opinionated man, he is much in demand for both radio and television shows.

To Russell Braddon all experience is grist to the mill. His prison-camp ordeal generated two outstanding books on World War II in the Far East: *The Naked Island* (1951) and *End of a Hate* (1958). His months in the hands of psychiatrists were used for a novel *Gabriel Comes to 24* (also 1958). Now, in *End Play*, bridge addict Braddon employs his favourite pastime to give his story of Robbie and Mark its shape; both brothers are modelled, with an imaginative double twist, on a ship's officer friend who was also a foundling. It was research for an article on the Spinal Injuries Centre at Stoke Mandeville Hospital in Aylesbury that gave him his insight into Robbie's disability.

Braddon is a professional who writes two thousand words a night and meticulously corrects each batch before starting on the next. When the work in hand is finished, he turns, for release from strain, to his other career—the broadcasting he so enjoys. Until the next book possesses him.

PICTURE CREDITS: THE FEARFUL VOID. Title pages Josephine Nelson/Camera Press; photo of Tombouctou Robert Harding Assts.

VV.79